ACCLAIM FOR

Dorothy Dunnett's

LYMOND CHRONICLES

"Dorothy Dunnett is one of the greatest talespinners since Dumas . . . breathlessly exciting."
—*Cleveland Plain Dealer*

"Dunnett is a name to conjure with. Her work exemplifies the best the genre can offer. It combines the accuracy of exhaustive historical research with a gripping story to give the reader a visceral as well as cerebral understanding of an epoch."
—*Christian Science Monitor*

"Dorothy Dunnett is a storyteller who could teach Scheherazade a thing or two about suspense, pace and invention."
—*The New York Times*

"Dunnett evokes the sixteenth century with an amazing richness of allusion and scholarship, while keeping a firm control on an intricately twisting narrative. She has another more unusual quality . . . an ability to check her imagination with irony, to mix high romance with wit."
—*Sunday Times* (London)

"First-rate . . . suspenseful. . . . Her hero, in his rococo fashion, is as polished and perceptive as Lord Peter Wimsey and as resourceful as James Bond."
—*The New York Times Book Review*

"A masterpiece of historical fiction, a pyrotechnic blend of passionate scholarship and high-speed storytelling soaked with the scents and colors and sounds and combustible emotions of sixteenth-century feudal Scotland."
—*Washington Post Book World*

"With shrewd psychological insight and a rare gift of narrative and descriptive power, Dorothy Dunnett reveals the color, wit, lushness . . . and turbulent intensity of one of Europe's greatest eras."
—*Raleigh News and Observer*

"Detailed research, baroque imagination, staggering dramatic twists, multilingual literary allusion and scenes that can be very funny."
—*The Times* (London)

"Ingenious and exceptional . . . its effect brilliant, its pace swift and colorful and its multi-linear plot spirited and absorbing."
—*Boston Herald*

"A lively, busy narrative that features an energetic hero in whom we find Ivanhoe's temperate nationalism, D'Artagnan's fine swordsmanship, and James Bond's unchivalrous way with women."
—*The New Yorker*

Dorothy Dunnett

The
DISORDERLY
KNIGHTS

Dorothy Dunnett was born in Dunfermline, Scotland.
She is the author of the Francis Crawford of Lymond
novels; the House of Niccolò novels; seven mysteries;
King Hereafter, an epic novel about Macbeth; and the
text of *The Scottish Highlands*, a book of photographs
by David Paterson, on which she collaborated with her
husband, Sir Alastair Dunnett. In 1992, Queen Elizabeth appointed her an Officer of the Order of the
British Empire. Lady Dunnett lives with her husband
in Edinburgh, Scotland.

The
DISORDERLY
KNIGHTS

The
DISORDERLY
KNIGHTS

VINTAGE BOOKS

A Division of Random House, Inc.

New York

In affectionate memory
of my grandparents Annie and Martin Halliday
and of my father, Alexander Halliday,
who was born in Valetta, Malta

First Vintage Books Edition, June 1997

Copyright © 1966 by Dorothy Dunnett
Copyright renewed 1994 by Dorothy Dunnett

Library of Congress Cataloging-in-Publication Data

Dunnett, Dorothy.
The disorderly knights / Dorothy Dunnett.
p. cm.
ISBN 0-679-77745-8
I. Title.
PR6054.U56D57 1997
823'.914—dc21 96-45599
CIP

Random House Web address: http://www.randomhouse.com/

Printed in the United States of America

10 9 8 7 6 5 4 3 2 1

THE LYMOND CHRONICLES

Foreword by *Dorothy Dunnett*

When, a generation ago, I sat down before an old Olivetti typewriter, ran through a sheet of paper, and typed a title, *The Game of Kings*, I had no notion of changing the course of my life. I wished to explore, within several books, the nature and experiences of a classical hero: a gifted leader whose star-crossed career, disturbing, hilarious, dangerous, I could follow in finest detail for ten years. And I wished to set him in the age of the Renaissance.

Francis Crawford of Lymond in reality did not exist, and his family, his enemies and his lovers are merely fictitious. The countries in which he practices his arts, and for whom he fights, are, however, real enough. In pursuit of a personal quest, he finds his way—or is driven—across the known world, from the palaces of the Tudor kings and queens of England to the brilliant court of Henry II and Catherine de Medici in France.

His home, however, is Scotland, where Mary Queen of Scots is a vulnerable child in a country ruled by her mother. It becomes apparent in the course of the story that Lymond, the most articulate and charismatic of men, is vulnerable too, not least because of his feeling for Scotland, and for his estranged family.

The Game of Kings was my first novel. As Lymond developed in wisdom, so did I. We introduced one another to the world of sixteenth-century Europe, and while he cannot change history, the wars and events which embroil him are real. After the last book of the six had been published, it was hard to accept that nothing more about Francis Crawford could be written, without disturbing the shape and theme of his story. But there was, as it happened, something that could be done: a little manicuring to repair the defects of the original edition as it was rushed out on both sides of the Atlantic. And so here is Lymond returned, in a freshened text which presents him as I first envisaged him, to a different world.

Author's Note

As with the two previous books in this series, *The Disorderly Knights* is based on fact. The attacks on Malta, Gozo and Tripoli took place in 1551 broadly as related, including the perfidy of the Grand Master, the trick by which Mdina was saved, the weakness of the Governor of Gozo, and the attempt by the Calabrian recruits to blow up the citadel of Tripoli, together with the part played by the French Ambassador in saving the garrison.

In the last part of the book, the feud between the Scotts and the Kerrs and its climax is authentic also, as was the betrayal of Paris by Cormac O'Connor. The rest is conjecture.

LEADING CHARACTERS

All of the following are recorded in history save for the characters distinguished by an asterisk.

Members of the Noble Order of Knights Hospitaller of St John of Jerusalem, Rhodes and Malta:

JUAN DE HOMEDÈS, Grand Master of the Order, 1536–53

NICHOLAS DURAND DE VILLEGAGNON, Knight of the Order

*GRAHAM REID MALETT, (Gabriel) Grand Cross of Grace and Hon. Bailiff of the Order

LEONE STROZZI, Prior of Capua and Commander of the King of France's Mediterranean fleet

FRANCIS OF LORRAINE, Grand Prior in France of the Order, and brother of the Scottish Queen Dowager

*JEROTT BLYTH, of Scotland and Nantes, Knight of the Order

GALATIAN DE CÉSEL, Knight of the Order and Governor of Gozo

NICHOLAS UPTON, Turcopilier or Officer of the English Tongue within the Order

SERVING BROTHER DES ROCHES, of the Châtelet, Tripoli

MICHEL DE SEURRE, Sieur de Lumigny, Knight of the Order

BAILIFF GEORGE ADORNE, Knight of the Order and Governor of Mdina

MARSHAL GASPARD DE VALLIER, Knight of the Order and Governor of Tripoli

SIR JAMES SANDILANDS OF CALDER, Preceptor-General of the House of Torphichen of the Order in Scotland

Other French, or in the French Service:

ANNE DE MONTMORENCY, Marshal, Grand Master and Constable of France

PIERO STROZZI, Seigneur de Belleville, Count de Languillara, Florentine colonel of infantry under the King of France and brother of Leone Strozzi

GABRIEL DE LUETZ, Baron et Seigneur d'Aramon et de Valabrègues, French Ambassador to Turkey

HENRI CLEUTIN, Seigneur d'Oisel et de Villeparisis, French Ambassador and Lieutenant-General to the King of France in Scotland

NICOLAS DE NICOLAY, Sieur d'Arfeville et de Bel Air, cosmographer to the King of France

Irish:

CORMAC O'CONNOR, heir to Brian Faly O'Connor, rebel Irish chieftain against England

*OONAGH O'DWYER, his former mistress

GEORGE PARIS, an agent between Ireland and France

Scots, or Closely Connected with the Scots:

*FRANCIS CRAWFORD OF LYMOND, Comte de Sevigny

*RICHARD CRAWFORD, third Baron Culter, his brother

*SYBILLA, the Dowager Lady Culter, his mother

*MARIOTTA, Richard's Irish-born wife

*KEVIN CRAWFORD, Master of Culter, Richard's infant son

SIR WALTER SCOTT OF BUCCLEUCH, Warden of the Middle Marches and Justiciar of Liddesdale

SIR WILLIAM SCOTT OF KINCURD, Younger of Buccleuch, his heir

JANET BEATON, Lady of Buccleuch, his wife

GRIZEL BEATON, Lady (Younger) of Buccleuch, sister to Janet Beaton and wife to Will Scott

ROBERT BEATON OF CREICH, Captain of Falkland, their brother

MARY OF GUISE, Queen Mother of Scotland, and mother of the child
  Mary, Queen of Scots

SIR WALTER KERR OF CESSFORD ⎫ Heads, respectively, of the two
SIR JOHN KERR OF FERNIEHURST ⎭ main branches of the impor-
  tant Scottish lowland family of
  Kerr, at feud with the Scotts

SIR PETER CRANSTON OF CRANSTON, a Border landowner, neighbour
  of the Kerrs and the Scotts

*JOLETA REID MALETT, sister to Sir Graham Reid Malett

*EVANGELISTA DONATI OF VENICE, Joleta's governess and duenna

SIR THOMAS ERSKINE, Master of Erskine, Chief Scots Privy Councillor
  and Special Ambassador

MARGARET ERSKINE, *née* Fleming, his wife

JENNY, LADY FLEMING, mother to Margaret Erskine, and former
  mistress to the King of France

*ADAM BLACKLOCK, artist ⎫

*FERGIE HODDIM OF THE LAIGH, lawyer

*RANDOLPH BELL, (Randy) physician

*ALEXANDER GUTHRIE, lecturer and humanist ⎬ Men and
  officers
*HERCULES TAIT, diplomat and antiquarian of St
  Mary's
*LANCELOT PLUMMER, engineer and architect

*ARCHIE ABERNETHY, former Keeper of the French
  King's menageries

*THOMAS WISHART, (Tosh) acrobat ⎭

JOHN THOMPSON, (Jockie, Tamsín) sea rover

HOUGH ISA, a friendly lady open to barter

English:

*KATE SOMERVILLE, mistress of Flaw Valleys

*PHILIPPA, her daughter

*CHEESE-WAME HENDERSON, their servant

Turks, or in Turkish Pay:

DRAGUT RAIS, Anatolian corsair in Turkish service

SALAH RAIS, corsair in Turkish service and joint lieutenant with Dragut

SINAN PASHA OF SMYRNA, General in command of Sultan Suleiman's expedition

THE AGA MORAT, Lord of Tagiura and ally of the Sultan Suleiman

*SALABLANCA, a Moor from Spain enslaved by the Knights

*GÜZEL, companion to Dragut Rais

*KEDI, a nurse

Heralds:

WILLIAM FLOWER, Chester Herald (England)

ADAM MACCULLO, Bute Herald (Scotland)

ROBBIE FORMAN, Ross Herald (Scotland)

Contents

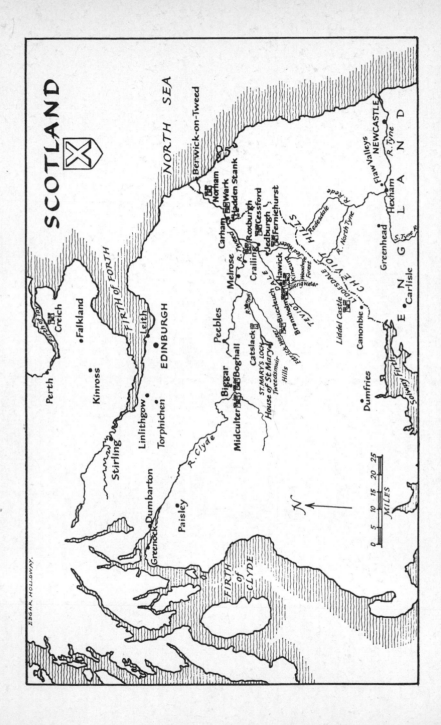

SCOTLAND

NORTH SEA

FIRTH OF FORTH

Perth

Creich

Falkland

Kinross

Leith

EDINBURGH

Linlithgow

Torphichen

Stirling

Dumbarton

Greenock

Paisley

R. Clyde

Peebles

Biggar

Midculter · Boghall

Catslack

ST. MARY'S LOCH

House of St Mary's

Tweedsmuir

Hills

Berwick-on-Tweed

Norham

Wark

Hadden Stank

Carham

Roxburgh

Cessford

Melrose

R. Tweed

Jedburgh

Fernieihurst

Crailing

Hawick

R. Teviot

Kinew

Branxholm

Buccleuch

Slitrig Water

Harehope Forest

TEVIOT

CHEVIOT HILLS

Redesdale

R. Reed

R. North Tyne

LIDDESDALE

Liddel Castle

Canonbie

Greenhead

S. Tyne R.

Hexham

R. Tyne

NEWCASTLE

Flaw Valleys

ENGLAND

Carlisle

Dumfries

Solway Firth

FIRTH of CLYDE

N

0 5 10 15 20 25

MILES

EDGAR HOLLOWAY.

The
DISORDERLY
KNIGHTS

Part One

THE SALTIRE AND
SUPPORTERS

I

Mother's Baking

(Catslack, October 1548)

ON the day that his grannie was killed by the English, Sir William Scott the Younger of Buccleuch was at Melrose Abbey, marrying his aunt.

News of the English attack came towards the end of the ceremony when, by good fortune, young Scott and his aunt Grizel were by all accounts man and wife. There was no bother over priorities. As the congregation hustled out of the church, led by bridegroom and father, and spurred off on the heels of the messenger, the new-made bride and her sister watched them go.

'I'm daft,' said Grizel Beaton to Janet Beaton, straightening her headdress where her bridegroom's helmet had knocked it cockeyed. 'And after five years of it with Will's father, you should think shame to allow your own sister to marry a Scott. I've wed his two empty boots.'

'That you havena,' said Janet, Lady of Buccleuch, lowering her voice not at all in the presence of two hundred twittering Scott relations as they gazed after their vanishing husbands. 'They aye remember their boots. It's their empty nightgowns that get fair monotonous.'

Being a Beaton, Will Scott's new wife was riled, but by no means overcome. The war between England and Scotland was in its eighth year and there had been no raid for ten days: it had seemed possible to get married in peace. Creich, her home, was too far away. So Grizel Beaton had chosen to marry at Melrose, with the tarred canvas among the roofbeams patching the holes from the last English raid, and the pillars chipped with arquebus shot.

Duly packed like broccoli into lawn, buckram and plush and ropes of misshapen pearls, she had enjoyed the wedding, and even the cautious clash of plate armour underwriting the hymns. Lord Grey of Wilton with an English army was occupying Roxburgh only twelve miles away, and had twice emerged to plunder and burn the district since October began. If the wedding was wanted at Melrose—and Buccleuch, as Hereditary Bailie of the Abbey lands, had fewer objections than usual to any idea not his own—then the congregation had to come armed, that was all. The Scotts and their allies, the twenty polite Frenchmen from Edinburgh, the Italian commander with the lame leg, had left their men at arms outside with their horses, the plumed helmets lashed to the saddlebows; and if there were a few vacant seats where a man from Hawick or Bedrule had ducked too late ten days before, no one mentioned it.

For a while, standing next to her jingling bridegroom, her gaze averted from his carroty hair, Grizel had thought the other absentees had escaped his attention. Then, as alto and counter-tenor rang from pillar to pillar, the red head on one side of her leaned towards the unkempt grey one on the other and hissed, 'Da! Where are the Crawfords?'

And Buccleuch, the bride saw out of the tail of her eye, sank his head into his shoulders like a bear in its ruff, and said nothing. For by 'the Crawfords', Sir William Scott meant not Lord Culter and his wife Mariotta, or even Sybilla, their remarkable mother; but the only man in Scotland Will Scott had ever obeyed without arguing: Francis Crawford of Lymond.

And it was then, as the Bishop bored on through the pages of print which were making these two man and wife, that the Abbey's chipped door-leaf moved and a man entered, in the blue and silver livery of Crawford, to speak quietly to one of the monks. From bent head to devout head, the word travelled. Lord Grey of England, guided by a Scotsman, renegade chief of the Kerrs, had burned Buccleuch's town of Selkirk to the ground, despoiled his castle of Newark, and was advancing, destroying and killing along the River Yarrow, through the trim possessions of the Scotts and their friends.

The wedding ended, hurriedly, on a surge of masculine *bonhomie* and relief. Five minutes later, followed by the red-eyed glares of their womenfolk, Buccleuch and his friends and his new-married son had plunged off to join Lord Culter, head of the Crawfords, and Francis Crawford his brother, to fight the English once more.

*

Sentimentally, Will Scott thought, it made his wedding-day perfect. Cantering, easy and big-limbed, through the bracken of Ettrick-side, with leaves stuck, lime-green and scarlet on his wet sleeves, blue eyes narrowed and fair, red-blooded Scott face misted with rain, he was borne on a vast, angry joy.

The lands of Branxholm and Hawick and all Buccleuch possessed in these regions had been a favourite target while King Henry VIII of England and his successor had tried to resurrect their overlordship of Scotland and seize and marry Mary, the child Queen of Scotland, to Henry's son Edward, now the young English King.

They had failed, despite the great English victory at Pinkie, and

4

timber and thatch had risen in Buccleuch's lands again, and the thick stone towers—his father's at Buccleuch and Branxholm, his own at Kincurd, his grandmother's at Catslack—still survived. After Pinkie, the English army had retired, leaving their garrisons to police the outraged land; and Sir William Scott had left Branxholm to join the roving force then commanded by Crawford of Lymond.

By the following summer, when Francis Crawford disbanded his company, Buccleuch's heir had turned into a tough and capable leader of men, and the child Queen Mary had been sent for safety to France, at six the affianced bride of the Dauphin.

In return, the King of France had filled Scotland with Gascon men-at-arms, Italian arquebusiers, German Landsknechts, a French general, a French ambassador and an Italian commander in French service, the last of whom was riding now at Will Scott's left side, his Florentine English further cracked by the jolt of the ride.

'The little bride shed no tears,' said Piero Strozzi, Marshal of France, in sombre inquiry. He rode with animal grace; a man of near fifty, just recovered from a hackbut shot outside Haddington which would leave 'one leg shorter than the other all his life. Beneath the umber skin, the basic shapes of his face were deeply plangent, denying his notoriety as a practical joker: only Leone his brother was worse. But today, riding against the muddling wind, in and out of the rain, his plumes dripping wetly from his bonnet and the black hair before his ears in wet rings, Strozzi's theme was the bereft bride.

'She has known you some weeks, it is true?'

'Grizel? I've known her a while, Marshal. Her older sister is my father's third wife.'

'There is sympathy between you?'

Will Scott grinned. Grizel Beaton had slapped his face four times, and apart from these four small misjudgements, they had never touched on a topic more personal than which of Buccleuch's bastards to invite to the wedding. But he liked her fine; and she was good and broad where it would matter to future Buccleuchs, which summed up all his mind so far on the subject.

'She's a canty wee bird,' said Will Scott now to the Marshal. 'But plain, forbye. Couldna hold a candle, ye ken, to Lord Culter's wife. You've met the Crawfords?'

So, duly turned from discussing the bride, 'I have met the Crawfords,' the Marshal Piero Strozzi said. 'The lord is most worthy and the Dowager mother enchanting. And the youngest brother Francesco is fit for my dearest brother Leone.'

A smile twitched Sir William Scott's mouth. As Prior of the Noble Order of the Knights Hospitallers of St John of Jerusalem and commander of the King of France's fleet off the Barbary coast, Leone

5

Strozzi, however practised with infidels, was not necessarily fit for Crawford of Lymond.

Will Scott said nothing. But he wondered why the Marshal Piero also smiled.

*

Sir Walter Scott of Buccleuch was happy, too, because he had caught the Kerrs at it again.

All over the middle Borders their land marched with his, and he loved them as he loved the Black Death. It was a Kerr of Ferniehurst whose timely murder had sparked off the holocaust of Flodden thirty-five years ago. Thirty-two years ago, a Kerr of Cessford had been involved in a little foray led by Buccleuch; and the Kerr had got himself killed. After that, despite damnable pilgrimages on both sides and eternal vows of reconciliation, despite Buccleuch himself, like his father before him, having to take a Kerr woman to wife (she was dead), the Scott–Kerr feud had flourished.

That it was discreetly refuelled from time to time by the English was subconsciously known to Sir Wat, but he chose to ignore his son's hints on the subject. A number of Scottish lairds, professing the reformed faith rather than the Old Religion of the Queen Dowager, were interested in an English alliance, and not averse to traffic over the Border. Others with homes at or near the frontier itself had had to give up the costly luxury of patriotism.

Still others, among whom the Douglases and the Kerrs could sometimes be glimpsed, were not exactly sure which nation would triumph when the smoke cleared away, and were prepared with spacious burrows in all directions. It had been a fairly safe wager for some time that Sir Walter Kerr of Cessford and Sir John Kerr of Ferniehurst, their sons, brothers and diverse relations had been selling information to the English ... so safe that, after the late brush with the English at Jedburgh, the Governor of Scotland had been persuaded to place the three leading Kerrs temporarily under restraint.

Unhappily, the hand of Buccleuch was rarely invisible. Suspecting, rightly, that the old man had engineered the whole episode, Andrew Kerr, Cessford's brother, had ridden straight to the English at Roxburgh, and showering Kerrs upon the welcoming garrison, had induced them to burn and plunder the whole of Buccleuch's country twice in four days, with a force many times the size any Scott and his son could muster.

And now, ten days later, a third attack had been launched, and to Buccleuch's ears came the confirmation he longed for. The Kerrs, the weasels, were on horse with the English. Swearing with great spirit from time to time, always a good sign with Sir Walter, he flew through the filmy splendours of autumn, primed to nick Kerr heads like old semmit buttons.

*

On the low hills above Yarrow, where the woodcutters of Selkirk had cleared a space among the birch and the low, fret-leafed oak, a group of men were working with sheep, the arched whistles coming thin over the ling, and the dogs running low through the bracken as the ewes jostled past staring glassily, the black Roman noses poking as the owners were hoisted rib-high in the press.

The two men lying prone on the heather were watching not the sheep but the valley below, filled now with a mist of fine rain. Both were bareheaded, blending into the autumn rack of the hillside, where the glitter of helmets and the flash of wedding plumes would have betrayed them. Their eyes were fixed eastwards, on the Selkirk road, where hazily in the distance black smoke hung in the air and there was a rumour of shouting.

Nearer at hand, dulling now in the rain, an aureole bright as a sunset showed where, over the next hill, something was burning. The younger of the two men stirred, and then moved backwards and on to his feet, still well masked from the road; and without doing more, drew the attention of the twenty men on that hillside to where he stood still, his yellow hair tinselled with moisture, his long-lashed blue stare on the vacant road, far below, along which the English would ride.

The noise increased. 'Here they come,' said Crawford of Lymond to his brother and smiled, still watching the road. 'Gaea, goddess of marriage and first-born of Chaos, defend us. The Kerrs and the English are here.'

Richard, third Baron Crawford of Culter, grinned and rose cautiously also. Square, brown-haired and thick with muscle, with skin like barked hide after a summer's campaigning about his Lanarkshire home, he believed his brother's present imbecile plan would either kill all of them or brand them as liars for life. It seemed unlikely, unless you knew Lymond, that twenty men could put an English army to rout.

News of trouble at Selkirk had met the Midculter party halfway on their long journey to the wedding at Melrose. Efficiently, the Crawfords had taken action. Their womenfolk were given shelter in the nearest buildings at Talla. A messenger was sent ahead to Melrose to warn Wat Scott of Buccleuch, and another south-east to the old castle of Buccleuch to summon the hundred German soldiers quartered there by the Government. There was no time to send to

7

Branxholm, Buccleuch's chief castle, where four hundred others stood idle.

By now, the Buccleuch Germans should be waiting in the next valley at Tushielaw. Sir Wat Scott and his new-married son, with perhaps two hundred Scotts, should have left Melrose and be entering the other end of that valley, where Ettrick Water ran between high, wooded hills from burned-out Selkirk to Tushielaw and onwards west. And here, above the valley of Yarrow, Lord Culter and his brother and twenty men from Midculter in their wedding finery with, thank God, half armour beneath, waited to intercept the English army on its plundering march, with two shepherds, twelve arquebuses, some pikes, some marline twine, a leather pail of powder, shot, matches, some makeshift colours, and eight hundred rusted helmets from the Warden's storehouse at Talla.

The English were slow in coming; not through any unfamiliarity with the route, but because the thatches were taking a long time to burn. They had taken a good few beasts and as much corn as they could carry, firing the rest. Most of the cottages they passed were empty, the owners either hiding up the glens or fled to one of the keeps. Lord Grey had paused to attack one or two of the latter as well, but with less success: the stone walls were thick, and needed the leisure of a good-going siege.

But Newark fell, which gave him great pleasure. They had attacked this castle in vain once before: it was the Queen's, garrisoned by Buccleuch. This time they used fire and got in, though four of Buccleuch's men fought to the end and had to be killed, and an old woman got under someone's sword. The Murrays at Deuchar held out, and no one troubled unduly with them; but Catslack was a Scott stronghold and they burned that, though the man Andrew Kerr who had stopped to rummage at Tinnis came spluttering up with a parcel of relations to complain that the assault party had made away with a Kerr.

'My dear friend.' William Grey, thirteenth Baron of Wilton, had been fighting in Scotland for months and disliked the country, the climate and the natives, particularly those disaffected with whom he had to converse. 'You are mistaken. Every man in this tower wore Scott livery.'

'It wasna a *man*,' said Andrew Kerr broadly. 'T'was my aunty. I tellt ye. I'm no risking cauld steel in ma wame for a pittance, unless all that's mine is well lookit after—'

'An old lady,' said Lord Grey with forbearance, 'in curling papers and a palatial absence of teeth?'

'My aunt Lizzie!' said Andrew Kerr.

'She has just,' said Lord Grey austerely, 'seriously injured one of my men.'

8

'How?' The old savage looked interested.

'From an upper window. The castle was burning, and he was climbing a ladder to offer the lady her freedom. She cracked his head with a chamberpot,' said Lord Grey distastefully, 'and retired crying that she would have no need of a jurden in Heaven, as the good Lord had no doubt thought of more convenient methods after the seventh day, when He had had a good rest.'

A curious bark, which Lord Grey had come to recognize as laughter, emerged from the Kerr helmet. 'Aye. That's Aunt Lizzie. She'll be deid then, the auld bitch,' said her nephew. 'Aweel, what are we waiting for? There's the rest of Yarrow tae ding.'

And so, jogging onwards with his mixed English and German light horse and the small, spare-boned party of vengeance-bent Kerrs, Lord Grey passed along Yarrow Water in the half-light towards St Mary's Loch, doing sums in his head connected with time, speed, and a quick return along Ettrick to Roxburgh in the early afternoon. Then his advance scouts came spurring. 'Horsemen on the hillside, my lord.'

Familiar words. He checked over the possibilities. Traquair was wounded in bed. Thirlstane wouldn't trouble him. Scott of Buccleuch and most of his relations were at Melrose, and Andrew Kerr had bribed every cottar in miles not to let the news through. There were plenty of steadings, of villages and keeps in the district, but none so crazy as to throw a handful of men against five hundred English, for the Scottish army under the French Commander and the Earl of Arran, the Governor, had withdrawn to Edinburgh.

Unless it had advanced from Edinburgh again. 'What colours?' Grey said sharply.

'Red and white, my lord. They seem in great numbers. Advancing down the Craig Hill from Traquair.'

From Traquair. From Peebles. From Edinburgh. And wearing the Governor's colours.

And then Lord Grey saw them, with his own eyes, through the veiling rain, glittering between oakscrub and thorn, threading through the wet beeches and the flaming clusters of rowan, pouring down the hillside like cod from a creel; steel helms by the hundred, with swords brandished among them, and pikes sparkling, and small firearms, let off here and there as his enemy paused to take aim.

If Arran had come, he wouldn't have less than a thousand foot, and at least a company of light horsemen as well. With all the impetus of that hill behind him, he would crush Grey's smaller force as he liked. Grey's men were tired; they had nearly finished their work; they had a criminal disadvantage of terrain. . . .

On his left, bruised mud running over the hill, was the Tushielaw Pass to Ettrick Water. Lord Grey called, loud and clear. His

9

trumpeter blew. And the English army, wheeling, started south at a gallop over the hill pass into Ettrick, followed by twenty men and eight hundred sheep in steel helmets.

By the time Lord Culter and his brother plunged down the last of Craig Hill to the road, the force of Lord Grey of Wilton was a thin ribbon coiled on the bare hillside, pricking faintly with steel. Lymond drew rein beside his brother. 'The wind is dropping.' It was true. Already, on the low ground, the white mist was thickening. As the twenty screaming men behind him jostled to a halt he added, 'We could follow and see the fun. If they hear us, they'll run all the faster.'

Richard, his face scarlet, was hoarse with shouting and laughter. He said, 'I was going to follow anyway, and I'm damned sure you were. Come on.'

Beside him, 'Come *oan*?' said a voice. 'Aw, but that's hardly right, master. That isna fair on the yowes.'

Through the reverberant air, Richard gazed at one of the two shepherds at his knee. 'On the yowes—ewes?' he repeated. 'We've done with them. They can go back uphill where they were. And I'll see your masters don't lose by it.'

'It'll take half the nicht tae put them back, they're that excited.'

'I'm sorry. But you won't regret it, I promise.'

'Ach, it's no that,' said the older of the two shepherds dourly, and a sudden grin cracked the furzy face wide open. 'But I'm awful anxious to get hame afore nightfall. The sicht o' eight hunner sheep in steel helmets is fairly going to put my auld dame off the drink.'

Thus, pursued by shadowy hoofbeats, my lord Grey, as he omitted to report that night to his loving friends, E. Somerset and J. Warwick, hurled himself up Megs Hill and down the Kip to meet Ettrick Water at Tushielaw; and to meet also Buccleuch's hundred Germans, rising fremescent from their ambush in the mist and thinly echoing, with frightening aptitude, the native cries of their fellow-countrymen under Grey.

There was a Teutonic crash of great brevity; then the English company set off east up Ettrick valley, hotly pursued by a small number of Germans on horseback, the Crawfords and a great deal of noise.

At Oakwood, soaked, exhausted, their cold flesh chafed raw by their armour, the English army careered round a hillock to see, looming up through the mirk, the porcupine spears of Wat Scott of Buccleuch. Hung with fur, feathers and jewellery, silver-buttoned and slashed and puckered and decorated over their armour like so many armadillo queens of the May, Will Scott's wedding party flung itself with evangelical fervour straight at its prey.

With a single accord, and no orders spoken, the army of Lord

Grey of Wilton broke ranks and rode belly flat on the moss for the haven of Roxburgh.

Much later, riding in rollicking company back to Melrose, Lord Culter expressed his regrets to Buccleuch on the death of his mother. 'Catslack was burning before ever we reached it,' he said soberly. 'But it was her own choice to stay, it seems. And she did some damage first.'

Sir Walter Scott of Buccleuch fumbled for a moment under his chin, and then pushed his heavy headpiece roughly back off his brow. He pointed. 'Did the same tae me once, the auld besom. I've got the scar yet. An auld de'il wi' a chamberpot. Huh!' He pulled down his helmet. 'She'll be able tae keep Yule in hell wi' her nephews, and they a' nicked already like targets wi' the aim o' their wives.'

*

'Andrew Kerr was with them,' Sir Wat counted afterwards, when the gentle festivities of marriage had been resumed at Melrose at dusk on the same day. 'And the Laird o' Linton was there, and George Kerr o' Gateshaw. And I saw Robin Kerr o' Graden, and of course the hale o' Cessford's household and natural bairns and bairns' bairns and cousins and them that owes him and Ferniehurst a tack all over East Teviotdale. There's some of them'll be nursing a guid scratch or two on their hinder-ends this night. . . . Man, it was a rout.'

'I imagine,' said Piero Strozzi, his dark face impassive, 'that my lord Grey's army would not relish their defeat either.'

'Oh, aye, the English,' said Buccleuch absently.

'We are, after all, at war with them and not with the Kerrs,' the Marshal said mildly.

To the Frenchmen risking their lives to drive the English from Scotland, such a feud seemed no doubt an ill-timed indulgence. To Buccleuch, any comment from a foreigner was a piece of damnable impertinence, no less. He said, 'And what pains the Marshal in that? Because we sit here in bows and silk sarks, it doesna mean we couldna jummle the English *and* the French off our own turf if need be, and mind our own affairs too. Ye didna fare so sweetly yourselves the other week in yon bicker at Haddington, after raxing yourselves in Edinburgh killing poor folk as they walked their ain causeway. . . .'

But halfway through this, Lord Culter had kicked the fiddler on the ankle and the fiddler, a man of sense, struck up a dance tune, while every Scott present rose hastily to his or her feet. Among them Sir William Scott, his arm in his bride's, leant over his father. 'You've a few quarts in you, Faither?' he said.

'No more nor him!' retorted the head of his house, surprised and irritated, with a wave at the Marshal.

'Aye, well. *He* isna going daft in the heid. Take a dance with Janet, Faither,' said Will Scott kindly, and whirled off with his new lady wife.

Looking round for sympathy, Sir Wat found himself indeed standing eye to eye with his wife. 'Fegs,' said the Lady of Buccleuch, fixing him with a calculating eye. 'If you're going to fight the English single-handed, you'll be needing your strength. I'll dance with Marshal Strozzi, if he'll have me.'

And as the Marshal, his face marvellously tutored, rose and made her a bow, Janet Beaton of Buccleuch took his hand and led him over to Will Scott and her sister Grizel whose wedding day, if memorable, was not what every girl would expect.

Later, the Florentine made a point of finding Lord Culter and congratulating him on the success of the day.

Richard Crawford, who was by no means a stupid man, smiled slightly and said, 'I am sure you realize the scheme was not of my devising. The peculiar imagination of the Crawfords is the inheritance of my brother Francis.'

'I am sorry not to see him tonight,' said the Marshal politely. Lymond, with the Midculter men, had ridden back to Talla to join his mother and sister-in-law and escort them safely home, leaving Richard to represent the family at the belated festivities. 'You are both of formidable calibre, my lord; you do not need me to inform you of that. I merely wondered whether, as the younger and therefore freer of you both, he had considered a captaincy abroad? The King of France, I know, would be happy to employ him, and I am sure my brother would press the claims of his crusading Order, were they to meet. Has he ambitions in Scotland, your brother Lymond? Or is he well-disposed towards France, or to the Religion? Or—' he smiled a little—'has he commitments quite incompatible with a life sworn to chastity . . . ?'

In the last few months, Richard Crawford of Culter had become very used to such questions. For sheer decency's sake, he seldom answered them. He rarely felt qualified to answer them, anyway. But here, from one of the great soldiers of Europe, was an inquiry without inquisitive intent.

He said carefully, 'Francis has led a company of his own, you may know, in this country and abroad. But as to the future . . . I have no idea of his plans, or his ambitions. He may have none. He has no ties here that I know of, other than what you might expect. As for religion. . . .' Lord Culter strove for tact. 'In Scotland, perhaps, we tend to extremes. There is a devotee of the Old Religion among us— you may have met him. Peter Cranston is his name—'

'—Who is so fanatically religious that he makes all men atheists. I have met him. I have met some of your Lutherans too, mostly in

12

prison. But it seems to me that your Government tolerates both, except where the Reformers threaten alliance with England. And your brother, after all, risked a good deal recently to keep your Queen out of English hands. I should judge him to be perhaps a man of humanist principles . . . ?'

He was offering more leeway than Richard, on his brother's behalf, was prepared to accept. The Order of St John, which had crept so obliquely into the conversation, was the supreme fighting arm in the known world of the Holy Catholic Religion. 'I should hesitate to attribute anything to him at the moment, even principles,' said Lord Culter, smiling. 'But you are free to try.'

Marshal Strozzi studied his well-groomed hands. 'There are three men I should like your brother to meet. One is my brother Leone, now in charge of the Mediterranean fleet in action against the Turks. One is the Chevalier de Villegagnon, a soldier and sea captain to equal any in the Order of St John. And the last is also in the Order: a Grand Cross of Grace named Sir Graham Reid Malett, known to a great many people as Gabriel.'

As he spoke the last name he looked up, in time for nothing but Lord Culter's habitually unexcited grey gaze. 'I've heard the Prior here talk about Gabriel,' said Richard serenely. 'He seemed at times to be confusing him with the Pope.'

'When you meet him, you will realize why,' said the Marshal simply. 'He is one of the Order's great names. You should be proud of him. His forebears were from Scotland, although he has no family now save a sister, a child of thirteen called Joleta, who lives in a convent on Malta. And in her also you would find something rare.'

A swift vision of his brother Francis posing as a man of humanist principles crossed Richard's mind. His voice wary, 'A beauty?' he asked.

The Marshal looked at him. Then, unexpectedly, he laughed. 'You are applying mundane standards,' he said. 'You cannot do that either to Graham Malett or his sister. Your brother will understand when he meets them.'

Richard was silent. He doubted it. If Joleta Reid Malett was as plain and as pure as she sounded, she was out of Brother Francis's territory, thank God. For Brother Francis's standards were mundane, all right. And high.

*

Not long after that, Sir William Scott took his bride by the hands, and drawing her from the throng said, 'Well, as you see, I came back. Were ye worried?'

'Worried? What about?' said Grizel, and as his mouth opened, added prosaically, 'Janet said that as a widow woman with no protector, I'd need to wed an Englishman or a Kerr.'

Her husband's features resumed command of themselves. 'And which would you choose?' he inquired.

'Well now. The English make bonny speeches, but they run to an awful wee man. And the Kerrs . . . there's something unchancy about a left-handed race.'

'I'm right-handed,' offered Will Scott.

'Aye.'

'And six foot three in my hose.'

'Uh-huh. I didna say I wanted to run up a beanpole. Nor have I heard hide nor hair of a speech, bonny or otherwise.'

'I'm saving it,' he said austerely, 'till I've the theme for it.'

'*Oh*!' said Grizel Beaton (Younger) of Buccleuch, with a squeal of delight. 'Will Scott! Are we having our first married set-to?'

They had come to the quiet wing of the house, and the suite where their chamber lay. 'Aye we are,' said her husband, a large hand closing round her arm, as he felt for the latch with the other.

'I enjoyed it. And what next?' she asked, doucely.

'We get reconciled,' said her husband, steering her through the bedroom door smartly and allowing it to close fast behind them. The tapers fluttered and straightened, bright in Grizel Beaton's wide, critical eyes. 'Are ye reconciled?' he inquired.

'I've been reconciled for eighteen hours, Will Scott,' said his aunt. 'And if ye don't win me ower soon, I'll be past it.'

II

Hough Isa

(*Crailing, May 1549*)

I N the spring of next year, when the Culter family were beginning
to find their younger son's presence a little wearing, the Chevalier
de Villegagnon, Knight of the Order of St John, came back to Scotland for four months, and not unexpectedly found his way to Midculter castle.

The war with England was then dwindling. Two Scottish strongholds had been recovered by their owners, and the occupying garrisons thrown out. In the remaining fortresses, the English and their
mercenary troops passed a formidable winter, deserting where
possible. Besides the bad food and the pneumonia and the boredom,
they had begun to suffer pinching from London, where the Protector
Somerset, with a political crisis on his hands, issued curt orders to
his captains in Scotland to lie as if dead.

Boredom was the great enemy among the French troops as well.
Depleted by the departure of Piero Strozzi and the rest recalled to
France, they were kept alive and fighting through the first part of the
winter by the Queen Mother's surgeons and the sale of her jewellery.
Then reinforcements and money arrived at last; and the problem
changed into one of directing the quarrelsome instincts of fifteen
hundred belligerent French towards the enemy and not to the
Scots. The country, ruled by Governor Arran in good Scots,
and by the Queen Dowager, the French Ambassador and General
d'Essé in their native French, became not bilingual but speechless,
and to hire a boat from Leith upriver at night, an interpreter was
essential.

In all this time, Crawford of Lymond devoted himself to refining
his professional skills to undue limits, to the affairs of his family, and
to keeping out of Sir William Scott's way, judging rightly that the
marriage so informally begun would best succeed if left to itself,
since a Scott, having got his bride pregnant, was apt to file her as
completed business for eight months at a time.

Then in the spring, when the Chevalier de Villegagnon arrived,
whose expert seamanship had taken the small Queen to France the

15

previous year, Thomas Erskine took him to see Francis Crawford at his brother's home of Midculter.

Instead, they saw the Dowager his mother. Sybilla, small, white-haired and timelessly chic, trailed thoughtfully into the great hall at Midculter where the two men were waiting and said, 'Dear Tom. How kind of you, M. de Villegagnon, to come and see Francis and how disappointed he will be, for you see both my sons are away. Richard is at Falkland with the Queen Mother and Francis. . . .'

Here the Dowager Lady Culter broke off and, rubbing her neck absently with a slender palm, said, 'But you must be seated instantly. Such an advantage of height must be *very* useful, M. de Villegagnon. And how is Margaret, Tom? And her mother in France? I'm afraid Francis is with Will Scott, dear, and likely to be gone all day,' finished Sybilla, her blue eyes owlishly on Master Tom.

Thomas Erskine at that time was a short, unremarkable man, whose chubby features concealed, as his neighbour well knew, one of the shrewdest negotiating brains in the hierarchy. Common sense was Tom Erskine's forte, and in his many diplomatic trips for the Scottish Crown he had made a number of friends, of whom Nicholas Durand, Chevalier de Villegagnon, was one. And at thirty-eight a brilliant exponent of arms and a knight of the great fighting and religious Order of St John, the Chevalier de Villegagnon had absolutely no use for common sense himself, but respected it in the laity.

Of such a militant lord of the Church, Sybilla was in no awe, but even Tom, least clairvoyant of men, noted that today she was having a little trouble covering her tracks. After two disingenuous guesses about Lymond's present whereabouts the Dowager finally gave way to subdued laughter and said, 'I'm sorry, Tom. But I think he and Will are at Hough Isa's.'

'Auhaizace?' said the Chevalier phonetically, in some confusion.

'It's a woman's daft name,' said Tom Erskine. 'She has a wee croft just out of Roxburgh.'

The Chevalier, topping Sybilla's largest chair, grinned unexpectedly. 'We may be under vows, my lady, but we are not unworldly. Isa: I know of her. Not all the ladies residing round Roxburgh and Lauder and even Ferniehurst have been reluctant prizes in the England forays. When the Roxburgh garrison emerges for a raid, there are a few houses in the district where they are made very welcome; is that not so? And this Isa's cottage is one?'

'That's right,' said Tom Erskine, removing his gaze reluctantly from Sybilla's face. 'They used to allow the country folk into the castle with eggs and meat and suchlike, until Hume Castle was taken by a trick of that sort, and now they let the men in only as far as the forecourt, and ban the women altogether. But not before they and the English garrison had become . . . acquainted. What's Francis doing there?' asked the Master of Erskine bluntly. M. de Ville-gagnon's eyebrows shot up.

'*Well*,' said Sybilla, taking her time. 'I'm very much afraid he's chastising the English. You see, if any Englishman serving in Rox-burgh actually felt homesick to the point of desertion, a friendly face and a roof nearby would be the first thing he'd want. So—'

'So Isa and her friends are helping English soldiers to desert?'

'They don't *help* them,' said Sybilla with dainty precision. 'They merely encourage the disaffection of their clients, and provide good advice and shelter to those who desert. Surprising numbers have gone, you know. Astonishing numbers, in fact.'

'With Francis behind the friendly ladies, I'm not surprised,' said Tom Erskine.

'And with Will Scott there as well, you can imagine,' said Sybilla calmly, 'that not all the English visiting Hough Isa survive the experience. They are not, to do them justice, all desperate to desert.'

'But when they do not come back, their fellow soldiers think they have. A most ingenious game,' said the Chevalier de Villegagnon. 'But not one which may continue for ever?'

'That's why Francis has gone,' the Dowager admitted. 'He thinks the English have begun to realize what is happening. Would you like him to call on you, Chevalier? He will return no doubt before long. He will find you at Leith?'

'Ah, but no,' said Nicholas Durand, Chevalier de Villegagnon, rising to his abnormal height and lifting his bonnet and cloak. 'I must meet him before then—I think at Hough Isa's.'

*

But it was Sir William Scott they met first, with a score of Kincurd men at Bonjedward, trotting cheerfully through green Teviotdale rehashing his last quarrel with Grizel. 'Use that word to the bairn's face and I'll clout ye!' Grizel Beaton had shouted.

There was no child—yet. He had said as much. 'Is there not!' had cried his bride. 'Is there not, Will Scott! And if it comes this night, what will I tell it, and its faither getting its kin in a bawdy-house?'

'Christ, I *told* ye why I had to go to Hough Isa's!' yelled Will Scott, his neck as red as his hair.

'Yes, you did,' agreed his lady. 'A matter of duty, ye said. And her cooking's rare.'

'Well it is! Better than the auld, done collops ye get at this table!'

'Then bring her home wi' ye, ye red-heided gomerel!' said Grizel Beaton, Lady (Younger) of Buccleuch. 'Would ye let us all starve? Doesna the Church tell us all, the act o' love is a sin, wanting a pur-pose?' There was a long, harassed pause. 'Or does she not like ye

17

enough?' Grizel had added and lumbered off, squealing with laughter as her husband chased her through to the solar. The odd ways of women were new to Will Scott, but some of them he was getting to like fine.

He was still thinking about it when he met Tom Erskine and his Chevalier friend, and they went on to Crailing together. At roughly the same moment, the English captain at Roxburgh fortress, six miles to the east of Hough Isa's, decided to pay the lady a visit.

It was a decision not entirely supported by the exiled English soldiery under his command. Those who still had voices with which to speak muttered. The rest wound and rewound the scarves round their jerkin collars and croaked. With each fresh command from the old man, their prospects for both tender friendships and a safe passage homewards to mother were dwindling. The captain had found out about Hough Isa and her friends. That is, the captain knew about Hough Isa already, but not about her specialized role *vis-à-vis* his vanishing garrison. And today the captain intended to act.

With a company of picked men therefore, about whose qualifications strange rumours were rife, Sir Ralph Bullmer with his cousin Sir Oliver Wyllstrop left the castle of Roxburgh and ventured into the enemy country around to visit the too-welcoming homes of single ladies of ample means.

The queen of these, Hough Isa, lived in a stone-built thatched house just outside the village of Crailing. Its windows, part board, were clean and neatly painted, her herb garden was trim, and her chimney place, with its blackened whinstone and its festive hooks and chains, smelt of good soup and mutton stew, witness to the fact that the local shepherds had hearty appetites and the means to satisfy them. There were fresh rushes on the floor of the kitchen, and in the next room a piece of painted carpet even, beside a double bed like a table, with the joiner's initials and Hough Isa's, though her English visitors did not know that, entwined on the headboard.

Nothing was entwined on the bed. The house was empty.

Sir Ralph Bullmer, seated aloof on his horse, ordered the residence to be burnt.

It was a bright, clear day in late spring, and the straw burned quickly, the smoke shadows trotting over the grass to their horses' hooves as they watched; the flames mere distortions of the blue air. A wave of anecdote went over the English troop as, scratching their necks and pushing back their helmets, they watched. They wondered, in an undertone, if The Bullock knew of the other two ladies who obliged, down Oxnam Water and the widow at Cessford village itself.

Sir Ralph Bullmer knew none of them, in the most congenial sense, but his military intelligence was so far adequate, at least. His pale, long-sighted gaze lifted to the road south beyond the cottage, and raising an arm, he waved his men past the crackling shell of Hough Isa's home and almost missed, so intent was his purpose, the fluttering movement of woe on the hilltop beyond. Then a woman's scream, blunted mercifully by distance, repeated itself like a seagull and there, on the rising ground behind the friendly Isobel's house, was Hough Isa herself, haloed in sunshine, her scarlet pattens sunk in the turf and her striped skirts tied up to her calves, shaking an arm like a rolling pin over the English soldiers below.

Nor was she alone. On one side, the ladies of Oxnam shouted curses, their mouths pale cavities inside red, painted lips. On the other, the lady of Cessford flung a stone. And behind, jumping and shrieking, were surely the comeliest lassies of Bonjedworth and Ancrum, Lanton and Bedrule, their bosoms veiled in sunlight but their voices unsheathed. What among the English had been disjointed talk turned instantly into babble. Sir Ralph Bullmer and his cousin shouted into it, silenced it, and wheeling, led their troops up the hill.

For a moment longer, the furious figures at the top skirled defiance; then they clung together, gown to gown, like silenced bells as the drumming hoofbeats approached. Then someone knelt; others sprang aside; some broke away and vanished altogether beyond the rise of the hill.

Useless panic, for where could they go? What farmer, in the shadow of Roxburgh, would defy the English and take them in? What farmer's wife would succour the flesh with whom she and her husband were three?

Sir Ralph Bullmer said to Sir Oliver Wyllstrop, 'Why d'you think they were met at Hough Isa's, Olly?'

Sir Oliver, trotting on, shook his head. 'If you ask the men to shoot, I fear they won't obey.'

In armour, no one can shrug, but the captain of Roxburgh castle laughed hollowly inside his helmet. 'So long as they die, I'm not going to watch how they do it.' An unoiled joint at his knee began to sob and he swore sulkily. There was a very sweet armful indeed, like a young cornfield in sunlit green silk, standing alone on one side of the hilltop, her pale face bathed in run mascara and tears. In the same moment she must have seen Sir Ralph too. She hesitated, turned to run, and then instead, trembling like a driven ship with her buffeting robes, stretched out a supplicating arm.

Five cannon, hitherto concealed on the hillside by heaped grass and Hough Isa's petticoats, fired promptly as one, blowing four hundred pounds of stone shot like an open hopper downhill through the packed men and horses of the English garrison of Roxburgh, killing one third outright with their eyes glistening still. Then, as the falcons' thunder deadened the ears, the tatters of Sir Ralph Bullmer's force saw the smoke lift and several kneeling ladies, their headgear knocked awry, touch a match to their hackbuts and fire. To one side of the guns, a broad-built wench with a beard let off a crossbow, and from just behind her a flock of arrows arched through smoke and shot and fell, thinly slitting, among the petrified troops. Then the five falcons fired again, and those English who could, ran like stoats.

Sir Ralph Bullmer, from pride and a burst girth strap, was the last to go. Bleeding from a scratch on his cheek, he recovered as the slipped saddle fell, kicked it free and bareback hugged his horse with his thighs and turned its head.

A light hand on his arm stopped him short. Below, her floating gown filthy, the girl of the hilltop beseeched him, her eyes anxious cisterns of blue. For the merest second, Sir Ralph Bullmer studied her. Her hands were empty and her thin dress innocent of weapons. 'All right. You'll tell me what it's all about, or I'll know why,' said Sir Ralph Bullmer hastily, and swung her behind him.

The horse careered down the hillside after his men. From behind, the arrows still fell although the firing had stopped. For the moment, it seemed, no one pursued. The girl behind him laid her cheek on his neck and began unlacing his armour. He knocked her hand away and then grabbed his reins as the horse danced, nearly out of control. The fingers stole round again. His cuirass was half off. The more intelligent of his men had slowed a little and turned to await him; still there seemed to be no pursuit.

He knocked the girl's hand away again and kicked out behind with his mailed foot, then floundered as, saddleless, he nearly lost his own seat. Melting behind him, the girl's limbs were untouched. She unfastened all the straps round his middle and undid his shirt; his swipe met thin air. Inward to his sweating body ran streams of cold air, through all the loosened flanges of plate metal. Clanking cuirass on thigh-piece, Sir Ralph Bullmer on his horse flew across the gentle valley of Teviot like a well-plenished tinker's curse, and did not know until he pulled up, dismounted, and his breeches fell down, that there was no one behind him by then.

Soon after that, a half-naked gentleman in breech hose knocked at a door in Upper Nisbet, requisitioned a jerkin and a pony with great charm, and went whistling on his way to Jedburgh, where by arrangement a second cousin of Will Scott's was to look after the homeless Hough Isa and shelter the ambushing marksmen, if need be, on the first stage of their journey back home.

Not long after Bullmer with his survivors had got back to the English fortress at Roxburgh, Will Scott and his men arrived at the tall wooden house of his cousin, peeled off their kirtles and bonnets and crowded into the kitchen where already Hough Isa and her two genuine friends were at the cooking pots. Then, having settled his men, Sir William dressed in his own clothes and took his two unlooked-for observers, Thomas Master of Erskine and Nicholas Durand de Villegagnon, upstairs to the small room to talk.

They spoke in French. It was not that the Chevalier's English was lacking, but simply that he mistrusted, that day, what he heard. That a Roxburgh deserter had warned Will Scott of the impending English raid on the ladies—that he understood. That this might be made an excuse to ambush the garrison—this again was clear. Wise also to have the five cannon dragged from Jedburgh—instant annihilation of superior numbers was thus made quite possible. And certainly, the sight of the ladies had brought the Englishmen half up the hill and within easy range, while the falcons were hidden by skirts. But, the Chevalier de Villegagnon had pointed out, they had been unable to ride pursuing the English, had not even tried to conceal mounted men behind that small hill, who could sweep over and kill...?

'Aye,' had said Will Scott on the battlefield, as they loaded the English wounded in carts and searched the dead for their money and weapons. 'Well, ye see, I got orders from the old Queen not to meddle. If I lost a man through defending a whore, she said she'd see me in jail for a year. So I made sure when the English came on,' said Will Scott simply, 'that my lads'd be after better sport than killing.'

'And what will the Queen Dowager say,' said Tom Erskine drily, 'if Crawford of Lymond is lost?'

'He'll be back at Jedburgh to meet us, you'll see,' said Scott a little quickly. And the Chevalier de Villegagnon, shrewdly observing, chose that moment to say, 'Will it please you to speak French?' and added rapidly, 'I understood on joining you that M. of Lymond had left the ambush altogether?'

Tom Erskine answered. 'He was in front with the ladies. He gave the signal to fire.'

'But he has not returned? Which was he?'

'The one in green that rode off with Ralph Bullmer,' said Will Scott; and without waiting for Tom's smooth translation added, 'And if Ralph Bullmer's still alive to tell of it, I'll wager he'd rather he wasn't.'

They were at their soup when Lymond arrived. A voice cut through the uproar below and Will Scott missed his mouth and got to his feet dripping; then sat down and wiped off his chin. Then the door opened on the tenuous girl in the green dress, now in staid brown hose under a tunic, the blond hair visibly short.

He was carrying a bowl of soup. As he kicked shut the door to the stairs, Scott spoke with reverberating gusto. 'Francis! What in God's name have you done with Sir Ralph?'

'Bullmer?' The voice was pleasant, the air one of mild surprise.

21

'I undressed him, I believe. Cousin Olly had a grin like a viaduct.' Francis Crawford laid down his soup and, without sitting, said to de Villegagnon, 'What would you have done, sir?'

M. de Villegagnon, Knight of the Order of St John, answered in French, one meaty shoulder negligently to the wall. 'Was Monsieur armed?' he asked.

'No.' Lymond used the same tongue. 'Or the captain would not have admitted me to his horse.'

There was a pause. 'Where there is a simple man,' said the Chevalier thoughtfully, 'the apt punishment is sometimes not death but shame.'

Cleansed of paint, Lymond's fair-skinned face was mildly forbearing. 'It is understood. We preferred not to expose those foresworn fools living round Roxburgh to the kind of retribution London would make if their captain were killed. Instead, we made a fool of him.'

'But Sir Ralph Bullmer, from what I hear, is not a fool.' M. de Villegagnon could flatter as well.

'Luckily, or he would have charged us. As it was, Nell of Cessford was the only person they hurt—'

'They killed her,' broke in Tom Erskine bluntly.

The eyes of the man Lymond and Sir William Scott met. Lymond said nothing. M. de Villegagnon, watching, saw the young knight flush; then Erskine, who in his own country preferred forthrightness to finesse said, 'She was a Kerr. Francis told you not to let Hough Isa bring her.'

Will Scott said angrily, 'Will the Kerrs take revenge for their whores as well?'

'Let us hope,' said Lymond, 'that they will look on you as her would-be protector, and that Grizel never hears of it with a blunt instrument to hand. If someone would introduce me to M. de Villegagnon I could sit down....'

*

Late that night with Tom Erskine (they drew spills for it) quietly asleep on the camp bed, and Will Scott's red head buried in his saddle while his soft palate buzzed and rattled with his dreams, Nicholas Durand de Villegagnon rose, and crossing the small crowded room the four shared, noiselessly paused at the hearth. In the glimmering red of the fire, the only light in the room, his height seemed inhuman, his bulk measureless, his silence uncanny, like the nesting owl with raked eyeballs pat to her claws. 'This play acting today, it entertains you?' he said.

In the depths of the carved chair where he had chosen to sleep,

Lymond's breathing did not change, nor in the toneless flood of red light did his face alter. He said briefly, 'It served its purpose. We are not all children of destiny.'

The solid body of the French knight was motionless also. 'I have heard a man whose lover has been killed speak like that,' he said.

Lymond's voice repeated drily, 'A *man*?' and in the buried red light, the Chevalier's face creased, as if he smiled. 'Perhaps not,' he said. 'But my premise remains. Not for all of us, the common dynastic toil. You, for example, have all the comfort you need at home and need seek no gentler company.'

'I am a great respecter of comfort,' said Lymond, and at the edge on his voice the Chevalier began to be satisfied. 'I meant merely,' he said, speaking always softly, 'that having none of the duties of an older brother, I saw a noble future before you at the Queen Dowager's side.'

'. . . And men of religion are not,' stated Lymond, as if he had not spoken. 'Furthermore, at each of the Queen Dowager's many sides, she already has a brother de Guise.'

Beside Lymond's chair stood a rush stool, warm from the fire. De Villegagnon bent and sat on it, his broad back to the dark room, and began at leisure to untie his fine shirt. He said, 'I know, of course, that a good many Scotsmen fear to become provincials of France. The Queen Dowager is not the Regent for her daughter, and yet she and the French Ambassador seem to make all the decisions that matter. Also, she and the King of France are of the Old Religion, and those of you who lean towards the reformed church would deliver Scotland to her old enemy England, with earth and stone and the clappers of her mills, rather than risk religious martyrdom with France.'

'You flatter us,' said Francis Crawford; and leaning forward to grasp the long poker, lifted the structure of the fire. Heat and light, silently refreshed, enveloped them both. Lymond, sinking back in his place, was smiling. He said, 'If you look, you may find Crusading consciences here, but not among the families that count. The Douglases and the Kerrs and the rest favour England because their land is near the Border and open to English attack, or else because under English rule they might have a chance of second-hand power.'

'And the Crawfords?' asked the Frenchman.

There was a second's pause. 'My brother, like Tom Erskine there, and the Scotts, happens to believe that until she has a strong Crown of her own, this nation will recover as well under French supervision as any other. We are too weak in manpower to be independent, even if our ruling families could combine and agree. And we are too poor to employ mercenary soldiers. France, after all, who can pay, puts the finest engineers and fortification experts, the best soldiers and seamen'—Lymond bowed gravely to the seated Chevalier—'at our disposal for nothing, along with the money to pay them.'

'And you?' asked de Villegagnon at last. 'If the Turk offered to protect Scotland on the same or better terms, would you accept them?'

The other man looked up, amused. 'We *have* accepted them, have we not?' And as de Villegagnon, caught unawares, was momentarily silent, for the secret alliance between France and the Commander of the Faithful was not yet common knowledge, Lymond went on murmuring. 'Tell me: as Knights of St John who are also honoured servants of the kingdom of France—do you and Leone Strozzi, for example, fail to find this alliance between France and Turkey troublesome? Or do you have all the comforts you need at Fontainebleau?'

The ensuing silence was abrupt. Then the Chevalier de Villegagnon, always in an undertone, gave a laugh. 'A hit. My answer is that the Franco-Turkish alliance is a paper one, to preserve France from the threat of the Emperor Charles V. The Knights of Malta are international. Whatever their allegiance by birth, their first duty is to Malta and the Bishop of Rome. We have all taken the same vows, soldiers and priests, of chastity, poverty and obedience, and have dedicated ourselves to the victory of the Christian world over the infidel.'

'To fight with a pure mind for the supreme and true King,' quoted Lymond. It was impossible to tell what he thought.

'If I made you leader today of fifteen hundred mercenaries, for whom or for what would you fight?' asked the Chevalier de Villegagnon suddenly. He was ready to wait for his answer. He only became slowly aware that the man in the chair was shaking with silent laughter.

'Not another! By the Blessed Gerard, father of the poor and the pilgrims, not another!' said Francis Crawford on a shattered breath. 'Is Europe desperate for second-hand captains, direct from the fripperers, that every courier seems bent on seducing me with a new-matched set of ethics? . . . If I had fifteen hundred soldiers, and tried to use them either for or against the Queen Mother, there would be civil war in Scotland in a week, and no Scots left to talk of it in another.'

'Then you must needs use them elsewhere,' said the Chevalier blandly. 'You are not a fledgeling. Where does your manhood suggest?'

'My manhood suggests,' said Lymond thoughtfully, 'that I should like to meet Sir Graham Reid Malett's sister Joleta, but not necessarily with fifteen hundred mercenary soldiers at my back.'

For a long moment, the knight stared at the Scotsman. In the end, slowly he rose, pulled off his creased shirt and stood dangling it, rosy-lit with the fire. 'Yes,' he said. 'Yes, my good sir. What you require in this life is a meeting with Gabriel and his sister.' And strolling off, he rolled himself in a cloak, settled into a corner, and in five minutes was asleep.

*

The house was quite still and the fire had gone out when Dandy Kerr of the Hirsell and twenty men hammered down the steep cobbles of Jedburgh and erupted into the lower room of Will Scott's cousin's house, to avenge the exposure to fatality if not shame of Nell of Cessford on the hill above Crailing.

They jumped off their horses as the town watch came running, broke the door and strode among the recumbent bodies, slashing and stabbing for some time before they noticed that these were merely bran sacks. Attempting then to run upstairs, they met sweet as a kiss with a torrent of Scotts, sword in hand, coming down. In the midst of them, yelling as loud as the rest, were Sir William Scott, Francis Crawford, Thomas Erskine and the Chevalier de Villegagnon.

The rout was spectacular, all the way uphill past the Abbey and out on to the glades and moors and little hills that rolled between Jedburgh and Cessford. At the ford across Oxnam Water, with the trees thick with summer life on either high bank, the remaining Kerrs turned at bay, and in the ensuing water battle, with peach-coloured mud up to the hocks, the horses splashed and drenched the mounted and the fallen, birds called and roe-deer fled, and swords rose and fell merrily until Dandy Kerr and his men, disengaging finally, shot off to Cessford Castle with the larger part of his company intact, which was more than could be said of his stock.

Lymond, grabbing Will Scott's arm in a hurry, prevented pursuit. 'Dammit, remember. We're supposed to be the injured party. I told you Peter Cranston would warn us to avoid an offence to the Almighty in spilling blood on a prostitute's grave.'

'The small gentleman with the wounded shoulder?' asked M. de Villegagnon sympathetically.

Tom Erskine answered, breathless with laughter. 'Francis asked him to stand watch this evening on the Cessford road, and he's very anxious to save Francis from sin.'

'A risk which does not unduly trouble M. Crawford himself,' said the Chevalier pointedly. 'He regards boredom, I observe, as the One and Mighty Enemy of his soul. And will succeed in conquering it, I am sure—if he survives the experience.'

III

Joleta

(Flaw Valleys, May 1551)

ALMOST two years had passed, and peace had been declared between England and Scotland, before the Chevalier de Ville-gagnon met a Crawford again.

For part of this period, Francis Crawford of Lymond had been living in France, repelling boredom with considerable success among those serving the child Queen Mary of Scotland at the French Court. He was there while the Queen Dowager of Scotland came to visit her daughter; and he was still there when his brother Richard, Lord Culter, came to serve the child Queen in his turn, and thankfully, in due course, left the French Court once more for home.

Boats for Scotland, in these days of brisk piracy, of offended Flemings and outraged English and well-armed Spaniards, were not frequent or cheap. At Dieppe, Lord Culter, a quiet but effective traveller, made a number of calls, and then sat back and played back-gammon until word reached him, one day at his inn, that a French galley was leaving for Scotland that night.

In half an hour, Richard had established that, as a royal ship of the King of France's fleet, the galley would take no paid passengers; that the master was not averse to money; that the decision to accom-modate one of the Scottish Queen Dowager's Councillors rested with a certain royal official now lodging with the Governor at Dieppe Castle; and that this officer's name was Nicholas Durand, Chevalier de Villegagnon. In an hour, neatly turned out in brown cloth and gold satin, Lord Culter presented himself at the castle of Dieppe.

The reunion was a civilized one. M. de Villegagnon, whose vows of poverty were elastic, wore a triangular jacket frilled at neck and cuff, to which were appended vast sleeves layered like cabbages. Richard, entering the private parlour set aside for the Chevalier by his host, became aware of a level of grandeur which had been present, but not obtrusive, in the cold harassed ditches outside Haddington. Several gentlemen in attendance and two pages in the Chevalier's livery rose as he entered. Further, beyond the Chevalier's portable prie-dieu, two nuns and an older lady in plain clothes collected their skirts, rose and curtseyed. M. de Villegagnon introduced one of the gentlemen as his secretary and another as his priest, and the elderly lady by name without any explanation at all. Then Richard, who knew when it paid best to be direct, broached his need of transport to Scotland, and consequent interest in the Chevalier's galley tied up at the quay.

In the old-fashioned room, hung with mementoes of Dieppois voyages, there was a busy silence, filled by M. de Villegagnon repeating the question to gain time. His eyes, Lord Culter observed, rested on the calm face of the old lady. She, apparently unaware of this, continued with a piece of fine sewing. Only, without looking up, she said, 'Mademoiselle would be the better of an escort, I believe.'

To live without property and to guard my chastity, thought Richard, and kept his face grave. M. de Villegagnon, however, smiled and said, 'Forgive me, my lord. The ship you speak of is about to convey to Scotland a special charge of mine, a young lady who has been placed in my care. Being convent-bred and very young, she is unused to strangers, which is why I hesitated to mention her name. But if Madame Donati is satisfied. . . .'

The old lady with the sewing, raising her powderless face, nodded her old-fashioned headdress and stared at Lord Culter.

'Then I think we might ask Mlle Joleta to give you leave.'

'She is at her prayers,' said one of the nuns breathlessly.

'I shall fetch her,' said the other; and with a heaving of black skirts she left.

'Joleta,' thought Richard. 'Where have I heard . . . ?'

Then she was in the room, and his mouth opened just a little, and stayed open. 'Joleta,' said the Chevalier de Villegagnon comfortably, watching him. 'Mistress Joleta Malett, sister of Sir Graham Reid Malett, Knight of St John of Jerusalem and my most famous friend of the Order in Malta.'

Madame Donati, who had risen, walked round and took the girl's hand. 'Gabriel's sister,' she said.

Joleta Reid Malett of the apricot hair was then just sixteen. Lord Culter never knew what she wore. The robe fell from childish white wrists, hazy with freckles, and veiled all her small bones from neck to floor. Above and over it, smooth as silk floss, the shining apricot hair fell back from the matt skin, flushed and speckled with sun. He saw her white teeth, exposed unconsciously like a child's below the soft upper lip, and her eyes, white-lashed aquamarine, filling her face. Then, because he was near suffocation, Richard Crawford, insufflating mournfully, refilled his lungs. Flushing, he caught de Villegagnon's eye, and then found it in him to smile. He was staid, intelligent, and not overlong married to a ravishing wife; but Joleta Malett would always stop your breath for a moment, unless you were blind.

27

Her voice was clear: firm-jawed like an adult's, and sparkling with small, over-careful sibilants. She said, 'This is the Master of Erskine?'

'No, Mademoiselle,' said Madame Donati, still holding her hand. 'This is another gentleman from Scotland, come to ask the Chevalier's permission to travel on your ship. His lordship of Culter . . . Mistress Joleta Reid Malett.'

Her hand was warm, with oval fingernails. He kissed it, and a vivid pleasure at once appeared in her face, followed by, he could have sworn, a flash of pure mischief. 'I told Gabriel about Lord Culter and his brother Francis,' said de Villegagnon from beside them. 'I think you would enjoy his company on the voyage, and I know he will enjoy yours. He has a new son to talk about.'

'A baby?' She sat down, studiously maternal, and said, 'How splendid it is to be surrounded by young life. I had a baby to look after once, at the convent, and Maltese babies are very happy-natured, although of course they do neglect their eyes. Do you have a kind nurse for yours? Perhaps your wife's own nurse? What is his name?'

The young, freckled face was completely solemn. With the echoes dimly in his ears of a hundred such exchanges with the old beldames of Lanarkshire, Richard Crawford said with equal gravity, 'His name is Kevin, Mademoiselle. Kevin Crawford, Master of Culter.'

'Your younger brother then no longer bears that title?' de Ville-gagnon asked.

'No. It is for the heir alone,' said Richard. And after a moment he added, for Joleta's benefit, 'But under the circumstances, luckily for me, my brother Francis does not mind losing it. You must meet him,' said Richard unguardedly, and then held his tongue. Francis, with his temper, his mistresses, his plunges into drunken adventuring, was alien to this kind of fun-loving innocence. For humanity's sake, indeed, it was worth making quite an effort to keep these two apart.

*

On that midsummer voyage to Scotland with Joleta and Madame Donati, Lord Culter confirmed that Gabriel's exquisite young sister was both quick and articulate. Every day, she and her governess ate with Richard and the captain, and then, clinging to poop and rambade, her mandarin hair flung like gauze to the wind, she would devise conundrums and riddles, puns and tales of fantasy to divert them both, which made Richard out of all character laugh aloud, while behind them, bench on bench, the rowers ravenously watched.

Evangelista Donati he also got to know. An Italian lady of unquestionable birth, Madame Donati had made her home on Malta for many years and had shared with the nuns of Joleta's convent the task of rearing the parentless child. Without resources of her own, she had been well paid for it, Richard assumed, by the girl's brother.

Of Sir Graham Malett himself, Madame Donati spoke sparingly and with embarrassing reverence. Like all fighting men, Richard Crawford respected the Knights of St John, the soldiers of Christ who cared for the poor and the sick in Palestine, four hundred years before, and protected the pilgrims against the Saracen on their way to the Holy Land. To fight the Saracen and care for the sick remained the essence of the Order, even after Jerusalem fell and Acre was lost; and instead of defending the Holy Land the knights found themselves pushed into the isles of the Mediterranean, taking their hospital and their fighting men to Cyprus, then to Rhodes, and now to the island of Malta, halfway between Gibraltar and Cyprus, in the Mediterranean Sea.

Twenty-one years ago, the Order had received the gift of Malta from the Emperor Charles V, 'in order that they might perform in peace the duties of their Religion for the benefit of the Christian community, and employ their forces and arms against the perfidious enemies of Holy Faith'. And so, men of all nations took their vows and went where in prayer and humility the Knights of the Order lived, nursed the poor and sick in their great hospital and fought to sweep the Turk out of the Mediterranean Sea and off the coast of North Africa.

From a land force, theirs became the finest sea-fighting school in the world. And from these medical knights, these pirate knights, these priestly knights with their holy vows and monastic seclusion on the sandstone rocks of Malta under the hot African sun, there came men like the Chevalier de Villegagnon, like Leone Strozzi, and like the knight Graham Malett, or Gabriel, Joleta's brother.

Gabriel, Joleta's brother, who after all these years was sending Joleta home to Scotland. 'Home?' said Madame Donati sardonically. 'The child's home is in Malta, in the sun. But he fears for her. There are always rumours, that this time the Turks will attack Malta, and that their fleet is so large, their Janissaries so ruthless, Dragut so invincible. . . .'

'Dragut is only a man,' Joleta had broken in swiftly. 'A Moslem corsair in the pay of the Turk. How could the knights, with their Faith behind them, fail to conquer?'

'Dragut is a seaman to match any in the Order,' said Richard drily. 'Your brother is wise to send you home.'

'Except that she has no home,' retorted Madame Donati, her faded eyebrows pushing up the thin, sallow skin. 'As you must know very well, Sir Graham's home near the Scottish Border was destroyed during the English wars, his lands wasted and his tenants dispersed. He has no possessions at all except what is allowed him through the

Treasury at Malta, and his jewels. He sold them to send Joleta here.'

And to pay you, thought Richard. He knew the rest of the story. The girl was to go to Sir James Sandilands, the head of the Order in Scotland. At his home in Torphichen she would rest from her journey before being placed, with the Order's powerful backing, in the best convent for her years. Madame Donati, staying with her, would continue to instruct in the gentle arts; and when the danger was over, Gabriel would come for her.

Richard, hearing these plans, had said nothing because he was nearly certain that Sandilands of Torphichen, lazy, rich-living and slipshod in faith, was the last person a Knight Hospitaller of St John of Jerusalem would wish to trust with the care of a young and malleable girl. Because he was conscientious, it worried Richard a great deal, for he was very aware that in the person of the child, small-boned as a bat against the east wind, he was bringing Pandora's box of vexing delights to his country, and he did not want to take the obvious course. He did not want Joleta Malett at his mother's home of Midculter, in case Francis came back.

Then the matter was taken out of his hands, for the fine weather broke, the wind rose, Madame Donati took to her bed, and the next day the child Joleta, unaffected by storms, who had stayed on deck as the gale blew and chanted Arab ballads until her dancing shadow crept up the sail, fell herself suddenly and inexplicably ill.

They were then off the north-east English coast, opposite Blyth. The captain needed little persuasion to land; and Richard, using all his authority, commandeered food, medicine and horses, and on being assured that the girl could manage a brief journey with safety, carried Joleta and her wan duenna to the nearest family he knew: the Somervilles of Flaw Valleys.

*

The Tyneside manor of Flaw Valleys lay on the English side of the Border, a mile or two north of Hexham. Since the war between England and Scotland had ended, Flaw Valleys and its owner Kate Somerville had welcomed many Scottish visitors, of whom Tom Erskine and the brothers Crawford of Culter were the most frequent. It was a strange friendship, grown out of fear and outrage during the war, when her husband Gideon was alive and these men had invaded her home. Long since she had grown to understand and forgive what they had done; but to her daughter Philippa, now a thin, brown-haired thirteen, Kate had never been able to explain the attraction of these two various-minded brothers. Since she was a child of ten, Philippa had been frightened of Richard Crawford and had hated his brother Lymond.

Nevertheless it was to Flaw Valleys, the kindly, unpretentious big house with its tidy farms and kept woodlands, that Lord Culter on a hot day in May brought Joleta Reid Malett and her governess to claim Mistress Somerville's charity. Mistress Somerville saw them come.

Since her husband's death two years before, Kate with her man of business and her excellent farm steward had run her own property. Not that the Somervilles were rich; but up and down Tyneside were farms and mills and cottages paying dues to Flaw Valleys, and in return receiving from Kate the services of her roadmakers, her wheelwrights and her smiths, her granaries in time of need and her shelter in time of war. No more than turned thirty yet, small, sharp-tongued and plain as a brown hen, Kate Somerville was priestess and nanny at once to her people, and a legend to her friends.

At the approach of the most beautiful creature in Europe, the mistress of Flaw Valleys was straddling her farmhouse wall, whither she had climbed to address a passer-by, a weeding-fork in one fist and a hog's yoke, on its way to the yard to be returned condemned to the maker, round her sun-browned neck.

Observing the Crawford colours through the trees, she waved the weeding-fork, called to Philippa to warn the cooks and hopped down, dragging off the hog yoke. Her hair mostly unfolded with it, so she stuck the fork in the ground and was packing her coiffure into its snood again, elbows akimbo, as the group of travellers trotted up.

It was Richard. She smiled widely none the less and held up her face for his kiss; then turned warmly to the two women whose presence he was explaining so earnestly. The older, a cool, Italian noblewoman labouring under some slight stress, offered a cold hand. The other, wrapped in Richard's cloak from head to foot, was being carried with great caution by Richard's mammoth manservant as if she were about to brim over.

This one, according to Richard, was suffering merely from the changed food and climate. 'Would you take her, Kate, just for a little—and Madame Donati? I have to go on to Midculter, but I'll send for them as soon as she's well. Joleta!' He raised his voice a little, and Kate thought, 'Paternity suits him, although it seems to have burst into full blossom rather soon.'

'Joleta!' said Richard again. 'Here is Kate Somerville. She'll look after you.' And as the bundle in his man's arms drew level, he reached out and gently turned back its hood so that Kate had her first good look at the contents.

A flood of rose-gold hair lay heaped over the wool, and within it two sea-blue eyes, bright with heat, lit a face disarmingly tinged with green. It smiled. Kate, finding her mouth slightly open, shut it again;

31

and then grinned and said, 'Excuse the bovine admiration. We consider ourselves lucky in these regions if there's an eye on either side of the nose, and a mouth underneath it.'

Joleta's voice, which had become very light, said, 'You forget. I belong to these parts. Or very near them.'

'You do?' Kate Somerville said. 'Then they either broke the mould, or gave it to someone to chew. Come along. You can have the Crawfords' room. The house is yours.' And Richard knew that, whatever her manner of saying it, she meant precisely that.

'Well,' said Kate to her daughter when at the end of that first day they were alone together at last, with Richard on his way home and the governess asleep in her charge's room. 'And what do you think of God's gift from Malta to the Crawfords?'

'I think Lord Culter doesn't want her at his own home,' said Philippa with accustomed unexpectedness.

Kate, thinking of six possible answers at once, said, 'Well, she can't go to Jimmy Sandilands, can she? He wouldn't have her anyway: she'd tell her brother far too much about what his lordship's doing with the Order's property in Scotland. And where else *can* she . . . ?'

'Lord Culter's mother may want her,' said Philippa. 'Even though his lordship doesn't. Or she could go to Tom Erskine's.' She waited, and said, 'You think Lymond will come back from France soon, don't you? I don't think it matters. Joleta will hate him.'

'Oh, *Philippa*,' said Kate, annoyed. 'He forgot his party manners once, when you were a child, and you'd think he was Beelzebub's brother. They'll get on perfectly well when they meet. Besides, he has someone he fancies in France.'

Incautious answer. It was only because it was running in her head —Francis and an Irishwoman, Richard had said: a woman called Oonagh O'Dwyer who had been mistress of some Irish princeling, and whom Francis had filched from her lover. Oonagh O'Dwyer, and beautiful. . . .

'*Someone!*' said Philippa hoarsely. 'Why, everywhere he goes he has hundreds and hundreds of—'

'—critics who are not old enough to learn tolerance. Oh, do learn tolerance, infant,' said Kate sadly. 'Or how are you to put up with your cross old mother when you're as old as me?'

For a day or two after that, Joleta Malett lay perfectly still, eating whatever she was brought and discarding it instantly. Only Madame Donati, brewing little morsels over the bedroom fire, seemed able to nourish her at all; and Joleta was happy, obviously, when her governess was there, although she managed a few words always for Kate, and a shadow of a grin for Philippa. Then Evangelista Donati, her impervious good manners unaffected by day and night nursing

32

in the first heat of June, came to Kate and asked if she knew of any woman in the district versed in herbal remedies.

'They all are,' said Kate with the utmost goodwill. 'Although if you want one of the real fewmets-in-rosewater school, the half-Egyptians are best. But really,' she said, studying the pale, aristocratic face, 'my own physician knows better. You still won't let me send for him?'

But, as always when pressed, Madame Donati retreated into icy politeness. 'Thank you, no. It is nothing. It will pass. If it does not, then we shall send for him. But Sir Graham has a superstition, you understand?' Across the wintry face passed a slight smile. 'Sir Graham does not care that the child should be seen by men. And she does not wish it. An instinct of innocence, Mistress Somerville.'

'Still,' said Kate, 'it won't do her much good to perish, however modestly unsurveyed. What do you suppose a herb woman can do?'

It was logical enough, in its way. Joleta's system, the governess explained, was used to Maltese remedies: the old brews common to nomads which even her convent, in all its medical sophistication, had allowed. And these a member of the queer sisterhood of gypsies might well know. 'Oh, dear,' said Kate finally. 'I suppose we'd better get Trotty Luckup.' She paused. 'She'll have to travel from Yetholm, and she's an old gypsy rogue. You'll have to pay her quite a lot.'

Donna Donati smiled, and with one cool hand took the liberty of straightening Kate's half-attached sleeve. 'I have dealt with many rogues in my years,' she said. 'Do not concern yourself.'

The widow Luckup arrived two days later on muleback, stayed the night with Joleta, and went back the next day without grumbling, accompanied, as Kate later found, by three silver plates and a pair of her dead husband's thick woolly breeches; which alone in her room she wept over, ridiculously, before blowing her nose and sailing forth to see how Joleta did.

Joleta, blessedly burning with new life, had eaten her first light meal for a week and was sitting propped up by her pillows, running her fingers over Kate's lute and singing, absurdly, the extemporized praises of Trotty. Richard had been right. Quiet and sick and very young, the vein had not shown. But the girl in her own right, and apart from the heavenly gift of her looks, was a person of character.

As the days of recovery went by, Philippa, at Kate's wish, spent a good deal of time with Joleta. Abrupt, forthright as her mother without, just yet, her mother's saving grace of humility and wit, Philippa sat at a loss and studied the other girl like a farm labourer at a flower show, while Joleta Reid Malett, whose courage was of the order of her brother's and whose self-discipline, on occasion, went far beyond her years, willed herself better, rose, walked, dressed and moved to the garden, sang, played and indulged in a ferocious gift of

33

mimicry, talking to all and everyone she met, from the kitchen boy to Kate's stubborn steward, and lit Flaw Valleys as with Mediterranean sunlight from within.

To Philippa she told a little of her quiet life on Malta, but otherwise spoke rarely of herself. It was Philippa she was eager to know about; Philippa's father and the war against the Scots; the coming of Tom Erskine to their door for the first time; and Lymond.

She asked Philippa directly, at last, why she disliked Lord Culter's younger brother and Philippa, hot-cheeked under three years' silence, told of the wartime raid when Lymond had broken into the house and had questioned her, a child of ten, against her parents' wishes. The long room; Gideon, whitefaced, begging the stranger to leave the child alone; and Kate hugging her on her knees, her cheeks wet with tears.

'But your parents overlooked it, didn't they?' said Joleta in her sane, friendly voice. 'And you aren't enemies now.' They were brushing each other's hair, Joleta's firm fingers dragging the brush swiftly and effectively over and over through Philippa's insignificant locks. Her own, in a single shining fall, reached to her hips over her robe; and her robe fell, as it should, over the soft rises of her young body. Philippa, flat as a kipper in front, said savagely, 'What's it matter? He could browbeat a child, whatever the motive. And he lives like a hog. I hate him.' And to her own horror, Philippa broke into tears.

Joleta's warm arms enfolded her, and Joleta's freckled cheek pressed against her own. 'Pippa, listen,' said the clear voice in her ear. 'Middle-aged ladies often imagine they have fallen in love. It doesn't mean anything. Your mother is very sensible, you know.'

Philippa Somerville's head jerked back, then her body, as she forced herself from Joleta's gentle clasp. Then, stuffing a not overclean hand into her mouth, Kate's daughter fled from the room.

She and Joleta continued to meet and talk after that, but never again lapsed into the topic of Kate's private affections. Nor, to do Joleta justice, did she give the matter more than a passing, fanciful thought. It was Philippa who could not bear to have her mind read.

*

Kate was relieved of her guests, in the end, by Tom Erskine himself, on his way back from weeks of negotiating the final terms of the peace treaty between Scotland and England at Norham.

Although he could not be said to understand Sybilla, Dowager Lady Culter and her two sons, Tom Erskine was haplessly fond of them all. And on receiving Lord Culter's request that he should return via Flaw Valleys and escort the recovered Joleta and her governess to the Culter home at Midculter castle, he had no trouble in imagining the arguments that polite request had provoked.

In strict fact, there had been the nearest thing to outright battle that had ever occurred at the Culters'. Richard had said, receiving a cramped and colourless note from Madame Donati, 'That Malta girl is better again.'

'Well?' had said his mother unhelpfully, while his wife, straightening out a smile, bent over her sewing.

'Where's she to go? Have you got her into a convent?'

'Why, is she entering religion?' had inquired Sybilla, her blue eyes amazed.

Richard had paused for a fresh breath. 'She has to stay somewhere until her brother comes for her. Do you want him to find we've put her into Sandilands's care, knowing what he's like?'

'Well then, she'd better come here, hadn't she?' said the Dowager absently, picking up some silks Mariotta had dropped. Her daughter-in-law shot her a swift look and bent again to her task. Experience with the Scottish family she had married into at least had taught her when to keep quiet.

'Mariotta has the child. To ask her to look after another—'

'Mariotta sees her son just as often as you do, and no more; and quite right too, with the best wet-nurse in Lanarkshire looking after him. In any case, I gather the girl is sixteen, not six months, and your real concern is in case we open a brothel?'

'*Mother*!' said Lord Culter and went scarlet, something only Sybilla could have achieved. His wife, in appalled ecstasy, dropped her sewing and gazed at them both, her hands over her mouth. Sybilla herself, after a moment, went on evenly. 'I cannot be hurt by Francis, my dear. What have you seen in France that makes you so afraid for this child?'

Lord Culter moved to the window and back: a square, hard-muscled family man with cares and responsibilities in plenty, wearied as he had been wearied all his life with the task of separating his brother's wake from his own. At length he said plainly, 'I'm afraid for them both. You wouldn't expect morality and restraint at the French Court. Licence is the mode and Francis has been setting the fashion. You've heard, I suppose, of Oonagh O'Dwyer. She was only among the more reputable of his indulgences. He has had a surfeit of that. He'll want something different now. Something,' said Richard, exasperation only half suppressed in his voice, 'like falling romantically into young love.'

Sybilla's pointed face, upturned to his, had not moved. 'Well of course. Why not?' she asked. 'The girl is quick and well-read. She won't stay sheltered for long. Or do you think she will take against him?' Sybilla cocked her head to one side, eyeing her older son. 'But, do you know, it would do him so much good if she did.'

'She's very young,' Mariotta couldn't forbear remarking.

'How old do you think he is?' said Sybilla placidly. 'To tell you the truth, I don't want him hanging about my petticoats for the rest of my life. He is, you must admit, a little *disruptive* in the home. What's your anxiety then, Richard? You think he has no self-restraint, and they will simply ruin each other before the grown-ups can prevent it? But, my dear boy, the child has been brought up in the Religion, with a brother in one of the strictest Christian Orders. She is unassailable, surely. And Francis. . . . Unless he has changed very much, Francis surely will respect her.'

It was unlike Sybilla to be complacent. In fact, it was only afterwards that Richard came to understand his mother's wilful self-deception in the cause of her younger son's need. At the time, unaccountably, he lost his head and said baldly, 'Then I advise you to engage some fat, presentable maids, or better, choose one or two grooms for their looks. Otherwise, I shall leave you the task of explaining to Sir Graham Reid Malett the Culters' stewardship of his sister.'

'*That's quite enough*,' said Sybilla. She had risen, her eyes level with his chest, but he stepped back a pace. There was no amusement in her gaze. She continued, 'What Francis does abroad is his own misfortune. What he does under my roof is what I and your wife permit him to do. I have never lacked authority over my sons yet; and to suggest that a guest in this house would be in danger is a stupidity verging on viciousness. The rest of your observations we shall consider unsaid.'

Her own face pale, Mariotta became aware that the incisive voice had stopped. Her husband, who could control without effort five thousand fighting men, stood saying nothing, his gaze on his mother, his temples moist as if the room were too hot. Then he said with difficulty, 'I'm sorry. Of course he won't touch her. But *she* might be attracted to *him*.'

'And so?' She would not compromise.

'Mother, she's too young for that kind of heartbreak. You talk of marriage. What do you think I'd give to see him married? What do you think it costs me to admit that marriage between Francis and any young, convent-bred girl is in all honour long past allowing?'

Sybilla's face changed. The arched, pale brows drew together and she sat, a little too firmly, in the chair she had just vacated. Then her straight blue gaze fixed on Richard again. 'Of course, he is too clever for his own good. But there is no vice there. None. I will not believe it.'

Lord Culter did not answer. There was a long silence, during

36

which Mariotta kept her head bent, her eyelashes wet, and the Dowager's face became whiter and whiter. Then at last, as the pause threatened to become unbearable, 'Then where,' said Sybilla evenly, 'do you suggest we send her?'

Richard's tremendous exhalation plumbed his shattering relief. He said, 'Would Jenny take her, at Boghall?'

It was the solution. Lady Fleming, exquisite widow of royal birth, was newly back at Boghall Castle from France, returned to bear a son out of wedlock to the French King. Of her seven children by the late Lord Fleming only Margaret, now married to Tom Erskine, could ever control Jenny Fleming; and Margaret, now in France with the Queen Mother, would soon be home. At Boghall, under the eyes of Margaret and Tom Erskine, Joleta Malett would be safe.

'Her brother will certainly not approve of Jenny,' said Sybilla thoughtfully. 'But then, if I know Jenny, she will be far too interested in returning to France to acquire another little insurance against her old age, to trouble about Joleta. Joleta would be virtually in the care of the Erskines. And the Erskines—'

'—know better than any the dangers of Francis with time on his hands,' said Lord Culter gratefully. It was, as a matter of fact, the first argument with his mother that he had ever won, and had he known it, the most useless.

*

So Tom Erskine called at Flaw Valleys to take the Malett girl and her governess home to Boghall, and saw and caught his breath at the child's looks, and noted that, since Gideon's death, Kate had lost weight.

She was the last person to seek pity. He treated her to a recital of Jenny's accouchement and the birth of the King of France's acknowledged son, and she laughed at that, but not at the little he told her of Lymond's presence at the French Court, and his wife Margaret's attempts to restrain him.

He was missing Margaret. Of their two years of marriage, she had spent eight months in France with the Queen Dowager, and it might be October before he would see her again. Kate, a perceptive soul, spent some time in talk of his wife before saying suddenly, 'I hope they come back from France soon, Tom. I have a feeling that child Joleta is going to need help.'

'She's pretty lonely, I would guess,' said Tom. 'We'll try to amuse her. She'll have the young men round her anyway like bees.'

'It's a safe guess,' said Kate, amused. 'I've had three fights in the stockyard already. If she hadn't been in bed ill half the time, God knows what would have happened.'

37

'Trotty Luckup cured her, I hear?'

'It looked like it,' said Kate uncompromisingly. 'She got her fee, anyway.'

'That's what I heard', said Tom, relieved. 'I came across the old dame the other day, in the cells for a drunken scold, and she had far more money on her than was likely—you know Trotty. But I was able to back up her story and save her a ducking. She's no beauty, but fair's fair.'

'That woman will make her fortune,' said Kate. 'Look at all the advertisement her cure has had. My apothecary is threatening to disown me. You wouldn't like to fall ill while you're here so that I can give him a turn?'

'Next time,' said Tom earnestly, 'I'll fall off my horse on your doorstep.'

'I wouldn't,' said Kate frankly. 'He's not very happy with bones. Something lingering with pimples in it is more in his line. Come when the apple trees are bearing, and help Philippa eat them.'

'She hates Lymond still, does she?' said Tom Erskine gently.

Kate nodded, and after a moment said, almost against her will, 'I don't think that other child would, though.'

'Don't worry,' said Tom Erskine cheerfully. 'Joleta and Francis Crawford are unlikely to meet. And if they do, I'll be there to see she's the same girl that she is now, when Gabriel comes to fetch her.'

And he smiled over his shoulder, at where Joleta and Pippa between them were tumbling last-minute possessions into the cart, Philippa laughing and Joleta singing snatches of rather rude lyrics; and did not see the shiver that overtook Kate.

Part Two

THE EIGHT-POINTED
CROSS

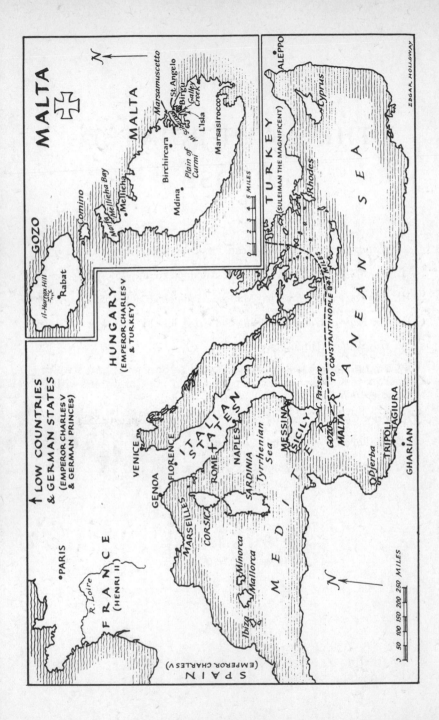

MALTA ✠

GOZO

MALTA

il-Harraq Hill   Rabat

Comino

Mtarfa   Mellieha Bay

Birchircara   Plain of Curmi

Mdina

Marsamuscetto   St Angelo
Birgu   Galley Creek
L'Isla

Marsasirocco

0 1 2 3 4 5 MILES

N

HUNGARY
(EMPEROR CHARLES V
& TURKEY)

↑ LOW COUNTRIES
& GERMAN STATES
(EMPEROR CHARLES V
& GERMAN PRINCES)

TURKEY
(SULEIMAN THE MAGNIFICENT)

ALEPPO

Cyprus

Rhodes

A E G E A N   S E A

EDGAR HOLLOWAY

●PARIS

FRANCE
(HENRI II)

R. Loire

SPAIN
(EMPEROR CHARLES V)

MARSEILLES

GENOA

VENICE

FLORENCE

I T A L I A N
S T A T E S

ROME

NAPLES

CORSICA

SARDINIA

Tyrrhenian
Sea

Ibiza

Minorca
Mallorca

MESSINA

SICILY

C. Passero

GOZO
MALTA

→ TO CONSTANTINOPLE 847 MILES

TRIPOLI   TAGIURA

●Djerba

GHARIAN

M E D I T E R R A N E A N   S E A

N

0 50 100 150 200 250 MILES

I

Sailing Orders

(Mediterranean, June/July 1551)

'AND this convenient Scotsman, where is he?' asked the Constable of France, pacing the floor.

The Chevalier de Villegagnon, closing the window against the midsummer heat, turned back into the rich little room. 'M. Crawford is coming. It is not yet the appointed time,' he said.

'We forget,' said a voice from the shadows in Italian–French. 'M. de Villegagnon is impressed by the gentleman.'

An older voice, in identical accent, answered drily. 'If the young Queen of Scotland has survived her sojourn here in France, it is partly due at least to M. Crawford of Lymond, you must admit. Youth and bravado, Leone, are delicious assets.'

'In the right place,' said Leone Strozzi sardonically, and strolled away from his brother as voices outside told the Constable's visitor had come.

Francis Crawford of Lymond, whose name, had he known it, was being bandied so freely at that time in Flaw Valleys and his own home, had then been in France for eight months; and his middling loyal activities during that time had brought him notoriety and a title, as well as the pressing interest of the Dowager Queen of Scotland, Mary of Guise, whose long visit to the court of France was nearly over.

When he appeared at the doorway of Constable Anne de Montmorency's parlour at Châteaubriant, France, on that hot June morning of 1551, only Piero Strozzi and Nicholas Durand de Villegagnon, who had known him in his native land, could assess the changes which the high living so forcibly described by his brother had brought. To the rest he was a slender, wheaten-haired foreigner in virginal velvet, with an affable expression. He paused on the threshold for just long enough to scan the four other guests in the room—M. de Villegagnon, the brothers Piero and Leone Strozzi, and Francis of Lorraine, brother of the Queen Dowager of Scotland—before entering to deliver his bow to his host and be introduced.

The Constable of France, broad, grey and matted with age and intrigue, smiled and lifted a great arm to the newcomer's shoulder. 'M. le Comte de Sevigny, is it not now?' he said. 'Let me introduce you to our friends. M. de Villegagnon you met in Scotland two years ago, he tells me, over a matter of a lady called—called . . .'

'Hough Isa,' said the Chevalier, smiling also, and gave Lymond his hand.

'And M. Strozzi you met also—'

'On the occasion of a wedding at Melrose. I remember, of course,' said Lymond docilely, and got a sharp look from the Florentine black eyes.

'But you have not yet encountered his brother Leone, General of the King's Galleys in the Mediterranean. With M. de Villegagnon here, one of the great seamen of the world,' said the Constable, throwing in some cursory tact.

'I had the misfortune to be out of Scotland when Signor Leone paid us his memorable visit,' said Lymond politely, and the second Strozzi brother, seal-like beside de Villegagnon's ursine bulk, younger than the Chevalier by five years and than his brother by fifteen, bowed till the gold ring in his ear winked in the shafted sunlight and said, 'I hear that you also, sir, have sailed in your time.'

With annoyance, the Constable saw that he was being left to retrieve this ill-timed reference to his guest's informal past. Wishing, once more, that Leone Strozzi were not the Queen's cousin, he said, 'Some of the noblest captains on our seas have rowed for a year or two under the whip, Signor Strozzi.'

'Such as Jean de la Valette,' said de Villegagnon coldly, offering the name of one of Malta's great captains.

'Or Dragut,' said Lymond cheerfully. 'I met him once, I remember, off Nice. A most cordial encounter. We were in different boats but on the same side, of course . . . as the Grand Prior will appreciate,' added the deprecating voice.

Francis of Lorraine, thus at last addressed, rose to his feet, scarlet to his soft hair line. At sixteen, the privilege of representing the Order of St John as Grand Prior of France was a prized and sensitive burden, as well as a lucrative one. Silent from youth and necessity, he returned the Scotsman's bow until, straightening, he thought of something. 'Whatever our allegiance to the King of France, Monsieur, our allegiance to God comes before it. I doubt if any member of my Order would call a murdering Turkish corsair *cordial*.'

'But I,' said Francis Crawford gently, 'am not of your Order.'

And Piero Strozzi, a man of humour and of no ties with the Order of St John, concealed his amusement and sat in a mood of silent anticipation. For this artistic performer clearly understood every nuance of his invitation to dine with the Constable, and for the

Constable, unused to ambush in the bogs of statesmanship, the auspices were bad.

So, as every man there realized, with the possible exception of young Lorraine, was his dilemma. For the de Guise family, whose eldest sister Mary was Queen Dowager of Scotland, was becoming also too powerful in France. And with the coming marriage of the child Mary of Scotland to the Dauphin of France, the de Guises would be supreme behind the joint thrones of Scotland and France.

To curb the Queen Dowager's power in Scotland were only a few strong Scottish families, dissatisfied with their French pensions, or with leanings towards the new religion and England. But these were hardly enough to keep her in check, so happily were they squabbling among themselves. And if Mary of Guise returned to Scotland with a new leader, a man of talent and panache, who would help her keep Scotland and maybe take Ireland too for the King of France, the power of her family would be beyond any control.

Similarly, if the King of France, so indebted to Crawford of Lymond for his services to the child Mary, chose with the de Guise family to make of Lymond an ally and a popular idol, the power of the Constable and the French Queen, silent in the daily company of her husband's mistress, silent on the subject of the pregnant Lady Fleming, would silently drain away.

And meanwhile—'As you have observed,' said the Constable at last to Lymond as the marzipan was cleared away and the rosewater brought, 'there are three Knights of Malta in this room. It is no coincidence. The Grand Prior and I have summoned M. de Ville-gagnon and M. Strozzi for the gravest of reasons.'

He paused. The Constable's grand-uncle, as no one present ever forgot, had been first Grand Master of the Order of St John in Malta. It was one of the most useful relationships the Constable possessed, in an age where nepotism was not only legitimate but compulsory. Thoughtfully drying his hands on the towel proffered, 'I cannot imagine why,' said Lymond, and laid the silk down. 'Unless the Sultan Suleiman is sending a corsair fleet against France?'

Piero Strozzi, commander and engineer, who had enjoyed every moment of his meal, caught the yellow-haired gentleman's wide stare and grinned. 'A little *too* disingenuous, sir,' said the Florentine, and ignoring the Constable's silence, continued comfortably.

'Of course, France has been an ally of Turkey for years. We are not supporting the Moslem faith any more than Suleiman is supporting ours. But in face of the Emperor Charles V, dear small man who is enemy to us both, an alliance, military and naval, does exist. Added to that—' Strozzi's dark eyes strayed from the sardonic face of his brother to de Villegagnon's steadfast stare, and from there to the

43

Grand Prior's flushed face. 'Added to that is the fact that Malta and Gozo were the Emperor Charles's gifts to the Order, which would be homeless without them. The Knights of St John have lived rent-free on Malta for twenty-one years on condition that they defend it from the Turks, together with its neighbour Gozo, and Tripoli, over on the African coast. So that those gentlemen of France who have taken the holy vows of the Order have on occasion the unpleasant task of deciding whether to fight for the Order in the interests of the Emperor against the Turk . . . or whether to defend France from the Emperor, despite the fact that France's allies are the very Moslems they are sworn to exterminate. . . . Am I right?' said Piero Strozzi, smiling, to de Villegagnon.

The Chevalier did not return the smile. He said stiffly to Francis Crawford, 'The Grand Prior has already made the position clear. To all Knights in the Order, whatever their nationality, allegiance to their Faith and the Order comes first.'

It was then that the knotted fist of Constable Anne de Montmorency fell; that the table rattled, chiming with abandoned silver, and the linen sprang grey with rosewater stains. Thick-built and grizzled; older than any man present, the Constable of France reared to his feet and stared at them all, jewelled and negligent round the small table in the leather-dressed room. 'Is it a time for toying with words?' he exclaimed. 'For parlour phrases and pettishness? Have ye forgotten?'

'*I* have not forgotten,' said Francis of Lorraine passionately, jumping up. Striding to where Lymond was seated he put his two hands white-wristed on the table and bent, the pale hair under the velvet bonnet falling flat over his flushed brow. 'If you are a man of no principle, leave us. If you are a man of no faith, abandon us. If you revere the infidel, go to him. But listen to this. *The Turkish fleet is at sea.* A hundred and twelve royal galleys, two galleasses, thirty flutes and more brigantines and troop ships under Sinan Pasha with Dragut, Salah Rais and twelve thousand men have left Constantinople and are sailing for Malta. The Chevalier de Villegagnon is leaving tonight for the island to warn the Grand Master. Signor Strozzi remains until there is a general call to arms, in case of attack by the Emperor on France. We wish to ask you, as a soldier and a man versed in ships, who has no national bias to affect his judgement and standing, to go with M. de Villegagnon and stir the Grand Master to Malta's defence.'

'*Against*,' said Lymond drily, 'Allâh's Deputy on Earth?'

The boy straightened. 'I have told you . . .' he began.

'Your allegiance is to God. I know,' said Lymond. 'But God knows the Sultan is going to be a little peevish when he notices that French knights are killing his Janissaries, whether in the Order or not. If I were twenty Scotsmen you might hide your perfidious political faces behind me, but I cannot see that you may hide behind one.'

'But you—' began the Constable, a little tardily.

'—are the equal of twenty. I believe it. But would your Treasurer believe it?' said Francis Crawford amiably.

There was a crisp silence. However couched, the demand was extortionate. It was contemptible. De Villegagnon frowned; Leone Strozzi smiled; and the Constable's face reddened with feeling even while he slowly agreed, as agree he must. Only Piero Strozzi looked thoughtfully at the speaker, knowing that Francis Crawford was wealthy enough to need no bribing, and sophisticated enough to find this kind of exercise mortally dull.

What he did not know was that the same Francis Crawford had found out only that morning that an Irishwoman called Oonagh O'Dwyer had just taken ship at Marseilles for the island of Gozo. And that if Francis Crawford reached Malta, it was because he always meant to reach Malta; not to fight, but to recruit.

In any case, it made no odds to the Order. The Order had got what it wanted; would have got what it wanted even had Lymond spurned them all and returned home to Scotland ... since it was for no disingenuous reason that M. de Villegagnon, Chevalier of St John, had placed on Lord Culter's anxious shoulders the responsibility for Gabriel's sister of the apricot hair.

*

With de Villegagnon and his suite, Lymond left that night for Marseilles. Before he went he did some brief leave-taking: of the King, of his friends and followers at court, of the Queen Dowager and Margaret Erskine, Tom's bride.

These last he got over quickly. Margaret, sober daughter of Jenny Fleming and herself a good friend in need, was pleased, he thought, even without understanding his motives. The Queen Dowager was angry.

'And what do I tell my child?' asked Mary of Guise. 'That you are now compelled to seek excitement and fortune among her enemies?'

'I do not expect,' said Lymond, 'to be fighting quite under the banner of the Emperor Charles. And if I were, I could hope surely for nothing better than to stand shoulder to shoulder with the Grand Prior of France.'

It was a nasty hit which, being Lymond, he did not particularly regret, even though he was fairly sure that the unworldly Francis of Lorraine would soon be sadder, wiser and several thicknesses of skin poorer under the lashing tongues of his brothers and sisters de Guise.

*

At Marseilles, imperial blue upon blue under cobalt blue skies, the Mediterranean lay fresco-still. The docks steamed with the smells and brown flesh of seamen and slaves; the rigging of brigantines, galley and galleass meshed the merciless sun. A galley had been found, with convict rowers and free sailors, little better; its master bought for the double voyage to Sicily, where de Villegagnon meant to take his first warning to the Sicilian Viceroy, Charles V's representative nearest Malta, sworn to help the Order in time of need. The knights might not go so far as to help the enemies of France, but it seemed that they were quite ready to call on France's adversaries to help them.

Before leaving, there was one visit to pay. De Villegagnon, with Lymond beside him, waited among the stream of traders, bankers and businessmen calling to see M. de Luetz, Baron d'Aramon, his Grace the King of France's Ambassador to Turkey, about to return to his post at Constantinople bearing, it was rumoured, four, six, eight, ten muleloads of gold to present to the Most Christian King's ally, Sultan Suleiman.

Rising to greet the monolithic bulk of the Chevalier, d'Aramon smiled his automatic, worn smile. Faded by the Levantine sun, he had watched his fresh young tenets, his forceful loyalties, his vigorous faith, bleach and shrivel with heat and distance until his homeland France seemed to him simple, noisy, bright as a toy. Despite the Court intrigue which lost him his lands to the King's mistress Diane, the Baron d'Aramon strove to do his best for France; but it was not the France of the missal and the anointed Christian King. It was merely an ambitious, quarrelsome country whose needs, unless tempered, could bring misery to herself and to others. In all the world, after all, there were only four nations who mattered: France, with Scotland dragged at her heels; Charles V, head of the Holy Roman Empire, with Spain, Flanders, parts of Italy and Germany; and the Pope in his pocket; England with Ireland under her thumb; and the Sultan, who possessed Turkey, Hungary, Egypt already, and who wished to conquer the world.

There were times when M. d'Aramon believed that life would be easier if he did, since he had verified what no man in France would dare to confirm: that the Sultan of the Ottomans was a good deal more humane than any Christian prince he had discovered.

Therefore M. d'Aramon, French Ambassador to Turkey, was apprehensive when one of the foremost French knights of the Order called on him, and fatalistic when de Villegagnon told him of the expected attack. But all he said was, 'Is Malta prepared?'

To which the Chevalier de Villegagnon replied with an explicit and no doubt sacred oath. 'With the Spanish Grand Master we have? De Homedès has done nothing. In fifteen years, Malta and Gozo and

Tripoli are as poorly fortified as when the knights first received them. Any fool,' said de Villegagnon bitterly, 'could see danger was coming. Didn't the Order help the Emperor last year every time Charles asked politely for the Order's galleys? The Emperor's Admiral cleared the Moors from half the African coast with the Order's help and chased Dragut temporarily off the seas; and it wasn't because Charles was over-concerned about the free spread of the One True Faith either. It was because Dragut was becoming a little too busy attacking Spanish-owned Sicily and Calabria, and he wanted to teach him a lesson. And now the Order will suffer.'

'And where is Spain's High Admiral?' asked Lymond. 'Still at sea?'

Brought down from his high dudgeon the big man hesitated, and then grudgingly smiled. 'Aye. After Dragut made a fool of him at sea in the spring, the Prince Doria found himself too desperately busy ferrying relatives of the Emperor back and forth to Spain to be able to fight.' The smile went. 'And so, since Sicily was unprotected, Charles got the Grand Master to send the Order's galleys under Pied-de-Fer to Messina to stand by. They're there yet.'

'To return, of course, if Malta is attacked ... backwards, if necessary,' said Lymond. 'Your one-eyed Grand Master must be a man of some character if he has your colleagues' support for all this?'

'He has a circle of Spanish knights like himself, more Imperialist than the Emperor,' said de Villegagnon curtly. 'With them, he can persuade the Supreme Council to vote as he wants. And he wants to obey the Pope and the Emperor and, if possible, to avoid accounting for any money he has spent in the last fifteen years. The real reason why he won't fortify and won't call in his knights is that the Treasury is empty. The Order has no money to keep it alive.'

'Dear me,' said Lymond mildly. 'I am being taken to an unfortified island, where half the defenders and most of the defence fleet are missing, to lay down my life in defence of an Order incompetently if not culpably led, wholly divided among itself, given over to fighting for secular princes and entirely denuded of money with which to pay me for my services. Where are Prudence, Temperance, Fortitude and Justice? Where are the Eight Beatitudes of that proud White Cross? Where are the Crusaders of yesteryear, chaste and highborn, dying in virginal joy for their vows? They sound,' said Francis Crawford abstractedly, 'just like the Kerrs.'

'You are forgetting Gabriel,' said the Chevalier de Villegagnon, and with a quick smile acknowledged that this was d'Aramon's own given name. 'Reid Malett—de la Valette—Romegas—the skeleton of the Order as it should be is in Malta still. Only there are not enough of us—yet.'

'And once you have been decimated by Dragut, there'll be none of you at all. Why not let Tripoli go?' said Lymond.

47

'Because the Order holds Malta by virtue of her readiness to defend Tripoli,' said the Baron d'Aramon. 'To give up Tripoli would displease the Emperor indeed. Do I gather,' he said, studying Francis Crawford, 'that the Constable of France has promised you a sum of money in exchange for your services in this war?'

'He has promised me a sum of money, clearly illusory, for my services, it seems, against the Grand Master,' said Lymond equably. 'He is also hoping, unofficially no doubt, to convey to your Excellency that any gifts of gold about to be dispatched from the King of France to Turkey would be better delayed.'

Over the pale brown, fatless skin of the Ambassador a tired smile appeared. 'Gentlemen, I am already late in embarking,' he said. 'And I may not even reach Turkey before the sailing season ends. But I know Dragut well. If what you fear comes to pass . . . and if I am in the vicinity, you can count on my help, at least to parley.'

'Should anyone, of course, pause to parley,' Francis Crawford pointed out.

*

Over the windless, hyacinthine sea, the galley *Sainte-Merveille* carried Lymond and de Villegagnon to Messina, the buzz and hiss of sheared foam on her beams. From the baked, frenetic shipyards of France, the white harbours of Ibiza and Minorca, the tawny shores of the African states, no corsair prince stirred from his palace; no lurking brigand hovered, hull down for a spice ship; no royal or imperial sea fortress set out to frighten the unwanted from the main shipping lane of the world. When the sea-wolves of Islâm were hunting, the small boats stayed on the beach.

Except one which nothing, not even Dragut, could deter; and assuredly not de Villegagnon's modest galley, leaving Marseilles on a breathless day under oar, on roughly the publicized date when the Baron d'Aramon, French Ambassador to Turkey, was due to embark with his four, six, eight or ten muleloads of gold.

The *Sainte-Merveille* met her fate long after the French coast had sunk in the milky haze of midsummer heat, far to port. It looked peaceful enough: a fishing boat lying ahead, tilting on the greasy slopes of the swell, the bright caps of the fisherfolk swinging, doubled, in the sea and the vaporous air; their voices, deadened with space, rehearsing a chant.

Lymond, who on leaving Marseilles had found a solitary spot of shade on the rambade and was occupying it, his eyes shut in thought, opened them suddenly and rose. The fishing boat, rowed in a desultory way, was making slowly towards them. Then, under his eyes, the bright, capped heads slid in unison as the rowers produced a sudden strong stroke, then another. Oars flashing, the tub shot forward into the bigger ship's path. At the same moment, incredibly, from her broad painted sides there slid the long black muzzles of cannon, and a voice from her poop shouted, '*Stop!*'

The command, in French, was heard by everyone on the *Sainte-Merveille*, including de Villegagnon who, running down the rambade, flung himself, an arquebus weighting each hand, on the deck where Lymond still stood.

From the rogue ship the command was repeated. '*Stop! Or we fire!*'

The *Sainte-Merveille* had neither cannon nor soldiers. The *Sainte-Merveille* had over two hundred chained slaves, a handful of nervous seamen, a number of conciliatory officers, including the Master, and M. de Villegagnon's party of six, including Lymond. There was also an assortment of bows, crossbows and arquebuses, which every ship in these waters carried, and which de Villegagnon's men were hurling on deck as fast as they could.

'We are within their range already,' said the Chevalier, peering lengthwise through the iron pins of the prow rail. 'If we veer or pass we shall simply make an even better target for those guns. I have issued orders that we run her down. If they let off their guns at close quarters, they'll suffer almost as much as we shall.'

'I don't fancy,' said Lymond, clearing his throat suddenly, 'that they'll fire at close quarters, or even at long range, for that matter. When they get broadside on, they'll trust to their hackbuts.'

'All right,' said de Villegagnon abruptly. 'We have the choice of flying and outstripping their aim, and shooting it out with hand weapons. I'd rather shoot.'

'Well, they're hoping that at least you don't fly,' said Lymond amiably. So far from accepting the weapon de Villegagnon had offered, he had remained standing, gazing over the rambade. Behind them, in the absence of reassurance, the rowers faltered, and abandoning the big beechwood sweeps, had broken into a cacophony of Arabic and dockyard French. The Master, taking responsibility on himself, exposed his head with sudden valour on the poop and yelled, 'Do not shoot! We stop!'

'Tell him,' said Lymond mildly to the bo's'n, above the subdued clatter of M. de Villegagnon handing out crossbows on the coursie, 'that the Baron d'Aramon is still at Marseilles.'

Across the glassy water over which, now bright and plain, the pirate boat was approaching, the frantic information was relayed. It had a cool reception.

'If that is so, throw your weapons in the water!' came the fishing boat's response.

'Neat,' commented Lymond, and looked down for agreement at

the railed platform where de Villegagnon now stood. But le Chevalier, at forty-one the survivor of more sea-fights than most, had already smelt the element of farce. And pinning his dignity to his instincts he rose to his full six feet four and, throwing his weapon uncharged to the deck, said, 'I think, sir, that you know this boat?'

Without turning, Lymond grinned. 'I know the joiner who fashioned the cannon. *Thompson!*' He cupped his hands round his mouth. 'Holà, Tamsín! Sing the next verse in French if you dare!'

Visibly, on the approaching boat, the oars paused. Then a sharp voice, in very plain English, said, 'Who the hell's that?'

'The guns—my God,' said the Chevalier de Villegagnon suddenly. 'The guns are painted rouleaux of wood.'

His smile deepening, Lymond hailed the pirate again. 'Francis Crawford. Have you still got my agate seal?'

A burst of magnified laughter jolted its way across the narrowing gap. 'I lost it at knuckle-banes in the old jail at Cork. Is yon hoited bairn's bath-boatie yours?' Close enough to see, the beery, black-bearded face under its cap radiated malevolent good nature over the corsair's rail. The wood and canvas guns, a little damp at the edges, were being neatly run in.

'It's yourself!' shouted the man in the cap, evidently locating Lymond at last, and downing his hailer, he placed both broad red fists with purpose on the ship's wide deal rail. 'Christ,' said Lymond amused. 'He's going to make a most superior etching in wood.'

But Tamsín, alias Thompson, or the liveliest Scottish pirate unhung on the roads between Argyll and Ireland, the Baltic, the Straits, or anywhere else for that matter, achieved faultlessly a leap over joppling deep-sea water that M. de Villegagnon did not care to contemplate, and landed head over heels on the *Sainte-Merveille* as his own ship, docile to anticipated order, retreated and kept her place a discreet distance off.

'Francis Crawford!' intoned Mr Thompson beatifically from the planks where he sat, and surging to his bare feet, wide-legged as a horse gypsy, embraced Lymond violently on either cheek. 'Continental habits!' shouted Mr Thompson, spitting neatly over the side, and stepping back, surveyed his friend. 'Man, you're a fine sicht. Hae ye a wife yet? I've got a lassie back there in Algiers that would dae ye a treat.'

'How much?' said Lymond instantly.

With an absent hand, Thompson pulled off the vile, salt-encrusted beret and scratched underneath. 'Tell you what. Ye dinna want all they arblasters. Throw in the hackbuts and six oarsmen, my choice, and ye can have her. She's rare at—' said Mr Thompson, who believed in a specific bargain.

The Chevalier de Villegagnon, unstirred as a rule by frivolities, suddenly found in himself an impulse to laugh. 'Thompson's oath?' Lymond was saying, looking interested.

In a lightning movement involving his nose, his thumbs and his breast, the pirate ratified the data. 'And other things too. It's a bargain,' he said.

'Thompson, you're a great friend,' said Lymond soberly, and shook him by the hand. 'It's just that my other wives would object. Come and meet M. de Villegagnon of the Order of St John of Jerusalem, who nearly blew your cannon into sawdust a moment ago.' And the man of commerce and the man of God, united in their devotion to chicanery at sea, clasped willing hands.

Much later, as the two ships, moving side by side, flawed a faultless opaline sea at the end of the long, hot day, and the masthead light pricked yellow in the invisible shrouds, the pirate Thompson scrubbed his full stomach, sighed, and said, 'Francis Crawford and I, we learned our seamanship the hard way, chained to the same rowing bench in a French ship, Brother. But we bear ye no ill will for that, him and me. Them that put him there . . . they've paid for their mistake. And me—I've taken full payment too for the slight to my name.'

'Thompson, boy; no man living has a worse reputation, or better deserves it,' said Lymond calmly. 'Spanish ships; Portugese ships; Venetian ships; Flemish ships . . . hovering round the Head of Howth; waiting for a galleass with malmsey or silver to run into Waterford. . . . How often have you been in Waterford jail, man?'

Grinning, the pirate shook his head while Lymond continued his disquisition. 'And Cork: we heard about that. He sailed into Cork on Christmas Day with a full cargo of wines and figs and sugar and *sold them*. . . . Where in God's name did you pick those figs, Tamsín? The Mayor and Council of Cork must be simple.'

'They asked the Lord Deputy's permission, and the Lord Deputy said they could buy, so long as the goods didna seem to be stolen,' explained Thompson.

'This,' said Lymond to de Villegagnon, 'was after he and Stephenson his mate had been jailed a dozen times for piracy—Where's Stephenson?'

'On board. He's sailing the old tub,' said Thompson. 'The secret was, it was Christmas Day, man. Peace upon earth, ye ken; and grannie coming for supper. They fairly needed those figs. Ye havena heard the great thing I'm starting with Cormac O'Connor?'

The silence lasted no more than a breath, and Lymond did not move, but it was enough to make Nicholas Durand de Villegagnon look up from his seat and say, 'Cormac O'Connor's just been at the French Court. You're talking of the big Irishman, heir to Offaly, whose father's been in London Tower for rebellion against the English?'

'The same. Ah, he would be in France all right,' said Thompson cheerfully. 'He's dead keen to persuade someone to chase the English out of Ireland for him. That's what he wants the money for.'

'What money?' said Lymond. 'Remembering that M. de Villegagnon is a pillar of the Church, and ought not to have more laid on his conscience than you've put there already.'

'Och, away,' said Thompson comfortably. 'It's only the insurance brokers that lose, and they're the lads who can afford it, anyway.'

'Oh God,' said Lymond. 'Don't tell me. O'Connor approaches a circle of merchants, insures their cargoes against loss by pirates at double the proper value; the ships are duly waylaid and emptied by you, and the merchants claim the insurance while you and O'Connor share the cargo.'

'You've got your ear to the ground all right,' said the pirate without rancour. 'Just that. O'Connor's man George Paris does the travelling, and we market the cargoes. I bartered the last one for a grand lassie in Algiers ... but I told ye about that. And where's Cormac now?'

'Lying incapable, I am happy to say, at Châteaubriant,' said Lymond briefly. 'He had an accident.'

'I heard about that,' said de Villegagnon. 'Over that black-haired mistress, I understand.'

'Oonagh? Had he Oonagh O'Dwyer with him?' Thompson was interested, but not surprised. 'I told him she'd be his death one day.'

'Unhappily,' said Lymond, 'she was not. She has left him; and I hope the string and clapper arrangement he calls a mind has been permanently put out of action. I can't rejoice in your choice of partner.'

'Evidently not!' said Thompson, utterly unperturbed. 'And where's the lassie, then? She's not on board?'

'No, you marinated tomcat,' said Lymond, exasperated at last. 'I hadn't got a God-damned fig left to barter with.'

Soon after that, the two ships drew together and Thompson unwillingly took his leave. To de Villegagnon he said, 'Ye'll no credit it, but I'm proud to know ye. Hard experience was all the teacher I had, but to learn the way of the sea, there's no school better than Malta.'

To Lymond he spoke in an undertone, the still lamps in the rigging showing briefly the thick nose and the clear, seaman's eyes. 'I'm no friend to Cormac, though I do business there when it suits me. Are ye for the sea-lanes yourself?'

Glimmering in the wide dark, Lymond's head moved in negation. 'I want to fight in Malta. I want to meet a man called Gabriel. And if I leave Malta, it'll be to go back to my own army in Scotland.'

'And your own ships?' asked the pirate Thompson softly.

'If I had a captain who would accept my command.'

There was a long silence. Then, 'Since we were galley-slaves, no man has commanded me,' said the man Thompson thoughtfully. 'But that's not to say I won't come to it yet.'

Again there was a pause. Then in the darkness Lymond suddenly smiled, and clasping the older man briefly on the shoulder, stood aside to let him swing over the rail. For a moment longer, on both sides, voices were raised in farewell; then the night echoed to the pipe of the whistle, the repeating of orders, the creak of timber and the rhythmic swish as the oars took their swing; and the *Sainte-Merveille* and the pirate ship, drawing apart, slid phosphorescent into the night on their different tasks. And by the time the new day's sun hung low and red in their faces, the Chevalier's ship was well on the way to Sicily.

Nothing more stopped them. De Villegagnon, with grave concerns of his own, found his paid companion sober, self-contained and less than talkative, and was reassured. They reached Messina at the end of their voyage after sundown, pushed at last by a faint following wind which took them through the darkly fretted Tyrrhenian Sea, the white feather of Stromboli hanging in the blue sky to port. Then, rounding the point, they hit the stream in the Straits an hour after low tide, and cutting through the patched and eddying water off the Porto di Messina, entered the green elbow of the harbour itself.

Inside, rocking cheek to cheek with their yellow lanterns, their serried windows and gunports, lay merchant ships, ferries on the Calabrian run, the armed Imperial boats which Prince Doria had left there and, as d'Aramon had said, the Great Carrack of Rhodes and nearly all the small fleet of the Knights Hospitallers of St John of Jerusalem, stirring like a poppy-field on the black water, the scarlet silk of their banners blooming lamplit like coals in the dark.

Earlier that day, when the first watch-tower had located them, and the small, fast boats from Messina had skimmed alongside to hail and identify, de Villegagnon had broken out on the *Sainte-Merveille* his blue personal standard with the three golden chevrons; and almost before the buffered sides of the galley touched the quay, a courier from the Emperor's representative in Sicily, his escort and lamp-bearers beside him, was waiting to come aboard. Late as it was, his Excellency the Viceroy of Sicily desired M. de Villegagnon to call.

Lymond, it appeared, knew Messina well enough to find his own entertainment for the evening. Clothed in light braided silk, bought in France, he set off unescorted into the dark while the Chevalier de Villegagnon, dressed at last in his black robe with the Eight-Pointed Cross on his breast, walked ashore with his entourage and was led to the Viceregal house.

When confined to a seaport town awaiting action, there are relatively few resources open to an Order which may not gamble, may not indulge in excessive liquor and may not exorcise its impatience in the ordinary way at an écu a night, as each of the humblest of their seamen was able to do. Either staying aboard, or with friends or, if they could afford it, at an inn, the knights passed their time in prayer, in argument, in rehashing old sea fights and designing new.

Jerott Blyth of Nantes, France, whose father came from the west coast of Scotland, was at the cathedral when Lymond finally tracked him down. Waiting in silence, his head gold as the angel harbingers of grace all about, the stranger was unnoticed by the handful of knights kneeling with Blyth, and Blyth himself, his handsome black head bent, his only ornament the gold ring belonging to the dead girl he was to have married, looked distant and unlike the intelligent, talented and spectacularly wild young gentleman he had been. Lymond waited, unexpectedly patient, until the other man rose, genuflected and turned. The flood of candlelight did the rest.

It was nine years since their last meeting; and they had been boys in Scotland then, though old enough to fight side by side for their country. Of the two, Lymond, as he probably knew, had changed most since then. Nevertheless it was for only seconds that Jerott Blyth, Chevalier of the Order of St John, stood, short, vivid, vital, and stared at the self-possessed stranger before him. Then he said slowly, *Francis Crawford!* And darting forward, seized those cool, relaxed hands.

It took a moment only to discover that Crawford of Lymond was in Messina with de Villegagnon, and leaving for Malta tomorrow. It took little longer for Jerott Blyth and his friends to carry Lymond off with them to the big white house of the Receiver of the Order in Sicily where, in moderation, they ate and drank; and where Jerott demanded the history of nine years' separation at once.

Lymond told it without detail and added, immediately, the news which was taking de Villegagnon to Malta. 'The Constable of France swears the whole Turkish fleet is on the move. It may well be against Malta,' he said. And as the other men, drawing breath, looked towards Jerott, Lymond added, 'Will de Homedès fight?'

'What with?' said Jerott Blyth bitterly.

'Then will the Viceroy here send him help?'

'And risk a Turkish attack on Naples and Sicily? The Chevalier de Villegagnon has one of the most persuasive tongues in the Order,' said Jerott. 'But if I were a gambling man, I should wager my purse against your pin that he'll get neither ships nor men out of either the Viceroy or his master, our dear Emperor Charles.'

'It's men you want, surely, not ships?' said Lymond, and watched them reluctantly agree. The flotilla now leaving Turkey was insuperable. With not only his own fleet but Dragut and all the North African corsairs under his banner, Suleiman was now supreme in the Mediterranean, failing the conjunction of the whole fleets of the Order and of the Empire, which Charles would never allow. What was needed were men and guns to raise bulwarks in Malta, at Gozo, in Tripoli, and defend them against a siege. And defended they had to be, said the Rule of the Order, through the voice of the Emperor Charles, the Order's landlord on earth.

'And *we* are men,' said someone in Gascon, standing up.

'Not to the Grand Master,' said Jerott Blyth sardonically. 'You and I are not even Knights of the Order—we are renegade French, liable to lead the Sultan personally into the Grand Master's room. Try sailing back to Malta without orders, and you'll find yourself despoiled of the Holy Sign as a prevaricator for offending our lord and master Charles.'

But after the meal, when the discussion, furiously raging, was beginning to spend itself, Jerott drew Lymond aside and said quietly, 'I have not heard the full story, I know; but I must ask this. Have you in mind that, one day, you may join us?'

Francis Crawford looked up from his clasped hands and smiled. 'The Constable would give a good deal to know,' he said.

Disappointment, unconcealed, was clear in Blyth's magnificent eyes. 'Then this is an intellectual gambit, nothing more? A specific for the Crawford career?'

'Not entirely.' That was direct. 'It was made easy for me to come, because I am temporarily an embarrassment in some quarters. I wished to come for a number of reasons. I am prepared, Jerott, in your language to serve the Order this summer. I have spent the winter, God knows, playing enough. Next winter, perhaps, I may serve best where I may embarrass most; if so, my time here will not have been wasted. In the meantime—' he smiled again, fleetingly— 'your truly dedicated brothers are free to convert me if they can.'

And Jerott Blyth, who was dedicated not to the Order but to the memory of a girl, accepted and passed over Lymond's knowledge of it, and said impulsively instead, 'You must meet Gabriel. He has heard of you. Did you know his sister was going to Scotland? I spoke of you—'

He broke off. Lymond said after a moment, amused, 'You've said too much, Jerott. Better go on.'

'—to a woman who heard me mention your name,' said Jerott slowly. 'She had just come from Marseilles. Her name was—'

'Oonagh. Oonagh O'Dwyer,' supplied Lymond as quietly.

'She was your mistress?'

'No . . .' said Lymond. 'Or at least, not as you mean. She was the mistress of Cormac O'Connor, the Irish rebel. She has left him now, to some degree my doing, and I'd sooner she didn't suffer by it, that's all. She's probably with another man now, not half her worth. Is that what you were avoiding saying, in your delicacy?'

'Not only for your sake—for the sake of the Order,' said Blyth with more than mock ruefulness. 'She's living with de Césel, the Governor of Gozo.'

'Valiantly vowed to Obedience and Chastity,' said Lymond. 'She would find a special kind of amusement in that. Will he be kind to her?'

'It's a question,' said Jerott Blyth angrily, 'of whether *she* will be kind to *him*. We're a seedy, spiritless fraternity, as will be clear. A weak Grand Master and his clique may do with us as he wants. The best of us have been lost already through the Order's mistakes, or through being dragged into Imperial wars under pressure, or because we've marched off home to our Commanderies, and de Homedès has had neither the guts nor the money to summon us back. And yet, believe me . . . there are great noblemen and great seamen among us still, serving their turn in the Hospital and ready to fight the Turk with their bare hands in between. *We* are the bulwark of Christendom. If we go, do you think the poor, ailing Emperor and his turkey-cock Doria and a scattering of ill-organized ships can take our place? The Sacred Law of Islâm would span the known world.'

He was shaking. And Lymond's cold voice following was as refreshing as spray. 'And you will all become converts and go to the Mussulman's paradise, where the climax of love lasts for ten thousand years. Consider it, Brother Jerott, if you dare.'

Brother Jerott, still scarlet, was spared the need to reply. For the door opened on a middle-aged gentleman who proved to be the Order's Receiver himself; an Italian banker who acknowledged Jerott's introduction with a courtesy barely concealing his extreme disquiet. At mention of de Villegagnon, he sat down suddenly, waving to the knights and to Lymond to do likewise. 'You've come from France with the Chevalier. Oh, dear. Well, you don't need me to tell you that he has just brought the Viceroy very bad news. Bad news. The Turk is preparing. He will soon be attacking these shores.'

'The French Constable's warning,' said Lymond mildly, 'was to the effect that the Turk was sailing rather against Malta and Tripoli.'

The Receiver heaved a nauseated sigh. 'That, M. le Comte, is what the Chevalier de Villegagnon said. His Excellency—I dislike having to say that his Excellency did not believe him. His Excellency, in fact, accused him of being the Constable's catspaw. The Viceroy, it seems, prefers to think that the warning is a French device to remove all naval defences from Sicily and Italy itself, to expose the Emperor more readily to attack by the Turks.'

There was a heavy-breathing silence during which Lymond's voice, unsurprised, said, 'And M. de Villegagnon replied . . .?'

'The Chevalier said "Christ" several times—he was exceedingly overwrought,' said the Receiver apologetically. 'Exceedingly. He reminded the Viceroy that, contrary to all standing treaties, the Emperor—with the assistance of all the knights, French, Spanish, Italian, German, English—had seized the Sultan's possessions in North Africa and had mortified the corsair Dragut to such a pitch that Dragut has not only petitioned but tried to pay for the privilege of launching an attack to exterminate the knights of Tripoli and Malta from the earth. He said that the Sultan was fully as angry as Dragut, and that when the Emperor excused himself on the grounds that he was, with the knights, simply clearing the seas of worthless corsairs of no concern to the Ottoman lords, the Sultan answered by heaping official appointments on Dragut and his friends, and by gathering them publicly within the framework of his fleet. ... He was most convincing,' said the Receiver doubtfully. 'Hard as it is for us to believe on this island, so close to Italy, that so great an infidel fleet could be built and commissioned simply to demolish a rock—'

'Was the Viceroy convinced, sir?' said Jerott's hard young voice. 'Since you clearly are not?'

The Receiver, who was merely doing his best in a state of some shock, said, 'I—there are difficulties in accepting the whole of M. de Villegagnon's premise, but I do so—I am prepared to do so. His Excellency has done the same. He has promised Tripoli two hundred soldiers from Naples, to be sent to Malta as soon as levied.'

'Under me,' said Jerott Blyth instantly, and in the ensuing babble of voices cut his way by sheer lung power. 'Under me ... and if anyone objects, they can argue with steel.'

'Since we are all to die together on our rock,' said Lymond's voice, pleasant as ever, silencing the argument, 'is there not one simple precaution we may take? The Turkish mind, after all, is far more subtle than ours. Our cruder subterfuges might even succeed. I take it that however near to Malta the Sultan's flotilla approaches, Charles is unlikely to release Imperial ships to help you?'

'He will never leave Sicily and Naples unguarded,' said the Receiver with simple conviction. 'Never. And without Prince Doria's fleet, our own galleys are useless against this monstrous navy of Sinan Pasha and Dragut.'

'And there is your one frail hope, surely,' said Lymond patiently to the circle of brown and bearded faces, shining with sweat in the lamplight. 'For although you know this for certain, Dragut does not. Say, if Malta were attacked, that the Turks intercepted a boat arriving from Sicily with ostensible news for the Grand Master that Doria was back in Messina, and that couriers had been sent abroad, to Naples, to Genoa, summoning ships and troops to help raise the siege. It wouldn't be true, but the Turks couldn't depend on it. They might take fright. They might retreat . . .'

They discussed it, the young men's voices rising in their excitement. The Receiver was doubtful. Could such a ruse mislead the Turks? How would he know that Malta had suffered attack? Whom could he send to Malta with a spurious message? And how ensure that the Turks would intercept it?

They argued a long time without reaching a conclusion, but Lymond, watching them, did not add to his point. Buckled to his fine belt was the thick purse, chiming with gold pieces, that Jerott Blyth silently passed to him. For though the Knights Hospitallers were not a gambling Order, they had their pride.

It was then two hours to dawn. As the sun rose, innocent on the innocent sea, the Chevalier de Villegagnon with his retinue, among whom Francis Crawford was modestly one, set sail in the Viceroy of Sicily's fastest brigantine for Malta, island fortress of Holy Church in the Middle Seas, and destined prey of Dragut.

II

The Tongue of Gabriel

(Maltese Archipelago, July 1551)

'UNTIL you have smoked out this nest of vipers, you can do no good anywhere.'

The words, long ago, had been the corsair Dragut's, speaking of Malta. And soundlessly Francis Crawford repeated them now, standing fanned by the striped triangular sail overhead, his gaze on those pink morsels of sandstone far ahead off the bows of the brigantine, a flaw in the shining blue twill of the sea.

Malta, Comino and Gozo, the three islands of the Maltese Archipelago. Melita, island of honey, navel of the great, tideless waterway. Comino, island of cumin and spice....

He had spoken aloud. 'And Gozo,' said the Chevalier de Villegagnon gravely at his shoulder. 'Isle of Calypso, the long-haired enchantress, alluring Odysseus with her voice at the loom.'

There was a respectful silence to the shade of Calypso, during which Nicholas Durand and Lymond were thinking of two quite different women. Then they were close enough to smell the hot sandstone rock, the dazzle of sea in their eyes; and under bare poles, the rowers drawing the brigantine through water like hazy blue glass, they slid into the long fjord with three left turnings: the historic deepwater harbour of Malta.

On their right, the scarlet flag of the Order moved, and then dipped ceremoniously from the watch-tower of St Elmo below the baked yellow heights of Mount Sciberras. The Order already knew, by fast boat from Sicily, that de Villegagnon was coming, and why.

But that was all. No galleys moved in or out of the long inlet, no metal glittered; no scramble of men building, digging, defensive, was visible on either side. On the brigantine, no one spoke save the master and the bo's'n, repeating orders, as she crept into Malta in the blazing midsummer silence; and Malta slept, sullenly, all around.

One precaution only the Order had taken. The chain was across Galley Creek, the hand-forged Venetian chain whose every link had cost the knights ten golden ducats. It sealed the mouth of the middle of the three blind seaways entering the long southern coast of the fjord, and from its vast capstan on the left to its rock bed on the right, joined the two tongues of land between which all the galleys and brigantines of the Order usually lay. On the left tongue was Birgu, the fishing village the knights had made convent and home of the Order, with the fort of St Angelo at its tip. On the right was the peninsula called L'Isla, with a watch-tower and scattered houses which stared across Galley Creek to Birgu.

Now, above the tiered, windowless walls of Fort St Angelo rising white from sea and rock on their left, a second scarlet flag dipped in turn; and a puff of smoke, followed by the dull thud of a gun, reported to the piled, yellow-white town of Birgu at its back that de Villegagnon had come. A skiff, running alongside the shallow boats supporting the great chain from side to side of the creek, freed the middle stretch from supports, and the taut line sagged and dipped as, invisibly, the slaves below St Angelo flung their weight on the capstan bars. De Villegagnon, silent in the bows, turned and nodded to the Master, and the brigantine slowly gained speed and slid over the line.

Slid, and then stopped, for the Chevalier, leaning over the rail, had seen the sloop turn and dart to the brigantine's side, and caught sight of paler faces within it among the olive skins of the crew, and a swing of black cloth. Neatly balancing amidships, a man stood and hailed the incoming ship.

Without approaching the rail, Lymond studied de Villegagnon as the rowers backpaddled and the big ship was stubbed to a halt. 'A welcoming party?'

A change had come over Durand de Villegagnon's face. For the first time you saw that, even to such a soldier—travelled, accepted, assured—coming to Malta was coming home; was coming to his Church and his friends, and to the only altar he knew where he could lay down his burdens for a space. De Villegagnon said, 'Yes. . . . It seems so. The knight on the left is the Pilier of the French Tongue. The man next to him is the Grand Master's secretary. The fat one is Nick Upton, the Turcopilier in charge of Malta's defences —he's English.'

'And the Grand Cross who hailed you?' Moving to de Villegagnon's side, Lymond watched as, below, the rope ladder swung down from the poop for the four knights to ascend. The man in question, already standing, was the first to lay hands on the ladder. He glanced up, grimacing: a tall, broad-shouldered knight in early middle years with hair brighter than Lymond's own—a brief cap, ruthlessly cropped, of guinea-gold, with a vein of his sister's apricot at the crown. 'Gabriel,' said the Chevalier de Villegagnon, with the tension gone from his voice. And so Lymond and Graham Reid Malett met.

Between these two fair-headed men; between Gabriel's Viking dimensions, his radiance, his serenity and the fauve, high-strung person of Francis Crawford, there passed no shock; no intuitive blaze of emotion. Coming to offer his hand after the great embrace he had shared with de Villegagnon, Sir Graham Reid Malett, Grand Cross of the Noble Order of the Knights of St John of Jerusalem; monk, soldier and seaman, of whom Strozzi, Francis de Guise and de Villegagnon himself had spoken with such exceptional warmth, conveyed simply a friendly interest that widened into a mock apologetic smile. Malett said, 'I'm going to hold prayers for a moment, I'm afraid: it's our rather repetitive custom. Could you pacify the Master for me? I know he's wild to get into Birgu's brothels.'

And thus released with courtesy from unnecessary commitment, Lymond was able to stroll to the prow with the Master while the four knights knelt on the beechwood deck where they stood and gave thanks for the Chevalier's safe voyage home.

Grace, intelligence, humour and great strength: these were the first impressions of Gabriel a stranger would receive; these, and the beauty of his magnificent voice. As prayers ended and the ship moved slowly up-creek to its berth, he spoke quickly and quietly of his arrangements. De Villegagnon and Lymond were to stay with him at Birgu. Unique among the knights, Gabriel had a house to himself instead of sharing the communal life of the Langues. Later, a meeting of the Supreme Council had been called, before whom de Villegagnon must speak.

At this point Sir Graham paused. In the sun-reddened face with its shapely bones, strong jaw and wide brow seamed with dry lines; in the sea-blue, cloudless gaze, a shadow of trouble existed. Addressing de Villegagnon, 'You're no novice, Nicholas,' he said. 'You know the weakness here, and how your detractors will work.'

'I had something of the same treatment from the Viceroy,' said de Villegagnon equably. The impotent storm of anger he had nursed from Messina seemed to have gone. Instead, he looked like a man restored to the cool legal terrain of his fathers; and all the emotion he had bred to sustain him slipped unneeded away. Lymond recognized that de Villegagnon had not only the confidence of Gabriel's support: behind Gabriel he saw God.

'Nicholas thinks I have the Grand Master in the palm of my hand,' said Gabriel tranquilly, picking up Lymond's tenor of thought. 'But no one here controls Juan de Homedès, least of all the poor gentleman himself. I pity him; I also fear for him. I fear for us all. He and his Spanish knights have weakened the Order. This season they may dishonour it in the eyes of all reasonable men.'

The soft bulk of Nick Upton pressed into the triangle. 'Gabriel, I am not a reasonable man. I say, throw out Juan de Homedès.'

Malett laughed, but unlike Upton, he kept his voice to a murmur. 'Throw out a Grand Master, appointed by Charles V and the Pope?

In face of his overwhelming Spanish vote in the Supreme Council? And with the whole Turkish fleet liable to besiege us? If ever the Order needed to be whole, Nick, it is now.'

'Better a wholesome half than a rotten whole,' said the fat Englishman dourly.

'You forget,' said Gabriel quickly, his gaze on the fast-nearing quay. 'We are hospitallers to trade. With the right medicine, even the rotten whole might be cured in time.'

'Even though,' said Lymond, since no one else seemed to be saying it, 'Juan de Homedès has been Grand Master for fifteen years?'

Gabriel smiled. 'Despite that. For Durand de Villegagnon has been absent for much of that time, and Leone Strozzi, and many more I could name. Nicholas is the first to come back. By tomorrow, you will see, there will be more.'

Upton, the fat Turcopilier, dropped his argument abruptly. 'And M. le Comte de Sevigny is to give us the benefit of his experience,' he said.

Again the wise, disarming blue gaze scanned Lymond. 'I did not care to court his already well-founded contempt by expressing it,' he said. 'But that, of course, has been all along in our minds. . . . Shall we go ashore?'

And, sparing Francis Crawford the need to reply, Gabriel turned and moving lightly, for all his great height, led the way on to the baked sandy clay of Birgu.

*

Less than an hour later, bathed and robed, the Chevalier de Ville-gagnon went to pay his formal respects to the Grand Master, and Lymond, left for the moment alone, changed quickly and in anonymous dark jerkin and hose walked into the steep, slatted lanes of Birgu.

From a breathless sky, the sun beat on the soft yellow rock; the long spit on which the knights had reared their tall, elegant houses, face to face in a network of alleys that climbed the steep ridge on either side from the water's edge, where the Maltese lived still, in cabin and hut. Emptied by the hour of siesta, Birgu presented itself boldly to the observer climbing silently between the splendour of grille-work and portico, cartouche, shrine and balcony; beneath the banners drooping still from the sunlight into the shadowy canyons where he walked.

First the private houses with their marble steps and beautiful knockers; the coat of arms fresh, the saints in their flowered niches bright with gold and enamel. Then the Auberges, Inns of the Eight Langues into which this Order of international knights had long ago been divided, so that each race could sleep and eat with its fellow nationals and speak, in the Inn at least, the same common tongue.

Since 1540, the English Langue had been nominal only. There were ten English knights left on Malta, of whom Nick Upton was one. In London there were, openly, none. When King Henry VIII of England renounced the Pope, he renounced the Order of St John of Jerusalem as well; seized the Order's rich Priory at Clerkenwell and all their possessions.

In Scotland the Priory was untouched, but only two of her knights remained in the convent: Jerott Blyth, at present in Sicily and now ranking as French; and Graham Malett, Knight Grand Cross and friend of the French, whose integrity that afternoon in support of de Villegagnon must sway even the Grand Master to believe that Malta and Tripoli would be attacked, and Malta and Tripoli must be saved.

Now, as Lymond, observing, quartered Birgu, only the Maltese stirred.

Between the palaces of the knights and those that served them; the convents, the elegant homes belonging to officers of the Church and the town; between the bakehouse and the shops of the craftsmen, the arsenals and magazines, the warehouses, the homes of merchants and courtesans, Italian, Spanish, Greek; past the painted shrines and courtyards scraped from pockets of earth with their bright waxy green carob trees, a fig, a finger of vine, a blue and orange pot of dry, dying flowers and a tethered goat bleating in a swept yard, padded the heirs of this rock, this precious knot in the trade of the world. Umber-skinned, grey-eyed, barefoot and robed as Arabs with the soft, slurring dialect that Dido and Hannibal spoke, they slipped past the painted facades to their Birgu of fishermen's huts and blank, Arab-walled houses or to sleep, curled in the shade, with the curs in a porch.

A great Church and a race of defenders had come to bless the peasants and noblemen of Malta, who possessed a rock and the language Christ spoke. Bitterly silent both about the privileges they had lost and the laws they were now to fulfil, the Maltese were apt to recall that the Church was already theirs long before the knights came; and that before the knights came, they had no need of defenders.

At the highest point in the little walled town, overlooking the canal which separated Birgu from the big white fortress built on the point, Lymond paused to look, the high trill of caged singing birds the only sound in the heat.

Over there, in the high fort of St Angelo where the Grand Master lived, the knights and their suites would withdraw in time of siege. The cisterns in St Angelo would be their only water supply; the stone-lidded grain tanks their main source of food; the slaves in the rock dungeons verging the canal their charge and their danger.

In the long journey from Marseilles Lymond had not wasted his time. He knew that Malta had no rivers, no wells and only one or two sweet-water springs, of which Birgu had one. He knew that, scattered pueblos apart, the only other city of substance, poorly fortified, was the old walled capital of Mdina, guarding a broad, dusty plain nine miles northwards. He knew that Malta's spoonfuls of Sicilian topsoil sustained cotton and melons, figs, vines, olives with difficulty; and that her corn, her biscuit meal, her meat, her wine, her powder all came from Sicily, or Naples, or Candia. Without her own ships, or the Emperor's fleet, a long siege would fall hard on the island.

Thinking; analysing; ignoring his soaked clothes and the baked stench of goat and stale food and human clothing, of oil and strong cheese and salt fish and the pervasive, peppery veiling of incense, he turned and looked between the fretted white houses to where Galley Creek, dazzling silver and blue, joined the long deepwater fjord of Grand Harbour.

Opposite and very near, on the piled rock of L'Isla, the scattered white houses hugged patches of green; the silver-grey of olives, the dense green of pine and carob, the serrated embroidery of date palms. It was a long way from the chameleon summer of the Scottish Border; from the costly and courtly graces of the Loire. In this community of dedicated knights, in this historic, tarnished Order, set among brothels and a devout, sullen archaic race of Phoenicians on their rock halfway between Europe and Africa, he had unravelled first all that was stupid and petty and high-handed about these complacent aristocrats, toughened and coarsened by endless coarse war; their intelligence besotted with the syrups of religion and by the anaesthesia of the Order's thousand rigid rules.

But then, equally of purpose, he had left the hospital and the Church till the last. Now he turned and walked back to Holy Infirmary Square and the big building fronting the street and running down to the rocks at its back where, by permission of the French Pilier, who was also Grand Hospitaller of the Order, Lymond was admitted to the halls of mercy of Birgu.

They showed him everything. He saw the kitchens where sweating men, desiccated with heat and work, ladled chicken broth from the copper vats into silver bowls; the dispensary with its rows of majolica jars, its apothecaries and quiet novices working without siesta, powdering and mixing to the chant of prayers. He walked past the rows of beds, past knights sick of wounds and crushed limbs, of dysentery and enteric, of pox and sweating disease. He passed through the rooms where Maltese lay uncomplaining, and Moors; slaves and free men; poor and rich; of any faith and no faith. In poverty, in chastity, in obedience, the knights and novices toiled, in their thin hospital robes, side by side with the surgeons, and did not even look up.

Then he left, and walked down through the sloping town square to the slumbering quayside and along the water's edge until he came to the steps, flight on flight to his left, leading up to the Order's Church of St Lawrence. He climbed these and went in.

Black vault in the white glare of the day, it gave him nothing at first but incense and coolness and a murmurous silence. Far within, something sparkled in a chance ray of the sun. Then he saw the pricks of tiered candles, the flowers and the flags, the painted ceiling, the gold altar canopy, the statues, the shrines and the tombs. And on the ranks of toffee-brown pillars, the Cross of the Order twinkling, pinned to the marble.

The church was full. On the diced marble floor there was no room even to kneel. And Lymond stayed there longest of all, without speaking, without moving; scanning the bowed heads among the gold and the marble; the raised faces showing age and patience, fear, compassion, timidity, conviction, strength. Of the five hundred Knights of the Sovereign Order of St John of Jerusalem, of Rhodes, of Malta, most of those living today in Birgu were here, praying for deliverance; praying for the survival of the Faith; praying for strength to endure. *Malta fidei propugnaculum;* Malta, Bulwark of the Faith, was before him, here.

As silently as he had come, Lymond left. Walking back to Gabriel's house through the graveyard and the steep sandy lanes, he marshalled dispassionately his information and his emotions on what he had seen. Centuries ago, appealing for a new Crusade, the cry had been '*Dieu le veut!*'—God desires it.

But which God? Francis Crawford inquired pensively of each silent street of closed doors. For if your Moslem is also devout and self-denying, loyal and fervent, courageous and tolerant, and believes that to dispatch a Christian in battle will send him straight to the Red Apple of Paradise, then in the forthcoming attack, with no professional, no ideological flaw on both sides, sheer weight of numbers must tell.

He said nothing of all this to the Chevalier de Villegagnon, whom he found already returned in Graham Malett's house. But presently Gabriel himself came in and, halting in the doorway, looked first at Lymond and then at his fellow knight. 'Have you told him?'

The Chevalier, rising, shook his head and Gabriel, gentle irony in his voice, addressed Lymond direct. 'You are to appear, M. le Comte, along with the Chevalier here in an hour's time before the Grand Council to corroborate M. de Villegagnon's report from France. You will see us, as I am sure you would prefer, at our worst.'

Durand de Villegagnon, a deeply passionate man behind a shell of militarism and law, looked uneasy. Lymond did not. He said, 'I try to rely not on feelings, but facts. At the cost, for example, of sundry murmurs from my insessorial arches, I have been surveying Birgu—all of Birgu. The Conventual Church and the hospital, as well as the magazines.'

'And you would not mind being carried into either? 'said Gabriel gravely.

'Not with eternity in Paradise assured for every Ottoman wound.'

'Someone,' said Gabriel, entering the room fully at last and kneeling, from habit, before the old and much-travelled shrine, 'once called us mercenaries of the spirit. True, of course. But we are all in life risking one thing to gain another. Is it better to fight for vanity, ambition, money, revenge, pique . . .?'

'Would you fight to cleanse the Qur'ân from the earth if the reward for death were the torments of Hell?' Lymond said.

There was a long pause. De Villegagnon, heated, drew breath to reply and thought better of it. Outside, as the violence of the sun subsided, life began to stir in the narrow street. The shadows moved. 'I,' said Gabriel at length, looking directly at Lymond, his eyes calm as a child's, 'have always sinned and never, consequently, deserved more than a hope of Paradise. But if I had, and by fighting the Turk I must give it up . . . then my answer is, yes. For those that follow me, that they might taste Heaven, I would fight, as I mean to fight; and suffer, as I should be made to suffer. No man could do more.'

'One man did not do as much,' said Lymond tranquilly, and saw Gabriel's fair skin stained red from neck to brow. But instead of replying he crossed himself, and turning to the crucifix on the altar, bent in prayer.

In a grip that bruised, de Villegagnon drew Crawford of Lymond from the room and in the dim white hall confronted him, outrage in his voice. 'What devil possessed you? The like of that man is not to be found in Europe, and you shame him before his own shrine?'

Mild surprise on his face, Lymond turned. 'I think Graham Malett can fight his own battles,' he said. 'It merely seemed as well to discover whether we are fighting for power or for Holy Church. For on our convincing the Grand Master on that one issue, the whole future of the Order in Malta and Tripoli quite certainly depends.'

And, 'He is right,' said Gabriel later when, brusquely, de Villegagnon conveyed explanation and apology together. 'On your integrity and mine, on the integrity of la Valette and de Lescaut and all the Knights of the French Langue—on our unshakeable faith in the Order will this outcome depend.'

*

66

'It is obvious to a child,' Grand Master Juan de Homedès was saying without moving, without turning his thin neck, his thin temples, his thin nose and eyeless socket clothed in a patch above the black and silver Aragonese beard, 'to a bantling, that Dragut has no ill intent towards Malta and Tripoli. It is France he visits with so vast a fleet—where else? D'Aramon, the French Ambassador to Turkey, awaits them, we know, with muleloads of gold. They wintered once before at Toulon—they do it again. Your master the Constable of France is mistaken, M. le Chevalier de Villegagnon— and so are you.'

In rank as great as a Cardinal Deacon; peer to princes; 'cousin' to the kings of Europe and answerable only to the Pope, the 48th Grand Master of the Sovereign Order of St John and Prince of Malta was an arrogant old Spaniard, dedicated to Christ, nepotism and the Emperor Charles V. In the byways of Rome he would have been a holy old man, no better and not much worse than the rest of the College of Cardinals. On Malta he was still holy and old, but he was also a selfish and unduly vain patriarch in a post requiring a saint; and he was dangerous.

Within the thick, chaste walls of the hall, lukewarm as the sun beat down outside on the white fort of St Angelo, the thirty members of the Grand Council—Bishop, the Prior of the Church, the Piliers of the eight Langues, several Priors and Conventual Bailiffs and four Knights Grand Cross—sat at two long, parallel tables, linked at top by the desk of the Vice-Chancellor, who with two priests at his side was their Secretary.

Beside the desk, and raised above it on a dais, was the canopied throne of His Eminence Grand Master de Homedès, the red silk banner of the Order with its plain, eight-pointed Cross hung above. Every man present, including de Villegagnon, erect in the space between the double rows of knights and facing the Grand Master, wore black. And alone of all the men present, the two priests and Lymond, waiting outwith the rectangle at de Villegagnon's back, did not qualify for the holy white Cross.

Malta and Tripoli have nothing to fear. It was all de Homedès would say. In vain de Villegagnon repeated the warning sent by the Constable de Montmorency out of the esteem and affection he bore to an illustrious Order which the Grand Master de l'Isle Adam, his uncle, had governed in most perilous times. In vain did Gabriel, with courteous good sense, remind the Grand Master that according to the Order's own brigantine, sent to Morea, all the rumours of the Levant agreed that Dragut had armed for an attack on the knights.

Lymond, who happened to know that d'Aramon's mission, far from welcoming the Turk to Toulon, was to return to Turkey and persuade the Sultan to relieve the Emperor Charles quietly of Bône,

North Africa, could not say so. And de Villegagnon, questioned narrowly and more acidly still about the true French relations with Turkey, could only reply too coldly, too loudly, that if the Turk was acting at the instance of the French King, none knew of it; but that Bône was taken from Suleiman, over the Emperor's pledged word and with the knights' help, and that Malta would suffer for it.

'Because of it,' said the big knight, straight in his robes, his high black hat tight in his hand, 'I have left France, abandoned my King, jettisoned my career, to range myself under the banner of this threatened Order, on this warning alone, without waiting for your Serene Highness's citation. I can do no more to express my unshakeable belief that the warning is true.'

'You have said, I think,' said the Grand Master's dry voice, in the old-fashioned Spanish he commonly used when Latin tired him, 'that Tripoli is poorly fortified, low in ammunition and garrisoned, as I think you put it, by a few sick old gentlemen retired there for tne air. It is also'—carrying on over the indignant murmur of Spanish voices—'surrounded on three sides by desert and enemy states. You think that Gozo castle should be demolished and the Gozitans sent to Sicily rather than defend their island. You think the two hundred troops the Viceroy, wisely or unwisely, promised you at Messina should be sent to Tripoli with an army of my young knights from Malta to replace the present weak garrison, while the Viceroy is pressed to send more soldiers and ships which in turn would leave Naples and Sicily bare. Does that seem to you just? And if the Viceroy sends no more than these two hundred men—and he will not, M. de Villegagnon, for I shall not ask it of him—does it seem right to leave Gozo empty, and Malta denuded, to half-strengthen Tripoli?'

'Call in the knights from the provinces,' said Gabriel. 'M. de Villegagnon had no need to suggest that. It is obvious.'

'And fortify Malta.' The French voice, its accent dulled with long years on the island, was Jean de la Valette's, Parisot to his friends; his grizzled face impatient, his shattered leg stuck incontinently at an angle below his parted black robes. 'We need mercenaries, cannon, bulwarks . . . a better fort at St Elmo, and one at L'Isla to cross fire with St Angelo across Galley Creek. If we work fast, there is time to do something.'

'But no men, Chevalier; and no money.' The dry voice of de Homedès was tinged with triumph. '*Yo lo siento.* As with you, the fate of this island keeps me sleepless at nights. Last year, as you know, the crops in Sicily failed. The Order was forced instead to pay for imports from France, from even further afield. We are not rich. We had no reserves. We had to pawn our plate to send even our last emissary to England. The Treasury, Brethren, is empty. We cannot

raise or pay mercenaries; we cannot finance even the summons of
our knights from their commanderies. By increasing our tax on these
properties we might later gather a little reserve for this purpose; but
that cannot help us now.'

'And will the Grand Master say,' said de Villegagnon, the veins
throbbing in his thick neck and all his lawyer's caution melting slowly
in the stifling candour of courteous authority, 'how the rest of the
Treasury money has been spent?'

The protest which ran round the room, he ought to have recognized, was not wholly disagreement and not wholly shock. It was,
however, an expression of rightful alarm that, against all the rules
of their devotion and their way of life, de Villegagnon should have
spoken openly to the Grand Master thus. Through it all Gabriel's
easy bass-baritone spoke. 'There are channels for accounting which
are none of your business, Brother Nicholas, as they are none of
mine, but which all the Order's officials are familiar with to the
point of nausea. In any case, don't let your distress lead you into
side issues. We are all sleepless, with prayers as well as with sailing.
We can only align and disperse solutions until we reach the right
one.'

'I need no protector, Brother Graham.' The Grand Master's face
under the black hat was thinly fleshed with his anger, but his voice
was unchanged. The black patch, unvarying, was bent on de Villegagnon. 'And I find you too ready to make M. de Villegagnon's
apologies. To have mistaken the King of France's intentions as he
has done implies a naïveté beyond understanding, or a knavery
beyond any apology. The Constable's message, I am sure,' added de
Homedès, who had played this game, monotonously, many times
before, 'arose from the warmest wishes for our well-being. But the
Constable is not France. The King is France, and with him the de
Guise family, *one of whose spies you have brought here, M. de Villegagnon, into this citadel!*'

It was neatly done: so neatly that, without hesitation, thirty-five
pairs of eyes, old, young, mature with long prayer, seamed with
years of sailing on bright water, lucid with sanctity and young
terrors overcome, slewed round to Lymond.

There had been almost no warning. But an instant before the
Grand Master's accusation was achieved, Lymond's own face
changed from the odd, waiting expression it had worn all day. Alight
with surprise and with discreet laughter he said, half under his
breath, 'Christ! The three mutes with the bowstring!' Then, as two
or three of the knights began, in the surge of talk, to jump to their
feet, Francis Crawford pulled himself together and moving forward,
addressed de Homedès, his voice clear and precise.

'I beg your pardon. Perhaps I may set your minds at rest most quickly by saying that I have no intention of leaving this island until the attack is over—if it comes. How could I, anyway? The brigantine that brought me has gone, and the Order controls the harbour in Malta. Even if I were an agent of France—which I am not—I could do nothing but report, if I live to report, how the Order bore itself under threat of the Turk. And the Order, I take it, has no objection to that?'

By the time he ended, he had silence to speak in. Gabriel's voice followed immediately. 'The Sieur de Villegagnon has laid down his career. Both he and M. de Lymond in coming here have offered their lives. We risk being called un-Christian if we ignore these facts.'

'We risk being called gullible if we look at no others,' said the Grand Master. 'What, for example, is to prevent this young man from betraying all our defences, should the Turk land?'

'Nothing,' said Lymond mildly. Gestured still nearer, he had moved a pace or two into the centre of the hall and stood relaxed, his head bare, his hands, holding his hat, lightly clasped at his back. He wore no sword. 'Nothing. Except that if the Turk lands, the King of France's warning is substantiated. And if the warning is genuine, why should I be otherwise?'

The eye patch stared at Francis Crawford's emotionless face. 'Shall we say,' said the Grand Master at length, his hands flat on his knees, 'that the Grand Turk is not wholly as yet under France's control, and that the King of France might desire an agent at hand in case affairs take an unlooked-for turn?'

'Let us say so, by all means,' said Lymond gently. 'So long as Malta is fortified against exactly such a danger, I should willingly place myself under irons for the length of any attack. All of my French colleagues would no doubt tell you the same. On her present resources, Malta can withstand only the briefest of sieges without outside help. You intend to bring Holy Church naked within reach of the infidel. For that, I salute your faith. Allow us to bolster it further with such measures as are within our means.'

There was a short silence. In one unexceptionable speech, M. de Villegagnon's companion had delivered a number of plain truths, of which the plainest was a challenge as well. 'Unless your fortify, you will fail. And you will not be permitted to blame that failure on your French knights or on me. . . .'

The Grand Master stirred. Under the grey brows his good eye shone, sharp and bright. 'I would remind you, sir,' he said, 'that alone of all those here present you have made no vows and are under no restraint. As to your . . . detention, I may well take you at your word. As far as your colleagues, as you term them, are concerned, I should attempt no such impertinence. I trust they will forgive you yours.'

He raised his voice. 'M. de Lymond, since you have chosen to come

70

to this island, you may not expect to leave it without our permission. M. de Villegagnon, we thank you for bringing our dear friend the Constable's dispatch. You have both our permission to retire.'

With nothing settled, nothing planned, these two dangerous men were being dismissed. De Villegagnon, his hat crushed to his thigh, said brusquely, 'Jean! Graham!' and took two impolitic steps towards the dais. One of the priests by the Secretary's table stepped in front of him; one of the Spanish Piliers, getting up in a hurry, knocked sideways his heavy chair with the painted crest on the back. De Villegagnon had probably no physical coercion in mind: his only idea was to approach de Homedès, man to man, and persuade. But the tension in the room, the taut consciences, the sour presence of prayer-drugged fear, dragged the situation suddenly out of shape. Lymond's eyes met Gabriel's and both men moved not forward, but back, towards the double oak doors from the hall, both with the same thought: to fling them wide and halt the scene quickly, by making it public.

Lymond, nearer the foot of the room, reached the doors first. But as he touched them, the timber shook with invisible assault; loud voices sounded outside and a guard shouted in protest. The handle rattled. Then, as Lymond fell back to where the knights stood, arrested in turmoil, the door burst open to admit Jerott Blyth.

'Oh, dear,' said Lymond mildly into the sudden extreme quiet. 'Sicily haven't sent their two hundred men.'

Blyth looked round. Visibly, a little colour returned to his handsome face, white with rage. His fists unclenched, hesitated, and then raising one, he removed his bonnet. Behind the long tables the knights lingered, shuffling, and then with a scraping of chairs slowly resumed their seats, leaving de Villegagnon again alone on the floor, his back to the Grand Master's dais, staring as the Grand Master was staring at Jerott Blyth's disordered dark figure.

It was de Villegagnon, his own anger forgotten, who echoed Lymond's words. 'They haven't sent the two hundred?'

The small, dark knight stalked, without speaking, from the closing doors to the foot of the dais. Arrived there, he hurled his battered black bonnet at the foot of the steps and folded his arms.

'They have sent them,' he said, 'I have come with them. Had they sent two hundred sheep, you could have eaten them. Two hundred goats, and you could have milked them. Two hundred cannon balls, and you could have killed Turks with them. What they *have* sent,' said Jerott Blyth, forgetting Latin, Spanish and decorum in his anger, 'are *rabbits*!'

'They promised us soldiers,' said de Villegagnon, his voice echoing in the silence.

'They have sent us shepherd boys,' said Jerott, the excitement

71

suddenly dead in his blood. 'Youths from the hills of Calabria. Woodsmen and goatherds, tenders of vineyards. Men wise in the stars and the weather and in growing grapes and melons and pomegranate trees. Boys who have been ill with fright all the way from Messina; children who have never seen a Turk; youths who have never held a sword or a gun. '*These*,' said Jerott, his voice shaking again, 'are to be the defenders of Christ's Church against the heathen in Tripoli.'

By then, moved as he was, he must have realized that his eloquence had struck no echo here: that he was to be permitted no fuel for his anger. The Grand Master had had enough of wayward emotion. Icily thanked, icily reprimanded, icily dismissed, Jerott Blyth found himself in the street without having heard a voice raised in comment; nor did he realize until joined almost at once by de Villegagnon and by Lymond, also dismissed, into what kind of crisis he had burst.

They did not know that the struggle within the Grand Council in which all three had precipitated went on all afternoon; that as the door closed behind the Chevalier de Villegagnon, the Grand Master had at last smiled. 'Either this Frenchman is the Constable's dupe, or he has a mind to make us his.' And against all argument, de Homedès's premise was unshaken. The Sultan Suleiman would never expend his wealth to take a barren rock such as this. And there must be firm news to the contrary before he would authorize a *grano* to be spent. The Turkish fleet was aiming at Italy, and the possessions of the Emperor Charles. And all this solicitude from France was no more than an attempt to denude Sicily and the Italian States of their defences by concentrating them uselessly on the knights.

To la Valette's renewed urging that he should garrison Tripoli with young knights under a wise and experienced Grand Cross, to put fortifications in order and evacuate useless mouths, de Homedès replied sharply that he had no intention of bolstering Tripoli at Malta's expense. By removing the older knights, they would merely deprive Tripoli of so much experience, as well as that stout, old-fashioned military spirit which never surrendered. The knights must stay.

'And Gozo?' Even one of his allies, Piero Nuñes, bailiff of la Boveda, was driven to ask. 'The castle is indefensible. The people must surely be taken off now and sent to safety in Sicily?'

Gozo, Calypso's island: the small, fertile rock to the north of Malta, looking across the forty-five miles of sea to Sicily, with villages, a small town and a castle, a crumbling ruin on a rock.

The Grand Master was quite explicit in his plans for Gozo. 'Heathens who have been trounced on flat ground should not be hard to throw off a rock. Men fight better, I have found,' said the Grand Master of the Noble Order of St John of Jerusalem, Rhodes and Malta, 'in the presence of their women and children. And I have the greatest trust in my Governor, the Chevalier de Césel . . . so brave, so skilful that there can be nothing to fear. To abandon Gozo,' said the Grand Master repressively, 'would merely ruin the Gozitans and dishonour the Order. Besides,' he added, offering with bored patience his coping-stone. 'If the Turks do not come, who will compensate the evacuated people of Gozo for their loss?'

The silence of accomplishment, of bewilderment, of surrender, was all the answer he received.

*

Through the windless airs of the Dardanelles the Mussulman fleet followed the high-banked oars of its flagship: galleys, brigantines, looming galleasses with their thousand fighting-men apiece; their cannon balls and powder and small arms; their stores of food, of water, of canvas and tents; their rolls of linen, their matches, their pots of sulphurous wildfire, their knives, their scimitars, their guns, the heavy cannon; the bamboo rods for the bastinado; the opium for the injured; the sorbet, raisins and lemons; the coffee, the bows and crossbows; the pennants and banners, the date cakes and the barrels filled with sweet grapes from Trebizond.

On the flagship travelled Dragut the corsair, and Sinan Pasha, the renegade Smyrnian Jew, in command. Because the Janissaries were on board, it was as if the Sultan Suleiman were present himself. Over its carved golden poop there stood the Grand Turk's own private standard: a square of beaten silver, aching-bright in the sun; and above that, the yellow crescent of Islâm and a golden ball, its long, horsehair plume streaming idly behind.

Spahís, corsairs, thieves and robbers, renegade Greeks and Levantines sailed westward with the Osmanli in their great fleet. Enslaved knights of Malta tugged at the oars; whistles shrilled; gongs pulsed with the strokes on, on, on through the lapis-blue water; and at the five appointed times, day after calm day, the *adhan*, the ritual call to worship, ululated from their packed decks.

The Twelve Thousand, the Followers of the Prophet, were approaching. Not to harbour in France; not to capture Naples; not to seize back Bône; but to drive the Knights of St John and all their works into the sea.

*

From the moment that he hurled himself, in a blaze of anger, on to Malta with his two hundred unfortunate shepherd boys, through all that followed, Jerott Blyth spent a good deal of time, out of curiosity, at Lymond's side.

No more than Gabriel did he attach any great significance to the encounter. But he wanted to find, and give nostalgic credence to the attraction he remembered as a boy in Scotland, before the years in France and his joining the Order: before Elizabeth's death.

The Blyths until then had always been lucky. Like the Culters they were well-born, well-favoured, and with money enough to give Jerott the finest tutors and the best training for war. He had not known Lymond well before the battle of Solway Moss against the English in '42; but he had allowed himself to be entertained, as had they all, by the kind of quick-witted fantasy which was Francis Crawford's trademark at the time.

For the rest, it was Richard, the elder brother, whom most people knew best. Until Solway Moss, the tragedy which ended in the Scottish King's death just after the birth of the child Mary who was to succeed him. In that messy rout, Jerott Blyth lost his father and saw Lymond, who had ridden and fought beside him with a kind of insane inspiration in the field unlike anything Jerott had seen before, removed a prisoner of the English to London.

Then on the eve of Jerott's wedding, amid the mourning for his father, Elizabeth too had died, and he had barely attended to the rumours of Lymond's wild subsequent career. Until, long settled in France, where his family were now in business, in course of taking his caravans and his vows to become a knight of Malta, Jerott had wondered now and then what the instant affinity had been that he had felt, nine years ago at Solway Moss, and whether, a man now instead of a boy, he would find it a childhood illusion.

In search of enlightenment, Jerott Blyth attached himself with great firmness that evening to the party which went to dine, after the Council meeting broke up, in the Auberge of France. As well as Lymond, de Villegagnon was there, and Graham Malett, with Nicholas Upton the Turcopilier, refugee from the non-existent English Langue.

For the sake of coolness the meal was set in the courtyard, visible through the crested doorway, its barrel arch lozenged in colour. For sixty scudi a year, the Pilier could clearly serve his knights' hunger most handsomely. The platter from which each quartet of knights ate was of silver; the food oily but surprisingly varied. Jerott Blyth listened, crumbling his brown, loose-textured bread, to Gabriel's level and accurate account of all that had happened in Council since they left. Nothing had convinced de Homedès of Malta's danger, and for his own reasons nothing ever would. He had given sanction for limited safeguards and, short of violence, could be made to do no more. It was for the knights themselves to stretch these as far as possible, and without equipment, without prospect of help from Sicily or the Emperor, to arm the citadel of Malta 'with straw and sea air', as de Villegagnon said bitterly, as best they might.

Throughout the heat of the argument Lymond had, Jerott noted, restrained comment. It was, after all, the Order's own dirty linen which was being turned over. A thought struck him. Leaning over, he said in an undertone, 'Have you been to Gozo yet?' From Birgu to the north tip of Malta was only a dozen miles or so, and four miles across the channel from that was the island of Gozo, where that woman was. Or where he supposed she was, if the Governor hadn't got tired of her.

Hoping for some observable reaction, he was disappointed. Lymond, watching Gabriel as he talked of fortifications, simply shook his head.

'It will be a little awkward now, surely, that you can't leave the island?' Jerott persevered.

He had spoken more loudly than he meant and Gabriel, who had a disconcerting trick of following conversations on several levels at once, broke off and said, 'If Mr Crawford wants to cross to Gozo, I can take him.'

With no perceptible pause Lymond answered as easily. 'I should like to see all the fortifications of both Gozo and Malta, but we should perhaps draw up our plan first. The Turcopilier and yourself have all the local knowledge we need.' And Jerott, noting the evasion, was rather gratified by the results of his impulse.

It was only later, as they settled down to the detail of the defence, that he realized that Lymond had spoken the truth, if not the whole truth. His grasp of the fortifications of Birgu and St Angelo was already uncomfortably accurate; his analysis damning in its lack of colour. Nick Upton, in whose bailiwick the deficient fortresses fell, interrupted once or twice, his colour heightened, until Gabriel in his deep voice said, 'Nick, this is the fault of no one but the Grand Master. If we are going to make the best of it we must accept the facts as they are. It is too late to make sea palisades; the hoops are rotten and there are no long chains in store. Soil must be brought from the Marsa for trenches—that means sacks, spades, wheel-barrows and boats. Water. . . . How many clay water bottles have you?'

Nick Upton pulled in a stool beside the four and lowered his great bulk. 'We shouldn't need bottles, Sir Graham. The underground cisterns will be enough.'

Graham Malett's eyes met Lymond's, and it was Lymond who answered the Turcopilier. 'Not if the cannon vibration cracks the rock,' he said briefly. 'You'll need seawater too, all the barrels you can spare. Sinan Pasha likes to use limpet fireworks, I believe, against men in armour. What about fire weapons of your own? Wildfire? Trumps?'

'We've enough saltpetre,' said Upton. 'Pitch, turpentine, sulphur, resin, oil. . . .'

'Where?'

Jerott didn't see the point until Gabriel said, 'In one of the warehouses you saw on the quay. We'll need hides, Nick; as many as you can raise, and some of those barrels of seawater.' For the warehouse, as Jerott realized, was itself a living bombard, which soaked hides at need might protect.

The discussion went on. Wheat, barley, oil, fish, cheese, wine and biscuit in the rock vats. Too late to lay mines, with only six feet of topsoil over the sand, and limestone below. Weapons checked—partisans, pikes, glaives, battleaxes and daggers and the knights' own two-handed swords; powder, balls and arquebuses, bombards and fireworks; the cannon and mortars at St Angelo itself.

The most easily quarried stone and earth to be brought to build up the outer walls of Birgu. There was no time to deal with Mdina, the other city, and de Homedès had refused guns, troops and defences to Gozo. Horses, to be placed at Mdina to keep contact with the north of Malta, Gozo and thence Sicily. Planks and brushwood to hide snipers. Some of the Order's remaining galleys to be accessibly sunk; the rest to be taken into the canal joining the fort of St Angelo with Birgu. The chain to be checked and maintained between St Angelo and L'Isla.

St Angelo, the only strong fortress and home of the Grand Master, would hold all the knights and, surrounded on three sides by sea and on the fourth by its narrow canal, would be their last stronghold. Birgu, and Mdina six miles away, the only towns, would have to hold all the refugee Maltese who, with their beasts and belongings, would be expected to stream for shelter as soon as the attack came.

Dragut, for this his fifth attack on the Maltese islands, would not risk sailing into the tongue of the sea, chain-stopped, between the St Angelo and L'Isla peninsulas. Instead, as before, he was likely to choose one of the sea inlets on either side—Marsasirocco on the south-west, or Marsamuscetto, the long inlet to the north hidden from Birgu and St Angelo by the spine of Mount Sciberras.

If Dragut chose this last place to anchor, he had only to climb Mount Sciberras to have the knights' headquarters below him, in full view across the water. He had only to drag his ships and his cannon across the neck of land between Marsamuscetto and Galley Creek to be able to sail right across to Birgu, *within the chain at the neck of the creek.* . . .

Plainer and plainer, as the talks progressed, was the knights' vulnerability. And plainer the queer congruity between Gabriel and Lymond: not in style or in temperament, but in coolness and, above all, in a sense of balance. Malett, the older man, with the peace of maturity within him, had a physical magnificence which had helped,

76

Jerott knew, to create his legend, but which was only the vessel for his special brand of power.

Beside him, they all looked pale. Even de Villegagnon with his honest passions and his brilliant career seemed slow-witted and crude; Nick Upton looked a sheepish, fat schoolboy and Lymond an ashen-haired, soft-voiced clerk, pattering solutions in court. Only Gabriel, Jerott noted, talked of the Maltese as if they were flesh and blood. Only Gabriel spoke of the hospital, and those who must serve there; and only Gabriel referred with simplicity to their strongest defence: their dedication to God.

And there only did Jerott's new-found enigma fail him a little. For none of the crusading zeal, clearly, was in Lymond's blood; and he did nothing, as Gabriel would have done, to avoid giving hurt. Instead, presently he remarked, 'Could we persuade the Order, do you suppose, to put their trust in the Lord and wear brigantines or plain leather jackets as the soldiers do? Or is a knight not a knight without his hundred pounds of plate metal, no matter how heavy or hot?'

Gabriel smiled, and forestalling de Villegagnon, said, 'There is no answer but armour to arquebus shot and scimitars, M. le Comte. Ours is made and seamed like glove leather in Germany, and in our armoury here. With the surcoat of the Order to protect us from the direct sun, we do very well ... have done very well, perhaps, for a thousand years.'

He paused. Lymond added nothing. Upton was busily writing on a dog-eared sheaf of notes and de Villegagnon was looking over the Turcopilier's shoulder. Gabriel said suddenly in a low voice, but with great clarity, 'Mr Crawford, you have come to us at a time when the Order was never in greater need of friends. You must understand that to men who have taken vows and offered their lives as these have, the Moslem faith is an insult to the Church we adore; a pit into which all that is noble in mankind may well fall and be swallowed. We here on this fragment of rock are the shield of Christianity, of culture, of humanity, of all the great arts for which men have died. Think of that, and don't despise us. We are not simpletons. We are not poor spirits fled to a cloister. We are men as you are, who have foresworn the pleasures of men; who will forego home and life itself if need be, to defend our heritage from the hosts of the fiend.'

Breathing quickly, Graham Malett suddenly stopped. Sweat, beading the fair skin, sparkled in the lamplight; and below his eyes, clear as seawater, dark shadows remained from the stress of the day. For a moment, raising his cupped hands, he masked his face from the circle of silent eyes. Then, dropping his hands open upon the table he added, his voice not quite clear, 'Do you not think that I am human too? Do you think my vows are simple to keep?'

For a long moment, alone among the silent men at the table, Gabriel's strained gaze sustained Francis Crawford's. Then Sir Graham stirred, glanced quickly round and said, his voice almost normal, 'God forgive me. I have embarrassed you, and myself too, come to that. What can I do? Gentlemen, I propose to take you back home for the finest wine my cellar can afford. After all, it may be the last chance we shall have to drink it. Nick—you can do nothing till morning. Come, man, and bring your lists with you.'

The passion which had brought Graham Malett to plead with a stranger was now well concealed. With talk sober but easy, Gabriel made the burden of that evening a light one; and later, when they were dispersing to sleep and Lymond and de Villegagnon had already gone, he put his light hand, restraining, on Jerott's arm.

'Wait a moment, if you will have patience with me. I think you are a friend of Mr Crawford's?'

'I knew him once,' Jerott said.

Gabriel smiled. 'Don't be hard on him. He is young. And he has been embarrassed quite enough. Jerott. . . . you seemed to know of some wish he had to reach Gozo. Don't tell me why. But,' said the great Graham Malett, making a quick, rueful face and holding up in two fingers a folded fragment of paper, torn and dirtied with much handling, 'this note came this evening from Gozo for Mr Crawford of Lymond, and I am sure he would be much happier if he thought it came through you rather than through me. Someone in Gozo, it seems,' said Gabriel gravely, 'heard with half the population this morning of his arrival from Sicily, and sent a hurried message to him addressed through me. Unfortunately, the superscription had been torn off and I have had to read it to discover its destination but, I promise you, I forget already all it contains.' And handing the dirty note with gravest formality to Jerott Blyth, the merest glint of amusement in his eyes, Gabriel bowed and wished him good night.

At a taper halfway up the stairs, being human, Jerott bent his handsome black head and read, quickly and surreptitiously, the note Gabriel had given him. It was inscribed inside to the Comte de Sevigny, which was acid enough in itself. As for the note, it said merely:

Do not come. I do not wish to see you. There is no danger I face greater than the miseries I have passed. If you believe any share of the blame may be yours, then serve me now at least by leaving me in peace.

There was no signature, but the thick, forceful writing was a woman's.

Presenting this missive a little later to Lymond, Jerott Blyth to his own surprise found himself incapable of a straight lie. When the other man, having glanced at the note, said, 'Oonagh O'Dwyer. How did this come to you?' the knight told him.

Lymond's fair brows rose. For the first time it occurred to Jerott that he would be an uncomfortable enemy to make. Then suddenly the other man laughed and said, 'Gabriel's thoughtfulness is unending. Or did he think I would suspect him of writing it himself? Recruiting ardour could do no more.' And then the whole thing was overlaid and forgotten in the morning news from St Angelo.

The Calabrians had revolted. Two hundred young men from the mountains of Italy, sitting sullenly in the straw of their stifling hostel, refused blankly to embark and fight the battles of the Order of St John in Tripoli. The Chevalier de Villegagnon brought the news, grimly, and Gabriel himself went to speak to them. For a moment only, the storm of complaint was quieted; but before he left, all Birgu heard the calls of 'sacrifice!' and the blare of country voices, hotly renewed.

When he did leave, Graham Malett took the captain of the Viceroy's bucolic army with him, direct to the Grand Master. There it all poured out as the young Italian, sweating with heat and stress, defended his men. They were shepherd boys and labourers. They had never seen a gun, held a sword in their fists. They didn't see, said the captain, a rising querulousness fighting through the deference, why they should go where the knights wouldn't go, to defend the knights' property and die in the knights' place.

Benign and barren of sympathy as the limestone of Malta, the one-eyed Aragonese face of the Grand Master de Homedès studied the young man. Tripoli, said the Grand Master, speaking in honour of the situation in appalling Spanish-Italian, was perfectly secure without his poor two hundred Calabrians. Did the captain really think the Order would abandon one of their own Marshals, their knights and their soldiers, in a fortress which could not defend itself? The Viceroy's army was simply required to travel to Tripoli because the Viceroy himself had commanded it; and the Grand Master was content, as the captain himself should be (if he wished to keep his post), to carry out the Viceroy's orders.

That worked for precisely five minutes, or as long as the captain took to get outside the audience chamber and face his men. The next moment, his Serene Highness was startled to see the doors of his chamber burst open before he had so much as left his chair of eminence, and three distracted men hurl themselves to their knees by his dais. Bathed in hysterical tears, the deputation begged his Highness to have pity on them and not to send them to butchery which, they pointed out with surprising cogency through their sobs, was what their ineptitude would mean to everyone they fought alongside, as well as themselves.

Then the guards got them out, and the Grand Master nearly succeeded in solving the problem by having the ensign in and promising him the command if he persuaded the two hundred to sail, when the captain, scenting treachery, got himself admitted again, the tears dried on his cheeks, and declared himself ready to march with his men if the Grand Master would send with them some of his knights, 'to teach and comfort us,' he ended with pathos.

'And so?' said the Chevalier de Villegagnon sharply when Gabriel, returning, called them together to convey the news.

'Tripoli is a defenceless husk,' said Graham Malett. 'As you all know. These children are right; it will be butchery. The Council advised the Grand Master, out of sheer humanity, to send at least a hundred knights with the Calabrians to Africa.'

'And leave Malta undefended?' said Jerott Blyth, grimly mimicking outrage.

'Is he sending any at all?' inquired de Villegagnon heavily. Lymond had not spoken.

For the first time Gabriel's eyes, as if he were weary, dropped to his closed hands. 'There are in the prisons of Malta,' he said, 'twenty-five young knights, thrown there by de Homedès for insurrection. They are to be released to lead the expedition to Tripoli. You and I are not to go.'

There was nothing to say.

None of them went down to the quayside to see the two hundred blundering youngsters pushed aboard the two galleys taking them to foreign deserts and death. Instead, they worked with Nick Upton, with straw and seawater as de Villegagnon had said, to make Birgu and St Angelo as secure as insane improvidence would allow, against the followers of Allâh's Deputy on Earth. And even the Spanish knights worked, sweating, at their sides.

*

Below the seven heavens—the green heaven of emerald, the heaven of silver; the heaven of red coral, the heaven of pearl, the heaven of red gold, the heaven of yellow coral and the seventh and last heaven of light—the armada of Islâm like a carpet of blossom swam over the seas to the east, and the grain of rock which was Malta came slowly plainer and close.

On the flagship, the spider shadow of the rigging was the only shadow there was. Struck by the African sun in its beaten gold, the brazen light shifted and blazed on jewelled turbans and scimitars, on enamelled clasps and brooches, on the shields of the Janissaries—dark, moustached faces above snowy caftáns—forbidden to marry

80

and dedicated to war; the rustle of their heron's plumes drowned in the grunting pulse, day and night, of the drums.

And beside the Imâms, in their dark robes and round-jowelled, chalk-olive faces, Dragut Rais stood, grizzled, scarred, hard-ribbed under his silk robes as a cask of tanned hide, and gazed ahead, his grey moustaches drooping to his grey beard; his flat, Anatolian peasant face blank.

Three times he had sacked Gozo, and once Malta herself; the old hound, the living chart of the ocean. Plucked from his mother's cabin, schooled in Egypt by arrogant Turkish benevolence, a Mameluke, a trained bombardier, a gunner on corsair ships, he had risen at length to own his own galliot, to sail with Barbarossa, to command his own squadron. And when, six years ago, Barbarossa died, worn out by his harem and by harrying Christians and merchants alike in the robbers' paradise of the African coast, Dragut had become his heir.

Corsica, Naples, Sicily, Djerba: his successes were legend while he lived. And now, no longer prince of corsairs, independent privateer of the Middle Seas, he had been placed by Suleiman at the right hand of Sinan the Jew, the Sultan's general; and Sinan had orders from the King of Kings himself to defer to Dragut's experience.

And ahead lay Gozo, where seven years ago the brother of Dragut Rais had been killed, and the Governor, so far from delivering the slain man for embalming and the rituals of his own faith, had burned the corpse like a dog.

Unstirring, Dragut Rais stared over the sea; and the islands grew plainer and close.

III

The Voice of the Prophet

(Maltese Archipelago, July 1551)

FROM the Governor's castle on Gozo, her black hair hot on her
shoulders, Oonagh O'Dwyer watched the striped sails, the
twinkling ships come.

High on its acropolis above the capital Rabat, the Gran' Castello,
her lover's citadel, guarded the centre of Gozo, a three-mile span of
sharp hills and patchwork plains, of carob trees and low, square
houses and stone terraces with the fishing nets drying and the gourds
seated, green and yellow and fat as aldermen on their walls.

To the south, beyond the sentinel cone of an extinct volcano, lay
the short sea channel to Malta. Within the fortress walls on this hill,
around and below her, all those who could of Gozo's seven thousand
people thronged and shouted. The thin scream of upset children,
like a mortal orchestra of gut and wind, took all the sense from the
ears. This balcony, overlooking the cathedral and square, was
empty. Her personal quarters, hers and Galatian's in this the
Governor's house were still undisturbed.

He was not there. What did a Governor do to protect fisherfolk
from the fire, the arrows, the cannon, the scimitars of twelve thousand
Turks? Whatever it was, thought Oonagh O'Dwyer with no emotion
at all, Galatian de Césel would not attempt it.

Years in Ireland as mistress of Cormac O'Connor, heir to one of
the great native houses, rebel, fighter, outlaw, struggling by any
means fair or foul, to throw the English out of his native country—
years of battle in Ireland and, exiled, out of it: years of supporting
the coarsening fibre, the blurred ideals, the ambition of the thick,
loud-voiced, black-haired man who had been the dark Fraoch of her
spirit, had sent her finally, soiled and disillusioned, to look for
freedom, space, sun, escape, loving wisdom if such were to be found;
kindness and friendship if it were not.

At Marseilles, in the courtly, middle-aged Spaniard she remembered meeting once in Ireland, Galatian de Césel with the clear oval
face and fair moustache, the perfect linen, the quiet silks, the dark,
monkish robes of the Order he wore over his jerkin at Mass—in this

man she found shelter. Kindly, he offered her passage, without payment, to his island of Gozo where, after a brief visit home, he was now returning. There were convents there; and one or two who would welcome her, for his sake, to their homes on Gozo and on Malta. And while there she could think, and plan, and decide where her future should lie.

And so, on board his galley, with the forked banner of his house streaming from the mast, she had lain passive in the sun as the years of brutish stress slid away and Cormac's shadow lessened and shrank; and the shadow of Francis Crawford of Lymond, who with such damnable detachment during his sojourn in France had shown her Cormac for what he was, and what he should have been. Lymond had been the agent, for his own ends—always for his own ends—who had divided her at length from the O'Connors and their fate in order to preserve the safety of the child Queen Mary. She wished to forget him.

Galatian had made it easy to forget. His kind touch brought her solace. The passing caresses reassured her even when, becoming gently constant, they stirred her to realize that, pathetically, he was craving more than her presence. She pitied his innocence and his lonely disciplines and out of pity, that momentous dark night, she had moved a little closer, as he touched her arm at the ship's rail, until her smooth shoulder lay under his hand.

His fingers had stopped, stricken, piteously unsure on her bare skin. Then suddenly as some desperate child's, his hand had plunged on, down and down, over the warm swell of her breast where, cupped and shaking, it rested.

She had not expected it. With a thud like a bolt in her buried flesh, need struck her, parted as she was for the first time from Cormac's brutal assuagements, and, unasked, her flesh sprang stark to his palm. Galatian de Césel moaned, a queer, desperate sound, and pulling his hand free to grip her, trembling, by her side, hurried with her, stumbling, to her cabin below.

They did not even reach it. In the darkness outside her door he started to sob, and a moment later, there in the heaving alley, they were charged with one another. He cried, she remembered, throughout.

Afterwards, lying on her pallet with his sleeping weight on her breast, Oonagh had framed silently, with compassion, the words she would use to comfort the tortured conscience she must face when he woke. But she drifted into sleep before he stirred, and awoke to his gentle urgency about her and presently, under his melting skill, her own breath suddenly lapsed. She met him, flesh to flesh in convulsive want, and raging, he took his fill of her again.

It was so all night and beyond, on that sultry voyage when, like drunkards, their only refuge day and night was the unmade pallet below the galliot's decks. But long before that, she knew that this had happened many times before; that Galatian de Césel was not a chaste nor a timid nor a fatherly knight, but a knight whose desperate hunger no religion could quiet.

Towards the end of the long journey spent, so much of it, in Galatian's clasp, Oonagh knew also that she was pregnant; and not by this monkish lover. A thick, black-headed Irish hog-child lay in her belly, to grow in dark and silence under the warm sun of Malta and ruin her new life.

Defying, for once, the furious fatalism that was part of her nature, she did what she could about that, but only made herself ill. She arrived at Gozo hardly seeing it, and was installed in the white-walled chamber off Galatian's room where, racked by more absences than she could bear, she realized that to keep him she must be well, and beautiful, and stirring to his easy flesh. For what he gave her so intemperately, she could not now do without.

Her pretence succeeded. For a month, inexhaustible, he stayed with her, and she hid that she was sick. Until last week when handling her, blindly ripe to his kindling, he became aware, as no monk should have been aware, of her sunken face and the first soft engorgement of her breast against his.

He had not risked his soul with a curse but freeing himself, had rolled from her bed. '*You can't blame your Irish bastard on me!*' he had exclaimed loudly and clearly at her door, and she heard it repeated, with open laughter, through the house and then the streets of the citadel.

But that day she had nothing left but a desire for oblivion. She had lain still on her bed, and after a while—after an age—after the whole afternoon had gone by, he had flung open the door, driven, as she had known he would be, by the pulse that they shared. But from then to now, he had used her often uncourted as Cormac had done; and she had not known until much later that he was burying not only his fever; but the knowledge of the fate approaching them all. She learned soon enough. They were to be sacrificed victims of Islâm, offered up by the knights to save their own skins; and de Césel, in his warm refuge, was afraid.

The knights, in their holy convent at Birgu, knew she was there. She had seen some of them: Jerott Blyth, who had been kind on Messina and to whom she had talked, stupid with sun and luxury, of Lymond.

At Birgu where they had first landed, she had seen the Grand Master, ancient and one-eyed, and the battle-scarred older man they called la Valette, and had heard of the quiet man with the beautiful voice and the guinea-gold hair, Graham Malett; and she had thought, fleetingly, that there was a man she could trust. Then the news came, as news always did, flying the short miles from St Angelo to the north and across the brief, teeming channel to Gozo, that the Chevalier de Villegagnon had come from France with warning of the Turkish armada, and that a Scotsman called de Lymond was at his side.

Then she had remembered her unwise talk with Jerott Blyth, and indolence and self-loathing burst into anger against this casual, indifferent man passing by, like some damned bailiff, to inspect the finished transaction. She was going to hell, it seemed, her own way; and she wanted none of Francis Crawford's cutting rebukes.

When later she heard that Jerott, who knew them both, had been on the boat they had glimpsed crossing that day from Cape Passero, she had written Lymond not to come. It would, she thought a little hysterically, be the last straw to be quixotically rescued by force from threatened Gozo, while her protector perished and the knights. in all their chaste ardours, found themselves saddled with a loose woman; and a pregnant loose woman at that.

Muffled through the thick walls of the house, the Rhodes clock on the battlements behind struck the quarter, as it had in all the long years of the knights' wandering since Rhodes. From the square below; from the narrow lane whose opposite walls she could nearly touch from her balcony, came the high, Oriental sound of wailing; an instant, childlike reaction from the men, with their barrel chests and curly mat of black hair, as well as from the veiled heads and squat shapes of the women. Drawing back, Oonagh O'Dwyer left the window and moving down the white marble steps to the landing, crossed the width of the house to open the back postern, crazily unguarded, and climb out on to those wide, commanding battlements where the rusted guns stood in their emplacements, and the Rhodes clock counted the hours.

As soon as the day's trial became unbearable, Galatian would come to her. Not to watch the sails, not to order the cannon, not to check his defences or his stores or to comfort his people . . . he would come running to her. She heard his hurried footsteps now, climbing the stairs, the rattle of the doors . . . and here he came. Paler than usual, his colourless hair stuck to his cheeks, his face familiarly suffused, he stopped when he saw her, half-transparent against the blue sky, and called her to come.

She heard him. She even started indifferently to walk towards him when suddenly she veered instead to the right, to the flight of steps which led down from the battlements to the street far below.

The noise had stopped. Below, from all those anguished, frightened throats, there came no sound but the routine sob of a child and the piping of young voices, pressing questions unanswered. Then she saw that every face was upraised to the watch on duty on the high battlements bridging the square. Turning, Oonagh fled to the parapet wall and looked.

The fleet of Suleiman the Magnificent, rank upon rank of silken sails flashing with gold, the crescent banners like cirrus against the blue sky, was still there, far in the distance beyond the sentinel hills. But it had not swung in the wide, so-familiar arc across the blue sea to Gozo. Instead it was moving, bright scimitar of the prophet, to the distant, rich, Viceregal shores of Sicily.

By her side, his craving forgotten, the Governor of Gozo in silence watched too. And out of that moment, that second chance, that respite from masochistic self-contempt, Oonagh saw something again clearly, with the hard, half-mystic certainty she had once had before she parted from Cormac.

Something should be done for these people, these children. Galatian de Césel would never do it: she was his drug and his curse but, failing her, he would find others no less willing in her room. Could she not teach him other comforts, though? The comfort of planning, of action; the great panacea of success. On this stricken island there was no one who could lead, no one who knew what a leader should be like . . . except Oonagh O'Dwyer, who had stood at O'Connor's right arm, and his father's before him.

'Praise be!' said Oonagh suddenly, her eyes cool and reflective as they used to be, the fall of her black hair resting kindly on her uncouth maturity. 'I wonder what your captains will say to this, my brave child? . . . I will have the Council room made ready for you.'

And he nodded, automatically, without touching her, his eyes on the dwindling surge of bright sails.

*

From Birgu to St Angelo; from L'Isla to the revived villages on each ledge of crumbling rock where the families, running back with their bundles, their babies, their goats, crowded the worn, white-walled chapels, the bells jangled in the suffering heat of the air, rejoicing in the miracle of their preservation. Like pale ejaculations of surprise, the mattocks hung in the unfinished trenches; the armourers' shops lay cold; the boats rolled idle with their empty casks on the shore of the Marsa. In the chapter hall of the fortress St Angelo, Grand Master de Homedès, relaxed on his crested throne, allowed himself to be mildly sarcastic at his Councillors' expense.

His knights heard him, torn between relief, uneasiness and, on the part of de Villegagnon, la Valette and those whom Gabriel led, with an apprehension verging on horror. Durand de Villegagnon sprang to his feet. 'But, Your Eminence, the danger, surely, is only postponed. The fleet may return at any moment.'

'They cannot now be said, surely, to be going to France,' suggested Gabriel's deep voice gently.

'Why not? Why not? We are not fools, gentlemen. We study charts,' said the Grand Master. He turned his head and his secretary, rising, spread a paper on the eminent knees. 'There,' said de Homedès. 'Along the Sicilian coast to Provence and their devilish meeting with the French Ambassador. If they follow the coast, they will shorten their journey by some two hundred miles. There, Brothers in Christ, is your proof!'

There was a painful silence. At length, 'It is one possibility, out of many,' said de Villegagnon curtly.

The single princely eye was bent on the Chevalier, and his very bulk reduced to a sin. 'Your suggestion is then, I take it, that the whole population of these islands should stand to arms; that the poor people we protect should remain crowded in Birgu and Mdina, spreading plague and consuming stores and water, while the food rots in their villages? Do you propose to let them out for the vintage, or must we house them here for ever, or until your precious Ottoman army comes, to eat, marry, squabble, breed, die in the convent of the Holy Order? I suppose from this year on, the Mass bell remains silent except for alarm; the Brothers are forever more exempt from their churchly duties in order to mix gunpowder and dig; the sunken galleys must rot? You have been too long in foreign waters, Chevalier. Our duty is not to glorify battle, but to enshrine and keep alive the fire of our Faith. The Order's galleys are at Messina. The power of the Emperor is in the western seas. For that very reason we have done our duty; we have not importuned him for untimely help. Be satisfied, Brother Nicholas, with God's grace as this day shown us, and do not anger Him with complaint.'

Which was all very well but, as Gabriel said with unexpected wry humour afterwards, it was not the Deity who seemed to be principally offended.

Sanctioned to ordinary routine; unable, even had they wished, to force Maltese and mercenaries to carry on the hopeless, arduous task of defence, the knights gathered in groups indoors as the new afternoon heat beat down, uneasily conferring, avoiding disloyalty and blasphemy as they might; praying always for relief. Outside, in the shimmering refractions of July, the hills and houses of Sicily hung all afternoon in the northern air, the painted sails of Suleiman's fleet suspended below them; and from the coast, creaming column after column of black smoke began to rise until it seemed as if all Sicily were Etna, and the sky itself a curdled ocean of lava.

Whatever their ultimate purpose, the Ottoman fleet was in no haste to leave these waters. Sinan Pasha, Dragut Rais and Salah Rais had landed in the lemon groves of Sicily itself, and were killing and burning unhindered across forty-three short miles of sea.

That evening, as the afterglow lay like watered wine on the long pool of Grand Harbour and stitched with pink the smoky seas of the east, two fishing boats came in past the point of St Elmo and laboured through the long harbour towards Galley Creek.

In the clear, rosy light there was a strangeness about them. More: as the sentries of St Angelo peered down from their blind Arab walls, they could hear sounds thinly rising from the flat water; an ill-tuned chorus of voices joined in shrill Christian praise. Crowding the battlements, they watched as the two high-prowed boats drew still nearer, rounding the point below Fort St Angelo and slowing before the shining chain across Galley Creek. The oars moved then, raggedly, to backpaddle, and the small lamps on the quay, in the gathering dusk, glimmered on the rowers, their brown faces upturned to the fort: on black, shawled heads and strong, knotted brown arms; on rolls and parcels and baskets and bundles which were silent and others which moved strongly and cried. It shone on a bent wicker cage in which a linnet lay dying; on a snoring child, clutching a doll sodden with tears; on the upturned eyes and untutored throats of the women and children of Gozo, who had rowed through the straits of Comino, past Mellieha Bay, past the bay where, fifteen centuries before, St Paul had been wrecked and had come, like St Paul, to seek sanctuary.

Gabriel took the news to the Grand Master. De Homedès, early in bed, found it easy to disbelieve him. After explanation, corroboration, delay, His Eminence at length had himself dressed and moved through his garden, past his menagerie and down to the rail overlooking the quay and the rocky ledge on which the great capstan stood for unwinding the chain. In the falling dark, the two boats far below could hardly be seen, except as two shadows barring the yellow columns of L'Isla's mirrored lights.

The ragged anthems had stopped. Instead, monotonously across the water, came the thin voice of a spokesman appealing, in the name of the Governor of Gozo who had sent them, for the Grand Master's permission to land.

'*Take the chain up?*' said the Grand Master testily. 'What nonsense is this? These are women and children.'

'They have come all the way from Gozo,' said Gabriel, sharpness audible even in that unshaken voice. 'If as you say the Turks have gone. . . .'

'Then they have no right to encumber us here. And if the Turks have *not* gone, as you are so fond of reiterating,' said Juan de Homedès with devastating precision, 'then what are these but useless mouths obstructing the garrison?'

'And if Gozo is attacked, and not Malta?' asked Gabriel bluntly.

The Grand Master turned away, his velvet cloak pressed peevishly against his thin flesh, the eight-pointed cross glimmering in the scented dark. 'Exactly my point, Brother,' he said. 'How do you suppose these poor men of Gozo will fight if we withdraw the very thing they want most to save? Send these people back.'

This last, delivered to the knight standing ready, lantern in hand, to signal for duty at the capstan, produced absolute silence. Even from the two crowded boats, now quite invisible in the dark, arose no whimper, no cry. The Grand Master raised his voice, impatient of their slow understanding, and repeated irritably what he had said. 'Hail them, sir! And tell them they are to go back to Gozo.'

'And if they refuse?'

Black patch and cold eye, turning together, expressed the Grand Master's unqualified disapproval. 'Then sink them,' he said.

*

'*That* for the Order!' shouted Jerott Blyth, hurling the ripped shreds of his robe of St John to the floor; and the circle of French knights about him, stirring, murmured and looked at one another, and at Gabriel.

'You are making it awkward for the Pilier, Jerott,' said Sir Graham sharply. He had just brought them news of last night's pilgrimage from Gozo and its outcome; and throughout the Auberge of France the knights, stunned, had come to hear.

De Villegagnon spoke, almost as sharply returning Gabriel's rebuke. 'None of us is shamed by M. Blyth's words. He is right. The Grand Master is insane. Let him go on, and we shall be the butt of Osmanli and Christian alike. For God's sake, Gabriel, take command for him. There isn't a man who would not willingly follow you. Damn humility! Damn modesty! Lead us, Graham!' And answering him, before Gabriel could speak, was a firm, an angry, a masculine rumble of assent: the deep voice of war, and not the ritual litany of the Order's daily utterance.

'May I ask,' said someone peaceably, 'why Sir Graham did not bring us this news last night?'

Calm within the clamour about him, Gabriel met Francis Crawford's neutral blue stare over the heads swirling between them, and smiled. 'Do you really think,' he said to that detached presence, 'that I would allow old women and young children to make that journey to Gozo without respite?'

'No,' said Lymond after some thought, and Jerott, sensing flippancy, pushed his way exasperated out of the crowded circle and gripped a windowsill, the light white on his face. 'What did you do?' asked de Villegagnon, his thick brows drawn.

'Put them in the sail loft overnight,' said Gabriel calmly. 'La Valette and a Serving Brother helped me. The Grand Master and the other knights are not aware of it, and the sempsters are sworn to secrecy. The Gozitans left this morning.'

'*Left!*' said Jerott, whipped from his sulks by the window.

'They have gone back to Gozo. Wait!' said Gabriel quickly; and his resonant voice for once was formidable. 'Wait before you judge. We have an obligation here: to all the people of Birgu and L'Isla, all the villages in east Malta, all the women and children who fled here the other day when we thought the Turk had arrived. And even that obligation we must dishonour if—as seems certain to me—Dragut attacks on his way back. He won't waste guns on Gozo; don't think it. His blow will be struck against us, the Order, where we are accessible to his ships. I would wager my hope of héaven if I had any such,' said Gabriel deliberately, 'that Sinan Pasha and Dragut mean to destroy *us*, here at St Angelo. You know our exact resources of food, our full store of water. We shall die fighting, I hope, of honourable wounds. The women and children with us will die of hunger and thirst, or will fall helpless to the Turk. The Order's duty is to fight Islâm, and in a last extremity, for the Religion, the Order has first claim on all reserves to survive. . . . They are better on Gozo.'

He had satisfied them, but he had not turned them from their new thought. De Villegagnon voiced it again. 'Lead us,' he said.

For a moment Graham Malett was silent, collecting his thoughts. Then with unaffected patience he answered. 'The Grand Mastership is dissolved only by death; and new Masters are made by the full Council, the Emperor and the Pope. This is an old, sick priest, given way a little to selfish concerns; unable now to bring balanced thought to his problems; unable to find comfort in prayer. To begin with, pity him.'

'Pity us!' retorted Jerott bitterly.

'Why?' said Gabriel swiftly. 'Because you are in your twenties and young and importunate, and the Order is four hundred years old and patient? The Order has survived weak leadership before. It will again. If we have complaints—' he held up his hand against the comment— 'the time to make them is after we have driven Dragut from Malta, and the place to make them is in full Council, in the presence of the Viceroy. I beg you . . .' he looked round, half rueful at his own rhetoric, half in pain with the sheer urgency of his wish to persuade, 'I beg you, do nothing now. Can you not see? The best leader in the world could not in the last weeks have forced the Emperor to give us ships and troops. The best soldier in Christendom, given our defences as they have stood this last month, could do little now to improve them. There is nothing material to be gained by rebellion now, and every possible loss, physical and spiritual. We should be accused of personal ambition, subversive nationalism, panic and cowardice in the face of danger. How could you deny it? Jerott—Nicholas—Brother Nick—dearest children in Christ. . . . Did you not say once, as I said, "*I vow to God.* . . ." ' And the tall, fair-haired knight quoted suddenly in his remarkable voice.

> 'I vow to God, to Saint Mary, ever a Virgin, Mother of God; to St John the Baptist, to render henceforth and for ever, by the grace of God, a true obedience to the Superior which it pleases him to give me, and who will be the choice of our Religion.'

Sir Graham Malett paused, and in the shared silence added the words heard for the first time by each of them on the day of his initiation. ' "Receive the yoke of the Lord, because it is sweet and light . . . under which you will find repose for your soul." Receive with humility, Jerott, the lessons you are taught, and do not lightly forget that we have a Leader who will not fail us.

'Let us go to Church,' said Gabriel quietly. 'And then work as we may on the defence of our island, to the last shred of our strength.'

*

On the morning of the 16th July, before the sun was more than a mellow radiance outside the white, sleeping walls of Birgu, the bells of St Lawrence started to ring and after them, erratically, slow, swift, shrill, sonorous, the jangling bells of every church on the island. The sound wrangled through the dark Arab windows: the grilled windows of the knights, the open shutters and the dark courtyards, and danced in the slumbering air.

Jerott Blyth, asleep dirty-handed where he had thrown himself in Gabriel's fine guest-chamber, looked across to where Lymond slept, worn as they all were with heavy, self-disciplined labour, his bleached head still on the pillow.

Then he realized that Lymond, too, was awake, and tensed. As he watched, the other man rolled to his feet and made for the door, snatching a cloak, for decency's sake, as he went. Jerott followed; and saw.

The bells were not for Mass. They were for the bright armada of Suleiman, sail on silken sail, moving past the mouth of Grand Harbour to anchor in Marsamuscetto Bay.

*

Before Lymond left with the others, Gabriel stopped him, a hand laid for a second on his shoulder.

Against the desires of the Grand Master, who wished the Order secure in the fastnesses of St Angelo and Mdina, presenting a barren country and a blank wall to the invader, Gabriel, de Villegagnon and la Valette in Grand Council had won their way. One swift and violent blow was to be struck at Dragut's hordes as they landed: one sally to let the Sultan feel the knights' steadfastness and anger.

It would only by a miracle cause Sinan Pasha and Dragut to draw off. But it would perhaps remind them that this would be no easy siege, and that two months only of fine weather remained in which to win the island and sail home in safety to Constantinople. One blow; and then, retiring to Birgu and its fortress, the knights would await what God ordained for them.

And the sally was to be a double one. Under the Commander de Gimeran of Spain, three hundred arquebusiers and a hundred knights on foot were to take skiff from Birgu across the Grand Harbour to Mount Sciberras, the rocky tongue separating the long water inlet of the Order from the Bay of Marsamuscetto, where the Ottoman fleet lay at anchor, to reconnoitre and do such damage from land as they could.

The other party, of thirty knights and four hundred Maltese on horseback, under Turcopilier Nicholas Upton, with Lymond at his side, were to ride round Galley Creek and crossing the neck of the Mount Sciberras peninsula, circumvent the end of Grand Harbour to reach Marsamuscetto Bay by land, to harry the Turkish landing parties as they arrived.

In the roaring chaos of the town square where the refugees, goats, hens, children, bundles of food and jars of water squeezed against the blazing stone of the houses to make room for the gathering knights, Gabriel moved his gaze from the dancing, sun-hazed droves of thick-bodied horses, the dazzle of plate-armour and helmets swinging with plumes, the shifting bright disks of shields of Auberge and Order, and the jerking pennants, congested with quarterings. 'Since you wear no armour and subscribe to no symbol of faith, would a soldier's advice offend you?' said Gabriel to Francis Crawford. 'You have not, I think, fought the Turk before.'

Always, though taller than most, Graham Malett gave away the advantage of height. Now, holding his linked hands, he presented Lymond with a lift into the saddle and also a space in which to frame his reply. And Lymond, who had no need of either, found, thoughtfully, the courtesy to use both and said at length, looking down, 'On the contrary. My experience has been in fighting *with* them. A kind of *bourgeosie de robe*.'

'Of course,' said Gabriel. 'I should have realized. With Turkish prisoners freed from Spanish ships. I wished to warn you about the scimitar cut, and also that your men may find it disconcerting when the Janissaries scream.'

No more than amused at the tact, 'I scream too,' said Lymond gravely. 'And louder. But it is kind of you to advise.'

Graham Malett said suddenly, 'Let me find you a breastplate at least, man. Their arrows . . . .'

'My dear Sir Graham,' said Lymond. 'I shall be behind a bulwark of three thousand pounds of plate steel, as worn by the Order. If their arrows go through all that, they deserve to succeed. My personal cargo is a twenty-five-pound helmet, a brigantine jacket and a sword, and I need only fall off my horse to dispatch someone flattened to his houris in Heaven. As for the Cross . . . my habit is to fight for the Saltire.'

'Then St Andrew and St John both guard you,' said Gabriel quietly, and let him go.

*

In Boghall Castle, Biggar, Scotland, Joleta Malett, who had been on edge all day, apologized for inattention to Lady Fleming for the third time and added, in extenuation, 'I feel there's something wrong. I don't know what. When I felt like this, it used to be Graham who was in danger.'

And Tom Erskine, Scots Privy Councillor and Ambassador, whose news from France was recent and specific, said, 'A professional soldier, monk or not, is always in danger. Try to forget. He has not become what he is by being vulnerable or stupid.' And thought uneasily that the same thing applied to Francis Crawford, who had also chosen to defend Malta on grounds known only to himself, which might procure him no dispensation in heaven at all.

*

The temperature was in the nineties; the sky removed a man's breath from the lip of the lung with its invisible heat. The northerly wind which had blown the fleet of the Faithful from Sicily had gone, and below the brassy blue arc of July the arid sandstone rocks, the crumbling houses, the stony terraces vibrated like blows on the nerves of the sight.

In their riveted armour, with the long, quilted leather jacks to protect from bruising beneath, the knights riding from Birgu round Grand Harbour were assaulted like an enemy by an element more formidable still: the single, burning sun which took from every chance encounter with salade, knee-plate or harness, with shield-buckle and sword, its penalty of blistered flesh. Fair skins blazed;

sweat, crusting thick with salt in straining eyes made worse the suffo-
cating blindness brought on by heat and pressure, by the nervous
stress, never lost, never admitted, of the hour before the attack.

This, through all the four hundred years of her history, was the
Order's penance, willingly undergone, below suns hotter than Malta's.
This was how they fought; this was how they suffered; this, when
they rode out to face the fanatical scimitars, was the other enemy
they must overthrow. By Lymond's side Nick Upton, vast as a
staved barrel, whom neither tiltyard nor rowing bench could diminish, said in his direct English voice, 'You'll find us none so monkish
on the field of battle.'

'I have nothing against monks,' said Lymond, his gaze scanning
the rocks and dry cactus ahead; his senses attuned to noise far away
from their galloping horses.

The bulbous, kindly face, fretted by the tongues of the Venetian
helmet, turned again, jerking to the horse's gait. 'Are ye a Protestant?'
inquired Upton in a mild shout.

Diverted, Lymond this time looked round. 'Because I haven't
clamoured to become a novitiate?'

The Turcopilier gave no direct answer. Instead he said, 'Gabriel
thinks a lot of you.'

'I thought I talked too much for his comfort,' said Lymond. 'But I
hear he has a ravishing sister. I must mend my ways.'

A surprisingly sweet smile crossed the Turcopilier's face. 'Nothing
on earth can surprise or defeat Gabriel,' he said. 'As you will find
out. But he would gladly welcome you—we all should—to our
Church.'

Ahead, minute in the shining air, was a sparkle of sunshine on
jewels and drawn steel. 'O England, thou garden of delights,' said
Lymond, lyrically intent. 'Set aside these thoughts of religion, and
let us go and chase Turks.'

*

The Janissaries screamed: that was true. Not when they were hit;
not when the two-handed sword slit through the puffed silk of the
turban, nor when the fire-hoops of wood rubbed with brandy
touched the light robes of muslin and silk and flared orange in the
white sunlight—robe, sash, beard, eyebrows and turban a white
cypress of flame. Then they called on Allâh, rapt in ecstasy, and died
fixed on certain Paradise and an eternity in the light. But before they
were attacked; when the parties moving inland from Marsamuscetto with their superb hackbuts from the Hungary wars, their bows,
their scimitars, their jewelled daggers, raced onwards from the firing
of a hovel, the burning of stored corn and carob seeds, the tearing

down of a lemon grove or a vine to see the knights approach—then the Jannissaries gave their high, wailing cries and gleaming teeth and black eyes, streaming herons' plumes and black moustaches under the golden crescent and three-cornered silk banners, airy as their white robes in the cruel heat, the Janissaries charged, and the dark Imâms urged on the Faithful.

With Upton, tireless in full armour, swinging sword and axe in the lead, knights and Maltese came across band after band on that ride, burning, destroying, plundering the poor wreckage of the empty pueblos on their way to the plains of Curmi to muster for battle. Because of Upton, the Ottoman landing parties came to Curmi not in well-groomed companies, but angry and harried by stinging attacks, by the small, orderly army of Upton's light horse.

And the knights endured remarkably well. Rarely conscious of them as faces, Upton was yet aware that both they and the Maltese like a single arm obeyed his desires; that no order of his remained ambiguous, that no slip went unrectified; and later, drawing them together among the low hills at the edge of the great plain, where to cries and drumbeats the white figures streamed and mingled, he realized that throughout he had directed through the mouth and limbs of the Scotsman, in his plated jerkin, riding back and forth at his side. And naturally, as it seemed to him, in acknowledgement of this powerful staff work at his shoulder, he said to Lymond, 'We can do no more, once they have mustered, unless. . . .'

'Unless we give the illusion of charging?' said Lymond, answering the bold thought.

The lunacy of the notion was plain: Nick Upton wanted to feel his hands on a Turk. But there was some sense in it, too. Behind them were thirty knights and four hundred Maltese; in front, the rallying-ground of twelve thousand Turks. Not all had landed; not all had reached the plain; not all were as whole or as single-minded as when leaving their ships. It was possible that, without horses and heavy cannon ashore, they might not relish yet a pitched battle against the whole strength of the Order, as it might appear. The Order they would rightly expect to remain tight in St Angelo until besieged. The Turk might run. He might equally stand fast and attack. Nicholas Upton had no intention of crossing that plain, but he stood a good chance, if his bluff were called, of being chased all the way back to St Angelo.

Before odds so great, there was no advantage in too much delay or too much thought. Shouting as loudly as their dry throats would allow, and followed by a thunderous torrent of brown figures screeching, 'Allâh! Allâh!' in the very timbre of Barbary; deployed to look like more than they were and the vanguard of more still, the Knights of St John pounded down the low hills.

They were seen. For a moment, swirled like pond life under a cataract, the Turkish troops leaped patternless about the wide plain. Then, perceptibly, they began to move purposefully, to coalesce, to stream slowly, scimitars flashing, in a single direction. Nicholas Upton put out an arm and, obedient, the cavalcade behind him reduced speed. There was no need to hurry; only to give the illusion of haste. The Turks were running away.

Leaving the plain, hazed with their dust, they ran back: back through the smoking ruins of Maltese farm and *casal*; back through Birchircara; back to the weedy rocks sliding under gloved feet, the salt crusting their gauzy brocades, the stinging air cracking gaped lips. They ran to their boats and rowed swiftly, accurately, sullenly (for someone had commanded them not to take risks) back to their ships.

Hearts thudding; parched with excitement, with heat, with relief, the knights followed. Not so fast that they overtook the main body of Ottomans, but fast enough to separate and squash each small company of stragglers, to gnaw at the slippered heels of the army until it slid into the sea.

They had only begun this work when Nick Upton, visible only as shining red skin between steel and steel of his helmet, gave a violent gasp and let all his plated bulk slither sideways, so that his horse stumbled and stopped. His hand quick on the bridle, Lymond twisted Upton's beast round and supported the man, pinning his own horse hard; feeling the steel burn his hands through Upton's fine scarlet surcoat with its dusty white cross. Then, as fighting broke out suddenly on their left flank and someone called him, he consigned the great burden, deftly, to other arms, and drew Upton's men onwards without him. There was no balm he could offer Upton but rest while the fighting continued. And the Turcopilier's company followed him, their swords bloody, their horses lathered with sweat, and beat the invader to the edge of the sea.

They came back, when it was over, to the same spot: weary, jubilant but with time now for concern. They had unbuckled Nicholas Upton's armour and he lay still on the ground, great belly upwards, eyes shut, his face puffed and glazed by the sun; his frame shaken by shuddering sighs. Francis Crawford knelt, holding his pulse for a moment; then rising without comment, gave all the necessary instructions. The Turcopilier did not waken when four men heaved his inert body into the sling, nor did his stertorous breathing change on the slow ride back to Birgu. To the knights who rode out from the arched gateway to greet him; to all those who pressed at their sides as they rode up the steep crowned streets of the town, Lymond made the same answer. 'Sir Nicholas has no wound. He is a fat man over-exerting himself under a tropical sun while carrying a hundred pounds of plate armour. Blame the sun. Blame the armour. Blame your own numbskull habits. Blame the courage of a man with a heart a good deal bigger than his body ever became. But don't blame the Turks. The Order of the Knights Hospitallers of St John of Jerusalem, Rhodes and Malta killed this one.'

In fact, Sir Nicholas Upton of England died later that evening, in his white-curtained bed in the hospital, his face turned to the doors of the Chapel of the Most Holy Saint. A moment later the French physician, laying down the silver cup engraved with the arms of de Homedès, rose and went quietly out, while the Prior continued in a low voice to recite the offices, and de Villegagnon, Blyth and the two knights closest to him in his years on Malta knelt beside the Turco-pilier and prayed.

The ludicrous death of the fat knight was the only loss that day. Lymond had brought back his company of three hundred and more without greater loss than scars and arrow-pricks; and Gimeran, in ambush across the water among the rocks of Mount Sciberras, had surprised the Turkish Admiral's galley itself sailing close in to recon-noitre, and had fired on it, causing the crew to drop oars in disorder and eventually to retreat. Sinan Pasha, furious, had ordered a landing on Mount Sciberras to engage the small party of knights, but having done what damage they could, prudently Gimeran's men had with-drawn, and re-embarking on their skiffs, had crossed safely back to Birgu.

Since when St Angelo, inspired by the Grand Master, had rung with the Spanish knight's praises. Jerott Blyth, who saw both home-comings and watched Lymond turn away, his men dispersed, after Upton's sagging stretcher had been borne through the pomegranate-wreathed door of the hospital, overtook him on the way back to Gabriel's. 'Well?'

Crawford of Lymond, Comte de Sevigny, who had respected Nicholas Upton, met this studied nonchalance blankly. 'For all I know, excellent. Hercules, as you observe, *brûla son corps, pour se rendre immortel*. For the rest, you could scarcely claim yet they were blooded. But they lost a prime lot of weight.'

*

Very soon after that a skiff, unseen, put off from the Turkish flagship at anchor in Marsamuscetto Bay; and presently, their jewels bright in the sun, Sinan Pasha and his officers climbed that rocky peninsula where, hours before, Gimeran's party had stood, and in their turn looked across Grand Harbour to the fortress of St Angelo, high on its sea-girt rock, with the town of Birgu behind.

And, 'Is *this* the castle which thou toldest the Grand Seigneur might so easily be taken?' said Sinan Pasha, white between turban and beard, to the square and silent Dragut at his side. 'Surely,' said Sinan Pasha bitterly, 'the eagle could never have chosen the point of a steeper rock for her eyrie.'

Then the seamed, lashless eyes of Dragut surveyed them; surveyed Salah Rais his fellow corsair and Sinan the Jew his general, and closed as the flat, turbaned face with its grey spade-beard clenched in a smile.

'Warriors of the Faith, why then are we here?' said the old man agreeably. 'The Unbelievers who harry the Edifice of God are within the Fort St Angelo, there before thee. Is thy quarrel with peasants and fishermen? God the Master of Worlds requires thee to cleanse that vile rock of its reptiles. God,' said Dragut coldly, 'and the shadow of Allâh on earth, the Sultan Suleiman Khan, son of the Sultan Selim Khan, son of Sultan Bayezid Khan, will meet failure with the righteous anger that slays.'

And in the council of war which followed, under the flagship's silken canopy, Dragut the Drawn Sword of Islâm and sworn enemy of the Knights of St John, partly prevailed. Tripoli was to be their main objective. Suleiman's order to his general had been to take Malta and Gozo if he could; but to risk nothing that would endanger the taking of Tripoli.

But first, the Emperor Charles was to be given a last chance. So, sailing beforehand to Sicily, Sinan Pasha had reminded the Viceroy of the treaties binding Charles and himself, and had asked to receive back in good faith the Sultan's former city of Bône.

Temporizing; all too clearly temporizing until the fine sailing days should pass and the fleet be constrained to set out harmlessly for the Sublime Porte, the Viceroy replied that having no advice on that score, he must refer the case back to his Master.

It was his last chance; Malta's last chance; Tripoli's last chance. Silently, the envoy had bowed himself out; silently, Sinan Pasha had heard the news and, lifting anchor that night, had turned south and burned and plundered his way down the Sicilian coast. Suleiman's orders had been to do nothing on Malta which would weaken the major onslaught on Tripoli. But they were not women, or bath attendants. To land on Malta and return empty handed would demean even these.

Dragut could not persuade them to attack Birgu and St Angelo; not even his tongue or his presence could stiffen Sinan Pasha to that. But he did convince them, at last, that they must march on Mdina, six miles to the north-west, where undefended, the Maltese nobles, their people and their riches would have recoiled in fright. And so, because of the courage of Nicholas Upton and Gimeran the Spaniard, the Chevalier George Adorne of Genoa, Commander of Mdina, with thirteen thousand refugees, three Knights of St John and almost no other soldiers at all, suffered Sinan Pasha's attack.

*

For thirty-six hours the little capital Mdina waited, gently mannered, classical in thought and in form; and perched like a rock-dove above the baked plains of Malta, looked for help which failed to arrive.

From the first indication of danger—the distant columns of steel, the hazy columns of smoke—they had done what they could. On the second evening, as prepared as he could ever hope to be, the Governor Adorne, with residents and refugees pressed into makeshift companies under his handful of knights, stood with his men and watched the Turkish army encamp.

Behind him were eight courageous attempts at ambush. Eight times he had sent out a knight with a troop of his ablest men to fire and harry the oncoming Turks. But three leaders were not enough; and he had no more. Bleeding, fly-coated, asleep on their feet, the knights were wholly spent. Sleepless himself for two days and a night and suffering, with them all, the spare allocation of precious water, Adorne began to feel his own grasp slackening. And in the thick-walled little city, with its five hundred square yards of quiet passages, of high walls and crested gateways and the squat Norman-towered cathedral packed with scared, silent people, hope was faltering too. At night, home-made ropes, despite all Adorne's warnings, trickled over the parapets and hurried shadows, swarming over ungainly, with bundle or baby, dropped to the ditches outside Mdina and ran . . . ran to disembowelment and slavery, for now the Janissaries were in place, ringing the city, drawing silently closer and closer over the plain. Of the three hundred men, women and children who tried to leave Mdina on these two nights, none escaped.

So, as the last pure light slid under the sea and the fires of Islâm, like marsh magic, danced unbroken below, the Governor Adorne of Mdina sent a first and last appeal to the knights at St Angelo.

And the courier, a grim little Spanish lieutenant he could ill spare, got through. With an arm strapped to his sword belt and a cut in his thigh that showed the white bone when he knelt, the dogged messenger from the besieged capital got to Birgu while the stars were still hung like lamps in the warm, sea-washed night, and presently, standing before Juan de Homedès himself, listened as the Grand Master, calm, dry and sarcastic, reduced to trivia the news he had brought.

'Insufficient leaders?' said His Eminence, gently chiding. 'But surely, great as is our calling, we must in humility remember that the

99

virtues of courage, leadership, faith, are not ours alone. Look among your native Maltese at Mdina, my child. Such an inducement to valour as they possess must rival our own deepest pledge.'

Monotonously, committed to incredible extension of his endurance, the lieutenant replied to each sally. 'The Maltese in Mdina are frightened. They are untrained. Under the knights of St John—under a leader such as M. de Villegagnon there—they will fight as well as any in the world. But not alone. No longer alone.'

'Each of us,' said the Grand Master, his voice melancholy, his patch staring affrighted at the wall, 'each of us in this terrible world must learn to fight, and to fight alone. This great Order of ours is the bastion of God in the eastern seas. By condoning the weakness of little men, we deny our sworn support to Holy Church. I can on my conscience send no one to Mdina.'

Soaking through breeches and hose, the dark blood rolled sluggish down the Spaniard's leg. His face, white beneath the dirt and the sweat, was a mask, but for the persevering, fixed eyes. 'Send M. de Villegagnon at least,' he said. 'Of all men, he will put heart into the city as she dies.'

'Certainly, if M. de Villegagnon wishes, he may go,' said Juan de Homedès unexpectedly. 'Someone, in any case, must take our message back to Brother Adorne and you, my poor man, have done enough. You have persuaded us at least, you may be sure, of your courage and virtue. M. de Villegagnon will go to Mdina. Rest assured. All will be well. See to him, Brother,' said the Grand Master lightly to the physician among those at his side, and made to rise.

He had underestimated the opposition.

'Your Eminence.' Determined and tender, it was Gabriel's voice. 'I beg you to spare the matter a moment more of your time. You are condemning M. de Villegagnon as well as the city of Mdina to death.'

The arid face was quite composed. 'I condemn M. de Villegagnon to nothing. I have said he may go to Mdina if he so desires.'

'He will obey your slightest wish, I am sure, whether he desires it or not,' said Gabriel plainly. Unspoken, the words hung in the air. *As will the twenty-five insubordinate knights you mean to send to sure death in Tripoli.* Aloud, he added, 'But if we can spare M. de Villegagnon, we can spare more. I wish to go.'

'And I! And I!' At last, skilfully, he had released them. The clamour of voices rose from the two long tables, from Pilier and Grand Cross, from all the Order's great officers.

Pityingly, Juan de Homedès looked at them. 'Send the flower of the Order to Mdina? Is that truly your counsel?'

'No,' said de Villegagnon strongly. Standing, his vast bulk towering over the forgotten messenger, he spoke at last for himself. 'No. I will go gladly. But if Mdina is to be saved, it will be saved not by peasants but by men who fight for religion and honour, by the Knights of St John who adopted these people as their children when the Order made Malta its home. Keep your great officers. Keep your defences. Keep your posts at St Angelo firm. But spare me a hundred knights— knights of no great seniority, but men who would willingly lay down their lives to defeat the Turk, and who would know how to make Islâm pay dearly. Give me a hundred.'

Back in his carved seat leaned the Grand Master, his black hat tall above the grey, passionless face, the patch insouciantly staring. 'I shall give you six,' he said with extreme care. 'Since to travel alone. and at such risk, is a burden I find I cannot lay on you, dear Brother. Take six, to be your companions.'

The sharp intake of shocked breath in the airless room was the only sound that met his remark. Suddenly Gabriel stood. But he was too late. De Villegagnon, looking straight at the Grand Master, had spoken his mind. 'You are laying nothing on me and on the six men you speak of,' he said, 'but death without honour.'

The Grand Master rose. Smoothly, swiftly for so old a man, he rose to his feet, and from his dais looked down on them all, his beaked nose pallid, his sunken cheeks drawn in noble distaste. And this time, in his edged voice, just anger showed plain.

'Brother Nicholas, hear this. In a Knight Hospitaller of the Order of St John of Jerusalem, whatever his age, whatever his rank, whatever he boasts of experience, I look to find valour. I expect obedience. I demand humility before the inscrutable will of the Lord. . . . Puling argument I do not attend. If you are affrighted by the prospect before you, with even six of my knights at your side, then I need only raise my voice to call on knights who believe that to die for their Order alone does them honour. I have no time,' said Juan de Homedès bitingly, 'for traitorous chatter. If you mean to leave, it had better be now, before daybreak. If you are afraid, say as much.'

'*Afraid!*' Not respect for the head of his Order, not discretion, not Christian humility as adjured, made de Villegagnon pause, but the steady message of Gabriel's blue gaze. Nicholas Durand de Ville- gagnon, his voice stiff with hurt, answered the Grand Master then. 'In speaking as I have done, I intercede for the city of Mdina, for the knights and the Maltese within her, and for the six wasted lives being abandoned with mine, that is all. My lord,' said de Villegagnon, staring straight at the one eye of this Aragonese who was master of them all, 'I give you proof that fear never made me decline danger. I go to Mdina tonight, and alone. So that the people of Mdina may die knowing'—and he paused, his voice heavy with ill-fitting irony— 'that through their sacrifice, the knights of this Order may remain secure in their castle of St Angelo to face the future with confidence, unscathed.'

He was allowed to leave, because the Grand Master had always hoped that he would leave; but not, after all, alone. Faster than the precious remnant of darkness, his shield, was melting away, the report of the Grand Master's pronouncement had spread. Six knights might go with him to beleagured Mdina. And when, corselet shining under his robe, helmet clapped on his rough hair, de Villegagnon strode down the steep ramp to the castle ditch, a handful of corn and an arquebus cord in his hand, and began calling gently to the mares tethered there, a touch on his arm turned him to face, not a riding horse's soft mouth but a knight of the French Langue, robed but without armour, a horse roughly bridled with cord at his arm, and behind him five other men. 'There was a ballot,' said a soft, vivid voice. 'And you lost.'

Jerott Blyth. Behind him, three French-born companions of long ago whose grinning faces warmed, suddenly, the raging ice at his heart. And behind them, two men already mounted, one splendid in height, the other lightly made and less tall; both capped in the moonlight with identical silvery hair. One of these was Francis Crawford. The other was Gabriel himself.

Halting at de Villegagnon's side, the Grand Cross bowed his golden head; and as if rebuked, de Villegagnon's bearded chin dropped, too, on his chest, and one by one, those of all that remained of the rest.

'Almighty God,' Graham Malett prayed, his palms tight on the mare's makeshift reins, his soft, deep voice reaching only the little band of whom he had made himself one. 'Preserve these your children who go with no thought of self to succour the weak in their hour of desperate need. We pray for this Order, that what we do may diminish none of its glory, and what we leave undone may be forgiven it and us. Guide us, and when we have gone, guide those that remain, who do what they do, O Lord, from most piteous love of Thee and Thy Son. Into Thy hands we commend our spirits: under Thy foot we lay, joyfully, our mortal flesh.'

The soft, fivefold 'Amen' lay like a presence in the air as they stirred, scattered and mounted. No Moslem watcher from Mount Sciberras saw the seven dark heads swimming the canal, nor the seven wraiths skirting the shore, the hot, salty air thrown back in the nostrils from the high walls of Birgu; nor did any stop them as they threaded through the dark night to the plain where Mdina's high citadel lay.

For to no seasoned Turkish captain, not even to Dragut himself, did it occur that any man, unless he came with an army, would desire to enter Mdina now.

IV

The Rape of Galatian

(Mdina and Gozo, July 1551)

SOMEWHERE on that arrogant ride to Mdina, as he listened to Ottoman voices at prayer, crouched, his mare's nostril's closed in his hand, or sprang from tussock to tussock of dusty grass so that not even the click of unshod hooves would offend the listening night, Jerott Blyth pondered on why they had come.

In the old capital where St Paul had walked, the chief city of Malta, shrine of her ancient laws and offices, they were to lay down their lives fighting the Turk. This, as knights of the Religion, was their duty. His three colleagues from the French Langue were there for that reason alone, he believed. He, who had joined the Order because a girl died, had come, he knew, for reasons that had little to do with the Turk. He thought of the Grand Master who, listening to his sorely honest account of his purpose in joining the Order, had said, 'Followers of Christ come to Him for strange reasons, my son. We do not choose the man who is already whole. We choose the man who knows his soul may be made pure in the service of God, and who will strive to this end. . . .' And that same Grand Master had allowed six of these seven men to ride to Mdina tonight in the hope that they would die, and in the knowledge that if Mdina fell, the shout of treachery might safely be raised.

Gabriel. . . . Why had Gabriel come? At the last moment he had stepped forward, laying his hand on the Frenchman chosen, and had said, 'No, Brother. You will live to make a better sacrifice than this.' And bare of armour as Lymond rashly was, without his beautiful Milanese cuirass or the famous helmet with its white plume, Gabriel had left St Angelo to join de Villegagnon with the rest in the ditch. Gabriel, who had buttressed the aged Grand Master with his own strength, was going to throw away his life at Mdina when the Grand Master, as he must have known, would have used force if need be to stop him. Why?

Why? It was then that Jerott's eye fell on Francis Crawford, who had a knack for leading, and who, Jerott thought, from a spoiled child's relish for gambling, had appointed himself, unasked, to the tiny squadron; and illumination struck him at last. Was it for Lymond's sake, for Lymond and the Religion, that Gabriel had come to Mdina?

On that same foolish journey, Lymond kept his own counsel. The skills learned on rock and on marshland in Scotland endowed him with silence and speed, and Graham Malett hardly saw him although, ignorant of the road, Lymond himself never lost Gabriel or de Villegagnon from sight.

Dodging by instinct, weaving, turning, too fast for caution in a race with the night, the seven men fled to Mdina: seven vulnerable men; the army Adorne was awaiting. And as, far to the east, the first slow rise of light spread on the sea, the Governor, sleepless on the high wall of the capital, saw something move in the ditch.

The bowman at his side had raised his elbow. A growing shudder of anger had begun softly to run through the guard when, in the darkness below the lip of the trench, a light sparked. It glimmered, faltered and flared; and in its yellow glow, grotesque, bearded, positive as a mask, was the face of the Chevalier de Villegagnon, the white cross at his shoulder. The army had come.

On the ramparts, dizzily staring, they were too wise to cheer. Swiftly, as they had practised, the lower cannon were rolled back from the gunports and new rope, cream against ancient cream, flung through the loopholes to the knights waiting below. They climbed like lizards, seaman that each of them was, and George Adorne, an agony of emotion behind his stiff face, counted as they tumbled inside.

Seven. The pause after the seventh man lengthened into a question that Adorne could not bear to put. It was Gabriel who, with a flicker of apology to de Villegagnon—a flicker that took in, Jerott saw, the whole waiting throng about them—said, 'The army follows, my friends. We are here to tell you that Mdina will be saved.'

And so, on the morning of the third day, the bells rang in Mdina. The people shouting and crying for joy mobbed the foolhardy knights who had brought them promise of rescue, and a great column of fire, lit on the Rock of St Paul in the faint light of dawning, told the Grand Master watching from the walls of St Angelo that de Villegagnon and the six had safely arrived.

Inside Adorne's palace, with the escorting crowds locked cheering outside the gates and the tapers smoking, tired yellow in the growing light within, the Bailiff turned, his arms outstretched, to clasp his rescuers, and the fatigue, the despair he had beaten down for three days in this moment of release and privacy, stole his voice and left the tears to stand, foolishly, in his smiling eyes.

De Villegagnon took his hands and held them. There was a growing pause, during which no one spoke. Then as the Governor, in that rigid grip, began at last to guess the incredible truth, the Chevalier broke into harsh speech.

'The people must not despair, but it is your right to know the truth. The Order lies at St Angelo to defend Christendom, and cannot spare but these seven men. We are here to die at your side in the breach ... and by our joint resistance, yours, ours, and that of the people beyond these gates, to make the fall of Mdina renowned in the world.'

'Forgive us,' said Gabriel gently in the half-light, as Adorne, released, slowly slipped to his knees, his two hands pressed to his face. 'We are not four hundred, but seven. We bring you, none the less, the prayers of Christendom and all the power of our faith. Miracles have been done with far less.'

And across the Bailiff's bowed and silent head, 'What miracle is the Grand Master praying for, do you suppose?' inquired Lymond's mild voice.

*

Mdina, isolated on three sides by a sheer drop and on the fourth by a ditch, owed its high sandstone walls to the Romans, and they had been little tended by anyone since. Proof against small slings, against arquebus shot, against scaling, these walls would crumble like powder before the cannon the Osmanli army was dragging, piece by piece, over the rocks from their ships.

Very soon, the Turkish gun-carriages had shattered on these bony tracks, with their ancient ruts chiselled by dead hands in the rock. So, fragment by dismantled fragment, the guns which would destroy them were being carried to Mdina on the naked backs of their Christian slaves, column after column winding through the baked plain; and their chant, rising and falling in the shimmering air, crept through the tight ways of the little city until the Bailiff's trumpeters, high on the walls, raised their silver mouths and piped brisk confidence over the plain.

The bells had stopped, but in the certain hope of rescue and the miraculous fleshly presence of de Villegagnon and his band, the people set to work to hold Mdina until the Order came.

Behind the flaking walls a ditch was dug, and in the rear of this a second wall was raised: a wall of earth and crumbling stone, a heap of friable rubbish ravished in this land of naked soil from the homes which stood that morning on this site. Craftsman, artisan, nobleman, judge—each family in that fated quarter of Mdina wrecked its house, and the dark, stocky women of Malta, the veiling stuck with sweat to their cheeks, carried the precious rubble cradled in their white skirts to the new wall. And as each section of entrenchment was finished, planks were dragged in for platforms and epaulments on which artillery could rest and arquebuses fire over the ditch.

It was while supervising this, his own powerful shoulder to the baulky wheel, shouting drolleries and encouragement in his deep voice, the guinea-gold hair bronze with sweat, that Gabriel looked up to find Lymond before him.

'I believe,' said Francis Crawford, 'that some of your inimitable eloquence would be balm on the western escarpment. The holy Augustinian brethren of these parts are threatening to slay us with thunderbolts if we knock their church down.'

Gabriel straightened. 'Explain to them,' he said.

Lymond shook his head slowly. 'I fear,' he said, 'that only someone on the most intimate terms with the Deity will answer.'

'Then I shall go . . . since that is what you would expect me to say,' said Gabriel, and a sudden, sweet smile crossed his face and was gone. He moved to leave, but at Lymond's shoulder hesitated, his face troubled. 'I wish . . . you did not need to mock,' he said, and rested his fingertips briefly, as once before, on Lymond's arm. 'For of all men, my God could love you; and I, too.'

At the brief council of war held when the wall was almost completed, no trace of this encounter was visible to the naked eye, or even to Jerott Blyth's lively intuition. From the fire, the bells, the loose mares in the ditch, the Turks must surely know, said Adorne tentatively, that some help had come.

'Of course.' De Villegagnon was impatient. 'But they don't know how much. And they may suspect from the signal fire and the trumpets—we hope they will—that more is on the way.'

'I wonder if anyone has escaped over the wall since we came,' said Lymond ruminatively. 'Unhappily, not very likely. They are all waiting now to be succoured, except perhaps. . . .'

'The Osmanli get their information by torture,' interrupted Gabriel sharply.

'. . . Except perhaps the Augustinian monks?' finished Lymond hopefully, in an inimical silence, and added undisturbed, 'Who would like to chalk a cross or two on black cloth?'

Gabriel smiled. 'The sheep-soldiers of Yarrow? I have heard of that,' he said, and as Adorne looked his question, amplified. 'We are ten knights, but the Turk will only count crosses. Dress every man, woman and child as a warrior. Helm the grandmothers; silver-paint muslin if you have no armour. Let's have sticks for arquebuses, rods for crossbows. . . .'

'. . . Logs for cannon,' said de Villegagnon, with a lift of his magnificent beard. 'Agreed most heartily. All that you say, I give in your charge, and M. Crawford's here.' He paused. 'I need not tell you that the Turk is not easily frightened, Sir Graham. Silver paint and sticks cannot overcome scimitars.'

'Then place your faith,' said Graham Malett, 'in the Eight-Pointed Cross,' and again, spoke to Lymond alone.

*

They knew how long they had, exactly, by the dragging march of the Turkish cannon. As the sun rose to its zenith the slave voices, echoing in tired unison, came clear up to the city, and the white caravan of lethal steel, the stone and iron balls linen-wrapped against the blistering heat showed clearly, like packaged ants, as the end approached.

All day, ortas of robed Janissaries, akinji, azabs, had been taking position just outwith Mdina's cannon range; and slaves, raw-naked to the sun, had toiled under Turkish sappers to build platforms for the great basilisk and the eighty-pound culverins, and to trench the recalcitrant rock beyond the ditch. As far as vision allowed, silken colour, slow-moving in the haze like some lethargic sea-exotica, unrolled at the city's feet; and the crescent of Islâm, like some heavenly mirage on every shield and banner told that, under the hand of the Most High, the army of the dispenser of crowns was at hand: the flaming sword and victorious blade of Allâh confronted the humble panoply of God.

Then all that could be done for Mdina had been done. Silent under the sun, knights, soldiers, servants, men and women of Mdina and the casals about—even, here and there, the best blood of Malta, the lord of Gatto-Murino, the Inguanez whose crest for a hundred years had been wrought in Mdina's great gates—persuaded at last by Gabriel's lucid power to help the hated, usurping knights, lay at their posts.

Beside the ancient cannon, beside the piles of slingshot, the vats of cooking-oil, the sparse bombards made from shredded cotton and chemicals, in their toy armour the defenders lay, watching as the culverins far below one by one crawled to their platforms and, the padding strewn like bandages on the rocks, were assembled each into a dark mouth threatening Mdina's high walls. Pavilions sprang up, looped with gold, and the horses tethered in the shade of the silk wore housings which flashed jewel-coloured as they moved. Dragut, Salah Rais and the renegade Jew of Smyrna called Sinan, or Devil-Driver, had taken up their command. The time was almost run out.

Jerott Blyth, on his last circuit of the inner wall, found Lymond and Graham Malett together, watching through bracketed hands the distant movements below. For a moment he joined them before, bitterly, he burst through their silence. 'And we have ten knights to

107

fight against that! The armies of Spain and Italy and all the Low Countries should be arriving unasked to stand here with us. My God, are we merchants, taking a keen risk for commerce, or rich men greedy for land for our sons, or blood-crazed soldiers killing for gold? Or are we preserving the soft white hides of the Emperor's Christian subjects at the cost of our lives, for the love of Christ and our fellow-men?'

'Is that why you came to Mdina, Sir Graham?' said Lymond; and Gabriel turned, his face changed.

It was the first personal challenge that Lymond had issued, and for a long moment Graham Malett studied him without speaking. Then, turning back, he let his eyes range over the swarming turbans below, tumbling like cottongrass in a boisterous wind, and his face was not serene. 'I came,' said Gabriel, 'to help force from the earth, foul body and black soul, the heathen hordes you see there.'

Lymond's tone remained gentle. 'An honest ambition. But after supporting the Grand Master so worthily, why deprive St Angelo of one of the few leaders who matter? Mdina is going to fall anyway. I came with de Villegagnon because, for one thing, with fewer suspects to blame, the Grand Master will really require to stretch himself this time. It seems superfluous to make the Order a laughing-stock before it vanishes.'

There was a prickly silence. Then Jerott Blyth said, 'I forgot, Crawford, you are an admirer of the Turk. Tell us; do you excuse Dragut *that*?'

There was no need to point. Before each gun-platform on the hot rocks below stood a row of roughly-hewn crosses with a naked, blue-white body nailed fast to each, limbs extended in pitiful parody of the Christian symbol, the heads gone. The men who had slipped over the walls of Mdina last night had found neither safety nor a quiet grave.

Without turning, 'Worse happened at home, before the Protector's wars ended,' Lymond observed. 'Buccleuch and his friends played football, as I remember, with his English prisoners' skulls.'

'These are vermin,' Gabriel said, his fair-skinned face taut. 'A plague which would infect the whole civilized world, killing all the good and gentle and virtuous things you and I know. Would you quarrel over the death of a rat?'

'Rats don't pray. And cowardice doesn't commend itself to Turks. Neither do they have the best example before them. Is it true that the knights sometimes fire their captives alive through the cannon?'

It was true. No one spoke. They were all tired and wrought-up with strain; they had, after all, only that afternoon and evening, probably, to live. Gabriel closed his eyes; then as Jerott made a troubled movement towards him, opened them with an obvious effort and after a moment addressed Francis Crawford in a quiet, steady voice.

'Forgive me. I have lost you and my own integrity both. You are right. I have betrayed the Order: vaingloriously thrown away what was not mine to lay down. . . .'

Lymond stirred and the fair knight, as if he had touched him, snatched away, averting his head. 'It is hard always to take the safe, the sane, the old man's path,' said Graham Malett. 'I hoped—it is not always wise to hope—for a miracle.'

'Who doesn't? But in miracles, as in hell, there is no order of rule. I recommend,' said Lymond pleasantly, 'that as Mdina is watching us, we all look enthusiastic about fighting instead. Handkerchief, Sir Graham?'

His eyes still wet, Graham Malett turned his back. Jerott didn't. With a swing of his muscled shoulder he brought the flat of his hand hard towards Lymond's cheek, and Lymond chopped it downwards halfway with a blow that nearly broke the bones of his fingers, and said crisply, 'If your godly offices stretch to praying as well as posturing, you'd better start reciting, *Brother*. Dragut has come out.' And as the call to arms rang out and from wall and tower and makeshift mound the masqueraders sprang to their posts, Francis Crawford rallied his knights. 'Come, comrades! Come, Brethren, and pray. Let us obtain, by our faith in the Sacred Sacraments, that contempt for death which alone can render us invincible.'

And, arrived at his post, the men allotted him in position about him, Francis Crawford laid his long yew bow against his foot and expertly strung it as the robed ranks below unrolled smoothly to a gong clearly heard and deployed behind the sinuous earthworks. There was a pause; and then with a hiss, as of a ship paying off to the wind, the arrows rose like vapour between the citadel and the sun, and began to fall on the town. Then presently the first cannon fired. Mdina's pretence, her show of false strength, was going for nothing. This was the preliminary to an attack in real earnest. And against scimitars, silver sticks, as de Villegagnon had said, were of little use.

A long time after that, when they were all a little deaf from the close-range bombardment, and the sandy grit was silting their mouths, de Villegagnon dodged past, vast, light-footed despite his armour, and pausing, said, 'Where is Gabriel?' And Lymond, lowering his arm, said in an unexpected voice, 'I thought he was with you,' and laying down the bow, still more unexpectedly, left the wall at a run.

About to follow, Blyth was brought up short by de Villegagnon's bark and returned hurriedly to his post. Two of their ablest leaders vanished was enough.

In all the prolific measures to prevent ingress, no one had thought to make it impossible to escape from Mdina. When Lymond reached him, Gabriel had made fast a rope and in a moment more was half over the inner, makeshift wall over the ditch. Then Lymond's hand closed over his, and the Knight Grand Cross looked up.

He had changed his dress. Stripped to plain tunic and hose, his cropped hair disordered, his face set, he gave a moment to dislodging Lymond's grip then, failing, flung his whole weight on the rope and on Lymond so that, for a second, the younger man was dragged head first in his wake. Then, going with the movement, without releasing his grip, Francis Crawford also swarmed over the wall and, arresting with arm, body and knee, locked Graham Malett to the rope. For an insane moment, Malett strove to fling him off; and in that moment, plunging with its double burden against the piled earth and rubble, the frayed rope gave way.

Had it been the outer wall of Mdina, they would both have been killed. As it was they tumbled, grappling still, head over heels down the grit and boulders and loose limestone blocks which the wrecked houses of Mdina had yielded half a day before until, slashed, flayed, squeezed blue with belabouring, they rolled together into the ditch below.

For a long moment, neither moved. In the deep trough it was dark, shaded by the wall. Ahead the outer escarpment towered, shielding them from view of the Turks. Incredibly, eyes strained towards the threat over the wall, none in Mdina had seen them drop.

Lymond was the first to awake. In a little while, Gabriel stirred. Slowly, patiently, the Grand Cross gathered his muscles, moved, straightened, and doggedly got to his feet. Beside him, tumbled prone on the earth, Lymond lay perfectly still. For a moment Gabriel stood, his hand inside his jerkin, his eyes dazedly searching the strewn stones about him; then taking breath, he wheeled round to run.

An arm shot out. His ankle was caught and held with the same manacled finality as the grip on his wrist, and falling headlong, he rolled over to find Lymond's cold stare fixed on his face. '*Are you sent me*,' said Sir Graham Malett, Knight Grand Cross of the Order of St John of Jerusalem, '*by God or the Devil?*' He made no effort, now, to rise.

'What were you doing?' Lymond's voice gave nothing away, but his eyes, accustomed to judgement, searched every line of the tired, steadfast face below him. From below the right eye to the jawbone, Gabriel's face was streaming with blood. His clothing, ripped like Lymond's, was blotched with it; you could see his chest heave, suddenly, as he said, 'They torture their prisoners. I could ask no one else to endure that.'

Lymond said, 'You meant to be caught?' And as Gabriel did not answer, 'I see. My gratuitous remark about the Augustinians. But

110

did it not occur to you that if Dragut tortured you for the news that vast reinforcements were on their way here, he might further torture you for the truth? You are neither immortal nor, forgive me, very like a Maltese peasant.'

'Under God, I feel no pain,' said Graham Malett, his eyes unseeing on the blue of the heavens as he lay. 'St Angelo I had deserted; Mdina I could no longer serve. By sacrifice, one may sometimes buy a miracle.' He spoke as if alone, as if the voice beside him were that of some dread and disembodied conscience, familiar to him all his days.

There was a long silence, which Lymond let pass uninterrupted. Then he said, 'Sometimes the sacrifice is not required. *Il y a des accomodements avec le ciel.* Look. I believe your miracle has happened.'

Slowly, the older man turned his head. Outside the great outer wall, the whicker of arrows, the drums, the gong beats, the cries, the shrill trumpets, had stopped. Instead, many voices shouted and others commanded; the earth shook with the movement of massed feet, and high above the noise sounded the chime which had rung in their ears all day, to halt at last in a silence worse than screaming, before the bombardment began: the sound of the great cannon being dismantled again.

From the packed walls of Mdina, from score upon score of parched, anxious, disbelieving throats a cry went up; then shout after shout of hysterical joy. From first one church, then another, the shaking carillons sprang. In the great ditch below, Graham Malett, drawn to his knees by the sound, dropped his disfigured face in his hands and chokingly prayed in a whisper.

The miracle had happened. The Turk was abandoning the siege.

Neither praying nor weeping, Francis Crawford stood absently nursing his bumps, and considered. 'If I were Dragut Rais, and Mdina lay ripe under my hand, what would frighten me off? Perhaps a mass attack from St Angelo. But he has no reason to fear one. What, then? What about false intelligence of another sort, Brother?' said Francis Crawford to the air. 'What about a little message from the Receiver of Sicily, ostensibly for the Grand Master, saying that Prince Doria with the Emperor's sea power has sailed to the rescue? That would fit. If I were Dragut, that would tear me away. And if I had neglected St Angelo and run from the shadow-threat of Mdina, if my Spahís were restless for booty, if I were the Drawn Sword of Islâm, whose brother lay in ashes on Gozo ... where next would I strike?'

And, 'Gozo,' Lymond repeated, committing the words above Gabriel's bowed head, and suddenly swore. 'Gozo Island, of course. The sacrifice is to be made after all for the Order, by Oonagh O'Dwyer and the women and children of Gozo.'

The result was the same, although his trick had succeeded and Gabriel's failed. Long before Gabriel had awakened, Lymond had guessed his intentions; had found them confirmed in the paper half-slipped from Sir Graham's tunic as he lay, stunned still, after their fall. One side was written in Turkish. On the other, Gabriel's big, well-formed writing conveyed a message in English. The Turkish siege was untenable. The Grand Master had sent word to Mdina. The whole force of the Order was on its way from St Angelo to trap Dragut like a rat between Mdina and Birgu. If it wished to survive, the Turkish army must fly.

The lies looked convincing. The Turkish side was more forcible still. Yet, aware now of Gabriel's calibre, Francis Crawford could not bring himself yet to acknowledge it, or his own malicious intent. The paper was crushed in his tunic. Gabriel, he hoped, would assume it lost in the fall. '*Da mihi castitatem et continentiam* ... Give me chastity and continence,' said Francis Crawford between his teeth, looking down at the Grand Cross of Grace at his feet. 'But pray God, not just yet.'

*

So the plan, prepared so lightly that evening in Sicily, became history. So the Receiver of Sicily's spurious letter announcing rescue fell into Sinan Pasha's hands as designed, and rather than leave his ships unmanned in Marsamuscetto and his cannon stuck at Mdina, the Turkish general decided to abandon the siege.

But on Gozo, the scrap of land to Malta's north, there were good farmsteads and one or two well-plenished palaces, defended only by the Governor de Césel's hilltop citadel, commanding the town of Rabat at its foot. Pleasing at once himself, his troops and Dragut, Sinan Pasha withdrew to his ships and set his tiller for Gozo. And this time, nothing stood in his way.

From the battlements of the citadel, her back to the square and the church, Oonagh O'Dwyer stood and watched Rabat become Turkish. Like husked seed the coloured turbans poured between the tall, flat-roofed houses, the felt caps and camel-hair cloaks of the dervishes wild in the van, and the walls rattled with the roll of the kettledrums and the screams of *Allâh! Allâh! Al-hamdu lillah!* as the Lions of Islâm broke through.

The nearer streets filled. You could see white teeth, flying *caftáns*, sashes ridged with daggers, the flashing mace, the crowded silver parings of the scimitar, the lacquered coins that were shields. Faces fair and dark: Circassian, Syrian, Greek and Bosnian, Armenian, Croatian as well as Turks; children of the House of Osman; soldiers of Suleiman the Lawgiver, forbidden to trample on roses.

She moved round to the east. Below the citadel walls the whips

112

cracked and the slaves ran as the culverins bit by bit assembled, grew, took shape, and bent their black mouths on the fort. To the west, and there below the steepest cliff of the fortress spread the other claw of the army, between themselves and the broad escarpment of il-Harrax on its strata of rock to the north-west.

They were encircled. And there were no Knights of St John on Gozo save Galatian de Césel, its Governor. There were four rotting cannon but only one soldier to fire them: an Englishman called Luke.

Oonagh never knew his other name. Irked by the deadweight of Galatian's fright and apathy, she had been roused to fury when, after the supreme effort of collecting and dispatching two boatloads of women and children to St Angelo, St Angelo had turned them back.

She had fought for action, for the simplest defence, the most rudimentary precautions, in vain. Luke, speaking up from ten years in the knights' service, had supported her, but the flicker of energy she had thought to rouse in Galatian had soon died. She took two helpers into their confidence: Luke, and Bernardo da Fonte, husband of her tirewoman Maria and a Sicilian whose voice counted among the few traders of the island. With their help she managed, in Galatian's name, to force some order out of the muddle. It might, she knew, stiffen for the moment the failing courage of the people and stave off the panic she knew must eventually come. It would do no more.

In the end, movingly, it was the people who stood firm when the first call for surrender arrived. When outside the gates the gong dimmed into silence and was followed by the peremptory Arabic of the standard-bearer, it was the people, depleted through the generations by the attacks of corsair and Turk, who screamed him down from the walls and spurned him recklessly with stones.

Then the Osmanli cannon opened up. The noise, drowning in its thunder the crash of breached masonry, was bedevilled with dust which rose in mantled clouds, silting into children's hair and the tender passages of nose and throat. Then through the haze they appeared, thicket upon thicket of attenuated silver crescents: Janissaries, Bostanjís, Spahís, blades raised, ready to pour from Rabat, up through the breached citadel wall and over the rocks to the Gran' Castello itself.

The smoke cleared for a moment, then the 80-pounder spoke again with its iron ball. It hit the wall foursquare as Oonagh watched. For a moment the stone deliberated; then the whole centre of the old masonry buckled and fell, a wilderness of severed life underneath.

And the people, for whom the alternative was slavery, ran *to* the breach, not from it. A single man, rallying at that moment, could have marshalled them; could have flung them the clubs, the crossbows, the old swords all rusting in the armoury so that for an hour,

113

the broken wall could be held, rebuilt, trenched—some pretence of resistance arranged. Luke, a common soldier, could not command them. Da Fonte the Sicilian, one of themselves, could not make himself heard. And Galatian de Césel, whose name they were clamouring, was here, adhesive as a frightened cur, on the pretext of quenching her fear.

From his grasp she saw Luke, his jerkin torn, run to the one intact cannon standing still by the breach. She saw him fire, and fire again, and heard the studied wail of the Janissaries turn to screams as the balls cut through the packed advance. The wave of robed, scrambling figures halted, hesitated, dropped; and as the smoke thinned it showed the red and white carpeted path of the shot. Then the whole Turkish battery spoke. When the smoke cleared this time, the walls of the citadel were down, and the men, women and children in the lanes and houses behind them were dead. Where the gun had been, and the English gunner, was nothing.

No one took his place. But one man, crazily, stepping out of the fumes and the bloody rubble, scrambled over the wrecked battlements, stumbled down the steep hillside beyond, and like an engine, marched straight for the Ottoman army. Even from the palace you could name him: Bernardo da Fonte, an arquebus tight in one fist, a crossbow in the other. At a good place he stopped, laid down the crossbow and with deliberation fired first one weapon and then the other into the enemy. Then, sword in hand, he raced into the dazzle of converging scimitars. Oonagh stayed, Galatian's arms around her, to see so much. Then, thrusting him abruptly away, she went to look for Maria da Fonte.

She found her, with her two daughters, on the threshold of their home. Before he had walked out to kill and be killed, her husband had used his sword with insane mercy. Maria and the children were dead.

By the time Oonagh returned to the palace, a priest had already gone at the Council's behest to indicate surrender, on certain gentlemanly conditions, to the commander of Allâh's Deputy on Earth. Hearing of it, she laughed and addressed the poor ghosts at her side. 'Chastity, Obedience and Poverty,' said Oonagh O'Dwyer. 'A knight engages, when fighting for Jesus Christ against the enemies of the Faith, never to shrink from battle, never to lower the flag of the Order and never to retreat, to surrender or demand quarter. A knight also,' she went on, rolling malevolently in her soft Irish voice the austere periods of the vow, 'or any other man for that matter, need not dream of laying down conditions, honourable or otherwise, for surrender, unless he has at least offered a brave defence. . . . what have you defended in the vale of Calypso, Galatian? Your chastity?'

And seized, like a fool, with the uncontrollable impulse to laugh, she leaned her brow for one indulgent second against the cold wall and sealed her mouth with the hard fingers of both hands, not to disgrace herself.

The answer which the priest, returning, gave Galatian stirred even that helpless monk with its disdain. Far from agreeing to preserve the Governor's liberty and gear and the property of the Gozitans, Sinan Pasha replied that unless the Hakím Governor gave himself up instantly, he would be hanged at the gate.

Hastily, the priest was returned to Suleiman's general. Would Sinan Pasha, commander of Suleiman, Lord of Lords, permit the Governor his liberty at least, and promise the freeing of two hundred of the island's greatest men?

Dragut's hand, not Sinan Pasha's, lay on the returning, curt answer. Provided there was instant surrender, forty of the greatest men of Gozo might go free. And, added the message repressively, if the negotiator returned, he would hang.

Then Galatian de Césel issued his only direct order: that the gates be opened to the Turks.

Senselessly, Oonagh O'Dwyer had run to her room as Moslem dress, light silks flying, appeared suddenly under her window, and the distant faces became characterful and distinct. She could see the heavy, oiled black moustaches, the trailing scarves, the jewelled daggers, the axe shining in the belt, the cocked tail of the turban over its *kavúk*, the high boots, thick with dust, into which the wide trousers were tucked. A man in a knee-length embroidered coat over chain mail paused on the steps by the house, wicker shield lowered while he studied it, and she backed from the window and ran.

Upstairs, Maria's sister found her, for, since the boats, the Hakím's pregnant woman was no longer given the Hakím's blame. So Maria's sister offered the Irishwoman a share in her most precious possession: a single, frail hope of escape.

Outside the citadel there was a hiding place: a tunnel leading underground to the abrupt, semi-conical height of il-Harrax Hill, where no one could find them. But first one must escape from the fortress on its steepest side, the side which would now, if the Fates were kind, be unguarded by Turks. And that meant crossing the whole of the citadel from south-east to north-west.

Galatian's whereabouts at that time were unknown. It is not on record that his mistress even hesitated. Oonagh, struck with the nausea of reaction; with the final stark impact of Galatian's cowardice, stumbled from the side door of the house with her rescuer; she who had been the swiftest rider in Ireland, the quickest wit, the most icy in vengeance, and ran from door to door, from lane to lane, from hide to hide until, with the screaming thick in her ears, she came to the well, the archway, the quick turn which led to the steep narrow steps to the battlements.

Here was a huddle of buildings, a wall, some steps, a gun-platform. And here, looking straight to il-Harrax, was a long, shuttered building whose door opened briefly to admit them. It was crowded with people: silent, white-faced people awaiting their turn to run across that sunlit platform outside, to seize the invisible rope, and to drop out of sight down the rock face. 'They are plundering now,' said her friend in her ear. 'They'll be too busy to watch.'

Her mind disentangling the Maltese idiom, Oonagh was, she found, staring also at a moving shadow in the steep lane below. A shadow which hid in other shadows, which hesitated, shrank and waited, trapped, in a distant doorway until a group of Janissaries, pushing an unclothed woman before them, disappeared in the dust.

The struggle between her pride and her will was infinitesimal: Oonagh O'Dwyer was a brave woman and had in her time been a great one. Noiselessly, without a glance at the woman who had brought her there, so near freedom and life; without a word to the others, the lucky ones who were on their way to escape, the Irishwoman slipped from the doorway and, with an agonizing care to avoid disclosing her refuge, made her way from corner to corner and down the steep steps to where, on his way to cowardly freedom, Galatian de Césel lurked.

She saw his eyes devour her, joyously, as she approached him. Signing danger, she seized his hand and he let her hurry him, soft-footed, back the way he had come, further and further into the citadel. When at length she stopped, he said pathetically, 'Have the Turks found out and stopped it? There's an escape passage over there. . . . Oonagh, help me reach it! We'll be free!'

'Free of what?' said Oonagh; and her cold stare, which he had never seen, raked him from head to foot. And seeing in the street a Believer passing, his *caftán* jewelled and his red scimitar hilted in gold she jerked Galatian in a single, shrewd movement into the sun, calling. 'Hakím! Governor! Behold the Hakím, lord!' And the Turk with the scimitar, turning, smiled gently, showing all his stained teeth, while from the houses others came running.

They made him, who had wanted to bargain with them, carry his own chests and furniture on his naked shoulders from the stripped rooms he had shared with his mistress, all the way to the ships. Then they peeled from him all his remaining rags and chained him naked on his back on the rambade, like a slave. Above him, Oonagh was set to sit with her wrists tied. By Dragut's orders she had been neither ravished nor unclothed, though neither would have mattered to her in the remote fastness of her thoughts.

Three hundred lived by escaping to il-Harrax. A thousand died. And six thousand three hundred men, women and children of Gozo were put aboard the Ottoman fleet, to be sold, at best, to slavery.

116

The forty greatest men on the island, whose freedom Dragut had so gravely promised, had proved, in bitter pun, to mean the forty most aged; since the oldest, Dragut mildly explained, should be looked upon as the principal. So, drawing away from the harbour, the sweet wind full in their sails, the Faithful called their farewells to the deserted island of Gozo, lying broken and smoking beneath the bright sun, with the reek of the unburied mixed with the thyme. And forty old men, sick, shaking, shocked near death and far beyond thought, stood silent there on the rocks and watched them draw off.

Into Oonagh O'Dwyer's quiet mind, as she gazed unseeing at the white flesh of Galatian there at her feet, stole the words of a grave-stone, seen once since she came, all enchanted, from France to Calypso's isle, and never forgotten.

> Ask thyself, cries Maimuma from the grave, if there is anything everlasting, anything that can repel or cast a spell upon death. Alas, death has robbed me of my short life; neither my piety nor my modesty could save me from him. I was industrious in my work, and all that I did is reckoned and remains. O, thou who lookest upon this grave in which I am enclosed, dust has covered my eyelids and the corners of my eyes. On my couch and in my abode there is naught but tears; and what will happen when my Creator comes to me? . . .

'But there is more,' said Oonagh O'Dwyer suddenly, roused to thought by a memory of her own. 'There is more, old woman, surely, unless my senses are lying? Where is that busy, bowelless gentleman now?'

*

Drenched in seawater and bleeding roseately from the stone which had felled him, Francis Crawford lay at the feet of Brother Blyth, who had knocked him unconscious; and Jerott Blyth waited without sympathy for him to recover.

The Turks had hardly gone from Mdina when Lymond had disappeared too. 'Where is he now?' Gabriel had said harshly, and Jerott Blyth had replied with exaggerated unconcern, 'Retrieving the Irish *amie*, I should suppose,' and then retreated into silence before Gabriel's visible dismay.

His skin paler, 'Of course. . . .' had said Graham Malett, going on rapidly. 'Tell Nicholas I've gone. It's hopeless. Francis must know it. No one can be saved from Gozo now. He must be stopped.'

'Not by you, sir!' It sounded firm; in fact a kind of horrified disbelief sharpened Jerott Blyth's voice. 'Are we *nursemaids*? He knows his own mind. Why should we stop him? Nothing here draws him or requires him now.'

'But I do, Jerott,' Gabriel had quietly replied. And had added, 'I will not add criminal waste to wanton wilfulness. He must be stopped.'

'Then I will stop him,' Jerott had said, and white with anger, had set off.

Tracking over the used grey grass and the knotted pink and chrome sandstone where Lymond on foot had struck out from Mdina, sighting him miraculously at length when all his energy had gone and pushing out, somehow, the extra effort needed to match, to excel, to overtake that cracking pace, he had come, parched and stumbling, to this northernmost shore. Here, green through the blistering haze, was Comino; and there, across the blue straits, the long ridge of Gozo itself.

In all the crazy, sun-beaten journey they had met no one. All north Malta had fled to the west, or was in hiding. Scrambling over the great stony ridges and down into the valleys hatched with terracing, Jerott passed their empty pueblos, square box-houses blending into the hillside, with their melon-patches bright green about them. Here some hens scratched. There, frightening him with the dull clank of its bell, a goat watched him, ears drooping, from the twisted branch of a tree. He passed white waxy stephanotis, its scent staining the air, and pink Fiori de Pasqua among the olives and carobs; and the prickly pears, yellow-green, beige, Indian red on their angular stalks, masked him from the man he was following, though not from the sun.

Then he was here at Marfa, on the grey grass and the tired grey sand above the northernmost beach, where the pitted yellow-grey sandstone ran out under the water like petrified sponges, water-moiled and ribboned with weed. There was one boat only in the harbour of Marfa, and by the time Jerott came, plunging downhill into sight, the one boat was launched and Lymond, the sun blazing on his unprotected head, was thigh-deep, ready to heave himself in.

Then Jerott, easing his powerful shoulders under the soaked shirt, had bent to scoop up a rock, weighed it for an instant, poised and threw it. He aimed for the back of the other man's head and did not greatly care how hard it struck. A moment later Lymond slid to his knees, his hands tracking down the skiff's sides, and Jerott, splashing through the shallows, had heaved him on to the hot, salty thyme. The boat, when he turned back to sink it, had already drifted far out of reach. Chest heaving, flesh viscous with sweat, Jerott Blyth flung himself beside his briskly felled victim and waited while the sea sucked on the sandstone and the crickets shrilled, high and pulsating; the only stirring of life on all that bare strand.

Then Lymond opened his eyes and rolled over, assessing Blyth's presence, and the far-off boat, and the aching wound in his scalp. He said, 'Gabriel sent you?' and as Jerott assented he added, icy rage in his voice, 'What a pity Sir Graham could not be present himself.'

'A great pity,' agreed Jerott grimly. 'He may see a soul worth redeeming where I may see only trash.'

Lymond sat up, his back rigid, perspiration in great tears on his lashes and jaw. 'And my God, you're revelling in it all, aren't you, out of sheer, schoolboy spleen. And how bloody offended you would be if I asked you how you'd feel if Elizabeth were there, and I'd stopped you reaching her. Even whores have souls, you know, *Brother*. . . . Why are we waiting, then? This is one game you have resoundingly won.' And standing upright, he turned back the way he had come.

He was the first soul Gabriel had called to them who, resisting, had hit back, and hitting back, had struck so sorely home. Only at Gabriel's order would Jerott have stirred a finger to save him: for Oonagh O'Dwyer he had no thought at all. And, indeed, the smoke haze spreading across the blue channel told that it was already too late.

V

Hospitallers

(Birgu, August 1551)

TWO days after this, the French Ambassador to Turkey, sailing from Marseilles to resume his office at Constantinople, was informed by a fishing boat that the Ottoman army had overrun Gozo.

The spokesman, whose name, oddly, turned out to be Stephenson, had a strange story to tell, and after listening to him with much interest, Gabriel de Luetz, Baron and Seigneur d'Aramon et de Valabrègues, invited him to sail to Birgu in his company.

Since Messieurs de Villegagnon and Crawford of Lymond had met him at Marseilles, M. d'Aramon had been a month at sea, and if he carried gold for Suleiman, it would be too tardy by now to finance the present Maltese attack. Lingering in Algiers, calling at Pantellaria, he diplomatically wasted time.

Three ships wouldn't save Malta. They would only endanger the King of France's tenuous friendship with the Turks, not to mention his substantial trading concessions. M. de Luetz, Baron d'Aramon, temporized; and only when he was fairly sure that Sinan Pasha had left Malta not to return, did he allow his captain to approach the Grand Harbour. Then he saw that the scarlet flag of the Order flew still over St Angelo, and despite his training, water stood, surprisingly in his eyes. Soon the welcoming salvoes broke over the still water, and in salute the Ambassadorial ships replied.

Close to St Angelo, d'Aramon observed more. The white walls of the fort were untouched. Birgu stood beyond, its stone unblackened by fire; and across Galley Creek, L'Isla was unmarked. Then the Order's boat drew swiftly alongside, and in it were de Villegagnon, the Chevalier de la Valette and Sir Graham Malett, the red sun coppering his hair.

Again, la Valette was unharmed, though de Villegagnon had a fresh scar and 'Gabriel', the man whose nickname, he remembered, was his own, wore a thin dressing over the bone of his cheek. They exchanged greetings with grave courtesy; then d'Aramon, ushering them into the poop pavilion where his own entourage waited, heard the story of the landing, of the repulse by Nicholas Upton and Gimeran, of the defence of Mdina under de Villegagnon, and of the sack of Gozo. During the whole invasion, the knights' only loss by death was Nicholas Upton; the only knight the Turks carried off was Galatian de Césel, Governor of Gozo.

That uncertain story, brought back quavering by a pack of senile old men, was corrected by the Grand Master himself. At supper at St Angelo, with the chain lifted and the galleys anchored snugly in Galley Creek, surrounded by the names all Europe knew; the incense in his nostrils from their black robes, the Eight-Pointed Cross repeated over and over in the candlelight, the Ambassador heard how Galatian de Césel had defended the citadel of Gozo with his life; how, so long as he was living, the people of Gozo, in obedience to his orders and in imitation of his example, had repulsed the attacks of the infidel with valour until at length their brave Governor had been killed on the ramparts by a cannon ball. Then the people, losing their leader and their courage at once, had been obliged to capitulate. The Grand Master, crossing himself, folded his hands in stricken prayer and M. d'Aramon, repeating the gesture, watched the other faces about the board with his shrewd, sun-pursed eyes.

The story didn't ring true. More, there was an air of unrest among the Order itself, noticed as soon as la Valette came aboard, which made him uneasy. He would not press the knights of France to divide their loyalties, and he expected no disclosures. But in all the detail, the tales of the grain ships sent for, the parties already on Gozo repairing the wrecked citadel and burying the dead, the soldiers working side by side with the Maltese to mend the shattered casals, the crowded hospital and the food, water, medicines taken daily to Mdina and the burned townships—he could not learn how many knights there had been at Gozo, or even Mdina, and why the whole Osmanli army had been able to move from Marsamuscetto to Mdina and from Mdina to Gozo unmolested.

Walking back afterwards with the Grand Master to his lodging, which with an attention he found almost too overwhelming, was in the Grand Master's own suite, the Ambassador said, 'I have a supplicant for you, Your Eminence, from the fishing barque whose false message from Messina caused the Turks to abandon the Mdina siege. The captain of the vessel was taken hostage, it seems, by Sinan Pasha. His lieutenant intercepted me outside Pantelleria in order to beg you to pay his principal's ransom.'

Beside him, Juan de Homedès's stiff walk had not faltered, but in the flare of the porters' cressets his face looked a little severe. 'There is no obligation on the Order to ransom this man,' he said at last. 'The boat is the responsibility of the Viceroy of Sicily, not ours.'

The French Ambassador waited a moment, then said reasonably, 'I gather that no seamen of the Viceroy's would take the risk. This boat, which had nothing to gain but a little money, was manned by a Scotsman.'

'A Scots fisherman in the Mediterranean?' said the Grand Master lightly. 'You astonish me.'

And by then, M. d'Aramon was fairly certain that the Grand Master was perfectly familiar with the identity of the captain who had taken the biggest gamble any Christian could: who had sailed into the hands of the Turks so that the misleading letter should fall into their hands. 'His name is Thompson,' said d'Aramon, with no hope of the Grand Master but a sudden very strong conviction of his own.

'The Scottish pirate! Dear me, M. d'Aramon, you speak of a man who deserves all the chastisement that this life or the next may provide. He is the scourge of the Order. I cannot count the number of times he has raided ships of the Religion.'

'He plunders us all,' said d'Aramon patiently. 'He none the less saved Mdina and most likely Malta that day.'

'A small remittance which will barely cover the least of his sins. No, no,' said the Grand Master, preceding d'Aramon into his chamber and signing him to be seated. 'I have much more serious affairs to discuss with you tonight. Here, in the privacy of this room, I must tell you what has reached my ears from the survivors of Gozo. We may not hope that the heathen, having done his worst, is sailing, distended with Christian blood, to his master at the Porte. No. Sinan Pasha, Dragut Rais and the Turkish fleet have gone to their real objective, Sir Ambassador; and their real objective is the taking of Tripoli.

'Therefore,' said the Grand Master of the Order of St John, standing old, tall and noble in his ancient office over Gabriel d'Aramon's head, 'Therefore in the name of Jesus Christ, in the name of the monarch your master who glories in the title of the *Most Christian King*, I must ask you to sail forthwith to Tripoli and to dissuade this wild and sinful pagan from his design. You, by virtue of your office, have been compelled to acquaint yourself with this vicious race,' said Juan de Homedès sternly. 'It is open to you now to make godly use of the commerce with which you have soiled your hands. Go to the heathen, sir, and order them to desist.'

*

Years of intrigue in his native France; years of exile as military attaché to the French Ambassador at Venice; years at the Porte, travelling all over Asia Minor in the Sultan's train, bickering over rights in Jerusalem and enticing concessions from viziers, had made the Baron d'Aramon's political senses very sharp. Long before this ominous walk with the Grand Master he had put in hand, discreetly, an inquiry among the soldiers, the mercenaries, the Maltese, to find out what really had happened at Mdina and Gozo, with no successes at all.

His train was big. Henri of France, ashamed perhaps at last of the treatment d'Aramon had received at home in return for long and painstaking service, had made him a Gentleman of the Bedchamber before he left and had given him two of the best-equipped galleys in the fleet, with Michel de Seurre, Knight of the Order, to accompany him in his galliot. Besides his own relatives and his captains, there were several noblemen, several Gascon gentlemen, the King's secretary, and three men who knew the Eastern Mediterranean as well as he did; of whom one was Nicolas de Nicolay, royal cosmographer to France and de Villegagnon's friend.

It was just before the famous dinner that the French Ambassador, courteously supervised into aseptic seclusion, called de Seurre and de Nicolay to him and said, shutting the door, 'I am a little mystified by what has happened here. We are not to be allowed, it seems, to ask questions in Birgu, and I will not ask M. de Villegagnon or his friends to betray their vows. But M. de Villegagnon has with him an independent observer, a Scotsman named Crawford.'

'I know him,' said de Seurre equably. 'He has a reputation in Scotland. A man of eccentricity.'

'I thought you had met,' said d'Aramon, relieved. 'M. de Villegagnon tells me that this Scottish gentleman is at present in hospital. The reason is not clear. It may even be,' said the Ambassador without stress, 'that the patient is not sick and does not wish to be in hospital. However that may be, it would be fitting if you were to visit him.'

'Would we be admitted?' The geographer's elf-like face jammed freakishly into ruts of perplexity, and he ran his hand through his short, rough grey hair.

It stuck up, and M. d'Aramon eyed him thoughtfully. He had chosen M. de Seurre because he knew from de Villegagnon that he had been on the Scots campaign, and because he was a Knight of the Order of St John of an absolute integrity. He had chosen the geographer because he knew Scotland, because he was endlessly inquisitive and a shrewd judge of character, and because he was the kind of innocent enthusiast who could get himself into (and out of) any corner he chose.

The Ambassador opened his mouth; but before he answered, Nicolas de Nicolay struck himself on the chest—an appalling blow, for he was a very little man—and reeling briefly in a circle with his knees bent, fell on his spine to the carpet with a thud that made his chair jump. As the others leaped to their feet, he lifted his head like a handle and said, 'I perish, *mes amis*. There is one hope only. The hospital!'

'You fool,' said de Seurre impatiently. 'They'd find out in five minutes. Get up. We are not children.'

'*You* are not children,' said Nicolas de Nicolay, sitting up to rub his bruised shoulder blades and then lying down again. 'But me, I am a child of Nature. Not for me the chastity, nor the poverty. And particularly, I do not obey.'

'That,' said M. d'Aramon, temperately amused, 'is obvious. Rise. If we must do this thing, let us do it—'

'With artistry,' said the geographer. 'With *élan*. And most meticulously charted.'

*

The Ambassador's guess had been predictably accurate. Lymond, conveniently for the Grand Master, was in the hospital. Inconveniently for the Grand Master, he was not ill.

Returning to Mdina after that impossible race to reach Gozo, both he and Jerott Blyth had been exhausted to the point of blindness by fatigue and heat. It had been a dogged test of endurance, achieved in wordless anger on both sides. Blyth by then was far too sensitive on Gabriel's behalf to see the absurdity of the thing, and Lymond, who probably saw it only too well, was having enough trouble keeping on his feet, considering that Jerott's stone had laid open the side of his head. Arrived uncertainly at Mdina, both were taken to the old hospital for the night and Jerott woke fully restored in time to accompany de Villegagnon and Gabriel back to Birgu.

Lymond, he learned with mixed feelings, had had a disturbed night and was still asleep. His state of mind was not helped by Gabriel who, visiting his rare anger on the unfortunate Blyth before he was well awake, had berated him thoroughly for his carelessness.

'How else was I to stop him?' Jerott had snapped. It was he, not Gabriel, who had worn himself out on that uncomfortable race.

'You might have killed him,' said Gabriel sharply, and turning his back strode away; from which Jerott received the comfort of knowing that logic was on his side, and Gabriel merely giving unusual outlet to his own anxiety. They set out, with Lymond still under care in the hospital behind them, and the people of Mdina ran at their stirrups and kissed their feet. Later, Jerott heard that Francis Crawford had been brought from Mdina by the Grand Master's orders and installed in the big hospital at Birgu, but he was not allowed any visitors, and even Gabriel was turned from the door. De Villegagnon, on Malett's advice, did not try. Nicolas de Nicolay, however, not only tried but succeeded.

The entire hospital was worried about Nicolas de Nicolay. In his first hour in the knights' ward he received visits from the Infirmarian, the Prior, the duty physician, the assistant duty physician, the surgeon, the barber-surgeon and two *barberotti*. No one knew what was wrong with him. With two hundred other sick, wounded and dying to care for, the hospital was conscious of other calls on its conscience, but could not wrest its nervous attention from the celebrated patient who, if harm befell him, would do the Order's reputation more harm than Dragut's galleys.

Nicolas, disregarding freely all d'Aramon's strictures about moderation, plunged into display like a mountebank. He screamed. He rolled about in evident agony. He clutched his stomach, his throat, flung hash at the curtains and upset soup on the novices. He wouldn't take his medicine and shrieked for de Seurre, who came to see him at regular intervals, by every conceivable route, but without discovering a trace of the missing Lymond.

After half a day of it, de Seurre brought news. 'You'd better give up the farce and recover,' he said, sitting impatiently holding the geographer's limp hand. 'We are going to Tripoli. The Ambassador has agreed to intercede with the Turk.'

Nicolas de Nicolay's brown eyes snapped. 'But the scraping-down of the boats, surely, isn't finished? And they will require time to water and provision.' Galleys, weed-coated, were having much-needed attention.

'D'Aramon will go in the Order's own light brigantine. The galliot remains. When the two galleys are ready, we follow.'

Nicolas de Nicolay sank back on his pillow and let out a mechanical yelp as an orderly passed. 'Then there's no immediate haste.'

The Chevalier de Seurre said irritably, 'You have the Ambassador's permission to abandon the search. It is not of importance.' It was not a business he relished. Of course, something was irregular; you could smell it, as d'Aramon had done. He appreciated the tact with which d'Aramon had refused to make this inquiry behind his back: as one of his party, it would have been intolerable. But he was afraid of what he was going to find.

And he had a shrewd idea, too, that the little, elderly geographer suspected it. For Nicolas de Nicolay said firmly, 'Turn my back on a new chart? Never!' and fell asleep. Or for all practical purposes became quite unresponsive. At length, as the siesta hour had begun, de Seurre went away out of patience. The hospital, relieved of its jumping nerve, settled down to sleep and routine, as long as its difficult patient's slumber would permit; and Nicolas de Nicolay, breathing heavily, waited bubbling for the hour when the quiet ward would be vacant of monks, and when a man in search of natural relief might find himself by mistake in several strange places.

When the moment came he rose, stuffed his pillow into his bed, and lifting the black cloak from beside the sleeping knight in the next bed, shrugged into it and shuffled off in the semi-dark of the veiled windows. Then, as was his business, he began to explore.

The mortuary of the hospital of the Knights of St John of Jerusalem was dug from the rock of Birgu: a cold, sweating rectangle, small and unwindowed, with a single taper burning below the crucifix on the walls. There on pallets of scrubbed wood the dead lay; and the priests of the Order, in their piety, strapped each corpse to its bed with thongs of leather, bound on the dead ankles and wrists and so wired that the slightest twitch of the dead limbs would set a bell trembling. So for twenty-four hours after death the knights lay, that no living body should be interred.

It was the last station on the geographer's lighthearted journey, and by the time he pushed the unlocked door open and pattered into the gloom, he had sobered a little. The person Crawford was not in any of the wards. He was not among the infectious, the wounded or the dying; he was not convalescing in the garden or under the knife. He was nowhere in the hospital, unless here.

And there, poor young man, he was. Nicolas de Nicolay closed the mortuary door silently and moved past the empty boards to the one which was occupied. Colourless in the gloom, the leather bands crossed at feet and wristbones, the corpse was undoubtedly the man of d'Aramon's and de Seurre's description. De Nicolay, a man of sentiment, swore carefully, and the corpse, interested, opened its eyes.

'*Diable de diable de diable*,' said the little geographer, with even more feeling, and with great formality bowed. 'Nicolas de Nicolay, come with d'Aramon's fleet, *mon cher*. So this is where they hide you? So *able*!'

'Quite. *Plûtot souffrir que mourir; c'est la devise des hommes*,' said Francis Crawford, unmoving. '*Vive le Corps Diplomatique* and all its friends; but for God's sake don't sneeze, will you? These bells are strung up so that they hear the moment I wake.'

'So that they may put you to sleep again, eh? You must have cramp,' said Nicolas with modest insight.

'I have,' said the other man. 'But if you—'

'—Stuff the clappers with my cloak, all will be well. Certainly. And now,' said the barefooted geographer, settling himself comfortably on the next pallet and closing his round eyes, 'Tell me all that the Grand Master is so anxious that no one shall know.'

Time was short; but it was enough. Succinct and damning, the story of avidity, incompetence, neglect and useless sacrifice was told. In the end, the Frenchman said thoughtfully, 'They do not kill you, for they do not wish a de Guise inquiry; and they are men of God, let us not forget. They merely silence you till we have gone, and thus buy a little time. What good will this do?'

126

'It will allow them to spread counter-stories abroad,' said Lymond. Reclining, ghost-like in white muslin, he was methodically rubbing life back into his cramped limbs. 'Already the Governor of Gozo has died on the ramparts. In a week, the Order will have manned and swept the Turk from Mdina, and sunk Dragut between Gozo and home.'

'Remind me to tell you about a Scot called Thompson,' said de Nicolay. 'And you are a little behind with the news. Sinan Pasha and Dragut haven't gone home. They have sailed to Tripoli, and M. d'Aramon and I—and a few others—are to follow and advise him against it. At the Grand Master's suggestion.'

'When?'

'Lie down. You frighten me,' said Nicolas. 'Today, in the Order's brigantine; but the rest of us follow, tomorrow possibly. Come with us. The Grand Master cannot stop you, and it may be your only chance to tell your story outside. . . . Tell me,' he said, his gnome-like face lit with sudden enthusiasm, 'are you not, you, the person who prevented the English soldiers following our little princess Mary of Scots, when M. de Villegagnon brought her safely from Scotland to France? A voyage of galleys round the wild north of Scotland, which these boats had never attempted before?'

Diverted, Lymond looked up. 'I had something to do with it.'

'I hear from M. de Villegagnon, who is my friend,' said Nicolas de Nicolay with satisfaction. 'The chart he used for this great voyage, I supplied.'

'A chart of the north coast of Scotland?' The tone was, recognizably, a shade too sweet.

'But no,' said Nicolas de Nicolay, giving up. 'But even better. It was made by your pilot Alec Lindsé for the voyage of your dead King James V, and fell into the hands of Lord Dudley, Admiral of England. The Admiral,' said Nicolas modestly, 'gifted this so fine chart to me five years ago. Later, when it was a case of tricking the English to get your little Queen away . . . I sent it to my King for M. de Villegagnon.'

'And so the Earl of Warwick,' said Lymond, beginning to laugh, 'was really responsible for Queen Mary's escape.'

'Yes. It is very funny, but I am cold. If we disturb our toes,' said the geographer, 'the bells will agitate—I shall unchoke them thus—and we shall be discovered, to great alarm. We shall be most hurt and most reproving, but what can they do to us but free us, as if all were in error? They cannot harm Nicolas de Nicolay,' said that gentleman with the utmost cheerfulness. 'Nor, now that you have told me all, are you in danger in my company. Come! Agitate the toes!'

They agitated their toes until the door opened and the aghast and ashen countenance of the mortician appeared.

The two white-robed figures on the pale slabs did not interrupt their conversation. 'I'm glad, in a way,' Lymond said. 'I couldn't quite bring myself to attack them, lunatics that they are.'

'You are sentimental,' said Nicolas de Nicolay complacently. 'But the tender stomach does not attack the pure—no—not even the pure in stupidity.'

*

Presently, when incoherent explanation and apology had been brushed aside and the Hospitallers, to their own relief, found themselves, if heavily mocked, at least unmolested by their victim and his rescuer, Lymond took leave of the geographer and, dressed once more in his own clothes, made straight for Gabriel's house.

Graham Malett, motionless before the shabby altar, did not hear him enter, or stand waiting by the door. At length he rose and genuflected, and turning, the cross half-gestured on his breast, saw Francis Crawford.

All movement stopped. His face, already serene from prayer, gathered light, and so transparent a joy that Jerott Blyth, striding after the half-glimpsed newcomer, stopped at the door. 'Thank God,' said Gabriel, and switched his tone, instantly, to an ironic apology. 'I suppose our mistakes are now proclaimed to the world?'

'Of course,' said Lymond. 'But why else did you make sure that M. d'Aramon found out where I was?'

'You learned that, did you?' The open face for a moment showed its fatigue. 'Jerott . . . come in. He is back, as bloody-minded as ever, I suspect. I desire,' he said abruptly to Lymond, 'to call you Francis. Is that permitted? It is out of affection and a . . . purely spiritual love.'

At the unexpected half-tone of mischief, even Lymond's blue stare relaxed. 'Of course,' he said.

'Then you forgive me what I have done on behalf of the Order?' said Graham Malett quickly. 'I *could not* let you go to Gozo.'

'It makes no difference,' said Lymond, after a moment. Then with an apparent effort he added, 'I am going to Tripoli.'

'*What*?' said Jerott Blyth sharply, and took a step into the room. The older man by the altar did not stir. 'Of course,' he said. 'To rescue the woman?'

'To save what I may,' said Lymond. 'Including a rascally hero called Thompson. Even, perhaps, to fight for Tripoli too.'

The silence this time stretched on and on. A burst of soft Arabic sounded in the street outside; a dog barked; voices, somewhere in the house, spoke in Italian above the chinking of pots. 'Then I go with you,' said Gabriel at last.

Jerott thought, It is the death-knell of the Order; a gesture of

128

self-destruction worse than Mdina. And fell into a surge of renewed hatred for Lymond, who had robbed their greatest hope so lightly of peace. He opened his mouth, but Gabriel was before him.

'No,' he said. 'Acquit me this time of easy heroics. The Grand Master has begged an emissary of France, no friend of his, to plead for the Turk's clemency for the Order, since the Order cannot fulfil its duty to defend itself. If he succeeds, he will need the Religion's help to negotiate. If he fails—'

'—He will become the fresh scapegoat,' said Lymond. 'Of course. But would you bear witness for him against your own Grand Master?'

'If we lose Tripoli,' said Gabriel, his beautiful voice grating, 'I will call the Order from the ends of the earth to sit in judgement on this sorry son of Christ's church.'

'Upon which all the Spaniards will come and vote for Juan de Homedès', said Lymond unspectacularly. 'Nothing but death, I fear, is going to rid you of your saintly leader, and a good many of his little flock are going to trot before him to the grave. What you need,' said Francis Crawford, his blue eyes guilelessly wide, 'is an assassin.'

It was almost imperceptible, the change in Jerott Blyth's face, the shadow of anxiety on Gabriel's. 'But I,' added Lymond with continuing calmness, 'am not the man.'

*

After only two days on Malta, M. d'Aramon's two galleys left again, on the heels of the Ambassador, taking with them two knights of the Order, Graham Malett and Jerott Blyth, and, to the Grand Master's anger, an unwanted observer in Crawford of Lymond.

Among those who wished them Godspeed was de Villegagnon, withdrawn from long vigil in St Lawrence's, where he had prayed beside Gabriel most of that night. 'You will know,' he said abruptly to Lymond, 'that I am not permitted to leave. And indeed, I may serve the Order best here. I commend your courage in doing what there is no call to do. I do not hope that even if God grants you life, you will come back to us.'

'I do not come to Malta for wealth or honour, but to save my soul,' said Lymond, quoting, his voice amused. It had been the inscription on one of the Turkish bracelets they had found after Mdina.

'You were perfectly honest about your reasons for coming to Malta. This I grant you,' said de Villegagnon. Under the tanned skin he had flushed, but his voice was level. 'You have earned your wages as a captain of mercenaries. I only wish our own hands had not been tied. There might have been more for you to do.'

'But in my other capacity, you must own I have been kept quite busy,' said Lymond. 'My post as an independent witness of the Order's troubles with a strong bias towards the French.'

There was a moment's silence. Then de Villegagnon said, neither confirming nor denying the implicit accusation, 'I am not in the running to become Grand Master.'

'But la Valette is, I believe,' said the independent witness. 'And Leone Strozzi, who is in French pay. And de Vallier, Governor of Tripoli, placed there I understand precisely to put him out of the present Grand Master's way. And of course, Graham Malett. Except that so long as Juan de Homedès leads an all-Spanish cabal in Council, no French man or French ally has a chance.'

After a while, 'Gabriel told me,' said the Chevalier de Villegagnon heavily, 'that you believed you had been brought here to rid us of the Grand Master by force. You accuse us now of inducing you to do so by guile. In the first assumption you are wrong. In the second. . . .'

The big knight paused. 'If to inform the world of the arrogance, avarice and cruelty of a would-be Christian is to do wrong, then the blame is mine. I have heard you talk to the knights, I have seen you watch and listen, and I have heard the questions you do not ask. You know as well as any of us where we are weak. I am not asking you to help as a kingmaker,' said de Villegagnon bitterly. 'I ask only that all who would save Christendom should help us make this breach whole.'

Face to face they stood wrapped in violence, deaf to Jerott Blyth standing burning at Lymond's side, and Gabriel waiting quietly at the door. Lymond, for once a fraction less than cool, wore an expression de Villegagnon could not interpret, and looked for a long time as if he wished to give no answer at all. At length, 'Quite,' he said. 'I know perfectly well what you want. You are to be honoured for it. But I am not at all sure that Christianity's best hope is not that the Order of St John of Jerusalem should disappear from the earth.'

VI

God Proposes

(Tripoli, August 1551)

I T took the men, women and children of Gozo three days to reach North Africa, for the Ottoman fleet, Turks and corsairs together, was big: a hundred and thirty sails, Oonagh guessed, although it was hard to count. After the first hours she was little on deck.

She and Galatian, she found, were not on the flagship but with Dragut, whose brother had burned like a dog on Gozo seven years before.

It was not a coincidence. For her, the squat old warrior with the powerful, peasant face showed only contempt. Towards Galatian he showed a child's capacity for taunting. With exaggerated respect, he had him freed when he complained of his fetters, and had the wounds rubbed, not with oil but with salt. When he was thirsty, he was given a sherbet of aloes; when he called Oonagh's name, and cried, they bandied among themselves, audibly, tales Oonagh had never heard of his supposed amorous prowess since taking his vows.

Afterwards, she realized such things must be common gossip among the Gozitans brought back so often on these raids. And when the Governor whined, Dragut said, with sudden violence, that the dog should suffer no longer from this unseemly itch, and Galatian was taken from her sight. When he returned, bloodsoaked on a litter, Galatian de Césel, Knight of St John, had embraced chastity at last.

It was Galatian's servant, Maltese and therefore an Arabic-speaker, who told her that they had stopped off Tagiura, twelve miles east of Tripoli. Wandering in France and Ireland, fighting for the sovereignty of her nation and ultimately of Cormac O'Connor her lover, Oonagh had yet heard of the great corsair Barbarossa who had extended the Sultan's empire over North Africa and the Mediterranean, to be made at last Beylerbey of Africa, with two thousand soldiers and orders from Constantinople to levy whatever army he might need from corsair, Berber, Moor or renegade and give them the standing of Janissaries.

So, with bitter fighting over the years, the great seaports of Africa

131

had been torn between Turkey and Spain; now the Emperor's and Christian: now Suleiman's and an infidel strength. Tagiura, rich oasis so close to Tripoli, was Turkish, and the Aga Morat, lord of Tagiura, was Barbarossa's successor and an officer in Africa for Suleiman the Magnificent, King of Kings. As the silken fleet floated inshore under the wide skies of sunset the batteries echoed from ship to tawny-green shore, and the banquet for Sinan Chasse Diable and his two naval commanders went on, they said, all night.

Oonagh saw nothing of it. Sometimes, at night, as she nursed Galatian in his fever, she thought she heard, stifled by decking, the whimpering of the people of Gozo, spread through the battered holds of the fleet. On Dragut's galleass there were none save herself and Galatian, with a servant apiece. Attending her patient with diamond efficiency, neither pity nor distaste crossed her face, reduced against its bone by heat, and strange foods, and pregnancy. Like a sea animal she could and did close in upon herself against affliction and shock, assimilate the suffering and show meanwhile an uncaring face.

For Galatian she felt only contempt. As suddenly as it had come, her own fever had gone. She felt an arid, fighting spinsterhood upon her, and glanced, with new purpose, at the fleshy, alien faces about her.

If Galatian lived, he would be ransomed back and she might be saved. If he died, she would accept her fate and wrest some pride out of it. Even while carrying the thick-skinned spawn of Cormac O'Connor. Francis Crawford had in any event passed her by, lightly and coldly as, of course, she desired.

For a few days, the fleet rested at anchor; then Sinan Pasha sent a message to Tripoli: a white-robed Moor on one of their small, swift horses bearing a white flag. Before the gates of the city he dismounted, and planting a cane in the pallid sand in front of the ditch, fastened to it the Osmanli call to surrender.

> Surrender yourselves to the mercy of the Grand Seigneur, who has ordered me to reduce this place under his obedience. I will allow you the liberty of retiring wheresoever you shall think fit with your effects; but in case of your refusal, I will put you to the sword.

The following day, the courier returned to Tagiura with the reply of Gaspard de Vallier, Marshal of Tripoli and Knight of St John, affixed to the same cane.

> The Government of Tripoli has been entrusted to me by my Order; I cannot surrender it up to anyone but to him whom the Grand Master and the Council of the Order shall nominate; and I will defend it against all others to the last drop of my blood.

*

132

On the brief journey from Malta to Tripoli, Jerott Blyth was able without undue trouble to avoid conversation with Francis Crawford. But during these same two days, from Gabriel who had seen service there, and Nicolas de Nicolay who had charted it, Lymond learned all he could about the knights' African home.

There was little that was good. Built almost at the end of the green and fertile strip of North Africa, Tripoli stood behind walls, on a plain, with five hundred miles of sand and salt marsh stretching to the east towards Egypt. To the west lay a succession of corsair strongholds, alternating with outposts of Spain. To the south lay the desert, broken by the blue ridge of the mountains of Gharian, a Berber stronghold. Beyond that was the Sahara, through which Tripoli offered one of the narrowest crossings. For Tripoli was the centre for three great African caravan routes, and at the mouth of the shortest and safest sea route to Europe, through Malta and Sicily. Because of this, Charles V had issued his ultimatum: If you wish to receive Malta as a home for the Order, you must defend Tripoli for the Empire.

It was a command of heroic proportions. The rough map scratched on the ship's rail by Nicolay's dagger showed a rocky corner, jutting out from the palm groves and enclosing a harbour, sheltered in that land of errant winds by a spit of rock with a fort on it where the corner, attenuated, ran out finally into the sea.

In the angle between spit and bay sat the city, ringed by sloping stone walls and washed by the sea on south and west; and within the city but cut off from it in turn by its own walls and battlements, was the square edifice of the castle, on its seaward side commanding the whole bay of Tripoli, and on its landward, overlooking the great wall and gates giving on to the eastern plain.

But the old castle of Tripoli, Roman, Byzantine, Spanish in turn, was a huddle of courts, rooms, passages and inadequate battlements for which neither Charles nor Juan de Homedès had opened their purses.

And its Governor, Gaspard de Vallier, was an old man: a knight of the Auvergne Langue who, having achieved the prime dignities and posts of the Order, presented a challenge to the Grand Master de Homedès, and thus had been removed here. Speaking of all this to Lymond, 'Everything depends on the Ambassador,' Gabriel had said. 'If he cannot persuade Sinan Pasha to give up the siege, then Tripoli will almost certainly fall.' He then stopped a moment and added, 'The lady . . . is she young? As young as yourself?'

Lymond, Jerott noted with satisfaction, did not take it at all well. He said, 'She is sufficiently young for the seraglio, if that's what you mean.'

Gabriel said gently, 'They are well treated, you know. The Osmanlis believe in marrying the wives and daughters of their conquered.

The mixed blood is their strength. You would do better to look for your pirate friend. They may take de Césel and the woman ashore, but they will leave the other captives with the fleet.'

'He saved Mdina with his false dispatches from Sicily. The Lord, surely, will look after his own?' said Lymond, causing another burst of anger, as doubtless he knew, not in Gabriel but in Jerott listening beyond. But it was Gabriel who bent forward and, leaving Lymond leaning back on the rail, the sea racing behind his bright, sardonic face, drew Jerott beside them. 'Come and be baited in comfort,' said Graham Malett.

Jerott Blyth shrugged his shoulders. 'Let him joke. Mr Crawford is here, I believe, to display his heroism in reclaiming a woman bold enough to escape from his bed. We are here to save souls.'

'Forgive me,' said Lymond. 'I thought that when you ran crying with your troubles to Mother Church, they put you under oath to fight. I run risks to improve my lot in this life; you to ensure your comforts in the next. You are under orders; I am not. The Turk worships and kills just as you do: what offends you in him?'

Just in time, Gabriel said '*Jerott!*' and added less urgently, 'I invited you to air your anger, not to resort to force.' And to Lymond, a smile in his eyes, 'You love malice, do you not, and to trifle with blasphemy? Most of us came to the Order for an unworthy cause. Jerott lost a bride; you need not remind him. I'—he hesitated—'had a power I was reluctant to use in case I became led astray. Some, like Strozzi, came I believe to train in the finest school in the world out of personal ambition. But when you say the Order should die, you are not thinking of that, or of the poor, silly leadership we have, or of our human frailties. You are not thinking of Galatian de Césel or Juan de Homedès, but of the weapon we make.'

'Against the Turk? He would like the whole world Turkish,' said Jerott. At Gabriel's reproach he had flushed. 'Can't you see our *muézzins* climbing St Giles's steeple five times a day: *Allâhu ákbar! Lâ ilâha Allâh! Lâ ilâha ílla'llâh!*'

Determinedly patient Graham Malett's voice cut off the warble. 'Consider that, unlike us, Francis has come fresh from Europe, and you will see. The struggle for power in Europe and Asia is being fought between four powers—England, France, Turkey and the Empire. This Order serves God. It also serves *per se* any power which for reasons good or evil wishes to destroy the allies of Turkey. Juan de Homedès is Spanish. He fears for the Order's possession of Malta, so he supports the Empire in her war against Turkey's ally France, Christian nation against Christian nation. We drive the Turk out of Bône not because we wish it, but because the Emperor chooses it, and we bring down on ourselves, not on Charles, the vengeance of Suleiman.'

'Thus, note, playing into the hands of the King of France,' said Lymond cheerfully. 'Because the Order, being badly led, badly organized and thoroughly demoralized, cannot defend itself let alone Tripoli, and has forced the Emperor to lock up half his sea and land forces in southern Italy and Sicily to protect the Emperor's lands from a possible break-through by the Turks, once Malta is overthrown. Since he is also being held in north Italy by France, attacked in Germany by the Duke of Guise and at war with Turkey in Hungary, the failure of the Order in the Mediterranean is about the best thing that the Kingdom of France ever witnessed. You are now what every sect potentially becomes when it loses leadership,' said Lymond calmly. 'A tool.'

'So we allow the Osmanlis to sweep the world,' said Jerott Blyth, his eyes bright.

'You either get out, and let the so-called Christian nations, instead of cutting each other's throats, unite and destroy the religion they all oppose; or you make yourselves so strong that you can dictate your own terms.'

'Under Juan de Homedès?' said Gabriel. His eyes had for a long time, never left Lymond's.

'No. Nor under Graham Malett,' Lymond said.

The blood, spreading under the golden skin, over the royal bones, stained Gabriel's face, as few people had ever witnessed it. Through it, Gabriel smiled steadily still, unaware of Jerott's hard fists at his side. 'You are hard,' he said. 'Who, then?'

'Until Juan de Homedès dies, no one,' said Lymond. 'After that, the list surely is very short. De Villegagnon is a born soldier and seaman but not truly a man of God, I think. Strozzi is strong but ambitious, with a personal vengeance to fulfil. Romegas is resourceful and gallant but without great personal power. Which leaves—'

'La Valette. I thought you had hardly spoken to him,' said Sir Graham. His colour was still high.

'I have heard of him from every knight I could reach,' said Lymond. 'It is sometimes better than meeting the man himself.'

'And Graham Malett, Grand Cross,' said Jerott's voice at his shoulder. 'What faults has the Master discovered in him?'

But Gabriel himself answered, his colour gone, leaving his face rather pale. 'For love of me,' he said, 'I can ask men to do all that I wish. I could grow to love this power too much.'

'You hear,' said Lymond placidly, into Jerott's icy face. 'We all love him too much.'

For the second time, swiftly, Gabriel caught Blyth's arm as it began to swing. Lymond did not move. 'Be still. Are you children?' said Gabriel, angered at last. 'Be still: your own destiny is behind you. There is Tripoli, there on the bow.'

135

They turned. Ahead, a white crescent of walls and towers within the single arm of the bay, lay the castle and city of Tripoli with the white Cross of St John minute on the ramparts. And outwith the spit, rocking gently at anchor in deep water, harnessing the sea with frail canopies and gilded tassels and long, reeling banners of scarlet and gold, were the Sultan Suleiman's ships.

'O Lord my God,' said Gabriel, his deep, quiet voice lingering over the waters. 'Take us, your children, into your hands; for we are losing our way.'

Blyth, his face hard and sick, closed his eyes with one hand. Lymond, his gaze on another fort, brave under the Order's flag, perched on the spit from the bay, merely began absently to whistle, choosing for the purpose a long, complicated and extremely bawdy song from the Scottish seaboard.

*

He repeated it at intervals as slowly, their seamen standing unarmed on deck and the lilies of France flying plain at the masthead, the two ships rowed slowly between the silent ranks of Turkish vessels to join the Ambassador's, lying alone in the alien fleet.

D'Aramon's standard, flying beside the French flag, showed that he was aboard. Much later, in a high, answering whistle from one of the Turkish boats, the pirate Thompson replied.

The gunfire as d'Aramon's brigantine came in was heard by Oonagh O'Dwyer, beside her sick lover's side in the Turkish encampment, and by the beleaguered Governor of Tripoli. To Marshal Gaspard de Vallier in his castle, it meant at first only that Sinan Pasha had opened fire, and his well-meaning staff, brash or ailing, had failed to inform him of it. Then he saw, as he hurried to the battlements, that the guns were not yet aimed at town or castle, but saluted an incoming brigantine, prominently displaying the royal colours of France. A moment later, as the brigantine gave tongue in return, he distinguished the colours of Luetz d'Aramon, familiar in the Mediterranean for six years as French Ambassador to the Grand Seigneur of Turkey.

Short of excommunication, the Frenchman could not intend to give active aid to his Turkish friends against the Knights of St John. He must be coming to intercede. When the skiffs put out and later, when the two other French ships sailed in and crept up to their leader, Marshal de Vallier felt a great weight ease from his overstrained heart. Help was near.

*

Patient, subtle, attuned by hard years of experience to the Asiatic mind, the Baron d'Aramon moved slowly. Every formality of arrival was observed. And then, before dreaming of requesting an audience, his gifts to Sinan Pasha, to Dragut and Salah Rais were dispatched. They came from the coffers he had brought to lay before the Sultan himself: a ruby and emerald brooch, a filigree purse full of gold, a belt of velvet wrought with Mexican silver and pearls, and length upon length of gold tissue and silk.

In due time, the courtesies were returned. By then the two galleys from Malta were in. Taking Michel de Seurre, Nicolas de Nicolay and Graham Malett with him, along with no more of his train than he needed to maintain his royal master's standing, His Excellency the French Ambassador to Turkey was rowed ashore as night fell to the Osmanli camp for his audience with the Sultan's general. As he went, the *ezân* rang out over the waters, proclaiming the Omnipotence and Unity of God. It rang out still as he stepped ashore among the robed and jewelled fighting arm of Islâm to the low rattle of the drum.

If he failed to move these men to give up their attack, it might mean the end of the Order in Malta. If he succeeded, his career as Ambassador for the King of France in the Levant was very possibly at an end, and *hiver sans feu, vieillesse sans maison* his reward.

Through the murmuring night, spicy with musk and honey and mint, between the lamplit tents and the coruscating, shifting shadows that were the children of the House of Osman, past the sudden odour of horseflesh that told where the small, swift animals were tethered, past the fumes of oil and fish and tripe soup and mutton where the Cooks of Divine Mercy prepared the evening meal, the Baron d'Aramon passed gravely through the ritual stages of welcome, and arrived at last at the great scented pavilion, transparent with lamplight with the sheet gold of the Sultan's standard planted outside, where Sinan Pasha greeted him. His train following, the French Ambassador entered.

The war-leader's tent was dressed, as he had expected, with the treasured care of a concubine. Under the precious filigree lamps the faces ranged before the fine linen hangings sewn with ribbons were not hostile; they were the faces of men with work to do, confident, competent, and showing a large patience before their importunate visitors. Seated on silk cushions piled over thick carpets, the Frenchmen were served with sweetmeats: sugared pistachios and ginger, Temesuár honey and rose jam, fresh dates and *halvá*; and drank from bowls of new milk, or full pitchers of *khusháf*, seasoned with amber and musk; the juice of Bokhara apricots and syrups of red-hearted peaches, served cradled in snow.

The thickened, sweet liquids, the robes of the eunuchs impregnated with jasmine, in the earliest days of his Embassy had sickened him,

137

waiting strung-up for the opening of the state matter he had come to discuss. Now, he felt nothing and spoke of nothing ('a very kiosk of Paradise') as the chased cups were filled ('rest to the soul; food to the spirit'), and when the time came, knew instinctively when to launch into the interminable, empty phrases leading insensibly to his master, the King of France; his master's regard for the Order of St John of Jerusalem, some of whom were born his subjects; and his master's willingness to regard it as a signal favour if the Grand Seigneur's great army would turn its eyes from Tripoli and pursue its courageous purpose elsewhere. This willingness to be marked, in the immediate future, by a display by the King of France of his famed munificence.

His flowing Arabic reached an end, and he waited, hearing behind him the effective suction of Nicolas de Nicolay draining his cup. Flanked on the heaped cushions by his corsairs—Dragut heavy and motionless, Salah Rais with his long, Egyptian hands lax on robed knees, the Aga Morat smiling—Sinan Pasha, Chasse Diable, answered agreeably. A man of middle height, the stiff folds of his *jubbé* rustled as he leaned forward, and the undervest of gem-sewn silk flashed in the light. His face, sun-darkened and lean, was dwarfed by the turban entwined with gold tissue which fell like a lock to one shoulder; but he did not use his hands, as an Arab does, to give point and space to his case.

He might have had no case to make. In the unexcited cadences of the Moslem, for whom it is unmannerly to raise the voice or to laugh, Sinan Pasha regretted that the Emperor (on whom may the blessing of God on High ever rest!) and the Order of the Knights of St John of Jerusalem (may God light up their tombs!) should have seen fit to trick and deceive the army of the Commander of the Faithful and the Lieutenant of the Envoy of God upon Earth.

The Emperor promised that the Sultan should receive the keys of Bône. The Sultan's officers sought them accordingly wherever the Emperor had representatives, to be met with either vain words or cannon fire; even at Malta, where they had looked for salutations and refreshments for their weary society. 'I am sorely aware,' said Sinan Pasha, with the unchanging expression of his hot brown eyes totally at odds with the commiseration in his voice, 'that the King of France (O God, be propitious to his house!) dislikes witnessing the siege by ourselves of a town defended by the famous and valorous Knights of Malta; but unfortunately,' he continued, his dark brows raised like flock in his sunken face, 'unfortunately, these brave men are always where, by the grace of the Most High, the Sultan would be himself.'

And since the Sultan intended to have Tripoli which was merely recovering, after all, his own; and had given him, Sinan Pasha, a sealed commission to that effect which His Excellency the Prince d'Aramon might peruse, it was as much as his, Sinan Pasha's, poor life was worth to disobey. 'Fight ye in God's true battle, says the Qur'ân,' ended the General piously; and d'Aramon drily answered, 'The Christian Bible says much the same thing.'

But he tried. And when, bruised against the wall of Sinan Pasha's indifference, he had to give up, Gabriel in his deep, rich voice continued: appealing less to Sinan than to Dragut, the old Commander; speaking with balance and humour; leafing it, even, with the twists of subtle, harmless malice that the mind of Islâm enjoys.

He drew, at last, a gleam from Dragut's sharp, seaman's eyes; but Sinan the Jew, clapping his hands, said, 'Thy silver tongue, O Lord, has won me quite to thy side; but of what use to thee or to me is a headless body? To disobey the King of Kings is to die. All the world shall honour you, who spoke for your religion. It is sad that Allâh does not show himself smiling to you, but to me. Let us eat, that there may be no ill will between us.'

The smell of *piláf* came thick on the hot air, driving out the jasmine and cloves and the underlying aroma of sweat-sodden clothing. The French Ambassador stood, his long tight hose wrinkled to the thigh, his neck and wrist-frilling limp. 'The blessing of God upon thee, O Ghazi, and my thanks,' he said. 'But we must return. You have heard us fairly, and what is to come will be revealed by God.'

For a moment there was absolute silence. Neither Sinan Pasha nor any of his company had risen, as courtesy demanded; no one spoke. Instead, reflectively, the white and gold turban inclined, and to a silvery rustle, the door curtain behind the Ambassador fell into place and swayed there, shutting out the fires, the tents, the moonlit dunes leading to Tripoli.

Then inside the pavilion there was a running flash of Damascus work round all the fringed walls, steadying into a trembling blaze. The Janissaries had lifted their blades.

'The Prophet, who is the Emissary of God, has already signified the path,' said Sinan's dispassionate voice. 'We fear the sea between this place and Constantinople is unsafe at present for the King of France's great lords. Nor may we permit them, such is our concern for their welfare, so lightly to violate the honour of nations. Honour us, we beseech you, with your company yet awhile. Eat, sleep, and seduce our poor ears with your voice in exquisite talk. There is no haste for either of us to leave this city *while it stands*.'

Behind the Baron d'Aramon the knights de Seurre and Graham Malett had risen to their feet, with Nicolas de Nicolay and the rest of the suite quickly after. They rose, their hands on their empty sword-belts, and then stood with stiff-lipped nonchalance as the linked scimitars shimmered and stilled. The trap had closed on them, and there was nothing to be done. The French Ambassador and his suite were to be guests of the Turk.

*

Silent under the African stars, the three ships from Malta waited for d'Aramon and Gabriel to return, and as the white crescent of Tripoli faded into the night and the light-shot black water around them lapped against the carved hulls of the Turkish fleet, strewn like night blossom on the warm sea, Jerott Blyth studied Lymond.

Since Gabriel and de Nicolay had left, they had not spoken. Just before night fell, for a long time, Lymond had been watching the Tripoli shore so that Jerott's own attention had finally been caught, and he had surveyed it in turn. Through the dusk he saw at length some shadowy activity: a dark bulk slowly moving on the weedy rocks between sea and castle, followed by another. Then, as night deepened, the rocks were full of prickings of light.

Then he knew what it was, and wondered briefly if the superior military expert at the poop was aware of the old Mediterranean trick. Galleys had been brought inland, on rollers, to serve as buttress and platforms for mounting the heavy cannon against the castle.

He worked out distances rapidly. The angle was too acute for the castle cannon to bear, and the hulks were not yet within range for arquebus fire. Arrows would not hurt them, and he guessed they were well soaked against incendiary shafts. But. . . .

'Question: Why isn't the fort at the end of the harbour offering cross-fire?' said a pleasant voice at his ear. 'There's a garrison there: I've been watching them. Do you suppose,' said Lymond, oblivious to Blyth's uncontrollable dislike, 'that the Marshal has put two hundred green Calabrian shepherds into it to perform feats of valour if so inclined, and if not so inclined, to insulate Tripoli from their gun-hysteria?'

'Or maybe the Irishwoman is keeping them busy,' said Jerott Blyth cuttingly, and went moodily off.

At two paces, he was brought back by a painful grip on his arm. 'Gently, little monk,' said Lymond, still pleasantly. 'Tell me: does your divine calling on earth teach you to swim?'

'Why?' said Jerott, not a fraction less sweetly, his long dagger brought lightly, with practised ease, between his fingers.

'Because an Osmanli boat is approaching us full of armed Janissaries, and of d'Aramon and the saintly Gabriel there is no sign at all. Something has gone wrong,' said Lymond cheerfully. 'Allâh's intervention, no doubt. If you are interested in going ashore, there is only one method, now.' He had released the knight's arm and was already stripping methodically to hose and shirt, tossing his doublet to the deck and unbuckling his dagger. Lymond threw it high, once, and catching it by the handle, began to move silently to the lee rail in the shadows.

The ship was quiet. The look-out, if he had noticed, had not interpreted the coming skiff as Lymond had done. Jerott hesitated and turning, Lymond observed it.

'Well, well, Mr Blyth,' he said, sympathy in the light voice. 'If you won't fight for money and you're frightened to fight for Jesus, you might as well come in for the bath.' He had a wrestler's grip the young knight recognized, but was far too late to prevent. Beautifully built and hard as iron, Blyth's compact body hit the sea side by side with Lymond's; and then he was on his tormentor, lurching wave-slapped through the water, the dagger high in his fist.

Below him Lymond twisted, dived, and as he was turning locked Jerott's legs in his own and pulled. As the water closed over his head, the black-haired man felt his right arm wrenched free of the knife and when he rose choking to the night air he found both arms gripped tight at his back. His legs, already numb, were still locked and immovable. He jerked once, and was treated instantly to a choking plunge under the water. When he came up from that, he couldn't speak, and the undisturbed voice in his ear said, 'Do that once more, and I'll duck you unconscious. The Turks are on the other side of the galley and can hear splashing quite clearly. Do you hear me?'

Blyth threw up, indiscriminately, the filthy inshore water and his last, meagre meal, but had understood well enough to do it silently. The ruthless hands let him go. 'All right,' said Lymond, suddenly bored. 'Kill me now, sweetheart . . . if you can catch me, that is.'

Jerott Blyth, cast suddenly free, lunged weakly as his knife arched towards him, handle first, and caught it. At the same moment, in a surge of black sea and a long green wraith of phosphorescence Lymond struck off, the water closing and unclosing in long strokes over his pale head.

The Chevalier Blyth did not pause. The recovered knife fast between his white teeth, he slid fast in pursuit.

*

It had been clear before they left the coast off Tagiura that Galatian would recover. Soon after he was carried ashore at Tripoli the fever left him and he slept instead a great deal—too much for Oonagh who, isolated by her ignorance of the language, waited with angry impatience for his awakenings.

His only residual importance to her was as a speaker of Arabic. He was also, she supposed, her sole prospect of returning to Europe. Of all the people of Gozo only they had been brought ashore to this double tent with its cushions and fine rugs and silent black servants.

She never went outside. Night and day the tent was guarded by the robed men whose shadows she saw on the silk walls, cast by the interminable sun through the day and the campfires by night. But they were hostages, clearly, not slaves; and Galatian was given anything within reason that he wanted.

It was he who had found out what the salvoes of cannon fire had been, and who had collapsed writhing in petulant despair when, on questioning their servants, he had learned that d'Aramon's intercession had failed, and that the Ambassador was being kept under restraint for the space of the siege. Even the rigging of his ships was to come down. If d'Aramon had been freed, he explained bitterly to Oonagh, he might even have persuaded Suleiman to countermand his orders. 'But no, but no, Sinan Pasha must not now be deprived of his conquest,' he railed, and took to shouting, to her icy mortification, each time he heard French voices in the vicinity.

When finally, late next morning, he was answered, he waited in a frenzy of anticipation for someone of d'Aramon's party to force their way in. 'Doesn't he realize they are prisoners too?' thought Oonagh. 'And does he really believe they won't know what happened on Gozo?'

She endured his presence as she might have endured a sick servant in Ireland whom she disliked, and was paralysed with anger when, having left Galatian asleep behind the curtains of the inner tent in the heavy heat of the afternoon, she heard the soft footsteps of many people approaching, an exchange of Turkish, and then the rattle of the tent flaps being pulled aside. There appeared the broad, moustached face of the guard she knew, axe in belt, clothed in the short-sleeved knee-length robe over a thin, cross-belted jerkin which was virtually a uniform, his feet in kid boots.

There were others behind him, dressed alike. They supplied an escort for a tall man in the black she despised, the white cross plain on his shoulder. Under the African sun, his hair was a cap of gold, and the blood emptied from her skin, leaving a cold imbalance which lasted some seconds. Then she saw, as he stepped into the shadow, that it was no one she knew.

Sir Graham Malett, on his part, saw a great deal that he did not expect that hot afternoon in the Osmanli encampment outside Tripoli. He saw that the Irish prostitute to whom adhered a poltroon Knight of the Order and also Francis Crawford, whose only weakness he had noted this to be, was an ageless black-haired woman with a straight back and accurate, ivory bones pressing hard through the fine skin. Her wrists were like a boy's, spiked with bone, but below the drawn face and slender neck the breast-line was thickly commodious. From her response to the guard's words she could know no

Arabic. He said to the black eunuch who had risen as he came in, 'Is she pregnant?' and the man nodded, baring his white teeth. In hospital and in seraglio, you learned much. He added a request, to account for the exchange, and smiling more broadly, the eunuch retired.

To Oonagh O'Dwyer he said, 'Forgive me. I could not announce my visit. I am under duress, as you are. My name is Graham Malett, and I hear that M. de Césel is here.'

She had heard of him, obviously, from Galatian, for she looked at him attentively from really extraordinary green-grey eyes, in that striking pale-skinned face, and said, 'The Lord guard us. Gabriel, who steered the Prophet's camel out of—'

'—Out of Mecca, in fact,' he caught her up gently. 'I have a feeling you were about to say Malta.' He paused. 'We've made a sorry mess there, haven't we? Did they curse us on Gozo?'

'Why didn't you send help?' said the woman. She had not troubled to rise, nor had she asked him to sit. He looked down at her from his splendid height, hesitated, and then kneeling abruptly, drew off his fine cloak and laid it before her. Beneath, he wore a plain thin doublet and hose, open a little at the neck for coolness. His rough-cropped hair, unregarded, emphasized the good structure beneath. He said, 'You must hate my cloth. Let us speak as man to woman. How badly hurt is Galatian? Do you know that in Malta he is being talked of as dead?'

He made no excuses nor did he exculpate himself from the Order's blame. Oonagh said, 'I do not hate it, nimble angel. I find it beneath even shame. Is the story spread that the Governor of Gozo died at his post?'

Gabriel nodded, kneeling still. 'The Turks tell a different tale,' he said.

'That tale is true,' said Oonagh indifferently.

'But he was hurt?'

'He was untouched on Gozo,' said Oonagh. 'He did their bidding quick as a girl; and when they got him at sea . . . they made him one.'

He did not flinch. On his face could be read what, clearly, was his thought: admiration for her mettle. He said, 'He will be ransomed, and you with him. There is nothing to fear.'

'Even though he is supposed to have died on the ramparts?' she said, her green eyes mocking. 'He will not be ransomed this year, or maybe the next, nimble angel. And meanwhile—'

He saw in her eyes what she was about to say, and saved her, his own face wiped free of shadow as she brought the matter, however contemptuously, before him. '—Meanwhile the child you carry will be born. Is it Galatian's?'

His deep voice, free of pity, struck at last the chord he sought.

143

With something of an old elegance and an old mystery, she widened her cool eyes. 'Are you of the opinion I have a lover for each month of the year? Until this year, I was no man's but an O'Connor's. Cormac O'Connor and I were going to conquer Ireland and remake the earth.'

'What happened?'

'Ireland belongs to the King of England,' said Oonagh. ''Twas Cormac who had the great idea that the King of France would pay a lot of money to place a puppet Irishman on the Irish throne; and after the great rebellion was over on French money, do you see, the puppet Irishman might have kicked the French out as well . . . King Cormac, we should have had.'

'And Queen Oonagh,' said Gabriel softly. She laughed.

'You think so?' And her long fingers traced, line by line, the inviolable seams of age on her face. 'I think not. He forced his bastard upon me, not his crown. Nor was it free Ireland that he wanted, in the end, but Ireland bowing to Cormac O'Connor. He and his father, young, were royal men,' said Oonagh O'Dwyer, her eyes far away. 'But soon wasted.'

'What stopped him?'

'A man called Francis Crawford of Lymond,' said the woman; and the last piece fell into place.

'I see,' said Gabriel slowly. 'A man of destiny who, God willing, will not be wasted.'

There was a long silence; but in the end, she couldn't resist it. 'He is in Malta, they say,' she said.

'He is here,' said Gabriel gently, and saw her crimson from breast to brow. 'He has risked his life twice to save you.' He waited, and then said into the helpless silence, 'The child is not Galatian's. *Are you sure it is Cormac O'Connor's?*'

Spreading black in her eyes was a memory she had driven out: a poignancy that held hope and horror and apprehension all in her speaking face. At long last, 'Mother of God, I pray that it is,' she said, and her voice was harsh.

His own was tender as the great surgeon is tender. 'Crawford knows you are with child?'

'No. *No!*' On her feet suddenly, breathless, she stared at his bowed golden head. 'Ah, *Mhuire*; and if you tell him, angel or none, here is my curse on you,' she said. 'I want no rescue; you know that. Even if that poor ruin'—and she jerked her head to where de Césel lay sleeping—'is let back, 'twill be the woman who takes the blame, who else? Leave me be . . . Leave me. I shall do as well here as anywhere.'

'Lymond won't leave you.' Rising, Graham Malett's face was filled with compassion.

'Ah, you are clever, are you not?' she said slowly, and the mer-

144

maid's eyes searched his. 'You'd make a monk of him? You'll never do that.'

'No. I only wish to see him live to choose,' said Gabriel quietly. His eyes, steady on hers, held for a long moment; then after hesitating, he raised both hands and rested them lightly on her two thin shoulders. 'Sin must be paid for, and better in this world than the next. Do you wish to save him?'

For a moment, a bleak smile crossed the pale face. 'I have no fear that he will suffer in any way except in his conscience, but it would offend me to be a burden on that,' she said. 'Is it a seraglio you will arrange for me? I doubt he will feel called upon to release me from that as well.'

'Have you no fear of the Turk?' he asked, and she smiled again at the searching blue eyes. 'I fear very little,' she said; and it rang true.

'I shall do all I can for you,' said Sir Graham. 'As for Lymond . . . He may reach you here, but I shall see he does not rescue you. And afterwards. . . .'

'Yes?' she said. Behind her Galatian, whom he had come to see, was stirring. She felt very tired, as if she had travelled far, and calm, as if the worst of her burdens were being supported for her.

Graham Malett's arms dropped. Gently he took both her hands in his and held them for an instant as in prayer, his clear eyes searching her face.

'If I tell him you are dead, he will believe me,' he said. 'But only if you give me leave.'

Her eyes did not leave his. 'I am dead,' she said. 'Mary Mother, I have been dead these long months.'

145

VII

But Allâh Disposes

(Tripoli, August 1551)

T O the people of Tripoli, the coming of d'Aramon's ships was a
promise of rescue. Far over the bay, they saw the skiff row ashore
and return. They saw the French Ambassador and his train leave
their brigantine for the vital meeting with Sinan Pasha.

They did not return. Nor did the Turkish sappers and cannoneers
working among the rocks in the lee of the castle slacken their labours.
The hulks were heaved into position above the seashore; trenches
were opened and cannon mounted in a triple battery of twelve pieces
each, pointing straight at the castle walls. Out at sea, a heavily armed
Ottoman boat could be seen visiting each of the French boats in
turn; immediately afterwards, the standing rigging of each of the
three slithered down.

Just before that, Jerott Blyth, clinging with aching arms to the
underside of a Turkish galleass, observed the release of the pirate
Thompson. He did not help.

Jerott Blyth had done his duty before in uncongenial company and
as a Knight of the Order he realized that the corsair had done the
Order a great service and was suffering for it. But by now he knew
that he not only disliked Lymond, he was afraid of him: afraid of
what his loose tongue might do to the Order and, more important he
sometimes thought even than that, might do to Gabriel. So he allowed
Francis Crawford to board this Turkish galleass on his own.

Granted that, together, Lymond and Thompson knew the workings of a Mediterranean cruising ship inside out, it was still quite a
feat to release a man chained by the ankle with fifty others in the
hold of a strange ship at night. The knifing of the right man for his
clothes, the axe for the shackles, the small, whistled signals that
located Thompson: that was Lymond's share. But how, at the right
time, was Thompson inspired to go berserk, biting and kicking fellow-
captives and guards, shouting and profaning in hideous Arabic until
removed kicking under special guard to a prison-storeroom on his
own?

There, soon, he had Lymond's knife, slid through a grating, and

146

his next visitor was his last. His fetters split, his clothes covered by the guard's turban and robe, he joined Lymond in the dark passageways and together, unseen, they slipped silently into the dark water where Jerott waited.

Topped by a streaming bundle of white, Thompson's bearded face surfaced beside him, split by a glittering smile, halved by the weapon held in his teeth. He bade the knight a polite good evening in Arabic, Spanish and French, and then swam off without pausing for answer to where Lymond had already struck out for the nearest spit of land: the tongue where the fort called the Châtelet was so unaccountably silent. After a moment, with more effort than he would have liked to admit, Jerott caught them up.

'And how,' he inquired sarcastically, 'were you proposing to break into a fortress of the Knights of St John without being shot?'

'Christ, you've a tongue in your heid,' said the man Thompson in equally muted register round the blade of his knife. 'And what've *you* come for? Tae hud wir jeckets, maybe?'

'You are addressing,' said Lymond, 'a Knight of the Order who is about to arrange dry board and bed for you. Be quiet. He's only here out of pique as it is.'

'I thought it wasna for my bonny blue een,' said the pirate philosophically. 'Damn me if I do any more dirty jobs for that lot. Ye get nae thanks for it in this world, and I'll be surprised if they havena blackened my character in the next. There's a brigantine out there with a queer look tae it?'

Jerott saw Lymond's head turn, and raised his own head a fraction to look. It was very dark in the bay, away from the rocking lanterns of Sinan's fleet. Against the black water between the swimmers and the dim walls of Tripoli only patches of deeper black showed where, here and there, the empty ships of the Tripolitanians lay at anchor where neither the owners dared venture to claim them, nor the Turks to sail them off under the long, wide-angled guns of the castle. Dimly, as his eyes got used to the dark, Jerott saw that one of them was indeed a brigantine and that, impossibly, there was a movement of some kind on the seaward board of the ship. Presently it ceased, and from its flanks a smaller shape slipped away.

'A skiff,' said Lymond, 'Making for the Châtelet, and high in the water. They've been loading, not unloading.'

'Could they fire from her on the shore guns?' Instinct and training had instantly driven all but this problem from Jerott's mind.

'They'd be blown out of the water before they'd done enough damage to matter.'

'Well,' said Thompson easily. 'If they're planning to up sail and escape through the whole Turkish fleet, they're mad.'

'Or men who know nothing of war and are frantic with fear,' said

147

Lymond. 'Look at the Châtelet. No one is covering their return. Whatever they are doing, it must be without the Governor's sanction. Is there a seagate on this side?'

'Yes,' said Jerott. They had been in the water a long time. With all the warmth of summer in it, he was not cold, but he felt the strength seeping from his muscles in the cunning way of the sea. He said, 'There's a military serving brother called des Roches in charge. I know him. We'll have to hope the guard holds his hand until I get close enough to explain.'

'You will,' said Lymond comfortably. 'They've got the gate open, awaiting the skiff. I think you'll find both the guard and M. des Roches are quite safely missing as well. All we have to do is walk in.'

And so it turned out. After a momentary confusion at the gate, where they entered unchallenged and then created hysteria by inquiring politely in Jerott's impeccable Spanish for the Commander, des Roches hurried to them with a genuine welcome and bore them to his rooms for towels, clothing and food. When their story was told, Jerott asked about his garrison.

'I have none,' said des Roches. As a serving brother, a man with no claims to nobility, attached to the Order with no other profession than war, he was straightforward to deal with: a tough, well-trained Frenchman with high colour and a frizzled chestnut beard. 'I have a litter of shepherds sent over from Malta by the Order, none of whom has ever seen an arquebus before, let alone a cannon.'

'The Calabrians,' said Jerott, and Thompson and Lymond, he saw with irritation, exchanged solemn nods.

'The Calabrians. The captain does his best, but we've wasted most of our shot and I've stopped the firing. The damage is done. We can't reach the emplacements over there with the size of guns we have now; and if we attract one shot in return, the whole garrison will drop dead from fright. I've already lost some who escaped back into Tripoli; they've put them on some simple guard duty at the castle. It's exposed here, you understand, under the guns of these ships.'

'And the brigantine?'

Des Roches, looking inquiry, was not aware of a brigantine. Jerott explained what they had seen. Halfway through, the Commander turned abruptly and began marching up and down the small room, his hands tight clasped behind his back, listening until Jerott had finished. Then he spoke standing foursquare, his arms still tightly held. 'I knew nothing of this. But you are right, I am sure. They prepare a way of escape. There is, as you know, no chance of sailing to freedom with the fleet waiting outside. It is suicide. But I cannot remove that hope. For if I do, I swear to you, these boys will surrender.'

'But if they desert you. . . .' began Jerott.

'They pay the price of death at the Turk's hands. And the fort is still intact, to be manned by better men. . . . War is a hard game,' said des Roches abruptly. 'Were I to beg them not to sail for their own sakes, they would not believe me. Seeming ignorance is better. Come, let us sleep while we may.'

Then he stopped, the breath pinched in his throat. Yellow, orange, flame in the black night, came the blaze of the first cannonade, followed by the ear-deadening shock of sound. Pushing through a wayward fabric of running, gesticulating men, des Roches and his three visitors reached the roof of the fort and looked towards Tripoli.

Jarred with light, the white walls, the flat roofs, the spire and minaret, the castle and arch flickered in gunfire which lit all the translucent water of the bay and defined the scattered, vacant vessels black and stark against the blaze of the batteries. From the castle, pathetically, came a crackle of arquebus fire and, caught in the light, the frail sparkle of arrows, falling harmlessly on the hulks that formed a bulwark for the entrenched Turkish cannoneers.

The shore batteries had begun and for two days and nights were barely to stop.

In the demoniac light, Lymond's face was lividly blithe. 'Well,' he said, and looked with raised eyebrows from one man to the other. '*Déjà la nuit en son parc amasse un grand troupeau d'étoiles vagabondes*. Du Bellay, by courtesy of Sinan Pasha. Shall we go?'

'No,' said Jerott Blyth.

'Eh. . . .' said Thompson; and Lymond stopped. 'Yes?'

'Yon's a nice little brigantine,' said Thompson. 'They poor Italian laddies couldna take a boat out to her now, in all this light, and they'll no can swim. It'd be a pity to waste her.'

'My dear seawater pickpocket,' said Lymond patiently. 'Even you couldn't sail that brigantine single-handed through a hundred and thirty enemy vessels without causing a little outburst of petulance at least.'

Beatific in the hiccoughing light, the pirate's brosy, black-bearded face split in a grin. 'Will ye wager?' he said. 'There's no telling at sea. This isna my fight, Francis Crawford. My trade is the sea, and I've lost one boat already through this poor, peely-wally Order. I'm making sure of my own while there's time. Forbye. . . .'

'Forbye,' he repeated, looking Jerott Blyth up and down carefully and returning his bold gaze to Lymond, 'some of youse might be glad of a wee boat before you're all done.'

Five minutes later he had gone—where, no one could say; and the dark knight was left with Lymond alone.

'All right,' Lymond observed. 'Go to hell your own way. Blyth, your Archangel Gabriel won't hurt for five minutes. Either he's dead along with d'Aramon and the rest, or Sinan's waiting to see what the

149

bombardment will do. With or without me, you can't stop those guns, and it's far too late to do any good here. They're going to need a garrison of experienced men later on, not one man now. All that being so, is there any religious objection to entering Tripoli that I haven't thought of?'

A moment's real reflection had told Jerott already how it would look if, instead of reporting to de Vallier in the besieged town, he joined the French knights in the Turkish camp. It made capitulation no easier. He said sarcastically, 'And what of the Irishwoman? She can wait five minutes, maybe, but will the Turks?'

'I haven't, naturally, given the matter a thought,' Lymond said; and with very good reason, Jerott did not say any more. When, presently, with one of des Roches's men as sponsor and guide, they made their way safely into Tripoli under the shattering roar of the guns, and from there to the castle down stolid, uneven, thread-like alleys between the sealed houses, Jerott knew that professionally Lymond was an impeccable ally; and that there was nothing else about him that he cared for at all.

*

By the time the morning heat was rising white off the desert, they were embroiled in the back-breaking work which was to occupy them for two days. Within the castle of Tripoli were the permanent garrison of twenty-five elderly Knights of the Order and a hundred Moors, Mohammedans but no friends of the Turk, who served the Order as soldiers. To these and their slaves had been added the twenty-five young rebel knights released from the prisons of St Angelo, and those Calabrians who had fled from the Châtelet and who now, exposed to gunfire much worse, were too scared even to go back.

The Governor, de Vallier, sunken-faced from strain and sleepless-ness, cried when two brisk young men from Malta were brought to him and Jerott Blyth, who had thought until then of little but the saving of Gabriel, transferred his shame-faced anger, with fine lack of logic, to Lymond. The sole comfort then was the news, brought by a fugitive camel-driver, that d'Aramon and all his suite were still safe. Sinan Pasha wanted no war with France. He merely wished to keep France neutral, by force if need be, until the surrender of Tripoli was accomplished.

As time passed, another gift of grace became apparent. The Turks were aiming all their fire, big and small, at the bulwark of St James, the best of the castle. Thick, well-mortared and terraced within, the wall received shot after shot without cracking or crumbling, and no sooner did a gap appear than it was stopped up by slaves working in the security of the great bulwark.

Labouring there with his fellow knights, with Moors, Turkish prisoners, commanding, cajoling, directing; masked with red grit and sweat, Jerott saw nothing of Lymond, whom he knew to be working on the other buttresses where no money had been spent, and where the old stone, dry and naked of mortar, was no more than a crazy fabric which the most skilled engineer could do little with now.

The Calabrians had been put as far from the gunfire as possible, and set to shovelling earth against the battered walls. Lymond moved there also for a while, and then returned to the bulwark of St Brabe.

Jerott wondered, cynically what he had expected to do. The problem with the Calabrians—the fundamental problem that had isolated them ever since they arrived—was lack of communication. When they troubled to listen, the lads could understand Italian's Italian; but no one at Tripoli except their own captain could make anything of the thick Calabrian dialect which was all that they knew.

After a day and two nights of continuous bombardment, during which they had done all they could to strengthen the town and the castle, and the slaves at the St James bulwark, working in shifts, were keeping pace evenly and without trouble with the damage, Jerott handed over his post to de Poissieu, one of the young French knights, and walked all round the fort.

The sun was reaching its height. Moving out from the shade of the awnings, slung between rooftop and roof of the high leaning alleys; crossing the sand-filled, ruptured paving from near-darkness into sunshine, it was like stepping into fresh, stinging hot water. After a while, beneath the breastplate he wore, in common with all the knights, over the black vest of his habit, he began to feel the heat as a weight on his sodden shoulders and limp legs, and his eyes, straining against the white glare, reflected through his nerves like a mirror the violent headache he had—they all had—from the ceaseless, relentless, inexorable pounding of guns.

Here and there, against the city wall, the slaves were still at work, naked ebony backs whitened with sweat and dust beside the stocky olive torsoes of the Osmanlis, their single lank lock swaying from shaven foreheads, the chinking of the iron chains that linked them by the ankle, two by two, surfacing quietly like continuous, gentle tambourines above the thunder of sound. In the second's space that came, now and then, between shots you could hear a child crying within one of the shuttered houses, its voice muffled by the thickness of sandstone. The alleys, crowded usually with water carriers, mules and merchandise, slaves and servants, beggars, goats, poultry, children, were empty; the street of the cook shops was shut.

As he stepped out into the open, past the ruined temple next to the big Roman archway, Jerott saw lying among the rubble the marble head of a boy, the rimmed almond eyes open to the sun, and wondered what the battered, fought-over houses of Tripoli would have to show of grace fourteen hundred years hence. He spoke to all the knights at the walls without seeing Lymond; the few Calabrians he had seen working on the western bulwarks had now gone. It was a Genoese knight, his face drawn stiff by the sun into lines of fatigue, who said, 'Your nimble friend, I believe, is in the hot-house.' It seemed ridiculous, but there was nothing but weariness in the other man's face. With no enthusiasm at all Jerott walked towards the square, anonymous building the knight had indicated, and pushed open the door.

The first thing that struck him was the heat. Thick as a blanket, airless, stinking, it closed in on him at the door and his overloaded lungs heaved; streamers of light flashed behind his dazzled eyes, and he halted, for the moment quite blind.

Out of the darkness, against a background of men's voices and a soft multiple fluting that bothered him by its familiarity, Lymond's voice said, 'Chevalier!' paused, and added something in Italian in which Jerott Blyth, who knew Italian, recognized perfectly a very coarse joke pertaining to himself. There was a general laugh, a spontaneous, wholly uncultivated laugh of genuine amusement. Jerott's sight cleared. Lymond had the Calabrians with him. Eight of them, half-naked in twisted white breechcloths and ragged vests, were scattered about the long hut, their unshaven, grinning faces turned towards him. Peasants. He looked round, noting the great apertures in wall and roof, glazed in and covered now with dirty blankets; even so, the heat through the glass was stifling. Along the walls and down the centre, on long benches of rough wood, were laid dozens of trays, and on the trays something moved.

Jerott Blyth took a step forward, and as he did so, Lymond moved forward and touched him. Something small and cold pricked down the young knight's classical jawbone to land almost weightlessly on his chest: the soft piping enveloped his head. His quick temper already up, Blyth took a swipe at it.

'Ah, be kind to them,' said Lymond mildly, on a wave of sniggering laughter. 'They think you're Mother.'

The minute, gauzy objects crawling over his elbows, slipping inside his armour, bumping down the planes of his sweating face, were new-born chicks. Yellow, beady-eyed, nodding, they filled every bench; Lymond's hands, as he stood before him, were full of them. 'Hatching chickens without hens,' he explained. 'An old Moorish trick. The people would have let them all die in their fright, but these fellows know about birds. They may not understand guns, but they'll help the garrison to survive, all the same. Are you going back? I'll come with you.'

He looked as fresh as the night he had swum from the French galley. Brushing the young birds from his clothing, Jerott wondered hotly what work, if any, the man had done this last day and night, and then saw that the well-shaped hands restoring the nestlings were as raw as his own. Lymond was a first-class mercenary: it did no good to overlook that.

On the way back Jerott said, 'It doesn't take eight men to hatch and rear a handful of hens.'

'They feel safer there,' said Lymond. 'It insulates their fear from the rest. And it gives them a meeting-place.'

'For rebellion,' said Jerott.

'Of course. There are two ringleaders in there; the rest are just boys. There may be some other dare-devils left in the Châtelet too—I don't know. As a matter of principle, I prefer to guess at any given time where my conspirators are.'

'They seem to trust you,' said Jerott carefully.

'They don't trust you, at any rate,' said Lymond. 'Defence work finished?'

Jerott said curtly, 'I'm going to suggest to de Vallier that half the knights should come in and rest. The older ones are exhausted with lack of sleep. They won't be much good against a fresh attack otherwise. The labour teams are already working and resting turn about.'

He was shouting, because of the gunfire. Inside the castle, the noise muffled by the thick walls, Jerott sneezed; shivered as the shadows enclosed his sodden body, and said, 'Thank God they're firing at the St James, anyway. We can hold on for a bit at least.'

'*We*,' said Lymond in the same deceptively mild voice, 'can hold on indefinitely. . . . Why has the rumour been put about that this is an indefensible city?'

'Dear Heaven,' said Jerott piously. 'You've just spent thirty-six hours propping up the St Brabe wall. . . . The mortar's mouldered from the magnificent walls with sheer age, and our Most Christian Emperor Charles has done nothing whatever for years to restore it. We have. . . .'

'You have stores for weeks, endless underground water, wells, fountains; thirty-six pieces of artillery in excellent working order, lance-grenades, *pots-au-feu*, a complete arsenal of gunpowder; and ditches, terraces and walls that may not be every pioneer's dream, but except for the St Brabe, could stand against anything the Turks have so far. Added to that, you have some of the best cannoneers in the world. Why wasn't the St Brabe mended and the defences put in order before we came?' said Lymond abruptly.

A first-class professional all right. The question was not one Jerott intended to answer. Lymond answered himself.

'Excuse one: because de Vallier expected big reinforcements from

153

Malta and Sicily to fight the Turks off. Excuse two: because he thought d'Aramon would persuade the Turks to go away. Excuse three: because he couldn't get his Spanish knights to do what he wanted anyway, because the Spanish knights want to surrender rather than be blown to bits and then tortured to death by the Turks. So far Allâh, aided by Fustern and Guenara, would appear to have a slight superiority over God, even when aided by Gabriel.'

'Blaspheme if you must,' said Blyth wearily. 'You'll get your wages all right. You'll survive.'

'I'm not going to die of laughing at any rate,' said Lymond, and Blyth nearly lost his temper again. Until, surprisingly, he remembered Oonagh O'Dwyer.

Jerott Blyth himself was a thoroughly competent commander. The list he put before de Vallier of the work done and still to be done, the assessment of man power and stamina, the list of the weak to be rested and the strong to be conserved, was the result of long training, high skill, and a love of his work that lessened, he knew, the love he should pour upon his Maker.

He thought de Vallier distracted. No more than any of them had the old man slept these last days, and the strain had begun long before that. A man who had seen long service in his time, and whose honest, plodding piety had put him at last among the contenders for Grand Mastership, Gaspard de Vallier found his triple duty—devotion to God, to the advancing techniques of war and to the frightening web of intrigue his great Order had become—increasingly hard to encompass. Now, hardly looking at Jerott; the wet, loosened skin of his face folded deeply round cheekbone and chin, he gave automatic assent to all the dark knight proposed, and only moved his blood-veined gaze upwards when a tap at the door ushered in de Herrera, his acting Treasurer, with a question.

'Put her in irons,' said the Governor of Tripoli wearily; and when the Spaniard had gone, rose and moved to the deep window, shuttered to keep out the noise. 'Open it.'

Surprised, Jerott stepped forward, and pushing the great bars, let the heavy wood swing back. Magnified, sudden as an attacking animal, the noise of the big-bore Turkish cannon roared at them. Smoke, grey-yellow and acrid, moved across the window space. Beyond, measured out against the castle wall, arquebusiers and archers, turn about, kept up the warning spray that forced the Turkish cannoneers at least under cover. Beyond, the sea sparkled like tissue beneath a sky of unsullied blue. A brigantine, her decks white and empty, idled in the bay. 'Our friend from Caraillon has deserted,' said the Marshal de Vallier; and as Jerott, obeying his look, reclosed the shutters, the room darkened to the dim amber of the oil lamps as if the light had failed with the words.

He knew the man the Marshal meant; a French knight from Provence long settled in Tripoli. He knew also the gossip: that the man had long since forgone his vows of chastity under the strong African skies, and had a mistress, a Moorish woman in the town. He was not alone there.

'The woman has told you?' he asked at length.

'She was made to tell us. It seems,' said the Marshal without expression, 'that he has been a practising Moslem in secret for some time. . . . He took a horse, and gave the guard some excuse to let him out at the desert port . . . but he took no food or water.'

'The Turkish camp,' said Jerott.

'Yes,' said the Marshal. There was a long silence. A long silence, and, slowly it came to Jerott, too much of a silence. He brought his dark, unseeing gaze up, and found the Governor's tired eyes fixed on his. 'Now open the shutters,' said Gaspard de Vallier. Jerott opened them.

Heat, sun, the dazzle of sea, the white walls, the silver armour of the knights: silence.

Silence. The guns aimed at the St James bulwark had stopped firing.

Jerott turned. Behind him the old man hadn't moved; only his tired eyes followed Jerott's stride back to the desk. When he got there, Gaspard de Vallier spoke. 'Tear up your list, my son,' he said, 'And order every man you can spare to the wall of St Brabe.'

*

In the stir of late afternoon, as the blessed shadows moved and lengthened infinitesimally towards the sea, and the sun striking the skin out of doors was more easily to be borne than the thick, airless heat of the tents, the guns started again. The meticulous rumble came distantly and pleasingly to the Turkish encampment, where the fringed awnings winging between palm and palm enclosed rugs, cushions, low tables, jewelled turbans and *caftáns* in shadow, like some ancient mosaic set in the white gravelly sand of the plain. Sinan Pasha and his officers reclined to take sherbet and sweet grapes as their cannon opened fire on the weak rampart of St Brabe.

'We have wasted too much time on what we now know to be impregnable,' said Dragut in his less than careful Turkish, breaking almond paste in his fingers to offer to the knight at his side. 'Our ships will also fire tonight on the fort at the port entrance they call the Châtelet.'

Gabriel, his face thinner but no less open, no less composed, shook his head, refusing the sweetmeat. 'How long, then, before the city will fall?'

155

The old corsair, his beard moving as he chewed, looked at the creeping shadows. '*In-shallâh.* . . . Tonight or tomorrow, perhaps. By then not the guns of Islâm but the poison of the infidel will have done its work. In two days, the city will be ours.'

'And the knights?'

'That depends on the terms of surrender. The lord Sinan Pasha is displeased.'

'Then the people of Gozo? They have no share in the terms.'

'They will be sold in the slave market,' said Dragut Rais with finality. 'Save, of course, the great *hakîm*, your governor, who will share the fate of the knights.'

'And the woman?'

It was a long pause. They had almost reached this point a dozen times before, but it had been unseemly that it should be said aloud, however well aware Dragut might be of what the Chevalier was asking.

The sage's far-seeing eyes observed him for a moment, then glanced away again. 'You do not ask about your friend the French Ambassador and his train, or about yourself.'

'I trust to your good sense not to offend the *fransuzja*,' said Gabriel. His Turkish was fluent, thank God; the fruit of all his years with the caravanisti.

There was a long interval, which he took the greatest care not to break. Then Dragut said, 'You say the man Crawford is your friend, and yet you wish to deceive him. I remember him well as a boy. You desire him for yourself?'

Unshocked, unshockable, the clear blue eyes smiled. 'No. I desire him, but not for myself.'

Dragut's head jerked towards the shabby black of the knight's habit, with its cross plain on the shoulder. 'For that?' He did not disbelieve Malett, but although courtesy would never permit him to say so, clear in his eyes was derision at the picture Gabriel had painted, of four hundred men enclosed in celibate life with none of the Moslem's more prosaic resources. After another pause, Dragut added, 'I have also no need of a woman, having all the sons I require. Moreover, in my house at present is a woman such as you have never known.'

'This one is pregnant,' said Gabriel. He had saved it to the end, the clinching argument which would preserve Oonagh from the public stripping of the slave market, the abuse which would kill her and her unborn bastard, the careless raping and death she might meet unprotected before the market ever began. A handsome, powerful son of good blood, to be brought up in the Moslem faith to fight for the Grand Seigneur, to be trained in warfare and the arts, to grow wealthy and powerful—even to rule—this was the future

156

that Turkey held before the cream of her conquered peoples, the dream of every father as he grew old. When the boy in time died, his wealth perished with him. No dynasties were ever formed in Turkey outside the Sultan's own; no hereditary power existed; no ducal families to challenge the throne. Only the young and ambitious aliens, converts to Islâm, who infusing their strength and their new blood into the land, would make of Suleiman in time lord of the world.

'Pregnant? *Hâmile?*' said Dragut. 'Of what stock?'

'Of the best stock there is. Of a line of black fighting Irish kings,' said Gabriel, and in his mind's eye saw all Oonagh had described to him of Cormac O'Connor.

'I will take her,' said Dragut. 'But if the son is yours, do you wish him back?'

'If the son is fair,' said Gabriel at length, and for the first time his eyes were lowered against the shrewd gaze of the corsair, 'if the son is fair, send to me, and I will buy him at any price you name. The woman need not know.'

'It shall be done,' said Dragut Rais, the Drawn Sword of Islâm, as across the white glare, in Tripoli, the guns made their first breach.

*

Twenty-four hours later, the Negro and Turkish slaves labouring to rebuild the bastion of St Brabe under a curtain of arrows and arquebus shot refused to do any more, and the order to bastinado went out. Jerott, armourless in filthy shirt and breech hose, heard the screaming above the gunfire and the noise of women shrieking in the castle halls, and anger fuelled his exhausted body like fire.

De Herrera, the Spanish knight, had come to look for the bamboo rods: the thin, whippy peelings used to tap feet and belly, monotonously, over and over until the agonized nerves gave way and the shivering tissues parted into internal haemorrhage and death.

Jerott had tried to stop him and so had de Poissieu, out of commonsense, not humanity. The devastation of the town behind its crumbling walls had turned the castle into a wailing wall of refugees, where Spanish knight and French knight eyed each other sullenly and the Calabrians whispered in corners.

St Brabe was broken. Because of the continuous firing it was suicide to work in the entrenchments behind. All right. What good would it do, said Jerott passionately, to kill the defenders publicly while the defences were giving way? Why in heaven's name didn't they do something positive? Re-site, re-angle the guns: counterattack. They had gunpowder, they had sachetti, they had trumps. Why not use fire on the Janissaries: grenades, pitch, catapults. . . .

'Because they would use fire in return, and fry us in our shells,' de Herrera had said briefly. 'So far they have been careful because they wish to capture the castle intact.'

'They will. They've only to wait,' Jerott had said, his face bloodless under the cracked brown skin and the dirt. 'They're having Tripoli handed them on a salver.' De Herrera had pushed past; and presently the screaming began, and there was nothing Jerott and his handful of French companions could do but go from post to post round the walls and battlements and into the halls and the sick quarters exhorting, cajoling, heartening, replacing weak links with stronger, sanctioning renewal of water, matches, shot, arrows and bolts, and listening all the time to the murmur of sedition.

When, at last, the brutal heat of the sun waned, to be replaced by the treacherous shadows and night, Jerott, irritated by a delay in the supply line, went himself to the magazine to find the reason and have a trolley loaded with sacks of shot.

He was not allowed inside. Striding along the dark corridors, through uneven passages, his way barred by great oaken or iron doors that had to be unshackled and dragged ajar by the serving brother at his side, Blyth reached the open space before the big underground magazine, whose veering oil lamps were hung on Corinthian columns and whose decaying walls were blotched with terracotta and chrome and the oval eyes and tight curled hair of Roman heterae. It had been a bathing-place, someone said. It was now a guardroom.

Three Knights of the Order were there; one by the door, the other two supervising the removal by Turkish slaves of a load of corn powder. The slaves were naked to their shaved heads. The guards did not leave their flanks until the double doors, of iron and then of timber, were shut and locked behind them. One of the knights went with the supplies. The other two remained, looking at Jerott. Both were Spanish, old fighting companions of Guenara's; both were fully armed with helm, breastplate, dagger and sword.

In the uncertain state of the garrison, it seemed a wise precaution. A pack of frightened soldiers could hold them all to ransom with a few sacks from here. It seemed a wise precaution until Jerott was informed that although his needs would be met, he might not enter.

'Why?' Hard, brown, his black hair in a soaking swathe across one grazed cheek, Jerott Blyth had his bare sword in his hands when he added softly, 'And by whose orders?'

'Control yourself, Brother. The Marshal has agreed that lest the French knights be tempted. . . .'

'Tempted to do what? Start a real defence against the Turks? By God, if I'd thought of it—'

'You are profane,' said the older of the two knights sharply; and

158

Jerott opened his mouth, and then discovering the sword in his hand, shot it back into the scabbard with his head bent. He took a deep breath and said, 'Forgive me. But there is sufficient distrust in this garrison, surely, without causing more?'

'These are the Marshal's orders.'

'The Marshal would never have thought of this idea unaided. Do you know that all the doors between here and the upper floors are shut and barred, and that supplies are taking twice the time they should to reach the guns?'

He could not shake them. 'There are sufficient reserves on the surface to keep all guns fully supplied. It is your job to ensure that these reserves are maintained.'

'Without being allowed into the magazine?' Jerott was sarcastic.

'The officers and soldiers at present raising the stores are under your orders. You have only to command.'

'Oh. They will obey, will they?'

'So long as I tell them to,' said the senior of the two knights. What he knew of him, Jerott had liked. But religion and politics were now in opposition, he suddenly realized. And politics had won. He could go to the Marshal, but what good would it do? The Marshal was hamstrung too. He turned away, and in sudden fear, raised his clenched fist and drove it home against the cold, leering flakes of fresco on the wall. 'What can I do?'

'Pray,' said Lymond's voice mildly in the gloom; and he saw him, just ahead, mocking, holding open the thick passage door for him to walk through. 'I came through an hour ago full of plans for an enchanting little shop of special grenades. They won't let me in either. Quite rightly.' Like Jerott, he had stripped to essentials. Down one arm was a series of frayed blisters from an arquebus or cannon barrel, and his shirt front was patched with brown blood, but he sounded still inhumanly fresh. 'Someone else's,' he explained when Jerott pointed to the stains, and left it at that. But as the next door closed behind them and the passage lightened, he added, 'The Calabrians, however, are allowed into the magazine. Interesting, isn't it?'

'My . . . .' said Jerott, and stopped.

'God,' supplied Lymond. 'I told you to pray. They haven't removed anything—yet, if that's what's worrying you. I've been watching them ever since I found out.'

'Why? What can they do except murder us?' asked Jerott blankly.

'What our panicky Spanish friends hope that they'll do, I imagine, is force us to surrender. That's all they want, isn't it?' said Lymond. And after a moment he said with genuine disgust in his voice, 'I tell you, if there were a few mòre of you and you weren't so damned holy, you could kick out both the Marshal and the Spanish crew calling the tune, get the Calabrians on to your side and let them

159

reduce us to a heap of sand before we had to give in. And we wouldn't have to give in.'

Jerott stopped. 'You tried on Malta to get Gabriel to revolt. He told you why he wouldn't, and I'm telling you the same. It would be open revolt against the Order. It would mean the end of us. I've taken an oath to obey. I'll do everything humanly possible to change this policy of suicide, but if they won't agree, I've no option but to obey. Don't you understand?' He pushed the thick hair out of his eyes and glared, his sight thick with tiredness, at the bland, importunate face. 'You follow the common laws of warfare, Crawford. Our service is to Christ.'

In the long, tolerant silence that followed, he became aware, outside his fury, of a sudden unpleasantness, an acridity, a thickening odour in the stone passage where they stood. He took a single step craning, towards the bend of the passage and daylight. A wisp of smoke coiled round and met him, and he hesitated, a question in his eyes, and looked towards Lymond.

Francis Crawford's blue gaze stared coolly back. 'The bodies of the bastinadoed slaves, burning,' he said.

VIII

Fried Chicken (The Yoke of the Lord)

(Tripoli, August 1551)

THAT night, for two hours, the Turkish cannon stopped firing again. As the great silence fell, and continued, the beleaguered garrison guessed that the halt was an enforced one. Constant firing in midsummer could play havoc with the guns. Almost certainly they were being rested, regreased and repaired, and the gunners were being given a respite.

They could afford to rest. Through the broken wall of St Brabe lay the first opening crack in the castle's defences. And the frightened slaves and dispirited soldiers who held the trenches behind, driven there under threat of torture, presented the slightest of obstacles. The greater the suspense the greater the likelihood that the defence would break down of its own accord. The Provençal knight with his Moorish mistress must have painted a shamingly accurate picture of the ancient Order's stand for their religion in Tripoli.

Meanwhile, at their posts, one in four of the defenders slept heavily in exhaustion in spite of the crack of the hackbut and the hiss of falling shafts that continued, in flocking bursts in the luke-warm darkness under the vast, glittering stars, to keep the over-eager on each side circumspect.

Jerott Blyth, so tired that he knew he was a hazard to the defence and to himself, dropped beside the men at the shore culverin and was wakened, by his own orders, at the end of an hour, sick and clogged with inadequate sleep. He made his rounds, his senses still sluggish, attempting to see that the older knights, the wounded and the less able were relieved, and only realized as he went into de Vallier's room to make his report that he had not seen Lymond. He mentioned it. Nerveless creature that the other man was, he was one of their most priceless assets at this moment with his hard expertise, and his harder detachment.

But the Marshal only gazed at him with his eyes filmed with recent sleep and said wearily, 'He is under lock and key. I do not know whether this man is a traitor or not, but he is an individualist, and in war the two are the same.' He paused, and added, 'He

161

countermanded the orders to bastinado the Moor, and when de Herrera interfered, he held him at sword point until the man was released.'

Jerott knew the Moorish prisoner he meant—a powerfully made man, second-generation exile from Spain who had fought for Turkey in North Africa until his capture by the knights. Since chivalry had obviously nothing to do with Lymond's action, Jerott said only, 'Why?'

The Marshal shrugged. 'We are all under stress. But we cannot have authority undermined at the moment when we are enforcing it. The Moor took his brother's place under the whip: it is not unknown. The Scottish gentleman thought it a needless waste of manpower. In any case, the Moor and his brother have escaped, and are probably hiding in the town, where they will almost certainly be killed by the cannon fire; so your friend has deprived us at one stroke of the services of two slaves and himself.'

In any man but Lymond, you would define that as crass incompetence allied to sentiment. Jerott said, 'I suppose I relish the gentleman no more than you do. But I can't see him unfaithful to the people who are paying him. And we can't afford to be without him, sir.'

'If I release him, the Spanish knights will kill him; or at the very least I shall have a revolt on my hands. He used rough measures. In public,' said de Vallier, and dropped the pen he was agitating as the big door crashed open. '*Dispense Vd. . . .* Forgive me, sir,' said his Acting Treasurer, his dark face drawn with sleeplessness and anger as the thick, hot air of the passage came with him into the lamplit room. 'If you speak of Señor da Laimondo, there is no need to release. He has escaped. Also, the arsenal has been broken into, and the guard slaughtered.'

Nothing about that made sense. As Jerott stared, the Marshal said, 'Search for him. What ordnance has been taken?'

'We do not yet know. The outer door is open, but the iron grille has been relocked and the key is missing.' There were men behind him in the passage; comrades, Jerott guessed, of the dead man. Whatever his reasons this time, Lymond's chances of survival were frail. The Marshal was enjoining silence and care, to avoid panic. True, the news that an unknown quantity of arms and ammunition was missing would hardly brace the garrison's confidence. A good deal more coldly than before, de Vallier was addressing him. Brother Jerott must now admit that his compatriot at the very least was a Turkish agent or sympathizer, intending either to lead a revolt or coerce them into surrender?

Brother Jerott thought of de Herrera, who was moving out, talking urgently, his hand on his sword. But he could swear there was genuine rage in his face. Besides, it was a Spaniard who had been killed. He visualized the team he had just seen, the murder party, splitting up and silently searching the castle through the hot night, the torch flares moving from rampart to rampart, the discreet questions which would elicit—which were bound to elicit—the direction of any small unexplained bustle, any unaccountable throb of running footsteps in the uncanny, exhausted silence.

Aloud, he said, 'I don't know. It seems unlikely. He is nothing if not professional. May I have leave to hunt also, sir?' said Jerott suddenly. 'I may be able to follow his mind. And on my Religion and my honour, I shall deal with you honestly.'

For a long moment, incredulously, he thought that the old man was going to refuse. Then the Marshal nodded, and with a wave of distaste, removed Blyth and the subject from the room. Jerott did not know, as he set off swiftly through the old castle, stopping at post after post, that he was being followed. His whole attention was on discovering the whereabouts of the Calabrians. Within a very few minutes he had satisfied himself that every man of them had gone.

Of all people, these country lads would never make for the Turks. For them there was one hope, revived now for the first time since the glare of the shore guns had ceased: the brigantine. To sail her, more than eight men were needed. Therefore the Châtelet must be involved: some kind of rendezvous between the soldiers in des Roches's isolated fortress at the end of the spit, and the few men in Tripoli. Somewhere, these men must be waiting with stolen munitions for the signal to join forces; perhaps men from the Châtelet were coming to help carry the powder and guns. . . . Where would they meet?

In Tripoli, the deserted city, whose walls now offered only token resistance, where there were no women to scream and point, no knights to hinder them. And in Tripoli, he knew exactly where.

To run, in the July night, was to slide through a glutinous coating of sweat, tracking down neck and spine and buttocks. For the sake of nimbleness and silence Jerott wore no mail, but had snatched up a dark jerkin to throw over his chemise; his sword belt and dagger he wore always. Because he had no need to avoid guards and gates and because, when he wanted to, he could move very fast indeed, he reckoned on reaching his destination very soon after the escaping Calabrians and long before de Herrera's men, grimly exhausting every possible refuge back at the castle.

If he had any doubts, padding through the uneven streets between the darkened houses, with abandoned awnings above broached with stars through their tatters and the rustle of rats and starving dogs in the thick blackness underfoot, he dismissed them. Whoever unlocked the arsenal doors had first killed the guard for the keys, and on that ring, he knew, was the key which had freed Lymond . . . Lymond, who alone of the garrison had been at pains to cultivate the exiles, who had just publicly championed the helpless. He ran through the empty slave market avoiding the dealers' empty platforms under the dark arches by memory, and out into the open.

Ahead, the square turret of the Lentulus Arch reared against the wide sky in a glimmer of Corinthian marble; and not far away, he could see the double row of pillars and the wreck of a tower which de Vallier had said had once been a mosque.

Beside it was the building he wanted, its strange big windows shuttered, and no lights to be seen. Slipping from wall to wall, he started to cross to it, blending into the dark, waiting for the sentry who would almost certainly be there. Then he saw him. There was only one, a shadow that had bulk, that breathed heavily against the distant flat popping sounds of desultory fire from the other side of the wall and the hush and hiss of the sea against the rocks outside.

The old tricks were often the best, especially with untried men like these. Jerott, groping, found a pebble at his feet and leaning forward, threw it as far as he could. It fell beyond the dark shadow with a thin chink, and the shadow moved once, and was still.

So was Jerott. Instead of stepping into the starlight as he had expected, his back presented to Jerott's ready blade, the watcher was still there, *facing him*.

To move was to be seen. Blyth stayed where he was, the sweat cold on the roots of his hair, the sword-hilt wet in his hand, and after a moment of incomprehension realized that the dim blur ahead of him which was the unknown man's face was now clearer; that in fact the guard, in conduct very far from that of a Calabrian peasant, was quietly approaching *him*.

The man had seen him; he knew he was alone. There was one corollary: the knife. As he saw the shadow lift its arm, Jerott flung himself sideways and forward, and a moment later with his left hand grabbed a muscular body wrapped in unexpected folds of cotton. With his right, he brought his sword down hard. There was a spark of fire, and his arm jarred. He had been parried by a dagger, a dagger which disappeared as Jerott, changing his grip, wrenched the fellow's right arm behind his back and adroitly kicked his feet from under him. The man crashed backwards taking Jerott with him, sword in hand. He did not guess the other man had shifted his knife already from right hand to left until the hilt hit the bone of his wrist with a crack as he rolled on top of his victim. Then Jerott Blyth dropped his sword and clutched for life at the upraised fist holding the dagger below.

Apart from the chink of metal and the soft flurry of their movements, there had been little sound. Neither spoke: Blyth because he could not afford to draw the attention of the men inside the building; his opponent for most cogent reasons of his own. Holding the other man's wrist stiffly at a safe distance, Jerott twisted violently to avoid being kicked off; tried and failed because of the man's robes to force him into any kind of lock; and after devoting a hard-pressed second to wrenching a gouging hand from his face, lost his grip, rolling over and over under the thickset body to come up, in a total exercise of strength, with his own knife at last in his hand.

At the same time, automatically, the forefront of his brain was assembling a number of extraordinary facts. This was a robed and bearded man, not a peasant boy in shirt and breeches. What he had just knocked off was a turban, and what lay under his hand was a naked scalp, from which dropped the slave's single, degrading hank of hair. It passed through his mind while he drew, fighting for his life, on the long, long training in close combat which he possessed embedded in his bone; and in three sudden, definitive movements he had the Moor disarmed and his knife at the dimly seen throat. At his shoulder a damnable, familiar voice murmured, 'How brave and clever, Jerott, my heart. Now let him go.' And a sword, delicately used, pricked Jerott Blyth's back.

Sick with effort, his chest heaving, every joint in his tired body sore, Jerott turned, and smiling, Lymond put a strong hand through his arm. 'Come, children,' he said.

The chicks were dead. Inside the hut the hot reek told it, and the silence, and the single bleared candle on the floor whose light wavered on the daffodil down in puffs and drifts all about it and on the benches above, picking out the waxy loop of a beak, the brown, half-open thumbnail of a wing, the skeleton claws. On one side they had been pushed back, in a tumbled ridge, to make way for boxes and sacks stamped with the mark of the Order. Beside them lay a young man with a large bruise on his ruddy skin, and cord round his legs and wrists. He was one of the Calabrians.

'From the arsenal?' said Jerott at length, his gaze on the boxes.

The big Moor, turbaned once more, his back to the closed door, was silent, his face expressionless, but Lymond answered. 'Of course. His friends will be back soon. They've gone to join forces with the garrison at the Châtelet. Then they hope no doubt to load guns and powder and matches from here into a small boat and make for the brigantine and the untrusty sea, no keeper of calms. Unfortunately'— he did not glance at the furious boy on the floor—'as I have already told our friend, the trip will be useless.'

A flood of Italian, nearly incomprehensible even to Jerott who knew Italian very well, conveyed disbelief and denial as well as uproarious fury. Jerott knew how the boy felt. Having, at some cost to themselves, spared the time to free Francis Crawford, it seemed unfair that Francis Crawford, along with his henchman freed from the bastinado, should then do his considerable best to undermine their little plot.

Jerott doubted if he himself would have had the stomach for it. Lymond clearly had no qualms. He said with gentle cheerfulness, 'We shall see. Giulio here says his friends will already be aboard the brigantine, ready to sail. I'm sure he's right, except that they'll find there's nothing to set sail with. As you would know too, if you'd been watching, the sails, oars, cables and everything else that make a ship move have been dismantled from the brigantine in the last two days. *And* from every smaller boat in the harbour. She's an empty shell, my friend. Your lads might as well take their guns to a floating tomb. Not,' said Lymond peaceably, 'that they're going to have the chance of taking the guns anywhere, for you and I in just a moment are going to blow them up.'

Jerott wished he had killed that damned Moor. He pulled himself together and said sarcastically, 'Of course, if you want to cut your own throat. You know these fellows killed a man to open the magazine and get you out of your cell. And you're being blamed for it. Surely the first thing to do is to report this, have the ordnance taken back to the castle, and have a strong party waiting for the Calabrians when they come back for the guns as they're bound to do, whether they get out to the brigantine or not. In their own eyes they're dead men unless they fight back. They don't know de Herrera has picked on you.'

'It's my French accent,' said Lymond idly. He was listening, Jerott realized, for any sound outside the hut. The Moor had slipped off again, no doubt to resume watch. Then, bringing his attention back suddenly, 'Look,' said Lymond. 'Nine times out of ten you may be right in extremity to make a public example by frying someone's liver in front of the vulgar—I won't argue. But here leniency is the only answer. You are threatened physically in that there is a breach in St Brabe whose extent no one yet knows; and unless the defences behind are properly manned there may be a break-through. You are threatened politically by the Spanish knights' fear of Turkish vengeance and the fact that, if they can find any easy way out, the blame has a good chance of being pinned on the French. Add to that mess two hundred peasant boys to be guarded day and night because they renegued and having absolutely nothing to lose by murdering the entire garrison and you get not only disaster, but a silly disaster.'

'What, then?' said Jerott. Lymond was speaking Italian, of a rough and ready kind but plainly, and probably understandable enough to the boy on the floor.

'So the Spanish knights are never allowed to discover what has happened. We return to the castle with our friend here, leaving a lit fuse to take care of the powder: poor little fried chickens, my dear. The Calabrians between here and the Châtelet, in the Châtelet or at sea can't help but see it, whatever they imagine caused it. No ship;

no weapons. They'll have to come back, if only to find out what has happened. And if they find no one suspects them, what can they do but return docilely to their posts and hope to God no one notices their feet are wet?'

Switching suddenly to English, he added something to that fast summing-up. 'De Vallier and des Roches must be told, of course. And trouble may well boil up among the men themselves once the firing restarts. But at least if the Spanish don't know, we'll avoid open insurrection and mayhem at this exact juncture, and have a chance of keeping them on our side.'

'And who,' said Jerott, 'is supposed to have knifed the sentry and taken the powder?'

'Salablanca,' said Lymond calmly. 'Our big friend outside. That was very nicely fought, by the way. He is no novice in any sense of the word at in-fighting.'

'I'm flattered,' said Jerott sarcastically. 'And a big, strong man, too. He carried all this alone?'

'No. His brother and a handful of slaves helped him. They'll be assumed, I hope, to have died in the fire. . . . In fact, they'll make for the Turkish camp.'

'So you have been unlocking a few more fetters,' said Jerott blankly. He had his sword again, he remembered, and his dagger. The Calabrian would help him.

'I've saved you two hundred soldiers,' said Lymond. 'In exchange for six slaves, one of them dying.'

'You'd have been a damned sight better letting them escape,' said Jerott sharply, 'and get themselves *and* the munitions *and* the boat blown out of the water by Osmanli guns. Then they'd be no further encumbrance on us as prisoners or as potential rebels.'

There was a brief pause. 'That, I am sure,' said Lymond, 'is what any man in the Order would have done. I am not a monk.' He was kneeling, a light flaring between his fingers, and looking up from the slow match, so efficiently led from powder to fuse, Jerott saw something grim in the underlit face. 'Let's get to the castle,' said Lymond, and rising, crossed to the prone man and cut his bonds. 'Do you understand? The powder will burn; your friends cannot leave by ship. If they come back now, no one will know what you have done. Go quickly and tell them so.'

The youngster was perhaps seventeen, certainly not more; and he could hardly sit, far less stand. Lymond propped him, adroitly, while the blood returned to his cramped limbs: the lashing had been sailors' work. But in spite of the pain, he was talking before he was upright.

Jerott grinned. What he could make of the language was picturesque even for that lusty countryside. 'He says he doesn't believe you. He says you are destroying the guns that would have saved their lives

167

and will betray them now to the Governor to save your own skin.'

'Well, it was worth trying,' said Lymond calmly. All that hate seething on his arm had not, it appeared, upset him. 'We'll take him with us to the castle. When he sees we aren't proposing to sell him by the slice, he may change his mind. The Moor can take the message meantime—the other lads will trust him. Come!'

The peasant backed and muttered. 'He doesn't trust you at the castle either,' said Jerott, who was beginning to feel a little more cheerful. 'He wants to go to the Châtelet after all.'

'Thank you,' said Lymond, staring at him, 'for the interpretation. Don't you think we had all better get wherever we are going, before the whole bloody building blows up?'

Whether the boy understood every word Jerott doubted, but he had certainly got the sense of what Lymond said. Ceasing to rub his cramped limbs, he launched himself like a dog at the door. And instead of letting him go, swifter even than the boy, in a single blur of movement, Lymond stopped him. Gasping, the lad wrenched desperately in his grip, trying to kick himself free. Lymond, holding him, suddenly turned his head listening, and then said sharply over the scuffling, 'We have company. You've been followed, Blyth. De Vallier doesn't trust you either, it seems.' And at the same moment, silent as an owl's flight, the door opened beside them and the Moor slipped in. 'We heard them. How many?' said Lymond, and the big man spoke low. '*Veinte, señor. Debemos pronto. . . .*'

'To get out. Quite. By the window, Jerott. There's a big one opening at the back. We can't fight twenty men, and we've got to get this lad out of sight—No, you fool!' to the struggling Calabrian. 'Look. If you're found anywhere near here, you'll be connected with that ammunition. You can't hope to get to the Châtelet now; the Moor'll do that errand. You'd better come back to the castle with us. . . .'

And as the Calabrian, with a sudden, desperate movement, twisted and half-jerked himself free, Lymond said resignedly 'Hit him, somebody. We'll take him unconscious if we have to.'

Whatever they had expected, the boy silenced even Lymond this time by his response. For now, pushed to it at last, hopelessly late, he began to talk. In the hut among the frail dead fledgelings he commanded utter silence; so absolute you could hear what Lymond had heard: the obscure shift of men gathering at a little distance—proably, Jerott thought with half his mind, the market. The explosion wouldn't harm them at that distance: there wasn't enough powder. Lymond said in Italian, carefully, 'Say that again,' and the hoarse voice, thick with fear, almost unintelligible in dialect, spoke again, while above his rough head the eyes of Jerott, Lymond and the Moor met and held.

The little explosion promised by the quiet fuse burning at their feet was only the forerunner, paltry as the new-hatched younglings, of the end of Tripoli. Before leaving the castle magazine the Calabrians had lit a slow fuse much bigger and longer and more important. It was timed to reach the first keg of powder once the rebels were safely afloat. It had been burning now for the better part of an hour. And the key to the locked iron grille which alone gave access to the arsenal had been thrown in the sea.

Lymond asked only one question. 'How much time have we left? How much time before the arsenal blows up?' And by that he meant the whole castle of Tripoli.

'It must be three-quarters consumed,' said the boy, and a shade of pride entered the sunburnt face. Lymond flung him from him.

'Let him take his chance,' he said. 'He knows now how to save himself. Salablanca, hide, and get to the Châtelet with the news if you can. If not, Allâh speed you. Jerott. ... Your conscience is God's. If you support me in this fiction, go to the market, tell them you have seen slaves here inside; tell them you've overheard them admit the arsenal has been fired. Before you've got halfway through that, I'll have this blown up. Then do what I'm going to do ... *run like hell*.'

'I'm going back to the castle,' said Jerott, his voice strained as he flung back the heavy shutters giving on to the lane at the hut's back and prepared with the others to jump.

'Bravo!' said Lymond sardonically and Jerott felt his anger rise and flood the vacant places of his fear. For Lymond had only said, run, and the implication of choice was worse than an insult: it was the last animal smear on his honour. Through all that was to cóme that night, Jerott Blyth behaved like a madman, hugging that single word to him.

No one spoke now. One by one they dropped to the ground and Jerott raced to his brother knights as Calabrian and Moor melted into the hot night and the lit taper in Lymond's hand arched back through the window and began to eat through the wooden cask. Then he lost sight of them all. As de Herrera met him, sword drawn in the shadows, and he shouted the news, the hatching hut at his back blew up in a corymb of vermilion and gold. Before the detonations ended, Blyth was running towards the castle, his message delivered, and after only a moment's hesitation the Spanish followed. For of all the knights, the Moors, the soldiers and slaves, all the worthy merchants and traders, the priests and serving brothers and Tripolitains, men women and children in the castle, only they and the three men who had found other business so tactfully behind, knew that in fifteen minutes the siege would be over. And that neither Islâm nor the Order would be masters of Tripoli, for Tripoli would not exist.

*

It was a case where numbers could not help, only skill. There was enough powder in the arsenal, Jerott knew, to destroy not only the castle but the city itself. There was no use shouting warnings, for there was nowhere to run to in time, and panic would only hinder the small chance they still had. Only they, on the perimeter when they got the news, had been safe, and they had thrown safety away.

He kept grim faith with his implied promise to Lymond. In the handfuls of words he flung to de Herrera as they ran, he said nothing of the Calabrians. And soon none of them spoke at all but merely ran, their throats parched, stumbling through the dark, broken lanes, ricocheting from wall to wall in the thread-like maze of alleys which lay between themselves and the castle.

To men who knew Tripoli well, in daylight, it was perhaps ten minutes' work. To Jerott Blyth and his fellow knights, it was a gasping nightmare of missed turnings and blocked passages and sudden, blind walls. A rotting barrow of fruit, jammed in an archway, held them up for precious seconds; and soon after that, hurling himself round a corner under a dark bridgeway blocking the stars, he found himself in someone's courtyard, blundering between lemon trees into a dry fountain, his feet clattering on the tiles. Outside again, casting about, his foot struck a tin bowl and he knew he was in the silversmiths' alley, and had been here before—my God, was he running in circles? And time—time was slipping away.

Then, at last, heart-bursting minutes later, they saw ahead the corner bastion and the high, dark outer wall leading to the main gate of the citadel. Ears straining, eyes aching, Jerott and his fellow knights crossed the open square to the big doors like beings demented and, cursing the guard for their questions, burst through into the castle. Then Jerott cried out.

Ahead, towers, walls, battlements sprang black across the sudden, burning orange of the night sky. A second later there was a roar; then another, and another, while the flaming air shook and writhed. For a moment, none of the little band moved or spoke. Then de Herrera beside him drew in a breath like a sob, and gripping Jerott's shoulder, launched forward again.

What they saw was gunfire. The Turkish battery had opened up again.

Afterwards, Jerott remembered bumping into a number of people without explanation; passing de Vallier himself standing looking oddly after them, and running very fast through a number of court-

170

yards, up and down stairs and then through an endless series of connecting rooms and down a stair, which led to more stairs, until they were in the long series of chambers and passages belonging to the Roman bath-house.

They were then, Jerott knew, in precisely no less and no more danger than they had been up above in the open air. It only felt, if possible, worse. In any case they had now no chance at all, for he reckoned, and guessed that the others knew also, that the time was up. Henceforward, every second of life was won from chance. And every door, every vast iron hatch between themselves and the burning fuse was closed and barred.

It was that discovery which nearly defeated their courage. Their strength, though they hardly knew it, was already spent. Then de Herrera said sharply in a high, exhausted voice, 'Will you let one heathen destroy the Religion in Tripoli?' and flung himself like a maniac on the heavy bolts of the next door. After that, they wrenched each open between them, silent but for their sobbing breath, and the slowest was left behind to slam them shut, to bring no transfusion of air to the speed of the fuse.

At the last door even Jerott hesitated. The lit match must now be so near the powder that a breath would dispatch it. The opening of this door in his hand was his entrance card, at twenty-five, to heaven or hell. The bolts were drawn. He remembered to pray for the first time, briefly and even with shame, and drew the door open.

In the quiet space before the great door of the arsenal the yellow lamps shone peacefully on the obliterated, weaving wall-dancers who in a thousand years had seen and suffered worse than this. The oak door unlocked by the Calabrians was ajar, unguarded: what need of a guard when the massive grille door inside was shut and its key at the bottom of Tripoli Bay?

But before it, two men were working; working feverishly, their movements surging in lamplit rings through the water spreading slowly across the tiled floor. Above the trample of soldiers' feet at his back, above the rampaging screech of a file, a familiar voice unfamiliarly crisp said, 'Blyth. I want a locksmith, a crossbow and bolts, some cloths and a lot more water. We have perhaps five minutes. Axes are causing too much vibration, and the file won't be in time.' And as de Herrera, behind, relayed the orders, Lymond added over his shoulder, 'Two of you come in. The rest stand by for orders. The corridor doors can remain open. We have tried drenching the floor, but the slope of the arsenal has sent it back to us. We have failed to reach the fuse with damp cloths on a rod: it is at the far side of the cellars and the other stores are in the way. I am about to try shooting soaked cotton. . . .'

And Francis Crawford, wasting no further time or words on them, finished binding his dripping, lightly wrapped arrows, and stretching the small Moorish bow in his hand aimed swiftly, and sent the laden shaft through one of the spaces in the grille. It floundered unbalanced through the air, above the stacked barrels and boxes, the stands of armour and spears, the stacked arquebuses and axes arranged in blocks throughout the wide vaulted cellars, with loading alleys cross-hatched between. Far across the room, from some bay invisible behind the crammed stands, a thread of smoke, thinly moving, was just visible in the dim lamplight within. And beyond the smoke, where like a monstrous clutch of marble and iron the cannon shot stood in pyramids against the far wall, a touch of rosy light appled the balls.

There were six arrows. Jerott Blyth watched them all leave the bowstring and spring through the latticed door. He also watched each in turn fall blundering against some cask or crossbar, or over-shoot to drape the cannon-ball stacks. The last one alone fell into the invisible chasm where the smoke rose, but too far to the right. The thread of grey wavered in its slow passage and went on, like the fin of some frail fish, towards the shining wall of packed crates filling a third of the arsenal on their left: the gunpowder.

And all the time, below him, the dark hands of the man patiently filing never ceased although the thick bar still held, and would hold, Jerott guessed, for ten minutes yet. It was, he saw, with no more capacity for surprise, the Moor Lymond had saved. And there were only three minutes of life left for them all.

At his back, jogging footsteps. The extra water casks had been fetched. Hoarse voices; splashing, pattering, fumbling. Cloths had been drenched and rushed in, and more arrows. He watched Lymond catch and fit them, wordlessly, his face totally without expression, his whole gimcrack battery of flourishes swept clean to concentrate on speed, on deftness and on—Jerott realized—his sense of hearing.

Suddenly Lymond threw down bow and arrow and turning, snatched. It was the crossbow arriving, and with it a man whose sobbing breath rang through the cellar as he threw himself on his knees before the iron lock, flinging aside the sweating Moor, and began with shaking hands to probe.

Lymond said only two words to the locksmith, but they filled the anteroom where, quite silent now, de Herrera and his men stood, ankle deep in useless water. 'How long?'

The smith did not look up, nor did he answer immediately. As life went ticking by, and the tang of burnt fabric filled the motionless air, there was no sound but the frantic rattle of his instrument. Then he said, still working, 'Five minutes, sir. It can't be opened in less. Is it enough, sir?' And as he spoke there was a little eddy, and the smoke, leaning forward, kissed the wall of stacked wooden boxes.

In front of the door, every man drew his breath. 'The smoke is a little ahead of the flame,' Lymond said. 'But it's passing out of the long alley running from left to right in front of us, and has got to the junction of the alley at right angles to it, fronting the gunpowder. I'm afraid we must risk this thing.'

'The crossbow?' de Herrera's voice was odd. The machine in Lymond's hands was wound and set.

'If the cannon balls fall the right way, they may crush the life out of the fuse before they break open the gunpowder. If they broach the gunpowder first, it's the end. Anyone play pelota?' said Lymond, a last, faint, grim smile on his lips; and for a second, a living flash of recognition and greeting and, he supposed, farewell, passed from his blue eyes to Jerott. Then he aimed, wound, and shot.

It was true. Accurate as a child's ball at a party, the heavy bolt hissed between shelving and pillars, clearing all the useless paraphernalia of war, and crossed the space where the long, charred trail of the match must be lying, to strike an outer ball less than halfway up the pyramid, with an echoing clank.

The ball started, in a cloud of white chipped splinters, and ramming its neighbours to the right, caused them in turn to start, pouting; to eject, miraculously, one of their number like a lumbering truant, bouncing and ricocheting to the floor. A frisson ran over the rest. Every ball, itself revolving, began to trickle from coign to coign, to hop, to rush, to spin until, buckling, the whole loosened, thundering pile dissolved into a colliding universe of spheres and showered bounding to the floor of the arsenal.

The roar, arched back by the vaulted stonework, was as frightening in its context as the roar of bursting dam water might be. For it was followed and accompanied by the crack and crash of splintering woodwork. Over the solemn ranks of nearer ordnance, crates heaved and trotted and threw jagged limbs in the air. Dust, a haze of spilled chemicals, a bursting rain of chipped stone filled the distant air like a tattered curtain; also, there were sparks.

In all the busy, boisterous confusion, the single tell-tale stream of smoke was quite lost. Jerott, clinging to the slippery bars with fists that were white to the bone, was praying with gritted teeth, the vibration of the smith's work running unfelt through his fingers. Beside him, Lymond was silent: utterly silent, for once.

Slowly, the thunder slackened and subsided. The gigantic, canonning stones collided, rolled, blundered and stopped; the last crate fell; the last wrenched cask gave out its shower of arrowheads or bullets. The wall of gunpowder boxes had rocked with the rest. Two or three had slid jolting from the high tiers to end rakishly on a lower. One was stoved, but not yet spilt. If the fuse had escaped harm, it would be licking the boxes now.

A long second passed. Another. And another.

It was hot. Within the arsenal, silence reigned; peace fell. Whether crushed lifeless or whipped and bent from its path, the fuse had been diverted.

Behind Jerott the Spaniard de Herrera laid shaking hands on Lymond's shoulders and said something, his voice cracked. It was lost in Jerott's cry. *'Wait! Something's happening!'*

Across the cellars, low in the falling veil of dust, to the right of where the live match had been and farther away, by two yards, from the gunpowder, a flush of pink flickered and eddied. As they watched it became more forceful in action and colour; limned itself with a flash of orange and a finger of charcoal mist, and identified itself with a thin crackling, as of ice fussing in the sun.

Except that this was no ice, but fire.

It began, no doubt, when the burning match, thrust by some chance ball back on itself, had been pressed into a wooden crate walling its passage: a crate harmless enough compared to the powder kegs for which it had been headed, but a pyre which could race to the stacked gunpowder as surely as the fuse ever did, and with twice the speed, if chance sent it first in that direction.

And even if chance did not, fed on acres of dry packing wood, the flames would get there in the end. In Jerott's ear, Lymond's voice said sharply, *'Shut the doors!'* and spoke again to the locksmith, 'How long?'

A ruddy man, the smith's face was glistening with sweat over a blotched hide of ivory and red, but his hands worked steadily, testing, failing, trying again. He said, 'Nearly ... God in Heaven save us. . . . Nearly, I think.'

And on that slender promise, they had to prepare. The sheets and hides were already soaked. Now they drenched their own clothes; handed out brooms and axes, sticks and shovels; aware as they did so that the red glow behind the fast door was brightening second by second until, with a rush and a creak, a sheet of fire rose high into their vision and the tops of the furthermost crates between the flames and themselves began, like lichen, to burgeon and run with low scarlet fire. Smoke, yellow and thick, rolled between the vaults and over the sea of boxes towards them and someone cried aloud. 'God save us! Mary, Mother of God!'

At that second, the iron grille creaked and swung open.

Where their eyes had stared upon the black iron pattern, like some template of hell, overprinting the gathering fire, now there was nothing but space, and thick clouds of yellow-grey smoke. Then Francis Crawford, axe in hand, a drenched cloth flung round his head, darted into the fog.

Jerott followed. De Herrera, a pace behind, stopped, alarmed by

174

some change in the air at his back. In that moment, against all his orders, the antechamber door was flung open; announcing, by the great swirl of air sucking behind, that every door in the arsenal corridor stood similarly ajar. De Vallier, too long left in ignorance, disturbed by rumours of running men and sudden orders, had sent a squad of soldiers, led by picked knights, to investigate.

Now, debouching into the antechamber, they stopped, paralysed, the glare coppering glazed faces; then, horror-struck, slammed the door shut. But it was too late by then. Fed on that life-giving air, the young flames around the two men inside the arsenal had leaped into full life, to become a single vast sheet of fire.

To Jerott, caught suddenly between a wall of serpentine and corn powder and an advancing surge, like a wave, of towering flame, it seemed beyond believing that now, with free access to water, sand, all the help that they needed, they were going to fail. Lymond, driven back also, arrived at his side breathing painfully; said, 'Cosy, isn't it?' and dragging off his smoking burnous, flung the wet folds over the nearest powder boxes and, coughing, dodged forward again...

The fire had spread between themselves and the door. Through it, Jerott saw faces, grim, terrified, sick, lit by the glare; and the sound of a weak hissing rose behind the crackle and roar of the flames. Sparks and soaring pieces of lit stuff in clouds of ash began to drift through the air. He pulled off his protective shrouding, like Lymond, and flinging it over the boxes, ran forward to join him.

The fire was running towards them, along a single line of stacks and casings; and between themselves and it was now only one stand, packed shelf upon shelf with armour. Lymond had made no attempt to get to the door. Instead, he was at the foot of the stand, hacking with all his force at the uprights with the sharp axe. After a second, Jerott took the other post and did the same.

Above them, the stand caught fire. The heat was scorching them now. Seared and blistered already by the stinging debris, Jerott worked now with timber crashing about him and pieces of flaming leather, jerked from above, falling flaring on his exposed back and head. A beam of wood, disturbed, glanced off his arm; he felt nothing at all. But for the wet cloths protecting them, the cases at his back would already have exploded in the heat. Already the thin, webbed folds were whitening; soon the fabric would be tinder-dry, a fuse in itself.

The stand rocked. He realized suddenly that the post Lymond had been working on was severed. In a moment the other man was beside him, adding his blows to Jerott's own. The wood under the blade creaked, then grated; the towering erection shuddered; and as Lymond said quickly, 'All right. As far back as you can!' the unwieldy thing rocked and heeled faster and faster with its vast

175

platforms laden with chain mail and plated metal, away from them, to fall with a clashing roar into the heart of the flames.

A tower of orange, roof-high, shot up from its far perimeter; then died low in rolling seas of black smoke, to fumble and mutter on fresh fuel. In a moment, such was the bed of heat, it would have found fresh, renewed life. But that moment was all that the men in the doorway required. As he pressed back against the lethal boxes, blinded, coughing, half-stunned by the tumbling metal as the rack fell, Jerott saw water run streaming across the floor at his feet. Men masked in wet cloth leaped over the fallen debris towards him in a whirling, feverish spray of water and sand. Sodden bales, thrown over and over, shrouded the naked, perilous boxes behind him, and as the teams began to move inwards, pressing, extinguishing, reducing in clouds of steam the diminishing circle of fire, he saw that the powder crates, one by one, were being carried outside. Then he looked at Lymond.

Lymond was looking at him. Beaten back against the crates they had saved, his shirt charred from his body, his face blistered, his tousled hair singed, Lymond opened bloodshot eyes on Jerott Blyth and intoned rashly, 'Receive the Lord's yoke, for it is easy and light. We promise you bread and water without any dainties, and a modest habit of small worth. . . . Are you adequately supplied with water, Brother Blyth? Your habit leaves something to be desired.'

Brother Blyth, fighting hysteria, pain and exhaustion, was in no state to interpret all that. He said in a harsh whisper, 'You should thank Him on your knees.' And as Lymond unexpectedly did not answer, Jerott added picturesquely, 'You draw your strength from the Devil to seduce men.' Then shutting his eyes abruptly, he buried his face in his burned arms.

Lymond stirred. Men were coming towards them. He would have to walk, to talk, to think, to act. He said, 'Oh Christ, Jerott, you've got one hero too many already. Stand on your own feet, Brother. It's good for the soul.' And stiffly, hauled himself upright and walked.

*

The post-mortem; the inquiry into the tomb in which nobody died, was held later in the Marshal's room, in the presence of a white-faced des Roches, the Serving Brother from the Châtelet; the silent captain of the Calabrians; the Spanish knights, including de Herrera, Fuster and Guenara, and, for the French, de Poissieu and Blyth. Outside the unshuttered windows, steady in precise cannonade, the Turkish guns fired, flushing the silvering sky of dawn and the still, opal seas with wavering flame. To Jerott, clothed and bandaged, dark circles under his sleepless eyes, it was as cool and remote after

176

the hell he had endured as watermusic heard in a dream. Through the rasping ache in his brain, he concentrated on the Marshal's words.

It was not des Roches's fault that the two hundred frightened lads had lost their heads in the Châtelet; nor was it the young captain's that he had failed to discover, until they confessed, returning panic-stricken from the dismantled brigantine, that the castle was in danger.

News of the revolt had been confined so far to themselves. Since escape was now hopeless, the Calabrians might indeed settle to helping the defence as the only alternative. Defending this viewpoint, des Roches said flatly, 'They will know for example, that if we allowed this hysterical attempt at slaughter to be known, the garrison would turn and kill them.'

'That which they intended was treason in the field and the whole-sale murder of innocent men, women and children,' said de Herrera. Like Jerott, the Treasurer showed the strain of the night's disasters, but through the weals and grazes on his face, the anger was plain. 'They are vermin, and should be shot like vermin.'

'If you want to help the Turks, that's exactly what you should do,' said Jerott grimly. 'How long d'you think the rest will hold out when they know that their own protectors have tried to kill them?'

The Marshal turned to the captain. 'The burden so far has fallen on you. Is there any means of controlling these men? Or must we treat them, as the Treasurer says, as tried and condemned?'

'They're boys, sir,' said the young man. Tears, Jerott saw, were not far away, though fright and pride were so far upholding him. 'The noise, the foreign tongues, the heat, the fear of the Turks and of the walls falling in on them . . . they're driven crazy with it, that's all. They wouldn't think what damage the gunpowder would do—they'd have no idea of the danger. They wanted to stop pursuit, that's all . . . cause a distraction, and pay back, if you like, the men who made them come here at all. They're only—'

'—Boys,' said the Marshal drily. 'And the men who risked their lives to put the fuse out were little more. Compare them, some time, in your thoughts. Des Roches?'

'For our sakes and theirs, be circumspect,' said the Brother. 'Keep silent. Spread them about the garrison with the strongest and bravest we have. Give them hope, and an example, and they may redeem what they did last night.'

'Or infect the rest,' said Jerott. 'That's the danger. You know that as well as I do. But if St Brabe is being damaged, we need all the men we can get for the entrenchments inside. I don't see there's an alternative. But I think you should see to it that if they're frightened of us, they're even more scared of the Turks. We'd look foolish if they threw the gates open and surrendered.'

'No one will surrender,' said the Marshal sharply. It was what Blyth wanted to hear him say. But watching the Spanish knights, he did not miss the glance they exchanged. The Marshal said, 'We shall do as our Brother suggests and disperse these men quietly among those we can trust. In the meantime—' his tired gaze softened—'you have all done more than any man could require of you, and you must be yearning to rest. You have leave to retire. Your posts will be held for you. Tell this also to the men who helped you. . . . Where is M. Crawford, for example? I trust he has taken no hurt. We owe him much.'

'He is well, but tired, like ourselves,' said Jerott. Answered like that, there might be no more questions meantime—not that he cared, but he was too damned tired to trouble; to tell them that Lymond wasn't in Tripoli at all. That after the fire, he had recovered to find that Francis Crawford and the Moor he had rescued had both gone, with a small band of freed slaves. And gone, he had realized blankly long ago, straight to the Turkish camp.

IX

The Invalid Cross

(Tripoli, August 1551)

'THE guns have begun again,' Galatian had said in the darkest part of the night when, thought forcibly suspended, she had willed herself to sleep despite the heat and the sand flies and the thickening opacity of her body through which, dully distorted, came the effervescence and pangs and plebeian protests of abdominal routine abused. Unthinkingly strong all her life; her flesh a mere vessel for the violent, untamed artistry of the mind, Cormac O'Connor's mistress had never suffered this indignity, or troubled to imagine it. But, keeping herself alive on goat's milk and fruit, and feeding too on the strange and deep resources of near mysticism which sometimes before she had called upon at need, she bore the days better than Galatian, who feared everything and voiced his fear. When just after dawn, the curtain trembled and Graham Malett quietly entered, she felt, however, nothing but relief.

In this strange world she was not foolish enough to expect security. But in Malett she had come to recognize wisdom, of the detached kind that pleased her best. He had, she discovered, a humbly used skill in social salvage which he used with delicacy. In the short periods he spent with her, his lack of sentiment, the absence of prying, moral or otherwise, his complete disinterestedness, were dearly appreciated opiates for her pride. Like all of d'Aramon's delegation, he came and went now at will. Sinan and Dragut gave them all at least a limited trust. On the surface they were treated as guests, although in fact nothing could have penetrated the guard surrounding the Turkish encampment, either from within or without. So, when the knight lowered his head and came in, Oonagh, who slept as she walked, in the clothes she had worn at the surrender of Gozo, rose and went to him. 'There is news?'

Cool-skinned, even in the milk-warm airlessness of after-night, he bent from his splended height as he sometimes did and kissed her brow, before settling her gently on the cushions again. Then he knelt, the white cross glimmering on his thin dark jerkin, and said, 'The news is bad. The Turkish battery is in full use again. Instead of taking advantage of the lull, as we had hoped, the Order has had to face a revolt inside the castle. It is over, but it may recur.'

'How do they know? Another spy from Tripoli? I hope he survived.' The last renegade to reach them had been clumsy. The Turkish outposts seeing him running from the city had shot him before he could speak. She remembered that he had once been a knight, like Graham Malett, and regretted her words when she saw his face tighten a little under its deep tan. But he only said, 'Some . . . legitimate refugees have escaped this time—Muslim slaves from the dungeons of Tripoli, led by a Spanish Moor from Algiers. They stole robes and turbans from the town to hide their branding and shaven heads, and slipped over the walls during the excitement. My child. . . .'

She had been thinking, but at the change of tone she looked up, the long, heavy hair fallen back from her fine bones. Always kind, he took her two thin boy's hands in his. 'My child, they have brought your friend with them.'

There was a long silence. Then, 'M. le Comte de Sevigny?' the woman said, ironically; and Graham Malett smiled suddenly at the show of pride. 'Francis Crawford, yes,' he said.

'Come, dear soul, to rescue the maiden from the dragon,' said Oonagh. 'He has been told, as we planned it, that the maiden is dead?'

'He had already found out that you were not, before I knew he was in the camp,' said Gabriel. 'Nicolay and I saw him with the others being taken into one of the big pavilions to rest after the interrogation. They are all spent and some of them are ill; there has been whipping at the castle. The Moor is apparently his friend.'

'Then what does your wisdom suggest now?' asked Oonagh. 'That I die forthwith?'

In the strengthening light, Gabriel's blue gaze was extraordinarily clear. Still holding her two hands he said quietly, 'He is here. The worst of the risks are over. He may even contrive to free you after all. There is apparently a brigantine waiting in the bay where you could be hidden until the outcome of the siege is known.'

'You have *spoken* to him?'

'He is in my tent. Nicolas and the Moor distracted the sentry and we got him away from the others in the dark. . . . My child, we talked of the risk to this man; we talked of his future. Now that he is here, how do you weigh these against a chance of freedom?'

Slowly, Oonagh O'Dwyer drew her hands from his; slowly she rose and walked to the far side of the tent. Behind the curtain, Galatian in the inner room slept, his mouth open, in a smell of sweat and dried blood and the oil they had used on his scars. She dropped the velvet and turned. 'You are the man of God. I cannot compete with the saints. If you want him, do as you wish,' she said. 'In these airs, anyone might sicken and die in a day.'

In turn Gabriel rose, his splendid presence filling the tent; the new sun spilled through the canvas on his cropped golden head. 'You should have been a queen,' he said. 'You who can maintain what is right when the man in question lies less than twenty yards from your bed. . . . My God is not so jealous or so harsh, my child, that he requires that of you. With our help and what he had prepared for you, surely you will escape from this camp. And when you are free, remember because of the sacrifice that was not asked of you that your future is not his.'

'I know already that it is not,' said Oonagh. 'But if you are caught helping us, the Turks will kill you. I cannot accept that.'

'I do not offer it to you,' said Gabriel gently. 'That is *my* sacrifice. Do you wish to see him?'

Lymond, whom had she been born ten years later might have been her first and only love; whom Gabriel with the rest assumed had taken her as a political pawn among the careless ranks of his mistresses, his loose-living libertine peers. And it was not so. For all their short knowledge of each other, they had been enemies, and had respected each other as enemies. Until at last for her own reasons and Ireland's, she had set out one night to seduce him, and he had forestalled her, and taken her soul.

One night. And they had never since met until now when, freshened as best she could in the meagre water allowed her, the glossy hair burdened in veiling, her soiled robes replaced by a snow-white burnous by Gabriel, whose guards smiled at him, and whose movements to and from her tent were not questioned—until, walking steadily at the tall knight's shoulder, she crossed the sandy gravel from her tent to his, and stepped with him into the masked light within.

It seemed at first empty of life: a travelling tent hastily furnished with rugs, cushions, a low table, Gabriel's few necessary possessions, and his shabby altar, a trace of incense lingering still. Then she followed his gaze.

At her feet lay Francis Crawford, lost for once to the world in a heavy, unnatural slumber, his oiled skin hardly hidden by a loosely-flung cloak. The limber body she remembered, muscled like a cat's, was griddled with burns; and there were fresh marks on the side of his face below the impeccable fair hair, barely ruffled. He must have lain unmoving where he dropped. 'Don't waken him,' said Oonagh, her voice harsh.

'I must,' said Gabriel. 'They will visit the tents soon.'

'What will you do?'

Graham Malett smiled. 'Being what I am, I am allowed my small altar in the most private part of the tent. Behind its draperies, there is room for more than one sinner. . . . He is wakening. The burns you

181

see are superficial; they have all worked without sleep for some nights. . . . Francis? I have brought someone to see you. I shall be just outside the tent if you want me.'

Silently he left. Oonagh did not hear him. She saw Lymond stir; halt a second, eyes closed, as his brain assessed the situation, and then continue the movement until her shadow fell full across his face and his hand lay lax close to his dagger. She said, 'There are none left to fear me in this world now, and yourself least of all. I hear Scotland is well lost for Paradise.'

Of a denser blue, his eyes did not cleanse with their candour, like Gabriel's. Instead there was the shock of his laughter: mocking, tantalizing, real. His face came to life with it, regardless of the stiffened skin and the exhaustion he had not shaken off. In three movements he was standing, his hands resting lightly on her shoulders, smiling at her as if they were playing against each other once more, duelling at her aunt's house at Neuvy. 'I hope to have both,' he said. 'Although in Ireland I have found Paradise already. . . . Does Gabriel offer you a chaste kiss on the brow?'

'Barely that,' said Oonagh. The desert, the hot breath of the seraglio, the gunfire, had all gone. 'But they tell me you're practising for the vows yourself. It seems a desperate waste of natural talent.'

'Then I'd better study the entire subject again,' he said, considering. It was a strange way to ask and be granted permission, but as he took her in his arms she had time to remember that he knew perfectly about her livid relationship with Galatian, and that in his immoral way he had a delicacy at least matching Gabriel's. Then he kissed her fully on her cold mouth, and the blood ran through her fine skin in pain and thankfulness; and she wept with her black hair fallen on his shoulder and arm, while the pulse of his heart beat quietly against her cheek.

And because of that thing, she found the firmness to draw off, her tears stopped, and say with something very nearly the same as her old brusqueness, '*Ah Mhuire* . . . nostalgia, the curse of the Irish. Were you in the way of addressing me on some subject, or are we both to crawl under the altar cloth when Sinan Pasha comes?'

He let her go, his eyes lit with delight, and said, 'It struck me it would be a stale, dull journey home without a lady, and a fine brigantine waiting out there with the biggest rascal unhung in charge. Would you come, at the cost of a risk or two, or are you perhaps more attached than I should guess to . . . the Turk?'

He did not mean the Turk, and she would not allow the euphemism. 'Galatian is safe. He will be ransomed eventually,' she said. And after a moment, as he still waited, she added, 'I have filled my debt there.'

182

'You would come? It would be a little troublesome.' He smiled.

'How?'

'The Moor with his party are to be sent to the shore batteries tomorrow. There they are within range of the castle fire and must fight or die. So Sinan plans to take no risks with their loyalty. You and I will be there, dressed as the other slaves.'

'Clothes?'

'The Moor will get them. No one will notice the change in numbers. At any rate, no one would choose to go to the seat of the fighting. And at nightfall . . . we take to the sea. It is warmer, Oonagh, than your damned Irish breakers. And on the brigantine, Thompson will wait for you. It looks empty and dismantled; no one will think of you there. And when Tripoli falls, I shall come.'

For a second, her mind filled with questions, she missed it. Then she realized what he had implied and said soberly, '*When?*'

'It can't stand.'

'None of us knows the Lord's will,' said Gabriel's quiet voice; and the sun blazed on the deep carpet and was extinguished again as he came in. 'Are you so sure?'

'My God, of course it's going to fall,' said Lymond, exasperated. 'Despite the knights running in and out of the chapel like hysterical mice. Sedition, suspicion and rivalry conditioned by passionate worship in church or out of it, or on a cannibal isle for that matter—they smell just the same.'

'You are not afraid, we know, of blasphemy,' said Gabriel wearily. 'The blame for that is the Order's. If Tripoli falls, it will be no more than another failure of the same kind. I am right, am I not? We have driven you from us? You mean to take the lady home, and you will not return?'

There was a pause. Watching the two men, both fair, both self-contained and prodigally gifted, Oonagh sensed that the query was more pressing than even it seemed; that more was at stake than the impugnment of what was the greatest Order of Chivalry the world had ever known.

Lymond knew it too. He said slowly, 'The only redress at present lies with the knights. Nothing more can be done until de Homedès is dead or discredited. That is not my affair.'

'No. . . . You will never return,' said Gabriel with bitterness, and was silent.

'I have to leave first,' said Lymond mildly. 'When Dragut is in Tripoli, ask me again. Oonagh. . . .'

'It is time for me to go. I am in your hands. Tell me when you are ready to leave,' she said. And after a moment, ' 'Twill be a queer thing, to fight on the same side at last.'

'We were always on the same side, you and I,' said Lymond. 'Only, *mo chridh*, you did not always know it.'

*

It was not enough, to sleep in separate tents with only twenty yards between them on this, perhaps their last night on earth. For how could such a masquerade deceive the Turks? Even muffled in robes, with her black hair wound under a turban—though she might pass for a boy, would her sunburnt skin pass for theirs? She had none of their language. If they were sent to their posts early, she had the whole day to live through without detection before they could slip into the sea—she who knew nothing of cannon.

Galatian was restless, as if he knew. And when at last, in the inner room, he had dropped into uneasy sleep, Oonagh O'Dwyer lay listening to the guns and thinking of Lymond, whose future she had lightly extinguished, as Graham Malett had forecast. And out of friendship, his kiss had told her. Out of friendship only. She had said to Gabriel, against her will, 'Shall I see him again?' And Gabriel had said shortly, 'He is not a child. If he wishes, he can no doubt find means of coming to you.'

But so far he had not wished, and she lay alone, under the fine lawn sheet Gabriel had got for her, her day clothes, full of grit and soaked already with sweat, discarded beyond. She could feel her body, only slightly rounded as yet, smooth under the cloth; her swathing hair was silk under her cheek. All to waste? All to waste?

When, late at night, the shadow darkened the starlight behind her silent shrouds, and the door, whispering, admitted a deeper shadow, soft-footed and deft, it found her already perfect as a flower brought to its full-breathing height. This was no frantic helpless Galatian; though speed was their master and silence, because of the sick man sleeping so near, a desperate essential. A stray beam from the closing curtain struck silver, once, from his fair head as finding her, he knelt. He said, '*Mo chridh* . . .' once, in the same whisper she had heard already that day. Air breathed on her aching body; and then she was no longer alone.

She sobbed once, under her breath, when Galatian, half-disturbed by some sound, called her sleepily by name. She need not have feared. Nothing could have stopped the man possessing her now. With him, she came nearer, reached and passed the threshold of delights against the clamour of Galatian's voice.

United in dazzling peace, they heard the sick man's voice at length trail unanswered into sleep. And presently the man at her side moved, murmured some half-ironic tenderness against her lips and was gone, the air stirring freely once more on her skin. For a long time afterwards she lay blankly content, thinking vaguely of the future, and Graham Malett's voice, long ago, saying '*sacrifice . . . sacrifice. . . .*' It sounded thin and monk-like and even pathetic to her complacent flesh, which could make an animal, if it chose, from laughter itself.

*

In later, soberer weeks, when bitterly she began to wonder if ever she had had the means to attract, she was to wonder if in that brief passage Lymond had hoped for oblivion, as she had once received it from him. For that afternoon de Seurre, a Knight of the Order and d'Aramon's other captain, walking like a drunk man through the joyous clamour of the alien camp, had brought them the news that the white flag was flying from Tripoli. Galatian, she remembered, had laughed. And Graham Malett, without a word, had risen and walked out of the tent.

Shortly after that, the guns stopped and they learned that two of Sinan Pasha's officers had transmitted the Turk's invitation to send deputies to the camp to treat. A little later, she and d'Aramon, Nicolay, de Seurre and Gabriel, watching silently in the background, saw the knights arrive, close-guarded by marching Janissaries. They had sent Commander Fuster of Majorca and the Chevalier Guenara, both Spanish, both enemies of France. Gabriel alone made the sign of the cross as they passed and Guenara, noticing, hesitated and would have stopped if the escort hadn't jolted him forward with some brusqueness. The Order, she supposed with remote pity, had never stood lower than that.

Soon they heard the terms. The knights were willing to surrender the city and castle of Tripoli provided that Suleiman's general would give the Governor, the knights, the garrison and the natives life and liberty, with ships to carry them and all their belongings to Malta or Sicily. And Sinan, black eyes cold, his dark Jewish face watchful, had laughed, and when he had done laughing had said, paring his nails, that he might begin to consider their wants when he had been reimbursed by the Order for all Osmanli expenses of the expedition. The knights were to pay the soldiers of Islâm for their trouble at Mdina, Gozo and Tripoli.

Even Fuster and Guenara could not conceivably agree; no man could. It was precisely why Sinan had asked it. It was Gabriel who waylaid Dragut, while tempers were rising, and as a businessman might, laid before him the facts Sinan Pasha had ignored. To prolong the siege might allow help to reach the city. Desperation itself might drive the knights to a last, costly stand. More: by ruining the walls, Sinan would expose himself when in possession. The knights might retake the city before its defences could be repaired, since the season was near when no blockade was possible by sea.

He added one thing more; and how much it cost him, no one was allowed to know. 'In any case,' said Malett, Knight Grand Cross, to the Turkish corsair Dragut, 'once the treaty is signed, his excellency the General is master, and can keep it or not as he feels inclined. In his place, none need deign to quibble.'

And Dragut, clapping the knight companionably on the shoulder with his broad palm, had gone off to intercept Sinan Pasha, who by Suleiman's orders must regard his advice. The delegation, chivvied from the General's tent at sword-point, waited drawn-faced under the canopies while Dragut and Sinan Pasha conferred. Granted leave, unexpectedly, to approach them, the Baron d'Aramon and de Seurre found that, for the moment, the barrier of suspicion and hatred had dissolved in their fear.

It seemed then unlikely that either knight would reach Tripoli again unless, shamefully, they agreed to the Turkish terms. Out, disastrously, came all that had happened at the castle since the Calabrians' attempt on the arsenal. Spreading the disaffected among the loyal garrison had only spread the sedition until, fired with promise of support, the young peasants had at last abandoned their posts, seized their commanding officer and threatened his life unless he forced the Marshal to surrender Tripoli to the Turks and save all their lives.

The Marshal, learning on the steps of his church that his soldiers refused to fight and mobbed by shouting mutineers, had fought his way to a hasty council of war where, once again, French and Spanish interests split the Order from end to end. In vain de Poissieu, spokesman for the French, maintained that the St Brabe breach could yet be guarded by good entrenchments, provided the soldiers did their duty. He was shouted down with all the old arguments, by de Herrera and the rest. It would suit France to prolong a hopeless fight. 'Under your protection, M. l'Ambassadeur, what can they lose?' said Fuster bitterly to d'Aramon now. 'Whereas we, the Emperor's subjects, can expect no quarter, as you see.'

In his wisdom, d'Aramon met this with silence; and, because above all things, the two delegates needed to talk, the tale was resumed. It had been decided to risk a daylight inspection of the breach provided the rebels returned to their posts. But even the promise of double pay, in the end, could not weigh against de Herrera's repeated insistence that they were being duped: that the Governor had no intention of surrendering, and would rather be killed in the breach.

At length, while the rebels huddled together, sheltering from the unceasing guns, Guenara himself had gone to the breach, since no French knight would be trusted.

'And?' said d'Aramon without expression, reflecting nothing of the Spaniard's low-spoken violence.

'It was without prospects,' said Guenara shortly. 'All that is left of the wall on that side would have been down before night. If we had tried to make de Poissieu's brilliant entrenchments we should have simply thrown away lives. The rebels understood that.'

'They forced you to surrender?' The irony in de Seurre's voice was barely concealed.

Fuster's, in turn, showed his resentment. 'They demanded that the white flag be shown instantly. Or they would let the infidels inside themselves.'

'So falls the Order in North Africa,' said the French Ambassador; and this time, the distaste showed.

A little after that, the deputies were sent for again by a thoughtful Sinan Pasha, Dragut at his side. The treaty as suggested by the Marshal de Vallier would after all stand, and Sinan Pasha himself was ready to swear by the Grand Seigneur's head to observe it.

On the Turkish side, he had only one condition to make. The General wished the Marshal de Vallier to come in person, to discuss the sea transport required for the great evacuation. An officer must be sent as hostage for the Turkish ships' safe return. At the same time Sinan Pasha would send a Turkish officer as hostage to Tripoli in the deputies' care.

The change of heart was too sudden, the terms too suave. Yet, what could they do? Bolstered only with pride, Fuster and Guenara at length left, with the so-called prisoner whose presence meant nothing in the Oriental philosophy of expendable life. 'You fools!' said the Chevalier de Seurre to the air as he looked after them. 'If you bring de Vallier here, you are digging his grave.'

So much only Gabriel had waited to hear. Returning to his tent he walked like a blind man, ignoring Lymond, deftly busy within, and dropped on his knees before the cheap, wrought altar, his head bent.

The other man also, it seemed, had heard the news. He finished the neat package of clothing he was making, and was proceeding with meticulous care to sharpen two most handsome Turkish daggers before he broke the silence, still without looking up. 'And is this the soldier rebuking the monk or the monk rebuking the soldier?' he said.

But, saint or fighting man, Graham Malett's face was invisible between his robed arms, and though his praying hands locked suddenly white on the altar, he said nothing at all.

Next day, returning to her tent from the permitted exercise in the milder heat of the early hours, Oonagh found a parcel concealed in the cushions where last night her lover had lain, and beneath it, a dagger. Inside the parcel were the cap, the turban, the tunic and belt, the kirtled robe and soft leggings she must wear as an Os-manli; and a note. 'Dress. The one who calls for you will arrange what you cannot. Afterwards, remember you are dumb.'

Thus simply her greatest fears, the turban, her lack of Turkish, were met. Before she dressed, she went for the last time to Galatian.

He was better; almost ready to walk. If he had been a man still, she thought, none of this would have been possible. Indiscreet, im-portunate, he would have driven Gabriel, every man, from the door. Yet he had cherished her on that queer and violent escape from her past; had installed her as his own, and fed and kept her since on Malta and Gozo. Even now, the food she ate was given her because of him. She said, seeing him jump as he always did when she entered, 'You will be safe now, Galatian. Every knight is to be ransomed.'

His heavy face was sulky, sticky already with the heat. 'There will be prejudice against me. Who knows what lies will have been told?'

If only the man would stand up to what he had done! She tried, in spite of her contempt, to find the right words. But she had not the patience, or the compassion which alone might redeem the Chevalier de Césel now. 'At least,' she said, her round vowels honey soft on her despising breath, 'at least you can fairly put your back into your vows of poverty and obedience, since there never was a knight in the Order so chaste as you will be now. Good-bye, Galatian!'

Another man would have cursed her, or even stirred himself, in spite of the pain, to confront and grip her. The knight of Gozo up-braided her like a disappointed woman, and the short-breathed phrases and unvarying pitch of it buzzed in her ears as she changed.

Gabriel, standing with d'Aramon's party at the door of their tent, saw the fresh contingent of Moors and Janissaries march off to the shore as the sun began to lose its first white shuddering heat that afternoon. Lymond he picked out beside the big Moor who had ostensibly led the escape from Tripoli. In unaccustomed white with the muslin bound expertly round his head, he looked quite at home; he did not glance over his shoulder. Oonagh he found finally walking behind, young and slight, her skin lightly stained, as was Lymond's, to deepen the tan. Without the veiling black hair all the Irish breeding of her face was exposed to the light, but no fear showed. Nor was it any spiritual faith which sustained her, as Gabriel well knew, but a fatalistic, mystical trust in Francis Crawford.

Shortly after that, the man sent as Turkish hostage to Tripoli returned to tell Sinan Pasha that his terms were agreed. Marshal Gaspard de Vallier, Governor of Tripoli for the knights, was coming to the Turks' camp to parley, with only his friend de Montfort to support him.

Long before the Marshal arrived, his harbinger had spread the news that the Christian garrison was rent now from side to side: that against every counsel of prudence and humanity the visit of the Marshal had been arranged, on the rebels' insistence, so that on this elderly, pitiable knight the strength of Turkish good faith might be tested.

No besieged group in such extremes of disunity could survive, the Turkish officer observed with deference to Sinan Pasha. Whatever the nominal terms of the treaty, in fact the General could make what conditions he chose.

*

Oonagh's task was to carry food, water, ammunition from the deep entrenchments by the shore to the forward ditches under the chipped and broken walls of Tripoli, and the emplacements where the cannon squatted, braced on the timbers of the beached and over-thrown galleys.

The guns were silent for the parley, but the drilled and naked servants of the guns were using every second of the respite like fairy gold, to cleanse, oil, replace, restock. All afternoon the work went on under the eye and tongue of their captain, and she wondered that she had ever been afraid of detection. These men were too busy for that. Only the captain, treating her as the mute lad of the Moor's styling, had taken a moment now and then to finger her as she passed and repassed until, suddenly alive to the risk, she arranged her route differently.

Lymond, she saw, worked at the Moor's side, thus relieved of the need to use much of his Arabic, and did so as if he had handled culverin all his life. He probably had, she thought; and wondered how he felt, repairing the mouth that had blown death into this stronghold, and might do so again.

A strange feeling began to grow on her that afternoon. As she darted from rock to rock and foothold to foothold with the leather flasks, the satchels, the sackloads of powder, she felt neither sickness nor strain. All her despised feminine feebleness had vanished, and in its place she had something as near happiness as she had probably ever attained.

When at last the light mellowed in the quick African twilight, she was dazed, realizing that the time of waiting was past. By then she had eaten, grinning wordlessly at the mimed cameraderie of sweating men, coarsely moustached, whom she had seen just now prostrate themselves in silent worship as nobly as the robed knights in St Lawrence. They treated her, now they had leisure, with a sly, teasing roughness to which her own hard fibre responded. She was not afraid. Dusk hid her identity; her wit had no frontiers. Then it was dark.

189

Lymond came for her very soon, laconic in Arabic, signing to her what to do. He had contrived some task at the waterfront, as he had had to do. They had spoken no word of English since they set out. Even now, holding her elbow as she stumbled over the tumbled rock, he said nothing that any man could not hear. Then, momentarily hidden by an escarpment, he pulled her down to her knees, and laying quick hands on her glimmering robes, began to peel them from her down to her shift. Then from his own clothing he pulled something dark and tossing it to her, left her alone with it while he stripped. Underneath he wore the same dark, tight tunic that she had just slipped on. It was, she recognized suddenly, something of Gabriel's. Then he took her arm.

At the edge of the still, dark pool that was the sea, at the brimming edge of freedom where no boat was to be seen, she spoke the first words of the few they were to exchange. 'I cannot swim. You know it?'

In the dark she saw the flash of his smile. 'Trust me.' And he drew her with a strong hand until the green phosphorescence beaded her ankles, and deeper, and deeper, until the thick milk-warm water, almost unfelt, was up to her waist. She heard him swear feelingly to himself as the salt water searched out, discovered his burns. Then with a rustle, she saw his pale head sink back in the quiet sea and at the same moment she was gripped and drawn after him, her face to the stars, drawn through the tides with the sea lapping like her lost hair at her cheeks, the drive of his body beneath her pulling them both from the shore. They were launched on the long journey towards the slim shape, black against glossy black, which was the brigantine, with Thompson on board.

She never knew how long a swim that was, for she had one task: to make his work possible. Her body limp, her limbs brushing the surface of the sea, she took air at the top of his thrust; learned after the first gagging mistake to close every channel to the sudden dip, the molesting wave that slapped suddenly over her cheek. The hard grip under her armpits never altered, nor did Lymond's own breathing for a long time vary at all.

Above the little plash and hiss of their moving, there was a deepening silence as the bustle of the shore fell away. The guns were silent yet. Above them, lit by a single, anxious lamp, the white speck of surrender hung from the castle battlements. Lymond lifted his head, supporting her, to judge his distance as he had done from time to time, and it was only when he spoke that she realized with a shock how much sheer will-power that level, timeless porterage had cost. 'We're nearly there,' he said; and sliding round supported her so that she too, upright, could see the high sides of the brigantine blocking out the dark sky at their back. As they watched, a pinpoint of light winked on and off again and he laughed, without any breath to do it with, and said, 'Thompson. If he tries to buy you . . . refer him to me!'

And in that second a skiff, its lamps blazing, shot out from behind the brigantine and, oars flashing, bore straight down on them.

Lymond said one word, '*Breathe!*' before the waters closed over her head. She had seen the robed, shouting Janissary in the prow of the boat, the glint of darts and scimitar and, between the rowers, the bound figure of a man in hose and shirt, his mouth sealed by a cloth. It was Thompson the corsair.

She went under on a strained gulp of air, thinking the brigantine was no use to them now. Exhausted and weaponless out at sea, they faced a boatload of armed men. . . . Then, her black hair fronding about her, she had no thoughts as her brain darkened without air. Suddenly, the cruel grip that had carried her down thrust her upwards again, and the collar of the sea found and broke against her head. Wildly filling her lungs she found that above them now was the brigantine, and that Lymond had taken them into its lee. Her hand, guided by his, touched cold wood, slimy with weed, and then something else, fat and slippery, that pricked in her palm. A rope.

In her ear, his voice was no more than a breath. 'Hold on as long as you can. I shall be back.' Then he was gone.

The boat was circling. Masked as yet by the hulk above her, Oonagh saw the tilting lamplight move sweeping round and retrace its path. The Janissaries had lost them, she realized, for the moment, and were searching again for the two heads, black in the shimmering path of their light. Then she heard a shout and, her heart shaking her numb, exhausted body, saw that the oars had accelerated, were moving swiftly and purposefully towards a sudden brush in the water: a revolving darkness which resolved itself into the head and shoulders of a swimmer brought at last to the surface for air, before sliding below the dark waters again. Above the speeding boat, a fan of silver particles rose, arched and fell, and kneeling men shouted against one another and pointed. Darts. And there, lancing the night like a silver needle, the shaft of a spear.

These were fishermen. And this living man in the water, their fish.

Living still; for casting suddenly at loss, the boat turned, a glinting fishbone of oars, and turned again before darting suddenly, propelled by triumph, at a tangent once more. The shouting, clear across the water, reached a climax and cut off again. The swimmer had surfaced and submerged once more.

It happened again, and then again; always in an unexpected direction, and always with a coiling speed that took him down before the missiles struck. And always, too, farther and farther away from the brigantine where the woman was hiding.

Later, she realized that he was waiting for something else too. But now, a paralysed debtor, she watched the game being played out. She could do nothing. Of what use to shout? It wouldn't save him; and he would sooner end, she guessed, in the sea. Now, drive himself as he would, his dives were briefer and less and less swift, so that he surfaced always within range, in that network of barbs. She heard the commanding officer laugh then and give an order, and a man holding a small bow of the Turkish kind came and stood in the bows.

There was something odd about the arrow. Then she saw the thin, tough cord at its base, and found that it was not an arrow, but a harpoon.

'*Stay down.*' Surely, from her Celtic breeding, she could transmit to him this silent anguish? '*Stay down. And I shall let go this little cord, and share your rest in the sea.*'

She saw him rise then close to the boat, all his skill worn out at last, his head flung back. Saw the archer take aim. Then saw the black sky, dressed at its foot with the sprinkled lights of besieged Tripoli crack across and across with red flame; flame which brightened and grew and took to itself other crackling small fires, all woven about the shore where the Turkish guns rested; where Lymond had spent the long, profitable afternoon.

For perhaps five seconds, the gaze of every man in the boat was on that blazing, unaccountable *feu de joie*. In that small space, with the last shreds of his powers, Lymond reached the skiff on the side where Thompson, bound impotently, lay. There was only time to slash once at the pirate's bound wrists; then Thompson himself was overboard, Lymond's knife in his hand, and below water like an eel, there to free his ankles, tear the seal from his mouth, and obey Lymond's hiss in their own tongue. 'The brigantine . . . *Get the woman.*'

Thompson was a practical man. No one in Turkish hands ever argued with a chance of freedom. No one, burdened with a man as spent as Lymond was, could do more than expect an early, cheap death for them both. He abandoned Lymond, since that was what Lymond wanted, and with the life-saving knife swam off in the darkness to the brigantine, where he was not pursued until far too late since Francis Crawford, from the limbo virtually of a sleepwalker, made his enforced boarding with enough spectacular venom to keep the rowers engaged for much longer than they enjoyed.

Unfortunately, when Thompson had finished sprinting about the ocean, in which he was perfectly at home, beneath or on top, he reached the brigantine to find it entirely deserted inside and out. After an interval of faithful casting about—for he remembered Lymond as a connoisseur in bedfellows—he gave up and drifted off to another boat he had fitted up in his spare time, before that little party had surprised him tonight on the brigantine. Before he went, he noted that there was another skiff missing. Possibly the guard they had left on board after capturing him had got hold of the woman and was rowing her ashore while all the games were going on, to capture the credit. Either that, or the poor bitch had drowned.

He got on board, shook himself like a pony, and peeling off his wet clothes, sat down in a towel, cup in hand, to sip wine and watch the fireworks on shore until they went out just before dawn. Then, not cold but pleasantly tired, he went off to bed.

*

It was the last dawn any of them were to see over Tripoli. For by then Gaspard de Vallier, Governor of the city, was lying in irons aboard Sinan Pasha's own galley after an interview in which the Turkish general, receiving the Marshal in his camp with the barest sketch of courtesy, had thrown the treaty in his face and demanded immediate payment, once more, of all the Sultan's campaign expenses by the knights. And when de Vallier, disbelieving, had remonstrated, Sinan Pasha's fury had burst. The Osmanli made and kept treaties with men of honour; not with dogs of Christians who owed their lives at Rhodes to the Grand Seigneur's clemency, and that on the promise that the Order should never in future attack the Sultan's subjects or exercise piracy on his seas, but should respect his flag in all places. 'But,' ended Sinan Pasha, and spat, 'no sooner free; no sooner settled in that robbers' nest in Malta, but the great and honourable knights returned to their old thieving trade. . . .'

It was not true, but the quarrel was long past dealing in truths. In vain the Marshal, gripping de Montfort's arm, offered to send to Malta for the original Rhodes agreement to prove that no such terms had existed. In vain, flaring up too weakly and too late, he had announced that he was ready to tear up yesterday's treaty if need be and resume fighting. Sinan Pasha's anger and also his interest had died. At a gesture, the Marshal was dismissed, against every code of gentle practice; in two sentences his companion de Montfort was told the terms he might place before his fellow knights on his return. Either the money would be paid to the Turkish general as he asked, or the whole garrison and city would suffer for it, and soldiers and inhabitants both would be sold off as slaves.

As de Montfort, sallow and staring, left with his escort his manacled leader called to him from the ground. 'My son . . . inform Commander Copier that it is my wish that he act in these straits as honour solely dictates. . . . And that he should regard the Governor of Tripoli as dead.'

This time, neither d'Aramon nor Graham Malett prevailed. In spite of all the Ambassador could do, de Vallier left that evening to be put in irons like a criminal on the General's flagship, while the knight de Montfort returned to Tripoli with the General's ultimatum.

Through all that night few of d'Aramon's party slept, and Graham Malett not at all. Sharing his vigil was Nicolas de Nicolay, the only Frenchman who had known of Francis Crawford's presence in the camp, and who had stayed with Gabriel since Lymond and the woman Oonagh had left.

Hands clasped over his comfortable belly, the little geographer was dozing on his pallet when the explosions began. He exclaimed, and began to squirm to his feet; but Malett was before him, striding out through the tent door to stare at the red sky over the sea; buffeted by running figures as the camp, like a shrouded anthill came suddenly alive.

They were still there when Francis Crawford was heaved into the settlement and tumbled on the coarse sand beside Sinan Pasha's pavilion, where he rolled and lay still. As the flares identified the sun-bleached, sodden head Graham Malett took a pace forward, and then stopped. It was d'Aramon, roused by the explosions and for his own sake ignorant of all that had happened, who thrust forward saying, 'I know that man. Where did you find him?'

From the darkness beyond a jewelled *caftán* glinted and the guttural, easy voice of Dragut replied. 'He was found by some of my men who had been attracted to the brigantine in the bay by a little unexplained activity the other night. There was a woman with him.'

'*A woman?*' There was no mistaking the utter bewilderment in the Ambassador's voice and Dragut, satisfied, permitted his bearded mouth a smile of serenest contempt. 'He was evidently trying to escape with the woman belonging to the Governor of Gozo. It seems very likely that he was responsible for the firing of the ordnance before he left. You say you know him?'

'He came here from Malta on one of my ships,' said d'Aramon after a pause. Whatever damage this misguided chivalry had done, it was too late to deny it. 'He is a Scotsman, a mercenary newly come to assist the Religion. He left the ship, I was told, after it anchored in Tripoli Bay, and presumably swam ashore.'

'Where he has remained hidden under the sea-shells ever since?'

D'Aramon shrugged. 'He may have joined the garrison in the castle. I have not seen him since.'

The ritual crescent bright on his turban, Dragut stepped into the torchlight and bent. Lymond's stained lids were heavily closed and his bruised and blistered skin sparkled with salt. They had had their fun with him, clearly, but no bones were broken—by order, perhaps. Below de Nicolay's uneasy gaze, Dragut took between finger and thumb part of the dark cloth that still clung to the swimmer and said, 'His presence here, at any rate, is not unknown to the Knights of St John.' And straightening, the corsair turned his jewelled slipper into the inert body and kicked, so that like a puppet it rolled spread-eagled to d'Aramon's feet.

De Nicolay, behind, drew in his breath with a hiss and held it, as the corsair's treacle-dark gaze fastened, first on him, then on de Seurre, d'Aramon, Gabriel . . . all the pale-skinned, silk-clad gentlemen standing about. 'He is thy lover?' he said. 'Or the mate of another among thee?'

From the darkness, Gabriel's deep voice spoke. 'In the Christian world, these things are forbidden.'

'Then who cares what becomes of him?' said Dragut. 'He is not a knight. If we find he is guilty of these unhappy accidents on the shore, my people will demand redress.'

He paused. Below him, jarred perhaps by the brutal movement, Lymond moved a little, his head back, pressing moisture on the small stones. In the east, the sky was paling. 'These things are bitter to the tongue,' said Dragut peaceably, 'where sweetness is pleasing. Have him washed and most carefully bound, while we inquire into this thing further. When the sun is high, it is most seemly that soul and body together should taste the reprimand of Dragut—ah, the dog wakens! Take him, then, inside.'

Lymond opened his eyes on Dragut. Then, confusedly, his gaze swept the murmuring circle above him, pausing nowhere, and returned to Dragut Rais again. Two soldiers moved forward.

Before they could touch him, d'Aramon said sharply, 'Wait!' And as Dragut turned he said, 'What injury are you planning? I warn you, this man is attached to the Order.'

'I understand it.' Dragut's tone was mild. 'And for instigating an act of war during the truce between the Order and ourselves, he would therefore forfeit his life. That, I believe, is just in all countries? And as I have said,' his beard twitched, 'his death will be sweet.'

'How?' d'Aramon demanded.

It was Gabriel's voice which replied. 'It's the old custom, Ambassador. The criminal is soaked in wild honey and buried waist deep in the desert, to die from the sun and the flies.'

In the ensuing uncomfortable silence Nicolas de Nicolay's carping voice shrilly spoke. 'But that is barbaric!'

Dragut turned. 'But you and I, *Hakim*, are barbarians. Or why else are we here?'

Nothing ever shook de Nicolay from a point. 'And the woman? Is she to suffer this too?'

'Ah, the woman!' Now, suddenly, Lymond's eyes were fully open, and Gabriel, watching without cease, saw his gaze and the corsair's slowly lock. Dragut smiled.

'The woman, I fear, suffered something less sweet, as her immodesty deserved. The woman is dealt with. When my men found her, she was sunk entangled in the brigantine rope, and already dead.'

There was a short silence. Under concentrated inspection, not a muscle in Lymond's bruised body moved. His face became not unpleasingly blank, his eyes open to their fullest extent, a beautiful and unusual blue. And then, lightly, he spoke. 'Dear me. And who is going to tell the Governor of Gozo?' he said.

'*Oh, my son*,' said Graham Malett quietly, and turned away suddenly, into the dark. The others watched while Dragut's two henchmen got Lymond on to his feet, and propelled him off to the tents. He walked too, stubbornly, until he got halfway there, and M. l'Ambassadeur du Roi d'Aramon had never been so thankful to see anyone drop to the ground.

*

When Lymond came to himself, he was alone in the stifling tent with Dragut.

Francis Crawford sat up, taking his time. He felt exceedingly sick. The sun was high. He was not bound. He had been washed, patched and dressed in thin garments, possibly of d'Aramon's. There was a guard outside the tent, but not within earshot. Oonagh was dead.

'Allâh be praised, *Emír Giaúr*,' said Dragut equably. 'We feared thou hadst withdrawn thy soul from this unequal world.'

'Not so,' said Lymond, gently surprised, his hands idle in his lap. 'Many doors open on God. To save a woman from shame can be in no way displeasing.'

'It may displease the woman,' said the old corsair blandly. 'But I speak of thy ill-advised cleverness by the shore. Much ordnance was consumed.'

'But none hurt,' said Lymond in the same tone; nor would anyone but Dragut have known that he could not possibly be sure of that.

'Thou art wise, indeed, in dangerous skills,' said Dragut Rais, and allowed the conversation unexpectedly to drop, sitting cross-legged in comfortable thought. The silence had assumed incredible proportions when Dragut at last smiled, and stirring, performed the grave salute he had omitted up till now. 'Thou hast great patience, as I remember,' he said. 'May thy woman find peace. In thine own land, thou wilt find fairer.'

Unsmiling, the other man performed the courtesy in return. 'I did not doubt you,' he said. 'Although the Drawn Sword of Islâm is keen and just.'

'If men of our race had died today, justice would have been done,' said Dragut cheerfully. 'They did not. Without proof, none can

196

convict thee of any crime save the rape of thine own woman. That she died is thy affliction. Thou wilt remain from sight and mind until the Order leaves, and I shall send thee with them.'

'Should I go?' Francis Crawford said. 'Should we all go?'

There was a little silence. Then Dragut said peaceably, 'You wish me to kill for you?' Then as Lymond violently said, 'No!' he smiled, and continued serenely to speak. 'There is no place here for such men as these. To me, thou art welcome ever. But an infidel, a *giaúr*, cannot fight for the Sultan.'

'You do not recommend, then, that I or another should stay?' Lymond said.

'No. I do not recommend either,' said Dragut, 'that thou spillest thy heartsblood for this order of cravens. To every man, his hearth calls. There thy duty may lie.'

All the little colour there was had left Lymond's face. He looked suddenly desperately tired, and sick, and in doubt. Without answering he rose and crossed the small tent. There he stopped and spoke to Dragut over his shoulder, obliquely as Dragut preferred.

'On Thursday, the fifth day of Allâh's creation, He made the angel Sigad id Din, who brought dust and air and fire and water to Allâh from the far corners of the world, from which Adam was next created. Then Sigad id Din entered Paradise with Adam, and taught him to eat the fruits of the earth. . . .'

'True. Thou knowest well our writings,' said Dragut's hoarse, level voice. 'Then Allâh, as thou wilt remember, ordered Sigad id Din to create Eve.'

Lymond, fingering his belt, head bent, said, 'It was a bad Thursday's work.'

'But in the end,' said Dragut peaceably, 'the peacock angel was made by Allâh lord over all the rest. Carry with thee this tale. A hunter went killing sparrows one cold day, and his eyes gave forth tears as he went. Said one bird to another, "Behold, this man weeps." Said the other, "Turn thine eyes from his tears. *Watch his hands*".

'I have always thought,' he added with sudden encouragement, 'that there are in thee the talents for a wondrous peacock.'

'My God, in *Scotland*?' said Lymond, swinging round, all the mockery back in his voice. 'An army of angels would merely dissolve in the rain.'

'Then take an army of men,' said the corsair, raising his thick, greying brows. 'Or was this not in the first place a part of thy mind?'

'And Sigad id Din?' Lymond said.

This time Dragut Rais also got up, smoothing his short coat as he prepared to go at last. 'I have already spoken,' he said.

A moment later and he had gone, having achieved all he intended to do; and Lymond, now lying quietly, his face on his wrists, received the mercy of solitude at last.

For him, the worst battle of Tripoli was fought then, alone on that last morning, when the decision that was to change the course of his life had to be taken, in fatigue and distress and with the echo of his own voice, then and always, bright and cold in his mind.

'Dear me ... dear me ... dear me. ... And who is going to tell the Governor of Gozo?'

Jerott Blyth, told that Lymond could be depressed by the death of a mistress, would have cackled with laughter. As it was, he was in no mood to be merry. For French knights and Spaniards had united at last, and the Order, outraged, had met de Montfort's shaming message with a unanimous decision . . . to fight to the death.

Had they done so, Europe might have echoed through the ages with the Order's martyrdom and fame. As it was, like de Vallier's resistance, it came far too late. The knights had chosen death with honour on the ramparts, but the garrison refused to obey.

Half that night, harangued, exhorted, threatened, with whip and bastinado freely used, the civilians and soldiers in Tripoli held out for their lives. And in the end the knights recognized defeat. At dawn, de Montfort would return to Sinan Pasha with the report that his condition could not be fulfilled, as the city held no money at all. But that, provided the besiegers allowed the Order's Brethren and three hundred people besides to march out freely, the knights would surrender, abandoning the Calabrians and all the rebel garrison to the Turks. Meanwhile, they decided the Moors, who had served the Order so faithfully, were to be given horses and such goods as they could carry, and allowed to leave by St George's Gate at first light to fly to Tunis or Goleta.

By that single act of humanity the defence reaped a strange reward. Some Moors refused to leave the knights they had served so long. Some left and escaped. Some left and were captured by Sinan's outposts before they could taste freedom. It was these, in their fear, who told Sinan Pasha that the knights' intention was to fight to the end, immolating themselves and the whole Turkish army in a final holocaust inside the city walls.

Sinan Pasha did not want to waste lives. Nor did he like to be robbed of his plunder. When, against all expectations, de Montfort appeared with his terms, Sinan Pasha received him cordially, and after the mildest haggling, agreed. Not certainly that three hundred, but that two hundred persons to be selected by the Order should be allowed with all the knights to return free to Malta, and that the Governor should be set at liberty as well.

It was an agreement laced characteristically with malice. When de Vallier, worn and trembling, returned to the castle, escorted with mischievous ceremony to the gates, it was to tell how Sinan Pasha had made his final demand for some kind of payment, and how the Marshal had pointed out that, without authority, he was helpless to comply.

'I told him,' said de Vallier slowly, his veined hands shifting among the useless papers on his desk, 'that I believed and hoped that my brother knights would never agree to his terms, and that I was ready to forfeit my life in that hope.'

He raised his eyes to the driven, sleepless faces about him and Jerott, his tired body propped by the window, sick to the point of vomiting with shame and fury, thought he saw a terrible kind of ragged pride sit on his unshaven face. 'My Brothers, the Lord has heard our prayers. At these words the Turk bowed his head before a greater will than his. Without further abjuration of mine he returned from his companions to say that, his honour being no less than ours, he would ratify the first treaty as drawn up in his camp. All Christians in Tripoli are to have instant liberty, only laying down colours and arms in the city before they leave. Ships are to be provided. I am here, Brethren in Christ, to lead you, every man, woman and little child of the Faith, to freedom. God in His mercy be praised.'

'Then God in His mercy has arranged that we should lead them from the rear,' said Jerott Blyth thinly from the window. 'The entire garrison of Tripoli has just marched away.'

They all talked at once after the first second until, crowding the deep embrasure, they saw that this, the ultimate irony, was true. The soldiers, the Moors, the Calabrians, the men, women and children of Tripoli had not waited for the Order to give its sonorous command to surrender. They had not even waited for the blockades to be laboriously shifted and the city gates, with grim courage, to yawn. Through the breached walls, bundles underarm, they streamed, over the sandy ditches, past the silent cannon, through the gaps of the crumbling buttress of St Brabe, and down to the shore.

'*Freedom!*' de Vallier had called as, mobbed by struggling Tripolitains, he had fought his way from the city gates to the castle. 'Freedom, my friends! The Turks' own ships are to come for you. Wait, and you shall hear!'

But since Sinan Pasha might easily change his mind, the occupiers of Tripoli had not waited. In all the ancient African stronghold of Christ, only the foreign knights of the Order remained.

The rest was bitterest farce. Attired in their crumpled robes over their armour, personal belongings flung together, unfed, unwashed and swordless as requested, the Knights Hospitallers of the Order of St John of Jerusalem rallied, bickering a little through strain, under their scarlet flag at the doors of the empty castle, and marched out through the ruined city of Tripoli and through the big harbour gates. There they were surrounded, neatly and thoroughly, by a shrieking body of Moorish cavalry under the Aga Morat from Tagiura, by prior kind sanction, as now was patent, of Sinan Pasha himself.

These, dismounting, closed cheerfully with the stunned Brethren; felled, stripped and robbed them in the rough proportion of eight to one, and laid them in neat rows on the sandy ground, chained like parrots in pairs.

To the impetuous soldiers and citizens of Tripoli, it appeared, the same treatment had already been meted out on the shore. Then, all herded together under the shimmering sun, the hilarious task of selecting victims for punishment was begun.

The sweet death by wild honey which Dragut had once promised Lymond was familiar to Jerott Blyth by the end of that day. He saw de Chabas, an old Dauphine cannonier and battle companion, thrust alive into the sand, nose and fists severed, and stuck full of arrows until he died. His sin had been to shoot off the hand of Sinan's favourite henchman. Others fared worse. In the end, blinded by heat, aching, sickened by the screaming, Jerott turned his head aside and abandoning all effort to apportion blame and honour wished simply and furiously that he were dead. Gabriel and the Frenchmen in the Turkish camp, he supposed, already were. He wondered, as at intervals for two days he had wondered, what cynical seraglio Francis Crawford had managed to set up for himself, almost certainly unharmed, unmoved and in favour with the reigning power, the willing mistress restored to his bed. The final irony, which struck him just before he lost consciousness, was that the honour and reputation of the Order would today be intact if he and Lymond had not laboured quite so hard that night in the arsenal.

He did not see, later, the crack infantry of the Turkish army—Spahis, Ghourebas, Ulafaje, Janissaries—marching in silent triumph, magnificently trained, below the great banners, drums beating, into the vanquished city, with Sinan Pasha at its head, mounted on an Arabian horse, turban flashing and sleeveless cloak falling stiff over the saddle above the long embroidered robe. The soft-booted feet of the infantry paced in unison, the white dust clouding the air and powdering the robes kirtled above gartered trousers, the laced tunics, the dark, bearded faces—almost every one smooth, fresh and scatheless, and fiery with scorn: the flower of the Sultan's army and all, save for a few gunners, the armchair conquerers of Tripoli, for which they had not had to strike a blow.

De Vallier watched them, lying on the ground like the rest, manacles again on his chafed wrists, and tears he could not control ran down his seamed, dust-coated face to the sand. Until, behind the Aga Morat's dancing horses with their booty-stuffed packs came the French Ambassador's party, walking between ranks of armed Janissaries; ranks through which the Sieur d'Aramon, reckless of risk, broke when he saw the iron carpet of human debris huddled, prone, raging, unconscious, stretching from his feet to the shore.

D'Aramon paused only to hear the Marshal's story, kneeling at the old man's side, his fingers on the clasped hands of the other; then he resumed his place in the derisive procession until, livid with suppressed anger, he was inside the abandoned castle and forcing an audience on Sinan Pasha himself.

It was the time then for plain speaking. 'The world will learn,' said the French Ambassador without preamble, 'of this act of injustice and of the tainted coin of the Ottoman oath. By treaty these men and two hundred more were to go free and unmolested provided they laid down their arms. This was done, yet they lie, robbed, naked, suffering insult, torture and death at your gates. My lord and most Christian Majesty the King of France,' said M. d'Aramon distinctly, 'will require reprisals for each of his subjects so treated. The Order will exact the same for its knights. From henceforth, each of your officers, when captured, may look to pay the price in blood for this treatment.'

To de Seurre and others of his party, waiting in silence, the childish battle seemed endless. With the forced artistry of any man dealing long at the Supreme Porte, d'Aramon moved from threat to compliment, from compliment to appeal, from appeal to coaxing. And at length, as Sinan had probably intended all along, for the price of all the remaining royal treasure in d'Aramon's galley, the General undertook to set free most of the knights and two hundred of the others arrested, provided that he chose these himself.

So, enthroned under the light canopies in the dreadful heat of the afternoon, Dragut and Salah Rais at his side, the Turkish General sat outside Tripoli and made his choice while the Ambassador watched.

Under the pointing finger the Marshal was liberated, to be lifted gently by de Seurre and d'Aramon's nephew and helped to walk. One by one likewise the older French knights were unbound, whose injury might with justice mean reprisals. Two from Germany were freed; four from Italy. Then, moving away from the ranks of the Order, Sinan began to select from the men, women and children of Tripoli and the castle the oldest, the weakest, the poorest, as he had done at Gozo. And in due time, these were all taken away.

The screaming of the hundreds still left behind woke Jerott Blyth in the end to sun, to noise, to the sharp bonds on his hands and feet,

201

to empty sand on either side of him ending, farther off, in scattered figures like his own—de Poissieu, who had so often urged a fight to the death; the youngest and fittest of the French; some Italian knights from Charles V's own states; and every knight of the Order belonging to Spain.

De Herrera's fears had been fulfilled. The full venom of the Sultan was to fall on the subjects of the Emperor, his greatest enemy in Christendom. . . . Then Jerott saw that Gabriel knelt beside him.

'Lie still, my son,' said Graham Malett, and guided the other man back to lie in the shade of his own body. 'D'Aramon is begging for your life. Sinan Pasha is threatening to keep back twenty knights who have roused his displeasure, to sell into slavery or to convert. If it's any comfort to you,' he added, in the loved and familiar tones of sanity and unshakable confidence, 'you must have done an extraordinary amount of damage before they felled you, in order to qualify.'

'I killed somebody, I think,' said Jerott thickly. He was thinking: total contribution to the Religion, one man. It was like being sent to Purgatory for crushing an ant. 'Are you all right? And everyone?'

'You've had a bad crack on the head,' said Gabriel gently. 'Don't you know? Your helmet has gone. D'Aramon and half a dozen of us are here to witness the . . . formal surrender. The rest have gone aboard the Ambassador's galley. Your friend is among them, I believe. Or *was* among them.'

'*Lymond?*' Jerott sat up, his ears drumming, his eyes blind, and after a moment was able to see clearly Gabriel's lightly-sunburnt, clean-shaven face, with the short, straight nose and the fine mouth in repose. Malett smiled.

'M. le Comte de Sevigny. No aspersions on his extreme ability: he was captured by pure accident while trying to free his lady friend. Luckily, I believe Dragut recognized him, and for past services appears to have overlooked this adventure. He is free, as we are. As you will be—somehow.'

'*Was* among the French party, you said,' repeated Jerott with a kind of monotonous persistence. His head was splitting. 'Where is he now, then?'

'No one,' said Graham Malett gravely, 'should ever be certain of reading that young man's mind, but if I were permitted to wager, I should expect to find him at this moment in the bay of Tripoli with a pirate called Thompson, preparing a deserted boat most effectively for sail.'

Afterwards, Jerott was to realize that in that short exchange Gabriel had shielded not only his body from the sun. Behind him, during this brief interval, the last shrewish discussion had ended between Sinan and d'Aramon on which Jerott's life and the lives of

202

the men lying around him must hang—men who, less fortunate, were watching in spite of themselves the angry face and sharp gestures of the Jew.

Then d'Aramon alone, his face stark with strain, left the canopy and moving towards the scattered men on the ground, halted and raised his voice. In French, Spanish and Italian he spoke seven words only.

'Brethren of the Order, you are free.'

By nightfall of that day, the 20th August, the Turkish ships lent by Sinan had taken on board the chosen two hundred, and most of the forty surviving knights of the garrison had embarked, Graham Malett and Jerott among them, on d'Aramon's own three boats.

D'Aramon himself was not there. Stiffly, he sat flanked by his entourage at Sinan Pasha's side in the great hall of Tripoli castle, lit from arch to arch as the knights had never dared light it, while outside turbaned Janissaries moved about the courtyard and battlements so lately crowded with six hundred Christian knights and soldiers and refugees; and hackbuts and cannon, destined to fight for the Religion, thundered and cracked in victory paeans to the skies.

On Sinan Pasha's far side, close to the other leaders, Dragut, Salah Rais, the Aga Morat in shining tissues and winking gems, sat de Vallier, the vanquished Marshal, with his entourage; commanded like the Ambassador to do honour to the treaty in this celebration banquet of Islâm. As the curds and steaming mutton went round; the fruit, the fowl, the almond paste and the Fezzan dates passing before the Governor untouched, Nicolas de Nicolay wondered if the old man was struck even yet by the orderliness of this conquering army, to whom drunkenness was a sin; whose soldiers might rape, loot, torture, kill under orders but were forbidden, marching, to trample on roses; who neither lightly shouted nor lightly swore but five times a day gave recognition and thanks prostrate to their God. And the French King's cosmographer thought of all he had seen crossing Tripoli that day—the turreted walls still fair and strong, with double ditches and false breaches; the wells and fountains, the food, the munitions, the artillery—and wondered how the world, bemused already by quarrelling reports, would judge the Order which had bloodlessly abandoned it.

They did not hear, through that interminable feast, the firing of the only guns still defending the Religion. At the little fort called the Châtelet, at the mouth of the bay, the Serving Brother des Roches alone had defied the call to surrender, and the thirty soldiers of the garrison who had replaced the Calabrians had rallied to support him.

It was, of course, suicide; but self-immolation with a purpose, selfless and gallant. Possession of the Châtelet meant virtual

203

command of the harbour, given possession also of the castle. Des Roches had three times refused Sinan Pasha's command to deliver the fort intact. Instead, he was forcing the Turkish fleet to level the building about them.

The roof had partly gone, ten men had died and ammunition was running low when, just after dusk, a low black boat arrived soundlessly at the sea gate of the fortress, guided by the finest sea-robber in the region, and with him a man des Roches, hastily summoned, recognized. Amid the smell of cordite, the dust of crushed stone and mortar, the fumes of burning wood, the crash of the attacking batteries and the splintering explosion of the massive balls, the Châtelet was silently evacuated and the little garrison, spent, lacerated and dazed still with their own good fortune, delivered in the concealing darkness to d'Aramon's own galley.

Thompson and Francis Crawford, with due modesty, came aboard last, swamped with low-spoken congratulations, and dropped with the others to concealment below, while the boat was lashed to the blind side of the galley's decks. No one had seen. With d'Aramon's own skiffs immobilized and the Tripoli shore guarded, no boat could have put out unseen that night . . . except one supposedly empty, already rocking deep in the empty bay, with the pirate Thompson aboard.

Jerott saw the two men briefly, Lymond's pale hair gleaming in the flickering lamplight, but he was talking quickly to others: to the lieutenant of the boat in Captain Coste's absence; to some of the senior knights. Then Graham Malett, from his fine height commanding the room, crossed to Lymond from where he had been speaking to des Roches. The two men briefly conferred. There was a swirl of movement, then men came running, and from the next hold came the sound of the storerooms being opened up.

With difficulty, Blyth burst through at last into the enchanted circle. '*What* . . . ?'

'Dear Jerott,' said Lymond warmly. 'Aren't you at the banquet? After we saved the castle intact for them? They'd give you a bagnio and three tails for that if they knew. Wouldn't you like three tails? I think we should go, Malett.'

'Yes. . . .' And as Lymond wilfully had not done, Gabriel swiftly explained. 'In return for his services, Thompson is to have some of our seamen and stores, and is going to try to sail the brigantine out tonight to Malta, with news of the fall. Crawford and I will go with him.'

And as Jerott started to protest he said calmly, 'My child, the Grand Master must know. The Turk may fall upon Malta next. We do not know. And he will believe me. If we do not escape, then nothing has been lost. But the fewer who try it the better.' His tranquil smile deepened. 'We shall meet in Malta, Jerott. Pray for us all. God has been good tonight.'

'Thompson has been rather splendid too,' said Lymond cordially. and waved a cheerful farewell.

A little later, setting course east to hug the far shore of the bay, remote from all the moored Turkish fleet, from the little company of French boats and the borrowed vessels with the freed two hundred on board, a black bulk slid silently from the anchorage and set off under the opaque black sky. Jerott, straining his eyes, thought he could just see the green sparkle of her oars, and knew that in a little, they could have her sails up, and the south wind would send her home.

No one else saw her. At the end of its long, dark spit, the Châtelet burned, red flames glowing behind the broken black teeth of its walls, and the attacking guns had fallen silent round its pyre. Within the bay, the rockets and gunfire had ceased although the castle still blazed, and lights in Tripoli itself showed where parties of soldiers, methodically searching lane by lane, were stripping the houses.

In the castle hall, the banquet was drawing to a close, and soon d'Aramon and de Vallier with their exhausted train would be allowed to retire for what little night was left before their embarkation at dawn.

And below, in the guts of the castle, among the corridors and mosaics where the stifling battle with fire had been fought such a short time ago, the prisons were full of the people of Tripoli and Gozo who had not been released; who might, some of them, be ransomed; but whose fate tomorrow or the next day was almost certainly to be whipped out through the purlieus of the castle and driven to the slave market to be sold.

Among them, but in a room apart because of his rank and ill-health, was Galatian de Césel, Governor of Gozo, who would see no Christian face for many years to come. And at his side, carried off and concealed so smoothly, so plausibly by the casual duplicity of Dragut and the gentle persuasiveness of Graham Malett, was the woman from whom Francis Crawford had been saved.

Oonagh O'Dwyer heard the cannonades; breathed like poison the air of scornful triumph; saw and was scarred by the routine, contemptuous conduct of the victors. Silenced, snatched from her rope that night before Lymond could return, she knew it all for a trap. She and Lymond had never been intended to escape, only to be separated so that she might convincingly appear to die. Only through the unexpected strength of Lymond's swimming had they travelled farther and run into more danger than anyone meant.

They were parted. The gentle, iron-willed man called Gabriel had achieved what after all he had never relinquished: an unblemished, perhaps a noble future for another man. Lymond was free, as she herself wished, and had nothing now to tie him to these shores, to womanhood, to human failings and pleasures. Lymond was dedicated. And she . . . she was the sacrifice.

Then she heard Dragut's step and rose dry-eyed, her black hair sheltering her inhabited flesh.

'Come, Cormac's brat!' she said aloud. 'You would not drown for me, and you will be sorry for it; for here I shall shape a scimitar for your fist.'

But when the step passed her door she lay down suddenly, sick, and closing her wide grey-green eyes, the colour of the sea, remembered a scented garden in France, and a quiet room, and Francis Crawford's soft laughter in her ear, and his hands cool on her skin.

And as the brigantine, stretched light to the wind, parted the dark seas and fled, Oonagh O'Dwyer lay hard-pressed, shuddering, denying her grief under the roof which, by the sacred miracles of Mohammed, Allâh had conquered from God.

X

Hospitality

(Malta, August 1551)

WITH silence for ballast, the three vessels of Gabriel de Luetz, Baron d'Aramon, recrossed the still blue sea to Malta twenty days after leaving it, bearing with them the forty surviving Knights Hospitallers who had sworn, with such fire, to defend the Religion to the death. Behind them under the flag of Islâm lay Tripoli, which had shown the white flag after five days' assault. And along with them, by Ottoman leave, were the borrowed Ottoman ships carrying the two hundred elderly Tripolitains so mockingly freed with which, it was unfeelingly suggested, the Order could set up an old man's hostel on Gozo. . . . It was not a talkative voyage.

*

The chain was across the harbour at Galley Creek when d'Aramon's galley made to anchor off Birgu. That was the first shock. Then, although in the gathering dusk they could make out the brigantine from Tripoli anchored in the bay, together with another strange boat belonging possibly to the pirate Thompson himself, there was no salute from Fort St Angelo; only a great deal of scurrying visible on the high battlements and a flash of steel, mysteriously, from the walls. The chain remained up.

After waiting, at the Ambassador's command, the three vessels and the Turkish ships with knights and refugees on board backed and dropped anchor outside the bar. D'Aramon's nephew said tentatively, 'It's late. They dislike admitting ships after dusk.'

'But the brigantine has arrived. They must know from Malett that we carry sick and wounded and the whole North African Command of the Order. . . . We have tempted fortune long enough,' said the French Ambassador, an edge of worry and anger fretting the diplomatic voice. 'M. de Vallier, can you reach the Grand Master in any way to request him to admit us immediately? We are here by the Turk's permission and against his instincts. He may well reconsider unless this operation is speedily transacted. And through the Order I

207

am already the better part of a month behind time in resuming my post.'

'God will reward you,' said the Marshal automatically, but his straining eyes were on the towers of St Angelo, with Birgu behind. 'I cannot understand it. For every returning caravan, however ordinary, the guns fire, St Lawrence is lit; the knights wait; the hospital is warned. . . .'

'A boat is coming,' said Jerott suddenly; and as small lights sprang to life all about them in the new-fallen dark, the Ambassador and his suite waited and watched.

It was Graham Malett, Knight Grand Cross, alone, in a boat rowed by Maltese, and as he came aboard, Jerott noticed with a cold paralysis of nerves that the lifelong serenity associated with this one man had broken. Blanched under the sparse lights, Gabriel's face was set with shock; his eyes darkened from lucid blue to near-black. Crowding with the others into the small poop cabin Jerott heard d'Aramon say, 'You have bad news,' without a query, and Gabriel answered, 'I am sorry. I have startled you.' And then, after a moment, 'I do not know how to tell you, or how to defend my brethren to you.'

The Marshal de Vallier's voice said harshly, 'What has happened? Why does the chain remain down?'

Graham Malett said, one steadying hand on the framework above his head, 'The chain will not lift tonight. The castle guard at St Angelo has been doubled and the Grand Master has ordered every knight to his post as if an enemy had arrived. If you are admitted tomorrow it will be to face imprisonment and worse, Marshal, as a traitor with your accomplices. And the Ambassador, to whom we should be on our knees in thanks . . . who has done all that man could do to persuade the Turk to raise the siege . . . who has delivered us all out of slavery and by God's grace has brought us safely here. . . . You, sir, are being cursed from house to house in Birgu as the cunning instigator of what they call *this scandalous capitulation.*'

There was total silence, which the Baron d'Aramon at length broke in his quiet French. 'This is the Grand Master's doing? What else does he say?'

Gabriel, cap in hand, bent his cropped head. 'That you obtained the Grand Master's confidence by pretending an interest in preserving Tripoli. That by exaggerating the weakness of the town and the strength of Sinan Pasha's forces you discouraged the men and led the Marshal to enter into dishonourable negotiation. That your presence in the Turkish camp was no less than a tacit sanction of Turkish conduct, as proved by the triumphal banquet, and by the vast treasures which passed from your hands to theirs. That your whole purpose in Tripoli was to end the siege quickly and so release

208

the Turkish troops the French King needed to help him in his present war against Charles V. They have questioned every man aboard my brigantine about this,' said Graham Malett, his straight gaze on d'Aramon. 'They accuse you even of inciting the Turk to plunder the knights' bodies once they had meekly surrendered.'

'How widespread is this story?' asked d'Aramon in the same quiet voice.

'It has been carried of purpose through the whole of Birgu. It will be in Mdina tonight. Already feeling is high against you.'

'I should not have believed it possible, even of the Order as it is today,' said d'Aramon. He glanced at de Vallier, who in a kind of stupor gazed back. Behind them voices, singly then in helpless counterpoint, chord, chorus, began to stir into affrighted life. D'Aramon said, 'For all our sakes, this must not be heard outside Malta. I shall ask to appear before the Grand Council and give a full answer to these lies.'

'You may,' said Gabriel. 'And be sure you will not be unsupported. De Villegagnon and la Valette have risked their lives to defend you. But it is too late. Three of the Order's galleys left this afternoon for Sicily, Naples and Bône with the Grand Master's version of Tripoli's loss, and bearing letters of corroboration written by the Spanish knights to his dictation to all the Order's commanderies in Europe. The Emperor is being well served. Also . . .' he hesitated.

'My God, is there more?' said d'Aramon bitterly, and dropping into a chair, leaned one elbow on the littered table and pressed his fingertips to his closed eyes.

'He will not pay for your hostages,' said Graham Malett, low-voiced.

But by this time the French Ambassador had jettisoned delicacy. He dropped his hand, and jerking it round the taut, incredulous throng about him said, 'And are we to send these men back to the slave market? I, their so-called enemy, humbled and impoverished myself to have them raised manacled from the sand and set free, and their own Order will do nothing to redeem their lives?'

'*What hostages? What payment?*' Jerott Blyth's shriek carried above the rest.

Graham Malett turned. 'When you and the Spanish knights lay unreleased, M. d'Aramon sued for your lives. He obtained them by paying all he had from his own private purse, together with a promise that the Order would in exchange release thirty well-born Turkish prisoners now in Malta. This the Grand Master has now refused to do, so that M. d'Aramon, who has to return to Constantinople to work, is being forced to dishonour his word.'

'He shall not be allowed to suffer.' It was the Marshal de Vallier's elderly voice at last. 'I and my brethren in Christ will refute this libel in person. Had the castle been garrisoned and fortified as it should

... had they sent us experienced knights, disciplined soldiers in place of these unfortunate peasants. . . .'

'If you enter Birgu, Marshal,' said Gabriel, 'it will mean prison. It may mean torture. It may bring degradation. It may even bring death. I do not consider that His Eminence will use impartial witnesses.'

Graham Malett renouncing all hope of justice and all prospect of the triumph of good was as close to ultimate horror as Jerott expected to reach. He said, 'Have you *told* them? Anyone in their senses will know you at least to be impartial. What about de Villegagnon? He won't support the Grand Master in downright falsehood. What about la Valette? Romegas? *Isn't anyone fighting?*'

'De Villegagnon knows everything I know. He will fight to the death,' said Gabriel. 'So will all the others you mention and their following. It makes no difference, as you should know. They are outnumbered. As for my being considered impartial. . . .' He smiled, a little bleakly. 'M. d'Aramon's mythical sins, I am told, are mine also. For sharing his sly duplicity from the safety of the Turkish camp, I have been warned that I return to Malta at my peril. You and I, Marshal, will be martyred together.'

'No!' The exclamation was instant and final, from both the Ambassador and de Vallier. The Ambassador added curtly, 'Martyrdom will not help the Order. I shall appear before this Council. Whether the Marshal does so or not is his affair. Be sure for my part I shall fully vindicate you. But your duty is amply done in stating our case and in bringing us this warning. To place yourself in the Order's power while the Order is crazed with fear, obsessed with this feverish need to excuse to the Emperor the fall of his city . . . desperate possibly to conceal misappropriation of funds which must be the Grand Master's blame alone . . . this is self-destruction. Leave de Villegagnon; leave Parisot who cannot at least be made scapegoats for Tripoli to fight what must be a long battle in the Order itself. I suggest to you your duty is quite other.'

'What is that?'

'Go with de Seurre here, who is also a knight. Take my letters to France informing the King what has happened. Remedy this spreading poison of falsehood. Tell the truth throughout Europe so that things are shown as they are. . . .'

'Betray the rot within the Order?' said Gabriel.

'Expose it, Hospitaller, so that it may be cut out,' said d'Aramon steadily.

'It is my life,' said Gabriel blankly, and it was Jerott, striding forward, black, furious, dynamic, who seized his arm and shook it. '*You must not go back*. It was my life, too. But if you will leave it, I shall go with you.'

Graham Malett shook his head, a dazed king; a man who had taken so many blows that even feeling had gone dead. 'If the Marshal and my brothers go, of course I must return. I know what efforts M. d'Aramon made in the Turkish camp. . . .'

'You have already testified to that: you told us. And the Grand Master, however much he may wish it, cannot harm me *within* Malta,' said d'Aramon. 'It is outside that I need your witness.'

'I cannot speak against the Order,' Gabriel repeated. He looked distraught. 'I cannot subject the Order to question in France. And where else can I go?'

'There is another ship in the harbour,' said Jerott; and Graham Malett turned his eyes over the craning heads, broken already into hissing, arguing groups, to where a dark brigantine, lamps ablaze, lay idly on the black water.

For a long time he stared at it, while the tide of dispute and anxiety closed around him; the voices of d'Aramon, the Marshal, de Herrera, de Poissieu echoing and re-echoing meaninglessly as Jerott pushed to his side. Then he saw that Gabriel's eyes were closed, his lips stirring, and realized that in anguish the other man had turned for his answer to prayer. So, he waited.

*

'There's something,' said Thompson, and jerked his unkempt head across the dark water.

For half an hour he and Lymond had been leaning idly on the brigantine rail, digesting an excellent dinner and exchanging small talk, while across Grand Harbour, the Lilies of France stirred at the masthead of the little cluster of boats which had sailed in at dusk and the round moon, slipping through her black arc, shone on the silver chain stretched hard across Galley Creek: the Order's whipping post for her fallen.

'Three rowers,' said the pirate, gazing. 'And gey low in the water. That'll be the gear.'

'How many passengers?' said Lymond, and Thompson, who knew better than to believe the sweet insouciance in the query, grinned in the dark. 'I canna see, just, no bein' a hoolet. Bide, son; bide.'

Behind them, the boat rustled with movement. Her crew from Tripoli, long since landed, had been replaced by Thompson's own men, awaiting him on arrival. She had been stocked for her long voyage without question all that day and was now fully laden: the Grand Master was not concerned with what credence the world would give a pirate. And Lymond, for excellent reasons of his own, had not made his presence known.

'Twa heads,' said Thompson suddenly.

'Colour?'

'Look for yourself.'

High on its prow, the approaching skiff bore a lamp. The swaying glow, low on the sea, shifted over two ghost-like faces, strained, silent, severely withdrawn; and over two heads, one black; one brightest gold.

'Malett and Blyth, ye unnatural bastard,' said the pirate Thompson without rancour, and feeling for his purse, threw it into Lymond's long waiting palm. Lymond caught it without looking. 'Of course. It's all been a chastening experience.'

There was a pause, while they both watched the nearing boat. 'Mind I'm still sailing tomorrow,' said Thompson at length.

'That's all right,' said Lymond. 'We'll all go.'

Thompson was frowning. 'It's a bonny mess for a monk to walk out of. If they're so damned handy wi' their whingers, you'd think they'd hae the auld devil out o' the head chair in a wink.'

'It's a matter of conscience,' said Lymond. 'They can't kill Grand Masters; only Turks. And if he's going to be found dead in his bed, I don't want to be there. Which is one reason, if you must know, why I personally am walking out also.'

'They'd accuse you?'

'I don't know and I don't want to find out. Remember, these fellows have sworn to obey the Grand Master. It takes a bit of nerve to break that oath and not fly to the other extreme.'

'So they fly home to mother instead.'

'If you like,' Lymond said. 'Blyth is cleaving to Gabriel and Gabriel is cleaving to. . . .'

'You?' said Thompson, and laughed crudely, having a joyfully crude mind.

'I was going to say, God,' was Lymond's equable answer.

'And what now,' said the pirate, a wicked gleam in his sharp eyes. 'What's taking the likes of you back to Scotland?'

'Reports,' Lymond said. He waved, vigorously, at the silent boat now resting below. 'Delicious, intriguing reports. Letters from home, and all points north and west.'

'A girl?' Thompson was taken.

'A girl. A girl,' said Lymond, exquisitely tender, 'called Joleta Reid Malett.'

212

Part Three

THE DOUBLE CROSS

I

Nettles in Winter

(Boghall Castle, October 1551)

O N the day Will Scott married, Lymond took, unwittingly, his first step towards the Knights of St John.

By the same subtle irony, three years later, Francis Crawford of Lymond returned to the suspicious bosom of his homeland on the day Tom Erskine died.

He died at Boghall Castle, where he was brought when the sweating sickness struck him on the road from Stirling south. He did not live to see his wife, Margaret Fleming, come home from France with the Scottish Queen Dowager. Instead he spent his last hours shivering in her mother's overdressed castle at Biggar with Lady Jenny herself, dressed in something pure and flowing, absently patting his brow with a cloth.

By then, although plied with every potion the Flemings could muster, he knew the end must be near. Fifty thousand people had died in England that year from this ailment. He had seen enough of it, as he rode back and forth to Norham as Ambassador framing the peace. The war he had helped to end had preserved his land from the scourge. The peace, it seemed, was to kill him.

Because of the peace, Philippa Somerville was at Boghall. A single-minded Somerville from the north of England, staunch allies of Lord Grey, would have crossed the Border eighteen months ago with an army, or not at all. Philippa, who at thirteen had every cell charged, like her mother's, with stark common sense, was in Scotland because she liked Lady Jenny, and her legitimate children, and her five-months-old bastard by King Henri of France.

It was Philippa who had sent for the surgeon-apothecary when Jenny's son-in-law was carried in. Jenny herself was far too busy ensuring the safety of her fully ratified prince. He was whisked with her legitimate children three miles away to Midculter, for the Crawfords to care for. Two counties heard him go (he was teething); and Tom Erskine, listening, squeezed an amused smile from somewhere for Philippa. Then Jenny, agelessly endearing in musty white linen, arrived to fondle his hand.

He was grateful, because she was Margaret's mother and he had no illusions about her, and he talked to her reassuringly while he could. The rigor had gone by then; only, dressed in one of Jamie Fleming's nightgowns, he felt the growing pressure in aching head and knotted stomach, and with it, the fire of fever. His affairs were in order; his indiscretions paid for; his father's estates and charges perfectly bestowed. All this he had arranged when Lord Erskine had gone to France with the child Queen Mary. Of his own marriage, so short and gentle, there were no children and never would be now. Margaret's son by her first marriage would be cared for at his father's home.

He had not seen his wife since the spring when he had gone to France on the Queen's business. To Margaret he could have said, 'I am not afraid of death. I am afraid to leave a pilotless ship. England and the Emperor Charles are exhausted by war and discontent; France is freshly belligerent; Turkey is aggressive and rich. All the old wars have stopped and new ones are beginning with new partnerships and new enemies: who will guide us through the maze in the long regency ahead? Under the Sultan, all Turkey is united. France obeys the divine will of the King; the English nobles will cleave to the Regent with wealth and power to share.'

And in Scotland, what was there? A divided leadership. The French Dowager fighting the Earl of Arran for the Governorship during Queen Mary's childhood and wittingly or not, with every French coin she borrowed, ensuring Scotland's future as a province of France. And since England dared not have another France over her border, England was ready to seduce any Scottish noble, from Arran downwards, who did not care for the Queen Dowager, or France, or the old Catholicism. A divided nation; a divided God; a land of ancient, self-seeking families who broke and mended alliances daily as suited their convenience, and for whom the concept of nationhood was sterile frivolity ... what could weld them in time, and turn them from their self-seeking and their pitiable, perpetual feuds?

A common danger might do such a thing, except that the nation was too weak to resist one. A great leader might achieve unity—but he must be followed by his equal or fail. A corporate religion might do it, but where did one exist which some foreign power had not seized and championed already?

There was another remedy. A decade of peace for quiet husbandry, so that every cottar should have his kale and his corn without stealing from the next; so that peaceful trade should offer rewards as rich as war, and rebuilt castles employ their hundreds without fear of burned harvests, or having to put foot in stirrup at sowing time, or finding their year's work of wool or leather or herring sunk by reprisal for Scots fisherfolk themselves driven to piracy. 'How would you set about that? How would you even stop a Kerr killing a Buccleuch, come to that?' Tom said aloud, and saw from Jenny Fleming's wondering face that she had been saying something quite different, for probably quite a long time.

Then she left, and he knew that instead of his nurses, soon he would have round him the embarrassed audience of the dying. He did not much care, for now the fire had reached every part of his body, and there washed from him in salty sickening jets the diseased sweat which would kill him.

There was nothing to be done. Water ran through the sheet and into the ticking. Dry sheet and dry mattress were drenched afresh, and again; then they left him as he was. When they brought icy packings soaked in well water he watched the white steam around him twist to the painted ceiling and was only mildly shocked when a clawed brown arm knocked them away and a shawled head, vaguely familiar, bent over him and hissed, 'Kill ye, wid they, afore the Lord has appointed?' And as he stared up at the seamed face of Trotty Luckup it relaxed its glare as she smiled and said, 'I'll win a little comfort for ye still, my dear, afore they lay ye cauld, cauld i' the mools.'

He drank what she gave him to drink and let her do with him what she wanted, and perhaps it helped. He listened too, to what she had to say and it came to him that Francis Crawford could make use of that gossip, except that he was dying, and Francis was abroad.

It was Philippa who found him alone in his room, without the cold bags, and learned, rushing out to flare at the women, that they had been forbidden under threat of the evil eye to replace them after Trotty had gone. Jailbird or not, the old woman was wise, and Philippa knew that Tom had always dealt with her gently. So she did not interfere, but went back slowly into the sickroom and sat by the dying man's side.

To Tom, stupefied with fever, she looked much like her mother, sitting straight in the uncomfortable chair, her combed brown hair clinging over the uncompromising front of her dress. There was no need for her to have come. Her mother had sat just like this at the deathbed of the girl he was once to have married, long before Margaret.

Since then, he had been often to Flaw Valleys, and Lymond sometimes too, until Philippa's hostility had driven him away. That, or the death of Philippa's father. And Philippa or Kate, or both, had often enough defied the rules of war and slipped over the Border to stay with him at Stirling or Boghall. . . .

Lymond, they said, had been fighting in Barbary and was due home soon. . . . Would Philippa stay so implacable? For a bemused second

Erskine wondered if, sanctified by near-dissolution, he could play the peacemaker . . . but no. Hatred shackled by promises to the dead was the vilest of all.

Time passed. The room was dark and his feet were famished with cold. His feet were cold, and it was too late for a death-bed peroration. Not that he had much of value to say. Or had he?

With great difficulty, on a breath that scarcely lifted his chest, Tom Erskine said 'Philippa?' and her voice answered him, steadily, from where she sat framed by the dull glow of the fire. He took a long, shallow breath and two others, and began and finished with them his message to Margaret. And then, while he could, he added the other message, for Lymond.

The gist of what Trotty Luckup had said was not hard to convey. He only wished, with the hovering desolation which all this day he had fought to ignore, that it had been Margaret whose quiet, sober mind should accept this unsavoury truth, and not young Pippa. He had the presence of mind, and just enough voice, to send her away after that.

As Jenny and the clacking herd of nurses and servants came to Philippa's call, the child herself fled. Downstairs, loyal to the family but huddled in whispering knots under the shadow of sickness and death, the kitchen folk answered her questions. Yes, Trotty Luckup had been here, and had a good sup by the fire, and gone out at dusk . . . on the Culter road, she had said.

In Philippa Somerville's mousy head that night was one thought: to catch up with that erratic old gossip, and hear more of what Tom Erskine had told her.

Trotty wouldn't move fast. With all the ale she would have drunk, she could probably hardly walk straight. Philippa didn't wait for her pony to be saddled; she found it rope-bridled in the big stables and cantered it out at the gates, a dogged stable boy, who knew what his job was worth, following on a hack, with a stick under one arm and a stable cresset in his free hand. Then they both set off headlong down the causeway through the dark bog.

They found Trotty where the soggy road lifted out of the marsh to cross the small rise before Midculter. She lay at the side of the ditch, and there was more fustian than flesh to her, as if a pedlar had spilled his pack in the gutter. She was dead.

It was not the first dead face Philippa had seen—this loose-jawed engraving in stark black and white, the old hooded eyes wavering in the torch-flare. 'Nae doot,' the boy said scathingly, 'she's skited inty the stank and bashed her auld pan on a rock.'

'No doubt,' said Philippa, her hands cold. The old woman reeked of beer. Her hands, that had gentled the birth-caul from unnumbered children, were crossed at her chest in a semblance of protection. The girl bent suddenly over the harsh autumn grass, latticed with shadow, and came up holding something: an iron bar. 'And this was the *rock*.'

The boy himself was only fifteen. He stared at the weapon, saying nothing; and from the brightening of his neck-muscles in the flame, Philippa knew that he had heard, too, the sound that had caught at her heart: the far-off drumming of horse-hooves coming west. Not, she knew, an anxious pursuit from Boghall, else they would be calling. But not, surely, the murderers of Trotty Luckup, who should be far away by now? Unless they had remembered leaving that blood-sticky iron bar. . . .

There were a great many horses. 'Put out the torch,' ordered Philippa sharply, making up her mind; and they stood in the windy darkness beside the corpse in the ditch and waited for the horsemen to come.

There were about twenty men, you could guess from the jingle of harness and the clatter of hooves on the stony road, riding in a thick band, torchless, by the glimmer of the afterlight on the path. If there were any commands, the trotting feet drowned them. They came at an even pace round the far bend and rode towards where she stood with the boy in the thick dark of ditch and hedgerow; drew abreast and passed by.

Half passed. Ten paces beyond her, the vanguard of the little troop, in uncanny unison, halted dead. The rear half, which had yet to pass her, halted as suddenly. And out of the darkness in front, a voice nauseating with underplayed authority said, 'There. Strike a light and bring them both forward.'

To struggle was useless. As she went forward with the boy, prompted by a broad hand on her spine, Philippa saw in the new torchlight that all these men wore good half-armour and helms, and she took renewed courage. Not, then, outlaws or robbers.

Outwith the torchlight their commander sat waiting, still mounted. He had not spoken again. Philippa turned to address him, the yellow flame bright on her thirteen-year-old face, and his horse stirred a bit, and was quiet. Then, before she could even speak, he said mildly, 'Why, the heir of the Somervilles, with attendant. You have a problem, I see. May we help you? Is that your old lady, or someone else's?'

She knew who it was before he rode forward; before the light fell on his hated face. His skin was dark brown, she saw, so that all its lines were imprinted in white, and his eyes and teeth shone as he smiled.

Philippa's eyes filled with angry tears. He was Francis Crawford of Lymond, the only man who could airily jest about an old woman battered to death in a ditch.

The boy started forward, blustering and explaining, but Philippa stayed where she was, her mouth shut, until suddenly he spoke to her direct. 'Remember me? Your favourite Scotsman,' he said. 'And don't pretend to be frightened. You Somervilles are as tough as old Romans. . . . Tell me one thing, Philippa. Did you follow Trotty here from Boghall?'

He had picked up the gist, then, of the boy's story. It was exceedingly awkward. It was the worst kind of coincidence. It was damnable, thought Philippa, miserably daring. She replied, after a pause, 'Yes. I'm staying with Lady Jenny. You *might have* called out to let me know who you were. I followed Trotty,' said Philippa austerely, through chattering teeth, 'because I was anxious to talk to her.'

She waited. Something light and warm flicked down over her shoulders—his cloak, she discovered. She had not quite the courage to throw it off. 'Jerott here will carry you safely back to Boghall and the Mistress of France. Did you see who killed Trotty, Philippa?'

'No. . . . They had gone some time before. I don't know anything about it and I can go home by myself, thank you.'

Lymond stared at her. 'I expect you can, but Jerott's dead scared of the dark.' And added the question that mattered, before she was ready. 'Why did you want to speak to her, Philippa?'

Philippa Somerville's large brown eyes became perfectly vacant. In Philippa Somerville's obstinate head was a message for Lymond, given her by Tom Erskine who had learned it from this busy old woman. To withold it would hardly harm Francis Crawford. It would, however, given luck, lower his conceit not a little, and she had followed Trotty Luckup with the intention of learning much more.

It was too late now for that. Philippa cut her losses, and without shifting the wide, disingenuous gaze told her lie. 'Trotty came to give comfort to Sir Thomas Erskine, and left before she could be paid or thanked, even. You know Lady Fleming wouldn't think of it. I had money for her, that's all.'

She had, luckily, in her purse. Lymond did not look at it. Instead he said sharply, '*Comfort?*' as she had hoped.

'Poor Sir Thomas is at Boghall with the sweating sickness,' said Philippa sadly, and would have earned short shrift from Kate for the shoddy ring of her tone.

She earned even shorter from Lymond. 'Since when?' he shot at her, and then, 'Jerott!'

The dark, cleanshaven young man behind stooped. Against the brief crack of Lymond's voice she felt herself swung into the stranger's saddle, while the boy hopped behind Francis Crawford; then the two horses swung round and set off at uncomfortable speed for Boghall, leaving the rest by the road.

Looking back at a bend, Philippa saw that, dismounted, they were already lifting the bundle of rags that was Trotty Luckup out of her gutter. In Philippa's soft heart was true compassion for Trotty and a real grief for the Master of Erskine. But when, arrived at Boghall, she found priest and cousins, tardily come, in pale conference outside the sickroom and saw Jenny Fleming, tears silvering her tinted cheeks, fling her arms round Lymond's neck, she realized first, that Tom Erskine was dead; and second, that Trotty Luckup's small piece of gossip was her possession alone.

Trotty had intended it to warn Jamie Fleming. Tom Erskine had seen beyond it to trouble for Lymond. Philippa, sitting on her own private powder-keg, merely hoped he was right.

*

For Jerott Blyth, who had acted throughout in a state of resentful boredom, it was no pleasure to be on the road to Midculter with Lymond again, with Boghall and its mourning mother-in-law in the darkness behind.

It was because of Gabriel that he was here. Graham Reid Malett, true to his word, had not spared himself since leaving Malta more than two months before. To virtually every Court in Europe he had presented, with force and justice, the story of Mdina, Gozo and Tripoli; blaming no one, but abundantly clearing of blame the French knights of Malta, the Chevalier de Vallier, and the French Ambassador to Turkey, M. d'Aramon.

Everywhere, except in the Vatican and the Empire, he had been given a hearing. His work and his reputation, preceding him to France, had ensured him an immediate welcome at Court, decently muted out of respect for that Turkish alliance. Henri II might not see eye to eye with the Baron d'Aramon, but he was willing to support him against the Emperor Charles any day; particularly as it was not difficult to guess, however biased Graham Malett might be, that the Grand Master was personally the scrapings of a particularly rancid barrel.

Gabriel had insisted on performing this pilgrimage alone. Banished from the Grand Cross's side, Jerott heard the sounds of his devoted success from his mother's home at Nantes and, in the end, could not forego a single heart-warming reunion with Sir Graham at Paris.

Thinner, his hair grown longer, his face tired, Gabriel had not otherwise changed. The sweet-tempered, steadfast crusader of Malta was still in him, smiling at Jerott's importunities, and saying at length, 'What next? How may any of us know what comes next? I shall go to London next month, and then to Scotland. I must see Joleta; and I think I must rest. My doctor seems to think it wiser, at

221

least.' And brushing aside Jerott's concern, he had said, 'Why not join me there? Why not go first and wait for me? You have still relatives there. You can meet Joleta and tell me if she and Lymond are friends.'

The horror in Jerott's expressive face had made him laugh again. 'That dismays you? I can think of nothing to please me better. Where I have failed, perhaps Joleta can win. Perhaps you too can help to persuade that young man that gifts like these are not be be wasted. Bury your distrust of him, Jerott. He will do honour to the Religion yet. The finest service you could render your Order would be to join him and befriend him now.'

'*What Order?*' had said Jerott Blyth bitterly; and Gabriel had smiled. 'Don't pretend that four hundred years of chivalry have ended with one misguided old man. You have been paid a compliment: Juan de Homedès does not like you. Let us show him how his work for Christ should be done.'

It was a winning thought, reflected Jerott morosely as he cantered through the cool Scottish night to Midculter. But it did not console him for the quality of Francis Crawford's smile when he had attached himself to his train on embarking for Scotland, or for the arguments they had subsequently had over Lymond's immediate plans. Lymond was on his way home to St Mary's, his property near the loch of that name. There he proposed to train men, as the Order trained, in the sweet arts of war; and Jerott had agreed to assist.

Whether this accorded with Gabriel's hopes of him he had no idea, but if he were to stay with Lymond he could do nothing else. He was out for a quick conversion, was Jerott; for the alternative—proselytizing by Gabriel's innocent sister Joleta—was unthinkable. Hence his distaste for the present journey to the Crawford castle at Midculter. They had been in Scotland for less than a day and in his view should make straight for St Mary's, where all Lymond's chosen men were assembling.

Instead, they were to call at Midculter, and he would be forced, in Lymond's presence, to meet for the first time Gabriel's sister, Joleta. And worse, to see Joleta exercise for the first time her tender sanction to win Francis Crawford to her beliefs.

Since leaving Boghall Lymond had not spoken. The death of Erskine was a pity, Jerott supposed. The Queen had lost a loyal supporter. Jerott said, 'The Somerville youngster has a stout heart for her size.' Even at the end, Philippa had not given way; and it must have been no joke, finding herself alone at night with a dead woman and a band of armed soldiers. She knew Lymond, it seemed. Why then, for God's sake, thought Jerott to himself with renewed irritation, hadn't the man shown some warmth or some decent concern for the girl? He added to his previous remark. 'But she's no beauty.'

At his side the dimly seen face did not alter. At length, 'God, I suppose, sends a shrewd cow a short horn,' said Lymond, and put his horse into a canter.

They were nearly at Midculter, although the rising ground hid the castle from view and only the sprinkle of cottage lights through the thinning October leaves told where the village lay. Archie Abernethy and the rest of Lymond's men would be there by now, having left Trotty Luckup, as Lymond had commanded, in the care of the Crawfords' own priest. Jerott became occupied with his own thoughts and jumped when out of the darkness Lymond's hand, strong and hard, fastened on his. A moment later he was on his feet beside the other man on the road, the two horses hitched to the bushes behind them, and was walking silently towards the trampling and shouting now clearly audible from round the next bend, above which the voice of Lymond's sergeant, Archie Abernethy, could be heard raised loud in complaint. There was a burst of laughter; and a moment later, Lymond and Jerott Blyth had caught up with their errant light horse.

It was a remarkable sight. They had mostly dismounted. The road, shiftily lit by the smoky cressets, was crammed with helmeted heads, all loud in debate but none advancing to the tree-enclosed causeway ahead, where the abused body of Trotty Luckup lay, a young man bent at her side.

The noise came largely from Archie Abernethy, veteran warrior and once chief Mahout to the King of France's elephants, who stood alone in the centre of the road facing his men and arguing plaintively with an Italian pistol two feet long which was pointed unwaveringly at his stomach. The holder of the pistol was a girl no more than sixteen years old. The torchlight fell on rose-gilt hair falling sheer from her intent golden brow to the dropped velvet hood of her cloak, and her face, in its jewel-like purity, shocked the senses like music with cymbals. She looked furious.

The likeness, even from the hedges where Lymond and Jerott Blyth, unseen, stood, could not be missed. It was—it must be—Gabriel's sister, Joleta.

A small, choked sound came unawares from Jerott Blyth's throat. Lymond's arm brought him up short. 'Control yourself, Brother. A peach, I agree, but a dangerous peach. Let me deal with it first.' And removing his hand, he melted into the night. Jerott took a step forward, and then a step backwards; and then stayed where he was, a handful of thorn in one fist. He was shaking a little, as one did when the cathedral doors opened and kneeling, one felt the bearers brush by in incense, and saw the still, loving smile of the saint.

His eyes were wet. And, God in heaven, his right hand was covered in blood. Pulling himself together, Jerott Blyth released the thornbush, jerked down his leather jacket, drew his sword, and took a professional step forward again.

The noise by this time was prodigious. As he listened to the ribaldry, Jerott soon understood. Riding from Midculter with her grooms, Gabriel's amazing sister had found Trotty Luckup's corpse in the hands of a group of armed strangers. That Joleta should blame them for Trotty's murder was no doubt natural enough. While one servant rode back for help, she had neatly isolated poor Archie and the next moment had hauled a pistol out of her saddlebag.

Any one of the twenty men present could have overpowered her. Archie himself, come to that, could use one of a dozen old tricks. But added to the minuscule risk (the girl, after all, might shoot the thing) there was a reluctance to end some good sport.

Their fun was not wholly unkind. Their trembling appeals for compassion, their good advice to Archie, hotly explaining, were all merely compensation for the facts that she was ravishing, well-born, and not for them. Further, that in their leader's most opportune absence, this was the nearest they might ever hope to approach.

Cuddie Hob was shrieking, 'He's an auld man! He's an auld man! He's got a weak hert and six mitherless bairns! Hae mercy, mistress!' and Archie Abernethy, bald head glinting in the flares, was saying angrily, 'We found the old woman; we didna kill her; we're on our way to Midculter now. For God's sake stop this nonsense. I beg your ladyship's pardon; that thing might go off. We're young Crawford's men, my lady: *Crawford* of *Lymond*—will you bloody bastards shut your mouths?'

Then Jerott took his one step and halted, for Crawford of Lymond had moved into the road twenty paces behind the girl's back.

They did not all at first see him, so the shouting died naturally. Only Archie and the girl at whose pistol-end he stood noticed nothing. Within the silken flame of her hair, Joleta's milk-white face was rosy with anger, her eyes brightly thicketed with shadow. 'So you say,' she retorted. 'Then why isn't he here? Or doesn't he care if his uncouth and uncontrolled following batter an old woman to death?'

'It's a lie. They've never battered an old woman to death in their lives,' said Lymond's cold, plaintive voice. During his long walk up the road to Joleta's back, not a pebble had shifted. He had taken no visible precautions; hands tucked into his sword belt, he had given the appearance merely of strolling into the scene, and his horsemen, after a sporadic attack of bemused silence, had shouted dutifully on, though in a noticeably innocuous vein, until he halted at last, a dozen steps from the girl.

'Young ones, now: that's different.'

It was a ruse so old that it was almost an insult. Archie Abernethy, by then aware of Lymond, should have been ready at the first sound of his voice to snatch Joleta's pistol as the girl started round. It didn't work because as Lymond moved into place, an eager torchbearer closed up behind him to give him more light. Before he opened his mouth, Lymond's shadow slid on before him, grey and revealing, up to Joleta and past her, and as he began to speak, Joleta whirled round and fired.

A scream, inhuman in its pain, tore across the ungentlemanly little theatre and died sobbing in a shuddering void, while a curtain of smoke spread silver before every motionless man.

It was impossible to see beyond it. Jerott, for one, did not want to see. She had fired, Christ preserve them, in a line dead behind. In a heavy silence he waited, rigid with the rest, and infinitesimally the veil spread, hovered, and began softly to melt.

In the distance, from the direction of Midculter, he was conscious of hoofbeats. Lord Culter, doubtless, summoned to rescue Joleta. . . .

From the lessening mists a voice spoke: the same voice as before, its tone vastly polite. '*Mortia la bastia, morta*, I hope, *la rabbia o veneno* . . .' And through the clearing smoke they all deciphered the singularly unconcerned person of Lymond, talking pleasantly still. 'That, Cuddie Hob, was your brown mare expiring. Give her a nice funeral. The torchbearer who moved, Archie, is to be flogged and turned off without pay. I should like to speak to you in my room when we get to Midculter. Ah, Richard. There you are. You've missed all the fun.'

That was his brother arriving, summoned from Midculter by Joleta to waylay her murderers, with some twenty or thirty men at arms with him. Remembering the Richard, Lord Culter of nine years before, Jerott Blyth saw little changed in this thickset, mild-mannered man with the shapeless brown hair. But the quality of his greeting to his younger brother was new, as was Lymond's response.

Then, 'Richard, introduce me,' Lymond was saying, in the same undisturbed voice; and he turned at last to where, dumb now, the child Joleta still stood, the smoking pistol dragging her hand. 'Attempted assassination counts as an unofficial introduction: I'm sure of it; but she might as well know who she's shooting at, apart from Cuddie Hob's horse.'

'Allow me to present my most heartfelt apologies,' said Joleta, and fainted straight off.

'*Francis!*'

'It wasn't my fault,' said Lymond doucely.

'How the devil was she fooled into firing in the first place? Don't tell me *that* wasn't your fault,' said Lord Culter, a familiar wariness displacing the warmth of reunion.

'All right, I won't,' said Lymond. 'Jerott, did you get shot also? No. Then kindly muster the lady in your monkish arms and ride with her to the castle. Yours is the only reputation that will stand it. And don't say I don't endow you with princely rewards for sitting on your bloody arse doing precisely nothing.'

Which was the manner of Lymond's homecoming from Malta.

*

Stepping over the Midculter threshold with his treasured burden like a penguin changing the habitat of its only begotten egg, Jerott Blyth missed the true homecoming.

Sybilla, Dowager Lady Culter, clucking over the unconscious Joleta, directing the disposal of Archie Abernethy and his twenty men, and dispatching her son Richard to entertain Will Scott in the castle's elegant hall, was largely unconscious of all these things.

Reality for her began when her absent son Francis, bright, sun-browned and vivid, stood deferentially at the door of her parlour and she was able to say, her voice sweet, 'Well, *mon cher*? I hear, Heaven preserve the counted, that you are a Count . . .?'

Then Lymond closed the door, and not even Richard would have intruded on them then.

II

The Widdershins Wooing

(Midculter Castle, the Same Day)

WHEN, under the direction of a stalwart Venetian madam to whom he took an instant dislike, Jerott placed his childish burden tenderly on her bed, Joleta was still unconscious. Her skin was so fine, he saw, that the veins ran like Sicilian marble over her temples and jaw. From her thinly framed nose to her invisible eyebrows, her sparely moulded pink mouth, her prodigious golden lashes, there was nothing coarse about her; and her hair, blown lightly on the lawn of her pillow, was insubstantial as new-loomed silk.

Stumbling slightly, Jerott Blyth removed himself from the room and the old madam's glare, and nearly walked into Archie Abernethy, marching along the corridor. From the colour of his neck it was clear that he, anyway, had had the promised interview with his lordship of Lymond. Then, tripping along the passage with her white hair and blue eyes and high-handed, small-boned elegance, came Francis Crawford's mother.

'Jerott!' said Sybilla, and clutching with her two small hands as much of his worn leather chest as she could reach, hauled down his head for an embrace. She smelt marvellous. '*All* the most beautiful men become monks,' she said. 'It's a oecumenical law or something. I can't imagine how they keep up the breed. What's wrong? Has Francis been rude? Then you must try to overlook it. I know you wouldn't think so, but he is thoroughly upset by Tom Erskine's death; and when Francis is troubled he doesn't show it, he just goes and makes life wretched for somebody.'

Smiling, she slipped her small, strong hand under his arm. 'How splendid that you and he met again. Come and be introduced, and tell me your news. Is your mother still so well and so shamingly *loaded* with energy . . . ?'

It was neatly done, and Jerott didn't try to resist. Setting aside his private reservations about a commander who, however disturbed, let fly at his lieutenant in public with no cause whatever, he followed the Dowager Lady Culter into her elegant hall.

In the year of Lymond's absence, Midculter had done rather well.

The Crawfords, like his own family, had always been wealthy, of course; less from their skill in war, though that was considerable, than from sheer intelligence and a native ingenuity in the handling of characterful experts. Sybilla, who made them laugh, had always been her people's idol. Richard, who risked his life for their sons on the battlefield, was respected and liked. Francis Crawford they must hardly know. He would possess, you could depend on it, a certain shoddy appeal for the womenfolk, which their men would not at all mind removed. If Lymond were to become the man Gabriel hoped, indeed, thought Jerott with satisfying logic, it must be removed.

In the painted hall at Midculter when Jerott joined them now were the third Baron, his wife Mariotta, and Sir William, heir to Wat Scott of Buccleuch. Richard, talking amicably while he waited for his brother, was aware that Mariotta, stitching furiously behind him, was listening to every foot on the stairs in a concealed froth of emotion. She had never been impervious to Lymond's doubtful attractions and would enjoy, he knew, having her feelings exercised once more, like puppies at gambol. Their marriage now was deep and firm enough to stand it.

Will Scott, also, was listening, his face flushed under his flaming red hair. Since his Kerr-infested marriage three years since to Grizel he had become the father of three and a man not to offend on the Borders. More and more as old Buccleuch, his father, grew wheezier, he had taken on himself the active duties of wardenship along the thief-ridden wasted frontier with England, dispensing international justice with one hand and with the other attempting to control the bloody bickering on his own side of the Border.

In the three years four Kerrs had been injured, and three farms burned down belonging to friends of the Scotts. He didn't always tell his father when it happened, because the old man's face turned mottled blue over his doublet, and unless Will got in first, he would send a runner round all the estates, and the threshing would stop while grousing, reluctant men straggled back for their pikes and swords and mail shirts, taking a long time about it, waiting for Buccleuch the Younger to come up, furious on his sweating horse, and tell them curtly to get back to the fields.

As the French grip on the Queen Mother and therefore on Scotland became tighter; as the danger grew that Arran, the Scottish Governor, would retaliate by siding with England, there blossomed among Will Scott's simple convictions the warning spoken again and again in the past by Francis Crawford.

If they thought their sovereignty worth keeping, the handful of lords who divided Scotland between them must unite. And unite before religious division caught and struck them apart for ever. For Lymond a year ago had maintained that, so far, the quarrel between

228

the old and the new religion in Scotland was nothing but useful ammunition for men who disliked and distrusted each other for other reasons entirely. The danger was that the thing, so lightly seeded, might take needless, schismatic root of its own.

All that, Lymond had said a year ago. Since then he had fought alongside Joleta's brother, clever, courageous and devoted adherent of the Old Religion for whom Luther and Mohammed were infidels both. And if Gabriel hadn't converted Francis Crawford, thought Will Scott gloomily, running a large hand through his blazing hair, the bloody girl certainly would.

These three diverse people however in Sybilla's fine hall greeted Jerott Blyth warmly enough, and made him welcome while Sybilla installed him in one of her vast fireside chairs. There was no sign of Lymond. While they chatted, Blyth inspected Lymond's family. They were presentable, he thought, and intelligent; and they knew their world, he would grant them that. Whatever subject they opened, and they had a range like a cadger's, Jerott was given a full share. They might almost, he would admit, have been meeting in France. Then the door opened and Joleta came in, followed by her duenna.

She was fascinatingly pale, the flood of rose-gold hair and wide aquamarine eyes the only colour about her. She was dressed all in white.

Jerott shot out of his seat. Richard, following more slowly, said placidly, 'You've had a shock. Shouldn't you stay in bed for a while?'

'No,' said Joleta flatly. She was not, as Sybilla had discovered, a person slow to make up her mind. 'To faint was childish. And to shoot was inexcusable. I might have *killed* Mr Crawford. I came to apologize properly. I should not like him to think me a child.'

'He won't,' said Richard gravely; and Jerott, with revived interest, shot him a look. 'But he'd like to reassure himself that you are well, I'm sure. Come and join us. He won't be long.' And, smiling, the child walked forward and choosing a hooded chair by the fire sank into it, while Madame Donati, with a sigh, seated herself far too near Jerott for that knight's absolute comfort.

Then Lymond came in. Suavely toasted and slender; all masked blue eyes and buttermilk hair, he moved forward without seeing Joleta in her tall, wide-backed chair, exclaiming, 'God, it's Buccleuch the Younger. I hear you are proliferating like mice, and every one of you with a skull like a marmalade orange. Have you no thought for the sorry state of the nation?' And went without hurry to hammer the big, grinning Scott's shoulders and salute, on one picturesque knee, the hand and cheek of his Irish sister-in-law. '*Mountebank,*' thought Jerott Blyth.

Last of all, Lymond bowed low to Madame Donati, and if his Italian disarmed her, she gave no sign, but answered austerely his soft inquiries about her charge's health. She had opened her mouth, presumably to direct his attention to Joleta's presence, when Sybilla cut in. 'And what did you think, Francis, of Sir Graham's beautiful sister?'

It was a risk that, knowing Lymond, Jerott would never have taken. He rather judged, from Will Scott's dropped jaw, that Lady Culter had alarmed him as well. Lymond himself, his back squarely to the chair concealing Joleta, said, 'She's a peach. I told Jerott she's a peach. He can have her. Some are clingstones. And some are freestones. But each dear little fuzzy fruit is packed full of poison. . . . Ah, there you are.'

'You knew I was here!' exclaimed Joleta. She hadn't knocked over her chair, because it would have taken two strong men to incline it an inch, but she exploded round the oaken rim of it like a charioteer, her hair swinging, the colour pink in her cheeks. She halted. 'I know all about you and your. . . .'

'. . . Nicolaitan practices? And I know all about you and your sanctity. Poor horse. Poor October horse, sacrificed to the God Mars. The fine in cows due from the murderer of a thane's son is sixty-three and two-thirds of a cow. The law of the Bretts and the Scotts. The fine for attempted murder,' said Lymond, moving round to the furious girl and leading her gently back to her seat, 'is not promulgated, but I imagine the odd two-thirds would meet it. The question is, which end of the cow?'

'You're talking nonsense, Francis,' the Dowager said with equanimity. 'And your manners are appalling. You'll make the poor child regret her bad aim. *Did* you know she was here?'

'I smelt the incense. So familiar with God, and such plenty of instructions from Heaven, she was a companion for angels. I trust she is. She's certainly a blistering nuisance in the company of men.'

Resisting, with remarkable strength, the thrust of his arm, Joleta was still standing. 'I frightened you,' she said, her little teeth sparkling before the great aquamarine eyes. 'I'm sorry. And you have a certain reputation for romantic violence to keep up. To be kind and conventional would be too dull, wouldn't it?'

'It's a lie,' said Lymond, releasing her. 'An unbridled liberty of lewd speech. I *am* kind and conventional. They pull their forelocks in the village cots, and call me the young master. How is Gabriel?'

Joleta's eyes sparkled. 'Well,' she said. 'I thank you. He writes of you often.'

'Does he, by God,' said Jerott, startled out of his trance and into unsuitable language. The Dowager looked interested and Will Scott, oblivious to nuances, was much entertained. 'What does he say? What *can* he say, missing out the swear-words?'

'Only,' said Joleta gravely, 'that in Francis Crawford he found an

230

armed neutral or even an enemy, so apprehensive was he of seduction by Mother Church.' And as Richard's eyes met those of his mother, 'And that I am not to be concerned if he shows the self-same alarm on encountering me,' said Joleta, ending, eyes downcast, in modest exposition.

Rarely, outside their own family, had a delicate situation been stripped to the bone, in the Crawfords' experience, by the supposedly oblivious victim. Never, in anyone's experience, had the protagonist made to look foolish been Lymond.

The reflex action was a foregone conclusion. Regardless of Sybilla's cry, the duenna's sudden, shocked protest, despite Richard's ejaculation or Will Scott's laughter or Jerott Blyth's angry clenched fists, Lymond pulled the girl to him in one hard, capable movement. 'But I,' said Lymond, 'am one of the new apostles, seeking nothing but voluptuousness and human pleasures, and abusing the world. . . .'

Her eyes closed as he brought his mouth down on hers. Her lips, a little apart, showed her sparkling teeth; her lashes were amber, and the long, apricot hair, streaming back to the floor, was born at her temples in powderings of golden down.

Francis Crawford drew a little breath, just before his lips touched hers, his eyes on that ineffable, heart-stopping face; then straightening, he opened his hands.

'No,' he said. 'No. I'm sorry. It's like kissing a chapel. Less a mouth, you might say, than a hole for the bell-rope. Sir Graham is right. I forego my option.' And, released from his hands and his attention in the same staggering moment, Joleta sat on the floor.

'*Francis!*' said Lord Culter hoarsely. Will Scott choked. And while Mariotta, her eyes round, looked from the dumbstruck governess to the flushed and furious Jerott and back, Sybilla Lady Culter, with erect hauteur, took the matter in hand.

'Madame Donati, I apologize. Francis, I shall speak to you later. Joleta, you can hardly be surprised at what has happened. If you had asked me, I could have told you, without putting yourself to the trouble of experiment, that no one, saint or sinner, is likely to seduce Francis against his will. Unfortunately.'

And as Madame Donati, monumental in anger, removed a white-faced and thoroughly shaken Joleta, Jerott Blyth, opening a grim conversation with Will Scott, found one satisfaction in the cheap little scene. Lymond, occupied in sitting staring at the floor, had an unpleasant appointment with the mistress of Midculter to match any he had made himself that day.

The Crawfords on the other hand were hugging a different discovery, equally pleasing. The simple village maiden was not about to fall under the young master's spell. 'And vice versa,' as Richard afterwards said. 'Vice, incredibly, versa.'

Later that night, having won his way, with some trouble, back into his family's good graces, Lymond answered some of their questions about Malta. And having listened, 'Well, they must be gey poor fighters, or ye were unco late with your warning,' said Buccleuch the Younger argumentatively. 'For they lost Gozo and Tripoli, whether it was the French knights' fault as they say or not.'

'They lost them because His Eminence the Grand Master is a two-faced bastard,' said Lymond. 'And having spent all the Order's money on himself and his nephews, he can't afford to fortify the Order's possessions as he should.'

'Depose him,' said Will Scott, astonished.

'The Grand Master's holy office terminates with his life.'

'And can nobody think of an answer to that?' said Will Scott.

'Riots, dry cuffs and straiks among God's priestly servitors, and when the dust settles, the French are in charge?' said Lymond. 'Charles would attack them, the Pope would spurn them, and four hundred years of chivalry would go for a groat. And don't tell me either there are murderers *and* murderers. If Juan de Homedès gets so much as a stuffed nose, heads will roll for it just now.'

Sybilla thought, And so you leave Malta at the mercy of this greedy old man and his retinue. That isn't like you, my boy. Presumably Francis, like Gabriel, knew too much about what had happened at Tripoli to be allowed to stay profitably on Malta. She wondered what part Francis had played in Gabriel's saintly retreat. Gabriel, they said, was a spell-binder . . . although it sounded, from Joleta's remarks, as if her son had proved more spell-resistant than Graham Malett had expected . . . which was a pity. She had no yearning to see Francis a monk—an involuntary smile crossed her face at the thought—but she believed him altogether too resistant to altogether too much.

Will Scott, dear, single-minded Will, said bluntly, 'Then what's Graham Malett going to do? What are you going to do, Francis?'

'Sir Graham, I understand, is coming back merely to see his sister and rest. I,' said Lymond, closing the lid of the spinet and sitting down again suddenly, 'am going to settle down at St Mary's and raise a little army.'

'A little army of what?' said Richard ironically, but his eyes were very wary indeed.

'Of masters in the art of war,' said Francis Crawford. 'Of trained engineers and pioneers and masters of ordnance. Sappers, billmen, pikemen, arquebusiers, strategists with horse and with foot. A virtuous little warband, highly trained and highly mobile, and nine-tenths of it officers.'

Once Lymond, with Will Scott at his side, had led a roving company in southern Scotland. Then there had been sixty of them, broken men and outlawed for the most part, because Lymond himself was outside the law. A camp such as Lymond now contemplated, on the other hand, could turn itself in two weeks of easy recruiting into an international force.

There was a respectful silence, broken by Lord Culter's agreeable voice. 'How exciting,' he said. 'And are we witnessing the foundation of the Order of St Francis, or is the Queen Dowager getting her standing army at last?'

'Not at all. You are witnessing the younger branch of the family being severely practical,' said Lymond, his blue eyes guileless in his tanned face. 'Brute force is the most saleable commodity in Europe today. In six months mine shall be in the market, washed, sorted and trimmed, and priced accordingly.'

'Strictly mercenary?' said Will Scott thoughtfully. 'My God, you'll be playing with fire.'

'No principles and no philosophy. For financial gain only,' said Francis Crawford. 'This year, I am travelling light.' And removing his gaze from his mother's frankly owlish regard, 'Now, dear Antony of Padua inform me, why should Mariotta be lugging about the Martinmas hog?'

For the door had opened on his sister-in-law, her black hair pulled curling out of its caul round her radiant face, and in her arms an animated bolster in a white, cock-eyed cap whose fat hand was wound throttlingly into its mother's agates and pearls. Its face was a pneumatic version of Mariotta's, but bountifully male.

Lymond, still talking, rose and went over. 'Don't tell me: the Master of Culter?' And he took the baby from her as he might have lifted a piglet, securely and casually, leaving her empty-handed, her gaze on Sybilla. The baby laughed and drooled, two milk-teeth shining in the wet. Lymond examined it, and it chuckled again. 'By all means,' he said. 'Born into this rout of robbers and hurly-burly of Lanarkshire vagabonds, you'd damned well better learn to spit or to giggle, or both.'

Until this child was born, the Master of Culter had been his own title. Mariotta did not forget: in four years she had matured. 'Thank you, M. le Comte,' she said gravely; and smiling, he threw the child in the air and returned it, fizzing with aerated mirth. Its eyes, coins of dark-blue iris, rolled round to follow him and Sybilla, felled by an unlooked-for discovery about this, her intellectual son, sat grinning back at a view of the door which was uncommonly blurred.

III

The Conscience of Philippa

(London, October/November 1551)

T HE day after Tom Erskine's death, Philippa Somerville finally
broke down, and was given a kindly escort home to Flaw
Valleys.

The occasion was the first news of Joleta's impetuous stand against
Lymond's soldiers and the sequel, willing or not, in Lymond's arms.
On hearing of it Philippa burst into ungainly tears and announced,
to any who could hear her, that if she also had had a pistol she
would have taken care to shoot Francis Crawford dead.

Within two days, Flaw Valleys received her. Kate Somerville, about
to leave for London on an errand of mercy of her own, took a quick
look at her daughter's angular face and decided, with a brief prayer,
to set out as planned and to take Philippa with her.

London, in an armed turmoil since the Earl of Warwick had seized
full power and flung the King's uncle and Protector into the Tower,
was not the obvious place, it had to be said, for a holiday. But her
husband, had he lived, would have been there, out of pure concern
for the safety of the boy-King he had served, and out of an exasperated loyalty to Grey of Wilton, his lordly general in the north,
now sharing the Protector's captivity.

A nondescript Northumberland widow, Kate could do nothing to
help the King or the thirteenth Baron of Wilton, but it seemed to her
that Lady Wilton might be glad of a friendly Somerville at hand.

So Kate stayed in London at the Somerville house, but took the
first chance of sending Philippa out of the city to Gideon's brother, an
ageing courtier with a toehold in both camps. Thus, in the last days
of October, Philippa Somerville found herself with her elderly nurse
Nell staying upriver with her uncle at Hampton Court Palace, where
he had, he said, Household business to contract. By no sixth sense was
it understood by either Philippa or her mother what shattering
results this family visit might have.

To begin with, it seemed to Philippa mournfully pleasant, wandering over the rain-drenched lawns and through the late Cardinal
Wolsey's big, beautiful palace, vacant but for the scattered perman-

ent staff and the small State offices, such as her uncle's, in sporadic use.

Uncle Somerville had little to say. He was busy, Philippa suspected with State business of his own, better transacted away from prying eyes in London. Visitors came and went in the back parlour of his house in the palace grounds, with its view of the smoothly flowing yellow Thames, while Philippa sat and read in the front.

Only once was he unexpectedly put out: when news came from the palace that the Queen Dowager of Scotland had landed on her way home from France, and was to break her journey at Hampton Court on her way to Westminster to be received by the King. Then Anthony Somerville, a high-coloured, placid man with thick, silvery hair, had asked one or two sharp questions, had appeared reasonably pleased with the answers, and had given orders for the royal boatmen, without livery, to be ready the following day to take a passenger up-river to London Port. The Queen Dowager, it appeared, was not due at the palace for four days, but Uncle Somerville was not taking any chances.

Philippa would not have been human, and certainly would not have been thirteen, if she had not taken good care next day to catch a glimpse of Uncle Somerville's private visitor. She saw him arrive about midday, after dinner, a tall spare man with a big nose and hollow cheeks exposing the muscular promontory of mouth and chin.

She knew then why Uncle Somerville had no wish that the Scottish court and this gentleman should meet. This was George Paris, secret agent between Ireland and France, and negotiator for those Irish lords who, paying lip-service to England, had never lost hope of persuading the King of France to help them overthrow English rule. She had met him once on a Scottish visit to Midculter: he had come straight from the Queen Dowager, whose fondest wish was to see France reign over Ireland as well. It would interest the Queen Dowager, now, to see George Paris, with a price on his head, supposedly sought high and low by the English Government as an enemy and a spy, in safe and secret conclave with an official of the English King's entourage. For George Paris was a double agent, it seemed.

Philippa wished, suddenly, that she had not witnessed the visit. Since the war had ended, she had given her friendships, as Kate had, on both sides of the Border without stint. She would take the problem, when she got back, to Kate.

But she had to take her own decision sooner than that. Hardly had her uncle and the man Paris launched into their business than she had a guest of her own.

For an instant, as her visitor paused on the threshold, Philippa thought it was Francis Crawford come to plague her. Then she saw

235

that this was a bigger man, splendidly built, with hair of a brighter yellow and clothes which were simply cheap without Lymond's expensive restraint. The face smiling at her was pink and pure-skinned, the eyes clear. Philippa, now thoroughly alarmed for a different reason, realized that confronting her was Sir Graham Reid Malett, Knight of the Order of St John, whose letters to her mother she had often read, sending his respects and his thanks for the hospitality Kate had given to his sister Joleta. And here he was, come to call on Joleta's young friend.

He looked much older than Joleta, but the family likeness was very marked. Stammering (heavens, how Kate would laugh!) Philippa introduced Nell and apologized for her uncle's delay. He neither blessed her nor became nauseatingly avuncular. Instead he said cheerfully, 'That girl's right: there's the essence of Kate Somerville in you. You don't deserve to be so lucky,' and she wondered if Joleta had reported so flatteringly of her mother, or if Graham Malett knew the Border hearsay of the Somervilles. His home, after all, had not been so far away long ago. Then he went on to chat easily about his journey from France in the Queen Dowager's ships and about his coming reunion with his sister, and she began to see how Joleta, whose quick brain held nothing sacred, could still worship him; and whence she derived some of her startling appeal.

Meanwhile, Philippa herself, making dutiful conversation, was in the grip of a notion. Cumbered with rather less than the usual count of desperate sins, she had been to confession all her life as a matter of course. Since returning from Scotland she had not visited church and Uncle Somerville, fortunately, hadn't noticed.

The trouble was, a dying man had confided a message to her and she had not conveyed it. Nor had she any intention of doing so. Philippa looked at Gabriel's calm face and thought that he at least, knowing what Lymond was, would absolve her from placing this weapon in Lymond's hands.

Her uncle would be here soon: the low murmur of voices in the next room was getting louder and moving towards the door. She said quickly, 'Are you sick of priest things, or could I ask you something do you think?'

Gabriel didn't laugh at all; he merely looked interested and said, 'It's non-priest things I usually get sick of, don't you? There's nothing I like better than putting my wits to work with a friend. What sort of problem is it?'

'It's a friend's, actually,' said Philippa cautiously, and in words as old as the language of Eden. 'There's this man she doesn't like.'

'And someone wants her to marry him?' said Gabriel helpfully. Startled into horrified amusement, 'Oh, no! No, no!' said Philippa.

'She just hates him. Everybody does. He questions small children and laughs about old ladies who are . . . who are hurt.'

'He sounds appalling,' Gabriel agreed. 'Womanizes too, I expect?'

Philippa went scarlet. 'Well . . . yes. So one believes. So, you see, he doesn't deserve to be helped.'

'Who would want to help him?' Gabriel asked.

'Oh, some people. There was this man who was dying,' said Philippa rapidly. 'And someone told him a secret which if it got known, would cause a lot of pain and misery and would do no one any good, except . . . except . . .'

'The man your friend dislikes so much.'

'That's it,' said Philippa thankfully. 'And my friend was asked to pass on the secret and she hasn't. She won't go to hell, will she?'

Gabriel's eyes, clear and steady, were fixed on hers. 'I don't think I've got a very unbiased story, have I? And I don't want to question you any more, or obviously I'd learn more than you want to tell me. But there are two things you must ask yourself. Did the dying man who passed you the secret recognize that it might be put to some wicked use? And did he tell anyone else?'

'No, he didn't,' said Philippa positively. 'I'm the only one who knows. And I'm sure he'd never think of the damage it would do. He was very deceived, you know.' She then went slowly scarlet.

'It's a useful convention,' said Gabriel comfortingly. 'But I'd rather guessed anyway. Do you know, from what you say, I don't think you owe it to anyone particularly to make trouble now by passing on this precious secret of yours. Will the effect on your unpleasant friend be painful if he doesn't know?'

Into Philippa's brown eyes came a speculative glint which Kate would have seen with misgiving. 'It might make him feel rather silly,' she said.

'Is that all?'

'It wouldn't *kill* him,' said Philippa. 'It wouldn't even *hurt* him, except in his conceit. It was only that a promise to a dying man. . . .'

'But the dying man, you say, didn't know all the facts. And if the truth would really cause such an upheaval, there is really no virtue in telling it. There are truths and truths,' said Gabriel solemnly. He smiled. 'You've been really upset about this, haven't you? No confession for weeks?'

'No,' shamefaced.

'Well, you may begin again now,' said Gabriel cheerfully. 'You've acted only for the best, and concealment of that sort isn't a sin, my dear child, that requires agonizing over, or even confessing. Make your reparation, if you still feel unhappy, by doing your best to swallow your dislike for this poor man, whoever he is. Keep out of his way, and try to be sorry for him. He doesn't know he's going to look a fool.'

Which was comforting. She was free to keep from Lymond the information Tom Erskine wanted him to have. And if Gabriel gave her his sanction without knowing the parties involved, how much more would he have done so knowing the truth?

Shortly after that, her uncle came in. No one had left the house by the dark little hall, so the inconvenient Mr Paris must have been smuggled out at the back. It had all been rather obvious, thought Philippa, and hoped that Joleta's brother was not inclined to regard the whole Somerville family as deep in weaselly intrigue. In any case, Gabriel stayed very little longer. What time he could spare had been already spent in Philippa's company, and he did not seem to regret it. Indeed, on hearing that Philippa and her nurse Nell were both due back in London almost immediately, he offered instantly to take them both with him in the barge waiting for him outside. Without Nell's long face she might have gone; but it wasn't really practicable with all the packing they had to do, and she had to let him go without her.

They met once more before Philippa went back to Flaw Valleys, when Sir Graham called at the Somerville house in London to pay his respects to Kate, and found Margaret Erskine there, off duty while the Queen Dowager rested before the royal banquet.

Margaret Erskine was on her way home after a year in France with the Scottish Queen Mother, and the costly ceremonies which were keeping Mary of Lorraine as a guest of etiquette in London were not grudged by the English Government half as much as by Tom Erskine's wife.

That for twenty days she had been Tom Erskine's widow was known to her mistress, to the French Ambassador in London and to very few others besides. Margaret Erskine herself was, of design, totally unaware of it, and would be, policy had decided, until she reached Scotland. The Scottish party must appear secure, sophisticated and carefree. The Dowager, in mourning white, had just lost her one living son, but her behaviour was handsomely gay. Margaret Erskine, normally a plump and prosaic young soul, was not only gay; she was sparkling with life at the prospect, at last, of rejoining her little son and her Tom.

Kate, going to her parlour door when Sir Graham Malett was announced, was frankly gloomy. To begin with, she thought it barbarous that Tom Erskine's wife should not be told of her husband's death, and she had said as much to the equerry who had arrived deprecatingly on her doorstep that morning from the Scottish Queen Dowager. However, she did not propose to interfere between the poor girl and her Queen, so she was forced, against her instincts, to greet Margaret when she arrived as if nothing had happened. Philippa, who showed a strong tendency to linger large-eyed in corners, was dispatched to her cittern to practise and Kate was grimly carrying out her part of the conversational bargain with no pleasure at all when the steward came to tell her she was wanted. Margaret, who had brought a chicken and was deep in detailed recipe-making, disappeared promptly and happily in the direction of the kitchens while Kate walked downstairs, meeting an inquisitive Philippa on the way.

Her visitor was, she found, that gallant crusading hero, Joleta's brother. Taking him into the small parlour she rarely used, Kate was civil and Philippa effusive. Kate had set up, her daughter knew, a characteristic resistance against the legend of Gabriel which had stiffened more than a little since Philippa's own glowing account, suitably edited, of the Hampton Court encounter. Sir Graham also had the misfortune to be staying with the Earl of Ormond, whom she disliked.

Kate had had much the same reaction to Joleta when the girl had arrived at Flaw Valleys in a cloudburst of reverent awe: only after she proved that Joleta was human did Kate unbend and become her usual sardonic self. Now, Philippa watching with an experienced eye saw that Sir Graham Malett was aware of this guardedness and was amused by it, even to the extent of apologizing for his noble Irish friend. Ormond, he agreed gravely over Kate's lavish refreshments, was a sorry young pensioner of his country's enemy, but one must be tolerant. He had to be so or hang.

Kate, who did not like being humoured either, switched the subject to Malta but did not succeed in drawing him either on the fall of Tripoli or on the conduct of the Grand Master. 'What, no harems unlocked, no spirited slave-girls carried safely to freedom? What a dull time crusaders are having these days,' said Kate at length. 'I shall need, obviously, to get the coarse side of the story out of Francis Crawford.'

'No,' said Gabriel with a moment's diffidence. 'That I shouldn't recommend.'

Kate, who had half her mind on Margaret Erskine helping to show the cook how to do a French chicken, jerked her attention back and said, 'Why? I'm sure he'd run anybody's white slave traffic with exceptional skill.'

She wished heartily that he would go away. Coming from France as he did, it was impossible that he should know about Tom Erskine, but she did not intend that he and Margaret should meet. Her own powers of dissimulation were not very great; his were probably non-existent. Nor did it seem fair to ask such a man to play a part in a deception.

In any case, he was deep in thought on some other subject entirely. After a considerable pause he said unexpectedly, 'I wonder, Mistress Somerville, if you know a man called Cormac O'Connor?'

'I know of him,' said Kate shortly. 'He's an outlawed Irishman who's been trying for years to get French or Scottish help to drive the English out of Ireland.'

'He was also the possessor,' said Gabriel without looking at her, 'of a very beautiful mistress. I met him in France the other week, in Ormond's company, as I was telling you. He parted with the woman in the end—he swears to our incorrigible friend Francis. In any case, it is a fact that Francis joined her in Tripoli, and lost her there. She was an unlucky woman; and the mistress of a knight of the Order for long months before that; but they had a real attraction for each other. I tell you only that you won't take the subject of women lightly, when next you meet.'

'I won't meet him ever again,' said Philippa forbiddingly.

Gabriel, seated in a chair too small for him, smiled at Kate, who merely lifted her brows. His smile grew broader. 'There seems to be a general disenchantment,' he said. 'Joleta writes in the same, if not stronger terms. I'm sorry, because I was relying on her to exert a little moral blackmail.'

Tact was not yet Philippa's strongest point. 'But Mr Crawford *kissed* her!' she said.

'Philippa!' Kate could hardly keep the satisfaction out of her voice.

'It's true! It was all round Boghall!'

Graham Malett was laughing aloud. 'It *is* true. Joleta wrote about it. But you haven't got the essential facts.' He looked at Philippa and sobered suddenly. 'This is a brilliant young man going to waste. I have failed with him; we have all failed. His career in France last winter is a sorry business, best forgotten. I had thought that Malta would change him . . . but he cannot do without women, he cannot do without wealth, he cannot do without admiration. He has come to Scotland for no better purpose than to raise a money-making army of mercenaries, just as he went to Malta for no better reason than that the Constable paid him to. I hoped that in Joleta's company he would learn other values.'

'On the whole,' said Kate bluntly, 'I feel that he would be far more likely to bend his brilliant mind to seducing Joleta.'

Gabriel's wise, direct gaze moved from Kate to her daughter. 'No man living could dishonour my sister. I believe in Joleta as I believe in the fount of my faith. But I would give her in marriage to this one man, if he asked it, provided that he brought as his marriage portion his new-made army, a holy instrument for Mother Church.'

'You would let him marry Joleta, knowing him as you do?' said

240

Kate sharply; and 'Poor Joleta!' said Philippa in a carping voice, and was quiet under her mother's glance.

Gabriel smiled. 'Joleta exercises a curious transmutation of her own. If she promised herself to him, he would become her equal in honour; of that I am sure. But it seems unlikely that she will. She challenged him, I think, and he felt impelled to show how vastly indifferent he was, and she became thoroughly piqued in return. . . . They are not elderly, passionless statesmen, these two. They would not be worth troubling over if they were.'

Philippa's eyes were suddenly shining. 'How nice,' she said genteelly, 'if your sister and Mr Crawford were married. Love often begins with a show of hate, doesn't it?'

'Only common mortals like the Somervilles have good old rotten hates, dear,' said her mother. 'Sir Graham manages to love everybody and wouldn't know what you're talking about. Have a bun.'

'He doesn't love the Turks,' said Philippa. 'He kills them.'

'That isn't hate,' said Kate Somerville. 'That's simply hoeing among one's principles to keep them healthy and neat. I'm sure he would tell you he bears them no personal grudge; and they think they're going to Paradise anyway, so it does everyone good.'

With some relief, Philippa saw that Gabriel was smiling. 'You have a sharp tongue,' he said. 'I think at bottom you approve of Lymond more than of me. You may be quite right.'

Starting from the collarbone of her least unfashionable winter dress and ending at the back of her ears, Kate flushed. Then, with Philippa's bright angry eyes fixed on her, she said, 'I merely know him better, perhaps. There is nothing wrong with his standards. He merely has difficulty, as we all do, in living up to them, with somewhat hair-raising results.'

'Whereas I succeed because my aim is more commonplace, and you find me smug,' said Gabriel gently. 'But we may only do our best as we are made. You will make life very unhappy for yourself and the child if you measure all your friends against this charming, undisciplined man.'

Kate's brown eyes were wide open to preserve her from any suspicion of weakness. 'My friends don't mind,' she said. 'Have a bun.'

At which moment, to Philippa's appalled relief, Margaret Erskine came in, smelling of chicken. She said, 'Oh, I'm sorry my dear: you're still busy,' and then looked surprised and pleased. 'Graham!' He had of course, Philippa remembered, travelled from France with her, although he had left the Dowager's party to come to London first. For the thousandth time, Philippa wondered how Jenny Fleming, the vivid mistress of Henri of France, could have produced this downy little person who, a war widow of nineteen, had found joy at

241

last with the Master of Erskine. Then Graham Malett, towering above them, said, 'Joleta has written me. What can I say, except thank God it was over so quickly?'

There was a terrifying silence, during which the three women stared at him as if he were an idiot while, hands outstretched, Gabriel took Margaret's floury fingers in his. Then Kate said quickly and harshly, 'Stop and listen. She hasn't been told yet. By the Queen Mother's orders. Break it quickly: she'll have to know now. Margaret, sit down.'

But Margaret remained standing, clearly unaware, to Philippa's frightened eyes, of anything but Gabriel's changing face. His grip on her hands became rigid as Kate spoke; there was a second's pause, then in a deep voice he said, 'Sit, for I must ask your forgiveness. I thought you knew. It is bad news, and from Boghall. Your husband was taken with the sweating sickness. He is with your father, at peace in God.'

There was a long silence while Margaret, her face perfectly livid, gazed composedly at Sir Graham. At length, 'He can't be,' she said. 'Not Tom. Not Tom *as well.*'

'Did you think life was always fair and always just?' said Gabriel. 'It isn't. You wouldn't be the person you are if it were; you would be a happy simpleton. But you are not, and today is your day of mourning.'

The words did what they were meant to do. After a single choked gasp, Margaret Erskine, now Margaret Fleming again, closed her eyes with her two hands and wept.

Shortly afterwards, finding herself unwanted, Kate crept outside the room with Philippa and drying her daughter's tears, set her to finish the French chicken. Then she sat down and had a limited cry to herself, within hearing of the low murmur of Gabriel's lovely voice. Margaret could not be in better hands at this moment. She only wished that his spell was less powerful where Philippa was concerned. She then faced, drearily, the fact that her own motives for this were heavily prejudiced; and further the fact that sometimes now she was able to forget: that Philippa's father was dead. '*Gideon,*' said Kate silently to herself on one noiseless intake of breath, and rising as if she had been shot, went to help Philippa with the fowl.

IV

The Axe Is Fashioned

(St Mary's, Autumn 1551)

CARRYING hods in Egypt, grimly, for Gabriel's sake, Jerott Blyth proceeded to the keep of St Mary's near the loch of that name in the Central Lowlands of Scotland, and remained there, professionally enthralled, the entire winter, while a legend was born.

Unlike the former Will Scott, Blyth was no inexperienced youth when he joined Francis Crawford. As soon as he arrived with the rest from Midculter in the district called Lymond, he saw that the land was already half-prepared for its burden. In fields newly fenced and hedged were wedders, rams and milk-ewes, all in good order. There were oxen for the table and plough, geese in the ponds and birds in the dovecots and coneys in the warrens. They passed barns stacked with oats, wheat and barley; a sawmiller's with cuts of oak stacked outside and new wheels leaning against their own shadows and silted full of October leaves.

Then the cottages and outlying buildings of St Mary's itself came in sight: the stacks of brown peat and charcoal; the forge with the air lively about it and the bell-chime of the hammer sweet above the thud of the horses. The stables, well-built rank upon rank, with covered horselines before, and a separate well. The bake-house, with its peel and tubs and tables and barrels of flour. The brewery, the warm malt-smell thick on the air, with the shining wortstands glimpsed through the windows, and the sweating five-gallon barrels of ale.

He saw the riding-school, and beyond it where the tiltyard had been laid out, and the butts and the practice ground for small and heavy arms shooting. Near these was the armoury, with crates and barrels outside still being unpacked. He had seen their contents being disembarked at Leith with a flaring interest that would not be denied: the shot and arquebuses and demi-culverins, the chests of bows and sheaves of arrows, the staves and dags and bills and axes, the lead malls for the archers, the pikeheads and powder, the touch boxes and flasks, the lint and the tar and the pitch and the halberds and the stacks of chain mail, headpieces, corselets; the wire for faggots, staves for ladles, hides, crowbars, harness buckles and prongs; the sieves, the ramrods, the handbaskets and shears—such was the marrow of war.

To assemble these things faultlessly, and from a distance, meant some very high-power organizing indeed. It also meant a long purse —a startlingly long purse, even for a man with two homes and a comté of unknown resources abroad. Jerott Blyth at about this point turned a conjecturing look on Francis Crawford of Lymond riding easily at his side and wondered what else he had overlooked during these hot August weeks on Malta and Tripoli.

The first person he met in the clean and beautiful courtyard of St Mary's was Michel de Seurre, Knight of the Order of St John. The second was the Serving Brother des Roches who had defended the harbour fort at Tripoli, and the third was the Moor Salablanca. Lymond in Africa had not wasted his time.

The task force which was to become famous in Europe began with two hundred men and eight officers. Later, other knights came to join it, and a number of exiles like Jerott who had made their homes overseas, bringing the total by Christmas up to thirty men all of whom had had at least a gentleman's training in war, and some of whom, like de Seurre and Jerott himself, were highly qualified.

To contain them, an excellent dormitory wing had been built on to St Mary's, which Jerott remembered as a war-crumbled keep untouched since the first Baron's day, and which had been completely restored to frankly Florentine splendours. Lancelot Plummer, the engineer and master-architect who designed it, was living there now, drawn by curiosity to become a pupil in his own new academy.

Jerott, who had met the exquisite gentleman in France, knew he was as hard as nails and had a whimsy of iron, and wondered, grimly amused, how Lymond thought he could handle him. Or Fergie Hoddim the lawyer, who knew more about vice than probably any man living; or Randy Bell the surgeon whose experience was nearly as wide and not nearly so academic; and Alec Guthrie who had lectured in Latin and Greek in nearly every university in Italy and Germany and France: a home-spun Humanist who would have had Socrates himself saying weakly, 'Take my case for example. . . .'

And Hercules Tait, antiquarian, diplomat, collector and businessman, who not only knew all the crowned heads of Europe but was related to most of them; and Adam Blacklock the painter, with his stutter and his wasted leg that he had taught himself to skate and ride and vault with, and his alcoholic fits of despair.

Jerott Blyth thought of the Knights of the Order with their violent, warring personalities reduced by the strict rules of the Church, by danger and hard work, by the rivalry of the Langues, the isolation from vice and free will and, above all, by the universal fire of their faith, and wondered cynically how a public warehouse for soldiers, with Francis Crawford as sole director and tout, could expect to succeed.

He found out during his first night at St Mary's. Used to communal living, he had early found himself a bed next to Randy Bell and stowed his possessions; then made himself roughly familiar with his fellow-scholars and with the chief technicians who were to run St Mary's and its equipment, and with the enlisted mercenaries who were to be the standing nucleus of its force.

It was a heavy day, and when at last he got to bed long after dark he was bone-weary; his mind deadened by new people and new impressions on top of the long journey to Scotland. The other seven in his room, some of them arrived only hours before and still unpacked, were equally worn. Few words were exchanged as one by one they came into the chamber and rolled, half-dressed or naked into bed.

At midnight, in a clangorous frenzy, the alarm bell rang. At first Jerott, clogged with sleep, thought it meant Turks. He struggled upright, the cold hilt of his sword to his hand, and then saw that he was in St Mary's, and that the cursing sleepers around him, slowly struggling to life under the single dim cresset, were as bemused as himself. Then a voice, a cultured voice which Jerott recognized as belonging to Salablanca, the Moor Lymond had rescued from Tripoli, spoke from the doorway in Spanish.

'Gentlemen. The apologies of Mr Crawford for disturbing you. Your presence is required, dressed, in the great hall in five minutes. I am asked to say that any gentleman later than this will be free to leave St Mary's at once.'

No one was late. But the quality of the silence when, seated grimly in rows in the blazingly lit hall, a bunch of dissident intellectuals awaited their leader, was corrosive in the extreme.

Lymond had been little in evidence that day: the sheer bulk of paper-work awaiting him on this his first visit to the altered St Mary's must have been daunting in itself. But now, when they were scarcely assembled, he came quickly on to the empty dais, bareheaded and unsmiling, glanced round, noting numbers, and then spoke, pleasantly and without unduly raising his voice.

'Gentlemen. . . . This is not the last time I shall exact from you unquestioning obedience. It is, however, the last time I shall do it without prior consultation.'

Clever stuff, thought Jerott sardonically. There was a fragile slackening of the outrage in the atmosphere and Lymond felt it, he was sure. He spoke again. 'By now you have met each other. You are all intelligent men, and men of consequence and ability. The others who will join you are of the same kind. Among you there will be no rank and no distinction. Any money this force may earn will be distributed equally among you. Your living expenses should we earn no income will be guaranteed by me. We are therefore a money-making unit, but the financial risk is mine, and these, which I am making clear to you now, are my conditions for taking it.'

Two conditions, said Jerott Blyth's wincing spirit. 'Worship me, and make me a rich man.'

As if he read his mind, Lymond's eyes rested for a moment on Jerott's, then passed on. He said, 'Your reasons for joining me are your own affair. You should know mine for having you. There is no standing army in England, although there has been an attempt to ensure one by paying noble landowners to raise and arm troops and to produce them at need. When the Government needs help it has to call in mercenaries under their captains from Germany and the Low Countries.'

He paused, testing their restlessness: no one moved. 'In Scotland there is no money for annual commissions. Even if there were, the natural leaders have been decimated by wars and divided by religious differences and rival claims to the throne. There have been proposals for a standing army of mercenaries; there is strong pressure currently to instal an official army of French. Both these would be operated for and through the Crown, and in my view both would be dangerous. . . .'

Below, someone stirred. Alec Guthrie, his greying hair thickly on end, said impatiently in his grating, lecturer's voice, 'May we speak? No one ever made a fortune protecting Scotland. If the French want to spend money that way, let them get on with it.'

'On the contrary,' said Lymond. 'If France or anyone else wants to spend money on that little job, let them pay us. Mercenaries and foreign garrisons we all know cause endless trouble. In any case the Emperor probably wouldn't release any more Germans or Swiss, and France has other uses for her troops, even if she could persuade them to go on fighting here. . . .'

'. . . So we are to become the fighting arm of the Queen Dowager,' said Hercules Tait lazily. 'I had a strange feeling it would come to that all along.'

'We are to become,' said Lymond, and suddenly his pleasant voice cut like edged glass, 'the strongest *independent* fighting unit these islands have ever known. We take work, for which we shall be paid, and we lay down the terms under which we carry out such work. If we think the work undesirable from any point of view, moral or material, we refuse.'

'M. le Comte . . .' It was the Chevalier de Seurre's bantering voice. 'May I point out that what you are proposing is to establish military

246

rule in your country? You are creating an *élite* of professional leaders to replace your vanishing noblemen. The Queen Dowager comes to you, very humbly, for an army, say, with which to invade England. You say, you, "No. I do not wish to attack England today. Instead we shall turn on our garrisons and push out the French." And so it is done. What can she do to stop you? You have the strongest fighting force in these islands.'

'And who takes these decisions in any case?' came Alec Guthrie's level growl. 'Yourself alone?'

Jerott found he was smiling a satisfied smile. So much for under-rehearsed empire building. Lymond said agreeably, 'Let's put another question before we start thinking of answers. Since when was the Queen Dowager at once a diplomat, a lawyer, an expert on political and military strategy, a seaman, a philosopher, a clear-minded and unprejudiced onlooker? I am none of these things. She, because in fact she is in many ways a good woman, is some of them. But we, as a unit, *are all of them*.'

'I repeat my premise,' said Alec Guthrie, but the fierce eyes under their hooded brows were narrowed on Lymond. 'You want to rule.'

His hands loosely behind his back, Lymond considered his answer. He spoke almost at once. 'My intention is to move among the battlefields of Europe and elsewhere and earn a great deal of money. My conditions are that at the same time we police and protect this nation as best we may, regulating the international squabbles, clearing both sides of the Border of the thieves and the lawless, carrying out justice where justice has up to now failed because of the threat of blood feuds. Beyond that I have no wish to usurp the authority of the Crown. For these services I should expect to be paid, by the Queen Dowager in Scotland and by the English Government over the Border. The payment, I can warn you now, will be in bags of tin pennies. But to your sons and grandsons the effects, if we do our work worthily, should be worth their measure in gold.'

Surprise, thought Jerott in the ensuing silence. Spiritual values have tottered into the discussion. He sounded as though he meant it. It doesn't matter whether he means it or not. He needs a unifying principle, and he's picked a crusade ... any crusade. Malta, thy wing is here.

'D ...' said Adam Blacklock, and smiling and dogged, tried it again. 'Dr Guthrie asked who would decide what the force will or won't do.'

Lymond loosed his hands. He was now, Jerott saw, truly at ease, smiling at the big artist, glancing to the back of the hall where Archie Abernethy and his senior sergeants waited quietly, and then running his blue gaze over all the heads, red, brown, blond, black, bearded and clean-shaven.

247

'When this winter is over you will be unbeatable in the world in the arts of war,' he said. 'More than that, you will have shared among you your judgements and your learning. Matters of policy will be settled by free discussion between us: who better could deal with it? I invite you now to criticize my views and my plans with your own. You are free to test on your own intelligence and initiative every step I take as your leader. The proviso is . . . that I *am* your leader. The casting vote is mine. The final decision is mine, and the unquestioned decision in emergency. And once I have issued my orders, however unlicensed the argument beforehand, I expect them to be instantly obeyed. There is only one punishment here for insubordination, and that is instant expulsion. I hope this is clear.'

'I follow you on these terms.' It was the quiet voice of the Serving Brother des Roches, who had held the Châtelet at Tripoli. 'I follow you on any terms, sir. You have my respect.'

'And ye hae mine,' said Fergie Hoddim levelly, 'if ye intend to argue every decision with this lot. Ye'll hae to pull straws for who's tae blaw out the tapers.'

'The legal mind,' said Lancelot Plummer caressingly. 'If we get bored in Scotland, may we depose you and go somewhere sunny?'

'I rather doubt,' said Lymond blandly, 'if you'll have the energy for long arguments. If you succeed in deposing me, you will certainly qualify for a trip somewhere sunny, or even merely, somewhere uncommonly hot. . . . For while I shall know all your tricks by the end of the winter, I doubt if you will know mine.'

'Why,' said the rich, agreeable voice of the doctor Randy Bell as he sat unmoving, thumbs tucked in his jacket. 'Have ye a sure cure for arsenic? It's a grand preventative for broken nights.'

'You should make the acquaintance of Archie Abernethy there,' said Lymond, unmoved. 'He used to give it to his elephants. You'd better come forward, Archie. . . . Am I to take it, gentlemen, that we are agreed?'

They were, Jerott saw: won over by the little display of disinterestedness and by the prospect of unlimited debate. They began to rise.

'Then you ought,' said Lymond painstakingly, 'to take note of the fact that Mr Abernethy has just released from their stalls two hundred and fifty of our young horses and driven them out of the grounds. They are worth sixty-five angels each and cannot be replaced locally. Every horsethief in the southern uplands will therefore be after them, and pretty well every other household worth its salt, come to that.

'Remembering that we have to live among these people without antagonizing them, you may begin rounding them up as from now. Archie will tell you directly what the stock markings are. You will of course have them here before morning: the training course proper opens at six a.m. in this hall. You might even manage some sleep. I,' said Lymond calmly, 'am going to bed. Good night, gentlemen. And good luck.'

It was a moonless night, and had just begun, grudgingly, to rain when his disbelieving audience found themselves outside the gates. Cantering round the soggy hilltops, lanterns jogging, and six furious mercenaries pounding behind, Jerott Blyth peered at somebody's ill-drawn map and then at the night before him, alive like a topiarist's nightmare with horse-shaped bush and twist, and cursed everyone but Graham Malett.

By four in the morning he had a dozen of the lost mounts, and had displayed furious tact through every kind of reception from farm and cottage in his allotted terrain. It was only now, approaching the last, that he discovered that Lymond in fact had not gone to bed. As he rode up to the porch, a tranquil voice in the darkness said, 'You may leave this house out. A baby is just being born. Who is it? Jerott?'

'Yes.' Through the rain you could just distinguish horse and rider, motionless against the wet thatch.

'How many have you recovered?' Lymond asked.

'Twelve. I'm expecting a report from the tally-centre.' They had a central depot established.

'You needn't wait for it, then. All the horses are in. You will find some of your colleagues collected more, but you had easily the worst ground to cover. Did you enjoy it?'

Imbecile question. Jerott Blyth opened his mouth to answer it as it deserved; then was struck, as many times before in his life, by a crazy discovery. 'Yes,' he said.

'Odd, isn't it?' said Lymond without surprise. 'It is the reason, if you would recognize it, why you enjoyed being a Knight of the Order. I'll look after your scout when he comes. If you go back now, you might just get half an hour's sleep.'

At six a.m., alert, alive, roughly cleaned up and talking hoarsely and indiscriminately among themselves, the twenty officers of St Mary's were all there in the hall. Lymond was there before them; not on the platform but amongst them, astride a chair and ruffling through a rainsoaked pile of notes. He bore no sign of having been out at all, but took them step by step through as nasty, and subsequently as hilarious a post-mortem of the night's ride that Jerott had ever attended. Then he gave out details of the day's work.

It was tough, brutal and typical of the régime they were to follow for the next six to eight weeks, with one exception. It ended at dusk. Then, over-extended and outplayed like worn guitar strings, the entire camp went to bed and slept for twelve hours.

The fashioning of a great corps had begun.

*

From the beginning it was clear to Jerott that Lymond could never have achieved what he did that evening with tyros. It was because these men, whatever their profession—philosopher, architect, lawyer, painter, doctor, artist and priest—were by force of the times they lived in soldiers also, and understood that speed and skill and toughness and above all self-confidence came from being pushed again and again and again past the edge of endurance until that limit became as elastic as an extra muscle, held in reserve. That crucial night they had their first taste of each other's quality and of Lymond's, and they found they could laugh.

They laughed a lot, breathlessly, that winter; but in between it was work: the hardest work Jerott had ever known in his life since the days of his caravans; more punishing by far than his novitiate, with the pious exercises, the swordplay and the shooting in ordered successions.

At St Mary's, perfection in every known branch of warfare was their professed object. Taught by queer initiates who sprang up out of the ground and then vanished, their exercise done; or by sharing their own considerable expertise, they shot and wrestled and ran and jumped; fought each other on foot and on horseback with every conceivable weapon; learned the use and practice and assembly and repair and transport of firearms from pistols to basilisks; absorbed strategy and field work and camp organization, large-scale feeding and medication, siege maintaining and breaking; pioneering and mining and mechanical means of assault.

They discussed armour and its uses and horses and their maintenance and listened to and shared a surprising amount of knowledge about other races and their methods of fighting. Salablanca continued to convey his master's orders in Spanish, and any other foreigner Lymond imported also spoke, without translation, his own tongue. There was to begin with a nervy scramble among themselves to find an interpreter. They usually did, and after a month or two were able thankfully to dispense with him: Lymond made no concessions on the grounds of language. If they fought abroad they would be expected as a matter of course to speak as their allies did. If they did not already know several European languages, then they must learn.

He would not, to begin with, let them ride their own hobby horses at all. If Randy Bell twitted him on the absence of feminine company, if Plummer bewailed his days filled with brawny antics and Fergie Hoddim tried to start an argument about their constitutional position or lack of it; if Tait struck up a travellers' private club with Archie Abernethy and Alec Guthrie tried to argue with Jerott about his soul and Adam Blacklock began to talk about Midculter, Lymond simply set them an exercise that lasted three days and unravelled their sinews like crochet work. When they came back they hadn't the strength even to curse him for it.

By then they were all caught up with it. When Lord Culter came once to visit them, bringing with him Will Scott and his father Buccleuch, Lymond stopped active senior work instantly, and instead had them all idly watching fifty mercenaries, for the tenth time that week, put up a complete camp, kitchens and pavilions and all, in two hours flat. Because none of them could keep away from it for very long, someone was arguing very soon about hackbuts with old Buccleuch, and the next thing anyone knew, targets had been set up and a lot of vigorous, loud-mouthed matches were going on.

Richard Crawford himself took part briefly in the archery and then retired, rather silent, to watch the doctor and Adam Blacklock shoot it out. Only Jerott, perched on a piece of fencing behind, heard him stroll up to his brother and say, abruptly, 'Not for the first time, you frighten me silly.'

Lymond, who had been watching the mercenaries and not the shooting, turned quickly. 'Why? You still shoot a good deal better than that.'

'Thank you,' said Richard drily. 'I hear you sent the Queen Dowager's gifts back.'

'Where did you hear that? It doesn't matter. I merely thought it might be inconvenient to have to pay for them some day,' said Lymond. 'So what frightens you?' And there was, Jerott noted, the slightest possible stress on the word 'you'.

His elder brother, grey eyes level, held his gaze. 'Perfection frightens me,' he said. 'They're too good, Francis. What do you want this axe-edge for?'

'*To cut with*,' said Lymond, his voice mild. For a moment longer they considered one another without speaking, then, abandoning the contest, Richard began to talk of other things.

Later, Will Scott joined them with something like envy in his eyes, and Lymond led him to speak of Grizel and the children, and from there to the unrest on the Borders. However much the three Border Wardens of Scotland and their counterparts of England met and wrangled and meted out justice, the trouble went on. Lymond said, 'If I were Warden, I'm damned if I wouldn't pair you off. For every Kerr head cut off, a bone-headed Scott gets the chop. That would either stop you or obliterate you, in time.'

'Well, well. Francis Crawford, in honest leather for once.' It was Wat Scott of Buccleuch, Will's father, scenting blood from afar. Bear shoulders braced and grizzled beard cocked, he straddled the wet russet grass. 'And with Tom Erskine gone and the Scotts gone and the Crawfords hell-bent on stooters, where d'ye suppose the Queen Dowager will get all her help from? France! And let me tell you I've been yapped at by enough musk-stinkit Frenchmen in the last three–four years tae gar me boke at the name.'

'Then for God's sake stop killing Kerrs,' said Lymond tartly. 'It's a signal for every other laird with inelastic opinions to treat a difference as a personal affront. A great and glorious nation of vindicated corpses: that's us.'

'That's what Janet says,' said Buccleuch gloomily. His energetic fourth wife (and son's good-sister) was a cross he bore in cheerful despair. 'Only in wee words.' His expression brightened. 'Have ye heard about Sybilla and the Italian woman?'

'Oh, yes.' Richard, visibly, was also cheered by a recollection. 'Remember Madame Donati, Francis? Joleta's duenna?'

'*La plus gaie demoiselle qui soit d'ici en Italie.* If you insist, I do,' said Lymond. 'What of her?'

Under Richard Crawford's benign eye, Buccleugh went purple, faded to scarlet, and when under normal aegis again said, 'Well, she spoke in Italian to Joleta one day, the cheeky besom, while your mother was in the room, and not knowing that Sybilla's fine little head is filled with useless information, she didna watch her tongue. So. . . .'

'So the last thing my mother would do is betray that she understood Italian,' said Lymond, amused. 'What anyway was the insult, Wat, that could make a Buccleuch blush?'

Richard, serene as ever, came to Wat's rescue. 'Spare him, my dear. It was the old story. She thought you and I were remarkably unlike.'

'And more, I would guess,' said Lymond, unmoved. 'So Sybilla found gentle revenge. How?'

'By telling the Signora that Peter Cranston had a fortune,' said Will Scott, and broke into howls of uninhibited laughter.

'Don't tell me,' said Lymond, his calm broken.

'Aye. She's after him like a deer at the rut,' said Buccleuch, satisfied. 'Takes a glass of wine at Cranston when riding near with dear Joleta, and lights enough candles on her hocks tae warm the cockles of his bead-clicking heart. He's daft. She's dafter. And isna Sybilla a wee love o' a bitch?'

'You say the nicest things about my mother,' said Lymond. 'Come in and have some wine, for God's sake, and tell us who in your opinion is sleeping with whom, and what capital you're going to make of it.' And they went in, Jerott following with Will Scott and moreover listening to him.

*

Lymond left St Mary's only once in those early weeks, to ride to Boghall Castle just after Margaret Erskine came home. The ostensible reason was to convoy a load of arms and saltpetre on its way inland from Leith, and Jerott went with him. By now it was clear that Gabriel, as usual, had been right. What he had proposed to suffer as a humbling martyrdom was proving a sharp satisfaction. He enjoyed working with Lymond. He meant, with de Seurre and des Roches to help him, first to make himself indispensable and then to educate this spiritual lout, to make . . . what had Gabriel said? A holy weapon out of a mercenary.

Lymond also took with him Bell and Guthrie for, it seemed likely, his own private amusement: the surgeon, breathing heavily, to stalk Lady Jenny, and Alec Guthrie to rationalize the event.

The meeting between Lymond and Tom Erskine's widow took place in private. Jerott, who had no interest in Lady Jenny Fleming, however pretty and however famous as the King of France's second-string mistress, set about getting the wagons loaded and the oxen hitched, with his men's help: thank God the weather was still open and the ground reasonably firm. Today, with the mild sun alight and the idle air removing, in quiet groups, the yellow leaves from the trees, Jerott whistled loud and secular tunes, and was grateful when Alec Guthrie, fully stocked with ground-up comment on Randy Bell's virility, came and joined in the work.

Lady Jenny, it seemed, had given them a charming welcome but to the doctor's disappointment was only interested in the news from France. Rumour said that she was desperate, now the royal bastard was several months old, to return before the paternal memory faded to engender another. Rumour further said that in order to make a licensed and legitimate reappearance in French royal circles, she was making a dead set at M. d'Oisel, the King of France's unhappy Ambassador; and rumour must have substance under its hat, for she was making a dead set at nobody else.

Except of course Lymond, whom she had fallen on with tender delight. But that, thought Jerott wisely, might have been to safeguard her newly widowed young daughter Margaret.

At that moment a man came up to him—a vigorous and efficient little man, whose exertions he had noted with half his mind while loading the crates—and said in the accents of Aberdeen, 'There's a beast with a bad leg we'll need to spare, sir. If you'll give me leave, I'll ask Lady Jenny up at the castle to loan us another.'

Something about the lined face and the nimble frame and the bronchial whistle under the breath seemed familiar. 'I've seen you before,' said Jerott sharply.

'Aye. This morning. Tommy Wishart—Tosh, they call me. I just landed yesterday,' the little man said.

'No. In France. Something,' said Jerott, tracking down a recollection, 'to do with a donkey.'

'You're right, sir. Tightrope work; that was the specialty.'

'It was the specialty in the area I was in all right,' said Jerott Blyth, an angry light suddenly dawning, and trapped the little man, before he could move, with a trained grip on the wrist. Tosh, blankly amiable, stood just where he was. 'You were following me before I came here, in France?'

'You're smart, though,' said Tosh cheerfully. 'I didna think you'd jalouse. It's all the same in the end, though; isn't it, sir?'

'*What's* all the same in the end?' said Jerott nastily, but he knew. While he thought he was fishing for Lymond, Lymond was fishing for him. Long ago he had been marked out as one of the men for this army, and Lymond with perfect logic had taken steps to keep him in sight. God knew how many other casual observers had watched his progress through France before Tosh took up the running at Paris. And he had played into the man's hands by voluntarily joining him. If he had not, what would Lymond have done? Various answers, all of them an insult to pride, rushed into his mind. He had assumed, without realizing it, that Lymond was aware that he at least, and de Seurre and des Roches surely also, held a watching brief for the Order. Could it be that Lymond, on the contrary, was under the illusion that he had made three easy converts to Mammon?

There was one way to settle that. Removing Tommy Wishart rather too briskly from his path, for he disliked anyone's spies, Jerott made for Boghall.

It was unfortunate that Joleta also was at Boghall that day. Lady Fleming, never the woman to invite stupid comparisons, had found life at Boghall castle without Joleta quite supportable; but her daughter Margaret, once she had come home, exceedingly silent, and renewed acquaintanceship with the son of her first marriage, who cried, and had paid a solitary and morbid visit to her husband's grave, from which she returned even more silent, if possible, had shown a neurotic tendency to live at Midculter instead of Boghall. Though Margaret listened to Lady Jenny's problems and offered very practical solutions, Jenny felt sometimes that her daughter preferred Sybilla's company to her own.

When, therefore, Margaret Erskine returned from one of these visits bringing Joleta to stay, Jenny greeted the child with sparkling affection and left her to Margaret to entertain. If Margaret thought it would lessen the tension at Midculter to have Joleta where she and Lymond couldn't quarrel, she was welcome to try. Privately, Lady Fleming thought it would do the little prude good to be the subject of Lymond's dislike.

It was too tempting, then, when she found Francis Crawford in her own hall, and Joleta unseen and unsuspecting in her solar above. Randy Bell Lady Fleming summed up without difficulty and got rid of, with guile, to her apothecary. Then she went, to Joleta's surprise, and sat with Joleta, after arranging artlessly that Francis Crawford, when free, should be brought to her there.

She could not, of course, prevent her daughter from warning him. It was the first thing Margaret Erskine recalled when all the intelligent, rational things about Tom's death had been said, and after, most unexpectedly to herself and perhaps to him, she had broken into a storm of tears in Lymond's passionless and steady arms. When it was over, 'You will hate it, Francis. I'm sorry, but Joleta's here in the castle,' she said.

'Why hate it?' Lymond asked. He had given her his handkerchief and she had used it unashamedly, blowing her plain nose scarlet on the still-warm lawn. 'Little girls are always throwing down gauntlets. Or worse. I don't have to pick them up.'

'You don't have to trample on them, either,' said Margaret Erskine with her customary directness. 'You spurned, in public, her spirit, her wit and finally her powers of physical attraction. You might have awarded her a minor decoration for trying, at least.'

'She's annoyed, is she?' said Lymond. 'Good. Let's find a nice convent for her. I have troubles enough without my name being linked with Gabriel's sister.'

Joleta Reid Malett was most certainly annoyed. When Lymond entered her room, expecting to take leave of Lady Fleming, and Lady Fleming at the same instant found urgent business elsewhere, Joleta was both startled and angry, and even Lymond was for an instant taken aback.

But after no more than a moment, he continued forward, raised his eyebrows for leave, and picking up a chair sat on it, saying, 'How awkward. And how like dear Jenny. We shall have to bear five minutes of each other's company. Never mind. Every absence increases respect. Are you respectable?'

Joleta had been stringing a lute, the apricot hair slung back out of her way and her quilted, loose sleeves rolled up. Her forearm along the ridge of the bone was powdered with freckles; underneath, as she laid down the lute, the flesh was white as curds. She had flushed. 'I am afraid to say anything,' she said sweetly, 'in case another of your dear ones has died.'

'No.' Despite the damp handkerchief in his doublet, he would not challenge her good taste a second time. 'It is the hatchet that has been interred. To save our friends' nerves, I suggest we meet on a plane of brutal courtesy. It need not interfere with our mutual distrust. Do you play that thing?'

'Not as well, I am sure, as you do,' said Joleta, her voice thin. 'And I don't intend to toady in public to someone who manhandled me as you did. Conceited men have no attraction for me. Shut the door as you go.'

255

'All right,' said Lymond pleasantly. 'But let me mention one thing. Margaret Erskine tells me she removed you from Midculter because of your pranks with my infant nephew. It is no doubt exceedingly hilarious to ply the wet-nurse with alcohol and Kevin cannot retaliate as Richard or my mother certainly would. But it is not the child's fault he is related to me. Pick someone your own size, my dear.'

The large, sea-green eyes sparkled with angry laughter. 'But he looked so ridiculous drunk.'

'And you,' said Lymond coolly, 'would look equally ridiculous in your petticoat-tails receiving a thrashing. Do it again, and you'll get one, from me.'

'*From you?*' Erect, glowing with incredulous fury, Joleta stared at her tormentor. 'I shall do what I like, when I please. If I wish, I shall teach your spying relatives a lesson. Wait till Graham comes! *Thrash me!* I'd like to see anyone in this beggarly country lay a finger on Graham Malett's sister!'

'Would you?' said Lymond lazily, and in one hard, purposeful stride was on her. As his right hand closed on her arm, Joleta, eyes blazing, bent. In two movements she had snatched the half-strung lute from its chair, smashed the fine wood into a jagged, needle-sharp club and was swinging it as he reached for her other arm. The chair went over with a crash.

It was a magnificent struggle. Jenny kept a large number of ornaments in her tower solar, and porcelain and silver, alabaster, soapstone and Venetian glassware beaded the carpet as the battle raged in the tiny room, and the small tables rained about. It took a long time, twisting and dodging and keeping his fingers sunk deep in the one arm, for Lymond to tear from her grip the battering lute, and he had more than one gash and a cheekbone well opened by the lashing gut before he had done.

Joleta, her hair in viperish coils round her neck, one sleeve off, and her feet bare and quick as a goat's, was marked dusky red like a schoolboy where she had sent furniture flying, and where Lymond's steely fingers, controlling by grip in lieu of breaking her bones, had discoloured the milky flesh. And all the time, her teeth set, she lunged from side to side, seizing what weapons she could. A pewter ale-mug hammered at his near shoulder and, wrenched away, was replaced by a sliver of glass, which slit both their hands before she dropped it. With windy sobbing, possessed by her fury, there was nothing she would not risk to defeat him, even to laying hands on his sword. For Lymond, that was the end. Holding her hard, he spoke sharply. 'Joleta. Don't be stupid. I'll have to hurt you.'

Her flushed face burned like a star. 'Try!' she said, and seized the hilt with both hands. His brows level, Lymond knocked her away

256

with the hard edge of his palm, and as she screamed, kicked her legs from under her. Light as she was, she went down like a gravestone, and drew down with her thick dusty skirts all the remaining shorn stumps of the furnishings.

His sword half out, Lymond looked down at her, breathing quickly as she lay in the Sargasso Sea of their wreckage, all the fight for the moment knocked out of her. 'By God, I ought to thrash you with this!' he said tartly in the very second that the door behind him heaved in with a crash and Jerott Blyth fell into the room.

He was quick, was Jerott, and trained to a hairsbreadth. Informed demurely below by Lady Jenny where he could find Lymond, he had heard on approaching the sounds of struggle deadened to the household below by the fourteen-feet thickness of wall. Moving fast with the force of his entry he saw the sword flash in Lymond's hand as he spoke, and below, white and bruised in the dust, the child Joleta, her gown torn, her feet bloodied and bare. Whiter under his tan than the girl, '*You nasty, lascivious little rat!*' said Jerott in astonishment, and jumped at Lymond, who knocked him down.

'Hah!' said Joleta, and scrambling to her knees began, a little shrilly, to laugh.

Jerott, scarlet now, his magnificent eyes narrowed, lunged again and got the flat of Lymond's foot on his hand. 'My God. Bring on the eunuchs. Calm down, will you? One adolescent at a time is quite enough.'

Without listening, the other man tore himself free, and gripping his scabbard, began hauling his own whinger out. 'Mr Blyth!' Joleta, on her feet now, nursing a cut foot in one hand, spoke like a harridan. 'Don't be a fool, and mind your own business!'

Jerott's hand fell, his face going blank.

'Neatly put,' said Lymond, approving. His hand, also relaxed, fell back from his hilt.

'And the same,' said Joleta, rounding on him, 'applies to you! Think twice, my smart friend, before you offer to thrash me. I'll give you something else to remember me by; and it won't be a scratch.'

'Your hands are bleeding?' said Jerott quietly. His chest heaving still from his exertions he looked from the man to the child and back again, his fists clenched, ready to act.

'She cut herself on the glass she was trying to gouge my eyes out with,' explained Lymond patiently. 'She cut her feet on the wreckage and she got bruised because I don't like being permanently mutilated on Thursdays. I may add that Friday is my day for raping; and I like it quieter than this, and they enjoy it.'

Still Blyth looked helplessly from one to the other. 'Oh, go away! said Joleta at last, losing what was left of her patience, and seizing the teetering door, jerked it open.

257

For the first time, Lymond laughed. 'I advise it, too. Armed with faith within and steel without, beat a retreat.' Thoughtfully, he looked down at Joleta. 'You are a violent, self-willed, well-shaped and dangerous creature, and I prefer your honest rages to your parlour archery. But who is going to explain to Lady Jenny?'

For the first time a smile also genuine lit Joleta's golden face. 'No explanations necessary. She'll think it must be Friday.' The smile on the face of Gabriel's saintly little sister became wider and more malicious. 'She'll be *furious*,' she remarked.

*

Never afterwards could Jerott clearly recollect that journey home. Waiting stiffly for Lymond, in a mental turmoil, he had tried to piece it out.

There had been a bitter struggle, in which Lymond must have been the aggressor. Yet the girl had shown no fear; had made fun of her rescuer . . . they both had, damn them . . . and had ordered him away. What had happened? Had Lymond prevailed? Was she, in her innocence, out of her senses? He saw her again, lying broken at his feet, and had resolved, against all his pride, on going upstairs once more, when Lymond appeared at his side.

'Come along. We've wasted enough time on that spoiled brat,' he said. 'Are we loaded?'

'She was hurt. What happened?' He had to know.

'Scratches. The Donati woman is slapping grease on them. She was making a nuisance of herself at Midculter, and when I threatened to thrash her she went for me. Enjoyed it, too. . . . Gabriel may think she's a sister-angel, Brother-in-Christ, but she isn't. It's worth remembering.'

'Why? For Fridays?' said Jerott nastily, and strode away. She had shouted at him—that delicate child, bred in the cloister. Gabriel had been wrong to trust the force of his faith. He, a man and a knight could stand up to this worldly professionalism. Joleta might not.

His irritation increased when, setting off with the toiling ox-carts for St Mary's, he observed that the gallant surgeon had been soothing his ruffled vanity with something out of the apothecary's bottle, and was strikingly gay. In the men's hearing Lymond said nothing, but the look on his face promised trouble when they got in: intoxication was one of the few cardinal sins at St Mary's and they had only had trouble once before, with Adam Blacklock when his leg was giving him pain.

Alec Guthrie, another man of moderate intake, dropped back from the head of the column to mention caustically that it had enlivened their tedious work to observe one of their leaders returning

258

from Boghall castle drunk, and the other fresh from a fight with some woman. This was by deduction, obviously, and Joleta's name was not mentioned, Jerott noted, feeling ill.

Anyone but Guthrie would have had his head snapped off. Lymond instead said briefly, 'You may leave Bell to me. The other issue was unavoidable. I haven't spent time and thought on building a reputable leadership in order to waste it at will.'

'The men, you appreciate, will want their indulgences too,' said the humanist drily.

'Why?' said Jerott. 'They're soldiers, not animals.'

'They can have them, when the time comes,' Lymond said. The backs of his hands were ripped with Joleta's fingernails, and the thin weal at his cheekbone was emitting a little blood. Brushing it with his folded handkerchief, 'Being men, and not monks,' he added, to Jerott.

'*A holy weapon*,' thought Jerott with contempt, and remembered all of a sudden why he had gone to Boghall at all. 'And will Tommy Wishart get special concessions?' he inquired. 'For services rendered?'

Lymond put away his handkerchief and changed his grip on the reins. 'You recognized him.'

'Yes. Did you have someone following de Seurre and des Roches as well?' said Jerott sarcastically. 'What happened if one of us promised to join you and didn't come? Did he get his throat slit? Or was he to be persuaded by the charms of Tosh's discourse?'

'My dear man,' said Lymond, 'he was keeping the numbers down. If we hadn't taken precautions the whole of the noble Order of St John would be disporting itself at St Mary's under the delusion that it was earning merit by converting us to the Cross. As it is, another half dozen are due any day. Alec, now you've kept us right, I'd be grateful if you would see if the head of the column knows what the hell it's doing without you. Jerott, it won't help us in an ambush if the rearguard is agonizing silently over Joleta's jeopardized soul. Forget the brat. Remember, we're common, coarse fighting-men, not a heavenly host in our shifts.'

The careless words set Jerott's teeth on edge at the time: they rankled still as he rode at Lymond's back into the courtyard of St Mary's, alive as a meat-market with the disorder of a big and vigorous camp.

On the wide steps a man awaited them diffidently; tall, quiet and badly dressed, but with authority in his stillness alone. As they got closer he began to move down the stairs and they saw clearly the clear-skinned, big-featured face, the good hands, the bare golden head. His eyes, lit with pleasure, rested on Francis Crawford alone. It was Sir Graham Reid Malett.

Overcome, Randy Bell vomited.

'Oh God, quite,' said Lymond. 'Christendom has caught up with us. My mistake. We *are* a heavenly host in our shifts.' And he rode forward without haste and dismounted, Joleta's fingermarks plain on his skin.

V

The Hand of Gabriel

(St Mary's and Djerba, 1551/2)

THE pressure of Gabriel's hand on his shoulder that first evening at St Mary's while Sir Graham introduced his small personal staff and humbly sought a night's rest on his way north to Joleta merely aggravated Jerott Blyth's uneasy conscience. But Francis Crawford's greeting, he noticed, was amicable in its astringent fashion; though Lymond listened without comment to Gabriel's generous praise of St Mary's and, next day, to his wholehearted amazement as he walked through the encampment and yards.

They all knew—but from a dogged obstinacy, a superstition even, would not admit it—that in a few weeks they had reached a standard that promised something exceptional. To hear it said, now, by an acknowledged master like Gabriel, was wine in the desert. Days and nights of unpleasantly hard work lay behind them with so far no break, and it was wonderfully good to relax that day in civilized company: to work for once in short spells in the neighbourhood and come back for meals; to see Blacklock, a board in one grimy hand, sketching the visitor as they both talked; to watch Tait, silent normally about his vast knowledge of Europe, exchanging stories about eating-shops in Algiers; to hear Gabriel greet Fergie Hoddim of the Laigh and laugh with him over lawyer's gossip.

Later, Lancelot Plummer the architect, precise, fastidious, sarcastic and the best engineer in Europe, was the man who helped Gabriel lovingly erect his portable altar, with Lymond's less than rhapsodical sanction, and was the first to kneel there. Alec Guthrie, an interested observer, raised his eyebrows above the bowed heads of the knights, of Plummer, of Randy Bell, flushed on his knees, and of Adam Blacklock, lurking hesitantly on the fringe. And even Guthrie's sharp eyes narrowed when, forsaking Latin, Graham Malett addressed his Maker and his audience simply, in the soft Scots of his home. 'Thou art my hope, Lord Jehovah; my confidence fra my bairnhood. . . . Look down on these Thy poor sinners, and grant us Thy grace. . . .'

Lymond also was there, watching. Jerott, lifting his head, disconcertingly found himself under that cold stare, and saw it move then to Plummer and to Randy Bell, where it rested awhile. Comparing, no doubt, his morals and his piety, thought Jerott bitterly. They would all doubtless find themselves tomorrow with the filthiest assignment in the camp.

They got it sooner than that, although not through any agency of Francis Crawford's. Before the service was over, a runner had burst in gasping to tell Lymond that the siege engine, the loved object of Plummer's and Bell's afternoon work, had outmanœuvred its blocks and run downhill into Effie Harperfield's farm, killing a boy in the byre and marooning the widow Harperfield and four children in her own back room.

They were all on their feet in the little chapel. 'I don't believe it!' said Plummer sharply. The tower and drawbridge, of heavy timber, was his personal triumph, and Jerott, who had worked with Bell on the job, knew how painstaking he had been.

By then Lymond was issuing orders, without wasting time on the cause; that would come later. At the same time Gabriel, hand on his arm, said quickly, 'Francis, will you allow me? De Seurre and Jerott and I have done a lot of this. We'll have it levered erect before your untrained men could manage.'

This was true. All the men of the Order were familiar with siege work. At St Mary's their mechanical training had only begun. And six men expert in leverage could save lives quicker than twenty unskilled. Lymond said briefly, 'Take over. It's yours. . . .' and in a moment, Plummer leading and Lymond and Graham Malett together behind, the members of the Order at St Mary's were making over the small hills towards the Widow Harperfield's farm, with the remaining officers, Abernethy, the carpenters and two smiths and their tools, and twelve picked men racing after.

It was a brief ride. As they streamed downhill in a sunlit river of leaves they could see the splintered skeleton of the tower above the thatch and rowan trees of the farm, while the hens flapped and screeched still and Thomas Wishart, who had made the discovery, reposed in an unlikely attitude, half in and half out of the roof, telling long Aberdeen jokes to the four Harperfield children stuck below. The byre was a rickle of stones, with an uneven heap lying beside it, its face veiled by a cloak.

The machine was erected, braced, and wheeled to flat ground inside twenty minutes. The orders came in a clear, steady flow in Gabriel's magnificent voice, pausing only now and then in deference to Plummer or to Lymond before making more demands on his men. The roof and chimney, properly strengthened, held firm and secure as inch by inch the great tower shifted, its swinging drawbridge safely strapped, its spine braced by iron. And as the hole was gradually cleared, Tosh swung his agile body and dropped, light on his acrobat's feet, to where the crying children crouched and lifted them to safety one by one, chaffing Effie Harperfield the while about the great new mansion she would be able to get off St Mary's in restitution.

Then at last, Gabriel was able to stand erect, the sweat running over his skin, and say breathlessly, 'It's safe now. Heavens, I'm tired. Francis, you'll never find a better set of men. I've worked them like dogs without even remembering that they're still on intensive training. . . . Can I on their behalf beg a break? I know you would intend to give them one soon. . . . I really doubt if they can go on without one after that.'

'You look exhausted,' said Jerott. 'Francis, he can't ride on to-night.'

'Old age,' said Gabriel. 'It's my second adventure in two days, in fact. On my first night at Flaw Valleys the kitchen chimney caught fire and then the room above; and Mistress Somerville, who appears as a rule to be most entertainingly level-headed, became extraordinarily upset at the idea of damage to her precious music room and we had to mobilize the countryside. Which reminds me, Francis. Her daughter Philippa is no friend of yours.'

'I know,' said Lymond. With the rest, they were walking to their horses. The Harperfields, with Tosh, had long since been taken to neighbours and the November moon was coming up in the dusk, smoky red and vast as a city.

'Then you know your own business best,' said Gabriel mildly. 'But I ought to tell you that she has some silly plan to shake your dignity. I don't know what it is and I'm not even supposed to know it's aimed at you. But my advice would be to give her a chance to forget you. She will, in time.'

'I can hardly wait,' said Lymond. 'You will, of course, stay as long as you wish after your magnificent endeavours, unless the household staff demand a holiday too.'

'You're going to declare a rest period?' asked Jerott. Leisure, with Gabriel there, seemed too good to be true.

'Rumour being what it is, I imagine it will have declared itself by now,' Lymond said. 'Yes. We shall take three days from our labours to relax. Provided Sir Graham understands that by midday tomorrow St Mary's will be empty and all the men at arms and half the officers whoring in Peebles.'

In the half-dark you could guess at Gabriel's smile. 'Do you think I don't know human nature?' he said. 'They are bound by no vows. But as they learn to respect you, they will do as you do.'

'That's what we're all afraid of,' said Jerott; and there was a ripple of laughter and a flash of amusement, he saw, from Lymond himself. But he had not meant to be as funny as that.

*

The following day, Gabriel left. Before he went, he sought out Francis Crawford and asked him, as a young lance might do, if he might later return to St Mary's and join his command.

The interview, by Gabriel's own contrivance, was private; but by some alchemy, on that misty morning, as they buckled on their cuirasses for the day's work, every officer at St Mary's knew of it, and speculated on what Lymond would say. And Jerott, for one, promised himself that if Francis Crawford's response was to humiliate Gabriel, he, Jerott, would walk out forthwith.

For what else remained for Graham Malett to do? His self-appointed task in Europe was done: Malta was a closed door. From the Knight of St John who had brought the Queen Dowager from France, Jerott already knew that the French Ambassador to Turkey had been vindicated by the efforts in Malta of de Villegagnon, though they had learned from Gabriel that a bitter struggle went on still for the life of the Marshal de Vallier, who had been thrown, a sick man, into the rock dungeon of St Angelo, and whose 'confession' under torture to treachery had been sent off to France. Rumours of bribery, of false trials and serpentine deceit by the Grand Master de Homedès were almost certainly true.

So without resources of money and land, his own Scottish birth-place destroyed, and too proud to hire his sword, as de Villegagnon and the Strozzis had done, to a foreign command, Graham Malett had come to his homeland. Torphichen Priory, for more than four hundred years the Order's centre in Scotland, would give him shelter but he could not strain Sandilands' kindness too far. As it was, were it known Sir James was on friendly terms with a knight called to justice, he would not remain Preceptor of Torphichen for long.

As they dressed, Fergie Hoddim and Tait and Blacklock speculated fiercely on Gabriel's reasons for selling his services to an obscure, half-trained corps such as St Mary's. And when presently they moved chatting into the hall and found there Sir Graham Malett, one booted foot on the hearth, waiting in idle talk with Lymond for a chance to depart, they paused, each trying without being obvious to read two unreadable faces.

Then Gabriel, his guinea-gold hair blazing in the firelight, looked smiling at Lymond, and Francis Crawford said pleasantly, 'Who's holding the wagers? Fergie? Then note, Fergie, that we are to be joined presently here at St Mary's by that well-known servant of Christ's poor, Sir Graham Malett. As the saying has it, if the Gods have woolly feet, they also have arms of iron. Sir Graham is one of the most ironic. I am delighted that he is coming and I wish only to point out that the Order is not taking over this army, nor is this army taking over the Order. It is merely, as always, following my command.'

There was a small silence.

'There is, I think,' said Gabriel, in his rich, gentle voice, 'nothing that any of us would ask better to do.'

*

'*Why?*' said Adam Blacklock later, when for the first time he and Guthrie were thrown together alone. 'Why the hell did he do it?'

'Do what?' said the philosopher without excitement. 'Throw down the gauntlet to the St John's men? He had to make his position clear, or they'd feel in conscience bound to convert or crusade or otherwise reserve their armchair in heaven. Why take Gabriel at all? He had to, my minikin fiddler with chalks; he had to, or he would have lost all his best men including Jerott Blyth who one day is going to be nearly as good as himself. Don't worry,' said Alec Guthrie comfortably. 'Don't worry. Of all men Graham Malett knows how to exercise patience and tact.'

'Of c-course,' said Adam Blacklock gloomily. 'But does Lymond?'

*

The last comment was made by Lord Culter when, riding to St Mary's in the first winter frost, he haled his brother swearing from the tiltground to entertain him before the fire. Sitting down, 'I don't care a damn,' said Richard Crawford calmly, 'if it's three o'clock and you've only got another bloody hour of daylight. *You* don't need the practice and the ground's like iron. You can lower their dignity some other way. What's the rush anyway? You can't fight anywhere till the spring.'

'We shan't be ready till the spring,' said Lymond grimly. He picked up the helmet he had hurled down on entering and gave it to his steward, who unasked had brought in mulled wine; then sat opposite his brother and running a metal-blackened hand through his hair said in a different tone, 'What a hell of a welcome. I'm sorry. But there's so much still to do outside before the weather closes, and we have to tackle all the dreary minutiæ on weapons and theory where all your knightly warriors start losing their tempers and you have to go through a deadly routine of light relief with competitions and war jokes and community singing, and long, long stories of rape and battle and Generals I have Known.'

265

'You're lying in your teeth,' said Richard cheerfully. 'You've hand-picked that little band of sophisticates, and you know it. Gabriel alone is pretty well worth paying to hear. Has he been back?'

'Twice. He had Joleta to see, and Sandilands has got him a house in Edinburgh, in one of the Order's tenements. He'll soon be able to spend most of his time at St Mary's.'

'I'm glad.' After a moment, as Lymond said nothing, Richard added, 'So is your doting mother. You certainly won't have noticed, but he is what you have always needed: your perfect complement at last. You may match up to this man, Francis, but you'll have to stretch yourself for the first time to do it.'

'Too late. You find me on the recoil,' said Lymond briefly. 'How's Mariotta?'

'Don't be a fool.' Richard wasn't to be put off. 'For God's sake, Francis, don't throw this chance away. Meet him halfway at least. He had Joleta *in tears* over having quarrelled with you, and he worships her and she him. . . . Incidentally, my friend, what was that disagreement about? Lady Jenny said the furniture was matchwood, and Joleta wouldn't explain.'

'She needed a lesson,' said Lymond shortly. 'So do you. I changed the subject a moment ago because if one more person thrusts the Archangel Graham Malett down my throat I shall vomit.'

'I daresay,' said Richard Crawford in the mildest tone he possessed. 'After all, he is the first master you have ever had.'

And was silent, abashed, as Lymond, his eyes wild with anger, rose to his feet like a cat and twitching the glass from his brother's lax hand, tossed wine and vessel into the fire.

'Drink to it, you and he,' he said.

*

In March, on her bed beside the spilling fountain in the corsair Dragut's beautiful seraglio, where the filigreed walls with their prayers to Allâh opened on the sunlit aviaries and the parks beyond, watered with cisterns and planted with pine and cypress and weeping willow and the blazing flowers of Africa, Oonagh O'Dwyer gave birth to her son.

Patience was something her Irish soul would never learn. But through the eternity of that winter, destitute in luxury, solitary amid hundreds, she clung to one thing. This was by her own will. Her own decision that she had cast off Cormac O'Connor, the debased son of kings, whose hectoring, black-visaged face she would see again in her child and his. Her own assent had freed Francis Crawford to return to Europe and his own arrogant destiny.

Dragut, old and princely corsair, had troubled her little and she had learned to respect him, and after Galatian, the pathetic weakling, to find no hurt to her pride in serving him. She had soon found that he was little in the palace, wintering near the Sultan and putting to sea at the first sign of fighting weather. In the seraglio she slept in silk and had pages and slaves black and white to fill every wish; and occasionally Güzel would come, whom she had never seen unveiled: Güzel the jewel of Dragut's old age, who alone went with him to Djerba, to Constantinople, to the winter palace at Aleppo; who spoke English and wherever she moved, in little clouds of serving boys, with her women, her slaves, her poets and singers, her artists and guards, her musicians and dancers, was surrounded, always, by laughter.

It was Güzel the anonymous, with her fleeting, uninformative visits, who had kept Oonagh's tough pride alive; prevented her from hammering the foul feet in her belly which thrust jumping through her tender skin day and night; the great skull and round buttocks and tight fists that squeezed and pressed the mills of her life into whining disorder; the interloper who deprived her of rest, of thought and of all delicate things.

Then, as the fretting crystals over her bed stirred in the first breeze of March, she felt her burden eased. She ate, and walked, and planned for when the swollen by-blow would be gone, and her mind and body her own. When the welcome, murmuring ache began she was inspired, relieved, exhilarated, and bore it in triumph until dusk. But when the gentle, timeous aches became elastic agony, and her monstrous young raped mind and spirit from her again, she wrestled alone in the dark under her silken sheets until, at the moment when suddenly she was afraid to be solitary, Güzel's voice said in Arabic, 'Now!'

And the room sprang into blazing light; and the commotion of many voices, the hiss of steam, the chink of china and silver, the grip of kind hands and the tone of friendly cheer, encouragement and delight suddenly warmed and melted her cold heart.

Time, excited, agonizing, magnificent time flew, to the lilt of Güzel's voice. The frenzy mounted, mounted and exploded in a vast, irresistible burgeoning. From between Güzel's ringless, capable hands came a string of brief, mellow cries; silence, and then a small, clear renewal of complaint, and two feet, blue-mottled morsels of flesh, kicked lost in the limitless air.

Oonagh's child had been born. It was a son, small-boned and perfect, with skin as white as new milk within a day of its coming, and hair downy gold as a chick's. It could not, in a thousand miraculous nights, have been begotten by Cormac O'Connor.

'*May God grant thee prosperity*,' wrote Dragut Rais to Sir Graham Malett in Scotland, fingering the smile in his grizzled beard as he paced up and down in front of his scribe. 'He that fulfils his oath is thrice blessed. The woman from Ireland, on being brought to birth of her child, has through the goodness of Allâh been granted a fair son with hair gold as corn.

'His breeding being therefore ignoble, I offer the child to thyself for the paltry sum of a thousand écus. Less I could not take for the trouble we have had to safeguard his life, his mother wishing him dead. Should misfortune divide thee from thy purchase, we shall permit her to kill him, since only Allâh knows in whose tent he was engendered. The woman I sell.'

The reply came when the baby was seven weeks old, naked in its basket of cotton, with new-grown golden lashes round newly-smiling blue eyes. The packet enclosed ten thousand écus. 'Keep the woman and treat her well,' the message enjoined, 'with this money for her well-being and as the price of the child. Rear the boy, I beg you, by the God we each serve, until I may come for him, or make further petition; and may the Most High reward you. . . .'

And firmly and clearly, Graham Malett had signed.

VI

The Hand on the Axe

(St Mary's, 1551/2)

CAREFULLY as a Hospitaller nursing his sick, Gabriel said no word to Francis Crawford of the birth of the child called Khaireddin; nor did he take any steps to send word to Cormac O'Connor, although he knew where he was. The only person he told, because he was closer to her than to any other alive, was his sister Joleta, as she sat brushing the brilliant hair back from her flushed skin, snatching periodically as tantalizingly he held her long ribbons just out of reach.

'*Brute!* Give me them! So he still thinks the woman died at Tripoli?' said Joleta, who as Lymond had found was not easily shocked.

'Yes. And it is better that he should. There is work for him here that matters much more. In any case, I believe the attachment was only a chance one: he did not look to me passionately involved. He could be, so easily, and with the wrong person. I wish you were on better terms with him, Joleta.'

Her colour high, she snatched at the ribbons again, and when she missed, flung down her brush. 'I have tried. I went down to that arctic encampment to apologize, and had to wait three hours to *see* him. He said I impinged on his Happy Hour.'

Startled, her brother loosed a shout of deep laughter. 'His *what*?'

'His Happy Hour. When he dries the tears of all the sad soldiers he chastised in the morning. Melancholy Man into Sanguine Man in an hour. He's good, isn't he?' said Joleta suddenly, her eyes bright.

Gabriel nodded, watching her.

Aware of it, she bent, in a stirring of gauze, to retrieve her hairbrush and, straightening, met his gaze with her own. 'Is the baby his?'

There was a pause. Then Gabriel said, 'It isn't Cormac's. That is certain. Nor is it de Césel's: it must have been conceived in France, before the lady and the Governor met. My charming Francis's behaviour in France last year was notorious, as you know; and Oonagh O'Dwyer was one of the favoured many. But even Cormac

O'Connor, as jealous an unseated princeling as any I know, does not accuse her of being any other man's mistress. Yes, the child is of Francis Crawford's blood, and the only one, I suspect. . . . He has taught you a lesson, has he?' said Gabriel gently. 'That not everyone is prepared to be entranced?'

Joleta sat upright, her blue eyes huge. 'He is the most conceited. . . .'

Gabriel laughed. 'Because he finds your friendship so easy to resist? Your charms, sweetheart, are ageing, or you haven't properly tried. Convert him for me,' said Graham Malett, and leaning forward, slipped the lovely ribbon under her hair, and closing it round her throat, drew his sister forward and kissed her. 'Convert him. But don't, Joleta, tell him of Khaireddin out of pique. Or I shall be angry.' And he kissed her again.

It had been a hideous winter. In place of the normal season in Scotland, the weather stayed open only till December, when the last of the knights from Malta arrived.

Then the frost came, from a metallurgical sky, and by dawn the last of the leaves, dry and fluted as walnuts, lay in unstirring heaps on the white roof of the forge.

An oven cracked, and the man responsible was flogged, for Lymond had made his provisions against the weather, as against everything else. What he could not protect were the knights with their thin blood, coddled with long years of Mediterranean sun. Even Gabriel was livid with cold, out night after night training and being trained until his child-like skin was roughened and raw with open sores, and his dry, calloused hands bled. In the end, since Gabriel himself would not, Adam Blacklock went to Lymond and said, 'S-send me tonight. Sir Graham has had enough. In any case, he has nothing, surely, to learn about strategic night work. . . .'

'Not in winter. Not in Scotland. Whereas you know about both; which is why you are not going. Has Sir Graham complained?'

'No.' Lymond, bright-edged at the top of his training, would be unaffected, thought Blacklock, if a new Ice Age arrived. He went on, his long, spaniel's face expressionless, 'He won't refuse, until he comes down with pleurisy. And if he does, you'll lose the goodwill of half of your men.'

'So I might,' said Lymond, taking thought. 'But I understood his portable altar had the matter in hand.'

The artist said nothing. Lymond, who was in his own room dressing to go out himself, paused, still holding the sword-belt Salablanca had handed him, and enveloped Adam Blacklock in an exceedingly shrewd blue gaze. 'But you don't think it a good idea,' he added.

'On several counts. . . . No,' said Blacklock.

'Well, thank God it was you,' said Lymond. 'If Jerott Blyth had brought me the self-same appeal I should have been strongly tempted to kick him out by the window. As it is, you may tell Sir Graham, Jerott, the other officers and as many of the camp as may care to take notice, that we *les executeurs de la justice de Dieu* hereby exempt the Chevalier from night exercises from now onwards, and from all other protracted training in the field. Plummer will lead tonight.'

'He won't like that,' said Adam drily. 'Lancelot likes his comforts.'

'Then he will require to place the blame, won't he,' said Lymond encouragingly, 'where the blame is due?'

The changed conditions, though a matter of bitter self-recriminations by Graham Malett himself, led to an instant improvement in his well-being, and the hard training did the rest to restore the tone he had lost since leaving Malta. With the challenge to his endurance withdrawn he also felt able, for the first time, to leave St Mary's as he had expected to do from time to time, to visit Joleta and Torphichen and establish some sort of centre at his chambers in Edinburgh.

Sometimes his absences were protracted as the weather grew worse, for by Christmas the snows had come, unusually heavy, and lay for nearly a month, renewing the white and grey landscape by foggy blizzards over the hills. Then sharp winds came and scooped the snow to its brown bracken bed, piling the rest in crusty drifts over cottage and tree. The training at St Mary's became practical exercises in rescue work, and the army made friends it was to keep through the summer. In January, in a snatch of open weather, Joleta came, defiant with her olive branch, followed by Madame Donati and a strong force from Midculter, where she was staying once more; to be spurned, as she was later to record.

It was one of the few occasions when Jerott Blyth fell out openly with his leader. Jerott had spent an upsetting winter. As a professional, he could not deceive himself or anyone else about the quality of Lymond's work. Nor could he deny that in his personal dislike of the man, he had let Gabriel down. Gabriel had sent him ahead to be his missionary, and had come to find the territory in command of the heathen, and all the spadework waiting for himself. It drove Jerott frantic to see Gabriel place himself under another man's direction, and to suffer so mildly what seemed to Jerott a crude and deliberate victimization as well.

It was Gabriel who pointed out that only the hardest of training would bring him back to the point where he could hope to carry weight in such an army; and as his prodigious talents proclaimed themselves, it was obvious that not even Lymond would expect any of them—Guthrie, Hoddim, Bell, Tait, Blacklock or Plummer, far less any of his own Knights of the Order—to regard Graham Malett as a fellow-pupil.

Nor, to do him justice, had Lymond ever attempted the role of

Grand Master here. He had allotted to Gabriel the tasks he needed for training, and the places where his expertise would be of use to the rest of the force. The other Knights of St John, who knew his methods already, were kept apart.

In theory, that is. In practice, whenever Gabriel was at St Mary's, the knights met for Mass, and for the gentler exercises of their vows; and their fellow sufferers, from conviction or curiosity, quite often came too.

Lymond was not told, but neither would Gabriel allow the serenity of the meeting to become the occasion for backbiting about their high-handed commander. Any unfortunate critic of Lymond, on the contrary, was liable to have a lecture from Graham Malett, an unaccustomed sharpness in his magnificent voice, until the complainant closed his ears in despair.

Gabriel himself had patience without end. Sophisticated Plummer the architect, hovering on the edge of the Faith, could expose, red-faced and drawling, his most secret dismays, and be treated levelly and with punctilio, as he craved. Randy Bell, afraid to confess the meetings in the byre that followed many a humane sick-visit round St Mary's, found there was no need: that Gabriel knew, and was tolerant. Hercules Tait, a collector first, a traveller and ambassador's secretary second, found a quiet listener to his catalogue of treasures, and unexpectedly, from Gabriel's worn baggage, was given an ikon from some Turkish hoard to add to it. And Adam Blacklock, hovering by the chapel door when his marred leg hurt, was found at length and made, in Gabriel's room, to take a drink.

Recoiling from the raw spirit, coughing, the artist had said, 'No, Sir Graham . . . I know it would help, but I've no head for it. Mr Crawford simply sends Abernethy to rub it, when the leg gets as bad as this. . . .'

But already the aqua-vitæ was glowing in his stomach, and he couldn't keep the appeal from his voice. Without speaking, Gabriel had poured out and handed him the rest of the drink, and had kept the lame man beside him until the effects had worn off that night, fibbing cheerfully when Lymond sent for him later. In the morning, seeing him off, Gabriel had said quietly, 'You are right. Spirit is risky. But there must be other drugs that would help. Come to me tonight, and any time that it's bad, and we shall see if Randy Bell and I can't find you something better than Abernethy's horny hands, skilful and hardworking though they are.'

Only Fergie Hoddim's love of legal analyses sometimes drove Malett to mock despair, and Fergie would wait for Lymond who would say instantly, before he could speak, 'I don't want the detail. I want the broad argument and the answer,' and force him to produce just that.

Alec Guthrie strained nobody's patience. With everyone in turn—sometimes with Gabriel, sometimes with Lymond—he would produce his premise, and sit back and wait for the argument. Then, with the subject closed to his satisfaction, he would pack up whatever impressions his acute eyes had been gathering, and slip off. After the first occasion, he attended no services but if Blacklock was sketching he could often be found, in silence, watching the chalk.

Jerott Blyth indeed fell over them when, storming indoors after seeing Joleta off on the day of her visit, he found the artist cross-legged in the hall, finishing the sketch he had made during her long wait for Lymond. Jerott was in a temper, and made no secret of it. When he paused for sheer absence of breath, Alec Guthrie, nearby on a stool, broke prosaically in.

'She's not quite royalty, Jerott. She came without warning, and it was her misfortune that her brother was away and Lymond primed down to belabouring mercenaries and not to being polite. What the devil did she have to make such a fuss about apologizing for, anyway?'

Jerott, striding up and down kicking, did not reply. Gabriel's sister had come through the snowy hills in her small cavalcade, mired with slush from their own horses' hooves, and had sought, flushed, ravishing and dripping, a kind word from Lymond.

He had sent word for her to wait. Certainly, she had been made comfortable, with a room for herself and Madame Donati to change in, and chicken and sweetmeats brought steaming to them before the roaring fire. The men of St Mary's, embarrassed, enchanted; grinning at her; recalling, shamefaced, the day she had shot at them on the road, had personally seen to that. But Jerott could not forget her dismay when Lymond's message arrived, nor the moment when Plummer, the fool, had said, 'He's shooting, against de Seurre and Tait and some of the men, in the snow. Can you see them? This window gives a good view.' And she watched, silent and hot-cheeked still, while M. le bloody Comte did everything but grow runner beans on his bow, and you could see the Venetian woman smiling at the girl's back and then round the room as if the child were some doting moppet of ten.

But all the same, when Lymond came in, bright, wet and imperviously cheerful, there was a look in her eyes that Jerott had not seen before, and her confidence, her quick-witted defensiveness, had gone. Jerott had time to think, 'On my soul, she can't have *enjoyed* the roughening-up he gave her? What possible glamour is there in that?' And then Joleta's voice, its sibilants so childishly marked, said purposefully, 'I wish to apologize for—for ...' And, her courage deserting her in the presence of Blacklock, Plummer, Guthrie, and Jerott himself, she became speechless almost at once.

It was never a failing of Lymond's. 'For trying to trade on your brother's reputation? I accept the apology, although as I understood the situation, once I had thrashed you we were even. However. And surely Madame Donati hasn't come all this way merely to chaperone you through that? Or is she to be our *vivandière*?'

There was an explosive sound from Mr Plummer, and Madame Donati became yellow. 'Believe me, Mr Crawford, I am here through no wish of mine,' said Joleta's duenna. 'After your disgusting behaviour at Boghall, I think the child is a saint.'

'No, no. Her brother's the saint,' said Lymond. 'Look at Mr Blyth, standing like Mohammed receiving the revelations: he'll tell you. The girl has a temper. Look out; she'll tear her dollies to bits. Joleta dear, you are forgiven. Go home now, will you? The gentlemen are busy.'

Alec Guthrie, observant on his stool beside the sketching Blacklock, did not move, but Plummer, casting up his elegant brows, made at this point a graceful departure and Madame Donati, blotched with anger, gripped Joleta's elbow. Joleta did not move, but simply stared, her sea-blue eyes pellucid with unshed tears; then lowering her head so that the golden hair swung over her breast, she let the duenna walk her to the door.

Lymond followed, talking unabashed, and after a moment Jerott strode out as well and seizing Joleta by the arm as, wrapped again in her snow-sodden cloak, she looked down from her mare, said, 'We don't deserve such a charming visitor. There is no need for you to go. Mr Crawford does not mean to be serious. There is a bedroom you and the Madonna may willingly have until at least your brother comes back to stay.'

There was a distinct pause. 'Then it must be yours, dear man,' said Lymond's voice with deceptive mildness. 'For there is none other in the castle that I know of.'

'All right. It is mine,' said Jerott shortly. 'Let me help you down, Mistress Malett?' And he held out his arm again.

'But I'm afraid you are *in* your chamber tonight,' said Lymond's voice deprecatingly. 'Didn't I tell you? To make amends for contradicting my orders. And three in a bed, Brother, is a touch overcrowded.'

He and Jerott stared at one another. Then Lymond added, the gentleness gone from his voice, 'We are not in St Angelo now. Mistress Malett has to ride a mere two miles to reach the home of some very good friends of mine who have agreed to put her up for the night. It is, on the whole, more respectable than retiring in a camp of armed men. It also leads to trouble among the said armed men, not all of whom are Knights of St John. Ask Randy Bell.'

It was then that Jerott turned on his heel and strode inside; and in due course Alec Guthrie showed him the uselessness at least of pursuing the matter with Lymond. Lymond himself did not again mention it, having already decided what course to pursue with the Chevalier Jerott Blyth. Only, in St Mary's itself, during her brief and unfortunate stay, the child Joleta had perhaps made more friends than she knew.

Then the snows came back, and the burns ran in spate hissing and bubbling under rimed ice, and there was, said Wat Scott of Buccleuch —square as a Tartar in a beaver-lined cloak, with a private fog in his curly grey beard—a damned yowe staring eye to eye with him through a second-floor window when he put his feet on the carpet this morning.

*

It was Buccleuch whom Lymond relied on, or rather Will Scott his son, when the freeze-up went on, without precedent, into March, and their fuel began to run out. Organized by Gabriel, newly with them after long absence enforced by the snow and Lord St John, the stocks of peat and firewood in the big, tarred-canvas stores outside St Mary's were freely drawn on to supply emergency fuel to the darkened farms and cottages around.

Lives were saved, but the heavy depletion, with no reserve for the future, left St Mary's itself in hazard and, driving himself to the utmost, Gabriel had taken no time to find other supplies. Even Jerott Blyth, informed one wintry morning by Tosh, whom he still disliked, of the sudden major withdrawal of stocks, was unprepared for the dark emptiness of the sheds. Gabriel had left early and would not be back until late; Lymond was away until at least tomorrow. Jerott, without comment, rolled up his sleeves and with des Roches's help worked out a temporary and drastic schedule of rations, while his spirit ached for Gabriel and his well-meaning alms.

It was an instance of the Hospitaller triumphing over the man of war for which it was impossible to blame Graham Malett. But out in every weather, using to the last trained ounce their skill and strength, two hundred and thirty men needed hot food and warmth when they came in from the bitter night; or they would go where they could get it. Despite the shallow coalition each had achieved, there was no doubt that on Lymond's return, Mammon and the Christian code of the knights were due to collide.

Francis Crawford came back that evening, unexpectedly, striding soaked, vigorous, sardonically cheerful, out of the snowy night into a cold and virtually lightless house. In the middle of his own hall he stopped, divested himself slowly of the last of his riding clothes and handed them to Salablanca. The group of senior commanders hugging the feeble fire moved apart silently, and got up.

The uncomfortable blue eyes swept them. Without moving, Lymond said, 'Jerott? When I left you last week, there was adequate fuel and lighting to last until summer.'

Jerott Blyth stood up, the smoky glow outlining his splendid black head, and said, without a glance at his fellows, 'It was reported to me this morning that stocks were quite low. I have cut supplies until we have more. The details are on your desk, if you will come and look at them.'

'You will show them to me in a moment, here. I want the gentleman you are protecting, whoever he is, to know all about it. Meanwhile, would anyone care to say *why* we now have no fuel?'

There was a heavy silence. Then, 'Because of God's holy charity,' said Gabriel's voice unexpectedly; and Graham Malett himself stood in the doorway, his blanched face seamed with tiredness and cold, and the melted ice from his clothes in a pool at his feet.

De Seurre leaped forward, one hand outstretched, but Gabriel shook his head at a proffered chair and spoke to Lymond, one hand gripping the door-curtain hard. 'Do you know what is happening, out there in the countryside? The woman whose baby you protected the night of the horse-chase is dead, and the child likely to die. Effie Harperfield is lying in bed day and night with the children in her arms, getting up to feed them cold gruel and bacon. They have no fuel and only enough light saved to let the priest give the Last Sacraments when the oldest child dies: she is coughing her lungs up already.'

Gabriel stopped and steadied himself and smiled, a long, rueful smile, at his leader. 'You gave me limited sanction to succour the countryside where needed. I have more than exceeded my sanction. But, Francis, I am not God. People are dying. I could not choose between soul and soul. While I could offer life, I had to give it to everyone. . . .'

His skin was raw with the cold. The melting snow continued to run sadly down his every garment; a two-days' beard, like gold thread, glistened under his skin. He said painfully, 'I have sacrificed your trust, and put your army's well-being second to others. You have my heart's apology. Now you also have my resignation.' And releasing suddenly his supporting grip, Gabriel reeled and, stumbling, slipped to the ground.

Above the sharp voices of the men gathered anxiously to raise him, 'Don't despair,' said Lymond pleasantly. 'I feel there is pleasure and profit to be had out of this little exchange yet. Don't take him away. Put him in the chair by the fire. He'll recover, I'm sure, with a little heat and the universal plaudits of all.'

In the inimical silence that followed, Alec Guthrie's grating voice said, 'I don't know your reasons for this, but the man is genuinely exhausted. His state is not assumed.'

Randy Bell who had been bending over Gabriel, now lying back in his chair, grunted and rose. 'He needs to be in bed, or he'll have trouble. You won't mind, I'm sure.'

Lymond's voice cut him exceedingly short. 'I do. He has trouble now. If he found my sanction inadequate, he should have consulted me. If I wasn't available, he should have consulted a council of his fellows. And, if he saw that either the cottagers or ourselves were to to be destitute, he should at least have attempted to obtain other supplies. With money, it is possible. Not all parts of the country have been so badly affected. It is one thing being a martyr,' said Lymond crisply, his eyes on Gabriel's pallid, closed face. 'It is another thing being a fool of a martyr.'

Across the white face passed a shadowy smile; a moment later, the sick man opened heavy blue eyes. 'I try not to be either,' he said. 'I came to tell you that I have the Queen Dowager's promise to send us any fuel we need. We have only to ask.'

Lymond flung back his head and laughed: a cold amusement that struck a wincing recoil from Gabriel and a growl of suspicion from Jerott Blyth. 'A tuppenny creel of peats for our independence?' said Lymond. 'You rate us low.'

'You overvalue yourself,' answered Gabriel, struggling suddenly upright, 'if you put your independence higher than the living crofters of Yarrow.'

'The lines of reasoning are getting a little blocked, are they not, by the excess of *Saint-Esprit*? I have no quarrel with your errand of mercy, but there is at least one other source of supply you might have tried with no strings attached. If you had approached Wat Scott at Branxholm, the fuel would have been here by now. He has plenty, and three thousand cousins who can supply him with more. Mr Bell can go and ask for it. He could do with some cold in his blood. Sir Graham, your resignation is refused.'

There was a sickening silence.

If Graham Malett left, as everyone was very aware, all the knights and a good many others would go with him. A good many others, but not perhaps all, for Lymond had used all his skill this past winter deliberately to bind his men to him, while Gabriel had been a great deal away. Neither leader, it seemed to Jerott, would be left with a workable force, and all the painful, invigorating, brilliant work of the winter would be undone.

Jerott Blyth wanted to be under Gabriel's leadership, not Lymond's. But he was also a professional fighting man, and he knew it would cost him something to walk out of St Mary's now if Graham Malett insisted on going. And he would surely insist. To a man of Gabriel's calibre, this cavalier treatment was nothing less than outrageous.

They all waited, their gaze fixed on Gabriel.

Malett's white face had flushed, and for a moment genuine anger showed in the tired blue eyes. Then he said steadily, 'Why? Why refuse to release me? Why this craving to dominate, to humiliate the Order? Look, I beg you, into your heart. You cannot dream of subjugating us to your ways. Is it jealousy because we obey a Master other than yourself? Or have you discovered the truth, that your army will not have physical unity without spiritual unity, and that it will not have spiritual unity without us and our Faith?'

The little fire had burned up. It flickered, hiding, revealing the intent faces of the men standing about it in the dim hall; it stencilled in long, rosy lines the person of Lymond, standing considering in front of it, and fell full on the strained face of Gabriel, sitting rigid in the big chair before him. And again, Lymond refused the challenge: refused as so often in Malta to show what lay under the armour. Instead he said, 'We are being imprecise in our terms, are we not? We are in free association, you and I. I can neither release you nor hold you. The only condition I have made applies to all, and not to the knights only. I lead. You may argue gold into radishes over how, where and why I lead, but the final authority must be mine. Two masters we cannot have.'

The carrying voice of Alec Guthrie said unexpectedly, 'But as Sir Graham has already pointed out, every practising Christian must serve two masters.'

'My God . . . *I know it*,' said Lymond. 'My nerves are on edge like a Dublin butcher over the conversation as it is. The situation is that Sir Graham's other Master and I are in perfect accord; whereas, being human, I am not convinced that Sir Graham and I should necessarily be.'

It was Adam Blacklock who began to laugh, and against his will, Jerott followed. It was impudence. . . . It was blasphemous impudence, come to that. But you remembered that never, at any point, had Lymond challenged any personal practice or principle of those within his command. His difference with Gabriel had been over an issue of ill-advised planning, not over the Christian services he had performed.

Against his will, Jerott laughed, and Lymond, moving forward, touched Graham Malett lightly on his bowed shoulders. 'Get some rest,' he said. 'Spiritual unity, you should know, can come from other things besides your precious religion. Don't despair of us yet.'

*

Within three days, supplies of fuel were coming through from all Buccleuch's vast territory, and St Mary's was lit and warmed and all the cold houses in Yarrow supplied. Calling at Branxholm to thank the old man in person, Lymond found that Sir Wat Scott and his wife Janet already knew of the confrontation between Graham Malett and himself.

'Aye, ye're an irreverent, loose-living man,' said the old man with satisfaction, rolling one of his grandsons along the settle and sitting down, unnoticing, on a rattle belonging to one of his sons. 'I hear ye stripped the Chevalier and put him into the stocks for over-doing his good works?'

'It's a damned lie,' said Lymond cheerfully. There was a kind of desperate elation about Francis Crawford that day that neither Will Scott nor his stepmother remembered seeing before.

'And called him God's own madcap ox tae his face.'

'Manners,' said Lymond reprovingly. 'Behind his back, maybe. Not to his face.'

'Why did ye risk it?' asked Buccleuch bluntly. 'He might well hae left ye. He's plenty of other pots on the boil. Jimmy Sandilands has sent him a few times to Council meetings since he was laid up with his quinsy throat, and he's fairly thick with the Queen Dowager at Falkland. Janet's brother Robbie says he's the only disinterested man of God she's got to advise her, and she knows it. She'll take him from you, and his knights with him.'

'No, she won't,' said Lymond amiably. 'She'll wait until she thinks she can get us all.'

'And will she?'

'Occasionally,' said Lymond, and displacing a Scott son (or grand-son) sat down himself. 'When it suits me, and not when it suits the Queen Dowager or Gabriel. . . . How is Peter Cranston's romance, Janet?'

'There's tact for ye, Janet,' said Janet's spouse with approval. 'There she is, heaving like a burstit horse tae get her word in. It's not about Peter Cranston—oh, he and the Donati woman are that thick it's no decent—but Sybilla could do with a visit. Richard keeps on at her about you and Gabriel quarrelling, and Joleta's pining, and Masterly ate something he shouldna and died.'

Masterly was Lady Culter's beloved cat, and his end was recounted to a pattern of screams from the elder Lady of Buccleuch. 'Wat Scott, ye big-mouthed auld thief. That was my news!'

Well, ye were too slow. Ye've a mouth like the West Bow. Use it!' said her husband complacently.

Will Scott's curious gaze hadn't left Lymond. 'It wasn't news anyway,' he said to his stepmother. 'Francis has called at Midculter and seen Sybilla—isn't that right?'

'Two days ago. I presided over Masterly's funeral and dodged the doting Joleta,' said Lymond. 'I gather they've sent for Philippa Somerville to entertain the child.'

Will Scott grinned. 'Aye. I've to pick her up at Liddel Keep on May Day and escort her the rest of the way to Midculter, avoiding you like the glengore.'

The ominous sparkle suddenly became a flame. 'Who says?'

'Your madcap ox. Gabriel. He called at Kincurd once, about Christmas, when he was benighted, and Grizel took him in and gave him a meal like I've never had before or since,' said Will Scott with resentment. 'He still calls in whiles, and she feeds him as if he's about to faint on the altar steps.'

'It brings out the mother in her,' offered Buccleuch senior unwisely.

'Then bad cess to it. The mother gets brought out in Grizel Beaton already as if some folk were crazy,' snapped Grizel's sister Janet and glared as her menfolk went into peals of stupid laughter. 'And why, pray, is Francis Crawford supposed to avoid Philippa?'

'She's out, I gather, to do him some damage. Flaw Valleys was a long time ago, Francis. You'd think she'd have come to her senses?'

'Coming to your senses is no asset in dealing with the Crawfords,' said Janet grimly. 'What's all this Will tells us of you visiting the Kerrs?'

'The *Kerrs*?' It was news, evidently, to Buccleuch. The shrewd eyes, hooded by the vast grey brows, stared at Lymond. 'Visiting the ailing poor, are ye?'

'Janet, you blessed fool,' said her stepson uneasily. 'I told you not to let the old man hear it.'

Janet stared back at him coldly. 'I'll hide any little murder you choose, but not commerce with the Kerrs. Your Da scents that out for himself like a rat after meat. You know that.'

From across the room, Buccleuch and Francis Crawford were staring at one another. Lymond said slowly, 'I have been trying to persuade them, as I tried to induce you, to drop your family feud.'

Wat Scott of Buccleuch rose to his feet. Aged before his time by hard living and hard fighting and a lifetime of Court machinations, he could still draw himself up like a bear, beard jutting, command in every gnarled joint. 'You presumed, ye brassy-necked jackanapes, to beg a truce of the Kerrs *on my behalf*?'

Francis Crawford stayed where he was. But he kept his gaze on Buccleuch, a cold, impersonal gaze that caused Janet to shiver suddenly and draw her youngest child close. 'Beg, Wat?' Lymond said. 'An axe doesn't need to beg. I have told him that the next Scott or Kerr to die in the cause of this feud will be avenged by St Mary's, not by the injured family. The same applies to every house on the Borders terrified to ask legal justice. I mean to break this crazy hermetic chain of slaughter, and I will.'

There was a brief silence. Then Buccleuch laughed, although between the curling grey whiskers his skin was purple; a deep, growling laugh with a grim note in it. 'Meddle with me, laddie, and your axe'll be blunt before summer,' he said. 'The Scott family fights its own wars.'

'I know. It's easier than fighting someone else's,' said Lymond curtly. 'St Mary's is still going to be the Warden's warden, Wat. I tell you now so that you may change your mind about our fuel if you wish.'

'You mean,' said Janet, casting a vicious glance at her husband who was spitting on the floor, 'that if Will here killed a Kerr, you'd see him hanged for it?'

'He wouldn't hang, if there had been provocation. If there wasn't, then he'd get all he deserved. I should see that he was brought to justice, that's all. Left to themselves, Cessford or Ferniehurst would take a revenge worse than any sentence a judge might impose.'

'Of course they would, ye wandering fool. And if they saw Will locked up safe out of their reach by a lot of mim-faced judges, they'd never rest till they'd killed a dozen Scotts to his Kerr, and Will himself on release.'

'They wouldn't, you know,' said Lymond pleasantly. 'For I should stop them.'

'With yon clecking of foreigners at St Mary's?' Buccleuch's nose and mouth, vocally paired, defined his opinion.

'You don't know what he has at St Mary's,' said Will Scott abruptly. He got to his feet, his hot blue stare fixed on Lymond. 'The training is finished?'

Francis Crawford inclined his head.

'It's military rule, then?' said Buccleuch's heir.

'No. We act within the law only.'

Buccleuch, his old eyes narrowed, had lost all his antic derision. 'This is a thrawn countryside, Crawford. There are folk who'll never thole that. They'd sooner call in the English.'

'They'd be too late,' said Lymond drily. 'The English have called me in first.'

*

Will Scott saw their guest off. Standing on the windy steps of Branxholm castle, looking over the wide fiefs of Buccleuch, with the slithering rush of the thaw in their ears, 'Ye ken there's no hope,' said Buccleuch's son to Lymond. 'The auld yin'll not change.'

'I know. Nor will Kerr of Cessford or of Ferniehurst either. But you will; given a chance to live; and the Kerrs who follow.' Lymond's horse and escort were ready. He turned suddenly, his eyes searching the earnest, carrot-topped face. 'You do understand what I'm doing?'

'Aye,' said Will Scott flatly. 'Aye, and I ken that you're right. It's just that life'll be awful dull without the antrin wee stint at making mince of the Kerrs.' He said wistfully, 'You'll have the new hackbuts, I expect, and pistols maybe; and a standard of marksmanship that's fair astronomical. I wish. . . .'

'Don't wish,' said Lymond curtly. 'Your work is here, guarding the name and the future of one of the nation's great families. Thank God for the strength to do your job, and the gift of wife and children to sustain you in it.' His voice cooled to its usual irony. 'Though whether the mass murder of strangers for one's principles ranks higher in virtue than attacking one's neighbours for the hell of it is a point I'm glad I don't have to settle.'

He was mounted. Will Scott reached up a hand, smiling. 'If you are patrolling the Borders for the English, I may meet you one of these darker nights.'

'For both sides, not only the English. We are the Wardens' mailed fist, to be rushed in where there's trouble.'

'And if there's no trouble, you'll make it,' offered Will Scott, his eyes bright, his cheeks red.

'No. At the moment,' affirmed Lymond grimly, 'I am having truck with nothing less than total calamity.'

VII

The Lusty May

(Dumbarton, April/May 1552)

FAT, perfected, and longing to bloody their weapons, the company at St Mary's obeyed with reluctance Lymond's decree that the spring and summer of their first flowering should be devoted to Scotland.

Some, like Gabriel, Guthrie and Bell, agreed that the work he proposed, the safeguarding, policing, shepherding, the patrolling of the Debatable Land, the thieves' waste between England and Scotland, was worth while in itself. All of them came to see, in the end, that the series of small, difficult actions into which he plunged them were satisfying, gave them confidence in each other, and were quickly hardening them into a team.

They did not, apparently, have any pressing need for an income, which was as well, for any payment they received was so far nominal. Their personal well-being continued to be guaranteed by Lymond, and this satisfied, it appeared, all his officers; although the mercenaries demanded—and received—promises of rich rewards for fighting on the Continent when the summer was over. Meanwhile, Jerott supposed, he and his fellow knights were living in part at least on the money Lymond had received from the Constable of France, and were doing work which might well have fallen to the King of France's garrisons in Scotland except that that unfortunate four hundred, had they attempted it, would have been sniped at by the united Borders as busybodies from an alien shore.

As it was, the Borders had a reluctant admiration for St Mary's, who had meted out tough help and tough justice that winter. Many an independent family, like the Scotts and the Kerrs, were hoping to pursue their own unlawful pleasures unnoticed and gave a guarded reception to the round of cool visits Lymond made that spring. He called, too, on Lord Wharton at Carlisle, and on the English Deputy Wardens who, with their Scottish counterparts, tried to keep order, stop thieving and exchanged miscreants between the nations.

Roads were drying out and Border cattle were fattening on the spring grass. With St Mary's help, they would calve where they ate.

The Armstrongs, the Grahams, the Elliots and all the broken men and freebooters of the Debatable Land might wriggle like eels in an ark to escape the attention of this forbidding new force, but as April began to grow towards May they began one by one to find themselves, to their own disgusted surprise, behind bars at Edinburgh or Carlisle, and with no prospect of a blood feud to recompense them when and if they became free. It looked nastily as if some of the fun was to go out of life, henceforth to be devoted to nothing more lively than raising sons, livestock and barley; and even the Trodds were to be policed.

Under this pleasant arrangement, the owners of stolen cattle were allowed to cross the Border not later than six days after the robbery to find them. If the loser failed, the stolen cattle belonged to the reiver. The hunt was therefore a feverish one: feelings ran high and heads rolled, leaving an uncertain judicial situation on both sides. A party engaged on a Hot Trodd, it was decreed, must notify St Mary's before departing. And in case it escaped their minds, Lymond had his independent observers from end to end of the Debatable Ground. He might be half a day behind the excited party, but the knowledge that he *was* behind was likely to cast a little restraint.

He visited, also, the few powerful landowners supporting the Crown in the south-west, and made sure that the Earl of Cassillis, Lord Maxwell and Sir James Drumlanrig knew exactly what he was doing. This meant long hours of riding, a brief call, and a quick return to St Mary's to control developing affairs, but it was done efficiently and without fuss, usually with no more than two officers and a score of men at his back. It was when Lymond was returning from one of these fast, scattered tours with something like nine hours in the saddle behind him, that he was greeted at St Mary's with the news that Thompson had been for two days at Dumbarton and must see him before leaving next day.

Thompson, that well-known sea robber, had been recruited, Jerott knew, to instruct in saltwater warfare that summer. It seemed to him, and he found to Gabriel also, that the business could wait. But Lymond, stopping only to change horses and issue brief directions, simply continued his journey to Dumbarton, a matter of eighty-five miles and a full day of hilly travelling.

Tait and Bell had been with him to Carlisle. Lymond left them at St Mary's and chose Adam Blacklock and Jerott to continue, to Jerott's disgust. And the tolerant counsel of Gabriel, to whom Brother Blyth had described with contempt Lymond's conduct at Dumbarton once before, reduced that young knight to impotent silence. All right: how would Sir Graham prise Francis Crawford from his bedfellows?

But once they left St Mary's, there was so much of moment to discuss and to plan that Jerott lost sight of his grievance, and even Adam Blacklock abandoned his stutter. They stopped at Midculter to pick up Lymond's brother, who wanted to discuss a cargo with Thompson, but to Jerott's profound relief saw no sign of Sybilla or Gabriel's sister Joleta.

By late evening they got to Dumbarton, and dismounted at the *Governor's Barque*, where the candles shone in the unshuttered casements of the inn's single hired parlour, to show that Thompson had come, and was waiting.

In eight years, Scottish pirates had taken a total of something like two million crowns in gold out of Flemish shipping alone. Jockie Thompson, who had a number of other imaginative sidelines besides, believed in making the most of his brief visits to land. Instead of his old leather jacket and stained, salt-rotted breech-hose, he was hung like a hoy with a six-pound furred gown, as Lymond noted aloud, and the gold chains like futtock shrouds on his chest. The black beard and the tough brosy face glistened with fat as he swallowed ox tongues swilled down with Bordeaux and groused about the lightage fees at Dover these days and the customars who, far from taking a gentleman's word, would drive an iron rod through your bales to see if you had hidden hackbuts.

'And had you?' said Lord Culter cheerfully. Relaxed, well-fed round their private table under the flickering tapers, they had disposed before the meal was half over with his personal business and, he guessed, were only waiting for his tactful withdrawal later on to complete whatever transaction Lymond and Thompson were entertaining. It was, he knew, a matter of arranging for Thompson to take the St Mary's officers, in groups, for sea training that summer. It did not need much imagination to guess that what they would practise was piracy, nor that what Lymond was here at the moment to receive was contraband stores, to keep Thompson sweet.

Richard Crawford watched his younger brother, who had spent the better part of a day and a night in the saddle without turning a hair, handle this explosive brute of a seaman like an artist while Blacklock, his stiff leg stretched under the table, looked on smiling and the other fellow, the handsome, smouldering knight Francis dragged with him everywhere, was despite himself drawn into the game.

'Was I smuggling hackbuts?' said Thompson now, moving the red wine aside and taking up the aqua-vitæ. 'By God's breid I was, but not in the cargo: in the fender casks. I tell ye, I had a dainty hand on the tiller yon day, drawing *Magdalena* off frae the jetty. Ae dunt on the planking, and guns would've burst from they fenders like a nursing mother out o' her bodice. . . . Man, are ye weel? Ye're not drinking!'

'I'm not drunk, if that's what you mean,' Lymond said crisply.

Thompson's voice, as always, had early grown thick. As always, it was not likely to get any thicker, since although Thompson's capacity was phenomenal, he had a head like an ox.

Now, he flung back his head and, without swallowing, let the blistering spirit run down his throat. Then he banged down his cup and refilled it, staring at Lymond. 'Better men than you, friend, have yet to see Jock Thompson drunk.'

He turned his seamed, seaman's eyes on Lord Culter. 'It's a grief, just, tae see a friend gone girlish as to the guts. I see *you've* not spared the flagon, my lord, and there you are, sober as one of the Pope's knights.' He had drunk just enough to be quarrelsome. 'So drink sends the wee fellow foolish?'

Blacklock, raising his brows, looked down at his long hands. But Jerott Blyth, a glint in his black eyes, watched Lymond. Last year in France, he well knew from the gossip at home, Francis Crawford had nearly wrecked his career and succeeded in poisoning himself with unbridled drinking. In Malta he had been moderate. Here in Scotland he had stopped drinking completely—taking no risks, it seemed clear, of being led into excess. It roused in Jerott, who had perfect self-discipline, an emotion of purest contempt.

'. . . And,' the old corsair was adding, pulling a face, 'you'll not be one nowadays for the lassies. Devil a rape; barely a wee lonesome damn. Jesus, it's a wonder ye'll sit with an auld hoor like myself.'

'I'll sit with you as long as I can stand you, but I'm damned if I'm going to bore myself to death launching imitation orgies to satisfy your sense of power,' said Lymond without visible emotion. 'If you've finished your unsavoury meal, then sit back and drink yourself into a coma while I attempt to dispose of our business.'

It was the signal for Culter to leave and he began to do so, with amusement, promising himself to find out later from Francis what had happened. Thompson's voice, raised unexpectedly, halted him. 'Aye. But I only do business with *men*.'

'Obviously. With drunk men,' said Lymond patiently. 'I suppose you know if you take any more yourself you'll be as full as a sow?'

'I can hold it,' said Thompson coldly, uplifting and emptying his cup in instant response. 'It's a right shame you're feart. Ye'll never know now, will ye, what the news is about Cormac O'Connor?'

Lymond's eyes met his brother's and Lord Culter, a little more sober than a moment before, achieved his withdrawal. Blacklock, who had not moved, said quietly, 'Would you like us to leave?' But before Lymond could answer, Thompson said jovially, 'Leave? What for should ye leave? We've only St Mary's business to discuss, if we even do that. I keep my gossip for a man who has a man's way with liquor.'

In the ensuing brief silence, Jerott saw that Adam Blacklock's attention was fixed on Francis Crawford, and that Lymond's blue eyes were blazing with irritation and anger. Lymond said, his voice soft, 'You've been too long at sea, butty. You need a lesson in shore drinking and shore manners both.'

And when Blacklock, his face anxious, made a sudden move to demur, Lymond turned on him, then rising, flung open the door. '. . . But let's clear out the ranks of the sanctified first, before we exercise our inordinate appetites against the Lord God Almighty.'

And in silence, Jerott Blyth and Blacklock both left.

Long after midnight, a man waiting patiently in the dark courtyard of the inn saw the lit casement window of the pirate Thompson's room swing slowly open, and Lymond stood silently there, his hand on the latch, the half-spent candles rimming his crisp hair with silver. The good smell of horses and leather, the stink of the midden, the night breathings of spring blossom and trees reached him out of the darkness.

Behind him, singing softly to himself, the pirate Thompson sat a little sunk in his chair, wet beard lost in wet beaver. He was not noticeably drunker than he had been over his supper: just a little hazy of smile and over friendly of manner. He had, in a sense, won. He had made Lymond drink with him, glass for glass, since the other three men had gone. Made him, in the sense that there was information which Francis Crawford badly wanted, and which Thompson's own good sense of preservation had already warned him it was dangerous to give.

Once before, at Dumbarton, when for the price of a sapphire, he had purchased the woman Hough Isa, he had eluded Lymond's questions on this preposterous ground. On the other hand, he liked the man. Lymond had done him good service at Tripoli, and he owed him an act of friendship. So, with his own brand of logic, Thompson had done the thing in his own way. If Lymond would let dignity go hang and crack a bottle—several bottles—with his old gossip, ending in whatever state of high foolishness he feared, Jockie Thompson would impart his tidings from Ireland.

And that was what he, Jockie Thompson, had done. He had started talking, in fact, a little earlier than he had meant, because they were drinking so blithely together, and his stories had gone over uncommonly well. So Lymond knew that he, Thompson, had been running arms and English harp groats into Ireland, and in the Earl of Desmond's dank castle had made rendezvous with Cormac O'Connor, that well-known rebel whose father was in an English prison and whose life till now had been devoted to trying to turn the English out of Ireland.

But Cormac O'Connor, that big wily brute, was also Thompson's own partner in a neat little swindle whereby merchants insured ships

287

and cargo they knew very well to be about to be robbed by Thompson and his friends, and afterwards got the insurance money and at least part of the cargo.

'So you told me,' had said Lymond pleasantly. 'You didn't tell me, however, that the Kerrs were clients of yours.'

He was a smart fellow, was that Crawford. 'They werena,' Thompson replied. 'Not then. They are now. But if they're boasting about it, I'll cut their gizzards.'

'They are, but I've warned them that you would do exactly that. You also said that George Paris acted as your joint agent.'

'Aye.' It was about George Paris, the well-known secret agent used so freely in the plots between Ireland and France to oust the English from Dublin, that he had to tell. 'There's a queer rumour come from the Irish exiles in London that's just come to the ears of Desmond. I was there when he told O'Connor. The story goes that George Paris is a double agent.'

'Oh?' Lymond did not seem specially impressed. Thompson repeated gravely, 'A double agent. Working for the English as well. Taking money from the Privy Council. Giving away, maybe, all the plans to throw the English out.'

'Well, who's worried?' said Lymond. 'France is trying to make friends with England; she won't try anything silly now, whatever friend Cormac is hoping. The only Irish conspirators George Paris could denounce are rebels already, and the Scottish Government, while offering their wholehearted moral support, has done nothing very active to promote the said throwing-out. But if you're anxious, why doesn't Cormac tell his friend the Scottish Queen Mother, and she can have Paris imprisoned on some trumped-up charge?'

'He's in France,' said Thompson, avoiding his eye.

'He is now. But he was in London at the beginning of the year, handing over gifts from the French to the English King. . . . Jockie, my gentle écumeur de mer, that of course would be when the Privy Council agreed to employ him. Then he came up here and conspired with the Queen Mother. I was told he even sent rings and messages and secret expressions of profoundest goodwill to Cormac's father in jail—the appalling deceiver,' said Lymond cheerfully. 'Why wasn't the Queen Dowager told then? Oh Jockie, Cormac wants the money from the insurance parties, and can't bear to lose Paris's help? Ireland, Ireland! Where are your true sons now?'

Thompson was not, for the moment, amused. 'I told him anyway that the woman O'Dwyer was deid,' he said carelessly. 'He didna ken she was taken to Tripoli, and he didna fancy the way he thinks you got rid of the lass in the end. I told him it wasna deliberate, but I doubt he's no friend of yours.'

'He never was,' said Lymond. It was then, Thompson remembered, that he got up suddenly and pouring out a whole beakerful of aqua-vitæ, opened the pirate's whiskered mouth with an iron forefinger and thumb, and emptied it in.

With the elegance of long practice, Thompson's epiglottis went into action and the spirit flowed placidly down. At the end, 'Ye didna need tae do that!' said Jockie Thompson indignantly. 'I can open ma mou' without being helped to it.'

His hand falling, Lymond looked down and against his will, it seemed, laughed. 'I suppose you can,' he said, and tossing the cup away, walked to the window.

He walked, perhaps a little carefully, and his eyes were a little too bright; but the corsair's gaze followed him, frankly admiring. What the embargo had been, who could tell? But there was no doubt about this. Francis Crawford could drink.

Then Lymond opened the window, and a man watched below.

*

If he had been watching still five minutes later, which he was not, he would have seen the candles snuff out as Thompson, fully clothed, rolled happily into bed; and just before that, the progress of a single taper from window to window as Lymond moved down the long gallery to his room.

From the shadows behind his just-open door, Adam Blacklock, who had had a long vigil, saw Lymond reach his own door, open it, and stop dead, the light from a hidden fire bright on his face. There was a pause, then Francis Crawford spoke sharply to someone within.

'*What are you doing here?*'

If there was an answer, Adam Blacklock couldn't hear it. Behind him, Jerott's light breathing went evenly on. Blacklock waited until Lymond's door silently closed, then shut his own with equal sound-lessness and went back to bed.

*

Had he been quite sober and quite fresh, Lymond would probably not have spoken at all. As it was, he had the presence of mind to shut his door, and leaning back on it, to gaze across the small tavern bedchamber at his unsolicited guest.

Seated in dogged discomfort by the hearth, her riding cloak clutched sweatily about her, her hair falling sheer to her knees and the colour itself of the flames, Joleta Malett was waiting. Lymond's icy blue stare fell on her; Lymond's blurred voice snapped, '*What are you doing here?*' and great, clear aquamarine tears sprang into

289

her eyes and fell sparkling down her pink baby skin. With a kind of strangled grunt, she put the back of one wrist to her nose, and scrabbling frantically in her skirts with the other hand, gave a real sob of anguish. '*My handkerchief!*'

Lymond stayed where he was. 'I haven't got one,' he said. 'Blow your nose on your bloody sleeve. I won't look. I suppose everyone in Lennox and district knows that you're here?'

The lorn apricot head shook. 'Luke and Martin came with me yesterday. I've got a room in another wing. Lady Culter and Madame Donati think I'm with Jenny.' She gave another sob, and cut it off. 'You've been *hours*.'

'My apologies, of course,' said Lymond politely. 'But I wasn't aware that I had invited you. How did you know I was coming?'

Wrapped modestly in her furry cloak, in the appalling heat of the room, she could look beautiful even when sniffing. 'Graham said that Thompson was waiting for you, and that you were in the south and would be sure to come soon. So I came to wait for you.'

'In the belief that no one would notice an unescorted female of good family putting up at a shore tavern with two grooms. You may as well divest your modest attractions of their outer wrapping. My hot young blood can stand it. And your reputation has presumably gone anyway. You came to wait for me. Why?'

Slowly, Joleta took off her cloak. Underneath, her dress was a young green: a web-like wool finely gathered under her breasts and covering her soft arms down to the wrists. Her little, sparkling teeth whose sibilants frosted her every phrase were sunk in her lip. Taking off her cloak was an effort, socially as well as physically: her golden skin was deep pink.

Lymond made no effort to help. Only, as the fur fell to the ground and she sat in her meadowland of green, twisting her hands, he drew a long, quiet breath and expelled it before he repeated, 'Why?'

'To say I'm sorry.' Her chin, so like Gabriel's, was up; her eyes, so like Gabriel's, were pleadingly, defiantly, on him. 'I'm sorry about Kevin. I'm s-sorry about losing my temper. I don't want you to hate me.'

Lymond shifted his position, fractionally, against the door. 'Sir Graham doesn't want me to hate you.'

She flushed again, and then paled, so that the ginger freckles contoured all the exquisite face. 'I know. But this isn't to please Graham. And you must know Graham wouldn't let me do this.'

'Why ever not?' said Lymond ironically. 'You're perfectly safe; it's only your reputation that's ruined. I be lightly drunken, as the man said, and have but little appetite to meat.'

Tears stood in her eyes but did not, this time, spill over. She stood up. 'You don't forgive me.'

'No, I don't,' said Francis Crawford lightly. 'I dislike you, Joleta.'

There was a moment of complete and cataclysmic surprise. Then the tears, unregarded, fell from Joleta's immense, open eyes, her jaw dropped and she said, 'But you *can't* dislike me!'

Laughter, remotely, stirred in the cool blue eyes. 'Well, that was genuine, anyway,' he said. 'Don't strain yourself trying to believe it. But I am a strange man to meddle with, that's all.'

Her dismay had fetched her half across the small room. In front of him, 'Don't you desire me?' said Joleta, and flushed scarlet again.

Against the door, his eyes heavy with wine, Lymond scanned her from her milky throat to her green-slippered feet. 'Dear Joleta,' he said. 'You've been reading too many Italian books. There's such a thing, you know, as seducing in hate.'

'I don't believe that,' said Joleta steadily. 'Love is stronger than hate. Love is stronger than anything. Where there's love, there can be no evil.'

'Maybe,' said Francis Crawford. 'But I am not, sweeting, in love.'

'*But I am,*' said Joleta Malett desperately. And pulling, tight-fisted, at the silken cord that bound her high-waisted dress, she dragged first girdle then buttons apart until the green stuff, gaping loose to the waist, slid from her bare shoulders and hung from her elbows, tight-sleeved like a courtesan's robe.

She wore nothing beneath. Her flesh breathed sweetness and warmth, and her sixteen-year-old breasts, round and rosy in firelight, lay high and ripe in their calyx of green. Three-quarters stripped, trembling, her eyes black with a queer ecstasy, half missionary, half not, Joleta caught Lymond's cold, clever hand and slid it round and over and down all her warm flesh.

There was a heady pause. She felt him steady himself after the first, quick-breathing shock; then the fingers which lay so passively in hers suddenly gripped like a vice. She gasped, and in the same moment heard what he had heard: distant galloping hooves which moment by moment became nearer and sharper until in seconds a neighing horse came to a jangling halt in the silent courtyard below. There were running footsteps, then a swordhilt hammered home again and again on the inn's big oaken door while a harsh voice yelled for admittance.

The voice was the voice of Randy Bell, and the name he was shouting was Lymond's.

The cries tore across the sleeping peace of the night: the roaring as the angry innkeeper stormed to the doorstep roused every soul in the wing. Across the corridor Jerott Blyth shot up in bed and a moment later Blacklock, grumbling, got out. He said, 'Christ, it's Randy. Look, you're decent at least. Go down and let him in before he breaks down the door. I'll tell Lymond.'

'Tell Lymond?' Jerott was cold. 'He could hardly help hearing that, unless he's stone dead.'

'He may not be dead but he may very likely be stone drunk,' said Adam with reason. 'Go on. You had the damned bedclothes all night. You ought to be warm.'

And, repressing a strong desire to curse, Jerott went. As he began to run downstairs Blacklock crossed the corridor and gave an almighty bang on Lymond's shut door. 'Francis? Send her out. I'll take her next door. The room's empty.'

Before he had finished, the door was open. Inside, Lymond, an extraordinary expression on his face, half of mischief, half of malice, propelled towards Blacklock a slender, golden-topped figure muffled in a great cloak. 'Look out, she's half naked,' said Lymond calmly. 'And if you force her, you lecherous scribbler, you can explain to Gabriel, not me.' And, half pulled, half carried, Joleta Malett was carted away.

Two minutes later, Randy Bell was upstairs, taking three at a time, with Jerott casting questions at his heels, and hardly taking time to knock on the door, they were both into Lymond's room.

Lymond, awake, alert and neatly dressed in London russet, laid down his book by the fire and gravely welcomed them in.

'It's the Hot Trodd!' said Randy Bell. 'Word came today from the Wardens to St Mary's. Someone's taken a great herd of Kerr animals, and Cessford and Ferniehurst are riding over the Border tonight.'

'How exciting,' said Lymond, staring at the panting physician. 'But not enough, I think, to keep me from my modest couch. Sir Graham, I take it, is leading a company after the chosen of the children of Benjamin?'

Randy Bell flung his helmet on a settle and sat down with a crash. 'That isn't all. The freebooters have been at Buccleuch beasts as well. Half the Scotts round about Branxholm are off to the Debatable too. All, thank God, except the old man himself. He's away at Paisley and hasn't been told.'

'Now that,' said Lymond, his voice changing, 'is news.' And rising swiftly, he opened the shutters. It was a clear spring night, with Jupiter bright as a diamond above. 'Give me an hour to finish what I have to do here. Jerott, get dressed and set off at once for St Mary's with Blacklock and Bell. When I'm ready, I'll follow. We should get directions there, and fresh horses, and with any luck catch up with Sir Graham before the Scotts and Kerrs find their herds or each other. . . . It's a pity it's such a clear night. Randy, I'm sorry, but you must come back with us. Could you arrange post-horses quickly below while the other two dress?'

'What remains to do here?' said Jerott Blyth. If you looked closely at Lymond's eyes and caught the smell of his breath, it was plain that Thompson had liberated him from his lofty principles all right.

'I,' said Lymond with simple truth, 'am going to bed.'

Five minutes later, Lymond saw Blyth and Bell off downstairs, and walked across to where Adam Blacklock was hastily dressing.

He had a bitten finger. 'She w-wanted to scream,' he said. 'So I stopped her. Her c-cloak fell off.'

'I expect it did,' said Lymond. 'And then she w-wanted to scream again?'

It was Blacklock's turn then to realize that he was not perfectly sober. Francis Crawford was not given normally to mimicry unless he wanted to wound. The artist said briefly, 'N-not on my account, I promise you.'

Lymond looked up suddenly, searching Blacklock's face; and his own expression altered. 'I'm sorry,' he said. 'I wasn't baiting you because of *that*, but you're a bloody fool, Adam. What happened, you couldn't sleep and saw Joleta earlier entering my room? In any case, you get the cup and the cash prize as well. Two minutes later and Blyth and Randy Bell would have been in the room, their eyes hung on jemmy-bands.'

'And now?' said Blacklock. From the stir below, and the clacking of hooves on the cobbles, they could hear that the others were ready.

He had left a buckle undone. Lymond fastened it, delicately, giving it all his attention, and stood back to admire. 'Now,' he said, 'I am going in my drunken lust to visit Gabriel's sister, *candidior candidis*, the virginal Joleta. And once there, to rifle at leisure her sixteen-year-old charms.'

Though the headache which had crippled him all evening, Adam stared back at the icy blue eyes. Lymond, worldly as he was, must surely have noted what he had noted. 'She's in love with you,' Adam observed.

'Is she? Perhaps. We'll know, shan't we,' said Lymond absently, 'in one hour from now?'

＊

But he spent longer with Joleta than that. As Bell, Blacklock and Blyth cantered out of the yard and the tavern settled once more to its rest, Lymond unlocked the room where Adam had concealed Gabriel's sister. Inside it was cold and dark and only dimly, by her hurried breathing, could one distinguish the child huddled there in her cloak.

Without speaking Lymond crossed the room and lifting her, quite unresisting, carried her in a crushed, silent bundle to his warm, bright room next door. There he laid her softly on the bed, spread out the

293

apricot hair on the pillowcase, and with gentle fingers laid back the cloak, unveiling once more to the firelight the bared silk of her beautiful body. Then he walked away and sat down. 'All right. Fascinate me,' he said, and settled back in his chair.

Joleta sat up.

'And a very pretty beginning. A little too spry, maybe, for the perfect effect. We mustn't bustle through the programme, you know.'

'*What programme?*' said Joleta. 'Who were these men? They tried. . . .'

'That was Adam Blacklock, saving your honour,' said Lymond comfortably. 'The newcomer was from St Mary's, to tell me that your brother has marched to battle, armed to the halo. I should be there too. I chose, sister-seraph, to be here.'

Sitting bolt upright in a tumble of green wool, golden hair and white flesh, she gave him back stare for stare. 'Even though you dislike me?'

'I'm a quick convert,' said Lymond. 'I thought I'd try love. Stronger than hate, if you remember. *Tant que je vivrai en âge fleurissant, servirai Amour, le dieu puissant.*'

Straight as a fawn, Joleta sat in the blaze of her hair. 'I thought,' she said, 'my reputation concerned you.'

Lymond laughed. 'After darting in and out of my bedroom all night with twigs in your beak? There's a love-nest here all right, sweetheart, as far as the inn is concerned, although St Mary's may not know of it yet. In which case, why not nestle?'

There was a short silence. Then Joleta said, masking her face suddenly in her long hands, 'Help me. Help me. I love you.'

'Good,' said Lymond encouragingly. 'Now you finish undressing.'

Slowly, her hands came down, hovered over the clasps of her girdle and then stopped. Two tears washed down her flushed cheeks. 'I don't know how.'

'Beautiful,' said Lymond approvingly. 'Now I should come over and unfasten it. I'm tired. You do it.'

She was crying harder, silently, the streaks silvering her firm little breasts. 'I meant . . . I don't know how to make love.'

'Joleta!' said Lymond. 'Magnificent girl. You deserve to be put in a play.' He got up, his eyes blazingly blue, his walk not yet quite steady, and began to approach. '*Then I shall have to teach you.* Isn't that what they all say?' And smiling, he brushed aside her hovering hands, and with smiling violence snapped the remaining clasps of her gown.

Below him, her white-lashed eyes were open and clear; the blood pulsed in her white throat. Wet with tears, the hair coiled round her neck and caught in the fine russet of his clothes. 'Be gentle,' she said, and Lymond, gripping her, shook his fair head.

'With you, no, angel-sister; not with you. For what you need, my Joleta,' said Francis Crawford, and his own teeth showed for a moment white against his hard mouth, 'is a master.'

Three hours later Richard Crawford in the other wing of the inn woke from the sleep of the healthily tired to find his landlord battering on his locked door.

From that anxious gentleman he discovered that two of the men from St Mary's had left the tavern at midnight, and that Thompson, on no doubt urgent concerns of his own, had also later departed, forgetting to settle his score. Having reassured the man with an English rose noble and the sight of some more, Richard got rid of him, robed, and marched to his brother's wing to investigate.

Lymond's door was locked, and his rap went unanswered, despite distinct sounds from within. Having made sure that Blacklock and Jerott Blyth had indeed vanished, Lord Culter returned to his brother's room and this time, annoyed, both rattled the latch and addressed him. 'Francis, you unmitigated rake. Put her down, whoever she is, and emerge.'

Behind the door something crashed, and Lymond chuckled. There was a short silence, then the sound of a minor struggle, and he laughed again. When he spoke, his voice was quite close to the other side of the door. 'It's all right, Richard. The others were called back and I shall be following them in five minutes. Pay the accounting if Thompson doesn't, will you? I'll put it right with you later.'

'If you live,' said Richard drily. Something hit the inner side of the door and fell, breaking. 'What's happened? Come out without your money?'

Lymond didn't answer. Instead, the key rattled. Richard heard his brother say something sharply and brutally, a tone of voice he had never heard him use in a bedroom before. There was one movement of extreme violence and a woman's voice, directly cut off. Then the key turned and the door blundered open.

Inside, eyes crazed, hair wild, a ripped sheet clutched round her naked sixteen-year-old body, Gabriel's beloved child-sister stood swaying.

Speechless, Richard Crawford stood stupidly staring, first at the child, then beyond her to where his younger brother, his imprisoning arm dropped to his side, turned abruptly and, kicking his way through the shambles, walked back to the fire.

In silence, his face drained of colour, Richard held out his two hands to the girl.

Joleta stared back. The sheet, unheeded, hung from her bruised arms and her cheeks were stained and dirtied with tears. 'It's too late,' she said. 'Too late for help.' And before he could move, slipped to the floor, lying quiet with her bright hair on his shoes.

Slowly, Richard knelt. He gathered up the light weight, folding the torn sheet softly about her, and carrying her into Lymond's room, laid her on the wrecked bed. Then he closed the door, equally slowly, and standing before it, as Lymond hours earlier had done, he said quietly to Lymond's still back, 'So this is the outcome of it all. This is why Tom Erskine preserved you; why Christian Stewart died and Gabriel has worked to redeem you . . . for this. Francis, I would sooner have discovered you dead.'

His brother turned. Fair hair tumbled, eyes blazingly bright, he was breathing hard still, his fine shirt twisted loose from its cords. 'I wish to God it had been anyone but you,' he said. 'Because for my sake and Joleta's honour you won't tell, will you?' His voice was bitter. 'You'll go home and mope like a dog, so that Sybilla is sure to wonder what's wrong. It won't occur to you . . .' He stopped.

Richard found that he was not only cold, but trembling with shock and loathing and fear. 'What won't occur to me?'

'That she was a bitch,' Lymond said. 'Just a bitch who needed a lesson.'

He waited without moving while Richard strode up to him, and did not lift his hands even when Culter took him in a double grip that must have hurt to the bone.

'It would help if I hit you, wouldn't it?' said Richard at last. 'I'm not going to. I merely want to point out that were she three-faced Hecate herself, she is Graham Malett's sister and a guest under your mother's roof.'

Loosing his hands, he stepped back. 'But she isn't Hecate, is she? She's sixteen, convent-bred and a little spoiled, and you are afraid of her brother, so you've used her . . . you've used her like an old dockside bawd.'

He halted, his voice suddenly out of control. 'I meant what I said. I wish you'd died first.'

A sort of deadly derision appeared for a second in Lymond's blank eyes. 'I don't think *she* does,' he said, and then stopped at the look on her brother's face. After a moment, he added curtly, 'Will you take her back to Midculter? Will you say nothing to Sybilla? The girl won't mention it if you don't.'

Richard, his flat brown hair fallen over his face, knelt by Joleta, the brisk, the clever, the bright, with whom he had journeyed from France, and took her bleeding wrists in his hands. 'You can rely on me, as always,' he said. 'You know better, of course, than to come to Midculter again.'

He did not look round, and it seemed a long time before Lymond's voice said, 'What, then, will you tell Sybilla?'

After a fashion, Lord Culter had clothed her, wrapping her in sheets and blankets, and then in the torn and crushed furry cloak.

Her eyes were still closed. Richard raised Joleta Malett again in his arms and looked up, the pink-gold hair streaming over his arm. 'That you are going abroad. I take it you are. I cannot imagine even you could face Gabriel again.'

'Then your imagination is uncommonly poor,' said Lymond with a kind of mulish bravura. 'I can face anyone except possibly Sybilla. I am going straight back to St Mary's. Why not? I've no more to do here. To market, to market, to buy a plum bun. . . .'

The door slammed.

'Home again, home again,' continued Francis Crawford genteelly to the strewn, empty room. '*Market is done.*'

VIII

The Hot Trodd

(The Scottish Border, May 1552)

THE only person who slept undisturbed that night on either side of the Scottish Border was Philippa Somerville, waiting at Liddel Keep with a small escort and one of Kate's serving women for Will Scott to take her to Midculter next day.

In fact, Will Scott had forgotten her, being at that moment briskly engaged. The previous night, the Kerr sheep and cattle had been lifted by a family of rogues called Turnbull, long since thrown out of Philiphaugh and now lodged uneasily in the Debatable Land. In the morning the family Kerr, led by Sir Walter Kerr of Cessford and Sir John Kerr of Ferniehurst with their sons, nephews and cousins, set off to recover their property, followed a false trail down Jed Water, and spent the day and half the night of the 30th unprofitably roaming round Redesdale.

They did not on this account meet the Scotts, who lost their beasts a little later in the day, the Turnbulls not being a numerous family, and set off eventually, under Sir William Scott, to rake Tyneside and Liddesdale. In doing so, they actually passed through the Turnbulls' squalid encampment, but found it empty of all but women, since the Turnbulls had not gone home at all, but had wisely kept their booty in a quiet little valley north of the Border until the first twenty-four hours had gone by, the interesting point being that if they could retain possession of the beasts for six days they could keep them for good, since the unfortunate losers were allowed only so long to hunt for them south of the Border.

The family Turnbull, therefore, smart as Chinese Checkers, spent the two days after the robbery moving nimbly up and down hills and keeping successfully just outwith the reach of either the Kerrs or the Scotts, but moving imperceptibly southwards ready, when the time came, to usher their tired beasts into the Debatable Land and home.

They nearly succeeded, but being stupid men, they were beaten by one thing: Will Scott had posted scouts. When, at dusk on the 1st May, the man watching the pass at Canonbie saw the slow-moving, bleating patch of shadow in a far valley appear and make its herded and painful way towards the settlement of Turnbull, he put spurs to his horse, and within the hour, the Scotts had taken the road.

By then, Randy Bell was with them. Neither he nor Jerott nor Adam Blacklock had particularly enjoyed the ride from Dumbarton back to St Mary's through the previous night, although the last two had slept at least since covering the same ground on the way north. They had reached St Mary's to find that, as they had expected, Gabriel had long since left with the company to police the Trodd. Messengers hourly told them that he had located the Kerrs and was staying with them, but that the stolen animals had not yet been found. He had not so far been able to trace Will Scott and his party.

Lymond's orders had been that all three of his officers should immediately join Gabriel. If the Scotts and the Kerrs were conducting a separate search, he had instructed that Gabriel, Bell and Jerott should stay with one faction, and Blacklock and Guthrie attach themselves to the other, with half of the remaining officers and the men of St Mary's with each.

It was clear however, when the three men arrived at St Mary's, that the double journey to and from Dumbarton without pause had been a good deal to expect from the doctor, tough as he was, without at least an hour's rest before continuing south. Further, they found that Scott's whereabouts were still unknown. So it came about that Jerott set off, after a brief meal, to join Graham Malett and the whole company of St Mary's with the Kerrs, while Blacklock stretched his weak leg and snatched an hour or two's rest beside the snoring form of Randy Bell.

The next messenger to arrive after they were astir had news of Will Scott. The stolen herd had been located in Turnbull country, and the Scotts were riding there. Bell and Blacklock paused only to send word to Gabriel, and followed them.

They caught up with the Scotts, riding through Liddesdale after dark, and Buccleuch's heir, already out of temper at their head, looked less than pleased to see them. Will Scott, it was plain, had hoped to manage this little expedition without any interference from St Mary's, and the news that Graham Malett and the entire company were on their way to help him retrieve his beasts was almost more unwelcome than the news that the Kerrs were sufferers also, and would be with him.

Adam Blacklock sympathized. He understood and was amused by the big, red-headed Scott with the small, snapping merry-eyed wife; and he knew that after a year with Francis Crawford, Buccleuch's heir could more than look after himself, and would set a high value on his independence. Yet he knew too that once Will reached them, the Turnbulls were likely to suffer swift justice, and that if the Kerrs and Scotts met unsupervised, one wrong word was enough to provoke a massacre. The Wardens' law must be preserved. Adam rode beside the taciturn Will, and wondered how near Gabriel was. It might almost be better for the Scotts to reach the stolen herd first, retrieve their beasts and start back for home, leaving dead Turnbulls in every ditch, than that the Kerrs and the Scotts should meet. He and Randy alone could hardly prevent the Scotts from doing just as they pleased.

It was in Gabriel's hands. If he thought it politic to delay, no doubt he would. Then for the first time in several hours, Adam Blacklock thought of Gabriel's young sister, as he had last seen her, white-faced, half-stripped, in the room next to Lymond's at Dumbarton, and recalled Lymond's bland voice: 'I am going to bed.'

Lymond hadn't come in an hour. Fully aware that two of the most explosive tribes on the Borders were ranging the land looking for trouble, Francis Crawford had stayed at Dumbarton while Gabriel took the sword in his place. Stayed, rather drunk, with Gabriel's sister Joleta.

Then at that point in his thoughts, the big doctor said, 'Adam? What's amiss?' and he tried to shake off the headache which had dogged him all day and smile. The moon was up, and very bright, and over the next ridge lay Turnbull land.

There were two Turnbull boys on outpost duty, but these were found and felled almost at once. Then as lights sprang and wavered in the mud-daubed sheds and turf-roofed cabins, the Scotts roared down like the fall of a beech.

The thieves hadn't expected it. Leaving behind the women and the old and the babies, they took to their horses in the brilliant moonlight and made for the hills.

They had no chance at all. Deaf to the shouts of Blacklock and Bell, Will Scott led his men after them, and where they could not capture, they killed. Adam saw old man Turnbull himself, built like a tree, back up his horse in the end shouting desperately to himself and the doctor, the only men among the attackers who were not Scotts. Randy Bell, nearer to him, did manage to fight to his side, but when Blacklock got there, the old man too was dead, and Randy Bell sitting on the young heather cursing Scotts; all Scotts and any Scotts of the name.

Then with the few prisoners they did take, the whole tribe cantered back to the settlement. The bulk of their own sheep and cattle they found where they had already noted them, in a big fold on the side of the hill. Furrowed tracks here and there showed where an opportunist granddad had made off with a heifer or two: a detachment of Scotts scouring the darkness soon rounded up all these.

The living remnants of the clan Turnbull, far from mourning their dead, seemed as ever practically inclined. There were calves in the woodpile and tupps under the bed, lambs in the chimneys and a milch-cow lashed to somebody's roof and thatched over. It was tricky work, but at length the Scott property, from Kincurd and Branxholm and all the long vale of Yarrow, marked with the Scott mark, was rounded up, and the owners were ready to go. It was then that Will Scott, flushed and exhilarated, ill-temper long since gone, clapped a big hand to his brow and yelled, '*Christ!* Philippa Somerville!'

He had been intended to meet her, it appeared, at Liddel Keep, not five miles away, and he should have been there this morning. 'I'll go,' offered Randy Bell. 'Take her to Midculter in the morning?'

Certainly, the sooner the Scotts left the district the better. Gabriel and the Kerrs had not yet arrived, but they might do so at any time. All the same, Adam Blacklock's gaze met Will Scott's, and Will said hastily, 'Thank you, but no. Kate would flay me alive if I didn't see to Philippa myself. She knows me, you see. I'll call for her now. I thought you said Francis Crawford was coming?'

'He may have gone to Graham Malett and the main company instead,' said Blacklock quickly. It was possible. He hoped it was true. Between them, Lymond and Gabriel could keep Dante's devils under control, never mind the left-handed chosen of Benjamin. It occurred to him that he had not yet seen any Kerr animals, although the scout who had first located the herd had reported that they were Scott and Kerr property mixed. Will Scott had been scrupulous, he had seen, in checking the burns.

They must be further away from the settlement. Satisfied, the Scott owners would have left the outlying valleys alone. Will Scott said now quickly, 'Well, I'm away. I've no itch, I can tell you, to see Francis Crawford, and get dog's abuse for not warning you all. Tell him he can come another time and hold my wee warm mailed fist.'

'You tell him,' said Adam Blacklock, and gave a cursory wave as the big young man, grinning, mounted and left. Randy Bell rode off with him. Adam, with half a dozen Scotts endowed him for safety, had elected to wait for the men of St Mary's and the Kerrs.

*

By the time Francis Crawford reached St Mary's from Dumbarton, riding alone, it was the afternoon of the 1st May, and he had been without sleep for the better part of two nights, and had covered something like two hundred and fifty miles since before dawn the previous day. He stopped at his own home for a meal and a flask of the strongest spirits he could find, to keep himself in the saddle and for no other reason, and after taking both, walking about the castle and talking to the few men who remained, set off immediately for Liddesdale.

He was, or had been at the outset, faultlessly hardened for this very purpose. He also knew exactly how much longer he could expect his mind to remain clear and his muscles respond without rest. It was probably long enough to trounce Will Scott for not having reported his loss to St Mary's, and maybe to view the winding up of the exercise. It seemed unlikely, with the whole company from St Mary's with the Kerrs, that anything undesirable could happen.

That, however, he knew at the back of his mind, was a rationalization. Had it not been for Joleta, he would have been there now.

As it was, he did not attempt to pick up Gabriel in the darkness, but rode instead straight to the Debatable Land where the Turnbulls had their base. There, instead of Will Scott, he found Adam Blacklock, comfortably installed in an empty shack with six Scotts before a big fire, awaiting the arrival of Gabriel, Jerott Blyth and the Kerrs.

Any constraint Adam might have felt before Lymond vanished when the other man strolled into the hut, hard, slender and hellish inquisitive. Adam talked, and Lymond listened until he came to the bit about the absent Kerr cattle. Then he said, 'Wait. When old Turnbull shouted, what did he say?'

'Nothing about Kerrs,' said Adam positively.

'What, then? Can you remember even a word?'

If the Kerrs had to ride all round the Border to find their benighted beasts, Adam couldn't see that it mattered. The Scott animals were away, with their owners, and the theft, God knew, had been fully avenged. He said nevertheless, 'He was frightened, that's all. He was trying to promise something, I think. Maybe restitution, of a kind. Whatever it was, we couldn't save him.'

'Randy couldn't save him. You didn't try. Who are left here?'

'About a dozen women,' said Blacklock stiffly. 'Two bedridden men and a cripple, and a few children. That's all. The Scotts took their prisoners with them.'

When Lymond spoke this time, it was face to face, and the smell of liquor was quite unmistakable, although his words were explicit enough. 'Find me a mother and child. For preference, a woman who has only one son.' And as Adam hesitated, 'I want to find those cattle, Blacklock. The wives must know where they are.'

'Do it yourself,' Adam said.

For a long moment, his eyes bright with cold temper, Lymond stared at the other man; then he turned on his heel and went out.

Adam counted only five minutes before he was back, leading two fresh horses from the Turnbulls' pastures. He flung the reins of one at Blacklock saying 'Come!' and as he mounted, shouted 'Follow!'

to the Scotts. Then the artist found himself riding hell for leather through the night at Lymond's heels.

It was a short ride. Blacklock never caught up with Lymond and so had no idea what he had learned. He only knew that swerving up a low hill and down the opposite side, he had to close his thighs sharply to avoid the man, who had suddenly reined, and then half-jump his mare sideways to avoid a large obstacle looming black on the slope. Next he saw that what he had taken for gorse bushes in the dark were other inanimate articles littering the whole valley before him. Then he heard, thinly and weakly through the spring air, the rumour of spent beasts in pain, and even then did not at once guess.

Dismounting, Lymond, Blacklock and the six men walked in silence from end to end of the valley, past every dead or dying animal that had once been the Kerrs'. Slashed, hamstrung, broken, stabbed or beheaded, every beast had been slaughtered or else uselessly maimed, with no regard for their agony or their value. Meat which would have kept Cessford and Ferniehurst all summer, and fed half of Edinburgh as well, lay butchered here on the grass. Near the beginning, Lymond struck a light from some tinder to look for the brand. They found it, marking each beast as a Kerr's. It was then that they saw for the first time the triumphant S which overlaid every mark, crudely cut in each flank by the butchers. And in these parts, S stood only for 'Scott'.

Shielding the flame in his hands, Lymond straightened and met Adam's taut gaze. 'You were with the Scotts before, during and after their attack on the camp?'

'Yes. They didn't do this. There wasn't time. They were only concerned about punishing Turnbulls and getting their own cattle back.'

'But you said that they came through Liddesdale once before, on their own.'

'Yes. But that was yesterday. This was done today. These beasts are still warm.' Adam added harshly, 'In any case, if the Scotts had done it, wouldn't they have taken home their own herd at the time? Why come back for it? Especially after signing their work?'

Lymond was staring at him. 'Well done,' he said. 'That takes care of all the arguments. Now tell me how we're going to prevent the Kerrs from going berserk when they ride over those hills and find this.'

At that, even the raised voices of the six men beside them were promptly cut off. Then Adam said slowly, 'We can't. But at least the Scotts will be well on the way home. That is—' Through the cloudy wastes of his headache, there came to him the thing he'd forgotten.

He went on, 'That is, they'd a call to make first. The Somerville youngster is at Liddel Keep, and Scott was going that way to escort the girl north.'

After a moment Lymond said, flatly, 'When did they leave?'

'Not ten minutes before you arrived.'

'With the animals?'

'Yes.'

'Then they won't be there yet. And when they get there, they'll stay overnight. It'll let the Kerrs get away, they would think, and rest the cattle and the men.'

Blacklock said irritably, 'What's so desperate? Gabriel may not bring them at all tonight. He knows by now that the Turnbulls are the culprits, but he may not tell the Kerrs until he's sure Scott is away. And even if they come, they may well miss this field until morning. You didn't notice it until you were told. And even if they find it, it'll be morning until they can trace the Scotts by the cattle marks. And even apart from all those things,' said Adam Blacklock with leaden patience, 'what hope have one undisciplined Border family, however wild, in fighting the whole of St Mary's?'

The light had gone out. Standing still at his side, Lymond said, 'Do you want an answer? Whoever slaughtered these animals will make sure the Kerrs know about it by now. That's why it was done. The actual killing, incidentally, was done by the Turnbulls themselves, for a fee. The man who gave them the money insisted on watching the slaughter, and, they assumed, was a Scott. So when the Kerrs come they will certainly kill all those Turnbulls still left. They will then by means of their torches follow Will Scott to Liddel Keep. . . . *It's too late*,' said Francis Crawford on a note that made Adam's skin crawl. 'It's too late. If I'd been even two hours before. . . . But we can try. . . . Adam, you must ride and try to warn Gabriel. He may guess where Scott is. . . . Christ, even I knew, if I had had the wit to remember. But if he knows what's likely to happen, he may be able to stop it. If not, and these wily old devils get the news first, they'll trick him if they can.'

'And you?' said Blacklock. 'You will ride and warn Scott?'

'One of his own men will do that,' said Lymond, and mounting, gathered the reins. 'For my bloody sins, I've got twelve women, a cripple, two bedridden men and eight children to hide first.'

*

Adam Blacklock had been right. After learning that the stolen herds were in Liddesdale, and that the Scotts were riding to find them, Gabriel delayed quite some time before imparting the news, with his congratulations, to the Kerrs. The two old men, Jerott noted, treated him with reserve. Walter Kerr and John Kerr, with justice, were suspicious of all the right-handed world; which was why they had reached the ripe years they had.

The younger Kerrs Jerott liked. Since joining Gabriel and his friends, the smell of Dumbarton had gone. He had enjoyed riding out among all the fierce, leather-jacketed young of Cessford and Ferniehurst, brash and vigorous and rough-cut as they were, hunting a herd which had been taken up into Heaven, it seemed.

Then, when Gabriel quietly told them the news, the first uneasy shadow appeared. Lymond had not yet arrived. When questioned, Jerott told the exact truth. Lymond had not been ready to leave the inn at Dumbarton, and had claimed to be following them in an hour. Further questioned, he added that Mr Crawford had been drinking, and presumably had other pleasures already engaged for the night. In any case, clearly, he had not followed. Without him, it was decided to defer disclosing the whereabouts of their herd to the Kerrs.

Then, as Lymond did not come, the Kerrs were told. Then and increasingly it became clear that Graham Malett was troubled, both by Lymond's absence and by his own assumption of command. The lesson of the rationed fuel had sunk, it seemed, bitterly deep. At every stage Jerott found himself, with de Seurre and Hoddim and Plummer and Tait and Guthrie, in round table conference over the next move. At St Mary's it would have worked. In the field, with several hundred robust Kerrs to be handled, it was uneasily wrong. Everything that Gabriel did or suggested was obviously and precisely right. But he would act on nothing before placing it, as Lymond had so caustically demanded, before his fellows. And always, they were looking for Lymond himself.

By dusk, and the approaches to Liddesdale, he still had not come. Afterwards, Jerott could never say when he realized that something was wrong. Only the air suddenly was cold, and full of whispers. The Kerrs who had been trotting in cheerful ferocity at his side drew off and could be found riding in knots, talking quietly. It was all the odder because a scout of Gabriel's, sent ahead secretly, came back to report after dark that the Scotts had clearly been to the settlement, recovered their cattle and gone, taking or killing every able-bodied Turnbull there first. He had not found the Kerr beasts at all.

This on the face of it nearly disposed of their obligations, on this trip at least. The Turnbulls had met their doom prematurely, but at least it could not be done twice. The Scotts were out of the way. It only remained to find the animals reived from the Kerrs.

Having reasoned so far, they all looked to Guthrie, who said, 'There's only one question that matters. Will the Scotts have taken the Kerr beasts?'

'No,' said Gabriel. And 'No,' said Jerott equally positively. 'You can rely on that. If it had been Buccleuch, perhaps. But Will Scott knows very well the feud had got to end.'

'Then,' said Guthrie, enunciating, as ever, to the class, 'If that's what the Kerrs are afraid of, and it must be, it'll do them a lot of good to prove otherwise. I think they think we're concealing something. I suggest we deal with it by setting them free.'

'Leaving them? I should be against that under any circumstances,' said Gabriel. 'But who agrees with you?'

They were having a break for bannocks and water, and perhaps a mouthful of wine, before the last stretch. After two days of it, although with adequate rests, they were a little stiff and looking forward now to an end. Here in the dark, with the dim shapes of their own men moving ahead and the concourse of Kerrs moving, muttering, munching beyond, they replied in undertones to Gabriel's question. No one thought they should abandon the Kerrs. But there was some agreement that they should split up.

Some time ago, Walter Kerr had approached Gabriel with the rasped suggestion that they would search a good deal quicker in small companies. Now that they knew for certain that the Kerr herds were not actually in the settlement, it was only common sense to search around.

Thus, when both Walter and John Kerr, pale with irritation at having to ask, required once more a gentleman's freedom to scatter and scour as they went, Gabriel gave his assent.

On the information his company then had, no one could have done other. But when Adam Blacklock, gaunt in the darkness, came racing up to them half an hour later, they realized, listening appalled, that the Kerrs knew the fate of their cattle—must have been told in secrecy, while they rode at their sides. And that all the Kerrs now out of their sight, including Cessford and Ferniehurst, their sons, Mark Kerr of Littledean and the rest, had gone straight to the scene of the slaughter.

It was then that Gabriel at last took command. He put under guard all those of the Kerrs within reach, and using the last of their torches, led the race to the scene of the butchery. Except for their black monoliths, wavering in the torchlight, the fields were empty of life.

Without stopping, Gabriel and the men from St Mary's rode through. Over two hills they came to the Turnbull family's cabins. They were ablaze, the window spaces lit with clean orange, the stench neutered in the bright flare of fire. In the light, bright as day, you could see the trail of the Scott cattle, leading west towards Liddel Keep.

The Kerrs could hardly have missed it. Silently, in their turn, Lymond's army, led by Graham Malett, followed as fast as they dared.

*

Philippa Somerville was annoyed. To her friends the Nixons, who owned Liddel Keep, and with whom Kate had deposited her for one night, she had given an accurate description of Sir William Scott of Kincurd, his height, his skill, his status, and his general suitability as an escort for Philippa Somerville from Liddesdale to Midculter Castle.

And the said William Scott had not turned up.

She fumed all the morning of that fine first day of May, and by afternoon was driven to revealing her general dissatisfaction with Scotland, the boring nature of Joleta, her extreme dislike of one of the Crawfords and the variable and unreliable nature of the said William Scott. She agreed that the Dowager Lady Culter was adorable, and Mariotta nice, and that she liked the baby.

By late afternoon she mentioned that his lordship of Culter was a very nice man, of quiet rather than vulgar colouring. He was also very wealthy. It was, indeed, to save him worry over his mother worrying over Joleta that she, Philippa, had agreed to come. Which being the case, it seemed only appropriate that the said Richard, Baron Culter should come and fetch her himself.

There was, however, no need to send for Lord Culter. Just after midnight Sir Will Scott arrived, and hammering on the Keep door, awakened the household. With him, milling round in the darkness, were three hundred yelling Scotts, armed to the teeth, and what seemed like the whole of a Candlemas Fair, bleating and bawling outside the walls.

Mistress Nixon's steward opened the door and after a while Johnny Nixon went down, in his nightrobe and in no very good temper. Philippa, her braids dangling over the banisters, could see that Sir William Scott, far from being nonchalantly superb, was covered with muddy chain mail and cattle slavers, and in a state of stupid, boisterous hilarity which she put down to drink, but thought later was just ignorance.

Shamed and furious, she heard Master Nixon giving cold permission for the crew outside to sleep in the yard, while Will Scott and two or three of his cousins tramped in along with a burly, slick-haired man with a cheerful face, referred to as 'Bell'. She heard them hammer up the tower stairs to the little rooms where Mistress Nixon kept her folding beds, and a little later a servant passed on his way up with hot water and meat and a jug of wine. Shortly after that, there was silence, even from the weary animals outside, although beyond the walls the starlight glimmered, now and then, on the helmet of the sentry Scott had posted there. Philippa went back to bed.

After almost no time at all, or so it seemed, another battering began at the front door; this time even more urgent and prolonged.

307

With imprecations embroidering the air, both outside the castle and within, the Keep heaved awake. Leaning over the stair rails again, Philippa saw Johnnie Nixon, his face scarlet, himself march to the door, while a red shock-head and a rattling sword debouching from the newel stairs to the tower proclaimed Will Scott's vigilant presence.

It was another cousin of his, a man he had left behind 'at the Turnbulls'' with five others and someone called Adam Blacklock. That meant as little to Philippa as it did to Johnnie Nixon, but the newcomer was heaving like a white whale in calf, and was the bearer, obviously, of sensational news. A moment later, they had it. Francis Crawford had arrived at the Turnbulls'. (Philippa drew back.) The herd of stolen animals for which the Kerr tribe were looking had been found butchered, for which the Scotts would be blamed. By now the Kerrs would have located the animals and would be following Will Scott's trail to the Keep, there no doubt to fight the Scotts to the death.

Lymond had sent orders. Will Scott and his men were to retire inside the Keep and draw up the ladder, taking with them as much water as they had time to carry. All weapons were to be taken inside. Anything that might be used as a battering ram was to be taken inside. They were to carry inside also as much fuel and inflammable material as they could. The horses and the herds were to be abandoned to their fate. And at the earliest possible moment, Philippa Somerville and all those normally resident at Liddel Keep, under the guidance of Nixon the owner, were to be mounted on the fastest possible horses and sent back to Philippa's home at Flaw Valleys, near Hexham, to await news to return.

The reason was, said Will Scott's cousin, coming to the end of his recital and his breath at much the same time, that Graham Malett and the whole company of St Mary's was hot on the heels of the Kerrs. Provided the Keep could hold out against assault, fire and battery for an hour, the most perfectly trained army in the island would relieve them.

Will Scott asked two questions. 'Do the Kerrs know that Gabriel is behind them? And where's Crawford of Lymond?'

'The Kerrs ken,' said his cousin, and choked. 'That's why they'll try anything to break in here quick. Crawford and the rest of us stayed to see to the Turnbulls, but they're coming straight on here after. They'll have a race with the Kerr clan, I doubt.' His face was green and running with sweat, but in the big, simple eyes there shone a terrible joy. 'Man, if ye'd clapped eyes on thae beasts. There wasna ae part of a coo that was next tae its usual. Cessford'll wet his breeks when he sees them.'

'Aye, aye,' said Will Scott drily. 'It'll be a grand fight.' And, raising his stentorian voice, roused the household to war.

When Francis Crawford and the five Scotts arrived, riding belly to ground, there were archers at every window of the tall grey tower and cressets burning bright along the yard wall. Inside, the first person Lymond's eyes fell on was Philippa.

In the words he had used such a short while before in Dumbarton, but in a voice very different, he snapped, '*What are you doing here?*'

Philippa's chin jerked. She was dressed, but not cloaked, and her flat chest heaved like a colt's. 'I'm not going. Somervilles don't run away.'

'Stay, of course,' said Lymond brutally, 'if you like men to die for you. Where's that fool Nixon?'

'I can't get her to go!' Philippa's host, white-faced, stood his ground. 'Her horse is ready. The rest are all mounted outside.'

'Go, then!' said Philippa. 'I'm not under anyone's orders. I know how to fight. I can fire a gun even. I'm as good as Joleta. . . .'

Someone said, from two floors above, in a wild skirl, 'They're coming!'

'You can keep away from Joleta,' said Lymond quickly to this other, plain child. 'You can leave Midculter in future alone. You can get back to Flaw Valleys when you're told, and stay there; and if you won't obey my orders you can take the consequences, *like this*. . . .'

He hit fast and precisely, and her jaw snapped shut under his fist. A moment later she was in Nixon's arms and down the ladder. Another moment and, homeless, gearless, the owners of Liddel Keep had vanished south into the darkness, leaving their home and everything that they owned as a battlefield for the Kerrs and the Scotts.

To the thundering approach of many hooves, the family Scott pulled up the ladder and locked and barred the thick oaken door; and Lymond turned to find Randy Bell grinning at his shoulder. 'Welcome,' he said. 'My God, you've a way with women, haven't you? You must let me teach you a thing or two, if we ever get out of here.'

'I know them both,' said Lymond pleasantly, and exchanged a long, wordless greeting that was not a smile with Will Scott, who knew everything there was to know about Lymond's way with women, and had done his best to apply some of it, to effect, with Grizel. Then they became very busy indeed.

No feud of many years' standing can keep at full pitch all the time. The rivalry between the Scotts and the Kerrs flared and died and flared with events, and there were times when an affront to a peace-loving member would bring no retort, while an imagined slight could cause the more choleric to burst out and kill. Probably never before, as tonight, had the whole Kerr family been wrought to such a white-hot pitch of fury when, fellow-sufferers in a common theft, the Scotts had taken the chance, they believed, of slaughtering all their livestock without cause. And had further had the confidence to proclaim it. With that shambles of beasts just behind them, the Kerrs were out for one thing: to reach the castle and kill.

The main door to Liddel castle was on the first floor and reached by a ladder now removed. On the ground floor there was a stone-vaulted room with a well where stores and stock could be kept, and where in time of need horses might also be hidden.

The Nixons kept their grain in this place. Into it Scott had pushed at least some of the fuel; the spare ladders; the new-cut tree in the woodshed that would have made a fine ram. There was no time for more. Bell had barely time to lock the big timber door over its stout iron grille and have himself pulled up with the rest into the keep, when the first Kerrs arrived at the gate.

They arrived in a grey, antique horde, mailed, malevolent, thirsty for blood as the red dogs of Hades, and poured screaming into the yard, hurling aside cattle and sheep as they came. They put the cressets out, plunging the courtyard in darkness, so that in those first moments Scott's men at every dark window found only shadows for targets: shadowy figures, well-briefed, well-organized, racing from building to building collecting what they required.

Lymond had been right. Cessford and Ferniehurst knew there was no time to waste. If Liddel Keep was to be taken, it must be stormed ruthlessly, and at once.

Swiftly, the assault began to take shape. The Keep was surrounded. The noise rose like a hymning of devils and added to it came the clatter of wood, as all that would burn was stacked round the base-batter. So far, the ground door was holding, although the Kerrs were now assaulting repeatedly and even attempting to climb to the windows, forcing the Scotts to man every room and waste shafts. Then the fire-arrows began to come from the courtyard, first into the windows, and then in streaming arcs against the two doors.

Inside, they stamped out where they could, and for the rest resorted sparingly to Lymond's precious water. Two men, leaning out to pick off incendiarists, had so far been shot dead, and there were some Kerrs in the yard who would never fight a blood-feud again. 'We'll do it,' said Will Scott comfortably, shouting over the tumult. 'If it's no more than an hour, we'll do it.'

'Christ, I believe you're sorry, you flaming maniac,' said Lymond. 'Don't I keep telling you that this is bloody childishness, and don't you keep agreeing?' He had given his bow to Scott, and was standing watching as the young, auburn-haired giant picked his mark for each arrow, steadily and accurately, as he had been taught.

Will Scott drew back the cord and loosed, and an agile gentleman clambering up the ale-house's low roof gave a squeal and crashed to the ground. 'Batty Home of the Cowdenknowes,' he said. 'A

310

cousin of Tom Kerr. Don't tell me you're not enjoying this fine.'

'Your blasted Nanny should have taught you what mine did,' said Lymond. 'The things you enjoy most aren't good for you. *Mauldicte soit trestoute la lignye*. I'm going to inspect the junior ranks.'

A second later he was back, with no words to waste. 'The impossible has happened. They've got in below. You'll have to lose some men, Will. We need a crossfire nothing can live through, or they'll set fire to the basement.'

They lost eight of their best men, shooting as fast as they knew how to prevent the stream of Kerrs dodging and rushing into the store-room with all the wood they could get. The big doors, oak and iron, hung drunkenly open until, with two blows of an axe, someone under Cessford's direction felled one to the ground and, dragged away, it became a shield for the ant-like traffic to and from the lower ground floor. Lymond called Randy Bell from the upper floor, where he had been in charge of guarding the rear. 'You can say your prayers now. Unless Malett comes soon, all they've got to do is set fire to their double boiler below and we frizzle. Or more probably suffocate first. Will: what's most inflammable of the stuff you put in yourself?'

'There was a vat of pure spirit out there,' said Buccleuch's son helpfully. 'I poured most of it into the well, but there's some to the right of the door.'

'Was there, by God?' said Lymond. 'That'll do, then. They've got all the ladders out, and they seem to be busy piling everything high so that the fire will have a chance of cracking the vault. There's a murdering-hole, isn't there, down to them?'

There was, locked and barred. 'Right,' said Lymond. 'If we surrender we'll get our throats cut anyway. Let's go out in a blaze of glory. Let's start the fire first.'

It was worth it, Bell said, to see the expressions, reflected in the red glare, on Cessford's and Ferniehurst's faces. Under Lymond's direction, the wooden floor over the basement was swilled with the last of their water. Then, when the noise below seemed at its height, the rusty bolts of the trapdoor were withdrawn. For a second, peering below, Scott watched while a dozen Kerrs in angry zest worked on their pyre. Then he lobbed down his torch. It fell full on the big jar of spirit, and the open door from the store to the courtyard was sealed off by a curtain of fire.

Will Scott didn't linger to see if any of his besiegers escaped. Slamming down and rebarring the trap, he got to his feet and followed the rest up the twisting stairs to the highest point of the Keep. There, crowding into the open air of the roofwalks, they prepared stoically to wait.

Once lit, nothing could put out the fire underneath. Soon the flames would search through the old stone until the floor above caught, and the smoke would press through to choke them. None of the Kerrs would attempt an assault on them now. They would simply stay outside and wait.

To surrender, to climb down one by one from that narrow door and these narrow windows, was death. Their lives now lay in Gabriel's hands.

Five minutes later, the crackling far below in the Keep had become a muffled roar, and looking out, Scott and his men could see the yard flickering red, and the fiery armour and long moving shadows of the Kerrs, standing well back and watching. No one troubled to shoot.

Very soon the smoke reached them, telling that the first floor had caught. It was black and acrid and the men on the battlements, to Lymond's discursive decree, gave way to an equal number of men from the upper floors. The allure of Liddel Keep could not carry them all. Throughout, Lymond himself, his voice husky with coughing, sustained a wildly impertinent exposition on the scene, breaking off only once to haul a choking youngster back from a sill. 'You have a small chance here, and none at all down there. Come upstairs and help us throw things instead. It doesn't do the Kerrs a bit of harm, but it'll relieve the Nixons of a hellish lot of poor ornaments.'

They loved him. You could feel it, despite the mess they were in; and most of all because he had started the fire himself, just to capture some Kerrs. Only perhaps Will Scott and Randy realized that if he had not done so, they might like lemmings have begun to rush from the Keep to die in the open, fighting, and perhaps take a few Kerrs with them still. This way, they might all live. If Gabriel came.

The flames were halfway up the stone walls when they heard it, the rumour of many hooves beating fast through the night. The Kerrs heard it too. An army was coming, an army which would round up and shackle them, liberate and comfort the Scotts, divide them for ever from their chance of revenge for the wrong done them that day. The door was burned down. The ladders were there on the grass. As Graham Malett led the company of St Mary's as fast as horse could run down the dark turf to the tower, the besiegers, impervious to hurt, burst into the burning building and over the broken, blazing floor to the stairs. When the company arrived, in perfect formation, surrounding the yard and sweeping all the remaining Kerrs into custody, the Keep was a fiery finger in the black vale, with the clashing of swords and the cries of the maimed within rising above the even roar of the flames.

Orders, more orders. Blacklock, Guthrie, Tait, Plummer, Hoddim, de Seurre, des Roches, controlling each their part of the jigsaw, proceeded with ladder and rope to enter every possible aperture, while a chain from the bailey wells was set up to safeguard their return. Inside, their bodies raw with chance burns, their spleen savage as ever, Scotts and Kerrs reeled and struggled in hand-to-hand fighting, in space hardly enough for the sword. Gabriel's men captured them, one by one, extricating each family and sending them willy-nilly down the ropes, or hurtling downstairs and through the charred door, over steps sticky with blood.

Lymond and Gabriel came face to face on the roofwalk, where ropes dangled from the deep crenellations and Tait was steering the traffic up and down. The fire was quietly progressing but the noise was much less. Isolated fighting only was going on still in the upper rooms, and even that would soon clearly cease. The only other sounds were from the hurt and the dying. The game the Scotts and the Kerrs played was a mortal one.

Gabriel smiled. He was pale, but his eyes in the flame-shot darkness were lucid as ever. 'So you got safely back,' he said. 'We were troubled for you.' Then he added, his voice sharpened, 'You're hurt?'

Inside Lymond's burst doublet, itself covered with dirt and smears from superficial cuts and burns, there was a line of dried blood on his shirt. Lymond stared at it as if he had never seen it before, and then said, 'I don't think so,' and Adam Blacklock, coming up beside him, said without thinking, 'No, you had that at Dumbarton,' and then held his tongue.

Gabriel, naturally, looked surprised. Lymond did not even register it. He walked past them both, and took up his stance again where Gabriel had found him, in a corner of the stone-flagged alure. In the rosy glow from the fire, you could see there were several men there already, kneeling or prone. Blacklock's eyes met Graham Malett's, and they followed him.

Will Scott was prostrate on the sweating roofwalk, his blazing hair touched to flame by the light; his face grey-white, with the boisterous, wilful vigour all gone. In place of his right arm and side was a mass of blood-sodden wrappings. On one side, Randy Bell, kneeling, held one wrist, while on the other Archie Abernethy, with hands used to gentling his animals, finished binding what was useless to bind.

A great silence fell, stirred distantly by occasional voices. The fighting had stopped. Gabriel said quietly, 'How did it happen?'

Lymond did not speak. Randy Bell said without looking up, 'He took the brunt of the rush for the stairs. I was in the middle, and Crawford at the top when they burst in, and he pushed past us all. It was his fight, you see.'

'On the *stairs*?' said Blacklock. 'But how could he lose his right. . .'

'How could he lose his right arm on the stairs?' said the big doctor, laying Will Scott's wrist down gently and rising to his spurred feet. 'You forget, Adam. You forget. The Kerrs are a left-handed race.' His gaze went from Gabriel to Francis Crawford and back again. 'Don't be sorry for him, though. He won't live to miss it. And he'll have died fighting the Kerrs. Isn't that their idea of glory?'

'No,' said Lymond suddenly and rudely. He added, 'Are we staying here until the bloody peel falls?' And then, 'Archie? What about it?'

'We'll have to take him down the stairs,' said Abernethy, gazing owlishly up from his task. 'Ye canna dangle yon frae a rope.'

And so, while the rest of the Keep was cleared of men, Lymond bent and with infinite patience lifted Buccleuch's oldest son. The sandy-fringed lids didn't open as Will Scott was carried from his last battlefield, nor when, slack in a horse-litter, he was borne in their midst from the yard.

He did not know how many Kerrs had been killed in this one night of savagery which he, of all his family, had been dedicated to prevent. He did not know how many Scotts had died with him on the stairs. And alone of all that silent company that set off back with Lymond to St Mary's, he did not look round at the last turn of the hill and see among its spilled wreckage, the tall brand of Liddel Keep, a cracked finger of fire in the empty black void of the night.

A little later, Gabriel collapsed, slipping wordlessly to the ground. The wound they found in his shoulder was not dangerous, but he had lost a great deal of blood. Lymond had him placed in a second litter, and with Jerott leading the company and Alec Guthrie in the rear, they resumed the long journey home.

With their cattle, their dead and their wounded, the other Scotts had soon left them for Branxholm. The Kerrs Lymond kept under guard until, two or three miles up the road, they came upon an old fort with a light at the window, and Lymond halted the troop to bring out all those of the family Turnbull that the Hot Trodd had spared.

Repeated to Cessford's face, the tale of the cattle killing; of the bribe paid by a stranger was not wonderfully convincing, but it was enough to give them all pause. It might have been some ruse of their enemies. They had plenty, God knew. And, cold after battle, both Sir Walter Kerr of Cessford and Sir John Kerr of Ferniehurst knew this night's work would exact its own price.

Shortly afterwards, Lymond freed the Kerr family as well.

It was high noon when they themselves reached St Mary's, and through all the journey Lymond had ridden back and forwards, speaking to the few who were wounded; discoursing, chatting. Trying, thought Jerott Blyth, irritated in his fatigue by the restless murmur, to recover lost ground.

Of course, in this, their first minor action, the new company had disastrously failed. The robbers they were paid to deliver to justice had been found and killed first by the robbed. The two families they were dedicated to keeping apart had fought each other with a fruitless loss on both sides. And Will Scott, only grown heir to all the lands of Buccleuch, was dying.

But for Graham Malett, every Scott in Liddesdale Tower would have been dead. Far from helping, Lymond's belated orders for the Scotts to stand siege had nearly sent them as a clan to their death. Better far to have let them meet the Kerrs in the open, man to man. Evenly matched, they might well have suffered less in the end.

So every man there would be thinking. Nor would these restive attentions erase what they had heard and had seen. . . . So Jerott Blyth thought until the dawn birdsong began, and with the first light he saw Lymond's face.

Lymond was very well aware of the situation, but he was not trying to handle it. He was merely fidgeting, Jerott saw without sympathy, because he was tired.

Much later, they rode into the orderly courtyard at St Mary's with the new, well-mannered buildings above them, flushed with spring sun; and Jerott checked, as he had noted Lymond checking again and again through the night, that Will Scott was unconscious but living, and that Gabriel was comfortable still.

Gabriel was not only rested, but awake, and a good deal recovered. As they slid from their horses he got himself out of his litter and, without help, walked stiffly to where Lymond sat, mounted still. Graham Malett laid a hand on his knee.

'Francis. Before we disperse; before we give our attention to other things; before our recollection is blunted, might we discuss what went wrong last night?' And as Lymond stared at him without speaking, Sir Graham added gently, 'It wasn't a notable success you know, in spite of all your fine work through the winter. We ought to know why. We are all tired. I know you are, too. But the future of the force may depend on it.'

'You are possibly right,' Lymond said. His voice was completely without timbre and his face, blank as a soapstone mask, was turned to the courtyard, where Salablanca should be.

Archie Abernethy came instead and said, 'Scott's alive yet, sir, although I've no great hopes,' and in the bygoing, offered his shoulder. Gabriel said, 'Francis?' and Lymond turned his head. 'Yes, I heard you,' he said. 'I agree. I have only to dismount, and be sick, and then I am, as ever, your man.'

A minute later and he had descended, one hand gripping Archie's shoulder, and crossing the courtyard was at once sick, his hands against the high, handsome wall. For a moment he rested there, without turning, and Gabriel, his wounded arm stuffed awkwardly into his doublet, began to drag himself after until Abernethy charitably barred the way. 'It'll just be something he ate.'

'Or drank,' said Jerott Blyth.

'Or the fact,' said Adam Blacklock tartly, 'that he has ridden three hundred miles and fought an action without any sleep?'

Gabriel said sharply, 'What?' And then, 'Why was I not told of this? He must rest, of course, and at once. I shall take the meeting, if he will permit me.'

'I'll live to take it,' said Lymond quietly. He had returned as coolly as he had gone, scandalizing Lancelot Plummer, whom he caught out with a turn of the head. 'A thick skin, and a certain misplaced sang-froid,' he added helpfully, turning Plummer's face scarlet. 'My sang at the moment is quite marvellously froid. Come along, gentlemen.' He smiled at them, with a shade of the old irony, and led the way in.

The analysis of their late action, or inaction as Gabriel ruefully put it, probably lasted less than an hour. During it, every aspect of their failure was thrashed out except one: the absence of leadership. Instead, Graham Malett took on himself all the blame for the central breakdown in the action: the decision to allow the Kerrs to search the neighbourhood of the Turnbull land for their cattle unguarded.

The others wouldn't have it. 'No.' Alec Guthrie, small eyes swollen with sleeplessness, turned his grating voice on Lymond. 'Sir Graham was against it. The rest of us persuaded him and he yielded to a majority judgement on your orders. There lay the essence of the mistake.'

Graham Malett's own voice cut in quietly. 'I disagree. As Mr Crawford once said, we are a council of experts, not a dictatorship. There is no room for a Grand Master here.'

'Really?' said Lymond's cold voice. 'What do you do on the galleys when a galleass with a thousand Turks aboard sticks her irons on you? Hold a conference first? In the field, one man leads, for good or for bad. In St Mary's, we confer, as we are doing now. To confuse the two situations is lunacy.'

There was a brief silence. 'Then I'm afraid neither of us distinguished himself yesterday,' said Gabriel ruefully. 'I'm going to abdicate in Jerott's favour next time you are . . . away.'

'It was a pity,' said Lymond coolly, 'that you didn't find the Scotts quickly, and divide your force between them and the Kerrs. The other flaws in the action, it seems to me, were outwith our control. Someone made quite unexpected trouble by paying the Turnbulls to kill and brand all those animals. And the Kerrs had a most unexpected piece of luck in breaking into that ground floor room at the Keep.'

'They'd batter the locks with hackbuts,' said Jerott contemptuously. 'Or the hinges were rusty. It's an old tower.'

'They didn't, and they weren't,' said Lymond. 'They used a key.

316

Maybe the Nixons keep the key under the doormat. I shouldn't know. But that was the third unfortunate occurrence, if you could call it that.'

'What do you mean?' It was Gabriel's voice, soft but severe.

'That someone doesn't like the Scotts or the Kerrs. I have no idea who—the English, would you say? Or one of their rival families on the Borders? I mention it with diffidence,' said Lymond, with no diffidence at all in his manner, 'and at the risk, I am aware, of misunderstanding. But we failed as we did for quite extraordinary reasons, nothing to do with our capabilities. Given the information we had, we acted rightly. I, for one, do not regret anything I have personally done.'

'Or not done?' It was Jerott Blyth again, but in an undertone. It did not escape Francis Crawford, who turned his head and smiled. 'I thought your objections were to my excesses, not my omissions,' he said drily. 'Sir Graham, if it seems to you that we have covered all the necessary ground, I don't think there is much profit in talking longer. Your wound must be causing you pain.'

Sir Graham rose, his face pale under his golden thatch. 'There are other things that pain me more,' he said abruptly. 'You are fortunate in having nothing of which to accuse yourself.' For a moment he stood, his clear, world-weary gaze on Lymond's impervious stare; then shut his lips tightly and left.

They all began to get up. '*Whatever* do you think he means?' said Plummer, drifting past, to Lymond's bent head. Lymond stood, so suddenly that Plummer took a step back. 'That surveyors there be, that greedily gorge up their covetous guts,' he said. 'What was it that you and Tait were so concerned should not be wasted in Nixon's chapel?'

Plummer's elegant body became rigid, but although his eyes flickered to Hercules Tait's and back, he did not flush. 'Oh, that,' he said. 'There was a very fine little Byzantine plaque on the wall, with a fragment of cross and some angels. The poor man had obviously no idea of its beauty—well, you had only to look at the rubbish he put on his plaster elsewhere. Probably stuck it up to cover a hole. But to anyone who knew. . . . You must take my word for it,' said Plummer, getting at last into his stride. 'It would have been sacrilege to let it burn.'

'I saw it. It was a silver-gilt Staurotheque,' said Lymond. 'About four hundred years old. With a figure of Christ enthroned in gold and enamels, and angels confronted. I travel too, sometimes, you know. . . . You were, I presume, going to present it to your own Church of St Giles?'

'I—Of course,' said Plummer slowly. His eyes, heavy with sleeplessness, took on an aggrieved glaze.

'But it is, of course, the property of Master Nixon, whom we shall in any case have to recompense for having allowed the destruction of his home. Since therefore you feel that the Church would be a more appreciative owner than Master Nixon,' said Lymond, his voice always pleasant, 'it only remains for you to recompense Master Nixon with the full value of the Staurotheque. If you and Hercules Tait will give me a bill on your bankers tomorrow, I shall delight in arranging it. And Plummer!' said Francis Crawford gently as the architect, pink-cheeked, turned away. 'Remember, theft is theft, whether committed by old man Turnbull or not.'

He saw them shuffle in time from his room, tired men all, not talking much, and watched Salablanca draw back the stools to their places and put away the board and place a light robe, without being asked, in front of the fire. The sunlight, dappled with shadow, shone in through his big window and fell on the bed, a plain one with white linen sheets, aired and turned back, and a cover of fine, soft blue wool. Lymond got up.

The big, soft-footed Moor, dropping what he was doing, came and stood beside him. '¿Quiere Vd comer? ¿Está servido un poquito, poquito . . .?'

'No,' said Lymond. He said in Spanish, 'Let me offer you some excellent advice. Never issue reproofs under stress. You say too much. On the other hand'—he turned a blank gaze on the Moor—'I believe the general discussion passed off well enough. I suppose it did. I have very little recollection of it, but I hope it did . . . ¿Cómo está el Señor Scott?' he said abruptly.

'That does not change,' said the Moor quietly. 'The Señor will sleep?'

'I will see him first,' said Lymond and leaving, walked through to the sick quarters.

Will Scott lay in the big room alone but for Randy Bell, sunk deep in a bedside chair, and Abernethy, cross-legged on the floor. Lymond said at once, 'Bell, you're exhausted man, and you can't do anything. Go and get some sleep,' and as the doctor, after only a token demur, moved slowly off, Lymond sat himself carefully in his place.

The young laird of Buccleuch had not far now to go. The carroty hair, the orange eyebrows, the sandy lashes, the white stubble of ferocious young beard were all the colour there was on the pillow, and the vigorous frame, reared by the old man at Branxholm to carry on his great name; trained to just deeds and informed by a simple and generous spirit, lay already as still as the Eildons.

But he was breathing yet. Abernethy, his scarred, nut-like face impassive, said, 'It may take long enough. But he willna wake now.'

'He might,' said Lymond. Once Scott had loathed him as some of his captains did still. No, that was an exaggeration. These were

318

clever, experienced men. They appreciated what St Mary's was, and he had made them laugh, but they didn't trust him yet as they trusted Gabriel, for example. . . . 'The very devil's officers,' said Lymond aloud, and from the shock to his nerves realized how near sleep he had been. He got up and walked slowly up and down the sunlit room.

Scott had more than trusted him, in the end. He had freed Lymond four years ago from his outlawry. And he had been ready to share any adventure, on his wedding-day even. Of his fourth wife, old Buccleuch had nothing but toddlers. And Will's sons were babies yet. But at least, of course, he had sons. . . .

Lymond stopped walking. There was a curious white haze in the room, and in his head an ululation, a singing of blood under pressure exactly like, he thought vaguely, a child's bleak, coughing cry. But there were no infants at St Mary's.

His sense of balance went quite suddenly then. He was conscious of the two violent blows, first on his shoulder and then on his knee, as his body struck the floor, and even that someone already there at his side had broken his fall. But after that, he knew nothing more.

*

Francis Crawford slept in his own bed until dusk. Put there by Salablanca and Archie, he was not conscious of it at the time, and would have lain longer still had he not been forcibly roused. His first impression indeed was of someone shaking him so violently that his exhausted body rebelled and launched him, half-conscious, into a fit of irrepressible coughing.

An outside agency stopped that for him, at once, with a jug of cold water slapped full in his face. Gasping for breath, Francis Crawford sat up, and with both hands cleared and opened his eyes.

It was night. He was in the loose robe that had been thrown in front of his fire: someone had undressed him. And the face before him, the grim, grey, rough-bearded face with every line a rut and every rut a channel of agony, was the face of Buccleuch.

Becoming very still, Lymond let his hands drop.

'Asleep, were ye?' said Will Scott's father, and laid down the empty jug in his grasp. Placing his hands behind his broad back he continued to stand, surveying the splendid blue bed. 'Well-drunken too, I see,' he said after a moment. 'At least ye fairly reek of a very nice make of liquor. Things going well, are they?'

Lymond did not speak. The robe he was wearing reeked of spirits, and in his face was the question he had lost the right to ask. Sir Walter Scott of Buccleuch answered it for him.

'You won't know: my son's dead. They were sorry ye left him so

319

soon to get at your drink and your slippers, though I'm sure ye deserved them. When he woke, seemingly, they couldna get ye roused tae speil off a kind word or two, just as he died.'

There was a long silence. Then Lymond said, 'I would have . . . I didn't know. They couldn't have tried.' He was white.

The grey, matted beard nodded. Buccleuch's face was covered with a marcasite of fine dust, where he had been riding hard and long against the May wind. 'His brain was soft a wee, mind. He asked for the Master of Culter, as if ye were his commander; and when they told him ye couldna come, he said you'd be by-ordnar plagued with things to attend to, and we were to tell you never to trouble. But he hoped all the time, they said, that you'd see past it and come. . . . But that's no matter. They tell me it was your orders that put him and the rest of them in the castle. There's just one thing I'll trouble ye to tell me: which Kerr was it killed him?'

'*Wat.* . . .' said Lymond, and stopped. All the time he had been speaking, Buccleuch's face had been bathed unheeding in a cease-less curtain of tears. He was quite unaware of it, it was clear as he plodded on with what he had to say. Nor was the bitterness of his words at all at variance with it. Only Lymond, wordless for once, had to control his own emotion before he could speak. Then he said quietly, 'I don't know, Wat. It may not have been a Kerr at all.'

'Aye.' The old man was not surprised. 'It's your heaven-given job, of course, to see there's nae prejudice between the two families. Are ye going tae manage it soon, do ye think? So it may not be a Kerr,' he said, the tears twinkling in his mirthless eyes. 'There's a lot of left-handed folk going up and down stairs in that part of the world, I warrant you. It'll be one of them.'

One could do nothing with that. Lymond left it. He said, 'Wat: will you let me tell Grizel?'

'The younger Lady of Buccleuch will know by now,' said Sir Wat, rising with his new, painful formality. The hapless, unnoticed weep-ing had stopped. 'Yon fellow Malett rode to tell her right away, wounded shoulder and all. I got him to say a prayer over the lad first. . . . He wasn't working for ye again, was he? Will?'

'No,' said Lymond.

'Oh. I thocht maybe he was, since he took your orders, it seems. Then ye'll hae no objection if his cousins and I take the body off home?'

'Wat. Stop it, for God's sake,' said Lymond. He swung out of bed beside the old Warden, and grasped the rigid, powerful arms. 'Another day I'll tell you what happened. But meantime, don't believe me indifferent. You could have had my right hand. . . .'

'But you had his, instead,' said Buccleuch.

The two pairs of eyes met, and held. 'All right,' said Lymond at last, and dropped his arms. 'But blame me. Not the Kerrs.'

'There's little, it seems, to choose between you,' said the old man carelessly. He picked up his bonnet and turned, but halfway to the door stopped to speak. 'That's two houses in this land ye needn't soil with your foot from this day on. Midculter and Branxholm. I hear your brother has banned ye the door.'

'Do you? *Who told you that?*' Lymond said, and Buccleuch, half-roused, looked at him blearily. 'It's the clack of Biggar,' he said. 'And the conjecture is fair making the Dowager spit. I hear that she and Culter are at odds about it already. The muckle Fiend fend ye; why don't you leave the country and let us all be at peace? What is there but untruth and heartbreak wherever you go?'

'I like to see friends at my bloodsuppers,' said Lymond with a sudden, intolerable venom. 'Pass the word round. To fight against me is to resist the Lord, who visits thy sins with such rods. . . . I am here, Buccleuch. I am staying here. Until winter, at least.'

'Are ye?' said Buccleuch. 'I think ye'll not. I'll wager my son's ring, in fact, to that sapphire ye wear, that the Queen Dowager has ye out before then. . . . This ring. It's a good one. Ye'd get a good bit for that,' said Buccleuch, and threw the band of thick gold on the bed.

It lay between them, glinting emptily, describing the young, big-boned finger where it belonged. 'Yon Gabriel,' said Buccleuch suddenly, and the water had begun running innocently down his surprised and angry face again. 'He gave me a line of prayer to say. I've said it, when I thought of it, whiles ever since. "God give me another lad like thee", it runs. "God give me another lad like thee . . . and syne take me to His rest".'

And lifting the ring, he went out, full of thought still.

Soon after that Adam Blacklock, alone in his room, jumped to his feet as the door crashed open on his commander, who slammed it shut and advanced, with what seemed to be a flask in his hand.

In spite of the violence of his entry, Lymond's voice was quite soft when he spoke. 'Adam? This has been left by my bed, and I've no use for it. Take it, and for God's sake throw that other rubbish away.' And as Blacklock's dilated eyes fixed on him, Francis Crawford added, still speaking quietly, 'Do you think I don't know? Or Abernethy? You're risking other men's lives, not your own.'

Adam flushed. 'If you think that, you can always ask me to leave.' The flask Lymond had given him held aqua-vitae. He added, 'Why the sudden crusade? I thought I wasn't to take spirits? Or don't you want to drink it alone?'

'I do,' said Lymond lightly. 'Oh, I do. But I have a sad, Calvinist conscience.'

'Not where girl-children are concerned,' Blacklock said. He hesitated, and then continued. 'If the men here ever find out about Malett's sister, there'll be hell to pay; you know that.'

'I know,' said Lymond. He was listening, expressively white, with dark, tangential planes under his eyes.

'Then leave her alone!' Anger and pity, queer companions, flared in the other man's eyes. 'Why risk all this for the sake of a—a romp in a cheap, tavern bed? If you can dispense with drink, you can practise self-control in other forms, too. Or do you simply like to live like a child?'

'Today,' said Lymond, 'if you must know, I don't like living at all. But that's just immaturity boggling at the sad face of failure. Tomorrow I'll be bright as a bedbug again.'

Below in the courtyard as he spoke, someone was talking; then a whip cracked, hooves clattered and a wheel creaked, taking the strain. A moment later they both heard quite clearly the rumble of a cart with a heavy escort of riders, crossing the uneven stones of the bailey below. It passed out of the gates of St Mary's and turned eastwards and south, where Kincurd and Branxholm both lay.

Eager no more: quiet and still in his empty farm wagon, grandly robed in Gabriel's own famous habit, with the Cross of St John on his breast, Will Scott had parted from Lymond for ever, and was going home to his own.

IX

Terzetto, Played Without Rests

(Flaw Valleys, June 1552)

AT the first possible moment after the Hot Trodd, but several weeks later than he would have liked, Lymond rode to Flaw Valleys, Philippa Somerville's home in the north of England.

Not surprisingly, in view of her experiences and what Lymond, in a wry letter to Kate, had described as his misrule both in wit, knowledge and manners, Philippa had not again attempted to travel to Midculter. The Nixons, generously recompensed and rehoused with ringing protest by the Kerrs and the Scotts as part of their fine, were back in Liddesdale, buying new ornaments in even poorer taste with the proceeds of the sale of the Staurotheque to Lancelot Plummer and Hercules Tait. The Turnbulls who survived were in the local almshouse, haggard over the only really nasty trick Fate had played on them: on recovering their blood money lovingly from the little hole hastily dug for it when all their menfolk were killed, they found every lying, smooth-edged bawbee was false.

Also, St Mary's had been busy. Damage had been done both to the company's conception of itself and to its reputation abroad. Giving them almost no time to recover, Lymond sought work, splitting them into details for smaller actions and using the whole force for larger, deferring for that reason the naval training which he had expected to start by now. Above all, he did not leave them himself again, nor did he delegate anything. The most striking change was there, for up to then, any one of his knights or his high-ranking officers might find himself in charge of an exercise or a raid, with specific and supreme responsibility. The effect was twofold. He drove them harder than they would ever have driven their fellow-seniors. And there was very little time in the twenty-four hours when he was not either in the saddle or at his desk.

He did not attend Will Scott's funeral, although Sybilla went, silent and dry-eyed, with her older son. Joleta she would not allow to go, on account of her youth and the recent unfortunate shaking she had received when her horse fell on its way from Boghall. Lady Fleming and the whole of Boghall, aware that Joleta Malett hadn't been near them for weeks, heard the explanation with barely-concealed interest; and Margaret Erskine, Jenny's widowed daughter, took Richard Crawford aside at the church. She was blunt.

'Lord Culter. . . . Since you brought her back, you presumably know where Joleta was, and how her horse fell. I ought to warn you that my mother apparently promised Joleta she would support the tale that she'd been to Boghall. Joleta hadn't, of course. Everyone in Biggar knows it. I have no desire to know where she actually was, but you know Jenny. Joleta won't explain the mystery, apparently, and my mother considers she hasn't kept her part of the bargain. She's furious, and very likely she'll question you.'

Since the departure of the French King's Lieutenant, M. d'Oisel, Lady Jenny had been deprived of the wherewithal to plot her own return to France. It would have pleased her, Margaret knew, to unearth a subterfuge of Joleta's. Joleta was young. The secret was probably no more than some surprise she was arranging for her brother Sir Graham; she might not realize the speculation it had caused. But Lord Culter should.

Margaret Erskine then noticed that Richard Crawford was unusually pale, and further that this was due to extreme anger. With a callousness quite foreign to her experience of him, Lymond's older brother said at once, 'If she does, she'll get no more for her prying than you will. Joleta's whereabouts that night are my concern.'

There was only one person who could unnerve him like that. 'Or yours and Lymond's?' said Margaret Erskine. 'You needn't explain. But you should think up a better story unless you want people to put two and two together. People will notice that he doesn't come home any more.'

'Thank goodness,' said Sybilla, arriving unexpectedly. With her white hair and white French mourning she looked very sweet and unreal, but for the dark circles under her eyes. 'It would be bad enough having the grooms fight like rams over Joleta without Francis being drawn to her too. Although she would be a very pleasing daughter-in-law, if a little difficult to live up to, and of course she has a temper—who hasn't?'

'I see her duenna is here, anyway,' said Margaret quickly. Sybilla in trouble was something she hated to see.

'Well, it's a funeral, of course,' said the Dowager Lady Culter, looking across the hazy candlelit interior of Biggar's new Collegiate Church to where Evangelista Donati, smooth black head bent and sallow face hidden, knelt at the side of an eager, small man in over-trimmed clothes. 'And Peter Cranston is here. The combination of religious misery and Peter Cranston would be quite irresistible. Anyway, Graham Malett wanted to talk to his sister alone, so she won't be missed. It's rather sad, in a way,' said Sybilla reflectively. 'I shouldn't miss her though. I don't suppose anyone would, in fact, except Peter Cranston, and he can always fill in by counting his beads or his money, or both. I must be kinder to her. I shouldn't like to be a person no one missed.'

Which, thought Margaret Erskine, was the height of charity, considering the lady and her charge had both been domiciled almost without a break at Midculter for something like nine months, and during that time Madame Donati's only contribution had been to make a disparaging, not to say suggestive remark in Italian about Sybilla's two sons.

*

In the middle of June, Gabriel left to represent Jimmy Sandilands at a meeting with the Queen Mother at Falkland, and since there was for once no immediate task in hand and some sign, by then, that his deliberate reign of terror was nearer provoking rebellion than the angry vigour he wished, Lymond allowed some of his staff to go on furlough, the knights, Bell and Fergie Hoddim among them, and supplied a modicum of work for the rest.

Then, with the Moor, Abernethy and a few men-at-arms, Lymond left for Flaw Valleys on a hot summer day that recalled the blue shores of Birgu, less than twelve months before.

On his way, he made a number of calls on all the big lairds of the Border and one woman: Janet Beaton, Lady of Buccleuch. It was not for the first time. Since Will's death, Lymond had never entered Branxholm when Will's father was there, although he had visited Kincurd at once, and face to face with Grizel Beaton, Janet's sister and Will's widow, had given her an objective and accurate account of how her husband had died. She had thanked him with her usual reserve, her eyes wet, and had added, 'I understand. It was bound to come. You have nothing to accuse yourself of.' It was a phrase with which he was not unfamiliar.

Soon after that, making sure the old man was away, Lymond had sent Tosh to Buccleuch's wife Janet at Branxholm to ask if she would see him. She did, and after castigating her husband and Lymond both for an acid five minutes, agreed at once to what Lymond proposed. When he left, Thomas Wishart stayed behind, ostensibly as a new body-servant. In fact he was there for one purpose only: to guard Buccleuch's life with his own.

That was four weeks ago. Today Lymond had called on Lady Buccleuch partly to reassure her, and partly to find out whether the old man, as Warden of the Middle Marches, was going to the Day of March in July. Touchy, well-fed, well-mounted and ripe with fine grievances, the denizens of the Borders flocked to these periodic summer meetings of Wardens to watch international justice being done; and if there were no quarrels to pick between the two nations, there were plenty to settle themselves. Swords and knives were allowed at March meetings: they were enough for murder, if not quite for war.

Policing the Hadden Stank meeting of Wardens was likely to be St Mary's next major task. Among others, Lord Wharton would be there. So would the Kerrs. So, undoubtedly, would the Scotts. It remained to be seen whether old Wat would be one of them.

'He will,' said Janet bitterly. 'I'll warrant he will. Sticking out his elbows and getting Kerrs to fall over his big toe and call him a bastard again, which considering his mother was a Kerr and his first wife was Ferniehurst's sister makes the Kerrs an easy-going lot. But they wouldna gag over an elephant, now. All they want is an excuse on either side to ding the rest good and dead.'

'If you were a dear, good little wife, Janet,' had said Lymond, 'you'd fall into a mortal decline that day, or at least hide his boots.'

'Francis Crawford, are ye daft! What ever kept a Scott from a fight? Women? Boots? If yon one were deid, he'd spend his time in Heaven sclimming up and down the Pearly Gates peppering Kerrs.'

'There is a sweeping assumption in that,' had said Lymond deprecatingly, 'which we needn't go into. Janet, if he hears we shall be there he'll cause a war for the hell of it. Let's make it all a beautiful surprise.'

'Oh, Dod, no bother about that,' said Janet grimly. 'That's what we're used to in these parts. Beautiful surprises.'

*

On the way south through the Cheviots, it was cooler, and on the higher reaches of the hills larks purred and trilled high in the summer sky, and the wind rustled the dried grass like the sea. Then they dropped into the pass of Redesdale and thence down green Tyneside towards Hexham. Then, a few miles off the town, they turned aside to Kate Somerville's rolling fields.

She had hoped, profoundly, that Lymond would come, ever since the breath-stopping day when the Nixon family with their servants and children had come flying wild-eyed in at the gates, bearing a silent Philippa, white of face, with a bruise the size of a fair-token on the side of her jaw.

Much later, when the Nixons were packed off to bed and she had Philippa to herself in her arms, she got the story, and the tears had come. Then Kate, in spite of her understanding, had felt anger, for again Lymond had embroiled them, willy-nilly, in his private affairs.

Philippa had been through enough: the corpse in the ditch outside

Boghall; the fire which had nearly trapped them at home; and now trapped again in a blood-feud, to be rescued in such a fashion as this.

Knowing Philippa, she could in theory see how essential that rough handling had been; and his letter of brief apology had further explained. But in her heart she ached for them both.

So, when she saw the blue and silver colours of Crawford with the engrailed bordure of the second son, Kate Somerville fled from the window and, strolling into the garden where Philippa was pouring soapy water on to her roses and intoning prayers for the greenfly, dispatched the child on some quest to the village. Then she returned, with no time, as fate always decreed, to tidy her blown parcel of mouse-coloured hair or change the gown she had bottled raspberries in, before her visitors had come, and her late husband's man Charles had seen to the comfort of the horses, Abernethy and the men at arms in that order, and Lymond was standing in the rebuilt music room, avoiding the virginals, avoiding the lute, avoiding all the instruments she and Gideon had once loved to play, and which Lymond had played in other circumstances, waiting till she should come.

He had not seen her. Soft-footed at the open door, she paused a moment, considering the delicacy which in such matters seldom failed, and was yet coupled with such wilful brutality. She studied his back. Had he changed? Perhaps his hair, bleached by stronger suns, was paler; perhaps, pacing from window to window, he had matured into a spare and harder frame. But he was trim as a cat, immaculate, although Charles said they had been on the move for three days, and in an hour must take the road back again.

Then, sensing she was there, Lymond turned, with the elastic smile and excessive charm which it was his habit to use, to provoke her to arid and more arid flights of sarcastic wit. 'Kate, my dear? Haven't your raspberries been marvellous this year? Come and be licked; I haven't dined yet,' he said.

Kate looked down at her stained gown. 'I know. I ought to leave it to the maids,' she said. Then, taking his hands as he came to her, she turned him round until the light from the big windows fell, inevasibly, full on his face.

There was a little pause. 'Your stains are showing too,' said Kate. 'Don't you trust your servants either, or don't they trust you?'

'Trust is a secular word in our part of the world,' said Lymond. He drew away slightly. 'We operate on Faith. The heavenly light from the navel. Fed on *recherché* meats to sacred melodies, like the lion of Heliopolis.'

'With a public whipping-post outside?'

'You know too much,' said Lymond. 'It's necessary. And applied with a fearful justice. Or the mercenaries, of course, would leave.'

'Don't your monks in armour complain?' said Kate, her voice

bantering; pure distress in her eyes. Even her concern about Philippa had gone.

'An Order that bastinadoes its slaves? They'd find it difficult, thank God. I have enough trouble with a growing tendency among the lower ranks to divide us into the forces of light and of darkness. I don't mind being labelled devilish but I do mind being regarded as unlucky. The only way to answer that is by a string of successes. Which we have had.'

'But not by luck. I know you don't want to sit down,' said Kate rapidly. 'I know you don't want to talk about what's happened. I know you don't want to distress me. I know you want to tell me quickly about Philippa and go. But if you will countenance an on-looker's opinion, I think you should *go to bed first*.'

There was an inimical silence. It might of course have been better put. But at least she would be spared the obvious response. In the end, Lymond said merely, 'Thank you, but no. I must go back.'

'To hold somebody's trembling hand?'

'To hold somebody's trembling hand with a dagger in it,' he said.

That was the point at which to leave it. Kate didn't. She said baldly, 'You've left St Mary's to itself for three days. If you daren't leave it any longer, after all the time you've devoted to it, then you must know you've failed.'

Lymond said softly, 'That is the only thing you may not say to me. . . . Kate, superb Kate: *I will not be mothered*.'

'*Mothered!*' Kate's small, undistinguished face was black with annoyance. 'I would sooner mother a vampire. I am merely trying to point out what your browbeaten theorists at St Mary's ought surely to have mentioned in passing. Health is a weapon of war. Unless you obtain adequate rest, first your judgement will go, and then every other qualification you may have to command, and either way, the forces of light will have a field-day in the end.'

There were two big chairs near him, one of them in the immediate path of the flood of sunshine creeping over the polished floor from her big western windows. Kate sat on the arm of the other and said, 'I know you better, by the way, than to suppose that you came here to do the sensible thing by persuasion. No one would be more stun-ned than I should if you agreed.'

'I haven't got that sort of pride,' said Lymond drily, and smiled. 'I'm going back, Kate, as soon as we have talked, you and I. I've spent six months and a small fortune training so that I or anyone else at St Mary's can handle and go on handling an emergency for quite a long time, and throw off fatigue reasonably well at the end. This is, if you like, an emergency. When I've dealt with it, I shall lie about willingly with a flagon of wine and a nymph.'

'I believe you,' said Kate coldly. 'Like Terminus: with no feet and arms. . . . In the meantime, I presume you may eat? Your hench-men are being fed, and you'll look a trifle quaint making a cere-monial stop to feed by yourself on the way home if you don't. I promise not to pollute the pork chops with drugs. I shan't even insist you sit down to it, although if you're not giddy with circling the room like a blowfly, I am.'

'Oh, Christ,' said Lymond rudely, and sat down in the other chair. 'Does that satisfy you? Kate, I came here to talk about Philippa. I know she got home safely from the tower. Did you understand my letter?'

'I understood that you were sorry you struck her unconscious,' said Kate. 'The rest was a little ambiguous. I gathered you wanted me to keep her at home and under my eye. I have.'

'You have. Where is she now, for example?' asked Lymond.

'In the v—— uh, henhouse,' said Kate with equal serenity.

'You're a liar. She's in the village, with Archie Abernethy after her. Kate, I don't like these little accidents that happen to Philippa. When I say under your eye I mean it. Until you hear from me, I want you to watch her, or have her watched by someone you can trust, night and day. Unless . . .'

For the first time, Lymond hesitated, and Kate set her teeth. If she had been a man, she would have clipped him over the jaw for his own sake, as he had done to Philippa. But Philippa was her child, and she was not a man. Seething with sullen anguish, she had to let him go on. He said slowly, 'I've hesitated to come, for it puts you in a thankless position. But for Philippa's sake I have to try. Someone hinted to me once, a few months ago, that Philippa had some infor-mation of detriment to me. I gather it was nothing particularly deadly. It sounded like some childish effort to puncture my undoub-ted conceit . . . and God knows, if it would exorcise her fear of me, I don't care who pulls the rug from under me. That doesn't matter. Except that more and more it seems possible that Philippa's dirty secret, whatever it is, may be the cause of these strange accidents. Suppose, Kate, that she has got hold of something that another person besides myself might want concealed?'

The surprise to Kate was total. She stared at Lymond, scowling. 'There's nothing that I know of,' she said. 'And heavens, of course she won't tell you herself now, less than ever. I think . . . I think in fairness you'll have to tell me who told you.'

'Graham Malett.'

'Oh.' Kate's brown eyes became fixed. Gabriel. She said, 'Sir Graham and Philippa met at Hampton Court, in my brother-in-law's house, and became sister-spirits. I wonder if . . . *George Paris's bribe!*' exclaimed Kate in a burst of discovery, and blushed crimson to the raspberry-stained collar.

There was a brief silence, during which Lymond's face altered, and she could see exhaustion flattening him like unwanted armour. He said, 'All right. I haven't heard that. I forget we are on two sides. It may help you to know that I knew it already, if you will believe that. If Philippa really has proof that Paris is a double agent and Paris knows it, then he may be the source of your trouble. Or . . . you ought to know . . . that apart from his spying activities between France and Ireland and England and Scotland, he is involved in a small private transaction of extreme illegality partnered by a man called Cormac O'Connor and a wily old seaman who would seduce Philippa with the greatest of pleasure, but wouldn't attack her, and affecting people like—my God,' said Lymond, coming to an abrupt halt himself. 'The Kerrs.'

Kate said icily, 'We are not on two sides. There was no need to spring into full national plumage and tell me all that. I was going to tell you anyway. George Paris was in Uncle Somerville's house getting paid when Sir Graham visited Philippa. Paris and Sir Graham left about the same time in spite of Uncle Somerville's efforts, and there was an accident on the river. Paris got into the water—he can't swim—and Sir Graham dived in from his boat and rescued him. Profuse thanks to God and Sir Graham, and eventually the two part after exchanging names, Paris giving a false one. So Philippa says. She knew who he was, but didn't tell Sir Graham. . . . We are *not* on two sides,' repeated Kate angrily at the look on Lymond's face. 'It only seemed politic at the time. In any case, when Sir Graham collected himself and his belongings again, wringing wet, and went to continue downriver, he found he had Paris's cloak. And in the cloak, a bag containing a great sum of gold, in English money, and some writing from the English Privy Council. . . .'

'Did Paris guess what had happened to it?' said Lymond.

Kate shook her head. 'It was very heavy. He must have assumed it fell safely to the bottom.'

'Then what did Sir Graham do with the cloak and the money?' asked Lymond.

'Tried to trace the owner, of course, under the name Paris had given him. And of course, couldn't find him. So he went back to Uncle Somerville and asked him if he would pass the cloak and the money on to his recent visitor. Uncle Somerville didn't recognize the name Sir Graham used, but he recognized the cloak and the money and the Privy Council's note, and said of course he would see they got to the right quarters.'

'And did they?' said Lymond expectantly.

'You don't know Uncle Somerville,' said Kate. 'Or the Privy Council. It went straight back to the Treasury. And when poor Paris appeared with his tale of woe, to squeeze another purse from them, they told him to learn to swim next time he went boating with gold in his pocket, goodbye.'

'Neat,' said Lymond. She could make nothing of his expression. If it had been anyone else, she would have said he looked flummoxed. He said, looking at her for the first time for a while, 'So you had to dry Sir Graham off and receive the gentle benison of his thanks. Did he pray a lot?'

At the tone, Kate's clever gaze sharpened. A moment's thought, and illumination burst on her at last. 'He was staying with Ormond, not with me. *Francis!* Is Graham Malett leading the forces of light? Is it *Gabriel* you are afraid of losing your disciples to?'

So much for her plans. As the soporific sunlight began to embrace his chair, Francis Crawford leaped to his feet with such force that the seat crashed to the floor behind him. He said, 'Sorry, Kate!' without stopping and flung away from her, the full length of the room.

There he halted, fighting for equanimity, and after a long, difficult silence turned, with obvious reluctance. Kate, standing, had been going to speak. Instead she stared at him, thinking numbly about hot milk and blankets, and saying nothing at all.

He misread her face. He said quickly, 'Don't be frightened. You look as if you expected me to strike you. . . .' And then, his eyes widening with tired shock, '*Did* you? Did you, Kate? Oh God, what does it matter then?' he said, and dropping to his knees beside the stifling windowseat, pressed both hands hard over his eyes, his elbows buried in Kate's old flock cushions.

Above the white voile of his shirt a pulse was beating, very fast, under the fair skin. After a moment he said, without moving, 'Would you give me a bed if I asked for one?'

'My dear, my dear,' said Kate, but to herself. 'I would give you my soul in a blackberry pie; and a knife to cut it with.'

*

In fact, he fell asleep, there where he knelt, and she had to persuade him to move. Once he had given in, he was too tired to undress; too tired to think any more. Kate had guessed rightly at overwork. He had said nothing to her of the useless, persistent, maddening trivia that disrupted his rest so that an hour uninterrupted was Nirvana; and several hours' continuous sleep something he had ceased to expect.

So he slept, in the end, on that same windowseat, with the shutters closed to keep out the sun: slept again, the moment he buried his head in the cushions. To Philippa, who stalked in defiantly halfway through these dispositions, Kate hissed, 'Say *one word* and you go to the Nixons.'

'I just came to make sure he hadn't hit you,' stated her daughter haughtily from the safety of the doorway, and marched out.

Two hours later when Kate Somerville, for the sake of her nerves, had found Philippa something to do elsewhere in the house, and was trying to fasten her own attention on something other than that silent room upstairs, the clack of hooves far off on the dry, dusty road told of two, maybe three riders coming south fast, obviously bent for Flaw Valleys.

One of them Philippa, materializing with astonishing speed, identified at once as Jerott Blyth. The others were soldiers.

At the gatehouse Brother Jerott, with his curling raven hair and hawk nose over a beautiful Florentine cuirass, wasted no time. 'Crawford of Lymond: is he here?'

As in some deadly cycle, due to move round and round to eternity, Kate saw her child run down the long drive waving. 'Mr Crawford? He's here!'

'He's here,' Kate repeated herself, to the unfriendly young man in her hall. 'But I am sorry, he cannot be disturbed until morning. You are welcome to the hospitality of Flaw Valleys until then, if you wish. Or I should be pleased, of course, to convey your messages.'

'I'm sorry,' said Jerott, his eyes elsewhere. What was the attraction here, in God's name? Not the little woman in the stained gown, surely? Or the plain fourteen-year-old who had been so courageous the night Trotty died? He said, having located the stairs, 'He's up there, is he? I'm sorry, but he's wanted elsewhere.'

'I'm sorry too,' said Kate at her most deceptive. By some miracle she was on the bottom step, and Charles, all six feet of him, two steps behind. '*Under no circumstances* can Mr Crawford be disturbed until morning.'

That got Jerott's attention. 'Why, who's he with?' he said, and Philippa, unseen behind, drew an enormous breath of sheer, crowing delight, and then choked on it, unuttered, in her throat. For there were tears of pure rage in her mother's eyes, and her mother's face, pale with controlled emotion, was turned towards herself. 'Philippa, go to the kitchen,' said Kate, in a voice her daughter never disobeyed. And to Jerott, 'Mr Blyth, has it totally escaped the attention of yourself and your other vigorous, efficient and devoted companions of the Knights Hospitallers of St John that your commander is ill with fatigue?'

'He's sick, is he?' said Jerott. He did not sound surprised. 'Still, he'll want to know, I expect. Next week's Day of March has been put forward to tomorrow. We were warned last week, it appears, but the news didn't reach us. Mr Crawford intended to go. But if he's ill,' said the dark young idiot cheerfully, 'then no doubt he'll send somebody else.'

'Oh,' said Kate. 'Tomorrow? That means leaving when?'

'Now,' said Jerott politely. 'I really must ask you to wake him.'

'And if,' said Kate desperately, 'Mr Crawford is too ill to delegate the command, how will his deputy be chosen?'

Jerott stared. 'There's only one choice, Mistress Somerville. If Mr Crawford couldn't lead, then it would fall to Sir Graham Reid Malett.'

'You'd better go up,' said Kate then ungraciously. 'He isn't ill—yet, but he's suffering from severe overstrain, in my view; and of course, lack of sleep.' Her sharp brown eyes sought and searched the brown face of this beautiful young man who had been kind to Philippa during that sickening episode of the old woman in the ditch, and who spoke so carelessly of his commander. 'You haven't known Mr Crawford long?' she said.

'We were boyhood . . . acquaintances,' said Jerott. 'And met again, last year, in Malta. I didn't intend to appear unfeeling. I have, I need hardly say, an enormous respect for Mr Crawford's ability.'

'But not for his character?' said Kate. 'Mr Blyth, you should remember one thing. A celibate island life fighting Turks is no particular guarantee of early maturity. Take a little crone-like advice, and don't rush your judgements.'

Jerott gazed at her with his splendid, cold stare. 'You are quite probably right. Sir Graham Malett, for instance, both admires him and holds him in deep affection.'

This Christ-like naïveté of Sir Graham's was, clearly, a matter for pain. Immune to the sarcasm, Kate suddenly pounced on the anomaly. 'The feeling isn't, I gather, reciprocal . . . Sir Graham isn't bent, then, on usurping the leadership?'

'*Usurping* it?' Jerott laughed. 'Mistress Somerville, Gabriel's one object in coming to Scotland has been to draw Lymond from his own recondite pursuits into a life worthy of himself and his gifts.'

'And the army?' said Kate. 'When Francis Crawford has taken his vows, what of the army?'

From the step above, impatient, Jerott Blyth looked down on her. 'The army is his. He would lead it, as now. But as a holy weapon. For great purposes, not for mercenary gain. To bring peace to the brotherhood of man.' He glanced upstairs and back, ironically, to Kate. 'He's flogged himself dizzy in a race that doesn't exist.'

All the same, forcing Lymond awake amused nobody; he was too exhausted for any gentle methods to work. It was a long time before he moved in his sleep, protesting at last; but soon after that he rolled over, his head in his hands, and heard Jerott's story. Then he got up and made ready to leave.

Kate had one last brief talk with Francis Crawford, after she had served a quick, generous meal to them all and had their horses made ready. '. . . About Philippa,' she said, as his pretence of a meal came to an end, and he waited for her to rise. Jerott and the rest were outside already.

'Yes?' said Lymond. 'You would like me to see her and apologize? I shall, of course. But I don't think. . . .'

'No, no. What possible good would that do? But I should like,' said Kate, ploughing on, against the clock and Lymond's own silent opposition, 'to hear the whole tale of the Hot Trodd. It might help to explain. What happened, for example, to the child you half-killed at the Turnbulls'?'

The blank cornflower gaze at her side came slowly to life. The fair brows rose to impossible heights. '*Kate!*' said Lymond. 'I know we luxuriate in every kind of melodrama, but I haven't started making a meal of infants, even Turnbull infants, yet. Who put round that extraordinary story?'

Kate laughed. 'Philippa picked it up from the big doctor—what's his name? Bell? When he came by one day to see how she was doing. She swore he said you had gone to torment a child in order to get the woman to confess where the Kerr cattle were. And you know that's Philippa's. . . .'

'*Bête noire*, I think, is the phrase,' said Lymond. 'She's not far wrong, in a sense. I got the facts I wanted from the mother, all right, but I didn't have to touch the child. Only told her that if she didn't help me, I'd take the poor half-starved object to Edinburgh and have it brought up a douce, well-fed solid citizen. That put the fear of God into her all right.' He shook his head. 'Give up, Kate. Whatever you tell her, she'll only believe now what she wants to believe.'

He pushed back his chair gently, and she rose. As he took her arm to walk out to the yard with her, she looked up and said, 'Why is the March meeting so important? It *is* important, isn't it?'

'For three reasons,' said Lymond. 'First, because old Wat Scott of Buccleuch will be there, aching to provoke the bloodiest kind of battle with the Kerrs who, he thinks, murdered his son. Second, because the cream of the English northern command will be there, and for all our sakes we must impress them. And third, because someone thought it worth while to see that two separate messages, from the English Warden and from Tosh, my man watching Buccleuch, about this change of date didn't reach us.' Arrived at the doorway, he stopped and turned. 'Kate Somerville, thank you. You did it against your will. But if you hadn't let Jerott in to wake me. . . .'

'Gabriel would have taken the command,' said Kate gently. 'Would that have been so terrible?'

'Yes,' said Lymond; and cold temper grated suddenly in his soft voice. 'Yes, it would.'

*

That night at supper, Kate found her daughter poor company. And since, nerving herself for the reasoned exposition she was about to make, she had remarkably little appetite herself, the meal was funereal in the extreme, and she was quite thankful when Philippa said, out of the blue, 'I didn't stay in the kitchen.'

'Oh?' said Kate, running her mind rapidly over several snatches of dialogue.

'No. I heard what that man said about the Hot Trodd.'

'Oh,' said Kate.

'You *believed* him when he said he didn't ill-treat that baby,' said Philippa.

'The gullible sort,' agreed Kate.

There was a pause. Philippa's small, sallow face with the ringed brown eyes was pale, and a strand of mud-coloured hair, unregarded, fell over her cheek. She said eventually, 'He thanked you. You wakened him, and it was horrible; and he *thanked* you.'

Kate hadn't known that Philippa was there during that little exercise in sadism. She said, 'He had a duty to do, chick. It was more important than sleep.'

'But he *came* here to sleep. Didn't he?' said Philippa.

'No,' said Kate, her stomach snail-like within her. 'Come and sit in the garden before you crumb the whole table.' And, sitting on the grass under the apple trees, with both their gowns becoming irremediably stained: 'No,' she repeated. 'He didn't come here to sleep. He came to make sure of your safety, and did without sleep to do it. He thinks someone is trying to harm you.'

'*Harm* me!' Philippa's lashes flew open, and her mouth widened of a sudden in a charming, uninhibited grin. 'But that's stupid! He harms me himself.'

'You heard why he did that,' said Kate shortly. 'He thought it too much of a coincidence that the Turnbulls' settlement and Liddel Keep should be so close together. And he thought our fire here was much too mysterious. So he wanted you away from the Keep quickly. It was your own silly fault you didn't do as you were told. . . . He was asking me,' said Kate, picking her way among her responsibilities and the fragments of her conscience, 'why anyone should want you out of the way. All I could think of was George Paris and his little secret.'

'So you told him?' said Philippa thoughtfully.

'Yes. He knew already,' said Kate defensively. 'So I wasn't exactly giving away the privy code book. But he didn't know you knew.'

'And does he think,' said Philippa cheerfully, 'that Mr Paris wants to murder *me*?'

'I think he finds it a little hard to believe. But it's not impossible. Anyway, until we know, I've promised to put you in irons, Philippa.

No more trips to the village without me. No visits at all away from home. And Charles or some other unfortunate sufferer has to keep an eye on you even in the garden. We're not taking any chances.'

Her heart sinking, she saw her daughter seize unerringly on the one reprehensible element. Oh, Francis . . . !

'But,' said Philippa, 'all Mr Crawford need do is denounce George Paris as a double agent, and the Queen Mother of Scotland would put him in prison, and I should be safe.'

It would be easy to say that, in belated patriotism, she had made Lymond promise otherwise. Kate instead baldly told the truth. 'One of the people in league with Paris over a little piece of chicanery is a friend of Mr Crawford's. He can't expose Paris without involving his friend as well.'

'Then why doesn't Sir Graham Malett expose Paris? He wouldn't care about Mr Crawford's criminal friends,' said Philippa.

'He doesn't know who Paris is,' reminded Kate patiently. 'Paris gave him a false name, remember? It was all very adult and tortuous.'

'I don't think it was very adult,' said Philippa after a moment. 'I . . . Oh, I see. Sarcasm again. All right. But then,' said Kate's daughter, pursuing it doggedly, 'why didn't *you* denounce Paris?'

'Because,' said Kate, getting up and shaking the cut grass and insects off her skirt, 'I have some shreds of respect left for my nation, if none for the extraordinary creatures who are attempting to run it at present. If George Paris is exposed as a double agent, he can't work for the English King any more.'

'I must say,' said Philippa getting up, 'Mr Crawford doesn't seem to be worried. He must think a lot more of his friends than he does of his country.'

'Um,' said Kate, eyeing her child in the mellow glow of late sunshine, prettily backlighting the apple leaves. Philippa looked terrible. She supposed she looked terrible too. She made up her mind to get a new dress and something that would contain her hair, and then changed it abruptly. Character was all. She said, 'If you think Mr Crawford isn't worried, you're blind. He's nearly out of his mind with worry.'

'About himself,' said Philippa. 'The trouble about Mr Crawford is that he has no social conscience.'

'The trouble about Mr Crawford,' said Kate, 'is that he puts up with his enemies and plays merry hell with his friends. Come on. Let's go inside, before my mother-love slips and I give you a bruise on the other side of your jaw.' And hugging her daughter rather desperately to her side, Kate Somerville went indoors.

X

The Hadden Stank

(March Meeting, June/July 1552: Algiers, August 1552)

THE Hadden Stank, a boggy meadow almost precisely on the Scottish–English Border and a few miles from the English castles of Carham and Wark, over the river, was not England's most popular spot for a meeting of Wardens. This dated from some twelve years back, when an English army of three thousand gallant horsemen was severely trounced on the low ridge in whose shadow the Stank unrolled. It was not popular either with the Douglases, who were on the English side at the time.

It was therefore with a great deal of unconcealed pleasure that Wat Scott of Buccleuch, riding north from Branxholm to the March, encountered Jamie Douglas of Drumlanrig, the Baron of Hawick himself, and the most active member now of all that great house, riding morosely ahead of him to take his place as Scottish Warden and Justiciar of the Middle Marches. Until two months ago, the appointment had been held by Buccleuch. He had given it up, with other public duties, when his son Will had died. Watching him ride beside her now, grimly jovial, chaffing Sir James, his wife saw that Buccleuch didn't regret renouncing this at least; a Wardenship counting near-sovereign power.

Her suspicions seethed. Over sixty, with a life of violence behind him, Buccleuch had been a broken man after the affair at Liddel Castle. More recently, however, the light of purpose had entered his eye, and, nimble as an elderly rectangular goblin, he had vanished and reappeared at Branxholm until they had all gone off their food.

Wat Scott of Buccleuch knew very well that to lay an unprovoked hand on the Kerrs would mean serious trouble for his house. The murderer of his son had never been found; and the law had ruled that the Kerrs, believing however incorrectly that the Scotts had killed all their cattle, were not to be blamed for retaliation. A heavy fine from Cessford and Ferniehurst had closed the incident.

Janet Beaton, Lady of Buccleuch, whose sister had married the dead boy, didn't think, in spite of her alarming forecast to Lymond, that Wat would provoke either Walter or John Kerr in person. In other respects she distrusted him to the uttermost, and her comely, uncompromising presence, planked sidesaddle on her mare between Buccleuch and Sir James Douglas and dividing a hard stare between both, at length drove Sir Wat into unwise speech. 'We're lamenting the price of auld stots. Will ye take your lang neb out o' my shouther?'

'I can hear ye. Ye're not lamenting the price of auld fools, Wat Scott?' said his wife instantly. 'Ye could be at home this minute with your doublet off and your slippers on and a stoup of good wine in your fist. What for are ye interfering in Sir James Douglas's business?'

'Because I wrang-wisely thocht I'd chaipit the auld bag at hame!' said Sir Walter furiously. 'Ye'll be the only female there, barring the hoors!'

Smiling, his wife nodded her handsome, positive head. 'Dod, Wat! It's every young lassie's dream!'

'Well, you're nae young lassie!' roared Sir Wat. 'Thrice merrit and six times a mother! They'll hae ye in and out o' their tents like a row o' fishermen gaffing a salmon, and ye needna look tae me for succour!'

'Wat, Wat!' said Lady Buccleuch with reproach. 'You're affronting Sir James. It's a perjink, weel-conducted March meeting we're off to attend, not a brothel.'

Sir James Douglas of Drumlanrig smiled, if a shade sourly. A slender, comely man, well and expensively dressed, he had been casting a shrewd eye, Janet knew, over the ranks of orderly Scotts and cousins following Sir Wat, each burnished as never Scott ever troubled to glitter before, and modestly armed with sword and knife. 'It should,' he remarked at length, 'be an unusually orderly meeting. The new army at St Mary's has been summoned, I believe, to keep guard.'

So much for Mr Francis Crawford's beautiful surprise, thought Lady Buccleuch, and caught the eye of their servant Tosh, riding discreetly behind. But, 'Oh, I ken, I ken,' said Sir Wat airily. 'Auld Wharton must fairly be past it, calling in yon giddy sprig o' gentrice and his pack o' priests. I trust they won't have to bestir themselves overmuch, that's all. I wouldna like my lord count to sweat up one o' his sarks.'

'*Wat!*' said his wife Janet warningly.

'Eh, my dear?' said Sir Wat. 'We're nearly there. I think ye should just take a hud o' my wee dirk. Your chastity is the Buccleuch honour, ye'll mind. And in case of contumaceous language, I'll just thank ye tae shut off your lugs.'

'Wat Scott of Buccleuch!' shrieked his wife. 'After all the contumaceous language that dirled in my ears and the ears of your poor innocent bairns from cockcrow to compline, is there a wee naked dirty word on the face of the earth that's no acquent wi' Buccleuch?'

'Hud your whisht,' said her husband genially, and rode past the first crofts of Hadden. Ahead, flat between river and hill, lay the Stank, the March banners flying. The Homes had arrived, he noted. Also the Elliots, the Armstrongs, the Veitches, the Burnets, the Haigs and the Tweedies, who were the mortal enemies, as it happened, of the Veitches; who were also at loggerheads with the Burnets. Plain in the middle of the field, bright with early sunshine, there flew also the standard of Richard, third Baron Culter, Lymond's brother.

*

On the stroke of eleven, the English Warden rode on to the field. By that time all the English families were there too: the Dodds, the Charltons, the Milburns and the other freebooting clans: the Ridleys, the Robsons, the Halls and the Grahams who inhabited both sides of the Borders. The banners stuck like gooseberry stalks out of the crowd, helmeted, cuirassed, and spilled like leadshot in heaps throughout the big meadow and along all the roads into it.

The tents were up by then, and the tented booths, score upon score, where anything from a whip to a copper kettle could be bought, at a price. In the middle was the platform under its awning, where the two Wardens of Scotland and of England, with their deputies, clerks and officers, would hear cases and pass judgements. Nearest to these, on the Scottish side, were the stations of the Scotts, and of the Kerrs. Behind Sir James Douglas's place on the platform there stood, ranged on the dusty grass, rank upon rank of Drumlanrig men. Behind the English Warden, stood dismounted the hundred light horsemen permitted Lord Ogle to discharge his duties.

But Lord Ogle, as they all knew, was sick; and Lord Dacre, whom he represented, was in the Tower. The office of Warden of the Middle and East Marches itself had been appropriated, at a salary of a thousand pounds per annum, by the Earl of Warwick, the Saviour of England.

Since the Earl, owing to pressing duties in London consisting largely of hanging the Government, was unable to attend personally to his office, this was normally occupied by a deputy. The deputy in this instance, brought hither by curiosity as well as duty, and accompanied by Sir Thomas Palmer and by Master William Flower, Chester Herald in person, was Thomas, Lord Wharton, Deputy Warden General of the Three Marches, straight from Carlisle.

Small, tough, self-made; a member of the English Parliament; one of the peers who tried and condemned the Duke of Somerset, England's Lord Protector, the previous year; veteran of every recent war on the Scottish frontier and ancient enemy of Lymond, Lord Wharton rode on to the field, his helmet pushed back from his grim, teak-coloured face, his hand held high in traditional token of good faith. Francis Crawford, who had been riding, chatting amiably, at his right hand, dropped behind and sat, still mounted, to one side of the dais while behind him the quietly shining ranks of St Mary's deployed alongside the Warden's men, officers, mounted also, at their sides.

The meeting with Wharton had been fortuitous. But the staffwork which had united Jerott and Lymond with the company and brought them here, fully armed and provisioned in perfect order, was not. Sitting beside Graham Malett, watching the Wardens cross the green grass, approach and embrace, while all around them the soft earth and flowers of high summer were metalled with armour, blinding under the kind yellow sun, Jerott was elated.

They had done the impossible. And Crawford was good: God, he was good. Good enough to do what had to be done and, in the middle of it, deliberately waste two hours on sleep. Two hours to the minute, and then the cutting edge was back. Christ, thought Jerott, Wharton must have wondered what was happening when they met. He hadn't tried to patronize after that.

Jerott glanced behind him at the still ranks of his own men. He lifted his eyes to the pale, airy void above him, and then across to the sunlit, classical profile of Gabriel, sitting still on his horse. At the same moment, Graham Malett looked round, and smiled.

Jerott's white teeth shone in an answering grin. Come what may, this was life.

*

A day of March dealt with crimes of the Border, too trivial to be referred to head Government. All thefts, robberies, depredations, homicides and fire-raisings and similar cruel, dreadful and iniquitous crimes committed by the inhabitants of these parts upon her Majesty's faithful subjects were in time referred to the Governor-General and Justiciar of Liddesdale, old Buccleuch. For as Warden of the Middle Marches he could both capture criminals and hold assizes to punish them, with all the clerks, sergeants and judges he needed.

In its day, a Wardenship had been a prize worth a small fortune, and handed out only to favourites. Even now, some thought went into the choice. In their hands lay negotiations that would daunt a first-class ambassador. One slip could cause, and had in the past caused, a war.

They punished criminals according to the law of the country in which the crime was committed. They had to hand over refugees if required, always bearing in mind the possible riposte from head Government for doing so with too great an alacrity. They had to arrange for reparation, and to crush trans-Border feuds.

It worked, in a perilous way. Before each advertised meeting, injured parties sent in bills of complaint to their Warden, who passed them to his opposite number across the Border. He in turn either arrested the accused men or summoned them to the next March meeting where each appeared with his two witnesses and his following and was tried, judged and sentenced or allowed to go free. In time of war, the Wardens took their own heralds, formally to demand and concede truce until sunset next day. In time of peace, as today, Chester Herald in his red and blue and cloth of gold merely had a formal exchange, followed by a good gossip in private with Bute Herald, while suits were being called and the rest of the formal fencing procedure got through by which the Warden's meeting was legally constituted. As the suitors filed in and took their places on the two long benches reserved for the victims, Scottish and English, of theft, bloodwite, spulzies, ejection and wrangeous intromission, as reeled off complacently in lawyer's Scots by Fergie Hoddim in an undertone, the two Wardens now settled side by side under the awning looked with careful indifference at the raw material of the day's work.

There were a great many women among them. Lord Wharton, the English deputy Warden, turning to big Tommy Palmer at his side, said in an undertone, 'Have you Ogle's list of pursuers there? Are these women related?'

Sir James Douglas of Drumlanrig, on his side, was also scanning the papers bequeathed him by Buccleuch, standing arms akimbo among his Scotts to the right. A certain irregularity in Sir Wat's beard led him to believe that Lord Wharton's question had not gone unremarked. He leaned over discreetly. 'Well? Are they related, Wat?'

'Only in misfortune, Jamie. Only in misfortune,' said that untrustworthy old knight, in deepest sorrow. Sir James Douglas sighed.

*

The morning passed, however, innocuously enough. There were one or two moderate cases of poaching, a theft of peats and oat straw from the stackyard, some off-season salmon fishing, and the ceremonial return of two loud-swearing rebels at the horn, caught in Kelso and handed back, with pleasure, by the Scottish Warden to their fate. The heavy guns, the horse and cattle stealing, the household robberies and thatch burnings and all varieties of slaughter, unpremeditated, chaudmelle or forethocht felony, were for the afternoon, when concentration had weakened and the more quarrelsome onlookers, touched by ennui, might have wandered away to the booths, the tents, the makeshift sports arena where attention and money were more seductively solicited.

341

Jerott, obeying orders, had begun circling the field slowly on horseback as soon as proceedings began, checking his men detailed discreetly on every part of the circumference, along with Ogle's hundred, thinly spread. Gabriel was doing the same.

So far, there had been no trouble. Lancelot Plummer, mounted with a strong detachment immediately behind the Kerrs, signalled nothing to report, but seemed uncommonly flushed about the cheekbones. Jerott hesitated, but rode on. Chester Herald ('Call me Billy') had elected to tour at his side, and he didn't care to expose something personal to the little Yorkshireman's shrewd gaze.

Fergie Hoddim, next on guard, was arguing law with someone dressed in black, and with only half an eye, Jerott saw, for his work. Latin flew like dubs from a puddle: '*continuatur ex partium consensu*', Fergie was saying heatedly, and '*essoin de malo lecti*'; and then began to press home a brilliant argument, no doubt, about litiscontestation and lawburrows. His tongue licked lawburrows into shape like a bearcub.

'Fergie!' said Jerott.

'And God give you the quartain!' said Fergie Hoddim precisely, turning his long, black-jawed face on the knight. 'My lord count of Sevigny has been visiting us on that tack already,' and in a surprisingly good imitation of Lymond at his most irritating: 'You can't swing a sword in a writers' booth, Fergie. Either the one or the other, Solomon; divide as you please.'

'He's a tongue, Mr Crawford has, hasn't he?' said Chester Herald in a pleased voice. 'We found that out in France. A proper lad. And what he got up to!'

'You should see what he gets up to here,' said Jerott, bored. 'Fergie . . . our gallant commander, it must be admitted, is right. Pay attention, man. You can loose your lawburrows on Gabriel afterwards if you want a thorough-going debate. . . .'

Hercules Tait was off duty, nominally to eat but actually buying something a little secretively from a packman's roll. Jerott couldn't see what it was. Alec Guthrie was grimly in position; and the biggest concentration of all, de Seurre, des Roches and Adam Blacklock, all in the vicinity of Buccleuch. '. . . Fought a boar single-handed,' Billy Flower, Chester Herald, was saying. 'At Angers. Single-handed.'

'You were there?' said Jerott. It was something to say. He had noticed Gabriel, off duty beside Buccleuch, sitting on the dry grass chatting to the old man as they both ate. Under the noonday sun his head was gold as a newly-coined noble and his engraved armour, his one magnificent possession, was still on but untied. He waved.

'That I was. And had the privilege of hearing the gentleman exercise his other talents as well, before their Majesties, you understand. Such an art; such an ear! I studied the lute myself once; in my youth,

342

that was,' said Chester Herald, swept away by his memories. 'But it sounded different. Yes, I must confess, it was in a different class from that.'

Jerott, dismounting, said without listening, 'So there were *two* bores? Chester—*Billy*,' said Jerott with distaste. 'Come and meet Sir Graham Malett and the Laird of Buccleuch. Proper lads both.'

And, cheerfully unnoticing, a smile on his rosy face, Chester Herald got down, just as Graham Malett, saying, 'Have you eaten, Jerott? No? I'm just going back on duty then. Wait and you shall eat here,' dispatched a man running for food. He brought back enough for Flower and Jerott both, and some wine as well, and Gabriel lingered a moment, talking to the herald, his shadow short and massive on the flattened grass as he refastened his straps. Buccleuch, struck by a thought, cut without ceremony through the chat. 'Is yon an Italian suit?'

'My armour?' Gabriel looked up. 'German, sir.'

'It's a grand fit round the houghs,' Sir Wat gave his opinion. 'Ye'll be having a set made for that sister of yours?'

'Joleta?' Sir Graham smiled, but his fair face held a look of faintly puzzled inquiry. Adam Blacklock, coming to life suddenly, stirred and got up.

'Aye,' said Sir Wat helpfully. 'Ye'll no have been at Midculter recently, maybe. The lassie came home in a right state the other day. Fell off her pony. She said.' Gabriel, wounded, had ridden twenty-one miles the other day to comfort Janet's sister Grizel. In principle, Buccleuch approved of Sir Graham. What stuck in his craw, now and always, was that St Mary's had failed to save Will.

Adam Blacklock, who could interpret as well as anyone the old man's tangled emotions, opened his mouth. But before he could speak, Gabriel said quietly, 'If my sister says so, then of course it is true. I have been to Midculter, as it happens. She won't go, even to Boghall, without a proper escort again.'

'But she *didna*. . . .' began Buccleuch and paused, as Blacklock laid a hand on his arm. 'I think they're due to start again, sir.'

'Are they?' Sir Wat craned round, his saddle creaking. 'No, they're not. There's Francis Crawford talking to Wharton, and Culter keeping himself to himself on the ither side o' the field. That reminds me. She didna. . . .'

'Wat!' said his wife Janet, emerging briskly from the tent into which she had been pushed, fuming, at the start of the break.

'I was just going to mention,' said Sir Wat, giving up, aggrieved, some part of his design, 'that I hadna seen the two Crawfords speak this morning. Culter must still be showing that ill-spawned young jangler the door.'

Anything to do with Lymond, Jerott knew and Blacklock now

noted, would always draw Gabriel's full attention. He said now, still quietly, 'I'm not sure what you mean. Is there trouble between Francis and his brother?'

'Wat!' said the voice of female doom over Buccleuch's shoulder. He ignored it. 'Oh, aye. They've quarrelled!' he said cheerfully. 'Culter's flung his brother out o' Midculter, and Sybilla's fair chawsed. Did Joleta not mention it? Biggar's exhausted with guesswork.... Ah, ye were right, Adam. There's the signal. Ye should have a word with your young friend about it, Sir Graham. A man of God such as yourself, brought up to entertain and nourish love, peace and unity and with a heidful of texts forbye should find no hardship in it.' And heaving himself up, Buccleuch nodded and offered an iron arm to his crimson-faced wife.

Graham Malett's fresh-skinned face, smooth as a sea-worn rock, smooth as an imbecile's, smooth as that of a man at complete spiritual ease with himself, reflected the shadow of trouble. But he smiled at the old man notwithstanding, and said, 'Do you think so? Somehow I don't think M. le Comte de Sevigny would agree with you.' And as Buccleuch, peching mysteriously, moved off, Gabriel sighed, and catching the eyes of Jerott and Adam Blacklock, ruefully smiled. 'I love my young friend, but this afternoon, I seem to be a little overwhelmed with his ineffable wake. Lancelot Plummer was having a stroke, nearly, when I found him, over some mild misdemeanour he and Tait had enjoyed at Liddel Keep, that all the Kerrs have been badgering him about today.'

The theft of Nixon's Staurotheque, thought Jerott, but didn't say so. Instead he remarked, 'Had Lymond told the Kerrs about it?'

'It doesn't seem likely,' said Gabriel. 'But Plummer thought he had. And then Fergie Hoddim was annoyed because he had been accused, virtually, of showing off his knowledge of law—not without justice, believe me,' said Gabriel, a shade of exasperation entering the rich voice. 'But if that same young man would apply his intelligence to delegating his work just a little and sparing his own health, he would be able to control himself and us just a little more easily.... Alec!' He turned, smiling, as Guthrie stumped up behind, ready for food. 'I'm getting old. I'm delivering lectures on the obstinacy of the young.'

'Criticizing the command, eh?' said Alec Guthrie drily. 'It's an ancient pursuit. Flamboyance, intolerance, cruelty are all faults of the young, true enough; but not only of the young. You knew what you were doing when you placed yourself under him.'

With calm speed, Gabriel was fastening his points. 'Of course I did. I wished to regain as quickly as possible all the skills I once had in Malta, and also perhaps to help Francis a little too. I think I may have done that. I know he has helped me more than he knows himself. It's only that . . . shut off from all affairs of the spirit, all art and all graces in the hard life he's led, it is sometimes a little hard to reach his understanding . . . over things I might feel are important, and he, perhaps quite rightly, does not.'

'A sensitive mercenary would be a contradiction in terms, don't you think?' said Guthrie. 'If he does nothing else, he makes us aware of our own weaknesses at least. I know I'm an argumentative old bastard who tends to hold up the action by talk. As now. Shouldn't you all be at your posts?'

He was right. They scattered, grinning; and Jerott, completing the circuit back to the dais, saw that Wharton and Drumlanrig were in their chairs with all their officials, and that Lymond, as before, was on horseback close behind. He also saw, now that he searched for it, Richard Crawford's family banner on the far side of the Stank and, finally, Lord Culter's grave, well-built person, exchanging words with all his near neighbours and not troubling to glance once in the direction of his younger brother.

It must be true, then. They had quarrelled. But over what? Ever since Will's death, Buccleuch had boiled with anger over Lymond. He would be ready to invent any libel. But why had Adam Blacklock been so anxious to intervene? And Lady Buccleuch? Jerott made up his mind to have a word with Blacklock, at least, before the day was over.

But, of course, the day wasn't over yet.

Jerott wondered, if it came to bloodshed, what the Wardens expected of St Mary's, and what each secretly hoped. Sir James Douglas, who knew a great deal about Francis Crawford, had been guardedly friendly. Lord Wharton, who had been tricked too often in the past to feel anything but pure dislike for Lymond, had been brought in the last few months, through exhaustive and contemptuous inquiry, to a grudging respect for his ability. They could converse, as they had talked all the way to Hadden, on matters concerning the conduct of armies. On personal subjects, and on everything to do with the recent war between their two countries, Lymond was tactfully and Wharton stubbornly silent.

Jerott noted further that Lord Wharton was one of the very few people totally humourless on whom Lymond refrained from exercising his wit. From which he deduced that, professional that he was, Lymond equally respected the little Cumberland man's grip of his job. On the whole, he thought that the Wardens would enjoy seeing St Mary's in action, for all their reservations about its commander.

The afternoon wore on. Now the more serious cases were coming before the tribunal: cases of wholesale theft and bloodshed; cases involving whole families, mainly of broken men such as the Turnbulls had been, who scraped an illegal living in the boggy wastes of

345

land which neither country cared to claim. There was a good deal of raucous shouting, some sound cursing and one or two drunken struggles, as well as a volleying orchestration of comment and insult from the watching crowd, but no mass movements had started, either for or against the defenders or pursuivants, and the feuding families, coldly oblivious each of the other's presence, kept to themselves.

Down by the river, the sport was well under way: wrestling, shooting, fighting with sword and cudgel. The booths were gradually emptying of their wares as the huckstering and peddling came to a hoarse conclusion and men turned to spend their money on the acrobats, the jugglers, the fortune-tellers, and on, of course, the jolly, well-built, sunburnt women who swaggered back-slapping through the crowds and gave as good as they got when the fresh hogsheads were rolled out dripping from the carts, and the well-worn quips undulated about their impervious ears.

In mid-afternoon Gabriel, whose splendour on horseback no restraint on his part could dim, observed to Jerott, 'We are, I fear, a subject for good healthy merriment along the river. Does it strike you, as it does me, that our respected leader is exercising his right once again to keep us alert? March meetings, in other words, are goodly things which remove dullness from little boys. . . .'

The thought had occurred to Jerott. Before he could speak, however, Adam Blacklock on his other side said, 'You w-weren't here two years ago. If folk from one side of the Border met the other, it was to fight; and pick the eyes from the naked dead afterwards. I've seen the Douglases and the Scotts play handball through the streets of Kelso with severed English heads for the ball.'

Gabriel's unclouded blue eyes turned on him. 'What were you doing there? Sketching them?'

The artist flushed.

Graham Malett noted it, but his voice was gentle. 'And what did you gain from that? Are you a better artist, Adam, for drawing only men of violence and acting in their brutal engagements? Do you expect to become hardened to it? You never will. You have too fine a grain.' Graham Malett's deep, rich voice hardened for a moment. 'There is nothing romantic about killing for money.'

But Adam Blacklock's lean, nondescript face with the untidy hair was blank. 'It depends whom you kill,' he said.

With a half-exasperated, half-amused groan, Gabriel clapped his free hand to his brow. 'Francis again,' he said. 'Do you *know* that you are all becoming copyists as faithfully mannered as the Chinaman who sat on the plate? I shall never redeem one of you until I have his ungodly heart.'

'He hasn't got one,' Blyth said shortly. 'Godly or ungodly.'

'He has something,' said Gabriel gently. 'Or why else do we follow

346

him? Why else is Adam here concealing what he knows? Something happened at Dumbarton, something so painful that Lord Culter has become estranged. Must I ask Culter myself?'

'Why not ask L-Lymond?' said Adam Blacklock, his gaze resolutely avoiding Jerott Blyth's.

'Because I think he hates me,' said Gabriel, and his gaze, drifting past them, rested on the distant, confident horseman, leaning down to talk to Wharton's clerk and then side-stepping to where Buccleuch stood to stoop chatting to him. Lymond's head, *jaune-paille* in the clear sun, was without a helm.

'. . . I think he hates me,' Gabriel repeated, bitterness for once in the deep voice. 'A fine churchman, a dexterous shepherd, is Graham Malett. This one man I cannot reach.'

The words were to remain, engraved leadenly on the air and on Jerott Blyth's memory. For just as they were spoken, the English Warden Thomas, Lord Wharton, reached the case of the three rows of women.

They were English women, with good Border names, of peasant and small yeoman stock. Not ladies of pedigree; nor, on the other hand, loose women or gypsies. They wore decent fustian gowns and long hair, to show they were unmarried, and they sat in the benches reserved for those lodging complaint. With them, bawling, squealing, fighting, slavering, and much occupied in casual regurgitation, were their children.

The fact became clear gradually as the clerk's weakening voice wheezed through the list of cases; and as he went on, the depleted crowd round the open-air court became markedly brisker, and in a kind of simmering movement, like oatmeal on the hob, began to thicken and bubble and spread until three-quarters of the total March meeting or all those not otherwise urgently engaged were standing watching the court.

The complaints, notice of which had been received too late to make known until now, were all the same. Nell Hudson, formerly of the Baxter Raw, Carlisle, did complain that Gilbert Kerr of Greenhead, having promised her marriage and got her with child, had heinously broken the said promise and had neither taken her honourably to his bed and board, nor acknowledged and maintained the child. Nell Hudson therefore prayed the Wardens to so judge that either Gilbert Kerr of Greenhead should marry her, with all goodly haste, or if constrained by virtue of prior wedlock, should admit to and maintain his son.

Gilbert Kerr of Greenhead, who was fifty-five and had eight children by his (living) third wife, had hardly done shouting his denials when the next case was reeled off.

Bess Storer of Little Ryle complained that Sir Thomas Kerr of

Ferniehurst, heir to Sir John Kerr of that ilk, having promised her marriage and got her with child, had broken the said promise and had neither fulfilled his engagement nor maintained the said child. ... Sir Thomas Kerr, who was seventeen, stood, pink as a flamingo among the squeals of his friends, and looked both surprised and pleased as he craned to see the aforesaid Bess Storer—pleased until he saw his father's black face.

Meg Hall of Screnwood blamed George Kerr of Linton; and Allie Lorimer of Haggerston, George Kerr of Gateshaw or Robin Kerr of Graden—she was not sure which. Sir Andrew Kerr of Littledean, a vast and sober citizen until recently Provost of Edinburgh, had sired two girls, it was said. Walter Kerr of Dolphinton, Gilbert Kerr of Primsideloch and Andrew Kerr of the same were each named as unwilling fathers, and the young laird, Andrew Kerr, Cessford's son, was accused of engendering twins, and was juvenile enough to crow triumphantly in the direction of Sir Thomas Kerr. The climax came when, half an hour later, Wat Kerr of Cessford himself was named as father of Sue Bligh of Bamburgh's four sons.

It might have been harmless enough save for one thing. Lying or not, each woman had brought two witnesses. And the accusation against Kerr of Cessford happened to be true, and everyone there knew it to be true, although no one had ever been able to prove it.

It was not surprising then that the clap of laughter which had begun, after the third or fourth notice, to greet every new accusation overreached itself in the case of Sir Walter and fairly frightened the moorhens off the Tweed a hundred yards off. Then it broke off, as a bottle shears at the neck, at the sight of Walter Kerr's blunt, battle-scarred face as the head of the Cessford Kerrs drew his sword screaming from the sheath and drove it into the ground before the Wardens' dais.

'De'il draw ye tae hell. Are ye daft? Is this a March meeting or the ribald outrage of children? The women are bought; the witnesses are plainly lying. The very malicious naming of near every member of mine and Ferniehurst's family is enough to prove falsehood and malice, and by God, ye won't seek far to ken whose it is!' And Cessford's eyes, seamed with apoplectic blood, veered to the bland, brosy whiskers of Buccleuch.

He finished in silence. As the words rang out, thin in the wide air, Lord Wharton said sharply from his chair, 'I must pray you, show the respect which this Chair demands. Clearly, the coincidence is not unremarked. The evidence must be sifted and the witnesses reheard. The source of malice, if proved, will be sought. Until then, you will judge as you expect to be judged, on firm evidence only.'

He got Cessford to unearth his sword and withdraw, just a little,

348

while the questioning went on. But the ranks of the Kerrs, of a sudden, had grown remarkably well-knit and grave; and the ranks of the Scotts, glittering with polish, stood trimly as they had throughout. Behind both families, deployed silently on Lymond's orders at the outset of the case, stood two thirds of the officers and men of St Mary's, markedly vigilant and, Jerott was sure, not so markedly memorizing names and addresses.

Jerott himself, back to the river with some of his men and facing the Warden's dais, listened fascinated as Wharton and Drumlanrig, carefully dispassionate, sifted the evidence, to an arpeggio of bawling bastardy. It had been well prepared. While no Kerr, not even Sir Walter, had been caught, it seemed, red-handed, the witness of the wronged maidens could not be proved false either.

There remained the evidence of the children. Running a desperate military eye over the squirming rows of bundles, breeched and breechless, of varying ages and small attraction, he ventured the mild opinion that since every Kerr was either married or promised elsewhere, it was in any case merely a matter of adopting and paying for the children.

'*Those!*' said Cessford in tones of undisguised loathing. And '*Those!*' repeated Ferniehurst with repulsion vaster still. 'I'd go to jail first.'

'You may,' said the Scottish Warden mildly. 'They are not, I admit, the flower of their race. But Kerr blood, for all we have been able to prove, may well run in their veins.'

'Pah!' said Walter Kerr of Cessford. Ferniehurst, more explicit by temperament, used a number of other words. 'My lord!' said Buccleuch, meekly.

The English Warden bent down. 'Yes, Sir Wat?'

Buccleuch murmured.

Lord Wharton straightened. 'An excellent idea. My good women, rise and bring your children forward. They are to receive a small gift. Some sweetmeats, to pacify their tempers and reward them for their patience. Pray allow the little ones to accept them.'

A bag of someone's comfits, hastily pulled from a saddle-bag, was passed to each small illegitimate child, and the crying stopped. The bag, nearly empty, was brought back to Lord Wharton, who took one and passed it to Drumlanrig. 'You will note,' he said drily, 'that every child accepted its sweet *in the left hand.*'

The uproar after that went on for a very long time, and in its essence consisted of Cessford's plea, repeated over and over, that without proof no one could force him to take and rear a pack of English bastards as Kerrs. When at last Wharton whacked on the board with his whip, the noise took a full two minutes to die away, and the Cumberland man, all too furiously aware that a monumental joke was under way, was in a foul temper. When he had reasonable silence, he snapped.

'The Scottish Warden and I have two solutions to offer.' He glanced at Sir James Drumlanrig, who nodded, and back at the quietly delirious crowd. 'There is no doubt that these accusations have been gathered from malice against the family Kerr. But we may not conclude from that, that the Kerr family is quite free of blame. In any case, the real sufferers seem likely to be these innocent children.' Lord Wharton, averting his eyes from the innocent children, glared at Buccleuch, who grinned back.

'Therefore we suggest either that the whole sanctions are continued to another March meeting, when more evidence may be forward and the matter may be argued again. . . .

'That's continuing the case until the next meeting *sub spe concordiæ*, in the hope that the parties may agree,' Fergie Hoddim was saying. 'An English love-day, they call it.' And gazed surprised as Lancelot Plummer at his side suddenly choked, and had to be thumped on the back to stop his coughing.

'—an English love-day,' continued Lord Wharton, less innocent than Fergie, glaring round him. 'That is one solution. The other has been put forward by Sir Walter Scott of Buccleuch. Since these poor women are incapable of rearing their offspring, and some of the best blood in Scotland may consequently (his phrase) weaken and waste, Sir Wat suggests that, failing support by their own putative fathers, he and his family will gratuitously, and for no payment other than his reward in Heaven, take these little children and rear them at Branxholm to bear proudly the name of Kerr.'

'Over my deid wambles!' yelled Cessford.

Wharton's face was set like brown wood. 'You object to Buccleuch's paying for these children?'

'He can pey for what he likes. . . . I see ye, ye canty de'il . . . but he'll not call yon bunch of louse-ridden, snotty-nosed hedge-gets by the proud name o' Kerr!'

Sir James Douglas's cool gaze swept the old man. 'Dinna be hasty,' he advised. 'Consider. Sir Walter is doing the State and ourselves quite a service. It'll be no cheap matter, laying out money for yon flock, Kerrs or no. If he supplies the siller, he can fairly call the tune.'

'Then I'll have the love-day,' said Cessford forebodingly, after a brief talk with his ally of Ferniehurst. Lord Wharton looked narrowly at the two.

'In order to terrorize the ladies or the Scotts? If that is your purpose, you will be disappointed, gentlemen. At Sir Walter's suggestion, we are asking Mr Francis Crawford to come lawburrows that the petitioners and their friends will be unharmed. That is, Mr

Crawford becomes your pledge that no illegal violence takes place, either to these women or their witnesses, before the next March meeting takes place. If the lawburrows are broken, Mr Crawford pays the necessary fine but is also, of course, entitled to obtain restitution from you. Mr Crawford, I take it that you are willing to do this?'

From across the flattened turf, Jerott saw Lymond's head move, affirming, but could not hear what he said.

'Well?' said Lord Wharton of the Kerrs.

Sir Walter Kerr of Cessford turned back from where he had been conferring in low tones with Sir John Kerr of Ferniehurst. Stiffly and without glancing at any person save his lordship on the dais, Cessford said, 'We have decided, my lord. We shall be responsible for the maintenance and upbringing of all these children. But we do not intend that they shall be known by the name of Kerr.'

Barely had he spoken when from the Scott side of the dais a cheer rose that sent the sentries at Wark castle to their arms. As the cheer broke down into resounding laughter and set off, down the field, a concatenation of comment and shouts, 'I think your conclusion is quite praiseworthy, under the circumstances,' said Lord Wharton, glaring around. 'The only proviso, to my mind, is that the mothers themselves must agree. The children are not to be named Kerr.'

The mothers, with difficulty hiding a certain jubilation, agreed. Before the approving face of Buccleuch, with his wife Janet hanging speechless on his arm, fourteen under-nourished, ill-advised children wavered, or were carried, from the litigants' smeared benches to the orderly ranks of the Kerrs, which opened yawningly to receive them, and then shut like a trap.

Weeping with laughter on Jerott's shoulder, Fergie Hoddim won through to speech at last. 'Suborning witnesses! Tracing cary-handit weans! Wat Scott of Buccleuch must have spent a fortune ... a *fortune*, man, to do it, but was it worth it! Nae provocation offered. All a matter of good honest law, with Buccleuch's name nowhere mentioned, and the Kerrs helpless ... helpless! And the cream o' the joke. ...' Fergie, to whom love-days were serious business, saw the funny side of this. 'The cream of the matter—Lymond, who fairly maddened Sir Wat by appointing himself Buccleuch's watchdog, has got the job of keeping the peace between the Kerrs and all the women Buccleuch bribed ... *including Sue Bligh of Bamburgh!*'

The meeting was beginning to disperse. The Kerrs, encircled by a solid wall of St Mary's men, were moving one way, the Scotts another. 'It was Buccleuch's day, all right,' said Jerott. 'While we all stood around in fancy armour like fools, waiting for mayhem, Sir Wat was baiting the Kerrs with impunity, and forcing St Mary's to protect him for it. I'd have given a good deal to have seen our efficient commander's face when the truth dawned.'

'Lymond? I saw it,' said Fergie. 'He had Gabriel on the one side of him and me on the other the whole time.'

'What did he do?' asked Jerott.

'Curled up on the neck of his horse and laughed himself silly,' said Fergie. 'Yon's no way to go on.'

'On the other hand,' said Jerott Blyth, 'rather shrewdly endearing, don't you think?'

*

It had in fact been an unfortunate luxury, that fit of irresistible laughter, and its after-effects were appalling. Sitting up, howling faintly still at Buccleuch's exquisite effrontery, Francis Crawford found that Gabriel had gone from his side.

Save for one quick half-circuit of the field in the opposite direction, Lymond had kept Sir Graham Malett beside him most of the day. He had noted, without comment, the distant interlude between Scott of Buccleuch and Graham Malett, and had perhaps read something of warning in Adam Blacklock's passing stare. In any case, missing him now, he looked for Graham Malett in one place only and found him instantly, on foot, his armour glittering, his helmet off, disclosing the splendidly-set head to the sun.

As the crowds waned chattering about them and the company of St Mary's, long since precisely briefed on its duties, split and muffled, with orderly calm, the smallest outbreak of dissension along the diverse homeward paths, Lymond sent his horse sharply trotting, after the briefest possible of farewells to the Wardens, along the boggy dip to where Graham Malett stood deep in conversation with Richard Crawford, his brother.

Lord Culter, standing reins in hand before the ordered bustle of his following, ready to mount and ride home, saw Francis approaching. He saw him, but although his colour became very high and his cold eyes colder yet, he did not interrupt the soft violence of Gabriel's tirade. Unseeing, his back squarely to the coming horseman, Graham Malett was saying over and over, his hands gripping Culter's leather sleeves, 'What can it count, some trifling misdemeanour, against kinship such as yours? Is it worth the misery on your mother's face, whatever it is? If it has meaning, surely Christianity means forgiveness?' He paused, and added, 'I have no brother, to my sorrow. But I have a sister, dearer to me than my soul, who is mischievous as well as wholesome, like the child that she is. . . . If the mischievous child grieves me, do you think I forget the loving spirit that lies behind? I forgive her before she troubles me, comfort her when she wrongs me; for she is my sister, and there is no act she could commit in this world which would estrange me from her.'

'You have great confidence in each other,' said Lord Culter quietly. Only those who knew him well might have guessed at the incredulous anger behind the flat tone: anger that, being committed to immoral silence, he should now be expected to maintain it in public before the well-meaning onslaught of the very man his brother had wronged. . . . And here was Francis, cheapening the impossibly cheap by coming to invigilate him.

'I have confidence in Joleta,' said Sir Graham, smiling, 'but not necessarily in the whole of womankind. She is fallible to the small sins of the flesh. And God has given her beauty: not an easy gift for a child. . . . If she had disrupted your home . . . if your parting from your brother is in any way Joleta's fault, I beg you to tell me? Indeed, I shall ask her myself. . . . I shall insist on an answer.'

'Well, is it Joleta's fault, brother?' said Lymond's lazy voice. Still gracefully mounted, he paced into Gabriel's view and stopped, between the two men. 'One of these small sins of the flesh, perhaps? Whither are you going, pretty fair maid, with your white face and your yellow hair?'

The long, silken hair of his bay's mane dropped, lock by golden lock, from his outstretched hand, leaving the fingers poised, elegantly cupped, in mid-air. Then smiling, he dismounted. 'Tell him, Richard. How jealousy hunted me from your door.'

Unhurried, Gabriel turned his head and studied Lymond's face. He said calmly, 'If I hadn't seen Mariotta, I might have believed it. It isn't because of any competition for her favours that Joleta looked ill the last time I saw her, and had a face white with crying. I think rather the reverse.'

Francis Crawford cried, 'She's in love with *Richard*!' and half a dozen people in the vicinity, including Adam Blacklock and Jerott Blyth, lingering uneasily for orders, looked at them. Invention blazed in Lymond's blue eyes. 'And contrived some reason for Richard to get rid of me!'

With one swift, unexpected movement, Graham Malett caught and gripped Lymond's two airy hands. 'I implore you . . . don't mock,' he said, and there was deep distress in his voice. 'She loves you. . . . She is pining for you. Don't you know it? And she is only a child. You must not be cruel.'

'*Tout animal n'a pas toutes propriétés*,' observed Lymond. 'Some like it cruel.' He raised his own hand, encased now in Gabriel's, and planted a solid salute on the other man's big, knuckled fingers. '*Io baccio la sua cortese e valorosa mano*—And some like it polite.' Gabriel removed his hands as if stung. 'And some think they like it

353

polite, but find they prefer to be handled rough. Tastes differ. . . .
You should find her a husband.'

'I thought I had,' said Gabriel, all the life gone out of his voice.

'But,' said Lymond, and chanted with gentle derision:

> The King of Spain is a foul paynim
> And 'lieveth on Mahound;
> And pity it were that fayre ladye
> Should marry a heathen hound?

'I have no reservations,' said Gabriel. He stood, his arms hung
rejected at his sides, his back a little bent, automatically, to reduce
his splendid height. 'With God's help, I have faith enough for all of
us.' He paused, looking directly at Richard, the fine skin seamed
faintly with tiredness. 'Won't you exert your faith also and take him
back? Won't you let me help you, at least?'

'I'm sorry,' said Lord Culter, his voice like pressed ice. 'I cannot
accept. If you want to know why, ask my brother.'

'Explanations,' said Lymond firmly, 'are a mistake. *I* am perfectly
happy. *Si non caste, tamen caute.* From me the seed; from Thee the
blessing that fertilizes. Grant it, grant it, O Lord!'

No one spoke. Beside him, Jerott heard the hiss of Adam Blacklock's intaken breath. Gabriel, looking at the speaker, wore for a
moment an expression of mild and puzzled distaste. But it was on
Lymond's brother that Jerott's gaze was fixed. Physical revulsion
was printed on Lord Culter's face: the stamp of an antipathy so
coarse and so sudden that he wanted to vomit. Instead, after a
moment, Richard Crawford spun on his heel and, lifting himself into
the saddle, forced his horse without a word away from them and
into the press of his men.

Gabriel's grave tender gaze followed him, and then returned to
Lymond's carefree stare. 'Forgive me. I have made you angry,' he
said. 'And that in turn has only made matters worse.'

'Yes, it has, hasn't it?' said Lymond. 'But then meddling inter-
lopers always do. Do you do this for a hobby, or are you writing a
book?'

Gabriel's voice remained steady. 'I have apologized. I am as
foolish as you would have me look. But I only wished from my heart
to help.'

'I,' said Lymond coolly, 'am a philocalist of independent means. I
help myself. If you can tear yourself away from my family's affairs, I
fancy there is a little work to be done. . . . Interested, Blacklock?'

Beside Jerott Blyth, and already as far from the centre of the dispute as the crowd would allow, Adam Blacklock flushed scarlet but
said hardily, 'I have a m-message for Sir Graham. The French

354

Ambassador is here, and would like Sir Graham's company back to Edinburgh.'

'Here? At Hadden Stank?' Lymond's eyes flickered over the crowd and returned, suddenly inscrutable, to the artist. 'Then he must be incognito. There is no banner. Are you sure?'

But Blacklock knew, as they all did, the tall, bony person of M. d'Oisel, the French King's Lieutenant in Scotland and Mary of Guise's right-hand man, who might well take the occasion, on his way back from the French Court, to slip into a March meeting and make observations thereon. 'It was M. d'Oisel,' he said.

Gabriel's voice was gentle. 'I saw him, I think. But I could not be sure; you will remember keeping me at your side most of the day. . . . He is a civilized man. He would enjoy Buccleuch's little joke with the Kerrs.' He hesitated. 'I need not leave with him unless you wish. I have come to know him rather well while pursuing Sandilands's affairs in Council, that is all.'

'What, disobey the French Ambassador!' said Lymond. 'Let us not tempt Fate with heresies. Go. Go by all means, and let thy mouth be filled with explanations, in French and English, of Buccleuch's little joke with the Kerrs.'

He did not join M. d'Oisel when that gentleman, with his two attendants, left the ranks of the crowds to pay his respects to the Wardens, and finally to ride off to rejoin the waiting train of his men, Gabriel at his side. More than anything that had so far happened, it underlined Sir Graham Malett's status and prestige.

The most powerful man in Scotland had not asked to meet Lymond. And if, as an afterthought, he had summoned him, Lymond would not have been there. For, no sooner had Gabriel left than Francis Crawford, without explanation, had handed over his command to Jerott and withdrawn from the field.

*

The blue and silver banner of Culter, dark against the westering sun, was far along the Kelso road, and the burnished helmets of his men at arms, following at speed, bubbled like quicksilver by the calm waters of Tweed when Lymond caught up with his brother.

Among so many pounding hooves Richard Crawford, travelling too fast too early in a lengthy day's ride, did not hear him approach; did not see him until at his elbow, where he had asked no one to ride, there came, neck outstretched, a bay horse as good as his own which—*God!*—he knew. His throat cold with unnoticed air, his abdomen lodged, it suddenly seemed, in his chest, Lord Culter drove his spurs, like a fugitive, into his splendid mare's sides. She widened her eyes, the rims white above her hard-breathing nostrils, and

355

lengthened her already stretched stride. Lymond's bay did the same.

Insanely, Richard did not even look at his brother. With more than a hundred men streaming breathless behind; with two hundred eyes watching, he put his horse flat out on the meadowland, and knew that he was forcing Francis to use his spurs without pity, too. For what seemed a space endless in time, they remained side by side. Then Lymond's horse, bearing a lighter man but not, Richard knew, in a childish thundercloud of outraged pride, better ridden, began to draw past.

It was not to be borne. His teeth clenched so that the ache of it, noticed later, drummed in every bone in his head, Richard forced the mare forward. She was a good beast, and he had cared for her. She responded, with a pumping heart, and they were level again.

When he felt the bay begin his next drive to the front, Richard was ready. With spurs, with whip, with knees and thighs like cramping-irons, he held his mare to her pace and past it until she matched the bay nose for nose, and then bettered it: nose forward; ears; neck clear of the bay's head; then shoulders in front. And finally, her great thighs revolving, she was a clear length in front of his younger brother.

Richard Crawford, his grip slippery, his breeches sodden with the sweat that poured like a gutter down his spine and dripped from jaw, eyebrows, nose, on to his cuirass, looked back and laughed. Far behind, in a pounding cloud of dust, his company laden with armour and weapons, were striving to follow. A length—two lengths, now, behind, Lymond had slackened his grip, the bay's flanks heaving and foam coating his bit.

Where Richard was limply dishevelled, Lymond's short, thick hair clung, fronded with sweat to his head; his eyes bright with the moment's exhilaration in a face as white as Richard's own. He waited. Then, as the leading horse eased, the race won and its effort expended, Lymond let the bay have the second wind he had been nursing so carefully all along. With an effort that was audible, the big horse pressed itself from canter to gallop again, and from gallop to full racing speed.

It was too late this time for Richard's horse to respond. In the second it took Culter to gather her, he knew she had relaxed too far already. When he pressed her she pecked, and a rider less excellent than Richard would have gone over her head. Then, although she recovered and put her foot forward bravely enough, the bay was close to her side. A moment later Lymond leaned over and gripping the mare's bridle hard by the bit, dragged them both to a halt.

By then, the two hundred men for whom Lord Culter was responsible, the familiar faces and the familiar names from all about Midculter were far behind; and towards the river, towards the rising ground on their left, and ahead at the approaches to Kelso were only strangers; distant hurrying groups; men with their own troubles to attend to.

For a moment, overcome by stress and no doubt by other emotions, the two men on horseback, so similar, so dissimilar, were silent. Then the younger brother took his hand away, his eyes brilliant still from the ride, and unexpectedly laughed. 'Poor Richard. Always suffering from being such a bloody bad actor; I thought you were going to be sick. I've got a question to ask you. Just one.'

It was then that one remembered that Francis very rarely acted without purpose. Lord Culter's horse was too spent to outrace the other. And now Richard had left neither the violence nor the will to silence his brother by force. For a moment longer, he stared in silence at his cadet. Then Lord Culter said, 'Very well. Since you have forced the encounter, ask the question. Then I have some news for you. If there is time.'

Lymond said quickly, 'Tell me your news.' But Richard merely waited in negative silence, his brows raised, while behind them both, the sound of hammering hoofbeats told how near were his men, and how slender their privacy was.

Then his lordship of Sevigny said abruptly, as he had to, 'All right. Richard, how is our . . . difference so widely known? Did you spread it abroad? Did Sybilla?'

Nothing of Richard's surprise was allowed to show in his voice. He said, 'Mother knew nothing herself until she began to hear rumours.'

'Started by whom?' Quick, level, precise, it hardly seemed the voice you had heard, a short time before, prostituting unspeakably the wise text of Islâm. Richard said, 'You, in your cups, I presume.'

'No. And if you said nothing, and I didn't either, how did the tale spread that Joleta spent an unchaperoned, unexplained night, and that next day you and I had occasion to quarrel? I haven't been noticeably absent from Midculter: there hasn't been time. Yet Buccleuch's heard it; everyone's heard it. Not everyone has yet linked the two facts, but they will. If Gabriel had been a shade more persuasive back there and I had been a shade less insensitive, the fair Joleta would have been ruined for ever.'

'I don't know. I don't much care either,' said Richard. The forerunners of his band were nearly upon them. 'Sybilla knows already. It's too late to shield her now. And everyone else will know soon. I would have told Graham Malett myself, as you feared, except that I couldn't bear . . . I couldn't bear. . . .'

He halted, rather than attempt the impossible. You did not try to explain goodness to Francis, or gentleness, or humility, or love. Or how you would break the news to a great and generous man that the protégé on whom he had set his heart had rewarded him by forcing his sister.

Against the darkening sky of the east, the Midculter horses were jostling, not yet within earshot but eagerly on the watch. There was only a moment more. 'So I believe you had better come home,' said Richard levelly. 'And soon. There is a certain amount to arrange.' And as Francis, very still on his horse, continued to stare without speaking, Richard had, with aversion, to put his news into words. 'It was your mother, you will be proud to hear, who made the discovery. Joleta is to bear you a child.'

Remorse, Richard hadn't expected to see. But shock, perhaps; and horror perhaps, and consternation certainly. Instead, he realized that the fair, fine-boned face opposite him was livid with pure irritation; an exasperation which not even the failing light could soften or hide.

'I thought so. God damn it, I thought so,' said Lymond bitterly. 'She's pregnant, the slovenly bitch.'

And sat, gazing frowningly after, as Richard rode precipitately off.

*

The dispositions of St Mary that day were quite perfect. Every man, woman and child for which the company were responsible reached home safely and remained safe. In hilarity at length all those not on guard duty returned at dusk to their base; and the line of torches, ermine-tails in the night, danced in the mirror of the loch as they approached St Mary's, song and laughter falling aside with their sparks.

Lymond led them. Of the malignant humour of a few hours before there was no trace. Rather he encouraged them to wilder and wilder humour, to chant, to whistle, to recite. To play, once back, on their loose-gutted fiddles in front of the fire, and stamp their feet, and sharpen their wits on each other.

And in their response to Lymond, Jerott noted, silent in the background, a bonhomie that had been missing before. It was not the success, for the latter part of the day had been a success; or the sense of efficient leadership, for this had been growing guardedly, since the mishaps of the winter and the disaster of the Hot Trodd. It was, Jerott suspected, precisely what he himself had found reconciling: the sight of Lymond in helpless laughter after watching Buccleuch make a complete fool of him.

Studying Francis Crawford now, bright-gilded by firelight, quick-voiced, restless, pursued wherever he moved by outbursts of laughter, Jerott understood, for the first time, a little of the machine.

Gabriel was away, so Lymond was soliciting their affections. But by the same token, licence was not without limits. Whether they realized it or not, no extremes of tongue or behaviour were being permitted, and no excess offensive to the Church. That would please Blacklock and Bell and Plummer and the spiritual faction; just as the sophisticated had been drawn by that prodigal joy at his own expense. . . . One step out of line and the edge would return to his voice. A respite, for a second, in the chorusing, and his eyes were chilly; hard as blue steel.

So he, Jerott, had been fighting the wind. You did not expect human values from a machine. You did not grow angry with a machine, or be disappointed or feel betrayed by it. You treated it with detachment and curiosity, as you would any soul-deprived object, and if it kicked you in the teeth, you side-stepped and kicked it back, harder.

*

At Algiers two weeks later, in the heat of August, the child Khaireddin was branded. The white-hot iron, with which Dragut stamped all his possessions, bore the first word of a famous verse from the Qur'ân, and the old corsair's initial. It was heated on a brazier just outside the women's quarters of the palace and impressed with care on the baby skin over the ribs and under the right arm. While it heated, the baby smiled, as he always did, up into the black face of the woman holding him, whose milk had fed him in his five months of life. The spare, curling floss on his head pressed on her arm as he craned upwards, blue eyes joyous, leaf-tongue jammed in the hinge of a pink-padded laugh. Then the eunuch, judging nicely with his eye, brought his hand down.

The uprush of screaming went on for a long time. It was followed by a monotonous throat-scraping squawk, like the hysteria of some large bird in anger that went on repeating all morning, thickening with hoarseness, pausing for a second, fifty seconds, as the baby slipped into sleep only to be pulled out again by pain, to scream and scream over again. The noise wakened even Oonagh O'Dwyer from her own fever, but she had not been told of the branding, and she was not likely to recognize her son's voice.

Her first and surest instinct, since he was born, had been to destroy him. For that reason she had denied herself every link with him; had hardly held him; had never fed him. Even had she wished, she had been too ill at first.

And then Dragut Rais had come to her, and had snapped his fingers absently over the infant and commenting lightly on his fairness, had asked her if Francis Crawford had sired him, or the Unbeliever who had visited her tent. And as she stared at him, stupid with weakness, she had discovered that nothing, indeed, had escaped the attention of her guards on those hot nights outside Tripoli.

One nocturnal visitor she had had; one treasured night of ultimate peace. And it was from Dragut Rais that she learned that her visitor had not been, could not have been, Francis Crawford.

After that, when she had made her first attempt to make away with first the baby, and then herself, she had botched it. The woman Güzel, coming too soon, had taken the child away and restored it, and next time, when she had persuaded the black woman Kedi to give him to her, the negress had run to Güzel and they had taken him from her again.

That time, she had looked at him; really looked, from the soft pulse that pattered in the silvery down over his brow to the curled fingers, each no larger than the top joint of her own. A line of milk, not her own, lay in the pink mouth under the sucking-blister and the lashes, that were to grow so thick and astonishing, were just beginning to spike the dark-blue, unfinished eyes. Then some wandering air-lock, toying with primitive nerves, sent one end of the milky mouth up in a merry, mischievous, sardonic grin. In four years, he would mean it. Now, he presented, innocently, the heart-breaking replica of the man whose son he was.

It had been a mistake to look. She had never been well after that, and they had kept the child from her, to live on alone into the barbaric unknown, if she died; to be a threat to the safety and happiness of his father, whatever happened. To Francis Crawford, this unknown son was a tragedy of which he must never learn. Oonagh O'Dwyer had let him think herself dead to free her pride from his pity. She had no desire to live on, in macabre comedy, as the fecund mother of his unwanted son.

But she did live on, and time passed, and the heat grew worse. Dragut and his household had moved elsewhere, but she was at first too ill to travel, then well enough only to be brought here to Algiers. She knew that somewhere in the palace Khaireddin was being tended, but there were other children, and nothing to tell her whether the bubbling purr she heard at night, of a baby full and content, was his.

Once or twice recently she heard, as well as Kedi's voice and her crooning, a baby laugh. It was an unexpected, deep, throaty chuckle which caught her breath and made the tears, stupidly, stream down into her black hair. But she did not know Khaireddin's scream, or the sound Francis Crawford might have made when once he too was branded for the galleys. So she did not guess. And when Kedi, her face bloated with weeping, told her one day that the baby was very ill, Oonagh did not ask why, but was merely stoically glad.

'Neither he nor I will live to burden his father,' she had said hardily to Güzel, standing above her cradling the unwitting morsel, months ago, in her arms.

And behind the veil, she had felt the other woman's level scrutiny, and heard her considered English: 'You believe so? In my experience, there is no person who does not blossom near to a child. You may find you have stolen what is most precious from your friend. Who will ever know Khaireddin's babyhood, except Kedi?'

And no one, she supposed, *had* known it, except Kedi, to whom he gave his first smile and at whom he laughed. Jolly, bountiful Kedi, who would do nevertheless whatever the eunuchs might order.

Soon after that Dragut called briefly on his way back to Turkey, and the third wife, who had ordered the branding, was turned off and sold. Güzel was not with him. The corsair, lighter by a stone for his summer raiding, went and stood over the silent cot where the yellow-haired baby lay, neither sleeping nor crying now, with silken, egg-blue stains under the strained, dark-blue eyes. He questioned Kedi, who gabbled, terrified, in faulty Arabic, and saw the maid who tended Oonagh each day. Then he retired to his own silk-hung room, and calling his scribe, dictated a letter to Scotland.

'The child is like to die, and the woman also. I return thy money since neither, being in poor health, seems worth the pain of preserving. As long as she lives I am ready, for the honour in which I hold thee, to allow the woman to stay. The child, if he lives, will be I fear of no value to his parents and of less than none to the Sultan. I intend, therefore, to sell him.'

And on Dragut's bearded face as he set his seal on the paper: the seal with his initials and the first word of a verse from the Qur'ân, was a most amiable smile.

XI

The Crown and the Anchor

(Falkland Palace and the Kyles of Bute, August 1552)

WHILE Dragut's letter to him was being written, Sir Graham Malett was still with the French Ambassador and the Queen Dowager of Scotland at Falkland, where he had been taken two weeks ago from the March meeting to bear M. d'Oisel company.

Mary of Guise set store by the big knight's advice. And when, at last, the subject of St Mary's was exhausted to her satisfaction, she found him intelligent on many subjects, and diffidently helpful on the matter of the St John revenues which Sandilands, crippled with sciatica, had gladly put in his hands.

The Queen Dowager of Scotland, no fool, had looked up from the pages, neatly covered with sums representing all the Knights Hospitallers' considerable income in Scotland, and had said, 'And the required tithe, you are saying, should go to Malta in the usual way? But how can this be done, when the English Priory at Clerkenwell is dissolved?'

'It cannot be done,' had said Gabriel, his clear gaze, smiling a little, on hers. 'Except by one of us taking it. A risky journey, and a destination no less . . . hazardous.'

Mary of Guise had heard all the reports of the Grand Master. She said, in a voice as calm as his own. 'Too hazardous, I should say. And meanwhile, the receipts pile up?'

Gabriel bowed. 'They are a constant anxiety to the Commandery. It seems to Sir James. . . .' He hesitated.

'Yes?'

'That since these are destined to uphold Mother Church, they should be placed in hands best qualified to do so. And forgive me, but in Scotland you have an outpost of the Religion besieged as virulently as Malta. For Holy Church, and His Most Christian Majesty who sustains her, the Priory of Torphichen would be content to make over all its tithe to Your Grace.'

'Instead of to His Eminence the Grand Master? You realize, Sir Graham,' said the Queen Mother, who liked to be sure of her income, 'that the Order may make serious protest, and even supersede yourself and Sir James?'

Gabriel's well-cut mouth tightened, and then relaxed again in a half-rueful smile. 'The day that the Order is strong enough to make a protest, and honest enough to carry it, I shall go back to Malta,' he said.

Mary of Guise, taller than most women, stood, and looked up at him as he rose. 'Good,' she said drily. 'Excellent. Then we shall have you with us, it seems, for some considerable time.'

*

Gabriel was still absent at Falkland when, following a string of small and estimable engagements, Lymond set out for the west, a full quarter of his company behind him, to join the pirate Thompson at last. With him he took the Moor Salablanca, Jerott, Alec Guthrie, Adam Blacklock, Fergie Hoddim and Abernethy. De Seurre and des Roches, practised seamen, were left at St Mary's, as also were Bell the doctor, Plummer and Tait.

Jerott, pointing out without modesty his own expertise, was told briefly that he was there as a tutor. Bell, who turned up unexpectedly at Greenock, was nearly sent back, but after explaining, red-faced, that there was a woman in Ireland he had in mind to visit, he was allowed to go, and Fergie Hoddim sent back in his place. Then they took a boat north-west, out of the mouth of the Clyde, and into the appointed place in the loch-ridden estuary, off the north end of the island of Bute, where Tamsín's roomy big merchantman, the *Magdalena*, was waiting.

The weather was good and Jerott, who had enjoyed the last few weeks, was grimly cheerful. As always, Gabriel's wise presence, his piety and gentle humour, and his infallible instincts in the field had been missed every day. The sharper discipline, the glittering tempo, of Lymond's handling was however a challenge that he liked, although on some the confident, cutting intelligence grated. Lymond made no concessions, to Tait, to Hoddim, to Plummer. At St Mary's he treated them as adults, and equal. In the field he demanded unquestioning obedience and got it, now, even from Alec Guthrie, with no arguments until later. Only the artist Blacklock, quietly mutinous, had begun to drink, and went on with it, in muddled defiance, in spite of warnings. When he began, obviously, to add to this some sort of drug, Lymond turned him out.

He didn't go. In silence, grim with embarrassment, the other officers of St Mary's went about their business aware of Adam Blacklock, his shaking hands locked together, sitting before the empty grate, alone with nothing to do; wandering through the stables, touching the horses, or standing, biting his lip, watching his friends as they shot.

At the end of the first day he went to bed as usual, but without his drugs, and woke shouting, his face like a child's. Bell got to him

363

quickly, holding him down, but Jerott went straight for Lymond.

There was no need to wake him. Lymond was still up, fully dressed, and Archie Abernethy with him. As Jerott began to speak, he heard Abernethy slip out, and in a moment he returned. Salablanca was behind him, with Blacklock in his arms. Then Jerott was sent away.

What happened in Lymond's room Jerott never knew; but next day the artist was back among them, paper-white but reasonably steady, and daily he improved. Taking him to sea was less, Jerott guessed, a staple in his training than a realistic acceptance of the fact that he never let Lymond, if he could help it, out of his sight. According to Randy Bell, grinning, it was because Lymond and Archie Abernethy between them were doubling his supply of drugs. In Jerott's own mind, it was another step in Lymond's battle to eclipse Gabriel. And since the machine was more and more engaging his interest, he opened the subject on the way to the west coast. 'Satisfy my curiosity. If you dislike him so, why did you bring Graham Malett from Malta? And if you are intent on outstripping him, why make no effort to supplant him in Malta? Until the last weeks, he tried to protect the Grand Master. You could have led a pretty revolt, had you wished.'

Lymond turned a solemn blue eye in his direction. Filing through the low hill passes north and west, the company was well strung out, with their scouts on all sides as a matter of course; and Alec Guthrie had been given the lead, freeing Lymond to move as he wished. Riding, at present, a little to one side of his men at arms and out of earshot, Lymond had a perfect opportunity to explain, if he cared.

And apparently he did, for after a moment he said, the laughter plain now in his voice, 'It's a tempting piece of analysis, Jerott. If I were as bloody jealous of our friend Gabriel in Malta as I appear to be here, what should I have done to supplant him ...? All right. What? Not oppose the Grand Master, for one thing. But the opposite. Infiltrate at the top, my dear. I should have made the Grand Master my indispensable friend.'

'You couldn't,' said Jerott bluntly. 'Juan de Homedès has truck with Spanish knights only.'

'Then,' said Lymond cheerfully, 'I should have treated him to my well-known imitation of a Spanish knight and, having gained his confidence, I should begin to throw doubts on both the sanctity of friend Gabriel's aims, and the quality of his leadership. And since no breath of criticism, of course, has ever touched him in either respect, evidence would have to be manufactured.'

'How?' said Jerott.

Lymond glanced at him. 'It isn't difficult to make someone look incompetent,' he said. 'If you really try. Recall how Sir Graham looked at Christmas, for example, when he ran us out of fuel supplies.'

'But—' Jerott began.

'That wasn't his fault, you were about to say. Exactly,' said Lymond, amused. 'Further, his friends must be suborned. Yourself, for example. If you had a weakness, which God knows you have not, I should pander to it, until you relied on me and no one but me.'

'Like Adam Blacklock?' said Jerott.

'Maybe,' said Lymond; but not quite so readily this time, Jerott happily noted, and the sidelong glance was pretty sharp. But he resumed, none the less. 'All right. I have undermined the confidence of his chief, his professional reputation, the regard of his friends. I take two other steps. I cast doubt on the purity of his morals, and I engage him and his friends in some activity detrimental to the Master's welfare.'

'But—'

'But his morals are impeccable, so we have to slip a nun into his bed and get him, perhaps, to do something faintly reprehensible to help a friend.'

'Like helping to police a parcel of English whores?' said Jerott.

'Perhaps. And finally,' said Lymond, with care, 'I should have consolidated my position as the Grand Master's right-hand man by getting rid of all rivals, or setting them at each other's throats, so that when the dust died away I should be sitting in the Grand Master's lodging at Birgu, invulnerable.'

'But you did none of this,' said Jerott. 'In Malta, you stood aside and watched. Why?'

Lymond, reined in to move along the line, looked back. 'Another time, Torquemada.'

A new voice said, 'No. I should like to know too.' And Adam Blacklock rode between them.

Speculatively, Lymond looked from Blacklock to Blyth. 'I see. How much of that did you hear?'

'All of it. Why didn't you fight on Malta? I thought you did.'

'I thought I did too. Jerott means, why didn't I throw over Juan de Homedès single-handed. The answer is, Jerott, that I went as an observer for France. And on my own account I wished to see the workings of your faith.'

Jerott's black brows were level. 'Rubbish. Or why turn from it now? You know why Gabriel is really here. You know why he persists against all the bloody insolence and heartache to win you. Would you fight at his side, then, to recover Malta?'

Across Blacklock's silent head, Lymond's gaze was turned full on the importunate friend of his boyhood. 'Did Malett direct you to ask that?'

'No,' said Jerott with anger. 'He didn't. I should still like an answer. Would you?'

'When Gabriel asks me,' said Lymond, 'I shall tell him.' He looked, to Blacklock's eyes, suddenly tired, but Jerott, heedless, noticed nothing. He opened his mouth but Lymond, smiling a little, forestalled him.

'I believe,' he said, 'that what will save Malta is a great and selfless leader, and a man of faith.'

The look of contempt which had crossed Jerott's magnificent face did not alter. 'You and Gabriel, side by side?' he said. 'For God's sake, let's keep our senses. Somewhere, no doubt, there is a great and selfless leader. But you are a mercenary.'

'I didn't think, somehow, that you approved of Gabriel's plan,' said Lymond, and smiled suddenly. 'But I challenge your definition, all the same. A mercenary fights for a living, and for love of battle.'

'Well?' Jerott was not impressed. 'You have, I suppose, other sources of easy money. But you love all this.'

He waved his arm. All about them, against the bright, sharp green of the bracken, the purpling sage of the heather, the brown roots and green mosses, twinkled the steel of armed men. All about them, above the trickle of stream and piping of curlew and trill of lark came the suck and pull of hooves in soft ground, the chink of sword and tinkle of bit and creak of leather, the jangle of harness and grumble of talking voices, with voices raised to call, to direct, to comment, to quip, criss-crossing the haugh. And all the time, as they rode, the brown faceless men up and down the valley watched where Lymond's horse moved, with his two colleagues. A hand raised, one sign, and they would move to his will: to stop a battle or start one; to save lives or to kill. 'You love all this!' said Jerott.

'*Love it!*' said Lymond, and Adam Blacklock looked up sharply.

Recalled to himself, Francis Crawford smiled, a little wryly, and dropped his voice. 'An overdose of applied conjecture. I'm sorry. The answer, Jerott, is that I don't find this particularly enjoyable.'

Jerott's gaze didn't move. 'What do you miss? Women?'

Lymond looked ahead. 'The point you always seem to be making, Jerott, is that I don't lack them enough. No, I don't miss fair company. Look what I've got instead.'

'Then what?' Jerott pursued, ignoring utterly Blacklock's silent advice to be quiet.

'Jerott, for God's sake! Are you doing this for a wager?' said Lymond, his patience gone at last. 'What does anyone want out of life? What kind of freak do you suppose I am? I miss books and good verse and decent talk. I miss women, to speak to, not to rape; and children, and men creating things instead of destroying them. And from the time I wake until the time I find I can't go to sleep there is the void—the bloody void where there was no music today and none yesterday and no prospect of any tomorrow, or tomorrow, or next God-damned year.'

He stopped. Adam Blacklock, saying nothing, looked down; and even Jerott, after the first moments, removed his troubled gaze. Then, as their horses paced evenly on, Jerott Blyth said blankly, '*Music?*'

But Lymond, whatever his motives, had by now had more than enough. Touching his spurs to the big horse, he shot ahead without answering, and Blyth and Blacklock were left in silence, riding behind.

*

Thompson, it was at once obvious, was doing well. The *Magdalena*, floating under bare poles in a leafy anchorage in the Kyles of Bute, was a large and roomy merchantman with holds for salt and pitch and potash and wool and hides and malmsey and salt fish, and a good false bottom for contraband. Jerott, looking her over as he awaited his turn up the ladder, thought that she might have quite a comfortable turn of speed to her, as well as God knew what hidden arms. From where he stood a brass falcon, not even covered, flashed in the sun.

Downstairs in Thompson's cabin, beside the one he and Lymond would share, Jerott sat next to the pirate's horny grey parrot, his feet on an Indian prayer rug and a chipped earthenware beaker of wine in his hands, and toasted the forthcoming voyage. Thompson, whose own cup was solid chased silver devoted to the nude female form, drained it and looked pointedly at the full mug idling in Lymond's hands.

'Oh, no,' said Lymond, putting it down. 'I'm not going through all that again. Jockie, I have one condition to make. I want these men to become good fighting seamen. I don't want them in Waterford jail.'

'Never heard of it,' said the captain of the *Magdalena* equably. Solid, changeless, brown as a pippin above the black, salt-blasted beard, he pinned Lymond with the shrewdest black eyes in the Irish Sea, and slapped his cup down.

'No. You damned near run it, you liar,' said Lymond. 'What cargo have you got?'

'None. We're on our way to Lambay to load. Linen yarn and some wool, for Antwerp.'

'I thought the Head of Howth was Logan's bailiwick,' said Lymond. 'And how in God's name do you expect to get into and out of Antwerp unhung? Every customar in the Baltic is ready to eat you out of a poke.'

'The *Magdalena*,' said the pirate Thompson, opening his black eyes wide, 'is no yin o' Logan's auld buckets to stop weans with and steal their sweeties. The *Magdalena* is a clean ship, that pays her charges and dips her bit flag when she should; and Stephenson there is her captain. In port, ye understand. . . . I was in Antwerp the other week.'

'And that's a bloody lie,' said Lymond.

'*And* shipped a cargo of gunpowder and fifty barrels of sulphur,' said Thompson.

'From *Antwerp*?' said Jerott, avoiding Lymond's eye. 'But that's impossible. The Emperor's desperate for munitions for all his own commitments. He stopped all exports of powder from the Low Countries months ago. Where in God's name were you taking it to? England?'

'No,' said Thompson, gratified. He sniffed, and lifting the flagon, slopped the beautiful wine into Jerott's cup and his own. 'Mind, ye'd get a fair price, for they're desperate too, but they ken baith me and Stephenson, ye'll understand. No. I took it to—' He stopped. 'Aye, aye. I forgot it was Francis Crawford. It was a rare bit o' dialogue, and ye fair had me going, at that. Mind your ain God-damned business. Yon Hough Isa was a rare cook!'

Lymond, unperturbed, raised his hand with the sapphire. 'You don't want it back?'

'No, no. It was a fair bargain. I'd gie ye another for the lassie ye had that other night, though.'

'Not before the children,' said Lymond, 'you damned inquisitive old rake. And you were in Djerba. The place stinks of carob seeds, and I know the man that put the dimples in the ladies' bottoms on that cup. .... It is not considered ethical to supply arms to the infidel. Jerott will tell you. But I'll wager anything you like they paid you in French money.'

There was a hoarse sound, which Jerott recognized after a moment as laughter, and then the pirate heaved himself up. 'Sharp as rat's teeth, aren't ye? We'll have a grand passage. I'll guarantee nobody'll jail Thompson this trip, but we'll no lack for fun forbye. .... There's a friend o' yours here. Stopped by at Brest, and wouldna be hindered from coming when he heard you were to be aboard.'

'Then I hope to God he's discreet,' said Lymond, staring. Thompson, stepping forward, flung open the door.

'I am a Frenchman, so therefore by nature discreet. Particularly,' said Nicolas de Nicolay, Geographer to His Most Christian Majesty of France, stepping through the doorway, his brown, inquisitive face alight, 'when agitating the feet. How are you, *mon brave*?' And jumping forward on his spry velvet toes, he embraced first Lymond and then Jerott on both cheeks.

But it was not to be a lingering reunion. One had time to remember the hospital at Birgu, from which de Nicolay had extracted Lymond from the mortuary; the Turkish camp at Tripoli; the fated homeward journey back to Malta. Jerott, catching the little man's bright eyes on him more than once, curious under the runic crest of grey hair, wondered if to an onlooker it was strange, and even despicable,

368

this abrupt departure from Malta of a knight dedicated as he had been.

But his principles had not altered. Malta had receded, because it was no longer the centre of his religion. It was no longer worthy of his allegiance: that was to an ideal, to his Faith, as represented by Gabriel here.

For the rest, his life was St Mary's. He found it satisfying; more than absorbing. He was proud of the company and of his share in it. He looked forward to what it could do. But it was purely secular in its objects, and in a way, as Lymond had shrewdly guessed, he dreaded this free brotherhood being forced into the mould of the Religion. And to restore Malta, he was beginning to see, as Lymond saw, you needed true faith—faith to soften the facts, as well as the risks. If you saw too clearly. . . . What was he thinking? He must bring his mind back to the *Magdalena*, and Thompson, agitating to be off. . . . But what he had been about to conclude was, surely, more important still. *If you saw too clearly, you might not wish to restore Malta at all*.

It was then that Fergie Hoddim, projecting his courtroom voice from a dinghy far below in the smooth waters of the Kyle, brought first Thompson, and then his guests out on deck. After an interval of shouting, a ladder was thrown down to him and he came up, with all the speed of a man trained at St Mary's. At the top, he stepped down on the deck, dug into his jerkin, and produced a folded packet for Lymond.

It was a message from the Queen Dowager of Scotland, written at Falkland, sent on to St Mary's and thence carried to Greenock where the bearer, Ross Herald, looking green in the pitching dinghy, had been thankful to find one of Lymond's own men about to return.

In it was a peremptory command to Francis Crawford of Lymond, Comte de Sevigny, to present himself at once, on pain of horning, at the Palace of Falkland, to answer to Her Grace for certain activities for which he had been recently responsible.

Tossing it to Jerott to read, Lymond turned to the *Magdalena's* captain. 'Have a good trip,' he said. 'You go alone. Jerott will tell you why. Adam, you will go ashore with me now, along with Salablanca, and ride with me to Falkland. Jerott, you have control, under Thompson, of the St Mary's men, and will act as the captain's officer between him and them. I shall meet the *Magdalena* when you come back, or send Adam if I can't. Jockie, I have some private advice for you, which you don't deserve. . . .'

To the men on the crowded decks, watching, the exchange between Thompson and Lymond appeared to take a long time and to be remarkably mirthless in character. By the time Lymond swung himself down the ladder, waving briefly to the rest at the rails, Adam Blacklock was already in the boat with his possessions, and Salablanca lending a hand with the dinghy's small sail, while Robbie

Forman, Ross Herald, sat rigid beneath. Then, in a moment, it seemed, the boom swung over, the sheet tightened, and the little boat veered off and vanished behind the green trees of Bute.

*

Because of the herald, Adam Blacklock kept his thoughts to himself during the journey upriver, and Lymond hardly spoke at all, except to make some desultory conversation with Forman and later, at the stables at Dumbarton, to ask Adam if the long ride to Falkland would be too much for his weak leg. Adam answered curtly, once he got the consonant out, that it would not; and they were off, riding as fast as he ever wished to travel again, with Salablanca and the baggage horses behind.

Night overtook them at Stirling; and to save the protesting bones of Ross Herald who had, after all, just ridden across half the Lowlands to fetch them, Lymond allowed a few hours' rest in a tavern bed. Then, with fresh horses, they set out again.

Just before they did so, waiting with Salablanca for Robbie Forman to come into the yard, Adam seized the moment to ask one at least of his questions. 'Why the hurry? Normal travelling speed, surely, is all the Queen Dowager would expect?'

'There is someone ahead of us,' said Lymond.

'You want to c-catch him?'

'I want to get to Falkland before him. Here is Forman,' was all Lymond said.

Two hours later, Ross Herald, grey with fatigue and the horrors of the Clyde estuary, fell by the wayside; and watching Lymond's expression as he took leave of him, tucked up moaning in a friend's bed at Kinross, Adam appreciated suddenly one at least of his reasons for speed. Patience being one of the prime requisites of the artist, he waited, riding in silence, until Lymond said briefly, 'You don't have to be so damned tactful. You haven't had a drink for four days. Have you?'

'No.'

'And Bell's little remedies are finished with. So you may consider yourself trustworthy. Ever heard of George Paris?'

Anyone who had been in France knew that. 'He was an agent,' said Blacklock, wasting no more time than Lymond did. 'For those Irish lords wishing F-French or Scottish help to throw off the English overlordship in Ireland. I don't know what he does now.'

'He's a double agent,' said Lymond. 'Now that French interest is falling off he's trying England for his pension. Thompson got wind of it through some old Irish cronies of his who heard from some exiled friends in London. Unhappily, Thompson's hands are tied because

370

he's mixed up in some illegal trading with Paris and one of Paris's Irish rebel friends, Cormac O'Connor. . . .' He glanced round.

'Oh,' said Adam Blacklock, just too late.

'I had forgotten,' said Francis Crawford with precision, 'what bloody gossip-mongering old women soldiers were. I take it the whole company knows about Oonagh O'Dwyer?'

There was a second's pause. 'I know that she was Cormac O'Connor's mistress,' said Adam.

'I'm damned sure you do, and enough to write a book about, besides. You realize then that Cormac O'Connor is no bloodbrother of mine, since I helped her to get away from him. When that attempt to set himself up as the saviour of Ireland failed, he resorted to petty intrigue and some quick ways of raising money, such as Thompson's insurance scheme. Because he's implicated in this, his friends in Ireland won't betray Paris, and neither will he, unless he's pushed to it. Paris has too much evidence against him in his insurance swindle. On the other hand, if Paris was going to be exposed anyway, O'Connor might get his oar in first, on the premise that no one will look too closely at a small swindle if he hands them a double agent on a plate.'

'And *is* Paris likely to be exposed?' asked Adam.

'It's not . . . unlikely,' said Lymond, pausing for the first time. 'I've told Thompson to sever his connexion with the pair of them and with all his other clients right away. Not that that's a great deal of good. Paris must have enough evidence against Thompson alone to send him to the Tolbooth for life.'

'And Paris lives in Ireland? Why doesn't Thompson or someone visit him and force him, if necessary, to hand over all the incriminating papers?' said Blacklock; and meeting Lymond's sardonic blue gaze, realized he had been naïve.

'Why the hell do you think I've been breaking my neck to get the *Magdalena* to sea with the lot of you this week? Paris is due in Scotland next month, and I'm willing to wager the *Magdalena*'s skiffs will be up every creek in Ireland hunting for him before Thompson brings her back. He was a worried man when we left him yesterday, which is no more than the crafty old profligate deserves.'

'And if he doesn't find Paris in Ireland?'

'Then we shall have to wait until Paris comes to Scotland, and persuade my favourite agent to give us his records then, won't we? Which will in turn warn him that exposure is in the air, and make us his criminal associates . . . syndication with Thompson is proving rather expensive,' said Francis Crawford reflectively. 'I feel that our wellbeing, yours and mine, is about to be sacrificed for the greater good, and I am not prepared to sanction it, just yet. Why do you stay with me?'

It was the kind of sudden question that made his stammer worse. Eventually, Adam got it out. 'I have a f-fancy to draw you. Let us say.'

'You've drawn me hundreds of times. You have a sixth sense for evil, haven't you, Adam? Gabriel was right when he said you shouldn't have been a soldier. Your eye tells your brain too much. I should have left you on board. You haven't sketched Randy. Or any of the lot at St Mary's now.'

'No,' said Adam. There was a long silence, broken by Lymond laughing softly. 'Your company is most disarming, Adam. How many rages would Jerott have achieved by now? But you are entitled to ask the obvious question and expect an answer, at least.'

Adam Blacklock smiled. 'I don't like t-trouble, that's all. All right. Who is the man we were following, and have now passed, since our pace has dropped to a little less than murderous?'

Lymond grinned. 'Yes, we've passed him. Didn't you see him, a thick black tree of a man at the last posting-station, on a broken-down hack? The poor beast is supporting a King's thigh, my boy. That great, bouncing basthoon of an Irishman on his way, too, to Falkland is my brutish friend Cormac O'Connor.'

'Ah. We are heading for an unp-pleasantness,' said Adam Blacklock.

'We are heading for that, anyway, I suspect,' said Lymond cheerfully. 'The Queen Mother doesn't send out orders of this kind just to make Robbie Forman sea-sick. . . . What do you think is going wrong at St Mary's at this moment?'

'Why should anything be going wrong at St Mary's?' said Blacklock, after a moment.

'Why indeed?' said Lymond. 'I panic easily, that's all. I don't know how long the Queen Dowager will keep me, but if Gabriel is still at Falkland, you had better find him and wait there until I come.'

'And O'Connor?' said Adam.

'Thompson brought him. He was on the *Magdalena* when she arrived, but disembarked, encouraged by Jock, before we came on board. Thompson thinks he has merely come to petition the Queen Mother for rebel money, and the visit will be short. On the other hand, he may be making up his mind to betray Paris soon. And if he is, I rather want to dissuade him . . . but without Ross Herald at my elbow, for choice. . . . It would be nice, Adam, if you could make a cartoon of Cormac O'Connor's resolves for me.'

'Why? Am I likely to meet him?'

'My dear man, Falkland is a village round a palace,' said Lymond. 'Nothing more. Put Cormac O'Connor in a back street in London, and you would meet him in a quarter of an hour. He's that kind of man.'

XII

The Crown and the Anchorite

(Falkland Palace, August 1552)

FALKLAND was full. The pepperpot towers of the palace, the statues and the handsome grilled French windows rose from a blue haze of woodsmoke. Every lodging and inn in the little burgh was filled with the Queen Dowager's staff and courtiers. Only because he had no need of a room and a lethal kind of charm when he chose to use it, was Francis Crawford able to command a meal for himself and his companions on arrival at the principal tavern in the little square.

He had no need of a room because he had found two invitations waiting for him: one from Sir Graham Malett, who was staying in the Order's lodging in Falkland, and one from Robert Beaton of Creich, Keeper of Falkland, who happened also to be brother to Janet Beaton, wife of Buccleuch. And he had leisure to have a meal because he had learned, on reporting to the palace, that the Queen Dowager was not yet prepared to see him.

There were people he knew in the tavern: a surprising collection of gentlemen of the chamber off duty, merchants, men of the Church, and lairds from Fife, the Lothians and the Merse. Salablanca had made himself scarce. Adam, sitting comfortably tired in the late afternoon sunshine outside the tavern door, a pot of wine and a wedge of bread and mutton on the board in front of him, was introduced to a number of strangers who came out from the smoky turmoil inside to speak to his leader. Twice a friend of his own came across to greet him.

Inevitably, after a while, he lost Lymond altogether to the company inside. Watching him through the open window moving desultorily, wine in hand, from table to table, Adam guessed that a little well-concealed research into the atmosphere at the palace was going on and stretching his booted legs comfortably, left Lymond to it. It was then that, idly watching the cobbled street that led past the palace, he saw a little group of horsemen shouldering their way through the crowds, and recognized in the lead the burly, black-browed hulk whom Lymond had called Cormac O'Connor.

He had a moment, perhaps, in which to wonder whether it was coincidence that Oonagh O'Dwyer's lover was making direct for the tavern where Lymond was. Then, as the group arrived, dismounted and silently surrounded him, he realized that Cormac O'Connor, too, had used his eyes on the journey from the *Magdalena*, and that he himself, sitting outside the inn door, had been as good as a signpost. Then the table, with his food on it, was kicked rattling to the ground, and a knotted, gloved hand travelled casually for the pit of his stomach. 'Faix, we know ye can run,' said the son of kings, while his companions laughed. 'Can ye jump now, as well?'

Adam Blacklock might have been tired, might have been heavy with food, did certainly have his weaknesses. But after a season at St Mary's, assault technique was not one of them. The big Irishman's fist didn't reach the cloth over Adam's hard belly. Instead, his wrist was seized in a triangle of iron: there were two quick movements, and before the grin was off his face Cormac hit the inn wall behind Blacklock with a crash, and Adam, his sword and dagger both out and the upset table between himself and O'Connor's six men, was waiting watchfully for O'Connor to pick himself up.

The inn door was at his back, but Adam didn't trouble to call. He took O'Connor's next rush with elbow and sword, and spun round in time to spike with his dagger point the man who came in at him over the table. The man screamed and O'Connor spat at him in Gaelic as he cleared the table with a kick and, sword out, came shoulder to shoulder with two others at Adam. A voice behind Adam's shoulder, gently rebuking, said, 'Cormac dear: you don't want to fight us *all*, do you? It's so hot for hopping about.' And Lymond, loitering in the tavern doorway with a growing crowd of spectators, raised his eyebrows at the Irishman, whose sword-hand slowly fell. 'Christ, it's the singin' acrobat, playin' the cat's melody behind the strong arm of his nurse,' said Cormac O'Connor, and ignoring both Blacklock and his men, waiting watchfully for orders, he walked slowly forward to Francis Crawford.

Lymond's level blue gaze did not shift from the big, bronzed, sweating frame. He waited, dry as ash, with his peculiar bleached elegance that Adam had long since given up trying to capture, and said eventually, 'Adam defends himself, not me; and does it most ably, as you have noticed. Would you care to pick your friend up? They get *hysterical* about litter. Brawling, too,' he added, as an afterthought.

'Do you tell me?' said Cormac O'Connor. He said it very softly, but each word fell like a small, starving leech into the gossip-gorged body of Falkland. 'And what do they say, my delicate fellow, what do they say of the little, whispering, crawling person that would steal a woman, and throw her aside, and leave her drowned in the weeds of a sea that is not her own, to roll from shore to shore of far-off lands for ever more? Do they care about tidiness in Tripoli,' said Cormac O'Connor, 'when they catch her finger-bones and her long black hair in their nets?'

Listening in silence, the Irishmen shuffling beside him, Adam Blacklock wondered if any other man there knew that they spoke of Oonagh O'Dwyer. Nicolas de Nicolay had called her a green-eyed morrow, and had told, too, of the misery of her life with this same Cormac O'Connor, and the blue bruises she wore from head to foot when she had sailed for Malta. Yet the tears stood in Cormac O'Connor's eyes, although Lymond's remained blue and openly contemptuous. Francis Crawford said, 'Of course. I had forgotten we had something in common. You know, by the way, that if you start a disturbance here, you are liable to be arrested?'

The Irishman smiled, and his big hand, covered with coarse pelt, fondled the hilt of his sword. 'It would be worth it,' he said.

'And your six friends? Do they think so?'

'This is between you and me,' said Cormac O'Connor.

'And George Paris,' said Lymond, smiling again with his lips. 'That well-known friend of Scotland and France. You have a red-head with you these days, I'm told. Yes? Then don't give her my address when the Queen Dowager sends for you; that's all I ask.'

But already the big hand on the sword-hilt had tightened, and the wet, round eyes narrowed. 'I should maybe remember my sweet Christian mother, and forget the wrongs others have done me? Is there ill-will in you?'

'Candidly,' said Lymond, 'I don't want to be arrested either. Suppose we let the dead rest, and you come and drink to red hair with me?' And warily, side by side, they entered the inn, pressing through a jocular crowd, while O'Connor's six men, the wounded one stumbling among them, shuffled off to the yard and Adam Blacklock, putting up his sword in some surprise, found himself the centre of a little group who righted his table, brought him food and besought him to throw them, one by one.

'How was it done?' said Lymond later when, O'Connor gone and the tavern emptied for the evening audience, they had the common-room nearly to themselves. 'How is anything done with that kind? Fear and self-interest, that's all. His betrayal of Paris is the coin he proposes to use to buy himself out of the insurance swindle. I left him in doubt about whether, in fact, the Queen Dowager doesn't know about Paris already. He isn't sure how much I know, but equally he isn't sure that, if he has picked me up rightly, he hasn't lost the only bargaining power he had to get the Queen Dowager's favour. It was,' said Lymond gravely, 'a very ambiguous conversation.'

375

'In these surroundings, it would seem quite plausible,' said Blacklock. The cunning of it shook him a little, as always. He said, 'You haven't exactly made him a friend, but you've certainly tamed him. And if he thinks the Queen Dowager knows all about Paris, he won't be very anxious to present himself at the palace now. . . . And yet he would have killed you, at the start.'

'He may change his mind,' said Lymond. Lying back in his chair in the flickering candlelight, waiting for Graham Malett to call, he sounded lazy as a cat. 'Or have it changed for him. That's your little task. Watch him for me. As for killing me—'

Lymond paused, and Adam thought, Of course. The expertise of St Mary's. Alone, O'Connor would have had no chance. And through him ran again the frisson of pleasure he had felt at his own sweet automatic response to violence, and the pang of fear that always followed, because of that joy.

'As for killing me,' Lymond was still saying, half to himself, 'O'Connor could have done it all right, in that first second, come hell or Adam Blacklock . . . if he had loved Oonagh enough. With one arm, with twenty against him, he should have run me straight through.'

For a moment, Adam was speechless. Then he said, 'Did you believe that when you came out of the inn at my back?'

Francis Crawford inspected him curiously. 'Yes, of course,' he said. 'Why? Dissimulation is a bastard art beloved of bores. All the same. . . .' He stopped, half changing his mind.

'What?' said Adam flatly.

'You do not know,' said Lymond drily, 'how close *I* came to killing *him*.'

*

Later that evening Graham Malett called to reaffirm his warmly offered hospitality; and on his heels Robert Beaton with his sister Grizel.

Watching Lymond and Gabriel together in the empty inn common-room, Adam heard that he was to stay in Gabriel's tall crooked house of St John, while Lymond lodged a dozen miles away at Beaton's castle of Creich. Lymond's audience would take place in the morning, Gabriel thought; and before the others arrived, the big knight, in his gentle voice, set himself to warn Lymond about this; about the Queen's desire to rule Scotland for her daughter with French help; about her readiness to hand out favours to every faction and ease the discomfort of all, friend or enemy, who might help her achieve this end.

'I've heard a rumour or two to that effect,' Lymond said; and

Gabriel struck his brow in despair. 'Of course. Your brother is on the Council. And you probably knew the Queen Mother quite well in France. . . . I am a fool. It is childish. My head is being turned by the illusion that I am at the centre of great affairs, and the truth is that I am nothing of the sort: merely enjoying Jimmy Sandilands's small shoes. I'm giving no more advice.' And, smiling up at Lymond from the low arm where he had perched himself, Graham Malett touched him gently on the arm. 'You are looking well. I'm glad. Thank God you are sleeping.'

There was a gloomy silence. Then, 'At the moment, I rather wish I were,' Lymond said, and removing his arm, walked to the tavern door where Blacklock was waiting, his colour high, to accompany Gabriel home.

Graham Malett stayed exactly as he was. 'No. Isn't it time we had all this out in the open?' he said quietly. 'Blacklock won't mind. You feel I am a rival, Francis; some kind of contestant in your personal popularity stakes. It reaches such proportions now that you cannot sleep without imagining I am wresting your leadership from you. . . . You realize, don't you, that if I had not arranged to have myself called away at intervals, such as now, you would have made yourself ill?'

'Your consideration,' said Lymond, 'is infinite. O how dear are thy thoughts towards me, O strong God! How great is the sum thereof! I would recount them, but they are more than the sand; and Adam, I believe, is quite ready. . . .'

Graham Malett rose then to his full, golden height. 'Francis. . . . You are St Mary's. You and no other. It sounds trite, but it is precisely true. I don't know your secret. There is no spiritual bond between you and your company: no common faith, no rites, no rules of chivalry. How is it done?'

'Charm of personality,' said Lymond. 'Allied to a generous wage scale. Blacklock and I are quite convinced that you have no designs on St Mary's. Do you mind if . . . ?'

'I mind,' said Gabriel. He was rather pale. 'God knows how I mind that you have no belief. You worship strength, do you not? Will you not believe that allied to faith, strength will increase itself tenfold? All the history of Holy Church proves it.'

Always before Lymond had resisted this particular challenge; always before he had remained outside Gabriel's arguments, a tolerant neutral. Now he said, calmly, standing still before the inn parlour door, 'History shows, too, great feats of endurance without mystery. What you leave undone, trusting to faith, you would be better to make sure of beforehand.'

'I hope we all strive for perfection,' said Gabriel. 'Shoddy work earns no miracles, surely. But we are human. We can achieve so much only. With our knowledge of divine grace within us, we may become more than human, that is all.'

'Why ascribe it all to the Divinity?' Lymond asked. He was speaking very quietly, without passion, and although he appeared to have forgotten Blacklock's presence, Adam wondered, suddenly if some part of this was intended for him as, the other day, riding in concourse to Bute, Lymond had talked circuitously for Jerott's benefit, and Jerott had not understood. So, 'Why?' Lymond said, and coming back, roved to the fireplace and turned, mild inquiry in his veiled eyes. 'Zest and power and exhilaration may spring from so much that is far from divine. Faith in one's cause, one's leader, one's love would equally do.'

Under Gabriel's pure, fine-grained skin a trace of colour had risen. He said in his deep voice, 'All these things are fallible.'

'Of course they are,' said Lymond. Outside in the yard they could hear the movement of feet and fresh voices which meant that Robert Beaton had come. 'But are the channels of Holy Church immune to error? Her priests, her offices, her very tenets are subject to doubt. Her interpreters are only human, and most souls, however aspiring, follow the human instrument, not the belief. ... If men's faith in Gabriel were shaken,' said Francis Crawford blandly, smiling a little, 'would men follow an abstract faith into battle so readily?'

There was a little pause. Then Gabriel said, strain showing for the first time in the beautiful voice, 'Francis. ... Of course the humble open their hearts to the simulacrum, to the identity they know of and understand. It is for them that the Saints listen, and Our Lady; for them the greatest leader of all time, who will never fail them: Our Lord Jesus Christ.'

The voices had reached outside the door. Lymond glanced at Adam Blacklock and strolling forward, lifted a hand to the latch. 'Well?' said Graham Malett. He had risen.

'Who is more important to Jerott Blyth?' Lymond said smoothly. 'You or Christ?' And ignoring Gabriel's wordless, wretched appeal, opened the door.

Grizel Beaton had met Lymond once since her husband was killed. Buccleuch, raging, had blamed Francis Crawford for his death, but Janet her sister had said roundly that Wat Scott had been leaping to conclusions as usual; horns blowing like a fuller's shop and both feet bang in the midden.

She was inclined to believe Janet. It had been a grand marriage, but in a prosaic way, taught by experience, she had not looked for it to go on for ever. Men had a chancy time of it, and Scotts more than most. She had her children. There were maybe two things she regretted. She had just about got him into her way of doing things and there it was, all to waste. And he had been an uncommonly dear lad.

378

So she gave her hand firmly enough to Francis Crawford, and greeted Adam Blacklock while her brother, at her back, was making himself known. And only then, looking further into the room, did she see the tall, diffident figure of the knight who had become her welcome visitor at Kincurd, and who three months before had ridden, wounded himself, to bring her the news of Will's death.

'Graham!' said Grizel Beaton, her definite voice diminished, even in simple surprise. And going forward, red in her face, she lifted her cheek to be kissed.

Women! thought Adam Blacklock disgustedly, and wondered if Lymond had noticed. 'Man is a being of varied, manifold and inconstant nature. And woman, by God, is a match for him.'

Shortly after that, when Beaton and his sister had gone, taking Lymond with them, Adam Blacklock left in his turn to accompany Gabriel to his lodging nearby.

Graham Malett looked tired. Nothing had been said, by Blacklock or by Gabriel himself, about that queer ten minutes back in the inn when he and Lymond had crossed metaphysical swords; but the light which had gone then from Malett's calm face had never returned. And although he attended Adam with every courtesy and installed him in his comfortable chamber with care, it was not long before the Knight Grand Cross excused himself gently and Adam, passing a moment later, saw him through the open door of his room, his shoulders bent, his face hidden, kneeling in silence before the old altar he had dragged over half Europe with his chests.

*

At eight o'clock the following morning, Francis Crawford was summoned to the Presence Chamber of Mary of Guise, Dowager of Scotland. And whether he wished then for Gabriel's advice, or his prayers, no one was likely to know.

Falkland Palace, the old royal hunting lodge where the Queen Dowager's husband had died, was all hers now: the lovely grilled French façade; the courtyard lined on three sides by the wings of her husband's father and grandfather with their medallions and their high decorated dormers; with the butts, the royal tennis courts, the stables, and the thick, flowery forest of Falkland with its echoes of Stewart voices between the lawns and the river. It was hers, and it was where she preferred to stay, above all else.

And because it was crowded, because it was private, because it was hers, her lords of the Privy Council and her Governor loathed it. But Mary of Guise was here, and her friend the French Ambassador was here, and his Grace the Earl of Arran, Governor of Scotland, had gone north in June and would be in Aberdeen for at least a month yet, so the Queen Mother had no intention of moving.

She had no intention, either, of allowing Francis Crawford to live any longer without enduring, for once, the full and forbidding dominance of the throne. But if Lymond suspected it, he gave no sign at all. He stood on the threshold of the Queen's Presence Chamber as his names were announced and made the first of the three required bows, the last of which brought him automatically to her feet below the dais of her chair. The usher closed the big doors. The Chamberlain, her secretaries, her women around her, the Queen Dowager of Scotland stared down at him, perspiring a little under her wired cap, her big hands on her knees. The dull morning light, filtering through the leaded west windows, jumped from ring to ring as her hands tightened. She said, 'You may remain on your knees, M. le Comte. It will remind you that we are royal.'

'Your Grace,' said Lymond obediently 'I have a glove belonging to our sovereign Lady your daughter which reminds me daily.' His eyes, slipping past the dais for a second, recognized the presence of Margaret Erskine, newly on duty that day, and then returned to the Queen's unfriendly face.

The allusion to his past services to the child Queen Mary was not, at the moment, what she wished to hear. In her strong French voice Mary of Guise said, 'You have, I am told, a fully trained armed force in camp at your home, consisting of thirty officers and now six hundred mercenaries, to whose numbers you are adding as necessary?'

At fourth hand, renewed all winter and spring, he had had her standing offer to buy himself and his company. It was the permanent army she craved. Behind her, a door opened silently and the Baron d'Oisel, the French King's Ambassador and Lieutenant in Scotland, slipped into the room. 'You have been correctly informed,' said Lymond.

The pale blue eyes scanned his calm face, and the hand lying open and relaxed on his raised knee. The little plume of his hat, held loosely in his other hand, lay quite still on the floor. The Queen Dowager drew air, hard, through the high, bony ridge of her nose. 'Then,' she said, and inclined her head to M. d'Oisel, arrived at her side, 'I have to tell you that your company must be paid off and disbanded, the officers dispersed and the mercenaries shipped back at your own expense to wherever they belong. Further, the buildings at St Mary's are to be pulled down, saving only the castle your home, and the arms stored therein confiscated by the Crown.'

Ten months' brilliant and bitterly hard work had dissolved with a breath. There was a moment of complete silence. Margaret Erskine's hands closed on the hardest thing she possessed, an engraved pomander, and gripped it achingly.

On Lymond's serene and respectful face there was no change whatever. He said, 'Is it permitted your Highness's humble servitor to know why?'

The Queen Mother glanced at M. d'Oisel again. 'We consider such a highly trained force, under a commander such as yourself, to be a threat to the public safety. Damage has been done through your livestock; lives have been lost through your machinery; minor cases of rivalry among the Border families have been magnified by the use of great forces into mass bloodshed in which the best of our young men have been lost. And those who consider themselves under your protection have taken the occasion to show insolence and disrespect to those whose duty it is to keep peace on the Borders. In addition—'

'Madam!' said Margaret Erskine, breaking every rule of the Court in one grim decision.

And because Tom Erskine's widow was one of the few intelligent and reliable women about her, as well as one of the better liked, the Queen Dowager stopped, and turning her head said merely, 'I was not aware that we had given Dame Margaret permission to speak?'

'No. Forgive me. I crave your pardon, your Grace,' said Margaret Erskine bluntly. 'But the Kerrs were sufficiently provoked to have slaughtered every Scott in the Kingdom, whether an army was there to stop them or not. But for the fear of St Mary's there would have been the same among many another pair of feuding families this year. And but for St Mary's, last winter, the families around Yarrow might have starved.'

'I heard about that errand of mercy.' It was M. d'Oisel's voice, but he was speaking to Lymond, not to Margaret Erskine. 'Carried out by Sir Graham Malett, I believe, against orders. We do not deny that some good might have been done. M. de Sevigny, after all, has had the most competent advice. What concerns us, however, is whether he is of a character to profit by it.'

There was a short silence. Presumably everyone present, Margaret thought, breathless with anger and fright, was thinking of Lymond's notorious behaviour in France during the Queen Dowager's visit. Everyone there knew that his own brother had since thrown him out. And at Liddel Keep, according to the Kerrs, before the battle which had cost Will Scott his life, Lymond had been drinking. Even Adam Blacklock, when challenged, had with reluctance agreed. The only person who, consistently, had championed Lymond through the last months had been Graham Malett, of whom Lymond—Richard Crawford had said it, and Adam Blacklock, once, and now, faced with all she had heard, she believed it to be true—*of whom Lymond was afraid.*

And as if she had picked up the thought, the Queen Dowager

suddenly added, 'In spite of all Sir Graham Malett has had to say in your support, we do not consider you either stable or sufficiently public-spirited to control these men in a small country such as this, particularly during those periods when they must be idle—you may rise,' said the Queen Dowager, and watched with perhaps a shadow of envy as he did just that, from his cramped posture, without faltering.

'On whose opinion, may I ask, is this estimate based?' Lymond asked. Behind the masked eyes there was still no hint of feeling.

'On the accounts of your neighbours and principal landowners. On the talk of your own men. On the observations of men of detachment such as M. d'Oisel here.' Mary of Guise paused, for the *coup de grâce*. 'And of my own observations of your temperament.'

Lymond appeared for a moment to consider, his eyes on M. d'Oisel; then he turned again to the Queen. 'The principal landowners as you call them, have been educated for years to believe that power and wealth comes not from a well-conducted nation, but from war or litigation with another principal landowner. They resent, naturally, anyone who interferes with this belief. As for my own men—' Lymond paused. 'I do not consult his manservant or his chamber-child if I wished a balanced view of, say, M. d'Oisel's character. They are the subject of his discipline and see only what touches their affairs, and that without necessarily understanding. Nor would I call M. d'Oisel necessarily detached. He stands in relation to the Crown, and the policy of the Crown in this country has been to divide and rule. Indeed,' said Lymond politely, 'I should fear all these judgements biased except for your Grace's, and there I venture to think that some past evidence of . . . public-spiritedness may yet occur to you.'

Patches of colour in her cheeks, Mary of Guise was unsmiling. 'Your intentions are possibly of the highest. But unless they are matched by your capabilities, this force is too prone to misuse. And were you Alexander himself, you are mortal. Into whose hands might not it fall when you die?'

'Sir Graham Malett's?' said Lymond with interest. 'There's public-spiritedness for you. Except that into whose hands might it not fall when *he* dies?'

'Sir Graham Malett has no wish to command St Mary's,' said M. d'Oisel a little stiffly.

'Oh?' Lymond was quick. 'So you've asked him?'

The Queen Mother broke in. 'It was hardly necessary. He has made plain his views over many weeks.'

'Then,' said Lymond quietly, 'may I be given the privilege of one day in which to do the same? St Mary's has achieved more, I believe, than you know. It is documented. I should like to be given time in which to present the facts to your Grace.'

The glassy, heavily metalled rings flashed; the pearls on her cap jerked, as the Queen Motner slowly shook her head. 'I have the only facts of significance. However well-intentioned, however successful, this army in private hands is a danger. It must be disbanded. And you, sir, will remain in our charge until it has done so.'

Watching Lymond, Margaret Erskine wondered what was happening behind that façade. If he did not disperse his company, it would be done for him, and all this great and formidable achievement would go for nothing. With his mercenaries scattered, and the confidence of his officers lost following this foolish indictment, he would never team them again.

And there was more behind it than that. He would know, as she did, that there was trouble ahead under French rule—or what would virtually become French rule if Mary of Guise was made Regent, and her daughter Mary's future husband was proclaimed King of both Scotland and France. She would then need all the armed support she could get. She had wanted Lymond to build her a personal army. She would not risk the presence of an army which might unite and even support the powerful families of Scotland against her. Thank God, thought Margaret bitterly, that Gabriel is what he is. But even Gabriel could not move against the pressure of national expediency.

And while she was thinking so, a whispered consultation at the doors turned into an announcement; a sharp question by the Queen Dowager and a comment by M. d'Oisel; and there, entering the room in his dark, cheap clothes, his burnished head bent, his expression grimly determined, was Graham Malett himself.

He glanced, once, at Lymond; and then in a moment was on one knee at his side. 'Forgive me, your Grace. If I offend you, punish me. But in the name of truth and in the light of my vows, and in token of the loving friendship in which I hold this man, I must speak. Francis—'

'Sir Graham!' The Queen Dowager's voice, when she chose, could grate like flaked metal. 'Afterwards, in private, we shall speak of this.'

Graham Malett rose and said, without answering her, 'Francis. They have ordered you to disband?'

'Yes.' Curiously, Lymond scanned the intent face at his side.

'There is another chance—'

'*Sir Graham!*'

Again, Gabriel ignored the Dowager. And such was his sheer force of personality that of all the entourage in the room, no one stepped forward to remove him. Instead, he went on rapidly. 'I didn't mean to tell you. But this is no time for hurt pride. At the request of the King of France, an expeditionary force is to be raised of Scots to

383

fight on the continent. I have been asked, and have refused, to depose you and lead St Mary's there myself. The alternative was to disband the company. There is a third choice. Prove to her Grace in the next month without a shadow of doubt that St Mary's is great, as you and I know that it is, and then lead them to France under the Queen Dowager's banner. On your conduct there, she can decide whether or not Scotland would be the better for your return. If she still cannot bring herself to believe that nothing but good will come of this idea of yours, then at least you will be free and with your army, and able to go where you please and name your own price.'

His face pale, the fire of appeal in his blue eyes, Graham Malett turned to the Dowager. 'Forgive me,' he said again. 'But you do not know what you are destroying. Will you not let us have this final chance? The King of France will receive a weapon for which he will be in your debt all his life. And I myself will stand surety for Mr Crawford until the expedition leaves.'

'You are eloquent.' The Queen Dowager was abrupt. 'The force you have seen fit to mention may not set sail until autumn.'

'Then will you not trust us, on my personal bond, until then?'

'My God,' said Lymond then, and the sheer incredulity of the tone betrayed, at last, the violence of his true feelings. 'May I speak, do you think? I don't recall having begged anyone to trust me, or to give me a last chance, or even to stand selfless bond to me. Nor do I negotiate at second hand.'

As suddenly as his temper flared, he had it controlled. 'It is even possible,' said Lymond thoughtfully, 'that the Queen Dowager might have been about to put forward this proposal herself?'

There was a little pause. 'Does this matter?' said the Queen Dowager at length. Within each eyebrow was a sharp line of displeasure. She had not wished, Margaret guessed, for the matter of the French expedition to be raised yet in public. Sir Graham would earn a reprimand, whatever his rank, for that.

'You are fortunate,' said Mary of Guise to Lymond, 'in having a friend so staunch, despite your discourtesy towards him. I put this to you at first hand therefore. Would you and your army join such an expedition, placing yourselves under my chosen leader'—('Cassillis,' said Gabriel, quickly, in Lymond's ear)—'and undertake both to refrain from all fighting in the weeks before such an army would leave, and to accept as final my eventual decision as to whether you and your company should return?'

To Margaret's amazement, Lymond appeared to be giving it thought. 'If during this interval we were attacked, might we defend ourselves?' he inquired.

'If you could prove that you fought in self-defence. Understand her Grace,' said le Seigneur d'Oisel et de Villeparisis forcefully.

'There is to be no trouble while you wait at St Mary's. You may help, yes. You may protect, yes. You may train as you wish, and prepare your arms. But no bloodshed. No hostile or criminal action. Or I shall be forced to muster my garrisons against you and, as her Grace has said, your men would be dispersed and you yourself taken into custody. As for the Scottish expedition, I can offer noble prospects and no small fees. Details I cannot yet give, but I can assure you that the King's Majesty's wars will be renowned, and full of honour to be won.'

'I am subjugated,' said Lymond drily.

'You would agree to those terms?'

'I should hate to disband Randy Bell,' said Lymond. 'The Flowers of the Forest would be Flowers no more.'

'*Do you agree?*'

'Yes,' said Lymond cheerfully. 'Provided that Sir Graham comes *formally* lawburrows that neither the Queen Dowager nor yourself will suffer for it. He's standing surety, remember; not I.'

Soon after that, it was over. Adam Blacklock, informed by Gabriel of the outcome, packed his bags and took his leave to meet Lymond, as instructed, at the livery stables. Lymond, having brought his baggage from Creich that morning, was already there, leavetaking behind him. He had spoken warmly to Robert Beaton and Margaret Erskine, and fleetingly to Gabriel himself. Graham Malett was to stay at Falkland for some days yet. Then, as he mentioned with a kind of anxious deprecation, he was to return to St Mary's to help Lymond maintain the Queen's peace. He did not say, and Lymond did not discover, that early that morning he had had a guarded exchange with the departing Cormac O'Connor; nor did he mention the name of Oonagh O'Dwyer that day.

When Adam Blacklock got to the stables, a hundred questions stuttering to his tongue, Lymond was standing inside, next to his horse, reading a letter with one arm on the pommel. Beside him was a lad Adam knew well from the group of messengers at St Mary's. 'News?' Blacklock said. And then, taking a closer look at Lymond's face, 'Trouble?'

For a moment more, Lymond read on, saying nothing. Then, quickly, he pushed the pages into his doublet, checked his girths, swung into the saddle, and throwing a silver coin to the boy said, 'Well done. Home tomorrow, when you've had a night's rest. Leave the girls alone—they've sorrows enough. Adam!'

'Yes?' He had led out his horse, and was busy saddling her. Silently Salablanca, slipping from Lymond's side, took the task from him and began methodically strapping on Adam's bags, his own mule and the spare saddle-horse waiting patiently, while Blacklock crossed to where Lymond sat.

'Trouble,' said Lymond, confirming. 'I've paid the reckoning for us both. Quietly through the town, and then ride for your life. For in this country be many white elephants without number, and of unicorns and of lions of many manners.'

'White elephants such as what?' said Blacklock, his voice insouciant, his hand suddenly unsteady.

'Such as Jock Thompson, pirate,' said Lymond. 'And Jim Logan, of the same brethren, who ran the Irish customars out to the *Magdalena*, off the Head of Howth. And half the officers of St Mary's, who might be in Dublin jail this moment accused of smuggling gunpowder to the Irish rebels, except that they sank the customs boat, burst up Logan's ship, killed six of Logan's best men, and sailed the *Magdalena* rejoicing back to Dumbarton with all Logan's cargo, including his contraband.'

Adam Blacklock's grey eyes were bright and steady on Lymond's. 'Sir Graham said that if there were any more incidents the Dowager had threatened to break you.'

'Yes. Well. This isn't an incident, it's a cataclysm,' said Lymond. 'It's more than that. It's the end of a nightmare. One way or the other. Come, Adam. You must be in time to draw the death mask of St Mary's.'

'How long will it take the news to reach the palace?' Adam asked. All three pacing soberly through the little town, spoke in murmurs.

'If the garrison at Dumbarton get to hear of it . . . say another day only. If Thompson is discreet, and I think he will be, it will go from Dublin to London, and thence here. Two weeks, then. If the expeditionary force goes in September—a month from now say—the Queen Dowager has two further weeks in which to—what's the phrase?—break us. If she wants to. And catch me. If she can.'

There was a short silence, during which they reached the open country, and then a long interval, filled breathlessly by some very fast riding indeed. At the first pause for rest, 'It really is exceedingly neat,' said Lymond, apparently in the belief that he was continuing the conversation, but without explaining in the least. His tone was one of deepest admiration. He said, walking round and round Adam as the artist lay, arms outflung in the deep grass, a bannock half-eaten on his chest, 'And Joleta.'

It was the last name Blacklock expected to hear. He raised a hand, removed the bannock slowly from his jerkin, and took a bite. 'Yes?'

'Oh, come on, Adam,' said Lymond with derision, standing over him. 'You're an artist. You saw her at Dumbarton. Sixteen, convent-bred and the light of Gabriel's life. Family pride kept my brother from breaking the awful news to Graham Malett, but you have no reason to hold back. Yet you haven't told him of my night with his sister, have you? Why?'

Some crumbs from the scone had got into his windpipe. When he had finished choking Adam sat up, scarlet, with tears in his eyes. 'It was none of my f-f . . . none of my business,' he said.

'Because you saw what I did,' said Lymond gently. 'What did you see, Adam?'

'All right,' said Blacklock suddenly and angrily. He got to his knees, brushing crumbs from the leather, and then rose face to face with Lymond. Neither man gave way.

'All right,' Adam repeated grimly. 'When I saw Joleta in Dumbarton that night she was pregnant, and it wasn't her first pregnancy at that.'

'Adam!' Lymond said; then stopped, and said in a more moderate tone, 'The eye of the master. You may have, from my personal storehouse, pens, ink, paper, colours, oils and pregnant women to sketch in unlimited supply from now until your dotage. She was not a virgin, and she had had a baby. She was also pregnant. Which makes her about five months gone with the baby she is going to foist on me. . . . No wonder Sybilla noticed.'

Adam sat down, confused. 'How do you know she's going to foist it on you?'

'Because she has done everything in her power, since I came, first to attract me, and then when that failed, to compromise me, willy-nilly.' He smiled faintly. 'That night at Dumbarton was a classic of its kind. She had hopes still, I think, of enslaving me despite myself with her charms. And I probably thought the same. We both found we were mistaken. It had its moments; but she has the mind and morals of a jungle cat. She didn't enjoy meeting . . . another of the same.'

'So she wants to take her revenge?'

'She has threatened that, unless I marry her, to Gabriel's fond applause, she will name me as her seducer. Grand climax to Gabriel's loving comradeship with Crawford of Lymond.'

'And to your control over St Mary's,' said Adam Blacklock slowly. 'She and Gabriel are mystic symbols of fortune to at least half your men. One whisper of this, and they'll leave you.'

'It'll be more than a whisper by mid-September,' said Lymond, calculating. 'Even if she wears tablecloths. . . . I wonder whose it is?'

'It isn't yours?' asked Adam. But he knew already, from that cool *What are you doing here?*' heard that night in Dumbarton, that it was not.

'No. And could be proved not to be, I suppose. But that doesn't matter a damn in an emotional crisis of that kind. It'll be too late when they turn out to be baby Berbers, or a litter of Moors. Poor bastards. Sybilla will do something for them.'

'My advice,' said Adam thoughtfully, 'would be to get your mother to immure her in a convent for a very long time.'

'The first thing Gabriel would do is visit her,' Lymond said. From defiant jubilation he had become quiet. 'It's odd to think that in four weeks, five at the most, it will all be over. St Mary's won't exist. Or it will continue under my command, without Gabriel. Or under Gabriel, without me. How would you enjoy fighting under Graham Malett, Adam?'

Adam Blacklock looked as levelly as he knew how into Lymond's bright blue eyes. 'So it's come, has it?' he said slowly. 'This is what you have been afraid of, all along? It has to be one or other of you; it can't be both. Graham Malett never will have you at his side.'

'Yes, it has come,' said Lymond. He had moved away again, without attending to Blacklock, and his voice was curt. 'The Queen Dowager has successfully brought it to a head, but the final choice won't be hers. It will lie with St Mary's, and the excellence or otherwise of our work there. If I have made men, they will act like men.'

'You may be a man, and fear God still,' said Adam steadily.

Lymond's face, too, was wholly sober as he looked away, over the low hills of Fife. 'I know But I, too, learned a lesson in Malta. *Never mind their eyes. . . . Watch their hands!* Adam, I have to go to Midculter to see Joleta. Then I am moving across to Boghall, where Margaret Erskine should be joining her mother shortly to wait for me. I have asked a number of other people to meet me there too. If you want to come with them, I should . . . welcome you. If you prefer to go straight to St Mary's, I shall understand. All I ask is that you say nothing of the gathering at Boghall. In any case, our ways part now. I am going home alone.'

Adam Blacklock looked down at his hands. 'Small, subversive gatherings in corners? Not St Mary's as we knew it.'

Lymond's answering gaze was disconcertingly sharp. 'But St Mary's never was an army,' he said. 'Only a battlefield. You must have realized that?'

XIII

The Axe Is Turned on Itself

(Midculter, Flaw Valleys, Boghall, September 1552)

IN the meantime, the unease which had settled on St Mary's, Falkland and several points on the Irish seaboard had assumed, at Midculter, the proportions of plague. Swirling furiously among the stairs and corridors of her exquisite home like a small and angry white bat Sybilla, Dowager Lady Culter, was not above spitting at her unfortunate son when he chose to sit down in his own great hall to take his boots off.

'If Madge Mumblecrust comes down those stairs *once again* for a morsel of fowl's liver with ginger, or pressed meats with almond-milk, I shall retire to a little wicker house in the forest and cast spells which will sink Venice into the sea for ever, and Madame Donati with it. The Church,' said Sybilla definitely, 'should excommunicate girls who do not replace lids on sticky jars and wash their hair every day with the best towels.'

'She's getting on your nerves,' said Richard perceptively. 'Why doesn't she come down and go out? It's a month since she immured herself up there. She'll make herself ill.'

Sybilla sat down. If her laughter was a shade hysterical, at least it was laughter. When she had recovered, she said, 'Yes. Well. She doesn't want to be seen, my dear.'

'Why not?' said Richard. He thought of Joleta as he had last seen her a month ago, when the child had first become noticeable, and Sybilla, grimly, had broken the news to him. Robed in white, her shining hair tumbling over her arms, by some magic the girl had kept intact that untouched, miraculous grace. In all those weeks she had said nothing that was not gentle about his brother Francis. And when Sybilla had questioned her, her own face stiff and pale, Joleta had answered simply, without recriminations. Only, when Lady Culter's anger for a moment showed through, the girl's eyes had filled with tears.

Then she had made them all promise to say nothing to Graham Malett until Francis had been told. But then Francis had been told, and had done nothing about it. So, 'Why doesn't she want to be seen?' said Richard irritably. 'In three months, everyone will know anyway.' Then, at the expression on his mother's face, he put down abruptly the boot he had just hauled off, and crossing the polished floor to her softly, knelt at her feet. 'Look . . . It *is* just possible to understand it, even if you can't forgive. She has a beauty that—that— Any man would want to do just what he did. The difference is that, being Francis and owning no rule and no master, he did it. And because she loves him, she gave him the chance.'

'Owning no master. That's the trouble, isn't it?' said Sybilla suddenly. In her lap, her hands, so like her younger son's, were pressed together, white and hard. 'He looked for one, I would guess, in Malta.'

'He found one,' said Richard quietly. 'But he cannot acknowledge it.' He smiled at her, and rising to his feet, put out his hands and drew her to hers. 'If he walked in just now and asked Joleta to marry him, what would you do?'

'Faint,' said Sybilla succinctly.

*

Later, in the balm of the open air, Richard was watching his ploughing, the oxen straining in the broad fields under the clouds of seagulls, the glistening, fresh brown earth slow-surging from the coulter, when the low drum of hooves in the clear air told of two horsemen coming from the east. A moment later, someone in a distant field raised a shout of greeting, and he saw the felt and leather helms of his trenchers bob and turn. Someone they all knew, someone belonging to the castle. . . . Francis, his yellow head bare, and the big, silent Spanish Moor behind him. Lord Culter wondered, his muscles aching already in anticipation of the ordeal ahead, what gay solution Lymond would produce to this problem. Adoption . . . abortion . . . or marriage, perhaps? Waiting, hard-eyed, for him by the roadside, 'You're a little late?' Richard said to his brother.

Lymond's face, so like Sybilla's, brightened into untrustworthy joy. 'Glory be, she's had a miscarriage!' he said. At which Richard, following silently on foot up to the castle, knew that they were about to have a particularly disagreeable afternoon.

The hall, with its painted roof and elegant carvings and its sad, bovine picture of the second Lord Culter, Sybilla's husband, was filled with sunshine when the Dowager entered at Richard's call. Barely glancing at her younger son she merely said, 'I think, Richard, that Joleta should be brought here before we attempt to discuss anything. Unless, Francis, you have any valid objections?'

Lymond looked astonished. 'I wouldn't dare,' he said. 'Here I am, lying about being amended in corners. It is my day for being humble.'

'It is your day, as always, for being impertinent,' said Sybilla sharply. 'Bring her, Richard.'

In the end Madame Donati brought the child down and, formidable in padded black, held her as she faced them all. Alone all the long day in her bedchamber, Joleta had laced white ribbons in her silk-apricot hair, and ribbons glinted in the pure voile of her dress. She was big with child. But above the turgid, womanly mound, shawled but cruelly undisguised by the white, childish dress, Joleta's face was blinding in its happiness. Setting aside her duenna's hands, with gentle care, she walked slowly and heavily towards Francis Crawford.

And cool, slender, expensive, that young man stared not at her but at that pathetic, white-bellied distention. 'My God, Mother,' he said, lively interest contending with horror in his voice. 'There's more than one small mistake there. She's setting a clutch.'

For their day and age, the Crawfords were a sophisticated family. But this was a callousness unknown in their halls. Joleta gave one short cry only, and then stopped it with her hands. Sybilla gasped as if he had winded her; and Richard Crawford, turning on his brother, brought his arm up in a gesture meant to drive some manners forcibly into his head.

Lymond who, after all, had more warning than anyone, ducked expertly and ran instead, with a stinging smack, into the flat of Evangelista Donati's hand. 'Whoremonger!' said Joleta's duenna in a voice rising to a scream. 'Anti-Christ! Wolf! Do we wish to see you? Do we wish to speak to you? Go die in a cesspool, misbegot hog!' And as Lymond, rocked by the unexpectedness of the blow, sat down with extreme suddenness in the chair just behind him and began maddeningly to laugh, Joleta ran, draggingly, to the door.

Lymond sat up, disregarding equally Madame Donati threatening at his side and Richard, his head flung back in anger, with Sybilla's hand on his arm. 'Come back! Oh, come back!' said Francis Crawford, and got up, one hand cradling his jaw. 'I am penitent. Only, if you indulge in numbers, how are we to get rid of the bastards?'

Joleta stopped.

'*Get rid of*!' said Sybilla.

Lymond turned to her, his blue eyes wide. 'Unless she wants to be a little mother to them? A little unmarried mother?'

'I am glad,' said Madame Donati, in the ensuing silence, 'that you do not insult the child, at least, with an offer of marriage.'

'Good Lord, no,' said Lymond comfortably, sitting down again. 'Do sit down, Joleta, sit down and take the weight off. . . . Heavens, girl, don't cry again. But, marriage to the right godly fresh flower of womanhood here would make me Gabriel's good-brother, wouldn't it? And I don't think Gabriel could stomach that. *Joleta*! We are *planning*!'

'Get out,' said Richard curtly. He had, incredibly, unsheathed his sword.

'No,' said Sybilla. 'No. He has come here to say something and you must listen, for Joleta's sake. Whatever you wish to do afterwards, I shall not stop you. *Lymond*: what are Sir Graham Malett's wishes in this matter?'

It was, Richard guessed, the first time in his life that Francis Crawford had been so addressed by his mother. It removed, for the fraction of a second, the smile from his face. Then it was back, with more malice than before. 'He doesn't know,' he said. 'What's the punishment for seduction? Pinned to a fiery wheel in the skies. But Gabriel is a kind monk. *Jeune, galant, frisque, dehait, bien adèxtre, hardi, adventureux, delibéré, hault, maigre, bien fendu de gueule, bien advantagé en nez*. Et cetera. He will ask only that I praise the Lord and marry Joleta.'

Joleta turned round. In the delicate face, her grey-blue eyes were liquid with unshed tears, her small sparkling teeth were sunk in her whitened lip. 'I would marry you,' she said. 'If you asked me.'

Lymond's reflective gaze stayed on her. '*Où est la très sage Helloïs*,' he said. '*Pour qui chastré fut, et puis moyne?* I have no intention of asking you,' he went on. 'I say it in the presence of the Fool Plough and the Bessy there. I don't take soiled goods into my bed, except to pass an hour slumming.'

Fortunately, perhaps, it was too much for Madame Donati's uncertain English. But as she stared, suspicious but uncomprehending, Richard Crawford looked from Lymond's mocking face to Joleta's white one and said, '*Soiled goods!* What filth is this now?'

'My dear man,' said Lymond coolly. 'Oüez, oüez, oüez. Et vous taisez si vous pouvez. Joleta Reid Malett is a promiscuous little lady with a foul temper, who is carrying a child whose father she probably doesn't know, even herself. It certainly isn't mine. That baby is due to be born a good deal sooner than three months from now. Let me assure you that, far from being deflowered at Dumbarton, Joleta Malett wasn't even a virgin. She was already carrying a child.' And as the girl, her face wild, suddenly flung out her hands to still the unborn, flagrant in its virginal voile, Lymond added, his voice metallic, 'And I wonder how Sir Graham Malett, Grand Cross of Grace of the Order, will enjoy being told *that*.'

Joleta's cry, 'He won't believe it!' coincided with Sybilla's quieter voice. The Dowager said, slowly, 'There is only your word for that, against Joleta's. Why, since you hate him so, have you not given yourself the pleasure of telling Sir Graham before now?'

'Because it is a lie!' said Madame Donati's shocked and furious voice.

'Because he wants it—don't you, Francis?—as a final, annihilating blow to strike Gabriel off from your heels. What did the Queen Dowager say to you, Francis?' said Richard harshly. 'We heard she had summoned you. Has she decided, too, that St Mary's under a man of no discipline and no principles is too dangerous to exist?'

'But *Graham* doesn't want St Mary's! He only wants . . . wants the best for you, because he admires you so.' Joleta, her tears dried, was staring wide-eyed at Lymond. 'You wouldn't give him such pain?'

'He's going to be a little pained, isn't he, whatever we do?' said Lymond reasonably. 'At least, this way he can retain his much-publicized respect for me while he proves that he doesn't want St Mary's.'

'That,' said Lord Culter softly, 'is blackmail.'

Lymond said agreeably, 'Yes, it is, isn't it? The weasel and the basilisk. It's a little troublesome, you see. The dice is loaded against me. *Nil est tam populare,* as you might say, *quam bonitas.*'

But Joleta, moving closer, her rosy hair falling disordered over her clear brow and cheek, said with a sudden, hurried intensity, 'You want Graham to go away? If Graham went away, right away—if Graham promised never to come back . . . would you marry me?'

And Lymond's bright, sardonic face, looking into hers, lost all its amusement; all its icy amiability; all its social charm. 'My dear sister in Christ, and mother in expectation, I may be what Buccleuch has called me: a harlot. But a *discriminating* harlot, my dear.' And, flashing out an arm, he snatched, lightly from below her labouring grasp, a fine glass vase of Sybilla's at her side. 'You don't sign your work twice,' he said softly. 'It's unlucky.' And watched as, dizzily, the child stumbled into Donna Donati's sheltering arms.

Holding her, the duenna stared above the silken head at Francis Crawford, her yellow, high-bred face hollow with rage and contempt.

'Your life, it is worth nothing,' she said. 'From now, every good-living man, as well as the blessed angels in heaven, will be cursing each breath you draw. We shall tell her brother. That good and holy man, in his suffering, may forgive what you did. His brethren will not. Whatever becomes of the little one and her baby, she will be avenged.'

The Venetian woman glanced at him once, with a kind of tired scorn in her cold eyes; and then shepherding the girl's swollen body gently before her, closed the door on them both.

No one said anything. Sybilla, the silvery nape of her neck bowed, sat staring unseeing at the polished floor, her thin fingers pressed to her mouth. Richard's square, quiet person, resting against the wall at her back, the thick brown hair fallen as it always did, straight across his ridged brow, was completely silent. And Lymond, his fair head flung back against his high chair, his eyes resting on the closed door, had not moved.

The door opened, on the lightest of scratches, and Salablanca the Moor came in, shutting it at his back. '*Señora . . . Señores . . . Están en el cuarto*,' he said.

Lymond answered in Spanish. 'Good. You may stand outside. Richard?'

Lord Culter said nothing. Lymond turned his head, and in a single, unexpected movement was on his feet, facing his brother. 'My God, don't you think I feel ill, too?' he said. And indeed, Richard, surveying him at last, saw with numb curiosity the reflection of his own sick anger in Lymond's white face. Then Lymond, looking from his mother to Richard and back again, said, 'I hope never to have to do that to you again. I hope one day you will forgive me. Try to remember, just at this moment, that my trade calls for acting. Try to remember, Richard, as I have told you, that because of your own honesty I can't confide in you. . . . Sybilla, all I must do depends on one thing. That in spite of what you have heard just now, you trust me for half a day more.'

Sybilla, Dowager Lady Culter, did not look up. Instead, opening and shutting her thin, shapely hands, one on the other, she said, 'Trust you to do what?'

Lymond said, his voice now quite emotionless and clear, 'I want to leave now, and go to Boghall. Margaret Erskine will be there tomorrow, and Janet Beaton, and some others you know. At midday tomorrow, I want you and Richard to leave here without servants, casually, and ride to Boghall to join me, mentioning to no one that I shall be there. If anyone asks, you think I have gone back to St Mary's. At some point, also, Joleta will send word of her troubles to her brother. Let her messenger go.'

'She won't beg Graham Malett to leave you now,' Richard said with sudden contempt. 'She'll let you ruin her publicly and be damned to you, rather than bolster your precious command. Trust you? I don't care what crawling plot you're involved with this time. We are free of you, and we're going to stay free. Go where you please. Graham Malett's friends will see Joleta amply avenged.'

Sybilla lifted her head. She was very pale, nearly as white as her china-fair hair, and there were rings round her blue eyes. 'There is something I should like to ask you,' she said. 'You claimed among other things, that you did not father Joleta's baby. Was that true?'

Lymond's answer was curt. 'Yes. She was already pregnant in May.'

'You called her promiscuous. Is that true?'

'Yes.'

'I am not a child or a cleric, Francis,' said Sybilla sharply. 'I wish to test what you say against some facts of my own. You called her promiscuous. Why?'

'Because of her practices. She is experienced,' said Lymond shortly. 'She appears to have a close relationship with her grooms. You could discover more, no doubt, if you care for the method. She marks her bed-fellows like a bloody bookmark: with a cross.'

'With a piece of glass?' said Sybilla, and for the first time, Lymond's voice took a little colour. 'Or a knife. She's a knack with weapons,' he continued evenly. 'And she has a temper. One of my men, Cuddie Hob, laughed at her once. She shot his horse.'

'She killed my cat,' said Sybilla dreamily. 'I didn't tell you, Richard. And until Margaret Erskine stopped it, she was never left alone with Kevin. A streak of natural cruelty. Her upbringing, I suppose. And always the example of the heavenly Gabriel. Anyone of her nature would rebel against that. . . .'

'*Killed* your *cat*!' said Richard incredulously, and Lymond said wearily, 'It's unbelievable, I know. It's a crime against all the marvellous things of the universe. You will never see anyone as beautiful again. She's sweet, and young, and lovely, and morally quite defective. Ask Mother. She was sitting there counselling marriage for the good of the family, and wondering all the while if she was going to have to spend all her life training her daughter-in-law not to kill cats. . . . I need you tomorrow, Richard, if you can bring yourself to come.'

'To plot with you against Gabriel?' said Richard. 'You can do that without me.'

But Sybilla had risen, and although still very pale, had crossed to where Lymond stood. 'We reserve judgement,' she said. 'But the facts about Joleta are a *little* in your favour; and we know your trouble about Richard's honest face. On the other hand, *I* am a great dissembler. You couldn't have a little conference with me?' And as Lymond shook his head, she sighed. 'In that case, I shall wait until tomorrow. I shall come to Boghall, Francis; and Richard will ride with me, if necessary roped by the heels.'

He was fleetingly amused, but left at once, after the briefest of leave-taking. It was then that Sybilla began to shake, and Richard, cursing with extraordinary vigour, lifted her gently from her chair and holding her tightly, took her to her room.

*

The next day, drawn by heaven knew what premonition, Gabriel returned from Falkland to St Mary's. The warmth of his welcome, as ever, brought light to his face and, his hand on Jerott's shoulder, he heard in silence the full story of Thompson's illicit voyage and the hounding of the *Magdalena* by the pirate Logan. His dark face blazing at the recollection, Jerott said, 'Thompson was magnificent. If the Irish boats hadn't encircled us, to finish with, we would have got free without fighting at all. As it was we did escape in the end, although he lost his guns. We may not have had much of a voyage, but by God, it gave them all a taste of the sea. They want to go back. Randy Bell says he's going to become the first medical corsair.'

'I saw him,' said Gabriel. His smile, as clear as always, had still something a little tired and a little anxious in it; and Jerott was reminded that of course, from authority's point of view, the incident had been damaging to St Mary's. His thoughts must have been transparent, for Gabriel said, 'The Queen Dowager is concerned about how we behave. She will learn, if we are careful, that we are to be trusted. . . . Where are the others who were with you? Where is Francis?'

Jerott grinned. 'We thought a little judicious dispersal might be a good thing, in case we were visited with any official complaints. As the respectable member of the sea-going party, I stay to rattle my rosary in their faces. Lymond. . . .' He paused. 'He should be here tonight. He sent word that he meant to call at Midculter on the way.'

'To see Joleta?' Graham Malett's face, suddenly, was cloudless. 'Then he is safe. The child will help him. He would let me do nothing at Falkland.'

'Was it unpleasant?'

'We have been given an ultimatum. No more slackness, no indiscipline, no brawling for a month, and Francis will have the opportunity of his life: to lead St Mary's in a great expeditionary force to France.' He was silent for a moment, and then said, 'It *was* unpleasant, for he is not humble, and he would admit to nothing; and the Irishman Cormac O'Connor, whom the Queen Dowager respects, quarrelled with him in public. . . . That must be resolved. In the meantime. . . .' He broke off. 'He *did* go to Midculter?'

Jerott was not, by then, the only one within earshot. There was a shadow of uneasiness, no more, in the big room. They were all aware of the rumour that Lymond was not permitted in his own home any more. Jerott said, after a pause, 'Possibly to see his mother. He may not spend much time with Joleta.'

'But he will hear news of her,' said Gabriel. 'If I'd known. . . . It doesn't matter.'

'What?' said Jerott quietly.

'Oh, I might have asked him to bring her back. There is so much to do . . . and we must have no trouble. I have to stay. What I am trying to say, so incoherently,' said Gabriel, smiling, 'is only that I haven't seen Joleta for a month. I miss her.'

'But that's simple,' said Jerott. 'I'll fetch her for you. Now.' And disregarding loftily all Graham Malett's protestations, he got up, there and then, and went out. In ten minutes his horse was waiting and he was ready. As he mounted, Cuddie Hob and his groom behind him, Gabriel walked up to his side and laid a hand on his knee. 'God go with you,' he said. 'And forgive me, I could have stopped you . . . I should have spared you the trouble. But she is my only haven on earth.'

He lifted his hand and stepped back: a big man, beautifully made, with the autumn sun copper-gold on his hair. 'But don't tell her that, will you?' he said, smiling. 'I don't want to be teased all the rest of my life.'

*

Long before Jerott Blyth reached Midculter castle on that bright-bronzed September day, Lymond's midday assignation at Boghall was over, and Francis Crawford had made the first moves towards turning the sharpened axe which he himself had fashioned of St Mary's inwards upon itself.

Sybilla was there, as he had known she would be, riding the familiar three miles from Midculter to Lady Jenny Fleming's big castle in its marsh, her son Richard silent at her side. Five years ago, in the great hall at Boghall with its tall windows, Lady Jenny's husband had held his last meeting before going to die fighting the English at Pinkie. From its roof, Richard had seen the smoke rise over the rolling bog when Lymond, with fire and sword, had made his first return to his mother's home.

Now, Lady Jenny, excited and a trifle apprehensive, ushering Sybilla up the wide stone stairs, was a widow, and the mother of the French King's son. Now her daughter Margaret, widowed first at Pinkie, had lost her second and dearest husband with the death nine months before of Tom Erskine, here in her mother's home. And in the great room upstairs, its strewn floor roused to sweetness by the booted feet of Lymond's guests, the coloured light fell on faces strange to these douce walls. Thompson was there, sea-robber, trader, navigator; sought by every harbour in the Irish Sea and the Baltic, and up and down the Middle Seas to boot; his black-bearded chin in the air, his arms folded across his salt-crusted chest. At his side, in a crackling haze of legal inquiry, sat Fergie Hoddim of the Laigh, who had not been on the ill-fated training voyage of the *Magdalena*, but clearly wished he had been.

Beyond, listening with gnome-like ardour to Janet Beaton, Lady of Buccleuch, was Nicolas de Nicolay, Sieur d'Arfeville et de Bel Air, cosmographer to the King of France; and next to him Alec Guthrie, humanist and philosopher, speaking to nobody; his big-featured fleshy face with the prematurely grey hair sunk on his chest, his thumbs in his belt. Margaret Erskine had already made her quiet way to his side, and sat down. Sybilla, after a moment's hesitation, took the vacant seat to the left of the chair and next to the lounging bulk of the corsair, who sat up with a half-salute and grinned as she settled her small, trim person at his side. Richard, she noticed, had found a place at the foot of the table, between de Nicolay and Fergie Hoddim; and Lady Jenny, her introductions made with the help of a tall, thin young man with a faint limp, described to her as Adam Blacklock, sat herself beside Richard Crawford at the far end. The vacant seat, to the right of the chair, was taken, with a little hesitation, by the man Blacklock as the door opened and quickly and quietly Lymond came in and paused. At his back, Archie Abernethy and the Moor Salablanca, closed and stood by the door.

Lymond's face told them nothing, nor did his voice when he spoke; although he had, to more than one experienced eye, the look of a man who has ridden far and fast. 'You are all here. I'm glad,' he said. 'Lady Jenny, this is your home. The place at the head of the table is yours, if you wish it.' He waited just as long as courtesy required for her flattered refusal, and then took his place, his feet hardly stirring the rushes, in the black carved chair Lord Malcolm had used.

In absolute silence, he laid his hands on the table and for the first time looked down the long vista of polished oak. Ten faces: ten expressions, varying through concern, suspicion, fear, anxiety and a controlled blankness which revealed nothing at all, returned the impersonal blue gaze. When, at length, he drew breath to speak, Sybilla was reminded irresistibly of the Collegiate Church at Biggar, and the priest leaning over the lectern, dropsical with earnest admonitions. 'We are gathered here, dearest children in Christ, for the purpose of praising the Lord.'

'We are gathered here today,' said Lymond quietly, his beautiful hands lying interlaced and still on the table, 'for the purpose of destroying Sir Graham Reid Malett.'

*

For more than two months now, through the best part of the summer, ever since the meeting at the Hadden Stank, Kate Somerville had kept her daughter Philippa at home; and if she moved abroad at all, had attached to her the largest, thickest manservant she possessed.

Nothing had happened, except that Philippa had won three pairs of boots and a man's saddle at dice, and had earned the respect of all their neighbours' children, who were not unnaturally convinced that the child

398

must be heiress to a fortune at least. If Kate herself chafed at never being able to arrange a simple outing without their feminine privacy being encroached on, she said nothing to Philippa, and if Philippa was beginning to be impressed, despite herself, by the fact that her practical mother thought it worth while following Francis Crawford's directions, however odd, to the letter, she said nothing at all.

She might have done nothing either if Sue Bligh of Bamburgh hadn't gone to market at Hexham to spend her regular allowance from Wat Kerr, and the handsome danger money she had got since Hadden Stank from Wat Scott of Buccleuch, and retailed, slightly overtaken in liquor, the latest gossip from the north.

It came to Kate's ears, carried lovingly, the very next day, and after breaking two flower pots and coughing herself silly trying to spread sawdust up the garden alleys in a gale, Mistress Somerville marched indoors and said to her imprisoned daughter, 'You're going to look a grand sight following Joleta up the aisle with Cheese-wame Henderson here in full armour in your wake.' And as Philippa, naturally, looked astonished, her mother said with irritation, 'It's hardly surprising, is it? Francis Crawford is marrying Joleta, they say. She'll want you there, I expect. You are the only creature of her own sex and age she has troubled to consort with.'

There was a long pause. 'When?' said Philippa carefully, at length.

'Rumour doesn't say.'

'Why?'

Kate Somerville turned her head slowly and looked her daughter in the eye. '*That* is an odd question. Am I mistaken, or do I remember you informing Sir Graham Malett in London that it would be wonderful if Lymond and his sister faced life, hand in hand together? We were all sobbingly moved.'

'Yes. But,' said Philippa, moving quickly to essentials, 'didn't Sir Graham say they didn't take to one another?' And with the clear, perfidious gaze that Kate could recognize with her eyes shut, the girl added, 'Unless she's *converted* him. Has she?'

'No,' said Kate. And after a moment, with reluctance, 'In fact, it's the other way round.'

There was no need to spell things out with Philippa. She got rather pale, which Kate was sorry to see, and then said, endearingly, 'I didn't guess or I wouldn't have forced you to tell me. He *has* to marry her?'

Kate Somerville, who had been playing with Philippa's pigtails, dropped the long brown ropes suddenly and turned the girl gently to face her. 'Why did you say that?'

'What?' It had seemed, to Philippa, the height of tact. She flushed. 'What do you mean?'

'You said,' said Kate slowly, 'so *he* has to marry *her*. Surely it isn't *Lymond* you pity?'

Philippa's face, already red, burned to a deeper scarlet. 'No. Oh, no,' she said. 'They deserve each other. That's what I think. Don't you think?'

Struggling between kindness and honesty, Kate's unremarkable face was a picture. 'No. . . .' she said at length. 'I don't think I think. Let's consider the subject exhausted except for choosing the wedding gift. Something tasteful with poison in it, perhaps. Although I can't think which of them deserves it the more.'

Two mornings later, entering her daughter's room, Kate was struck by the flatness of the bed, and then by the sight of a folded paper laid dead centre of the untenanted pillow. Unfolded, it proved to be a witty and delightfully-written apology from her daughter for upsetting the household, coupled with the information that, having some business of vital importance to transact north of the Border in the immediate future, she had taken the liberty of leaving for a few days without permission, as she just knew that Kate would make a fuss and stop her. She would be back directly with some heather, and Kate was not to worry and not to speak to any strange men. She had, Philippa concluded, taken Cheese-wame Henderson with her: thus becoming the only known fugitive to persuade her bodyguard to run away, too.

It was a typical Somerville letter, and in other circumstances Kate no doubt would have been charmed by the spelling alone. As it was, she roused the neighbourhood for ten miles around, and there was no able-bodied Englishman within reach of Flaw Valleys who slept in his own bed that night or the next.

To no avail. With perfect thoroughness, Philippa had managed to vanish. And riding back and forth, frightened, on her grim, fruitless search, Kate Somerville saw, but did not comprehend, that the big tinker who had spent the summer mending ironware under a huddle of rags in her meadow had now picked up his belongings and gone.

Philippa Somerville disappeared on the Feast of the Holy Cross and was missing still next day, the 15th September, the day on which Jerott Blyth rode north to bring Joleta home to her brother.

On that day also Cormac O'Connor called at St Mary's, in unwilling response to a sharp summons from Gabriel himself, and brought with him as a peace offering a special cartload from his contraband warehouse at Leith.

*

By then, a hundred miles north at Boghall, Lymond's coldly purposeful attack on Graham Malett had reached its inevitable end.

'We are gathered here today,' he had said, 'for the purpose of destroying Sir Graham Reid Malett,' and their ensuing deliberations began with the crash of a chair as Lord Culter thrust himself upright. '*By God, are we?*' said Lymond's brother, and Sybilla's quick breathing faltered. Beside Alec Guthrie, unmoving, Margaret Erskine's eyes filled with tears.

It was Fergie Hoddim, next to Thompson's comfortable solidity, who said drily, 'It'll all come out in the evidence, man. We're none of us all that simple that we'll condemn a man out o' malice—either one man or the other. Let him have his head. There'll be no hope for St Mary's else.'

'Sit down, Richard,' said Lymond without looking up. 'You have quite adequate support, as you see. The onus is on me to convince you. I am attempting to do this now because time is against me. I have three somewhat depressing handicaps. I do not have the goodwill of any of the Knights of the Order, who might otherwise have been here to substantiate Gabriel's actions in Malta. De Nicolay is the only detached observer I can offer, if he will allow himself so to be used. Secondly, I do not at present have all the evidence I need to overthrow Graham Malett. If I had, I should be speaking now to the Queen Dowager, and not to you. And thirdly, I have, by my own history, every possible motive—personal, religious, professional— for wanting Graham Malett out of the way at any cost, which will in itself discredit nearly everything I say.

'You may conclude from that,' said Francis Crawford, looking up without change of expression, 'that knowing the risks, I am putting before you something I think is more important than individual failure, or even individual life and death. And that if by any chance at the end of this meeting you are convinced'—a smile fleetingly appeared in his eyes—'you can rest assured that against these odds, your decision must be correct.'

It was an impressive opening, thought Adam Blacklock, sheltering his eyes behind one long, big-knuckled hand. And then Janet Beaton's voice, deeply unimpressed, said, 'Well, one way or the other, ye'd all better make up your minds. He wants to marry Grizel.'

'*Tu dis!*' Nicolas de Nicolay, listening open-mouthed, was startled into speech. 'But the vows of celibacy, those?'

'Churchmen *may* marry nowadays, you know; isn't it interesting?' said Sybilla unexpectedly. 'And if he can't get back to Malta while Juan de Homedès is Grand Master, he may well settle for a secular state. And in any case, as Francis is dying to point out. . . .'

'By marrying Will Scott's widow, he will have control of his children, and of all the Buccleuch lands, should Wat die. It is logical,' said Lymond courteously, 'if you note that he already has virtual control of the Order's possessions in Scotland. Sir James Sandilands is ill and lazy and most unwilling to speak, but I have learned that

401

the Queen Dowager is being given some of the revenues already, as a sop. With the Queen Dowager's support, with the revenues of the Hospitallers, or even a tenth of them; with the lands and offices of Buccleuch in his hands, and with the weapon of St Mary's behind him, Sir Graham Malett has, it can be agreed I would think without any prejudice, the prospect of becoming a major power in Scotland; particularly if, for example, the other major landowners such as the Kerrs and my own family became discredited or extinct.

'The question is,' said Lymond, and his eyes, impersonal as his voice, wandered round the long table, 'if, however innocently, he acquired such power, do we believe he is a fit person to wield it?'

'For many years, in the Mediterranean,' said Nicolas de Nicolay unexpectedly, 'he is known as a great and godly person. He is certainly of a courage unmatched.'

'There is no question,' said Lymond at once, 'of his courage. Or of his ability. I have tested both over and over again. I wish there were. . . . Lady Jenny, what is your impression of him?'

Taken aback, the little red-haired woman, plump and pretty, her china-blue eyes wide on his, clasped her hands under her chin. Her rings flashed and dazzled and the King of France's cameo, occupying the whole of her forefinger, stared balefully at his employee de Nicolay. Jenny Fleming might not be noted for her brain, but her emotional independence was considerable. 'He looks like God,' she said simply.

Alec Guthrie, his face cracking involuntarily in a smile, cleared his throat. 'He sounds like God, too,' he said. 'You'll never get the women on your side, Crawford.'

'You think not? Margaret?' said Lymond.

Margaret Erskine, very pale, raised her eyes. The tears in her brown eyes had dried, but strain was marked on her brow, and in her tight-clasped hands. She said, 'He unwittingly broke the news of my husband's death to me. It was not his fault; he had no reason to believe I didn't know already. But I can't help. . . .' She broke off, and then resumed in a very steady voice, 'I can't help, obviously, associating him with my feelings then, although he was painstakingly kind. I'm sorry, Francis. I am not fond of him, but for no practical reason. I must rank myself simply as biased.'

'Or more sensitive than most of us,' said Sybilla suddenly, in a queer voice. Up to now, she had neither spoken nor looked at her son in the chair; only, her back flat and straight, she had studied the rows of Fleming paintings on the opposite wall, her small face set. 'Graham Malett knew that Tom's death had been kept from you, Margaret. The Queen Dowager sent to inform him before he paid you that visit. I spoke to her messenger, quite by chance, when they came north.'

And as Margaret Erskine, a new expression on her face, stared at the Dowager, Lymond said slowly, 'So . . .' and then breaking off without warning said, 'Margaret, I'm sorry. I didn't know. There's no reason for you to endure this kind of experience unless you are anxious to stay.'

'But I am,' said Margaret Erskine; and surprisingly there was a new firmness in her voice and her round jaw. 'More than ever, I am.'

'Then . . . yes, he was cruel, this man of God,' said Lymond quietly. 'Surprisingly cruel, and surprisingly amoral in his dealings with his erring brethren. We all have our weaknesses, and for all his preaching and his praying he seems to have done little to overcome them. . . . Is that true, Adam?'

Adam Blacklock, seated, inescapably, on Lymond's right, took down his sheltering hand and watched it shake. 'Is this a public degradation?' he said.

There was a pause. 'Of course,' said Lymond's passionless voice. 'It is the very fabric of degradation. For all of us. For myself most of all. It is a count of small nastinesses; a long, sordid, petty-minded tale aimed only at destructiveness. I regret,' said Lymond, his voice sharpened for a second beyond his level, deliberate key, 'that I cannot offer you, this time, the noble anguish of some magnificent hell. Only the embarrassment of mentioning now, in the privacy of this room, that Graham Malett made you drunk and kept you drunk, whenever he could.'

Adam, his betraying hands trapped between his knees, did not reply.

'*Is that true?*' said Lymond, and turned to look him full in the face.

Adam Blacklock lifted his head. 'Yes. Yes, it's true. But only because Abernethy's treatment was so slow, and the pain was. . . . Oh, God. I'm not going to make excuses. Make what you can of it,' he said. 'It wasn't his fault, anyway. He tried to stop me.'

'But being addicted to spirits, as he must have known, once you started you couldn't stop. So in the kindness of his heart, he switched you to drugs.'

Adam said nothing. The silence stretched on. 'Provided by whom, Adam?' said Lymond quietly. And as Blacklock didn't answer, he went on himself. 'Randy Bell, wasn't it? Who is, Archie Abernethy tells me, an obvious addict himself, and possesses imported drugs in quantities usually unobtainable except in Mediterranean countries. Whatever you may say, Gabriel's part in that was not kindness. It was not even intelligent. If he had appealed to your brain instead of to your emotions, he would have had you off it in a month. As you now are. And as you are going to stay, whatever the outcome of this. There is also Plummer.'

Alec Guthrie said, 'The theft at Liddel Keep?'

'Yes. How, as a matter of interest I wonder, did you hear of that?' said Lymond.

'It was all round yon March meeting. The tale was that you had let it be known in order to keep him in his place.'

'I have other, more direct methods of keeping Lancelot Plummer in his place,' said Lymond. 'There is nothing wrong with either Plummer or Tait, except that they have rather esoteric tastes for an obscure country retreat in Scotland. Instead of putting this into perspective, Malett chose to sharpen their cultural exile by creating a craving for things material and immaterial which he knew could not be satisfied at present with me. Hence the theft of the Staurotheque from Liddel Keep. Every chance he had, Tait was in some little hole or corner hunting for a bargain, and that's only one step from contraband. Plummer came down, eventually, on the side of the angels, and in a month or two wouldn't have stirred off his kneecaps, if it were the time to be on his kneecaps, if Ghengis Khan and his horde had appeared at the gates. What were you offered, Alec, that you have withstood so admirably?'

'The opportunity to analyse Francis Crawford,' said Guthrie's level voice. 'You guessed that, surely.'

'Yes.' Abruptly, Lymond pushed back his chair and, rising, walked to the windows. He turned, the heavy tassel from one of the tapestries in his hand. 'You had better say, then, why you are here?'

Alec Guthrie raised his eyebrows. One stocky booted leg cocked on the other; his thumbs tucked into his belt, his spine curved at the bottom of his chair, he was the most relaxed man there. 'You're the cleverest drunken lecher I know; and the only one who'd stand there and give me the chance to say it,' he said.

'Wrong,' said a thick voice mildly.

Guthrie grinned.

Thompson the corsair, lifting his matted beard out of his jerkin, stared back. 'Wrong,' he said again. 'Dead cold sober to the point of ociosity.'

'At Dumbarton?' said Lord Culter's cold voice.

'Once,' said Thompson calmly. 'In the better part of a year. I have a wee rule. I'll do no business with a sober man. I'll tell ye this more. I'll no do business with Francis Crawford again, drunk or sober. I had a stound in my brain-pan the next morning and a second-hand feel to my own affairs that I didna relish. I talked. I dinna doubt it.'

'Some of it to purpose,' said Lymond, smiling a little, and came back and sat down, as Janet said flatly, 'If we're to be as fussy as yon, I might mention that according to Wat ye fair reeked with whisky that night ye know of. Not that I blame you.'

The night that Lymond, their brilliant archer, had given his bow at Liddel Keep to Will Scott, Adam thought, because his hands were not to be trusted. The night Will Scott died, and Lymond had brought through a flagon of neat aqua-vitæ, full.

'If I can speak?' said Archie Abernethy woodenly from the door.

'No. You are partisan,' said Lymond quietly.

'But,' the brown, scarred little man persisted. 'Mr Hoddim there will recollect. We tried to rouse you, when the laddie was dying. The spirits got all over the place. That was Sir Graham.'

'Someone,' said Lymond slowly, 'left the flask beside me?'

'That was Sir Graham,' Fergie Hoddim, his face absorbed, confirmed. 'But a reasonable thing to do, under the circumstances.'

'Under the circumstances,' said Lymond, 'an act of God-damned calculated bloody-mindedness that. . . .' He halted.

'That completed the alienation of Buccleuch, you would say,' said Alec Guthrie blandly. 'But Graham Malett, surely, has never knowingly caused you pain. His affection for you has never been hidden. He stood up for you in all his talks with me; he's sometimes been the only one who did. The only grief of his life, we all know, is that he canna bring you to the light as well. You've proved maybe that he's ower skilly with other folk, and maybe ambitious, and maybe with a quirk or two in him he tried to conceal. But you've proved little more.'

'*I haven't started yet*,' said Lymond, and the soft intensity of it silenced them all. 'Bear with me. . . . Only bear with me.'

The sun moved. Inside the great hall, the coloured light moved over the ten intent faces and the centre of their attention as he talked, watching them all: referring occasionally to one or other of them; making each point with cold clarity.

'Let us consider the siege engine,' he began. 'The siege engine, built lovingly by Plummer and Bell, which had run out of control and capsized, killing a boy and trapping Effie Harperfield and her four children. The siege engine which had required Gabriel's special skills to raise and free them. Thomas Wishart had discovered the accident, and had helped to free the unfortunate family. . . . Tosh?' directed Lymond.

Buccleuch's bodyguard, nimble, grinning, got up from his hunkers beside Abernethy. He'd examined the engine. The brake had been off. He'd also looked for the wheel-marks. It had been left standing at a level point near the top of the small incline. From that position, the ridged earth indicated, it had been levered to the top of the hill and allowed to run. 'Yon was no accident,' said Tosh with positive enjoyment. 'Yon was engineered, and be damned to Effie Harperfield and her weans.'

'It may have been, but Sir Graham had no chance to do it alone,' said Fergie Hoddim sharply. 'Someone was with him all that day.'

'Agreed,' said Lymond. 'However, let us turn now to the curious matter of Philippa Somerville. Philippa discovered, never mind how, that George Paris is a double agent, working for England as well as ourselves. I hope you've severed your connexion with him, Thompson my friend, for his time is running out very fast now. She knew also that Graham Malett was aware that Paris was an English agent. She did not know, as I did, on Tosh's advice, that Malett had seen Paris several times in France and knew that he was supposed to be working for Scotland and Ireland as well. For some reason he does not wish it known, it seems, that he possesses this knowledge. For one thing the Queen Dowager would be upset to think that Gabriel knows of Paris's treachery, and has done nothing about it.'

'Have you?' said Richard Crawford, and Guthrie smiled.

'I might have done,' said Lymond. 'Except that the Queen Dowager's activities *vis-à-vis* Ireland in the past year haven't mattered a damn; and it seemed a good deal more important to guess Gabriel's game. Also I could hardly move without discrediting Thompson and hence St Mary's through the Thompson connexion. All my precautions in that direction have now been nullified, obviously enough, by Thompson's fool behaviour in Ireland. But that's something else again. The point is that Philippa seems to have constituted a danger in Graham Malett's eyes. He made one or two unsuccessful attempts to escort her here and there, and while staying with her on one occasion was much disturbed when the building nearly burned to the ground. The rendezvous at Liddel Keep with Will Scott was his suggestion, and it seems more than a coincidence that the Turnbulls, who lived so conveniently near the Keep, were paid to do what they did *when* they did. Which brings us to the Hot Trodd.'

'But Will was killed by a left-handed man,' said Janet Beaton of Buccleuch suddenly.

For a moment Lymond said nothing. Then he asked softly, 'Why did Will take the route he did when he followed the Turnbulls, Janet? It took him two days and a night to discover them. Granted they dodged all over the place, but his tracking used to be better than that.'

'It wasna a matter that was troubling him on his return, so we'll never know, will we?' said Janet uncompromisingly. 'I mind the rest, though, saying something about new hoofmarks coming smack in your eye at every bend of the road like horse-dashings.'

'You would almost think, wouldn't you, that they were deliberately being led astray?' said Lymond. 'Would a few questions among the men who were on the Trodd do any good, d'you think, Janet?'

'I could try,' she said. A big, stalwart woman with a mind of her own, she had caught Sybilla's eye and was frowning, thoughtfully.

'Alec? Fergie?' said Lymond. 'You were both with Gabriel. Was it possible that for these two days he was leading you away from Scott?'

Carefully, 'It's possible,' said Fergie Hoddim at length. 'But if you'll remember, the real hindrance was your own absence and Sir Graham's reluctance to usurp your command, after that affair of the fuel supplies.'

'My absence. . . . Yes,' said Lymond briefly. 'Adam, this is where you come into your own.'

Adam Blacklock laid hold of the arms of his chair. His sharpened voice saying, 'I don't want to say anything of that!' clashed with Lord Culter's, as Lymond's brother sprang to his feet at the foot of the table and said, his voice harsh with angry disgust, 'My God, we don't have to listen to this. Haven't you smeared Graham Malett with mud enough, without dragging in his sister?'

'But don't you think,' said Lymond pointedly, 'that Graham Malett has been remarkably successful in maligning me? At every opportunity my drinking, my morals, my ability to organize and my general fitness to command St Mary's have been called into question. Will's death was laid at my door; Philippa's, no doubt, would have been due to me also. In his brotherly concern for me, he did nothing to change Philippa's own dislike and distrust of me personally, and he made quite successfully worse the unhappy relationship that was developing with Jerott Blyth. If events at Dumbarton had turned out on that occasion as planned, Jerott Blyth would have precipitated the crisis that ended my career at St Mary's. As it was, Richard bore the brunt, and being my brother, kept it to himself. Which didn't suit Sir Graham at all. He nearly succeeded at the Hadden Stank in badgering Richard into proclaiming my shame to the world, but not quite. Although I had to be bloody obstreperous, Richard, to get you to break off the encounter before the worst befell. If apologies are any good to you, I offer you mine, publicly, now. If we ever get out of this bloody mess, the credit will be yours. Adam, your natural delicacy does you honour; but in the matter of Gabriel's rare and lovely Joleta, you are the only witness for the defence.'

Lymond paused. Round the long table, the hardening of their attention was plain to see. He was approaching the inexcusable: something that all of them, except for de Nicolay, knew or suspected; and they awaited it with shrinking revulsion. Only among the women, Jenny looked less than disturbed, and Thompson, with a chuckle, shuffled lower in his chair. Margaret Erskine, her face deliberately calm, sent a silent message of support over the table to the Dowager of Culter.

Lymond continued, his cold voice unaltered, 'Two of the prime moves towards usurping power, it seemed to me, would be to attack on two fronts at once: to rouse the Government—in this case, the Queen Dowager against me, which he has done—do you really think, Thompson, that Logan's attack on you was a coincidence?—and to discredit me, finally, with the company. The one person associated

407

with him who walked also in clouds of sanctity, and possessed as well extreme youth and extreme beauty, was his sister Joleta.'

'Ah, the golden child. I know her,' said Nicolas de Nicolay lingeringly. 'But you suspect Sir Graham Malett, you would say, of accusing you of molesting her? Your exposition enchants me, but this I find hard to believe.'

'You needn't. It's true,' said Lymond drily. The clinical blue gaze looked for the recoil and found it, from face to face round the table. 'The point being,' he continued, staring at them, 'that Sir Graham has almost certainly been accusing people of debauching Joleta since she became eligible for seduction. Joleta is not a virgin. She was experienced when she came here from Malta. In addition, she has, as Adam will confirm for you later, borne at least one child. She is pregnant now, though not by me. These are facts, however unpleasant. There are, also, other traits of character which some of us can put before you which might lead you to agree that she is not the winsome vessel she appears. What you must also bring yourselves to understand . . . is that Gabriel knows it.'

'*Gabriel knows it!* But this is sacrilegious rubbish!' The voice, the contempt, were Lord Culter's. But Alec Guthrie's followed immediately after. 'You'll have trouble substantiating that. If it were true, he would never have brought her. Too much of a liability.'

Lady Jenny sparkled. If her attention had wandered through some of the discussion, it had become remarkably vigorous at mention of Joleta. 'A liability? With Francis?' she said, the lightest malice in her tone. 'I should think Joleta was Sir Graham's greatest asset.'

Unexpectedly, Lymond smiled back. 'He thought so,' he said. 'No effort was spared to press home the point that Joleta was to be my redemption. So that I became enslaved, he was prepared to contemplate marriage—anything. It would have saved him a remarkable amount of trouble, obviously, to have me a doting member of the family. Joleta did her best. . . . My God, it was a display. Fiery, disdainful, contemptuous, and as inviting as hell. That was before Gabriel arrived. I refused the invitation, much to her surprise. There was always the chance, still, that when he found out he couldn't do it the easy way, he might not come. I didn't quite know the full extent of his vanity then. He must have written back trouncing her, and she abandoned the intellectual approach and came trailing nubile misery to St Mary's, where if she didn't manage to stay the night, at least she went on record as being innocently adoring. In fact, she was furious, with him and with me. Then he installed himself finally, and battle was joined.'

'Dumbarton?' said Adam Blacklock. It fitted so neatly, you could see them all thinking. It fitted so neatly that only a master strategist could have devised it. But which of them *had* devised it? The gentle, maligned Gabriel, flying from Malta? Or Francis Crawford, who had met his master and would not admit it?

'*Mille douceurs, mille bon mots, mille plaisirs:* Dumbarton. To which Gabriel was so gently insistent that I should not go, that I fell into the trap. So Jerott, Adam, Richard and I arrived at Dumbarton to take counsel with Thompson. Joleta was already there, and able to insert herself into my room before I got there myself. How did she know I should be there? Richard left after she did. But it was Gabriel who relayed to me the message that Thompson was waiting. Gabriel could have told her, well in advance. Gabriel could also have paid the Turnbulls to make their cattle foray at precisely the right time, so that Bell's arrival at Dumbarton with the news interrupted the happy union between myself and Joleta. That was, in fact, precisely what happened. But for Adam, who hid her for me, the whole sordid business would have been exposed there and then, and to Jerott, Gabriel's adoring disciple: poor bloody Jerott, torn in two. . . . He was to be Gabriel's Baptist and oust me before he came, did you realize that? Luckily Jerott is an intelligent man as well as an honest one, and it didn't happen. One of the things I have promised myself is to get Jerott out of this safely.'

Lymond paused. Often before, at St Mary's, Adam had seen this kind of marathon. Properly projected, Lymond's voice did not tire, and his concentration was sustained with no obvious effort. Even now, when what he was saying was both disagreeable and emotional in content, and so momentous for his own future, he talked as if giving them yet another of his precise, coldly documented briefings. Adam wondered where in the Culter family had gone all Sybilla's vast store of warmth. Wit was there—yes, when it suited him; as the whipping-post was there also. If the tale about Joleta were true—and Adam, more than anyone there, had cause to believe it might be true—he pitied, if he pitied either of them, the promiscuous bitch which was Joleta.

The door clicked. Such had been the pressure that no one there had noticed Margaret Erskine rise and go out. Now she came back, and behind her the Moor Salablanca bore into the room a tray of pewter cups and a flagon. Silently he distributed them, and in the little release from tension they scraped back their chairs and stretched, and uttered commonplaces among themselves.

At the head of the table Lymond did not move, staring down at his hands; nor did he lift the cup when it was put at his side. Margaret, pausing at his chair, said crisply, 'Yours is water.'

Then he turned round, and the blue eyes, alarmingly, blazed into laughter. 'My dear, my dear. You are the queen of women,' he said. 'For this, you are right, I need to be either entirely sober or very drunk indeed.'

On his left, Sybilla had heard. 'I think, on the whole,' said the Dowager, looking levelly at her son, 'I should prefer that you kept sober and *we* got exceedingly drunk.' And that, Adam on his other side noticed, effectively silenced Francis Crawford.

After that, there were no more interludes. Thompson, brisk after his third cup, began it again, jocularly, by remarking, 'And so ye bedded the lassie at Dumbarton and left me on my lainsome, ye rat. But why, now, if ye jaloused a trap? There was a loon on the watch in the courtyard that night who was gey interested in your window. Did ye not see him?'

'The Master of the Revels. Yes, I saw him,' said Lymond. 'Look, the moment that girl walked into the inn, never mind my room, I lost the chance of preserving my laughable reputation. The damage was done. I didn't see why she shouldn't pay for it. And there was always the chance, an unlikely one, I admit, that *I* might have converted *her*.'

'And did you?' It was Lord Culter, bitterly disingenuous.

For a second, the line of anger between Lymond's fair brows showed; then his face smoothed, controlled again. 'Obviously not,' he said. 'From her performance when you walked in and afterwards. You didn't spread the rumours about my conduct that night, Richard; nor did I. And Gabriel was in no position to appear to know what had happened—not yet. It must have been done, in some artless-clumsy way, by Joleta herself.'

'It was,' said Lady Jenny brightly. 'For a clever girl, I never heard anyone *quite* so bad at lying.'

'And she was very good at lying,' said Sybilla. 'I can confirm that, if it has any value. But why spread the rumours at all?'

'To prepare the ground. She is, as you know, to bear a child. It is not mine, and could be proved, I suppose, not to be mine, but I shall be accused of having fathered it, and in an atmosphere so emotional that reason must be swept away entirely. That will be the last move—or nearly the last move. And it must be done, for effect, soon. Joleta's condition will become public any moment now. For Gabriel to be mortally hurt by the revelation, the blow must come first. He will know, by now, from our little scene yesterday at Midculter that he is safe; that I have spurned Joleta and alienated my family without apparently having any suspicion of himself. That, indeed, up to now has been my only strength—that he is vain, and has conducted his campaign without truly examining his pawns, except for their faults.

'Fortunately, perhaps,' said Lymond with a wry smile which did not touch his eyes, 'among the throng of mine he missed my only virtue, which is persistence. Joleta cannot travel, but the news will be brought, any day now, that whoever lay by the rose has emphatically borne the flower away, if not the bush. By that time, the news of Thompson's little affair will be reaching the Queen Dowager and she will do what she threatened—descend on St Mary's to clean it out. Instead, she will find, I should guess, St Mary's under sole control of Sir Graham, bitter but brave. *You* may not object,' said Lymond pointedly, 'but if I am to lose my life in the same way as Will Scott, I should like it to be clear why.'

There was a little silence. Then Janet Beaton, speaking carefully, said, 'Will died on the stairs at Liddel Keep, defending it from the Kerrs. He died from a left-handed sword-thrust that cut off his right arm.'

Lymond looked again at his hands. 'Adam,' he said. 'You were there. Do you remember Randy Bell's account of how Will died? It was quite accurate. He said, "He took the brunt of the rush for the stairs. I was in the middle and Crawford at the top when they burst in, and he pushed past us all." Is that right?'

'Yes,' said Blacklock.

Lymond looked up, and now in his narrowed eyes they saw some of the temper concealed up to now. ' "*I was in the middle*," Bell said. A left-hand sword-cut from below, Janet, is quite indistinguishable from a right-hand sword-cut from behind . . . except for the angle of the cut. Will Scott was killed by a blow that cut *downwards*.'

'*Bell!*' Slowly, Alec Guthrie got to his feet and stared, thick hands on the boards, at the head of the table. 'Will Scott was killed by *Bell*?'

'Of course,' said Lymond. 'Think, my butty. Who supplied Adam with drugs? Who worked with Plummer on the siege engine that nearly killed the Harperfields? Who came with such magnificent timing to Dumbarton to interrupt my *tête-à-tête* with Joleta? Who killed old man Turnbull just as he was protesting, no doubt, that what he had done was done under orders, and that killing Turnbulls was no part of the scheme? You didn't see a Scott kill the old man, Adam. You only assumed he did. It was Bell's hard luck that I actually got to the Keep from Dumbarton, and he couldn't slip out before the attack, as he'd planned. The Kerrs wouldn't have got into the Keep without that cellar key. Who left them the key? Who bribed the Turnbulls? Bell would know, as well as Gabriel. It was Bell who tried to delay leaving St Mary's in order to weaken Scott's alibi still more for the cattle killing. Philippa should have died too, if I hadn't got her away. As it was, the Scott clan was nearly cooked like pies in an oven, and the herd slaughtered, thus alienating Buccleuch from the protection of St Mary's. Tosh has been with Wat as you know, Janet, ever since. For Gabriel is manipulating the concerns of the Scotts and the Kerrs. But for Tosh, the two families would have come face to face without our protection at the Hadden

411

Stank: two warnings concerning the date failed to reach us, confiscated by Gabriel's men. In fact, because Buccleuch confined himself to his farce with the children, the March was unlikely to have any lethal outcome. But that was merely Providence's own little joke. For the next step, surely, is the death of Buccleuch.'

Politely, but firmly, Nicolas de Nicolay cleared his throat. 'There is something I would ask in all this. You say, and I believe you, that you were afraid when you left Malta that Sir Graham Malett meant to come and take your place at the head of your finished army. Why, then, did you permit him to stay at all? If you had turned him away, so courteously, at the first, he would have had time neither to make disciples nor to undermine your authority. Is this not strange?'

This time there was a long pause. Lymond's face, again without expression, was turned to the long windows, where the cooling lacquers of dusk had overlaid the bright colours. 'Turn away this great, militant monk, famous throughout Christendom? Yes, I might have done that. I would have lost most of my best men, and all the Knights of St John, and the others would have every reason to believe me afraid of his stature. But remember—or try to imagine—that I knew him, incredibly, as a man of evil intent: clever, powerful and basking in his gift for inspiring and handling his fellow-mortals.

'Perhaps, once, he was all he appears to be. Perhaps he plumbed too early the false places of religion and of violence, perhaps he grew bored with his great skills; perhaps, as he once confessed to me, the sheer love of power corrupted what was never very difficult to corrupt. . . . Perhaps he is insane. But he is not what he seems. He is a great and dangerous man; and if I had turned him from St Mary's do you think he would have accepted that for a moment? He had no fear, even on the dramatic night of the fuel crisis, that I would allow him to go. On the other hand, if I hadn't taken a firm hold of the command on that night, I should have lost it to Malett. From then on, he was bound to try to get rid of me. He has refused an offer by the Queen Dowager to depose me, but only because he will be surer of the support of all St Mary's when I have gone. His prize after all is to be Scotland, so ludicrously vulnerable during the Regency, so strategic in position, so potentially powerful. Failing St Mary's, he would have found his army elsewhere, and fashioned it out of men less expendable than I am, or less intelligent than you.

'I had,' said Lymond, his eyes still remote on the glass, 'really only two alternatives. I could have killed Graham Malett, or fought him. I should perhaps have killed him; but it would have been without proof and without reason, and I don't, I suppose, any more than the next man desire to trespass out of this uncertain world through a noose in New Bigging Street. And it would have been the

412

end of St Mary's and I had—I have—great hopes of St Mary's. So—I elected to fight. I have probably lost.'

The faces round the table now were ghosts in the dusk, only shapes: long and short-haired, bald, snooded, above shoulders padded, buckled, sheathed in worn leather. No one spoke, though Thompson shifted explosively in his chair and pressing one hand on the table, looked round. '*No principles and no philosophy*,' said Sybilla, Dowager Lady Culter suddenly, her voice soft and derisive as she quoted his own account of the aims of St Mary's. 'And for money alone.'

'Dragut Rais knew, did he not?' said Nicolay. 'You have not asked me what I know of Malta and Tripoli.'

'Later, if you will,' said Lymond, his voice flat. Speaking, suddenly, was an obvious effort, but his manner was still, like Sybilla's, uncompromisingly cold. 'Dragut Rais knew, yes. After all, Malett was working for him. But only Jerott, perhaps, would fully understand. The case here must stand or fall by what we can prove in Scotland. The case for the Government is a different matter. But I cannot move without proof, and I have come, at last, to the point where I cannot get proof without help. It is too near the end for me.'

'I see.' It was Guthrie's quiet voice. 'Naturally. If what you say is true, he can't afford to let you live, can he? Your death would be persuasive, of course, but a pity.'

Lymond's half-smile could be felt in the dusk. 'I must confess, it would be more . . . convenient if I could convince you now. If not, there is one thing at least you can do. Richard. . . . If anything happens to me, Lymond will be your property. Do what the Queen Mother has threatened to do. Blow it up. Dismantle the cabins and all the encampment, disperse the stock, destroy the weapons. It was created with my money; it is not Graham Malett's or the Queen Dowager's, it is mine. I would forgive no one, least of all a man of my own blood, if something I had created became a knife at the throat of my own country. And if you are then convinced, pursue Gabriel; pursue him to the ends of the earth, for wherever he is, there will be nothing but waste.'

'*No*,' said Lord Culter, and stood up.

The emotionless voice beside Adam Blacklock stopped, and he felt, in the gloom, Lymond give some movement, at once controlled. It was odd, Adam thought, that Lymond's harshest opponent should be his brother, and that each man had such power to hurt the other.

A sound at the door made him look round again. It was Margaret again, with the three men, each bearing a taper. Light ran round the room from bracket to bracket, garlanding the tapestried walls, turning the table into a ruddy pool round which the bright, fleshy faces calyxed in linen and gauze and fancy Swiss bobbin-lace looked

413

with surmise and relief, each to the other. 'How would the other verdicts run?' thought Adam. Margaret Erskine, pale and big-eyed, was already biased against Gabriel, and was a loyal adherent of Lymond's, Adam knew, for many years now. Sybilla, for all her sharp, unsentimental brain, was a kindred soul with her younger son, and Lady Jenny from jealousy alone would support any man who maligned Joleta. Add Janet Beaton and a natural wish to find someone—anyone—who would exorcise the misery of her stepson's death, and you could say that the women were on Francis Crawford's side.

One might have expected as much, and in the counsels of the Dowager and the power they could bring him in men—the Flemings, the Grahams, the Scotts—this was not a trifle. But Adam knew, and Lymond knew, that unless he had convinced these men—Fergie Hoddim, Alec Guthrie, Thompson who had no principles you could appeal to, his own brother Culter and, Adam supposed, he himself whom Lymond had trusted some of the way at least, and whose self-respect he had rescued by trusting him. ... Unless he had induced these men by logic, by half-proofs, by the compressed, powerful current of the prosecution thus coldly concluded to believe that what he said was correct, he was beaten at last.

And on Lymond's face, clearly seen for the first time since Richard had made his disclaimer, you could tell that he had braced himself to meet the first proof of his failure. Elbows on the table, chin propped on his two thumbs, he sat quietly, his lashes lowered, his lips pressed against his interlaced fingers. He did not move again when Richard repeated more clearly, 'No. There will be no call to pursue Graham Malett then or any time in the future. We must cut him down *now*.'

The heavy lids lifted. After a long moment, Lymond lowered his hands with great care from his face to the table, and said, 'Why?' Beside him, Adam noticed, Sybilla's blue eyes were running with tears.

There was mild impatience on Lord Culter's pleasant, undistinguished face. 'Because you have done all that skill could devise to present a detached case, and failed. Because you are asking for help, and you hate asking for help. Because of our mother's evidence, and Blacklock's evidence, and Margaret's evidence, and the fact that you asked Guthrie and Hoddim and the fact that they came. This may be,' said Richard with unexpected wry humour, 'a crusade conducted by the Culter family solo in a band of dissentients, but I am with you.'

'Reasonably well put,' said Fergie Hoddim, 'You could add that the arguments were extremely cogent; and that we have the further testimony, not yet put forward, of a most estimable witness in M. de Nicolay. There is a basis for further examination; there is no doubt of that. Even a case for forethocht felony, forthwith.'

414

'Blacklock?' Richard said.

'I have known for some time,' Adam said. It seemed as if he had known it for ever; and that with trust had gone all that he had ever believed.

'And Guthrie?'

Alec Guthrie, whose profession was arms and whose first loves were honesty and justice and human rights, said, 'I have weighed these two men also, long before today. What we all must remember, and keep remembering, is that this is not the Church against the rebellious intellect, just as it is not a struggle of Christian values perverted against a great faith.' Alec Guthrie paused and, his eyes on Lymond's still face, grinned.

'The argument got a bit specious to my mind at times: if there's a man in the district with a soul white as a burde claith, it's not Francis Crawford. But in Graham Reid Malett goes a monk who is false as a diamond of Canada. I'll join your verloren hoop.'

'And I!' said Thompson, and crashed his knotted fist on the board so that the empty cups rattled. And as Richard sat down, satisfaction on his face, and the women nodded agreement, Lymond spoke calmly.

'We are, then, unanimous. We are high-handed together; and if we do the Church wrong, then we cough together in hell. There are questions you will wish to ask of myself and de Nicolay, and tasks I have to burden you with. These will do later. There is food coming, I am told. Let us forget Graham Malett, briefly, till after that.'

It was over. Stretching painfully, Adam wondered if his aching back were his alone, or shared by them all. The tension had been at times as much as he could stand; the summing-up, now he came to think of it, deliberately brief.

At his side, Lymond rose. They were all getting up, stamping their feet, smiling, a little subdued because of what they had learned and what they had undertaken. Thompson, heaving up from beside Sybilla, reached out a hairy wrist to thump her son's back.

But Lymond had gone, moving unnoticed between chair and table and the disordered, discoursing company in the flickering light. The door clicked and Adam, shouldering swiftly towards it passed Archie Abernethy, thoughtfully chewing a chicken bone. The former Keeper removed it, revealing the gap-toothed cavity of his mouth, and said, 'In a moment, sir. He hasn't gone far.' Adam opened the door.

It was true. A little below him, where the stair widened to accommodate a window embrasure, Lymond had stopped to look through the panes, one hand gripping the woodwork.

The fingers of that hand were white with pressure. Adam Blacklock stepped back quickly from his vantage point, and silently closing the big doors, walked round the table to find Sybilla, and salute her.

XIV

The Axe Falls

(St Mary's, September 1552)

CHEESE-WAME HENDERSON was a big man, despite the pot-belly that gave him his name. He was not the first of his family to serve the Somervilles; he had grown up with the kind severities of Gideon and worshipped his widow Kate. But most of all, he was marshmallow in the hands of Philippa, whom he had taught to look after her ponies and pets, and who had taught him in return the family brand of acid and affectionate humour.

When Philippa had first demanded his help in eluding Kate and travelling to St Mary's, he had indignantly refused. He was there now because he had discovered, to his astonishment, that she was desperate, and perfectly capable of going without him. Why she had got it into her young head she must see this man Crawford, Cheese-wame didn't know. But after pointing out bitterly that (*a*) he would lose his job; (*b*) the rogues in the Debatable would kill them, (*c*) that she would catch her death of cold and (*d*) that Kate would never speak to either of them again, he went, his belt filled with knives and her belongings as well as his own in the two saddlebags behind his powerful thighs, while Philippa rode sedately beside him on her smaller horse, green with excitement, with her father's pistol tied to her waist like a ship's log and banging against her thin knees.

They had a long way to go. For September, it was a mild night, and the reeking warmth of her horse and the steady trot pioneered by Cheese-wame, who had no desire to be caught by his fellow-servants before the lass had got whatever it was she wanted, kept Philippa warm. Riding beside the waters of the North Tyne, the fallen leaves sodden below her mare's busy hooves and Henderson's comforting bulk beside her, and his big hand ready to steady hers on the reins, Philippa felt her stomach turn, again, at what she had decided to do.

After mature reflection; on information received; from the wisdom of her encroaching years, she had reached the conclusion that she had made a false judgement.

Once, long ago, Francis Crawford had reduced her to terror and, the episode over, she had suffered to find that for Kate, apparently, no reason suggested itself against making that same Francis Crawford her friend.

He was not Philippa's friend. She had made that clear, and, to be fair, he had respected it. He had even, when you thought of it, curtailed his visits to Kate, although Kate's studied lack of comment on this served only to make Philippa angrier.

He had been nasty at Boghall. He had hit her at Liddel Keep. He had stopped her going anywhere for weeks.

He had saved her life.

That was indisputable.

He had been effective over poor Trotty Luckup, while she had been pretty rude, and he hadn't forced himself on her; and he had made her warm with his cloak.

He had gone to Liddel Keep expressly to warn her, and when she had been pig-headed about leaving (Kate was right) he had done the only thing possible to make her.

And then he had come to Flaw Valleys for nothing but to make sure of her safety, and he had been so tired that Kate had cried after he had gone. And then it had suddenly struck her, firmly and deeply in her shamefully flat chest, so that her heart thumped and her eyes filled with tears, that maybe she was wrong. Put together everything you knew of Francis Crawford. Put together what you had heard at Boghall and at Midculter, what you had seen at Flaw Valleys, and it all added up to one enormous, soul-crushing entity.

She had been wrong. She did not understand him; she had never met anyone like him; she was only beginning to glimpse what Kate, poor maligned Kate, must have seen all these years under the talk. But the fact remained that he had gone out of his way to protect her, and she had put his life in jeopardy in return.

A year ago this month, on his deathbed, Sir Thomas Erskine had given her a message for Lymond. It was his right to have it. And whatever his anger at the delay, whatever danger they faced on the journey, she was firmly resolved to deliver it. Lion-hearted; her tremors braced with virtue, Philippa trotted on.

At Tarset they stopped for some bread and cheese that Henderson had prudently packed in his saddlebag, and drank burn water although Cheese-wame had, she noticed, been providential in this respect also and provided himself with a serviceable corked bladder from which he drank by the little flickering fire he had made, his Adam's apple moving up and down. But for the gentle sound of beasts cropping in the commonlands they had passed, it was totally quiet, now their ears were free of the noisy river, bubbling and shearing high in its banks. Picking their way back to it after their rest, Cheese-wame halted once, his hand on her arm, and they both listened, but the sound, whatever it was, had stopped, and soon they remounted and went on their way.

They were to ride all night, Cheese-wame said; and by dawn they might be past the Cheviot Hills and into Scotland itself, where they could look for a small inn in Liddesdale to rest. If Mistress Somerville sent after them, she would never think of looking so far. Then to-morrow afternoon, not to tire the little mistress, they would ride to Hawick and stop at Buccleuch's house of Branxholm, where she would be welcomed and not made to go home. Then, after a night's rest, they would take her to St Mary's.

It seemed to Philippa a good programme, apart from the allowance of rest for the little mistress, which was excessive, she felt. But long before her mare, now slowed to a walk, had begun to climb the long, grey reaches of the Border, she found creeping into her mind a little, gem-like fantasy of herself, in her thickest white nightie, and even her bedsocks, and even a hot brick as well, curled up on her mattress filled with Bass Rock feathers, under her striped woollen blankets and her silky cotton-stuffed quilt, with the curtains run all round the rods and a candle beside the bed, and a book, and nothing else except her own warm, breathed-out air. 'I've got a blister on my bottom,' said Philippa. 'Let's sing a long song. A rude one would be nice.' And because Cheese-wame Henderson was a simple man, as well as a nice one, they sang.

The big tinker had a hill pony, unshod, with feet like a baby's. On the soft ground the little, slippered beat could hardly be heard, and he had wrapped the bit and stirrups with fragments of rag. He travelled light; all his worldly possessions buried carefully in a marked spot by Tyneside, and carried only a bit of sacking with some food in it, and a long knife, and a blackthorn club, tied to the saddle.

He took his time. He wanted to think about Cheese-wame Henderson, to begin with; and he liked privacy for his violence, well away from the commerce of Northumberland, where sheltering nature did half the job for you. So he followed carefully, and drew back at Tilsit where, not far away, the cottagers were too nosy; and then, dropping back as the river thinned and quietened, he pattered gently behind Philippa and Cheese-wame, waiting his moment.

*

At Boghall the meeting was over very quickly, once they had eaten. Lymond had left first, to go straight to St Mary's, and Nicolas de Nicolay was to follow shortly. Janet, with Tosh in attendance, had wanted to return to Branxholm, and Lady Jenny, knowing her anxiety about Wat, let her go. Alec Guthrie had gone with her. And Thompson, Hoddim and Blacklock had dispersed also, with business to do.

Riding home with her older son silent beside her, Sybilla showed despite herself the strain of the past hours. She had been bitterly concerned about Francis returning to St Mary's now. Collect your evidence by all means, she had argued; and when you have it complete, take it to the Queen Dowager and let her act. But why go back yourself, when you know that the trap is about to close? Gabriel is about to make his definitive bid for leadership with the help of Joleta. The Queen Dowager, when she hears about the *Magdalena*, will be forced for the sake of peace with England to support him. Why risk your life?

'I like my fun,' Francis had said briefly. Pressed, he had given other reasons. His strength had been, and still was, his supposed ignorance of Graham Malett's nature. Until the proofs he needed were gathered, such as they were, he must not put Gabriel on his guard. Then, since messages had to pass between Joleta and St Mary's, and between London and Falkland, there were probably a few days in hand before anything could happen. Joleta, obviously, was unable to travel. The news—the shattering news, said Francis ironically, his eyes hard—would break with maximum impact, when he and Gabriel and as many as possible of the disaffected were present. In Gabriel's eyes, Lymond must realize now that Joleta was about to confess to her brother what he had done to her. If Lymond stayed away now, it would be open cowardice, from which Gabriel could make any capital he liked. On the other hand. . . .

'It is always possible, you know, that he may overreach himself,' Francis had said calmly, tucking her skirts round the planchet for her. 'He's not the only *rhétoriceur* in this cringing district. And although I can't expose Joleta for what she is, she may expose herself. It is, in any event, a battle I have to face and survive if I can. Because I cannot, in the end, ask these men to follow me unless they know what they are following. They are hand-picked, after all, and not fools. All I have to fear is the hysteria of the moment, and I think I can deal with that.'

'One blessing,' said Sybilla now reflectively to her other son as they rode. 'I needn't try to like Madame Donati any more.' And as he continued silent, she said sympathetically, 'You liked Sir Graham, didn't you? It seems a pity, but I had really rather have you friends with Francis.'

Richard said drily, 'Like you and Evangelista Donati, I suppose I felt I should like him. He is the only man I have ever met who had the stature to handle Francis, and the only one of whom I knew Francis afraid. It is a tragedy to Francis as well as to the Order that this is the outcome. If he survives this at all, it will leave him in unquestioned command. *And he needs a master.*'

'Or a mistress,' Sybilla remarked.

*

419

Very near the Border, they were seen crossing the Kielder Burn, but Cheese-wame said it didn't matter. By that time Philippa was almost too tired to keep in the saddle, and Cheese-wame, it would seem, had lost some of his confidence as well, or he would not have turned off the main route across the high fells to take the wheel causeway to Wauchope Forest.

The scrub and windblown pine trees, black in the greying light, gave at first the illusion of warmth and shelter from the little, pestering dawn wind; but then Philippa began to shiver again, and Cheese-wame, suspecting at length their direction, stopped both horses, and lifting her down from the saddle, built a roaring fire for them both on the steep slopes of the hill, the flame blown in guttering tassels against the black pines, while they waited for light.

The soft, resinous pile underfoot made for quiet pacing. The first Cheese-wame knew of the tinker's presence was a great blow on his back that tumbled him head over heels. It was not until minutes later when, clipped man to man by knee and elbow and wide, muscular hands, they threshed and bounded and crashed among the oak scrub and thorn that he isolated the thin, needling pain within the fading ache of the buffet and felt the tinker's grasp slide across the thick wet of his leather back, where the blood poured from the tinker's knife.

Philippa saw the knife between Cheese-wame's solid shoulders. As the two men rolled downhill past her, their voices lifted in snatches of wordless, guttural anger, she plunged to her feet, and snatching a blazing stob from the fire, ran jumping after them. She saw Cheese-wame's face, lithographic in grey and black, rear puppet-like over the tinker's great bulk and the tinker's shoulders begin their surge from the ground. With all the force of her arm, Philippa brought the flaming wood down on his head.

It burst like a catherine wheel. Blazing slivers, leaping into skin and sour clothes and hair, sprayed the tinker with fire, while the unburnt stock, a club in her hands, belaboured him as he struggled, both hands to his face.

Face averted, eyes nearly shut in a grimace of insane fright and sheer Somerville resolution, Philippa went on hitting until the man, now really shouting, managed to roll over on to his front and, blazing still, hands to his raw face, to begin to lurch to his knees. Then, dropping the branch, she ran to Cheese-wame.

He was on his feet, swaying. In the dim light the black channels and patches of blood reduced him to shapeless mosaic: even his face, where it was smeared, had acquired grotesque, different salients. Philippa said, her voice shaking, 'It's a lot of blood, but that's a good thing, you know. It washes away the dirt. I think if you could get on your horse I could perhaps hold you on for a bit until . . . until we get help. Unless,' said Pippa Somerville, a good deal of the conviction suddenly leaving her voice, 'you would like to use my pistol?'

But it was evident, first, that Cheese-wame Henderson was far from aiming and letting off her pistol, and secondly that unless they got away soon, the bleeding, dizzy madman crashing through the scrub would suddenly come to his senses and finish what he had come to do. With fibreless fingers, Philippa somehow managed to tighten the girths on both horses and help Cheese-wame to mount, jammed between her body and a thick, twisted pine. Then they set off.

She did not know where to go. She asked Henderson but he spoke in tight, compressed phrases which she could hardly make out, and since it obviously gave him pain to breathe, let alone to speak, she dared not ask him again.

He needed help. But whom could she safely ask? That had been no chance attack: she knew that unshaven bulk too well. For weeks he had made his camp at Flaw Valleys, scouring the in-fields for scraps; begging in the village. He had followed them in order to kill.

Her young arm round the sagging body of Cheese-wame, aching with the switching pace of their horses, Philippa forced her tired brain to think. Downhill. If she went on downhill with the sun on her right, she would be in Scotland, if they were not there already. There should be crofts and farmhouses in the lower reaches of the hills, and later, she might strike the Slitrig Water, which led straight to Hawick. There were Scotts everywhere inside Hawick, and Branxholm itself a little outside. Then she would be all right.

The main thing was to keep going. She had no idea how badly, if at all, the tinker was hurt. She had seen Cheese-wame use his knife. But he might come after them: they could follow hoofmarks. And she had to get the big man some sort of help.

Philippa removed her arm, and fixing his hands somehow on his own horse's pommel, hunted for and found his flask. He drank from it as they rode, and although a good deal of it went over his stained jacket, he seemed a little stronger than he had been. The bleeding where the knife had been had stopped, but she undid her saddlebag and stuffed a shift under the stiffening leather to make sure. He looked odd with a hump to his back, and he had whimpered a bit while she did it, but afterwards he rode on in silence, and she only had to hold him now and then. 'It won't be long,' said Philippa cheerfully, her mother's ring in her voice. 'You know what Bess says. There's nothing in this world a drop of aqua-vitæ in a sheep's bladder won't cure. Stop the Somervilles with a *knife!* It needs *artillery*.' And she blew her nose hard.

*

Gabriel's return to St Mary's after an absence, like the return to class of some revered but exacting headmaster, was always a comfort to its officers and men. His massive competence spelt security even when, as now, he worked them like dogs.

The efficiency of St Mary's had been questioned. Therefore, before any emissary of the Queen Dowager or her French Ambassador might descend on them, their house must be put in perfect order. The moment that Jerott Blyth left, charitably to bring the gentle Joleta to her brother, Gabriel called his men before him and set them to work.

Inevitably, in his absence and Lymond's, the impossible standards they had both set had fallen off. With easy certainty Gabriel set about their repair, issuing formidable orders; walking and riding round all the big establishment to see them carried out; to advise and to help. He demanded that they finish it before Lymond came; and the pace was back-breaking. When darkness fell they continued, by torchlight, eating as they worked.

By midnight, everything in St Mary's was in order. In all its domains there was no wall broken or fence unrepaired; the beasts were tended and bedded in clean straw, the stores and weapons re-inventoried, the buildings whitewashed outside and washed and painted within. The big house itself reeked of soap, and all the mild disorder of everyday living had gone.

It was done willingly, for Gabriel; but with some private resentment as well. 'To hell with the Queen Dowager,' said Lancelot Plummer at one point, flinging down pad and penner. 'I didn't join this groat-sized model army to count herring barrels and hay and elevenpenny hogs, and how many bolls of barley we've sold to the neighbours at ten shillings under market price. Our lewd friend Crawford got us into the old woman's black books with his habits. I don't see why we should get him out.'

The Chevalier de Seurre, working with him, looked up from the sacks. 'I'll give you one very good reason,' he said. 'Because Graham Malett asks it.'

Cormac O'Connor, spectating, found much entertainment in the sight. He had come, with great reluctance, to visit St Mary's. Francis Crawford made his hackles rise; and he was afraid, moreover, for his position *vis-à-vis* Thompson the pirate. But, as with them all, Gabriel had somehow reassured and soothed him, and under that benign presence he was willing to wait, he did not know quite why, until tomorrow and even suffer Crawford's presence, if he came. When, their work exhausted at last, the company foregathered out of the starlit September night and, summoned to the castle itself, found waiting for them by Gabriel's orders a vast supper set out in the great hall, its savoury steams rising to the fine timbered roof with the heat from the great blazing fire, Cormac, his heavy face bland, took his place among them at the long officers' board at the top. Gabriel, from his place beside Lymond's empty chair, stood waiting to welcome them and then as, by his command, they seized their meat, he thanked them in his magnificent voice for what they had just done. Everything that should be said was expressly said, with no word of blame for their leader's lapses, and unstinted praise for themselves. Then, having eaten sparingly, he retired, leaving them to unrestricted enjoyment.

'That's a gentleman,' said Cuddie Hob approvingly.

'That's a saint,' said someone else, examining his callouses. 'But all the same, when I get to Heaven, I don't want to be in his bloody work-party.'

Then Cormac O'Connor unloaded his gifted contraband, which consisted of twenty puncheons of raw sherry-sack.

*

Ninety minutes later, with the noise ringing over the dark hills from Ettrick to Yarrow, Graham Malett rolled from his narrow bed, and tying his doublet quickly over his creased shirt and hose, went next door where the officers slept. In the first room, de Seurre's bed was occupied; the knight, his head buried in a huddle of blankets, had not wakened. In the next he found three others, two of them from the Order. There was no sign of the rest. He ran then, light-footed for all his height, down the stairs which led to the Hall.

The big room, finely tapestried and until now used on the rarest occasions by St Mary's mercenaries and men-at-arms as well as themselves, was so bright, after the cool dark of the dormitories, that the eye ached. With the light came the impact of noise. Between three hundred and four hundred men were talking, shouting, singing, stamping, and arguing noisily in groups. On one of the tables, his boots lobbing cups like quail into the air, someone was dancing a vigorous jig. In a corner, in very slow motion, two archers were fighting in a solemn and concentrated way; and, not unfortunately in a corner, someone else was being sick. Here and there, on or under the benches, the weak-headed had already succumbed on limp heaps. Everyone was very happy.

Unnoticed, Graham Malett stood in the doorway and looked. Then swiftly moving to the top table, the Knight Grand Cross found and laid a hand on Randy Bell's broad muscled shoulder. The doctor was singing. He looked round, still intoning, and for a moment, meeting Gabriel's clear eyes, his voice faltered. Then, a look of uncertain nonchalance struggling across his blunt features, he leaned back, carolling again. He was very drunk.

So was Lancelot Plummer. Mingling with the broad golden streams of sack coursing down the fine broadcloth, his tears dropped unregarded on to his hands, turning and turning the empty goblet before him. 'No one,' he was saying heavily, 'can call himshelf man and not mushroom, and fail to cherish the Artsh. Arts. *And lousy beggary hangs upon us!*' he cried, enunciating fiercely at his neighbour with sudden passion.

Hercules Tait looked up from his arms. 'We *are* lousy beggary,' he said distinctly, and shut his eyes again.

Serving Brother des Roches, who had been standing over him, straightened, and seeing Sir Graham, strode over, in rueful relief. 'It's a shambles,' he said. 'I'm sorry. I've done what I can, but they're in no mood to be moderate. It was O'Connor's wine.'

'The sherry-sack?' said Gabriel sharply. 'I said they might share it, by which I meant one serving per man. I gave no orders that they should empty the wain-load down their throats.'

'Then O'Connor and the rest didn't understand, sir,' said des Roches directly. 'The belief was that they could finish it. They just about have.'

Gabriel's examining gaze returned to the serving brother, and he smiled. 'Children, aren't they? Cunning and foolish at once. Let's see what can be done with them.' And, stepping again to his place, he collected a pewter wine-pot and with it, banged on the board.

All his life, des Roches and the few who were sober were to remember that talk as a faultless example of handling under adverse conditions. To begin with, Graham Malett hadn't even silence to speak in. Shouts and drunken laughter interrupted the shifty apprehension of those still able to recognize him. Only, as the speaker went on, his voice deepening in force and anger, these died away, and he spoke into absolute quiet.

He began by telling them, dispassionately, that all that had happened that night would be reported to Lymond when he came back. They knew what that meant. They had no reason to complain. A supremely trained force such as theirs could neither operate successfully nor defend itself against others unless it accepted the severest standards of authority within itself. It seemed to him, said Gabriel, looking at the ruined tables, the stained and stinking floor, the rucked and spattered tapestries and the crooked flares, that like common soldiers they had gone about their work that day, content to grumble under orders, without any thought of the purpose behind it.

'You,' said Gabriel quietly, 'are the many blades of the fine instrument we call St Mary's. Called into being a year ago, a bodiless force, a secular force, no more than an idea in your leader's mind, it has now become a company worthy of renown throughout Christendom.' He described, in the waiting silence, some of the things they had done: their services to the countryside; those actions where they had succeeded best. He made no mention of their failures but stressed Lymond's name, over and over again, as the man to whose vision and ability they would owe their great future.

It was the fault of no one, said Gabriel at length, that the Queen Mother had found it necessary to demand proof of their competence and their integrity. They possessed both. For a month, no longer, unless the work they had done together was to be wrecked, they must be seen to possess both. They must do exemplary work and lead exemplary lives and regard it, if they must, as penitence for past misdemeanours. 'No one,' said Gabriel, smiling a little at last, 'is proposing to ask you to continue so unnaturally when your probation is over. Men who trade in danger and hardship find it less easy than others to resist sin, or I have found it so, and I accept it. I only suggest, for the sake of your own peace hereafter, that when you go with the Queen Mother's army to France, you carry your sins, as you do to me, to someone you can trust, who will ease you of them. I would wish to think of you as gay and gallant and light-hearted as you should be now, with all these toys, these childish excesses, left behind.'

'But you will be with us!' said des Roches; and his startled words, unintentionally clear, rang through the hall.

Graham Malett looked down. 'I—shall not be with you in France,' he said gently. 'Or afterwards. I am leaving St Mary's.'

There was a surge of motion. Afterwards, Plummer, watching squint-eyed, remembered it as the breaking of a long, sullen roller, pouring ashore, to stub all its length on a reef. Gabriel stilled the commotion with one hand. 'I know. St Mary's has become a part of my life as it is of yours, and it is hard to remember that I promised myself to come only while I could help, and to leave it then to the man whose creation it is. I have taken vows. Thanks to you all—to your leader especially—I am fitter than I have ever been to keep them. I hope, one day, to lead the crusade my Faith is awaiting. In the meantime. . . .'

Sir Graham Malett paused, his shoulders thrown back, his clear eyes surveying them from his magnificent height, and like a schoolboy, passed his fingers through his badly-cut golden hair. 'Meantime, foolishly, I must find something to live on. The Order impounded all I have, and although my needs are nothing, there is my sister.... But these are troubles that need not concern you. They concern me very little: my God will not desert me. So I shall take my sword and sell it wherever it may be needed to preserve Christ's Church.... Perhaps, one day, I shall find a company to match this. I doubt it. I shall miss you all.'

Sir Graham Malett drew a deep breath. His blue eyes, over-brilliant, left the rumbling, rising throb of responding impulse and settled, slowly focusing in pleased astonishment, on the back of the hall. 'Jerott! Already?' And then, his whole face lambent with delight, 'Joleta is here?'

You would expect Jerott Blyth to be tired. He had, after all, covered the ground between St Mary's and Midculter twice since the afternoon. But he looked, to those who craned round, resenting Gabriel's lost attention, like a man set on by thieves. Des Roches thought, 'The girl is dead.' And then, before he could help himself 'Ah, now he will stay?'

Then the young man at the door, the grey blindness still in his face, said, 'I couldn't stop her. She should have stayed.' And realizing, perhaps, from the altered expression of Gabriel's face that he was making frightening nonsense, Jerott made a sharp and visible effort, his hands cramped to his thighs, and said, 'Could you spare a moment, Sir Graham? Your sister is with me, but she is not. . . .'

He was saying 'well' when Joleta Malett, walking slowly, dreamlike in fatigue, came and stood by his side. Above the furred cloak she wore, its muddied hem dragging the ground, her face was pale as a windflower and misted with fine sweat. Her long hair, a tangled skein on one shoulder, was bronzed with it. 'You haven't told him,' she said.

Her voice was reasonable, and just a little higher in pitch than was usual. Jerott said, 'We shall tell him together, when he is alone. You mustn't worry him here. Come to his room.'

'No.' Although addressing Jerott, Joleta's filmed pale blue eyes were fixed on her brother. She said, 'Tell him.'

There were two steps down from the dais. Graham Malett took them in one stride, and was halfway towards them when Joleta cried out. 'No! Stay where you are. I want every man of them to know!'

'Joleta!' said Blyth desperately. She was unfit to travel. She should never have come. He had been through hell with her and then through worse than hell, anticipating this moment. He had carried her in his arms through the night from Midculter and she had said over and over, 'I will tell them all. I will tell them all. They will all know what he has made of me.' Sick with loathing, sick with revulsion after shouting, in the midst of his shock, at the useless duenna, raging over the absence of Sybilla and Richard Crawford to revile, he had been subdued by Joleta's terrible need.

Now, leaving him at the door, she began to walk down the long hall. On either side, uneasily, admiringly, lasciviously in the last fumes of the sherry, the watching men scanned her; the child sister, the little flower of the nuns; Graham Malett's translucent Joleta. Then, facing her brother, she stopped, and her white, kitten's teeth sparkled. 'I have a saint for a brother,' she said. 'Do you not envy me?' and laughed.

Gabriel, his baby skin suddenly white, took a step forward. 'Oh, no,' said Joleta, and stepped back. 'A saint for a brother. Who will say, "This poor young man who still lives by his senses can be taught by us both to lift his eyes to greater things".' In her fresh, sibilant voice, the cadences of Gabriel's rich one sounded harsh. 'Take time, my child. Learn to know him, for I know he will learn to love you. And if, one day, you find you love him in return, there is none in this world I should rather have for my brother. . . .'

Her voice faltered then, and broke; but her eyes, staring distended at Gabriel's stunned face, were perfectly dry. 'You said that of Francis Crawford,' she said, her voice shaking. 'He came. And I learned to love him, oh yes. And he taught me to comfort him in my bed for the holy power of his love for me that did him such violence when we prayed. . . .'

Joleta dragged herself forward and, freeing one childish arm from her cloak, she brought it unavailingly, like a thin flail, across her brother's smooth cheek. Gabriel did not move. 'That is for my maidenhood,' she said. 'Do you want him still for brother? I have asked him to marry me—there is all the sum of my pride. He laughs and says the landscape has lost its novelty. Look, Graham. He planted his bastard on me, those days at Midculter; but that is all he troubled to do.'

She dropped her cloak. Twisted over her pathetic girth, her nightsmock was grimy with travel and sweat. Bodily she looked worn and ill and abused. But her face, despite the stains of fatigue, had kept all its pure beauty. The skin was lovelier than Jerott had ever seen it; her fine brows and long lashes and thin, shapely nose added to the poignancy of what lay below.

Never shifting his eyes as she talked, Gabriel swayed once, and Jerott thought he would faint. But then, he stayed silent, listening, although every few moments he would draw a long, shuddering breath, as if in the intervals the machine of his body had lapsed, and the lungs refused their office. At the end he said, his voice low, 'You are very tired. But I am glad you came. You know there is nothing to fear now. I am here.' He put out his hand, tentatively, and laid it on her thin arm. 'Come and sleep.'

Concentrated completely on Joleta he was ignoring, Jerott saw, the noise of comment mounting around them; and for Joleta, it did not seem to exist. In the hot, crowded room, thick with the raw fumes of wine and humanity, their emotions at loose, enlarged and played upon by alcohol and adulation both, every man there felt, as Jerott did, the shock and outrage at Joleta's pitiful tale. Like some helpless audience at a play, they heard Joleta say, with the same obsessive clarity, 'Where is he? He should see your nephew, shouldn't he?' And suddenly breaking out again, with tears of anger for the first time streaming down her damp skin: 'He hates you! Won't you realize it? That's why he has done this! He hates you and all you stand for! And you thought you could *convert him!*' And, standing in her dirty gown, she laughed and sobbed at once, her hands hanging loose.

It was Jerott who, seeing that Gabriel dared not touch her, picked up her cloak and held her, wrapped again, against his travel-stained shoulder. Gabriel said, the magnificent voice uncertain, 'I didn't hope to . . . convert him. That would have been too officious. Joleta . . . Joleta, I only wanted him to worship you as I did. With that light in his life, he would have achieved nothing but good.'

'His achievements are obvious,' said Joleta bitterly. '*Where is he?*'

'*We* shall go before he comes,' said Gabriel quickly. 'I was leaving anyway. We need only go a little earlier than I thought. Grizel Scott will take us in.'

With the girl's weight heavy on his arm, 'She can't travel,' said Jerott flatly. 'And for God's sake, you're not going to let Lymond turn her out? Or turn you out, for that matter.'

Slurred still, but intelligible, Lancelot Plummer's voice intruded. 'So this is his little pastime—our fireball Count who's so finicky about other gentlemen's manners. I don't think,' said the architect with precise loathing, 'that I care to continue in his unedifying company. De Seurre?'

'He'll find a few to his own taste, no doubt,' said Michel de Seurre abruptly, called from sleep, like the rest, by a silent des Roches. 'I shan't be among them.'

'Nor I,' said Tait, and the growl was taken up and echoed along the strewn tables, where in knots and groups the men of St Mary's had begun to move forward.

Gabriel lifted his head. 'Wait. . . .' he said, but there was no conviction now in his voice, and urgency and new force in Jerott's as he said, 'Wait? What for? Who will follow Francis Crawford after this? What fool would trust him?'

And Randy Bell, standing grimly beside him, said, 'You didn't hear Sir Graham address us just now on the dangers of loose living and lax discipline in a fighting group. He didn't talk about the times our gallant leader has failed us already. He hated Sir Graham all right. Mistress Joleta is right. Think of the winter campaigns Sir Graham was forced to take part in and suffer; think of the night he came back from his work of mercy with the fuel. Think of the Hot Trodd when Crawford left him to do all the work and face all the danger—do you know why? Do you know that was the night, the night before Will Scott died, that Lymond was forcing Gabriel's sister in an inn in Dumbarton?'

For a moment he paused; for a moment in that ugly drunken

assembly there was silence. Then as pandemonium belaboured the air, Randy raised his voice to a bellow. 'Think of that, and think how again and again, Sir Graham has saved Lymond and protected him. But for Gabriel, would Effie Harperfield and her children have escaped yon day the siege-engine ran off? Would we have succeeded even so far as we did at the Hot Trodd; would we be blessed by the Church and have the regard of M. d'Oisel and the Queen Dowager? I tell you, if Gabriel hadn't spoken out at Falkland the other day there would be no St Mary's now, and no future for any of us.'

Inflamed with drink and an overmastering rage, Randy Bell glared at the roaring concourse around him. 'How much of all the great work we've heard of has been *Graham Malett's* doing, *not* Lymond's? Graham Malett's, aided by God?'

'God knows,' said a lazy voice, cool and familiar, from behind. 'But looking round the policies I can tell that either Gabriel or the *Saint-Esprit* is a past master at housework. . . . Good evening,' said Lymond politely to all the hostile faces as they turned. 'Wouldn't you prefer to stab me in the front, rather than the back? I am here, like the Blessed Gerard himself, ready to fall like a fruit, ripe for eternity.'

In the second's flinching silence, it was the girl who spoke first. Pushing herself off Jerott's shoulder, Joleta turned, and with her eyes fixed on the speaker, moved to her brother's side and clasped both frail hands, hard, on his arm. 'It's Francis Crawford,' she said, her young voice harsh. 'Kill him for me?' And as, around them, the sluggish noise climbed of men nursing their anger through drink and oratory and resented fatigue, Jerott Blyth bent his head, and drawing his sword smoothly from its long, leather scabbard, turned, last of them all.

Profoundly unexcited, Francis Crawford stood framed in his own carved doorway and gazed, in polite inquiry, at the receding rows of dishevelled tables crowded with hostile, sullen faces; the long raised table at the far end where Plummer stood watching, with Tait and Bell at his side; and Cormac O'Connor sprawled at ease, a tight-lipped smile on his fleshy, unshaven face; and lastly at the small knot of people standing alone between himself and the dais: Gabriel, with his sister's slight, swollen figure on his arm, and Jerott, his sword balanced delicately between his two palms, facing him at their side. Then, raising his hands to his short, square-collared cloak, Lymond unclipped it and threw it aside, followed, a second later, by his sword belt.

'That's in case anyone feels nervous,' said Lymond. 'I take it *all* of you are drunk?' And looking round at the thronging men and the ruins of his elegant hall, his long mouth twitched. 'Ah, yes,' said Lymond. 'Our dear Masters, the sick. Mr O'Connor has been too generous.'

Jerott, his purpose fractionally interrupted, said sharply, 'How did you know that?' And then, 'Your cloak is dry!'

'The look-out, unfortunately, is not,' said Lymond agreeably. 'I have been here for half an hour. I passed you on the way. I thought I would allow Sir Graham rather than myself the pleasure of upbraiding the fallen under the circumstances. ... It is not a question, Joleta, of squabbling over your honour. There are verifiable facts about that of which even Sir Graham is unaware. He won't be much happier for knowing them, but then this public exposé isn't my choice. He and I no doubt later will make our peace. ...'

'*Make our peace!*' Graham Malett's easy voice was stripped to its warp. He did not move, his face turned, stiffly blank, on his chosen novice. He said slowly, using the words of King Clodoreus to his son, 'Thou cursed harlot! If this is true, then nothing else in this world is of moment. And other courtesy than death you will not have.'

The sword in Jerott's hands flashed as he caressed it. 'It *is* true, isn't it?' he said. 'Thompson's women were a little coarse in the grain. You preferred to teach a fifteen-year-old to serve you, and carelessly got her with child. Would we ever have known, if I hadn't called at Midculter today, and your precious mother and brother hadn't been out? What were they planning to do with it when it was born? Drown it? Threaten Joleta to keep quiet?'

'My dear Jerott,' said Lymond. 'Lemand lamp of lechery I may be, but neither I nor my family are naïve. To get Joleta with child meant the end of my career at St Mary's. Even if my family weren't the solid pillars of virtue they unfortunately are, no one could possibly conceal the birth of the child, whatever fantasy you are proposing. My God, half the Lowlands of Scotland is alive with rumour already. Use your head, Jerott. Surely, if the child had been mine, I would have married her?'

For a second, Jerott's black brows drew together. Then he laughed, his teeth flashing in his white face. '*Married* her? You heard her. She wants you dead.'

'Don't shout. Naturally,' said Lymond. 'Because I won't marry her. Could we all sit down?'

The point of Jerott's sword, swung smoothly round, sparkled before Lymond's soft, exposed throat. 'Not yet,' said Jerott tersely. 'Do we understand that Joleta ever dreamed of marrying you?'

'Ask her,' said Lymond. 'Ask my mother and brother. Ask Madame Donati. Ask yourself if she cried out for help when you found us at Boghall, or at Dumbarton. She had only to scream at Dumbarton and you would have caught us hand-havand, as Fergie Hoddim would say. And as he would also say, under these circumstances we have a clear ruling in law. *Volenti non fit injuria*, Jerott. No injury may be reckoned done to a consenting party.'

'Ah, would you hear him,' said a mellow Irish voice from the background. Across the strewn table on the dais, Cormac O'Connor leaned forward, his hirsute hands clasped, his brown, fleshy face eager. 'Give him the great occasion, and he will put a thread of Latin round it. Was it a case of *volenti non fit injuria*, would you say, when he wiled away me wife Oonagh O'Dwyer?'

Lymond's head slowly lifted, until his gaze met and crossed the big Irishman's. 'You have no wife, O'Connor.'

'You have the right of it. Not since you killed her,' said O'Connor agreeably. 'Left her to sink in the waters of Tripoli Bay, while you saved yourself in a Turkish boat. Full of kindness and sympathy the Turks, I'm told, and saw that none laid an uncivil finger on ye. But then, that great old fellow Dragut and yourself were slaves together, they tell me. The King of France paid a smart sum, they tell me too, for the likes of you to warn the Knights of St John that the Turk was coming. And in spite of all a noble prince like yourself could do, Gozo was slaughtered and Tripoli fell . . . the great warrior that you were!'

'A traitor . . . a traitor in the convent. Is that why you tried to stop me climbing the wall at Mdina? Is that why you tried to join the Turks at Gozo? Is that why you gave all your time to the Calabrians at Tripoli—pretended to save the fort to safeguard your name, knowing all the time it would fall?' Lifting his dazed, magnificent head from his sister's rose-gold hair, Graham Malett's voice rang out, and deepened and hardened until it was clothed, at last, in the timbre they all knew from the quiet chapel at St Mary's, where he led them in praise.

'Of course. Thompson was your associate, but the Turks didn't touch him, did they? Oonagh O'Dwyer knew what you were, so she had to die. Did Nicholas Upton recognize you, too, for a damned soul?' And all the serenity gone from his eyes, Graham Malett laughed shortly.

'What a fool I was, harnessed only in my Faith, believing you fought, with me, to repair the flaws in the Order. I offered you here my heart and the work of my hands, and when you seized the one and laughed at the other I thought, this is young arrogance and youthful cruelty; both will pass. And so I trusted you with Joleta . . .' His tone changed.

'Oh, be quiet!' added Gabriel abruptly, swinging round, and the men he and Lymond had both led, who, surging from bench and table, roused and threatening, now filled all the space around and behind them, saw his strained face and the two shining tracks made by the tears on his face. 'Be quiet! Is this a matter for drunken soldiers or for any of the common laws of society?'

'It is a matter, I think, for the "fine instrument we call St Mary's",' said Lymond's undisturbed voice. 'Leaving all our disillusionments

431

aside, you cannot change leaders in a drunken brawl in the middle of the night and still hope to remain a company—what was it?—"worthy of renown throughout Christendom". I shall not escape you. I have, I think, an answer to most of the accusations that trouble you, and it is very much to my own advantage to stay. Then you may hear the case on both sides in the cold light of sobriety and justice.' His observant eyes swept them all, resting finally on the men who silently had approached his sides and stood now, breathing heavily, at his shoulder. One of them stepped back.

'I am no more than one man,' said Lymond mildly. 'Whatever your decision, I shall honour it. And it will give you an opportunity to persuade Sir Graham, if you wish, to stay as your commander. At the moment, as you see, his only desire is to leave.'

With a hiss of steel, a second unsheathed sword joined Jerott's before Lymond's eyes. 'No,' said Randy Bell brutally. '*You* will be the one to leave.' And knotting tighter and tighter, the circle about them moved inwards. Standing behind and between Jerott and Bell, a hand on each shoulder, 'You should have married me,' said Joleta in a low voice.

'Regrets, Joleta?' said Lymond. Dressed for rough riding, in his white shirt and sleeveless leather jack, the soft deerskin boots pulled high over his hose, empty-handed and bareheaded, he looked, beside their dishevelled turbulence, patiently authoritative. No one yet had laid hands on him. His blue gaze, diamond-hard, rested on the girl's breathtaking face. 'Why not tell Sir Graham the truth? It won't be pleasant if he finds out when you are together and alone. Here, you have three hundred protectors.'

'What truth?' said Graham Malett slowly, and turning his own head, he studied his sister's thin face. And still in the same slow, almost caressing voice, 'Why did you not call for help, Joleta?'

Nicolas de Nicolay, arrived unnoticed behind them all, took a breath just in time to save himself from suffocation. *Diable de diable de diable de diable* . . . the boy was going to do it. My only hope, he had said, is to drive a wedge between Joleta and her brother. But how to do it, without revealing that he knew all? Launch into half-proved excuses for his behaviour here and on Malta, and they would lose patience and attack. He must have time, for his witnesses and his evidence to be brought in unmolested. So . . . if only this powerful Gabriel might be led to think that he could not trust his sister . . . if only his sister might be brought to realize that once alone, her brother might turn against her, she might—she just might—desert Sir Graham for a safe and winning side. . . .

'You see,' Lymond had said, towards the end of that meeting at Boghall, 'she was meant to expose me at Dumbarton. Blacklock didn't silence her. She should have called out.'

432

'Then why didn't she?' Lady Jenny had asked with tremendous decorum. 'Did she have reason to hope, perhaps, that she might . . . tame you yet?'

'It is probably what she told Sir Graham,' Lymond had replied thoughtfully, his wide eyes on Jenny's small, handsome face. 'Myself . . . I doubt it.'

Youthful arrogance, Gabriel had said. There was something in it. Francis Crawford knew his own powers very well. And yet he had never, from the beginning, underestimated Gabriel. He was afraid; he had spoken cold-bloodedly at Boghall of his fear of Graham Malett. Not of injury, not even of death, except that if he died, Gabriel would have won. In the duel now reaching its unavoidable climax here, only Lymond, fighting with all the arts he possessed, knew what depended on the outcome. To Gabriel, contemptuous, loftily confident as he must be, this must seem no more than the final brushing aside of the pawn he had selected and toyed with, and which had proved a little more troublesome than he had anticipated. So, 'Why did you not call for help, Joleta?' asked Sir Graham; and Lymond, his gaze still locked in the girl's, said gently, 'Because she didn't dare. Adam Blacklock, when he comes, will tell you. I'm sorry, Sir Graham. I was not the first. And I shall not be the last. The child is not mine.'

Nicolas de Nicolay swallowed and, for a moment, he himself felt a twinge of unaccustomed coldness. Lymond knew that this was not the reason, and that both Gabriel and his sister were aware that it was not. Yet he put it forward, deliberately, as he might be expected in his ignorance to do, thus rubbing, rubbing on the one small spot of friction between Gabriel and his sister. Had she, somewhere among the wildness and the cruelty, found an affinity with Lymond? Would she betray her brother? So Gabriel must be thinking.

And then, at once, the big, golden knight showed his mastery: showed that Lymond had been right to be afraid. He drew Joleta towards him, and holding her close to his shabby doublet, her silken hair pressed to his breast, he said huskily, 'They are trying to drive me from you. It isn't true. I will never believe it. And I will prove it on his body.' And, looking straight at Lymond above Joleta's still, downcast profile, he said, 'Give him his sword.'

And that could have only one result. The vociferous, calling voices around him rose in raucous dissent and Jerott, a rock in the struggling tide, said, raising his own voice, 'You can't lead St Mary's dead or outlawed. We should present this man to justice for justice to deal with.'

'Provided,' said de Seurre's thin, cutting voice at his side, shoulder to shoulder with Plummer, with Tait, with even a white-faced des Roches, holding back with their broad shoulders the impatient, violent surge from behind, 'Provided that St Mary's is allowed to execute its own justice first.'

Only Jerott Blyth hesitated. He did not see de Nicolay begin, burrowing like a desperate mole, to fight his way, sword in hand, to Lymond's side, knowing that it was too late; Lymond must have known that nothing he might say would be listened to now. Jerott hesitated, and in that second caught a half-smile, incredibly, as Lymond's blue eyes rested on him for a moment, and a fractional shrug of the shoulders as if he accepted, with resignation, the foolishness of man. Lifting his sword, on equal impulse Jerott reversed it, and slammed it home in the scabbard. Then, turning, he thrust his way back through the crowd until he reached the dais, and leaped up on it.

'Dear Jerott,' said Lymond. De Nicolay, stopped not far away, saw that he was rather white, but that his eyes, brilliantly blue, were as calm as his voice. 'He's going to tell everyone, for the sake of their souls, to put their little hatchets away and use their good, honest Christian fists instead. There he goes. St Mary's mustn't murder their commander. An excellent point. I seem to remember making it myself. Nor could they leave the offence unpunished. Pity. The influence of friend Gabriel and his awful, golden face. So. . . . Oh, Jerott,' said Lymond, talking half to himself and half to the unfriendly faces straining behind his officers' linked arms. 'I thought of it myself, but I hoped you would have an imagination a little less trite. *Not* the whipping-post!'

'But yes,' said the Chevalier de Seurre; and releasing Randy Bell's hand, he stepped aside, followed at once by his fellow-officers, to let the men who had obeyed Lymond for a year pour through to where he stood.

Or had stood. For suddenly he was up on the table behind him, a candlestick in one hand and a heavy pot in the other, swinging them experimentally, the flame of battle and a kind of wild laughter filling his face. 'Convicted,' said Lymond, 'of using unreverent language to the bailies again, the prisoner resisted arrest, bestowing three bloody noses and a sprained pinky. . . . Come along, children. You have to get me from here to the whipping-post—oh, Jerott! How conventional!—without killing me on the way. A bagatelle. *Vive la bagatelle!*'

But by that time, they were on him. He did more damage than his officers, watching, would have thought possible in the few seconds available. Then they all, Gabriel, white-faced, with Joleta close in his arm, followed the struggling, drunken mob slowly out of the hall and downstairs to the great doors, as they dragged their talkative commander feet first, bumping and rolling, down to the cool darkness outside.

The post, a massive, manacled cross of oak, stood severe as a schoolmistress in the wide shining reaches of the yard. The rain had stopped. The cressets brought by the provident burned twice, clear and bright, in the still air and on the dark, river-like paving underfoot. The din, so ringingly loud in the hall, became thin and bodiless, interlaced with its own echoes in space, and more frantic as the fresh air began to work on the sherry-sack.

Twice Jerott and once Lancelot Plummer had interfered when the assault on Lymond had taken a savage fervour that offered small hope for the bagatelle. Jerott thought of that mocking phrase as he beat his men off, cursing. He had looked, as he uttered it, like a man who had won a contest, not lost it. There was about him, in all his viciousness, his waywardness, his insolence, an aspect of sheer, blistering courage that caught Jerott by the throat. It recalled other times to him—he *had* risked his life in that underground hell in Tripoli, risked it ten times over—and, you could tell by the numbers who now, their passion lessened, dropped from the crowd and hesitated, as he did, on the fringe—you could tell that others were reminded, too, of other occasions here at St Mary's. But at the core were those whose bitter resentment on Gabriel's behalf still carried them forward; who had suffered from Lymond's merciless tongue; who had themselves paid at this post. And those, like Bell and Plummer and Tait and the Knights of the Order, who seeing the finer implications of all he had done, could never condone it.

Through it all, Francis Crawford himself was quite conscious. They were keen, in any case, to revive him if ever his handling proved more than he could bear. He had half lost consciousness a few times but continued, automatically with a highly specialized form of resistance that taught them a few things, embarrassingly, that even at St Mary's they had yet to learn. Then they got him to the post and kicked him to keep him quiet while they chained him, and he did call out then, once, and choked, strapped inescapably in their view, with the nausea of the blow.

'So you receive your wages,' said Graham Malett's low, beautiful voice. The crowd by the post parted, their work done, and stepped back a little as Graham Malett came forward, a fire-stick in his hand, and relinquishing his sister to Jerott's arm, walked round to face the man he had befriended.

Spreadeagled on his own post, his breathing tumultuous, his face livid under its bloodstreaked and battered skin, his jack gone and his fine shirt in shreds, Lymond stared back below his long lashes, choking still from the last blow. '. . . And the world is witness of your lightness, loveless friend that you have been,' finished Gabriel sombrely.

'Do you wonder,' said Nicolas de Nicolay's accented voice quietly at Jerott's elbow, 'do you wonder, perhaps, why M. Crawford chose to come back at all?'

'Wait,' said Jerott, without listening. Gabriel's voice, it seemed to him, had gone unaccountably flat, and the big man, his guinea-gold hair bright in the torchlight, was looking, not at Lymond's face pressed to the wood but below: below the long throat, starkly lit by the torches, the collarbones outlined in gold and smudged black, the chest exposed where the shirt had been torn back to the shoulders, above the strong, leaved rib-cage and the hollow diaphragm, black and brilliant by turn as his disarranged breathing for the moment defied control.

Cut into the fine skin of the breast, the new scar sharp and black in the light, was a crude attempt at an Eight-Sided Cross. Jerott did not know its history, although Adam Blacklock might have told him, and Lymond's own family at Midculter certainly could. He only knew, as some of them did, that Lymond had borne the mark, whatever it was, since the day of the Hot Trodd and Will Scott's death.

It was perhaps the reminder of that occasion, and of Lymond's drunken débâcle, that made Graham Malett's gentle face change in the torch-light; made him draw himself up, as he seldom did, to his great height and stretching his hand, take himself from its hook the strong, knotted thong Lymond was accustomed to use, in time of need, on the backs of his men.

'Pray,' said Graham Malett to the man chained alone in the dark night before his own house, his own men in a shrinking, shuffling ring of bright faces around. 'And repent. For we are here, a small sort of knights and squires, to bring you in your vilety to fear God and greet pain as His mentor. Let us taste,' said Gabriel, his white teeth suddenly clenched, 'this lewd elegance, this hauteur, this Olympian irony now.'

And from his great height, his forearms ridged through his sleeves, he brought down the whip.

XV

Death of an Illusion

(St Mary's, September 1552)

IT seemed almost certain that Cheese-wame Henderson was dead. He had not replied for a long time when Philippa spoke to him, and when she prodded him as he lay, doubled forward on her horse's neck, he did not move any more. It would have been sensible to have shouldered him in a respectful way down to the ground and then mounted herself, for her shoes had fallen apart and she was walking among the papery bracken and wiry heather of these trackless Scottish hills in her bare feet. But if he proved not to be dead, Philippa didn't think that, without his help, she could ever get him back on to the mare. And unless she got them both food and shelter soon, she felt she would probably die herself. And Kate would not approve of that.

At the thought of it, a watery grin crossed Philippa's white, swollen face and she stopped again, as she often did, to rest herself and the horse, but mainly to check a childish wandering in her thoughts, and to remind herself sternly of her plans and her duties.

She had got herself lost on leaving Wauchope Forest: that she knew. Long before now she should have met some kind of cabin or keep: even the homes of thieves like the Turnbulls who infested the district. But she had met no one, and the sun had appeared briefly and gone early, leaving a grey noon that had deepened, with unbelievable ill luck, into fog. In the end she had simply sat down, and although Cheese-wame was very weak, she had got him dismounted and he had started a fire, and they had eaten the last of the food.

They had stayed by the fire in the dank gloom until the heavy moisture that beaded her hair and sparkled in Cheese-wame's brown beard turned imperceptibly to rain, and she got Cheese-wame somehow, with his help, on to the mare, which was fresher, and through the clearing mists to a belt of trees, dimly seen in the distance.

She was walking then, because it was the only way she could hold him properly in the saddle, and it hardly mattered at the time when Henderson's horse, with a freakish impulse of energy twisted his reins from their knot and vanished soundlessly through the grey web of trees.

When the rain stopped, visibility was better, or else they were viewing the nameless, rolling land to the north from a different angle; for Henderson, full of constant, hoarse apology and harsh breathing which angered and frightened her both, thought he recognized the terrain. He pointed out a line of march, which was just as well, as he shortly ceased to take any interest and Philippa was left, doggedly marching, with her shoes falling to pieces.

When night fell, she was still marching, steering by her own good sense and the stars. Tinkers or not, enemies or not, Philippa Somerville was going to stop the first stray cottager, the first stray pedlar, the first gypsy, the first human being on two legs she met, and beg them for help. It was her own deserved good luck, and by no means the incredible coincidence it seemed, that the first person she actually met that September night was Adam Blacklock.

She met him because he was on his way from that heart-searching meeting with Lymond at Boghall straight to the last meeting-place of the Turnbulls, of whom he intended to ask some very cogent questions indeed. And he found her because he was trained at St Mary's to read geography with his body at night like a bat, and heard but could not interpret the stumbling step of a tired and heavily loaded horse, accompanied by the shuffling, clattering tread of a walker also tired, and short of leg, and most lamentably shod.

Adam Blacklock turned his horse from the causeway and rode gently, his hand on his sword, in the direction of the noise.

It stopped. But the tableau he saw silhouetted against the pale rocks of the hill was that of a drooping horse with a man laid across it, and beside it a slight figure which must be a woman's. He said, pitching his voice clearly and quietly across the small, wild sounds of the night, 'Are you in trouble? Don't be afraid. I mean you no harm. But if you are, perhaps I may help.'

The tone was civilized, the voice kindly, the offer unimpeachable. Philippa Somerville, whom little daunted, laid her poor swollen face on the wet flanks of her mare and burst into uncontrollable tears.

*

After the whipping had gone on for quite some time, Joleta was sick, and Randy Bell, after a hesitant glance at her brother, took her to lie, exhausted, on his coat on the cold steps. At the same time Jerott Blyth, one hand on his arm, tried to make Gabriel stop.

It was necessary. Doing his caravans in the Mediterranean, Jerott had seen men flogged to death. He knew the process, stage by stage, and remembered that Lymond, too, must know it; must often have seen men die, and must have suffered flogging himself, often enough, in his days at the oars.

So, unlike most men, he must know exactly what he could bear. You had privacy, to begin with. Your back was to your chastiser. As long as you could hold your head up, pressed hard against the cold post, your agony was your own also. You braced yourself for each stroke, and in the end exorcised the pain with your voice.

Francis Crawford did not move when Gabriel raised his arm for the first stroke; only his closed lids tightened, a fraction, as it fell. Before Jerott's fascinated eyes, the thong rose and then, curling, fell again, and then for a third time with no more effect. Lymond must, surely, be experiencing the agony—the three livid weals across his back, slowly welling with blood, testified to that. But he had, it would seem, divorced himself by some effort of will from the context.

Gabriel, perhaps, had reached some such conclusion too, but it did not suggest to him that his arm should falter. Divine as some punishing God, his fist rose and fell, and around him, released by his own violence from his own rules, the sherry-sack reappeared joyously, and sank from throat to throat, and the whole restored *salon des singes*, observed Nicolas de Nicolay, watching wanly himself, in some druidical frenzy, flung themselves capering and bawling and singing round the bright silent post, and roared at the sound of each blow.

For how long, thought Nicolas de Nicolay, had Graham Malett longed to do just this thing? For twelve long months Lymond had held out against him. For a year he had resisted the mightiest blandishments known to man; returned all Gabriel's advances with raillery; obstructed all Graham Malett's confident plans and finally, shown a courage and a stamina under constant, devious attack that must have maddened this great god of a man, so contemptuous of his fellows.

And through it all until now, neither man had betrayed his true mind. Rather than spread this evil, Lymond had fought it himself, until he had the means to destroy it. And only now, secure in his triumph, borne on this wave of hatred, of drunken emotion so neatly pre-formed, with Lymond's standing here at St Mary's almost totally destroyed and the Queen Dowager's wrath pending—only now was Sir Graham able, in public, to void some of his impotent anger in open chastisement.

Contentedly, the whip whined and thudded until, at last, Graham Malett had what he wanted. The immunity broke, or could hold out no longer. When Gabriel's next, careful blow fell Lymond moved, in spite of himself, his face suddenly taut, and Gabriel, his lips drawn back in the smile known throughout the Christian world, increased at once the speed of his blows.

From then on, the progression was routine: were you a man of iron, you could not avoid it. The recoil, in silence, that could no longer be controlled; the shuddering intake of breath which was all one's mechanism could contrive between each blind onslaught of pain . . . the nausea and the dizziness, coming more and more often, and cured, sharply and drowningly, by shrewdly applied pails of cold water, coursing down, meddling curiously with the exposed red sponge of one's back.

It was then that Joleta was ill, and Jerott, saying *"That's enough!"* seized Gabriel's iron arm and got, for his pains, the thonged lash full over the face.

Jerott fell back gasping, his hand over his cheek. He saw that the blow had been perfectly automatic, that Gabriel was hardly more conscious of it than if he had brushed off a gnat. And to a chorus of harrowing groans, some encouraging, some mellowly pained, Graham Malett, his fine face all suffused, turned back to the post, and raising his arm, with all his might brought down the thong, again and again, on his enemy's back.

That was what Philippa Somerville saw when she rode in Blacklock's arms out of the darkness, out of the rain that had begun, patteringly, to hiss on the torches and drum on the paving and on the pewter and on the soiled leather shoulders of the shouting, gesticulating figures before the big castle, in the crowded courtyard blazing with lights; and on the central, superb figure of Gabriel, all-powerful, unflagging, avenging his wrongs.

She jumped from Adam's pithless embrace and, like a decapitated hen, ran squawking straight for the post.

Through all the noise and the pain, Lymond must have heard her. He opened his eyes and Jerott, released from an icy limbo of shock followed their direction and lunging, scooped the screaming girl into his arms. 'What the hell are you doing here? He's seduced Joleta, *that's* what's wrong. Get back into the. . . .'

And then he realized what she was saying.

Gabriel, too, had heard it. His hand arrested, he seemed to freeze where he stood, an awakening horror on his face. Then Graham Malett fell back, staring, to where Jerott and Philippa stood, and stammered, 'What have I done? Jerott. . . . Oh, God, it is a spreading evil. I think its spores have entered us all. . . .'

But he was looking at Philippa, and Philippa, her lips trembling, her mouse-brown hair plastered in mouse-brown streaks on her neck, was recounting at last the secret that old Trotty Luckup had confided, in gratitude for all his past favours, to Tom Erskine as he died. She had told him knowing that Jamie Fleming was fond of Joleta. And the dying man had wished Francis Crawford to know, and to be forewarned.

The truth was a single fact—de Nicolay knew it already: the fact that Joleta's illness at Flaw Valleys was nothing less than the results of an abortion; and that, as Trotty had learned from her ravings, Joleta had already borne a child, already known many men when in Malta. A simple fact, but substantiated now, with all it implied, by this distraught girl who had no cause to love Lymond, it withdrew with one bloodless pull the barb from all Lymond had done. And by the same token, drew all the listening, curious faces to where Graham Malett stood panting, sick-white in the torchlight, his dilated eyes on the far steps where his sister was crouched.

'Philippa!' said Lymond's voice. Nicolas had used the interval, with spry effectiveness, to unshackle and lower him, talking all the time fiercely, thoughtlessly, in French. 'Do you hear me, Francis? You were right. Someone was afraid of Philippa's secret. But *this* was the damaging information she possessed, not Paris's stupid affair.' Pausing, Nicolas de Nicolay clucked his tongue; then leaning forward on wet knees, put his warm hands over Lymond's icy ones, cramped on the wet flags as he lay. 'It vindicates you. Do you see it? The baby Joleta expects might be anyone's now!'

'You sound as if you ... didn't believe it before,' said Francis Crawford's voice, muffled, but not missing by much its usual note. He raised himself a fraction and said more clearly, 'If that's blood, I ought to be dead: oh God, no: it's raining ... I can't turn round. Tell me what's happening.'

'Jerott is coming over here. Gabriel is saying nothing, simply staring across at Joleta, and Joleta has got up, hurriedly. Bell's got well back.'

'She's right to be frightened. He'll cast her off now. He's got to, for his own sake. Shock, Christian outrage, shattered love—all the rest. Either that or admit he's been pimping for the woman all along.'

It was then that he called Philippa and she came rushing to him; then hesitated and, scowling, knelt slowly down at his side. There was blood, streaming rosy with rainwater over the bruised white skin of his face, and blood, liquid and black, shining through the light cloak de Nicolay had laid over his back, but he turned slowly, his weight on his elbow, and said, 'You knew you might be killed if you rode out of Flaw Valleys. .... You wouldn't have made Kate very happy. Or me.'

'You have to pay for your mistakes,' Philippa said hardily. From white, in the dim light, she had turned poppy red.

Lymond said quietly, 'You had good reason to hate me. I always understood that. I don't know why you should think differently now, but take care. Don't build up another false image. I may be the picturesque sufferer now, but when I have the whip-hold, I shall behave quite as crudely, or worse. I have no pretty faults. Only, sometimes, a purpose.' He paused, and said, '*Est conformis precedenti*. I owe the Somervilles rather a lot already.'

441

Philippa's unwinking brown gaze flickered shiftily at the Latin and then steadied. 'I should have told you before. You don't *mind*?'

'If you had told me before, you might not have decided to have me for a friend. I don't mind,' said Francis Crawford and told, for once, the bare truth.

They took her indoors then, dazed with reaction. Cheese-wame was safe, left in a house Adam knew of. And she had come in time—surely in time, to undo a little of the harm. And she had made a friend.

The moment she had gone Lymond moved, his soaked fair head heavy, first to his knees, then back on his heels, then, laboriously, pulled by Blacklock and the geographer, to his feet. As his spine took the weight he drew a long, sobbing breath and stood perfectly still. '*Le malheureux lion, languissant, triste et morne ... Peut à peine rugir*,' he said, though his eyes were closed. He opened them. 'He didn't much like seeing Joleta's trade-mark, did he? I wonder if I could walk to where Joleta is?' And glancing in passing at the sodden revelry around him where, like children in a fountain, the drunk cheerfully frolicked, 'That makes me feel very old,' said Lymond, and stopped trying to walk. 'Here's Jerott.'

It was an uneasy encounter. Francis Crawford, his hand gripping de Nicolay's shoulder, met Jerott's bright black eyes with very little expression, and Jerott said thickly. 'You've heard? According to the girl, Joleta is ... is ....'

'She is, too,' Blacklock said briefly. 'I saw her at Dumbarton.' And he added a small, carefully chosen epithet.

'Oh, God, don't waste time on her,' said Lymond wearily. 'Don't you suppose she's going to get all, and more than she deserves?'

And shaking off Blacklock's helping hand, with sudden impatience, he limped quickly and crookedly to where Gabriel, moving at last, was walking clear through the pressed-back, murmuring crowd, to where his sister stood on the steps.

On the stairs, the profiled triangle leading up to the great doors of St Mary's, Graham Malett and his sister Joleta stood quite alone. Whatever leering glances the soaked grotesques capering still in the courtyard might cast up to the staircase, none of Gabriel's brothers-in-arms wished to intrude on this, his pitiless disillusionment.

Quick as the flooding water in the darkening courtyard, the word had gone round. It was true, what Lymond had hinted. The Somerville girl, whose dislike of Crawford was notorious, had come barefoot from Hexham to tell it. The pure and lovely Joleta, lodestone of Gabriel's life, was a wanton, self-willed and careless as a young animal. What he had worshipped was defiled. What he had cherished had secretly mocked at him. No wonder that, in the light from St Mary's big doors, he seemed to grow in height, to stiffen and harden

442

in anguish, the water running unregarded down his broad shoulders, soaking his wide sleeves, his long tunic, the hose of his strong, beautifully-turned legs.

Graham Malett lifted his heavy, leonine head till the rain beat on his throat, and his closed lids, and his wet, ruddy gold hair. Then, his throat pulsing, his chest swollen with air, he gave a great cry; a wordless call from the heart that stopped them all, half-sobered, half-limp with convulsive fatigue, where they stood. Standing there, his clenched hands outflung, his eyes slowly opening on his sister, 'I would have given you my heart to eat,' said Gabriel's low, carrying voice. 'And you have paid me in filth. Go inside. Go.'

Soaked through cloak and night-smock, hollow-cheeked with fatigue, braced against the nameless bulk she was carrying, Joleta stared back, dark rings under her eyes. The straight, sodden mass of her hair, coiled dripping round one thin shoulder, showed like some delicate cast the perfect shape of her head, the lovely line of jaw and neck. She said, harshly and suddenly, in a voice no one there recognized, 'No! I prefer to stay here.'

There was a pause. Then Graham Malett said softly, 'You are untouchable. No one here would presume to interfere between us.'

'One man would,' said Joleta. In her bloodless face her eyes were as Jerott had seen them once, at Boghall, screaming from the floor at Lymond: wild with anger and a kind of unstable excitement. 'Shall I speak to him, Graham? Shall I ask him for my brother's living heart for my Morgengab? I would let him whip me, Graham. That would be only fair, wouldn't it?' And as Gabriel, his face suddenly quiet, made a small movement towards her, Joleta said, 'Take care, Knight of the Ass. Knight of the Ass, stuffed with cotton and shown in a cage with two monkeys, St John and St Andrew.' She laughed, and still watching him, began to climb, sideways, the steps above them that led to the big doors. 'It is great sport, in Francis Crawford's yoke,' she said, and laughed again. Graham Malett began to climb after her.

Below, Adam Blacklock released a long breath and took another. 'She's crazed. She'll drive him to attack her.'

'She merely warns him,' said Nicolas de Nicolay, in prosaic voice, 'that if he harms her, she has it in her power to betray him. She does it with unwise violence, I think. It is possibly her nature.'

Jerott had not heard. He was staring, like a man in a nightmare, at the vanishing figure of his dream. Joleta, to whom her brother could cry aloud as he had. And who could answer, brightly and cruelly, that cry with a jibe.

Then Lymond arrived incredibly, by some blind obstinacy, at the foot of the same steps, looked up and called, on a long, painfully-gathered breath. 'Joleta! *Come here!*' And as she stopped, hesitating,

Francis Crawford said reasonably, 'You must not put upon Sir Graham the sin of harming you. Come here. Jerott . . . take Sir Graham to his room.'

It was an order. And cold, wet and tired as they were, no one demurred. Few people, thought Adam Blacklock, his throat tight, could have looked less a leader than the man holding himself upright with such an effort at the foot of his own steps—a man they had just manhandled and flogged. Why then did no one laugh at the command? Because, whatever else might be proved against him, he had not wilfully despoiled the innocence of Gabriel's child-sister? Or because, as he had, they had seen Gabriel's face when, whip in hand, he stood back and looked at Lymond prone on the ground?

Jerott had seen that look too. He moved slowly forward, but before he reached the foot of the steps, Gabriel turned round. God-like in his despair and his agony, he looked at no one but Lymond. 'It is great sport, in Francis Crawford's yoke,' he said, his deep voice blank of expression. '*Is it?* Francis Crawford, having found what she was, would make no effort to redeem her, would he? He would confide her to no one that might repair her, body or soul; he would, so tender is he of my peace, give me no chance of saving my own flesh and blood. He took the gifts so marvellously offered . . . he took a lust-crazed woman and. . . .' His voice thinned and choked.

'Send her down,' said Lymond.

'If you will come up,' said Sir Graham Reid Malett huskily.

What happened then, none of them ever forgot. As Lymond hesitated, his eyes on Joleta, motionless on the top landing, her back pressed into the railed outer corner between landing and descent, Jerott moved swiftly forward. '*I'll* take her down.'

'You fool. He'll kill her first,' said Lymond, and took the stairs at a limping run, Jerott behind him.

Gabriel laughed. It was a mirthless, heartbreaking laugh that stopped Jerott dead in his tracks, and Blacklock and de Nicolay and the rest just behind him. He was bargaining only with Lymond, they all saw, for Joleta's life. And only the initiated knew why Lymond was risking his own life to save her. For if Joleta lived and confessed, Gabriel was defeated.

But Francis Crawford, this time, made two frightening mistakes. He overestimated the strength he could summon. And he underestimated by far Gabriel's inspired opportunism in the face of attack. His face mask-like with the drive of his will, Lymond got up the stairs somehow, and kept ahead somehow of Jerott until he was within Gabriel's reach.

And against all expectations, Gabriel did not try there and then to seize him, to strike him, to vindicate on his flesh all the passion stark in his face. Instead, Gabriel's famous arm, bearing his naked sword, swept round and hurled the persistent, unsteady young man at his heels, with the flat of his blade, up the remaining steps and back into Joleta's arms. She cried out as Lymond crashed into her, his own breath coming in great sobs from the blow on his pulped back; then she gripped him, an opportune shield, her back pressed into the angle of iron which railed the high platform overhanging the crowded courtyard below, as Gabriel, flinging after them, smiling, presented his sword a yard, no more, from Lymond's bared breast.

To Blacklock and de Nicolay, watching, his intention was never in doubt. To kill Francis Crawford, licensed by these appalling discoveries, while Lymond protected Joleta. Or to force Francis Crawford to play craven now, in full view of the crowd, and by saving himself, expose Joleta to that murderous blade. For Graham Malett would want rid of Joleta, who might yet betray him and confess. And Lymond's only chance of ensuring her safety was to die himself on Gabriel's sword.

From among all the faces below, intent, aghast, 'Oh, my God!' said Plummer suddenly. 'Jump!' There was just room, Blacklock judged, his face grey, for a slender man twisting round to drop between the rails to the ground. For a woman, a pregnant woman, there was none. And so the choice, as the great sword in front of him steadied and behind him, dyed with the blood from his back, the cruel, untameable child called Joleta pressed herself sobbing against the rail of the platform, was Francis Crawford's.

Bright-eyed and colourless, his hair sea-wet with the rain, Lymond left it pitifully late: the vital decision, the last turning in the road he had chosen, thirteen months before, alone in Dragut's quiet tent. He could live on, to fight Gabriel at the cost of this perverted child's life; at the cost of throwing away all that Philippa had risked her life for. Or he could die, and trust that Joleta would live under Jerott's strong arm, and would add her own damning testimony to the evidence against Graham Malett which he had now set in train. Either way, Gabriel had proved himself master indeed.

Jerott Blyth shut his eyes. Then, with all the power of Graham Malett's great shoulders, Gabriel's sword began its drive home.

Quick, quiet, light and unfleshed as a gull, Lymond dropped downwards and sideways, and with a thrust of his long hands, rolled between the lowest two bars of the railing to fall, a loose, undisciplined heap, into the courtyard below.

Above and behind, the sword he had escaped drove on, unhindered, into and through the heart of the girl.

No one moved. Below, a desert of shining pavement around him, Lymond lay where he had dropped. After the first unbelieving reflex, jerking back his sword arm, with the clotted blade already clearing with rain, Graham Malett stood, his back pressed against the castle

445

wall, frozen also in stillness. Joleta screamed three times, a thin, breathy kind of scream, with her hands spread rigid, like shining, flesh-eating plants before her. Then, collapsing forward and sideways, she hit the top step with her shoulder at her brother's feet, her rose-gold, rain-heavy hair whipping her cheek, and with a grotesque slowness tumbled from step to step, clumsily, downstairs.

She would have passed Jerott but, falling to his knees, he arrested her with his strong hands, and unfolding the tumbled clothing and putting back the silken hair, found and looked at her face. The eyes were open, and a look of surprised fury, terrifying in its malevolence, lit the dead face. As he watched, it vanished. Jerott laid down, heavy on his hand, the loveliest child in Christendom, and got to his feet. 'She's dead. Go inside,' he said abruptly; and after a moment, Gabriel stirred, like a dead man himself, and moved without speaking into the castle.

Jerott turned round. Below him Adam Blacklock, his face turned away, was gripping the lower rail. Beside him, the geographer, his face unusually pale, said incomprehensibly to the vacant air, 'It was right. What use proof, if he died? The man Gabriel was crazed. He would have killed the sister too, or she would have fallen. Is it not so?'

Blacklock, his face invisible, shook his head. The others, behind said nothing. Only their eyes, Jerott found, were turning, first one then the other towards himself. His hands shaking, his bowels water within him, Jerott said steadily, 'Bring Mr Crawford here and take him indoors. He is still a prisoner, with charges to answer. What he has just done . . . is not, of course, a matter for law.'

But it was not, either, a matter that the men of St Mary's, new to Gabriel's demented violence, new to Joleta's reported perfidy, could stomach. Before their officers, without hurrying, could reach the unconscious huddle in the dark rainswept courtyard that contained the lewd elegance, the hauteur, the Olympian irony of Francis Crawford, the men had got there first. And although Plummer and de Seurre and Bell and the rest used their voices, cuttingly, to promise retribution of the unpleasantest sort, they did nothing much to prevent Lymond's own men from dragging him, bruised and bloodied afresh by the fall, witlessly yielding, from below the rain-washed railings to where the whipping-post stood, and fastening round wrists and ankles the chains he had so recently left. Then they threw a few things, but by that time, however dilatory, their superiors were on them, and cuffed them out of the way and across the courtyard in the drumming rain at last to their own quarters.

The last of the torches by then had gone out. In the dim light from the castle windows and from the lanterns kept alight at the gatehouse and on the far walls, Jerott checked with his colleagues that no drunken reveller remained, asleep in the mud, to be found raving in the morning.

By his orders, Randy Bell had gone indoors to Gabriel; and two of his fellow-knights, their hands gentle, had faced the task of lifting Joleta and carrying her indoors to his bed. The debris in the great hall, also by his orders, was being cleared. No one went near the dark post in the centre of the courtyard or looked at the man bound there. After a sharp exchange, Adam Blacklock had walked off, grimly, in the opposite direction. So Jerott, by his own design, was alone when at last, his eyes sunk in his head, every nerve throbbing with tiredness, he walked slowly across to the post.

The rain had stopped. In the castle, only two or three lights now remained to beribbon the cobbles. Far off you could hear, under many roofs, the thinning rumble of tired men's talk.

In the courtyard the silence was absolute. He tried to conjecture how much blood Lymond had lost, between the flogging, the rough handling, the fall. They had been careful to break none of his limbs and he had fallen loosely; he had fainted, Jerott thought, before he touched ground.

Randy would have to care for him: he might not like that. And they would have to guard him from Gabriel. If Graham Malett had wanted him dead before, how must he feel now? They would have to guard him, too, from his men. Except that, by morning, they would want to think of very little but their headaches. They would hardly remember, he hoped, that they had left Lymond here, in the rain.

That had been a good point Adam Blacklock had raised: that old Trotty Luckup's death should be looked into. He would question Philippa. Better, he would take her to Midculter with him and see Joleta's two grooms. Philippa was all right. He had sent indoors half a dozen times since it was all over to see how she was. She had fallen asleep, steaming, before the big fire, and someone kindly had replaced her wet cloak with a dry one and had wrapped a rug about her. She had not wakened. He wondered, briefly, in passing why Nicolas de Nicolay had insisted on staying at her side, but decided that Frenchmen were odd, and this one could be trusted.

Walking slowly in the dark, Jerott Blyth thought, at last, of all his stirring hopes when he had rediscovered Francis Crawford in Sicily. And after, at Birgu and Mdina. And then the brilliant, shadowed affinity they had nearly found in the arsenal at Tripoli. And lastly, in watching Lymond fashion this force.

Gabriel had hoped to catch and tame this exceptional spirit. Gabriel instead had been reduced to killing it with his bare hands. Jerott wondered, flatly, if he were a worse Christian than Gabriel, or a less exacting one.

The post was here. He braced himself, putting one scarred hand on

447

its cross-branch and groping forward with the other for the man chained there in the dark.

His fingers met nothing. He moved closer, running quick hands over the wood, then on the ground, in case by some fantasy the links had broken and the prisoner in his weakness dropped to the earth.

The ground was empty. The whipping-post was vacant. And, when he ran for a lantern and looked, the chains which should have secured Lymond, above and below, were all unbolted, neatly, from their place in the wood, leaving the padlocks intact.

But that was half an hour's work. No man in the whole of St Mary's had been alone at the whipping-post for so long since the whole unbearable business began.

Except one. 'How *conventional*, Jerott!' Lymond had said, his eyes hilarious, as Jerott had made that pompous speech from the dais. Lymond had passed himself and Joleta on the way. He knew, very likely, what might happen. And he had amused himself, during that half-hour's wait, while Gabriel, playing disciplinarian for him, had scolded his men, in half-unshackling the chains.

Which meant that, had he wished, he could have escaped the flogging, at will.

But no. Surrounded, he could hardly have fled. But this time it was different. It must have been an odd feeling for Lymond, thought Jerott, to find himself on awakening in the one place from which he knew he could vanish. Or perhaps it was no coincidence at all. There had been some familiar faces, he realized, in that unruly herd.

So Lymond had taken his chance. Wherever he was, whatever he might be doing, Francis Crawford was no longer at St Mary's.

That was all that Jerott cared about and more, too, than he thought was anyone's business to know. Abandoning the empty whipping-post, its ingenious chains dangling, to the night air and the stars, Jerott Blyth walked across the bare stones to St Mary's, and climbed the dark stairs.

XVI

Jerott Chooses His Cross

(The Scottish Lowlands, September/October 1552)

NEXT day, in the bright russet sunshine of late morning, Philippa Somerville rode to the haven of Midculter, her nose thick with recent weeping, her eyes red with tears and fatigue. With her went Jerott Blyth and Nicolas de Nicolay, accompanied by no more than their personal staffs.

Behind them they left a chastened St Mary's. Graham Malett, found that morning collapsed before his worn altar, had been forced to lie open-eyed and silent in bed, and had made no comment when Jerott had explained their purpose in going. He had said nothing about Trotty Luckup. Adam Blacklock had left early that morning on unexplained business and Archie Abernethy and Salablanca had both discreetly vanished when Lymond did.

Visiting Gabriel hesitantly in his room that morning, to broach the subject of Joleta's burial and the report that must be made of her death, Jerott found that word had already reached him of Francis Crawford's escape. To what authority might say of Joleta's death Sir Graham seemed totally indifferent, sunk in a lethargy where no emotions still lived. And it was true, even had it been no accident, he had small need to fear. Whatever their sin, Knights of the Order were judged first by Malta, and not by the common law of their land.

Jerott, rising silently to leave, decided privately to seek Lady Culter's wise help. For there was no aid for him here; only the acrid smell of distrust and disaffection. Drunk; loose-living; incompetent—Lymond had received a damning indictment, and his ultimate act of self-interest, the preserving of his own precious life at the cost of Joleta's, had made even the least squeamish draw back.

But, on the other hand, some of Joleta's tarnish had stuck to her brother. There were some who said that no man of God should have used such unbridled violence first on Francis Crawford and then on the girl; that he had had no right to force on Lymond such a choice. The company was divided, no longer brutally single-minded as it had been before Philippa arrived ... as he, in his heart of hearts, was beginning to be divided.

For that reason, perhaps, the silence in which he rode to Midculter was weightier than it need have been, so that his two companions several times exchanged glances; and then Philippa, the little geographer's gaze encouraging her, said disarmingly, 'Sir Graham is a very wicked man, isn't he, to try to put a sword through someone unarmed like that, without even a trial?'

'Like what? Like Lymond?' said Jerott irritably, brought back from his own worries. 'You know what he did to Joleta.'

'Of course. But we know now he wasn't the only one, though she made out he was. It was *Joleta* who deserved to be thrashed. And a good deal earlier,' said Philippa, nervously falling back on an echo of Kate to defend her from the memory of what had actually happened to Joleta.

'Don't be silly,' said Jerott Blyth shortly. 'He's only human, Sir Graham, like the rest of us. You can't turn and rend in a moment a girl you've adored all your life. Lymond should have told Gabriel, somehow, what his sister had become. Instead, he pushed her back in the gutter.'

'But Sir Graham *knew* what his sister was,' said Philippa perseveringly. And as Jerott swung round, impatient and scornful, she went doggedly on. 'He sent her the drugs that brought on her miscarriage. Ask Lord Culter. He told her, once when I was at his home, he hoped she'd thrown away the box her brother had sent her that had brought her seasickness on. Trotty spoke of a box, too. She had been shown it, when Joleta thought she was dying, and recognized what the drug was.'

'You're obsessed by the thing,' said Jerott roundly, but not without kindness. 'Look, think of something else. Whoever is to blame in the whole bloody mess, it's not Graham Malett.'

Then they reached Midculter and found that elegant residence in a state of unusual confusion; for someone, on an early errand to the stables, had found half their valuable horses cut loose, and two grooms clubbed to death.

The grooms had been Joleta's. Impressed into silence by this piece of information, Jerott led his cavalcade with increased urgency from gatehouse to castle, and once inside the door, de Nicolay and Philippa at his back, met and withstood with difficulty the shock of Madame Donati's onrush. 'Mistress Joleta? Why have you returned? Is she with Sir Graham safely? Madness! Madness!' said Evangelista Donati harshly. 'To travel with the baby so near!'

Behind were the stairs, and at the top of the stairs, her small spine erect, her face firmly controlled, stood Sybilla. Jerott pushed past the agitated Venetian and climbing, came to rest a step or two below Lymond's mother.

'I did not think,' said Sybilla without moving, 'that you would cross this threshold again?'

'I am wiser,' said Jerott, in a subdued voice. He had forgotten to prepare for this interview, coming on the heels, it must seem to her, of the visit he had made in her absence, screaming at Madame Donati and riding, raging, with the weeping Joleta, back to St Mary's.

'What do you say?' said the duenna's sharp voice at his elbow. 'Where is Joleta? What has happened?'

'The stairs,' said a definite Somerville voice from below them, 'are no place for emotion. You could get a nasty fall. It's Philippa, Lady Culter. May we come up?'

And Sybilla, a little spark of humour back in her eyes, said, 'My goodness, the woman of sense is with us again. Of course. Come up. And M. de Nicolay, isn't it? We have met at Court. David, wine in the hall, please. . . .' And she led the way up.

But before the wine came, Jerott Blyth took his stance by the windows, his thick, Indian-black hair flung back out of his eyes, his beaked, flaring nose jutting into the air, and said uncompromisingly, 'Joleta is dead.'

Evangelista Donati, her hands folded genteelly in her lap, opened her prim mouth and screamed.

'How?' said Lady Culter shortly; and as the screaming went on, drowning Jerott's reply, she rose, administered a sudden, painful slap on the side of the dariolette's face, and sat down in the suddenly restored silence. 'Did she lose the child?'

Jerott found, enraged, that his voice had lost half its power. At the second attempt he said, scrapingly, 'There was a . . . struggle at St Mary's in the courtyard. She . . . was killed.'

'*Killed!*' Sybilla's voice, unusually high, clashed with Evangelista Donati's 'Killed! But who has killed her?'

'I'm sorry . . . it was Sir Graham,' Jerott said, and Sybilla's hands dropped to her lap.

Into absolute silence, '*Killed her? Sir Graham?* But this is the last thing he would do,' said Joleta's governess slowly. 'She is *not* dead! This is a falsehood! A falsehood to frighten me into. . . .'

She broke off herself, on that rising note, as Nicolas de Nicolay said, 'It is true, Signora. We had discovered, what you must already know, a little of the poor girl's sad history. Such was Sir Graham's horror at his sister's deception that he drew his sword on her and stabbed her to the heart. She lies there in the chapel, poor child.' And de Nicolay sighed.

Jerott, staring at him suspiciously, considered this edited version of the girl's death. It did not mention Lymond. But in Sybilla's presence that was perhaps as well. Only it gave the impression. . . .

'This is true?' the woman's harsh voice was pressing. 'Mr Blyth, this is so? Her brother killed her because of her . . . past?'

'Because she had borne a child, and lost another before ever she reached this present sad state,' said de Nicolay sadly. 'Young Mr Crawford would have protected her. He opened his arms to her, and she would have gone, because she was greatly afraid.' His arms fell to his side, his face owlish in its gloom. 'But it was too late.'

'*Sia maladetto*,' said Evangelista Donati in a soft voice, and sat down. 'Her poor, helpless craving for love became known, so he must discard her, unsullied himself. And he must more than discard her, lest in revenge she let all the world know what this glorious gentleman, this upright monk, this godly Knight of the Order truly is!' And she rolled her Italian tongue on a word which took even Sybilla by surprise.

Very carefully, Lady Culter settled back in her chair; and Jerott, bewildered, found himself, with Philippa, silently assigned to a seat. 'Tell us,' said Sybilla gently, her tone of friendliest interest, 'what Sir Graham is like?'

*

Afterwards, when Jerott, feeling as if he had shared, for a short time, Francis Crawford's whipping-post, was standing by the tall windows, looking blindly out; when Madame Donati had gone, her face ugly with weeping, to take her exhausted fury to bed; when Philippa, carried off by a startled Mariotta, had been taken below for some food, Sybilla said, with studied care, 'But you have said nothing of Francis?'

'He escaped,' said Nicolas de Nicolay gently. 'This was right. He could do nothing further and many are sufficiently roused at St Mary's to endanger his life. Also, when news of this and of the *Magdalena* reaches the Queen Dowager, she will send to arrest him. That he cannot risk until the case against Sir Graham Malett is complete. You understand?'

'We understand now,' said Jerott Blyth bitterly, and turning faced her, his clasped knuckles, in a childish gesture, pressed on his lips. 'I have been a thick fool.'

'I know. But there's such a comfort in numbers, don't you think,' said Sybilla, without really thinking. 'Could you tell me, do you think, just what happened?'

And at the end of that recital, which exhausted him more than he would have admitted and left Sybilla looking like a princess in paper, Nicolas de Nicolay broke his considerate silence again. 'There is another thing perhaps you should know, since Thompson does, and the rumour of it you may find in every Mediterranean port.' Uncharacteristically, he halted.

'About Malta?' said Jerott baldly. 'Sir Graham said Lymond betrayed us on Malta.'

'Did he? But you would expect him to, would you not? My experience,' said the geographer, 'was different, and no doubt so was yours. But no. This dealt with the woman, Oonagh O'Dwyer.'

'They say she was O'Connor's wife,' said Jerott quickly. From Sybilla's face, it was clear that the fate of Oonagh O'Dwyer was no secret.

'I do not know. I should regard that, if I were taken to task, as a small misapprehension on O'Connor's part,' said de Nicolay easily. 'But I meant something other. They say she did not die.'

'She drowned!' said Jerott. 'When Lymond. . . . When Francis was forced to swim away from her.'

'I am glad that you accept his story,' said the cosmographer, his smile glimmering about the mouth. 'It is a true one, I am sure. But I am told that she did not drown, though he was intended to think so, but was most carefully rescued by Dragut Rais, and tended in his harem after the knights' ships had gone.'

'Why?' said Sybilla bluntly, her face white, her breathing painfully short.

De Nicolay raised his shoulders. 'Who knows? Perhaps he was paid. But it is true. I have met someone who saw her, months after she was said to have died. A white woman, an Irishwoman, in Africa could not long, you may imagine, be hidden. And especially not a white woman with a child.'

There was a shade of deprecation in the voice: a hint perhaps deliberate which had already put Jerott on his guard. But Sybilla, silent for a single, blocked moment, simply said, brightly, 'Dear me. Of course. The offspring of the bereft Mr O'Connor. So she was pregnant when she was captured, was she? Poor child.'

Nicolas de Nicolay hesitated.

'Well?' said Sybilla, and her lip suddenly trembled.

'I am told,' de Nicolay went on, his exuberance absent; his voice very flat, 'that the child, a son, has none of Cormac O'Connor's size or girth, or his or Oonagh's black hair. I am told that it is the fairest ever seen in or out of Africa, with blue eyes and hair pale as flax. She will not say who the father is, so it has been called Khaireddin.'

In the long, ensuing silence, neither man looked at Sybilla. Then, 'Does Francis know?' said the Dowager, clear-voiced and dogged, with the tearstains spreading dark on her dress.

'No, ma'am,' said de Nicolay shortly. 'The young man, I believe, has anxieties enough. I had no intention when I came to Scotland of telling him, or informing you. But this I now say. It is nothing if it is not a weapon. Be on your guard. Say nothing. But pray to your

453

gods, and the gods of the Turks, that Gabriel does not know what we know.'

Soon after that, Alec Guthrie arrived, very wary of Jerott at first, and then exceedingly business-like. He came from Lymond, to whom he had reported when his work at Branxholm was done. They had traced Gabriel's connexion with the Hot Trodd. The route taken by St Mary's and by the Scotts in their search for the lost herds had been anything but fortuitous: they had found the men bribed to keep each force, by false clues, on the wrong path. If Adam Blacklock succeeded in his interrupted quest with the Turnbulls, they could prove how the Trodd was planned to take place and fail.

He had further news. A large force of French troops under M. d'Oisel, with artillery and dogs, had arrived at St Mary's, sequestering the buildings and placing their inmates under detention; and a country-wide search for Francis Crawford had been launched. News of the *Magdalena*, obviously, had reached Falkland. Guthrie had orders to tell Nicolas de Nicolay, and the Chevalier Blyth, if the circumstances were right, that Cormac O'Connor had left for Falkland again. Further, that only Nicolas de Nicolay, on whom no suspicion rested, might return, if he wished, to St Mary's again. All the others who had been with Lymond the previous day at Boghall were to remain at large, since at St Mary's their liberty might be curtailed by the Ambassador. Their continuing absence Gabriel also would put down to this reason.

'Mr Guthrie,' said Sybilla. 'Tell me. How did you discover Francis?'

The soldier-lecturer grinned. 'Forethought, my lady. He drew up a route, just before he left Boghall, and tacked it all into us like soling a floor. A day in this cabin and two days in that cave, two days on the journey, and three in a friendly farm. We all know where he is any day you like to choose, and can report to him, and get our orders. And those who are watching St Mary's report, too.'

'How is he?' said Sybilla with equal composure. 'I am told he received a thrashing. I am sure he has one or two owing him.'

'Yes. Well, not one of this order,' said Guthrie, glancing up at Jerott and de Nicolay. 'Someone thought they were taking dust from a floor-claith. Ye'll no can pat him on the back for a week or two. But otherwise he'll do. He's food and drink and all the blankets he needs,' he added kindly, for the Dowager's benefit. 'And a purpose that'll see him through, were he holed like a thurible. I'm afraid, ma'am, a high-handed young despot is what you've bred, you and your husband.'

'I suspected as much,' said Sybilla. 'Gaineth me no garland of green, but it ben of withies wrought. Don't look so nervous, my dear. If I had a woolly shirt and a tin flagon of medicine you could have

454

them with pleasure, for the amusement of seeing him laugh himself sick. Tell him ... I have a new cat.'

'Is that all?' said Jerott, standing up uncomfortably. Guthrie was to take him to where Lymond lay.

'And that George Paris landed at Dumbarton today, I'm told,' said Sybilla. 'And means to leave shortly for a lodging in Edinburgh.'

'So!' said Nicolas de Nicolay, suddenly vastly interested. 'The sensible one downstairs and her story fall into place after all. Is this, would you think, one of Gabriel's final moves?'

'I hope so,' said Sybilla coolly, and there was no ambiguity in her meaning at all.

*

This day, in his provident itinerary, Francis Crawford was spending in a daub and wattle shepherd's hut, deep in the Tweedsmuir hills.

Archie Abernethy, his sun-dried face impassive, was on guard. Passing him, with Alec Guthrie leading the way, Jerott was seized with a desire to be anywhere but here.

The evidence against Graham Malett, his lifelong hero, was overwhelming. He was prepared to believe it with his head, if not yet with his heart. His feeling for Lymond, on the other hand, echoed a little what his own men had felt last night. An illogical resentment that he, with all his failings, should be the *deus ex machina* to destroy Gabriel's great name.

To Lymond's cool brain it was inevitable. He must have set out deliberately to expose Graham Malett a long time ago. He had spared nothing. He had had the hardihood to play the third, vulnerable hand in the last knife-edge game between Joleta, Sir Graham and himself, in the hope that Joleta would be frightened into confession; he had even, with the same mechanical single-mindedness, offered himself as whipping-boy to induce Gabriel to give full rein to his passions.

So he had come to the place where Graham Malett, finding both Lymond and Joleta his sister troublesome, had found a witty solution at the top of the steps to St Mary's.

Again, it was logical. It was logical that Lymond had sensibly saved his own life at the expense of the girl's. By Joleta's orders, the old woman Trotty had been killed. He knew, from Sybilla's quiet account, of what else Gabriel's sister had done. She was wild and cruel and corrupt. By taking that murderous thrust in his own body, Lymond would have done only what Gabriel coolly hoped he would do. Jerott could admire his good sense, but he did not particularly want to meet him now or indeed ever again.

He had not been announced. So, hesitating on the threshold and peering into the murky interior, Jerott heard Lymond say in his ordinary voice, 'Come in, Alec. I regret the redolent gloom; the sheep-stank had a little more style about it. But Archie stamps on my fingers if I venture outside . . . *Jerott!*'

He stopped speaking for a moment. Moving forward, angrily aware that Guthrie had found something unexpected to do outside, Jerott distinguished a candle guttering in the near corner of the windowless cabin. Papers covered the makeshift table on which it stood, with Lymond's hands spread upon them, full in the light of the blown flame. His face, in the reflected glow, was to Jerott's dazzled eyes merely a pale mask of inquiry, its framework and cavities engraved in depth by the light. Then he said, unexpectedly, 'I am deeply sorry.'

Jerott Blyth let the hide door fall to behind him, and moved farther in. 'Madame Donati has told us everything she knows about Sir Graham,' he said, 'But the groom who killed Trotty Luckup is dead. Your brother thinks he can find out who did it.'

Lymond looked down, and picking up the pen he had been using, balanced it thoughtfully between his two forefingers. He said, without looking up, 'And you believe Evangelista Donati? She was devoted to Joleta, remember.'

'She couldn't have invented . . .' Jerott's voice failed him. 'I believed her,' he said shortly. 'I have heard also about the Hot Trodd. And there are other . . . discrepancies.' He paused. 'He has set mastiffs after you.'

'Yes.' Lymond laid down the pen with care. 'At Martinmas I kill my swine, and at Christmas I drink red wine. An act of rather less than Christian charity. But war on the infidel is the Order's prime rule, isn't it, Jerott?'

'So also is chastity,' said Jerott, his strong voice blanched still with distress. He took a deep breath and added, 'I have come to tell you that I am rejoining Sir Graham at St Mary's.'

Under the candle flame, brightening as the hills outside dimmed towards night, Lymond's hands moved slowly together and united, with great care. When he looked up his underlit lashes starred his face with spiked shadow, like a doll's. 'No, Jerott,' he said. 'Some of us might deceive Gabriel; but you, never.'

From his rare advantage of height, Jerott Blyth stared down at the seated man. 'Yes, of course, that's what you would think,' he said. 'That I was proposing to spy for you.'

The hands in the candlelight lay still. Lymond said, 'Surely there are only two intelligent reasons for returning to Gabriel now. One is to spy for me. The other is to betray me. I assumed you would hardly visit me in the latter case to tell me so.'

Jerott Blyth's black brows were straight above his shadowed eyes, and his lips pressed together before he answered at last. 'My reason is not an intelligent one. I have seen what intelligence can do.'

'Ah, yes,' said the pleasant voice. 'My heart mourneth sore of the death of her; for she was a passing fair lady, and a young. Also a cold-blooded little trollop. Desert me, Chevalier, because I dodged, but for God's sake don't feel called upon to wash the stains from the murderer's hand.'

'For God's sake,' said Jerott Blyth, 'I am called upon to care for Graham Malett's impaired soul, not to drive him to further excesses.' With an effort, he made his voice level. 'I shall give him no information, naturally, about your whereabouts or plans. And I shall have the hunt for you stopped.'

'In the teeth of the whole bloody French army, M. l'Ambassadeur du Roi d'Oisel included? Don't be a raving fool, Jerott,' said Lymond. 'It's out of Gabriel's hands now, as he meant it to be. Use your brain. This isn't a giant strayed. It's a clever and powerful man who can find pleasure in a vast, despotic scheme like this and work towards it secretly for years if necessary. The Order taught him to kill his infidel, and by heaven, he's using the knowledge on every one of us standing in his way. I've great respect for the power of prayer to dislodge devils, but in this instance, I'd prefer to use a hundred pounds or so of round stone shot, at close quarters.'

'As St Mary's teaches,' said Jerott. 'Really, there isn't much to choose between you, is there?' His dark eyes rested on the mess of papers on the bright table. 'He will hang when you have your evidence, without a thought for all that is great in him. You would have killed him yourself, I know well, except that it wasn't convenient to martyr him. You didn't see him in Malta in the great days, preaching, fighting. . . . His name rang round the Mediterranean.'

'Before he gave up hope of deposing the Grand Master. So,' said Lymond, and unclasping his hands, he lifted the table away with a movement of unexpected violence, and got up. 'As soon as you begin to lead him into the paths of righteousness, he will do one of two things. He will kill you, because of what you obviously know, or he will promptly become converted for exactly as long as it suits him to achieve his object. Either way your respective souls are going to emerge a little dog-eared. You are risking innocent lives to indulge in a quite hopeless piece of missionary work.'

There was no heat in the hut. As the shadows gathered and the candle began to flicker low, Jerott saw his opponent only as a lit shirt-sleeve and long, smooth line of dark hose, leaning back against the tough mud wall, his hands tucked into his trunk-band. Breathing hard, his face flushed, Jerott did not feel the cold. He said, 'Have you counted how many have lost their lives since *you* took the great matter of Graham Malett in solitary hand? He accused you of pushing Joleta back into the gutter. What chance have you given him?' His voice shaking, Jerott said, 'He might have been entrusted to the wisest hands in the Order to save. Now I—*I* have to. . . . His only hope is in me. *Do you think this is easy?*'

Head bent, Lymond was studying the invisible floor at his feet. After a moment, he said, 'It is very sad; but no one with theological training is ever going to believe that nine times out of ten, what is best for one's character is the primrose path, not the thicket of thorns. You realize, of course, that knight or not, he will die in the end for what he has done. And that if he is to die shriven, you have a week or two only in which to make your conversion. I shall have all the proof I need by then; more than he can possibly refute.'

He looked up suddenly. 'Do you mean him to pay for his crimes, Jerott? Or do you plan to take him south, where he may see the light of repentance in prayerful peace, and return one day to illumine your Order? You are still under his spell, aren't you? A man no worse, you may say, than others who rule today, who stops at nothing to achieve power and has all the virtues of courage and leadership and a wide-ranging mind. But a man, too, who could sway nations with the power of his voice and the religious fervour he can inspire. My God, Jerott: think of the damage a good and simple man can do under these terms. What do you suppose an evil and most damnably intelligent one would do? No, *mon Chevalier*,' said Lymond, speaking clearly and slowly. 'You are not going back to Graham Malett now, or at any other time.'

Afterwards, Jerott realized that, blinded with anger, he had missed the small sounds Lymond had been waiting for: the approaching, hesitant footsteps of Archie Abernethy and Guthrie, waiting with impatience for the long interview to be over; stirred finally by curiosity and then by suspicion to come close and listen. Moving quietly as he spoke, Lymond had reached at length the dark corner of the hut where Archie Abernethy had made up his bed of dry heather, the blankets turned back where he had left it. Beside it, lying unseen in the failing light, as Jerott should have known it would be, was his sword.

Now Lymond made one sudden movement and straightening, the hilt in his hand, backed swiftly, still speaking, between Jerott Blyth and the door. 'Your sword, Jerott,' said Francis Crawford quietly to his boyhood friend, and Jerott Blyth, unbelieving rage rising within him, found himself looking along the steady, silver blade of Lymond's own steel.

With an instinct sure and swift as the Order could make it in all the years of his training, he flung himself sideways and gripping the makeshift table, flung it rocking towards Lymond as he drew out his own blade with a hiss. Lymond, expecting it, hurled himself sideways. The table, teetering, crashed on to its back where he had been, fully blocking the curtained doorway of the hut.

There was a moment's pause while the two men stood, breathing fast, long swords ready, on opposite sides of the cabin; then the hide door-cover was ripped away from outside and Abernethy, with Guthrie behind him, laid hands on the overturned table to heave it aside and jump in.

'All right,' said Lymond. He was very breathless, but his eyes did not move from Jerott's wild face. 'This is my affair. Alec, these papers contain the case against Graham Malett as I know it so far. You know what to do with them. Archie, wait outside with Mr Guthrie. You understand that whatever happens, the Chevalier is not to return to St Mary's. Nor is he to suffer any harm. It isn't his fault that he's surrounded by vile engineers and commercials. Jerott, in this space neither of us can possibly miss. Put down your sword.'

'Talk!' said Jerott Blyth between his teeth. 'I have had my bellyful of talk, without respect of honour or oath. I don't forget that you would use a living woman as your shield rather than lay down your life for the justice you talk about. I risk no one's life but my own, and if I succeed, my prize will be a man whose stature you would not even begin to comprehend.' His dark eyes brilliant, the young knight stopped, and raising his heavy sword high in both hands, hurled it suddenly to the opposite corner of the hut, where it fell thudding against the bare wall, and thence to the floor. 'Stop me if you dare,' he said, and walked steadily towards Lymond and the door.

For a second only, Lymond hesitated. Then, a moment before the other man reached him, Lymond also lifted his sword aside quietly and dropped it behind the overturned table at his side. Behind him, Alec Guthrie's voice said sharply, 'Crawford! Let him go!' and Archie Abernethy called out.

Jerott paid no attention. He saw Lymond standing in the open entrance to the hut, his hands gripping the overturned edge of the board at his back, and the dimmer figures of Guthrie and Abernethy against the storm-dark sky behind. Then he jumped.

They were the same age, of the same build, and they both knew all the possible grips which would throw a man down and keep him down, and also if possible ward off outside interference as well. Lymond, his eyes wide and dark, sidestepped as Jerott thought he would, and so instead of crashing at full pelt into the dark bulk of the table, Jerott heeled off it; got clear, all but a glancing blow, when Lymond from behind it jerked it on to him; and was already round and behind Lymond before he had straightened, and finding a purchase, with knee and two toughened hands, to twist his leader's arms back with all the strength he possessed and throw him in Abernethy's face.

He might have done it, despite a kick in the ankle that made him gasp, if Lymond had not chosen precisely the right moment to bend sharply and, using his trapped hands as leverage, to somersault the other man to the ground.

His breathing soft and quick, as it should be, Jerott bounced to his feet like a cat. Bit by bit, he was losing his anger, in the sheer artistry of what they were doing. He crouched, ready to engage, just as the candle went out.

And Lymond, he realized, was prepared for it: had in the last second of light already marked his next grip, and from the force of the onslaught Jerott now received, hurling him back willy-nilly into the far corner of the hut, had determined to subjugate him, with the darkness as his ally, here and now.

Then Jerott was down, as he had so often been down, suddenly, in the days of training. He answered it properly. He used his strength, which was suddenly invincible, to free the one hand that could chop, with its cast-iron edge, at the throat rising from the open-necked shirt above him; and as Lymond rolled sideways to go with the impact of the blow, Jerott surged up, kicking, and with all the force he possessed, flung himself on top of his commander and then, his hands hard in his shoulders, propelled him over and over the uneven ground until Lymond crashed back, under Jerott's passionate thrust, straight into the spiked bulk of the table. As his back took the full force of the blow, he exclaimed aloud.

There followed absolute silence, ringing with the reverberations of someone's shouting, abruptly cut off. From Lymond, spreadeagled under his hands, there was no further sound and Jerott, kneeling back abruptly, pushing the hair from habit out of his eyes, was able to review what he had done. It had been deliberate. He was, after all, an *homme de métier*.

A dark figure dropped from outside over the table edge and thrusting past Jerott, still kneeling, got out a candle and lit it. In the new light under his fingers, Archie Abernethy's face was a demoniac mask: Koshchei the Deathless. 'I wad flense ye here for the gulls, gin there was time,' said Archie. 'But there's nane. Get ye gone.'

'Now. Not so hasty, Archie.' Alec Guthrie's admonishing voice from the doorway struck cold into the little hut. 'We were told that the Chevalier was not to be let go back to St Mary's, *whatever happened*. It's just Mr Blyth's good luck that you're lighting the candle and I'm standing here gaping with my chaft-blade in the air, all fit to be walloped.'

It might have been Mr Blyth's good luck, but he was doing nothing about it. Instead, gasping still, he was looking at Francis Crawford, lying still at the foot of the table, his skin flushed, his lids heavy, his lips cracked with fever.

Jerott shifted his feet. Archie Abernethy swore, and, sponge in hand, dropped beside the man Jerott had felled so handily, while Jerott uneasily drew back. He said angrily, 'He chose to fight. Did he think I'd come crawling back, overcome by remorse?'

'The charitable assumption,' said Alec Guthrie's grating voice, 'is that he didn't intend his friends to be hurt in his quarrel. Also, he had reason to believe he could teach you a suitable lesson with a raging temperature and all four limbs paralysed. He was wrong, that's all. . . . Are you going, or do we have to kick you out?'

'He'll be mad,' said Archie in a low voice. Under his careful hands, Lymond made a sudden, wordless sound, and his closed eyes tightened.

'But on the other hand,' said Guthrie coolly, 'he'll be in no condition to put his madness into effect. I'm sure Mr Blyth is right. To add remorse to Mr Blyth's present burdens would, I am sure, be intolerable. Let's keep it simple. Get out.'

For a moment more, Jerott Blyth hesitated. Then, his face grim, he rose to his feet, retrieved his weapon, and went.

Shrewd, competent, hard-headed professionals that they were, neither Guthrie nor Archie Abernethy had anticipated anything like the storm that broke upon them when Lymond came to his senses at last to find Blyth had gone. Swaying with weakness, Francis Crawford described to the two silent men exactly what they had done. And even Guthrie, sustaining those flaming blue eyes, recognized the time had come to be silent, listening, and to hope merely not to be dismissed.

But in the end they were of course dismissed, totally and finally, to go, in More's bitter words, to kill up the clergy and sell priests' heads as cheap as sheeps' heads, three for a penny, buy who would. It was Abernethy who spoke as the tirade ended and Lymond turned aside to the wall, shaking with foolish exhaustion.

'Oh, ye've a temper,' said Archie consideringly. 'And ye had a rare old time losing it, and ye were like enough justified at that. But take a thought, too. Are ye to accuse Graham Malett in the law courts from the flat o' a bier-claith, or on two sticks like a wife wi' Arthretica? If ye're tae walk upright like the fine, testy gentleman ye are, ye'll need some nursing, I'd say. So I fear Guthrie and I had best bide.'

He was prepared, philosophically, for a savage response. In fact, dropped from abrupt necessity among the tumbled rugs of his pallet, Francis Crawford sat with rock-like obstinacy and shivered, while from above, Alec Guthrie's harsh voice went on gently, 'Archie's right. My dear lad, you need all the help you can get; don't cast it off. We were wrong to let Blyth go. I admit it. But he knows now what he risks. I think he'll come back to you. I think they'll all come back to you. But you and Gabriel stand opposed in all this sorry battle. Not one of us can take your place.'

Lymond turned. His eyes were brilliant with fever. He was smiling. 'Why should they come back? They're not all simple-minded. If I could let Joleta die, what fool is still going to trust me? Who is going to separate cowardice from moral expediency when even I, looking back, can't now be sure . . .? *That* is what has driven Blyth away. Nothing but that.'

'That's nonsense,' said Guthrie sharply. 'There was no possible guarantee that the case against Gabriel would be complete on your death. It was far more likely to lose all its impetus. If you had never run up those steps, Joleta would have died at Gabriel's hands just the same. It was opportunism—pure, brilliant opportunism to force you to do what you did, and undermine all the doubts the Somerville lassie had sown. Nobody would have been more stunned or more contemptuous than Gabriel if you had stood firm. . . .'

The grating voice hesitated. Guthrie said kindly, 'As you said . . . we are not all simple-minded. What you have to face now is something a good deal more difficult than accepting Gabriel's sword-thrust at the top of those steps. What you chose was not the easy way out.'

'No. The thicket of thorns,' said Lymond, with the flatness of utter fatigue. 'Some day, I must take my own prolific advice and contrive to drop dead.'

Then Guthrie's eyes met those of Archie Abernethy, moving forward with a cup in his hand. And very soon after that, doctored by something more drastic than Archie had ever had occasion to administer to him before, Francis Crawford was profoundly asleep.

*

Then the net drawing Gabriel and Lymond together began at last to close tight.

For two weeks, with men and mastiffs, the law officers of Scotland, aided by the Seigneur d'Oisel and his Frenchmen, hunted Francis Crawford and his friends among the small hills, green and soft with deep mists, long-shadowed with apricot sunshine, where the corn crowded fat in the sheaf, as it had not stood for nine warring years, and two since. It was a strange, plodding game, in which French curses and Scots rose intermingled to the mild skies, and only the chief actors were dumb.

For Lymond, it was a time to recover, despite the almost daily moves expediency demanded. And evidence continued to come in.

462

Adam Blacklock, back triumphant from Liddesdale, brought with him an insalubrious Turnbull who could identify a steward of Gabriel's as having paid them to kill the Kerr cattle. And, stuttering, Adam produced something else: the sworn statement of the big tinker who had attacked Cheese-wame Henderson, and whom he had found, logically enough, lying sick in one of the Turnbulls' appalling mud cabins.

It was Fergie Hoddim on duty that day. When Blacklock had finished his recital, Fergie took him up sharply, 'As to evidence, now. Unless ye brought the said steward to Liddesdale to be identified, how could yon auld thief tell it was him? Did ye pay him siller to swear it?'

For answer Adam slipped from under his arm and laid on the floor the leather case he was holding. From it, he drew several sheets of thick paper, each bearing, delicately done in red chalk, the drawing of a man's face. That on the first was, recognizably, the steward they were discussing. 'It comes in useful . . . sometimes,' he said, and met Lymond's eyes, smiling.

Fergie's face also had cleared. 'Aye. That's better. It's a clear case o' deadly enmity and feud. A clear case. So we need all the independent proof we can gather—evidence without fear or favour, if ye take me.' He gazed thoughtfully at Francis Crawford's unimpressed face. 'Ye could even get bloodwite off him for yon beating. Nae mair nor fifty pounds, of course; but it's not to be sneezed at. Aye. I'd advise on bloodwite; you'd be perfectly safe there.'

There was a moment's pause and then Lymond, to Adam's relief, began quite genuinely to laugh. 'Well done, Fergie,' he said. 'Yes, of course. Whatever happens, *ad lucrandum vel perdendum*, let's make sure of our bloodwite. It'll do to buy a bloody memorial with.'

For no one was the waiting easy. Philippa, resolutely ensconced at Midculter despite Sybilla's gentle pressure to return home, busied herself silently with helping Mariotta and the baby and merely appeared, a grim and bony changeling, when Adam Blacklock came, as he often did, with a fragment of news from his leader.

Kate had been told, as soon as Lady Culter could send off a horseman, of her daughter's safety and of all that had happened; and being Kate, she had stayed, gnawing her nails, where she was, and had left Philippa to do her growing-up without interference.

Sybilla lost her nerve only once, as Adam was leaving one day.

She began mildly enough. 'It hasn't occurred to Francis, I take it, that there is nothing now to prevent him from awaiting the full indictment against Graham Malett from the relative comfort of prison?'

Adam Blacklock glanced at Philippa and away again. 'He wants Gabriel arrested first,' he said. 'And he won't allow that until the evidence is complete. He's an extremely clever man, Graham Malett. Mr C-Crawford won't risk any loophole being left. That's why we are waiting now for Jock Thompson's report. The official complaint from England about the arms-running into Ireland must have come now, and we may be faced with a major charge of civic disobedience as it is. At least if we can show Gabriel's complicity, the Queen Dowager won't give him her trust and the leadership of St Mary's at once.'

With one long, slender finger, the Dowager traced the ferny pattern of her gown. Without looking up she said, 'And, of course, if you or Mr Guthrie or Mr Hoddim or my other son were to come forward now with your evidence, your lives would be exposed to attack by Sir Graham. While you are in hiding, you are safe too.'

'He has that in mind. Lady Culter,' said Adam Blacklock, his brown eyes direct. 'If we believed it would serve any purpose, my friends and I would have accused Sir Graham long since.'

Sybilla flashed him an abstracted smile. 'What an obstinate band of young men you are,' she said. 'The leadership of St Mary's! What does it matter? For leading an unruly assembly, for disobedience, for causing trouble in Ireland, what can they do to him? Fine him, perhaps; keep him in prison until his temper cools. Even if the worst happens and Gabriel goes free, Francis is most unlikely to be asked by law to forfeit his life. So that all this endeavour and all this danger is endured for one reason: the leadership of one excellent small force, which Francis cannot bear to see fall into the wrong hands. *Does* it matter?' Turning, she confronted the artist, her neatly capped white head cocked, her brows straight. 'Or is Francis merely bewitched by his own little creation?'

It was Richard Crawford, standing solid and quiet just inside the door, listening, who answered. 'Francis knows very well what he has done. He has bred a terror in a small nation such as this which could jeopardize the balance of nations and overthrow kings. And he has placed this power in the hands of Graham Malett. Should Gabriel learn what is being plotted against him and fly, he would still be able to take this force with him, virtually intact. This axe may be poised yet to the glory of Gabriel over more defenceless heads than we dream.'

'It won't happen,' said Adam Blacklock abruptly; and bending, he kissed Sybilla's idle hand, pressed it, and left. And as the throat-constricting silence after that threatened to continue. 'Don't think about it,' said Philippa quickly. 'Look, here's Kevin.' And diving for the door, she lifted from the surprised hands of his passing nurse the vibrating red bolster which was Kevin Crawford, Master of Culter, and sat him on his grandmother's lap.

'Mother always says,' said Philippa, 'that when the worst is happening and your knees are rattling like Swiss drummers, there's nothing like a baby to give you a sense of proportion.'

She did not know then why it misfired. She only knew that at her side, Lord Culter stood dumbly staring at his son, and that Sybilla, her arms embracing that small rotundity, with the red cheeks and black feathery curls and deep, blue-black Irish eyes of Mariotta his mother, bent her head on his dark one and cried.

*

At Boghall and at Branxholm, they also waited. Jenny Fleming, chained by her history to Boghall castle, far from Court, paced her room and visited her royal bastard in his nursery, and wrote long, placating letters to the Constable of France. Her daughter Margaret, waiting in silence for news from the arsenal which was St Mary's, knew that her mother was obsessed with the need to return to France, to love and power, and gaiety and admiration. Anything, even the courtly respect with which M. d'Oisel had treated her, was fuel to her determination.

As the wife of the French King's Lieutenant in Scotland, she could return with him to France and to a place in society which would surely include the attentions, however discreet, of the King. Diane was old. The Queen was becoming stouter and plainer. Or if Francis Crawford had been a less fickle child of fortune. . . . He was wealthy. He had a comté. . . .

'Don't fret, child,' said Jenny Fleming kindly to her daughter Margaret as for the third time that day she found her staring unavailingly out of the window towards the rooftops of Midculter. 'Once Sir Graham is put down, the Queen Dowager will ask Francis to take his company to France. He will make his name, I'm sure of it.'

Margaret Erskine's sigh was noiseless. She turned round. 'You weren't thinking, by any chance, of going with him?' she said.

Lovely still, Lady Fleming's vivid face sparkled. 'Why, dull child? Do you think he'd object?'

It was a long-standing conspiracy. 'I know he won't,' said her daughter briskly. 'I've discussed it for you, in fact. He said he wouldn't mind, provided you put your rates up. Villeconnin's mother, he said, got two hundred thousand crowns in the bank from the last King of France for a son.'

She knew her mother too well to fear any damage to her *amour propre*. Jenny Fleming merely looked exasperated. 'That young man,' she said, 'ought to be plucked out of his pride and impaled on a thornbush. He introduced me to someone as the Controller of the King's Beam, last time we met.'

Which at least had the merit of making her daughter laugh, if a little wildly.

*

At Branxholm, Janet Beaton had the whole matter strictly in hand.

Bit by bit, her husband had been allowed to learn of Gabriel's iniquity, and of Joleta's shortcomings. Of his share in Will's death Janet said nothing. Lymond had said only, 'Put him on his guard. Tell him a little. But nothing, for God's sake, that will send him frothing off to St Mary's with a noose in his hand. We don't want Buccleuch dead or Gabriel vanished.'

It was a matter for nice judgement, but Janet knew her Buccleuch. The first time she raised it, he called her a havering ninny, and advised her that the dust was standing in bings under the draw-bed, and she should mind her own feckless business before kilting up other folks' tails for them.

But he thought about it, and though he poured scorn on the idea at the next airing too, she knew he would surely come round. And soon enough, brows jutting, he was saying bluntly, 'Yon fellow Crawford's made a right hotch-potch and mingle mangle o' it, then. And Sandilands is as bad, by God, letting the de'il stroll in.'

'Jimmy Sandilands is a creishy wee fox,' said Dame Janet with emphasis. 'He'd like fine to line his pockets with the Order's revenues, and he thinks he sees a way of getting someone else to take the blame for it. Francis had a fair shot at hinting the way things might go, on the way home from Falkland, but the fool whined over his gouty foot and quoted the Scriptures until you would think he was mad. Francis couldna shift the Kerrs, either.'

'I should hope not,' said her husband indignantly, allowing a grandchild to drop off his knees. 'A good-going feud like yon isna put out like a spit on a match. It was going fine long before Graham Malett got his hands on it.'

'Oh, we all ken that,' said Janet angrily. 'Flype a Scott and you find a wee man thumbing his nose at a Kerr. But he pointed out, all power to him, that the lot of ye were no more than playing into the hands of anyone that wanted real power for the asking next to the throne, and no awkward questions from the gentrice. Cessford said,' she added absently, 'that as the Scotts werena gentrice, it would make no difference when the Kerrs loused down their points and ran them greetin' out o' the land.'

It was next day before she was able to touch on the subject again, and Buccleuch's feelings were still uncommonly ruffled, but he did agree, growling at last, to take care in all his dealings with the family

Kerr. And also, with greater reluctance, to lend an ear, when the time came, to the discourse of Crawford of Lymond.

'Thank God,' remarked Janet at this stage, fanning herself with an infantile garment. 'Ye're a dogged au'd besom, Buccleuch. But you're namely for sense, in the end.'

'Sense! With the blood of me rotted with nagging! Can ye no envisage a decent reticence, woman, but you've to knock and chop hourly like the chapel-heid clock? Sense!' bellowed Buccleuch. 'A purseful of auld sousis for all the sense that ye'd ever spy in this house!'

But Janet was satisfied.

*

And so the time drew to a close, and at St Mary's Gabriel received and dispatched messengers, and played chess smiling with M. d'Oisel, and watched, with the French Ambassador, while the cream of his men, confident in training and skill, outpaced their French custodians in every exercise of the jousting ground and the butts. For M. d'Oisel was being allowed to discover what kind of weapon Sir Graham had sheathed at the asking, and how smoothly it fitted his hand.

And all the time Jerott Blyth stood at Gabriel's side. Resisting the easy course, Jerott had come back to justify at last all the Order had given him, when he had nothing to give in return but a past to be buried. He had told Lymond what he intended to do. He meant to save Graham Malett: to give Gabriel the chance no one had given his sister. And yet, to keep his implicit promise to Lymond, he must do it without betraying what he knew, or how close the hounds were at Gabriel's heels.

It was not possible. It could never have been possible, although Jerott kept his word and in their prayers together, in the long discussions he forced on all the great issues of religion and ethics, he gave no sign that Graham Malett's own spiritual welfare was his concern.

But by the same token, nothing he could do carried weight. Looking at Gabriel's unclouded face, that could so easily darken with pain at mention of Joleta or of Lymond, Jerott found it incredible that any man could maintain such a pretence; could kneel, his arm round Jerott's shoulders in chapel, and pray for Francis Crawford's black soul. And that such a man, asked to countermand the order to track Lymond by bloodhound, could say quietly, 'Jerott . . . have you not learned that the flesh and its ills are less than nothing? His crimes against my sister, the bitter effects of a shameless ambition . . . these mean disorders of the soul far more desperate than any harm his

467

body might suffer. He is sick ' said Graham Malett gently, and pressed Jerott's shoulder. 'Don't deny him the healing he needs.'

Then, gazing up into those candid eyes, He *is* sick, thought Jerott Blyth grimly. And I *have* denied him the healing he needs. But in body only, Sir Graham. There is nothing wrong with Francis Crawford's sense of the major moralities, and a good deal that is admirable. Whereas. . . .

Whereas in Gabriel, he recognized, sickeningly at last, a power for evil, effortlessly sustained, which could come only from a mind totally warped.

Against this, no living Knight of the Order could hope to succeed. To plead, to reveal what he knew, would merely allow Malett to flee and would place the fate of all Malett's future victims at his, Jerott's door. He had been wrong, and Lymond right. The task of returning Graham Malett to the light of grace was the dream of a fool.

Jerott did not go back to Lymond. Only, after two or three days of brutal self-examination, he found out Nicolas de Nicolay who had returned to St Mary's, secure in his famous name and led by his native, long-whiskered curiosity to watch the duel end. And Nicolas de Nicolay, spry on a keg in a corner of the brewery, watching the big vats toil and ream, turned and said with satisfaction on his gnome-like face, 'Ah: the cow turned back into Io again. You have come to ask me, I hope, about Malta. I have much about Malta to tell you. And of Tripoli. Come. Let us walk.'

And so, walking head bent over an empty Scottish moor, with the young, cold wind of October running fresh through his cloak, Jerott Blyth was taken back to the blue misty seas and brazen skies and the hot powdery walls, cream-pink against both, of his convent in Malta, and heard the story of Dragut's attack as Francis Crawford and de Nicolay had pieced it together.

It was the story, when you thought of it, of a cold-blooded pursuit of power without absolute parallel. There was in Graham Malett none of the dynastical ambition that had made the House of Guise great, and that had made of the Queen Dowager's brothers an amalgam of priest, diplomat and ruthless man of affairs. Nor was he, as Popes and Cardinals had been before him, a man of religion who had formed a taste for secular power and intrigue. 'This,' had said Nicolas de Nicolay at the outset calmly, 'that you worship, you, like a champac tree, is a clod of undeveloped Nature, no more. There are in him, we find, no sinks in which one may trace any particle of feeling for his fellow-man. If he has not this, then all he is and all he does is spurious; and most of all, this blasphemous mummery before the altar.

'Think, *mon ami*,' Nicolas de Nicolay had said, wandering from tussock to tussock, hopping a burn, stopping to pick and twirl the straw fingers of willowherb from the hedgerow. 'Think of it. A man may make his vows and his life may move into other paths, so that the vows are overlaid and forgotten. It is sad, but common. But here is a man who daily, hourly renews his vows and his protestations on his knees, who searches out God as his dearest confidant and friend and by nothing, by no amazement or defeat or tragedy, will let for one second the sacred mask slip. This is a true prince of darkness, is he not? A man worthy of fear.'

'For of all men, my God could love you; and I too.' So Gabriel had told Francis Crawford in those early days when, with magnificent artistry, he had crooked his finger and passed on, smiling, expecting Lymond to follow.

'Why?' Jerott said suddenly. 'Why, when Sir Graham saw that Lymond was going to resist both himself and his Religion, did he simply redouble the pressure? Why try in the first place to make Lymond of all people a disciple? A personal challenge?'

'A challenge?' The little geographer, stopped in mid-flight, turned and stared at him. 'Does such a thing exist? Not to Gabriel. Or not to Gabriel then. Ah no. One thinks this was merely one of many gambits our friend Sir Graham was playing, in his growing disillusionment with the Order. He is a Grand Cross of Grace. He might legitimately have expected to be considered for the Grand Mastership and then the world should shrink and bow the knee! But here is this old man de Homedès, who will not die, who is draining the Treasury and weakening Gabriel's rightful patrimony so that, when the Turks have finished with it, what will there be in Malta for him? And worse, new names are coming forward: la Valette, de Romegas, even Leone Strozzi. It is by no means sure that he will even become Grand Master in the end. So he looks at the possibilities. There are two. The Grand Master may die, or Gabriel may seek his advancement elsewhere. Where? By crossing, first, to the Turk. If the Turk is to win Malta, then Graham Malett would be well-advised to be on the Turk's side. Or he could look for a niche elsewhere: another principality which one day he might make his own.

'So he was interested in our young friend for two reasons. He might, by evangelical fervour, incite Lymond to kill the Grand Master, or start an insurrection which would lead to his death. Gabriel himself could not do this and hope to obtain the appointment himself either from the Emperor or the Pope with his hands sullied so. Or, he might discover from the young man all that was possible about his own land of Scotland, and whether a welcome might await a long-lost son who might be forced to leave his life-long vocation. In this case, there was more: he found Lymond knew Dragut, and was able to size up that old corsair long before he met him with his offer.

Graham Malett might have thrown in his lot with the Turks, had he not learned of Lymond's plan for this army of St Mary's. He had already made approaches. That was why he advised against fortifications, why he persuaded the knights the Turk would attack St Angelo, and not Gozo as he did. That was why Sir Graham was one of the seven men—the seven brave men, my friend—who went with de Villegagnon from Birgu to beleaguered Mdina. If Lymond had not kept him in sight throughout the whole of that journey, Dragut would have known by morning that only seven men had entered Mdina. If Lymond had not stopped him, at the risk of his life, Gabriel would have scaled the wall of Mdina next day to warn Dragut that the message about reinforcements would be false. And in Tripoli, you will remember, Graham Malett was most carefully outside the citadel, and not within it—in other words, in the encampment of the Turks, where he and no other must have warned Sinan Pasha about the weak bastion. You thought, you in the citadel, did you not, that an escaping renegade had betrayed it? But that renegade was killed before he could speak.

'For Gabriel wished the downfall of the Grand Master,' said Nicolas agreeably. 'While giving him such magnanimous support, he was gently, gently undermining the foundations. The Calabrians who objected so unhappily to leaving Birgu—he could do nothing to soothe them, this golden-tongued priest. He left them in worse case than before, and stressed merely the Grand Master's cruelty by insisting that Tripoli was defenceless. But it was carefully done. Sir Graham had no wish to lead, you see, if the Order was heading for defeat and disaster. On the contrary, he wished the credit for appearing to hold it together.'

They had reached the hills above Yarrow, and the long cleft of the Craig Hill where on a misty October day, four years before, twenty men and a flock of sheep dressed in helmets had put Lord Grey and his English to flight. Now the river, brown and merry, wound through the meadows still green in the autumn sunlight, and Nicolas de Nicolay, with an exclamation of pleasure at the sight, put his arms on the rough wood of a sheep-stank and stood, Jerott at his side, gazing while he talked.

'But he did not forget, Sir Graham, that the services of Lymond might prove more valuable still. He took steps to remove his competition: all that might hold the other man, or interfere with his plans. He has told me about, and you may remember, a note from Mistress O'Dwyer, carefully delivered, which Gabriel had so innocently opened. You yourself were instrumental, I believe, in preventing him, at Gabriel's request, from crossing to Gozo where he might either have lost his life to the Turks or rescued the woman and become saddled with her forthwith. It was through Gabriel, it offends me to think, and not myself solely, that Mr Crawford was brought safely from the hospital in Birgu where the Grand Master had hidden him, I am sure with the worst possible designs. Mr Crawford was not to be a victim of Juan de Homedès. He was to be a bright little tool in the brazen fingers of Gabriel.'

'So Oonagh appeared to die,' said Jerott. Throughout, his face pale, he had offered neither question nor comment on de Nicolay's crisp and kindly discourse.

'So she was persuaded that in the interests of Lymond himself, she must appear to die; or having conveniently disappeared, she must continue to let him think her dead. You and I both know how Lymond rescued her at Tripoli. They nearly lost them both. He swims marvellously well, and they had not expected it. But who could possibly have known of that attempt at escape? Only two people: Gabriel and the pirate Thompson. But Thompson was not likely to be the traitor. His life was in Lymond's hands; he owed his own escape from the Turk's galleys solely to Lymond. Therefore it was Gabriel who decided that Lymond was to return to Scotland alone, was to prepare this great army for him, and having trained it, to become either Graham Malett's disciple, or his victim. You know the rest.'

For a long time, Jerott Blyth did not speak. Then at length, his voice husky, he said, 'You say Lymond watched him. . . . How could he? How could he guess, more than any of us could, what Gabriel was?'

Compassionately, the little man watched him. 'It is hard, that? He has no fervour, no intuition, and yet he smells something wrong, something too perfect, something that makes one ask, "If this man is all he seems, why have all the prizes of the world not fallen at his feet? Why is he not the lodestar of all the Order, Spanish or none? Why is Juan de Homedès not abased, ashamed, before him?"' The little man's sparkling eyes searched out Jerott's face, and his dark, printed brows danced. 'Is it because there is something a fraction inhuman about these perfectly controlled responses, this unearthly radiance?

'Shall I tell you,' said Nicolas de Nicolay, flinging out his elderly arms, 'why Lymond first began to hate—to *hate*, mark you—your monastic friend? He has told me. It was when, whatever haven he offered them overnight, Graham Malett allowed to return all the women and children of Gozo.'

'He couldn't have prevented it,' said Jerott blindly. 'The Grand Master was in charge. The Spanish knights alone more than outnumbered us.'

'Mr Crawford does not dispute it,' said de Nicolay gently. 'He says, merely, that if Gabriel were all he appeared to be, *he should have died on the landing-stage.*'

471

There was another long silence. And then Jerott asked his third and last question. 'His son. Oonagh's son,' he said. 'Who has the baby?'

Nicolas de Nicolay, geographer, explorer, recorder of men's monuments in sand and marble through inhabited Europe, turned again to his post; to the wind and the sunlit vale of Yarrow.

'I do not know,' he said. 'I can discover no one who knows. Lymond has not been told of its existence, and, I trust, will never hear. I should advise you to pray, if you have faith still in prayer, and if you know who might heed you, that the baby is dead.'

*

After that, they took their time in returning to St Mary's; and got in, at midday, to find the place in a turmoil. There was reason to believe, said Graham Malett curtly, his face disturbed, that Francis Crawford had been seen in Edinburgh, with his disaffected friends. In any case, M. d'Oisel had deployed his French troops in the district long enough. The immediate search for Lymond was to halt, and the whole company of St Mary's, with the French force riding with them to guard against incidents, was to repair to Edinburgh.

'Where is merriest cheer, pleasance, disport and play,' said Lymond, when told some three hours later by Jerott's servant in the crumbling tower he had adopted as home for two days. 'But I am not in Edinburgh, and I have not been in Edinburgh; so why should Gabriel want d'Oisel there? What does Mr Blyth think?'

'Mr Blyth thinks that it is a trick,' said Jerott. A final constraint had made him send his man in, instead of himself. But Lymond was alone, and quite recovered. At Jerott's appearance, armed, in the castle doorway Francis Crawford rose from the window embrasure where he had been talking, and walked slowly forward. 'Ah. A conversion,' he said flatly. 'De Nicolay, I presume.'

'Yes ... I am taking steps to renounce my knighthood in the Order,' said Jerott with equal lack of expression. 'I have not approached Sir Graham about this or any other matter concerning his conduct. I shall leave at once for France.'

Lymond turned, and roving abstractedly across the straw-scattered floor, resumed his seat in the glassless window. 'You won't get there by any orthodox means,' he said. 'You were on the *Magdalena*, remember? No one is going to let you out of the country until the English commission has reported. Luckily, Thompson got here just about the same time that the English complaint reached Falkland. Logan was paid to interfere. . . .'

'So your case is complete,' said Jerott. 'And the dogs have been called off, so you are free to travel to Falkland to present it.'

'Do you think so?' said Lymond. 'Perhaps. In any case, Thompson will be sailing in two days. Horning notwithstanding, I am sure he can convey you to France, if suitably paid.' He paused. 'I'm exceedingly glad to know about the evacuation of St Mary's. About your intention to leave the Order I have, and should have, nothing to say. One of the things Gabriel and I seem to have in common, as you once remarked, is the fact that between us we have stripped you of your religion.'

'No. Neither of you could do that,' said Jerott, his dark-drawn gaze suddenly steady. 'But you have shown me, between you, that I have no claim to be more than a limping novice on that journey. The Order requires more than I have to give.'

'They ask more than anyone can give,' said Lymond, his manner suddenly altered, and got up. 'Is this true? You see beyond Gabriel's shadow to the ideal of the Order? And beyond mine to ... what I mean to do, rather than what I do?' He smiled, though not with his eyes, and coming forward, stood with Jerott in the doorway. 'You will find your place, Jerott. Good luck. And God speed you to France.'

He did not touch the departing man, nor did his eyes have in them any of Gabriel's lucent candour; but Lymond's voice was as Jerott had rarely heard it, pared of all mockery, and a little of the warmth he was suppressing, despite his effort, showed through.

And for some reason, this brought Jerott's whole mechanism for speech, emotion and deed to a shuddering halt. He stood, his stomach turning within him, and heard Lymond add, his voice cool once more, 'How unimpeachably shifty it sounds. What a fate for the tongues of the world, that after Gabriel all that is true and simple and scrupulous should sound like primaeval ooze.'

It was then that Jerott took heed at last of the knot in his belly and the ache in his throat, and announced, regardless of every plan he had made, 'I should like to stay. May I?'

'Oh, God, Jerott,' said Francis Crawford, and the blood rose, revealingly, in his colourless face. 'Yes ... but ... oh, *Christ* I'm glad; but if you touch my back once again you'll have to see the whole bloody thing through yourself.'

*

He was only just in time. Half an hour later, word came from Midculter that, so said Madame Donati, the Kerrs had received some sort of summons from Graham Malett, and Peter Cranston had gone off to join them. They were Edinburgh bound.

And hard on the heels of that, pounding up to the hingeless door with a handful of broad Scotts behind her, was Janet Beaton, Dame of Buccleuch herself, with grim news that put all the rest into place. Thomas Wishart had been killed—Tosh, whom Lymond had put into Branxholm to guard Buccleuch with his life. And Buccleuch, ignorant of the murder, casting off escorts and lacking Tosh's persistent protection, had gone off alone.

Questioned, Janet stumped about the floor of the keep, scraping her head under the upturned brim of her hat. 'I was over at Andro Murray's place with Grizel, ye understand. Sybilla's idea; and the lassie's taken to him, thank the Lord. I heard none of this till I got back. But the bruit was that the Lord Provost had sent for him, on the Queen's instructions from Falkland.'

'Sent for Buccleuch to go where?' said Lymond. 'Falkland? Hardly. He would have taken a train. Yet he took no one.'

'He didna take so much as a poke with a sark in it,' affirmed Janet in her powerful voice. 'Now that wad argue maybe a place where he had childer and linen? He's a house in the High Street weel furnished with both.'

'The High Street where?' Jerott's voice was quick with excitement.

'Edinburgh. *Edinburgh*,' said Lymond. 'You have heard Gabriel's trump. Gabriel is prophetic. D'Oisel is in Edinburgh; my own troops are in Edinburgh. And the Kerrs. And Buccleuch, poor self-willed gallant old man, unguarded and on his cantankerous own. So of course. . . .'

'You're not going,' said Jerott quickly.

'I want Nicolas,' said Lymond, ignoring him. 'And the three officers and my brother. Is the man from Midculter still outside? Archie and Salablanca will be reporting directly. Richard to bring Madame Donati and Philippa. . . . Is that fair? Yes, I think Philippa needs to be there. And Janet . . . will you come? But with only the men you have here guarding you, no more. . . .'

Jerott caught his arm. '*You are not going!*'

Under his hand, Lymond had become perfectly still. 'What in life, do you suppose,' said Francis Crawford precisely, 'would sweeten the knowledge that another Scott of Buccleuch had died when I might have prevented it? Oh, Gabriel knows that the news of Tosh's death will take me to Edinburgh after Buccleuch. But he doesn't know that I'm bringing his death-warrant with me.'

Jerott dropped his arm as Janet's powerfully harassed voice broke in. 'The Kerrs are in Edinburgh, did ye say? Is this another of Gabriel's moves?'

'Yes. You see,' said Lymond, and bending, he heaved his light saddle on the wide sill and began, with quick fingers, to buckle and fill the bags that strapped to each side, 'George Paris is in Edinburgh, in some lodging, and Cormac O'Connor is in Falkland with the Queen Mother, beguiling her with the news, at Gabriel's request, that George Paris is not the faithful go-between she has always found him, but is really a double agent working also for England.

'And since George Paris almost certainly has in his lodging a large number of documents incriminating not only himself but the Queen Dowager and the Irish lords in their conspiracy to kick out the English, she will be very anxious indeed to make sure these papers don't get in English Government hands. So she will probably send to Edinburgh at the first opportunity to have Paris arrested and the papers seized, probably by a civic authority, by her Ambassador from France, or even, if O'Connor suggested it, by some loyal and independent nobleman she could trust to bear her own part in the affair. And for the sake of secrecy he might be told, for example, to take no servants. . . .'

'Buccleuch,' said Janet. She blew her nose. 'I sent some of the men after him. If they traced him as far as Edinburgh, they'll go to the town house.'

'He'll be at Paris's lodging,' said Lymond. 'Discovering Paris's papers. And have you forgotten what else is in Paris's papers? International treachery, for a part. For the rest, the documents, very likely, about Thompson's great sea-insurance scheme, and the names of his fellow-tricksters, *among whom are the Kerrs.*'

*

After that there were orders, a great many orders, with the Midculter man and two of Janet's big Scotts brought in as messengers; and in the middle, Abernethy and Salablanca appeared and were told what to do.

Then, moments later, it seemed, they burst apart on their various errands like a firlot of lentils, and Blyth and Lymond, with the two men behind them, were riding without respite or concealment straight into the net.

475

XVII

Gabriel's Trump

(Edinburgh, October 4th, 1552)

THE Kerrs, left hands longingly fondling their swords, were very angry. Rankling in their minds, never forgotten, were all the old murders and recent insults: the rout at Ettrick, the killing of Nell of Cessford, the slaughter at Liddesdale, the farce of the children at Hadden Stank. And today, it seemed, the old thief Buccleuch would surpass himself. He had gone to Edinburgh, so rumour said, expressly to expose to official gaze the Kerrs' unsavoury share in the scheme run by Jock Thompson, Cormac O'Connor and George Paris, whereby through insuring your cargoes and allowing the pirate to steal them, you got your insurance money and maybe even some of your cargo back for good measure.

So the Kerrs were on their way, this fourth day of October, with their friends and allies for company, through the gentle country that lay between Cessford and Edinburgh, with the full harvest gilding the fields under the pink sky of sunset and the cottar smoke filling the hollows and misting the trees by the wayside, so that the silver-blue harness of winter seemed to lie on their breasts.

When they reached Edinburgh, it was dark. Sir John Kerr of Ferniehurst and his brother Walter of Cessford were shrewd. A grim company, fully armed and in Kerr colours, would be stopped at the Bow. So they filtered through slowly, in couples, and the first to go through were those detailed to find out George Paris and kill him, and destroy all the papers they might find.

So, through the West Bow and up the steep wynd to the Lawn-market, there walked eleven Kerrs, among them Cessford and his son Andrew; Ferniehurst and his brother and good-brother; and Dandy Kerr of the Hirsell, now owner of Littledean, and his son. There were some servants, a number of men related by marriage, Sir Peter Cranston and three members of the family Hume, also great on the Borders, which had no desire to fall out with the Kerrs.

Robert Kerr with two others made their way to Buccleuch's house. Ferniehurst, with Andrew Kerr of Primsideloch, George Kerr of Linton and Littledean and his son, made for George Paris's rooms in the Lawnmarket. And Sir Walter Kerr of Cessford, the old man himself, with John Hume of Coldenknowes at his side, strolled down the main street of Edinburgh, the castle wall at his back and the towers of Holyrood beyond the Nether Bow Port part-way down, and kept well clear, for once, of the weak lanterns slung on each side, flushing the timber jowls of the high, chimney-like tenements, and the outside stairs, their narrow flights vanishing high in the gloom.

On the square stones of the causeway, their soft deerskin boots made no sound; nor did they have a light borne before them, as was the custom. There were few people abroad. After eight o'clock, in October, a fresh little wind blew from the west, pleating the Nor' Loch; and Frenchmen in taverns drank too well, and came looking for trouble. There was a woman or two in the street, and a light or two, and the noise of laughter, clapping silent and loud as a tavern door swung. An officer of the burgher watch passed, swinging his bowet, and observed them curiously.

Behind them, no brawl had broken out in the Lawnmarket, dirling among the under-carved eaves: the work with Paris must have gone off well. Pacing without haste, Cessford and Hume passed from the wide market into the narrow channel of the Queen's High Street of Edinburgh, choked by the straggling line of locked timber shops, the Booth Raw down its middle. There they took the foot-passage, narrow and dark, on the right of the Luckenbooths, where the tall bulk of the Tolbooth, prison and seat of justice and Parliament House at once, loomed dark in the night, two of its dim windows lit. And next to it, as they passed, a lamp hung in the Norman porch of the great church of St Giles, the queer masks carved in its nested archways yawning and leering, and the odour of incense preached at them from the big, stately fabric, with its high crown of groined stone, and its great bell, that had rung out the nation's grief at the disaster of Flodden; and tonight and every night, at ten o'clock, would toll its forty strokes, in warning to the citizens of Edinburgh to keep off the streets. They had to do what had to be done, and leave the city by then.

At nine o'clock precisely, Kerr and Coldenknowes had reached the east end of the Stinkand Style, past the booths and the church, and were in the open High Street, with the Mercat Cross on their left, and on their right the entrance to Conn's Close, running down to the Cowgate, where George Hoppringle, with a boy, happened to be having his horses shod in David Lindsay's smith's booth. Below that on their right was the Tron, and beside it the tall house with its corbelled oriels, the slatted flats rising crooked above their heads, where Buccleuch had his lodging.

Then the lights went out. Until nine o'clock, the law said, lanterns must be exposed by each householder; and the householders, with the price of lamp oil in mind, made sure that the servant girl ran down the forestairs with not a moment to waste. At the same time, a patter of footsteps coming down-street the way they had come heralded a servant of Ferniehurst's, who slowed when he saw them in the last extinguishing lights, and in a low voice gave them his master's message.

They had found George Paris's lodging, and forced open the door. But they had been too late. Paris had gone, and his papers with him, in the custody of the law officers of Edinburgh under the Lord Provost himself, with Wat Scott of Buccleuch with him.

The Kerrs' complicity with Paris could no longer be hidden. But there was time for vengeance: all the time in the world.

Neither Hume nor Cessford this time hesitated. Watched over by the pious mottoes and unseen, benevolent statues of the elderly land, they ran lightly upstairs to Buccleuch's house, the servant following, and raised their fists to bang on the door.

They were forestalled. Robert Kerr, Ferniehurst's brother, moved out of the shadows, his friends silent behind him, and spoke in a low voice. Buccleuch was not there. But Robert Kerr and his friends were prepared to wait for him, and all night if need be. Leaving him there, Sir Walter Kerr of Cessford and his ally John Hume returned to the street, and retracing their steps, walked slowly up the High Street towards the Stinkand Raw again.

Wat Scott ran into them just there, after leaving George Paris under guard in the Tolbooth, and crossing round the graveyard at the back of St Giles, which he rounded at Our Lady's Steps on his way to walk down to his lodging.

He was alone. Cessford and Hume saw him first as a stocky dark shadow trudging past the pale grey bulk of the church; then, as they came closer, the feeble light from the Virgin's statue in its niche above the church's north-east doorway showed the familiar, broad-bearded Warden, his brimmed bonnet flat on his head, his wide, short gown swinging as he strode, spurs clinking, over the causeway.

He saw their faces quite clearly as they threw themselves on him, John Hume in the lead; and given a second longer, could have raised that stentorian voice in a bellow that might have saved his life. But Hume's thick hand cramped over his bearded mouth, and Hume's and Cessford's combined weight heeled the old man like some recalcitrant cargo to the ground, kicking and stumbling, spinning among the booths and into the High Street and back among the booths again. Then John Hume drew his sword.

Buccleuch was a strong old man. But his son's death had told on the fabric of his body as well as the vigour of his mind. He rolled on the ground, kicked, half-throttled, voiceless, and probably saw the glint of Coldenknowes's blade and the sudden movement as Kerr of

Cessford, seized with caution, fell back, and Hume, his voice furious, called low-voiced, 'Strike, *traitor!* Ane stroke for your father's sake!'

With one violent movement, Wat Scott of Buccleuch got to his knees just as the sword came at him, and grasping the other man's thighs with his knotted hands, tried to hold John Hume off.

It was too late. As Cessford hesitated, Coldenknowes swore, and thrusting Buccleuch off with his left hand, drove the sword clean through Buccleuch's body. It was a cruel wound: mortal, but lacking the mercy of an instant death. For a moment he floundered, there at their feet, among the stinking rubbish of the Luckenbooth trash; and then with a grunt he lay still, his blood ebbing fast with his life.

Bending, his sword sheathed, John Hume fumbled for and found one stout booted leg, cursing as the spur slit his palm. Then, heaving with both hands, he slung Wat Scott's inert body behind the broken-hinged door of a booth, with the reek of decayed food and animals thick in the darkness. 'Lie there, with my malison,' he said softly. 'For I had liefer gang by thy grave nor thy door.' And with Cessford silent behind him, he made his way swiftly and quietly out of the Style, and down Conn's Close to the Cowgate, where the horses were ready.

Half an hour later, tired of awaiting Buccleuch, Robert Kerr left his house next to the Tron and with three men, Kirkton, Ainslie and Pakok, who was a man of Hume's household, began to quarter the High Street looking for him. At the same time a boy, well bribed in advance, left the Cowgate Port on the heels of Cessford and Hume and riding round to the south-east came across the night encampment, just outside the walls, of the French Lieutenant-General, M. d'Oisel with his French troops, escorting the whole company of St Mary's. The message he brought to the pavilion where the Seigneur d'Oisel and Sir Graham Malett were sitting at supper, was that Buccleuch had been murdered. Five minutes later, Sir Graham at his own request by his side, d'Oisel was riding fast through St Mary's Port and up to the High Street, half his band of French light horse at his tail.

Lymond missed them by perhaps five minutes, because he took the direct route to the West Bow, to bring him quickly into the Lawnmarket where George Paris was lodged. By that time the great bell of St Giles had rung its forty brisk peals and all the many gates of Edinburgh were locked to the casual; but Francis Crawford had brought his own entrée: the robed and gout-stricken person of Sir James Sandilands of Calder, Grand Prior in Scotland of the Order of St John, roused from his comforts at Torphichen by all the urgency Jerott could muster. And Jerott, too, wore over his cuirass the black robes of the Order, packed flat in his box ever since he left Malta, with the Eight-Pointed Star glimmering faintly on his left shoulder.

The three men, the Grand Prior's train of twelve men-at-arms riding behind them, swept up to and through the Bow gates, and cantering up the steep slopes to Castle Hill, deployed down the street. Paris, they found in their turn, had departed. Leaving Sandilands to rouse the Tolbooth, puzzled, angry and a little afraid, Lymond, followed by Jerott, set off down the wide Lawnmarket to call on Buccleuch.

They passed the Luckenbooths as Robert Kerr entered them, with the three men at his back, searching for Wat Scott of Buccleuch; searching and hearing presently the sound of growling distress; the low whining breath that might be a dog's, but which proved to be the high heart of Buccleuch, stirring in his blood, whispering for help and for vengeance. Then, as Lymond's hoofbeats grew fainter, with Jerott's, down the long hill, Robert Kerr drew his sword and entered the booth.

With sword and dagger the three men with Kerr finished the work begun by John Hume, three and four times over, plying blade over blade until the mess of clothed flesh in the stall was indistinguishable from the filth round about. Then pulling from the hacked body the bloody remnants of cloth, with its familiar jewelled clasps, chipped and dulled over with use, the grey chopped hair pressed in the folds, they too made for Conn's Close in the dark, running.

Few people in Edinburgh in that hour and year would have cared to stop a party of men hastening past the Mercat Cross in the dark, one bearing a bundle of rags. Adam Maccullo, Bute Herald, on his way from Holyrood to Castle Hill was the exception. As the light from his bearer's lantern fell first on two horsemen riding swiftly downhill, and then on the men who, emerging from the Booth Raw, slipped quickly downstreet to Conn's Close, he called out at once, 'What's the matter?'

Only John Pakok, Coldenknowes's man, had the hardihood to reply. 'There's a lad fallen,' he remarked, and walked on, whistling, after the others down the sharp descent to the Cowgate.

But already Maccullo's lantern and the sound of the voices had brought Lymond back, in a wide arc, from the Tron by Buccleuch's deserted house. Jerott, following, found Lymond dismounted and running, with Maccullo at his side, towards the dark, jostling booths, their paint blistered, their dirty ribbons fingering the air under the jerking light of the lamp. Swinging in turn off his horse, Jerott tied both loosely to the stone pillars of the nearest arcade and was moving quickly after the two men when Maccullo cried out.

Now, cautiously, lights glimmered in the high lands above the booths and the church; shutters creaked back, and candlelight on first one high balcony, then another, glinted on the brass rail and the peering flesh of the owners, craning above. Then Maccullo's boy, without the lantern, came running out of the Booth Raw and turned up towards the Tolbooth as if all the ghosts in the graveyard were after him, and Jerott, arriving at last, nearly fell over the herald, standing mute at the broken door of a booth where, the lantern light rimming his hair, Lymond silently knelt. Beside him, in the dirt, lay the disjointed carcass, wet, warm, grossly squandered like soft fruit, which for the better part of seventy years had answered the heroic spirit of Walter Scott of Buccleuch.

Jerott saw that Maccullo had recognized Lymond: was staring at him as he knelt, his hand uncertainly on his sword-belt. Lymond himself paid no attention, and although the line between his eyes was drawn black in the stark light, his voice was quiet when he spoke. 'He is barely two minutes dead. He was alive when we passed him.' He looked up, his eyes blazing. 'There is a blood-feud for you, Jerott,' he said. 'They would dispatch a stirk cleanly, but a living offence to their pride, never. What old man in the world would merit such hatred?'

'*There he is. Take him,*' said Gabriel's voice, ringing, hoarse with emotion, out of the darkness. '*Take him, in Christ's name, with his hands red yet again in another man's blood.*' And suddenly, with a hiss of drawn steel, the trampling feet of an army seemed to converge on Lymond; and the High Street, the booths, the Stinkand Raw and the dark graveyard leading down to the Cowgate were all peopled with soldiers.

Jerott waited just long enough to see Lymond jump to his feet, white and lithe, his sword out, and to be glad that he himself was not in the party which was to arrest Francis Crawford here and now. Instead, Jerott turned, and facing the doorway, his black eyes alight, he struck with his sword the first blade that fell into the lamplight while at his back Lymond crossed Buccleuch's body with a bound and, striking through the rotten back of the booth with blade and shoulder, burst through into the jostling darkness beyond.

Jerott held them at bay for a matter of seconds. Then he was thrust aside as Maccullo was, his cry unnoticed, as d'Oisel's Frenchmen poured after, shouting. His cloak half-pulled from his shoulders, the young knight straddled Buccleuch's helpless body, buffeted on all sides, and strained to see, through the milling bodies, whether Lymond was through, while using the flat of his blade viciously to keep the trampling feet clear and to protect himself from rough hands.

He saw Bute Herald, caught in the swirling tide, suddenly reach a decision and, fighting his way through to where Jerott had left the horses, untie one and set off down Conn's Close, with two or three men at his stirrups. The boy must have come back from the Tolbooth with a sergeant and some men. The Kerrs, if the Kerrs had been responsible, would not get far. Then Jerott himself turned to follow

481

Lymond and the French to where the shouting was loudest; and there came the sound of snapping timber as the booths crashed; and smashed glass as men reeled back into the little windows of the lower lands. So the Chevalier Blyth came face to face with a massive shadow standing silent in the gaping back of the stall: the shadow of a tall man whose white plume stirred in the night air and whose cuirass glinted bright, like his own, under the long black robe, starred on the shoulder, of a Grand Cross of the Order of St John.

'My poor lad,' said Sir Graham Reid Malett gently. 'You wear your robes, who have broken every vow of chivalry the Order requires. You have chosen to follow that headstrong and lonely young man, and no prayers can save you now. . . . Are you listening?' For behind them, swirling up the Lawnmarket where every window was crowded and every stair laden with people, the noise of night-blinded pursuit had reached a screaming crescendo. 'I doubt,' said Graham Malett gravely, 'if he will reach the Tolbooth prison alive.'

Then for the first time, Jerott truly believed all that he had learned of Graham Malett: would have believed it even had he not seen, a spark in Gabriel's hand, the dagger he had brought to use. Afterwards he knew he owed his life to the burgher watch and the law men from the Tolbooth, who stumbling just then into the wrecked Luckenbooth, shone their lanterns on the old man who lay at their feet, and then summoned the monks from the Maison Dieu at the head of Bell's Wynd to carry the heavy, disfigured body into their quiet chapel.

But by then Jerott had gone, fighting through the throng to reach its wild and disputing centre, aware all the time of the tall magnificent man moving smiling behind in his wake. How many of Gabriel's men lay ahead? Of course, Gabriel would make it his business to see that Lymond did not reach the Tolbooth alive. But Francis Crawford had the night on his side. He knew every wynd and vennel in Edinburgh, and provided in those first seconds he had obtained the lead he required, he had at least a chance of escape.

Escape to what? To Gabriel's assassins, *les enfants de la Mate*, as Lymond ironically called them? 'Other courtesy than death thou shalt not have,' Graham Malett had once said. Here, in the emotion of the chase and Buccleuch's slaughter by a hand still unknown, Gabriel had his most effective chance of encompassing what he wished.

It was then that Jerott realized that he, and Graham Malett a few yards behind him, were being carried past both Stinkand Raw, church and Tolbooth, and that the crowd, swirling round the west corner of the tall prison, had debouched along the graveyard path beyond, spilling among the grey tombstones, flickering in the manifold lantern-beams and stumbling among the grey buttresses of the side and back of St Giles. It remained, and was thickest, before the wide steps leading up to the south porch of the church. Pushing and thrusting, Jerott Blyth reached those steps. D'Oisel stood at the top, his lieutenant beside him, and an officer of the city guard, his face red with worry. Crichton, the Provost of St Giles, was not there, but you could see two or three frieze cassocks, and the cloth of gold and blue velvet of the Deacon, clearly quick to assume office. With a little help from the French men-at-arms and the city officers, the crowd stayed, swaying and jostling, at the foot of the steps.

Then behind him, clear among a thousand others, Jerott felt the presence he was waiting for. Patient, undisturbed, a little amused, Graham Malett moved to his side, and laid his fine hand on Jerott's shoulder. 'Sanctuary,' he observed amiably in his rich voice. 'The foolish young man has sought sanctuary. The church will shelter him, of course, for as long as he cares to remain. But unless he means to die there, he must know that one day he will emerge, and the shackles will close. . . . Poor, foolhardy creature. Shall we go in, you and I,' said Gabriel, the pressure of his hand increased suddenly on the fine tendons of Jerott's strong neck. 'Shall we go in and guide his soul to take the true, the selfless course?'

His hand dropped. And side by side, their robes airy behind them, the two Knights of St John of Jerusalem climbed the wide steps, between the clustering lamps, and entered the great church of St Giles.

*

From more than forty altars the long, white tapers pricked to life with their small flame the dim treasures of jewels and paintings, of silver-gilt and delicate, hand-sewn fabric and queer, painted faces that graced the aisles and chapels of the long two hundred foot nave, and lent their bouquet of light and incense to the rows of thick stone pillars that upheld the groined stone arches, far above.

Entering the murmuring silence of the church; leaving behind, thinly removed, the raucous excitement of the crowd; dismissing from his mind that circle of craning, avid faces at the south porch, Jerott Blyth walked with the man he once worshipped, past the carved font where he himself had been christened, and turning his back on the seven chapels of the west corner and their scattered, kneeling suppli-cants, he paced with Gabriel up the stone floor of the nave, past the Norman door, past the chapel where hung the Blue Blanket under which the citizens fought for their city, past the great stone pillars with their coats of arms and their altars, past the aisles and the altars of St Duthac and St Mungo, St Christopher and St Peter, St Columba and St Sebastian—the altars maintained by the skinners, the surgeons, the masons, the wrights, the shearers, the bonnet-makers and all the great of the past with a great achievement to be thankful for, or a great sin for which to atone.

They passed the organ, and the fine carved stalls for the prebendaries in the choir, where the officers of the church, the chaplains in their robes and the men and women who had come solely to pray and were caught up in the night's strange events stood aside, in ones and twos, whispering. Then Jerott could see the steps to the high altar, its chandeliers blazing with light; its vestments of black and red velvet and of cloth of gold; its pall of red satin hangings blatant in heraldic pattern behind.

On the steps of the altar, above the shifting heads of the half-dozen soldiers d'Oisel had allowed in, Lymond was standing. He had seen them, and across all the intervening space let fly a gleam of deprecating mockery in Jerott's direction.

'I am here,' said Lymond amiably. 'A refugee from pollarchy. Come and let us inspire that great Greek saint Giles to cast the demons out from us all.'

For a moment Jerott in turn looked up at the painted face of the tall statue, vested in cloth of gold and red velvet pendicle, placed above the jewelled casket bearing his relic: a hand and armbone, drily anonymous, with a diamond ring rattling loose on its finger. Beside him, Gabriel crossed himself, and Jerott did the same, aware that people were moving in softly behind them, filling the aisles and the stalls.

He turned round. The Sieur d'Oisel had come forward, and the chief magistrates with him, among them the Lord Provost himself. There were faces he did not know: French faces, and Scots faces; and then suddenly one very familiar indeed: Adam Blacklock, with a hooded girl on his arm. Philippa. Then Henri Cleutin, Seigneur d'Oisel, moving down to the altar rail, said crisply, 'This nonsense will cease. Mr Crawford, I am required by her grace the Queen Mother to remove you to the safety of the Tolbooth until your status and your loyalty have been examined. You need fear no injustice. In defence of your own innocence, I suggest you place yourself in my charge forthwith.'

'Truly,' said Lymond, his voice still mocking over the strain, 'I would rather live maligned than die justified. *Vive la bagatelle*. I am here, my lord Ambassador, for the blessing of the cultivation of peace, union and brotherly affection among honest men and fellow-Brethren. Will the Lord of Torphichen permit me to speak?'

Beside Jerott, Sir Graham Malett became very still. 'Aye,' a thick voice said, a little harshly. 'Sandilands is leal to his word, and a chiel namely for justice. Ye have the Order's permission to cry out.'

Sir James Sandilands of Calder, Grand Prior in Scotland of the

Order of Knights Hospitallers of St John of Jerusalem, flung his black robe around him and sat down. 'I have heard an indictment,' he said, glaring at d'Oisel and nowhere near Graham Malett. 'Whether Mr Crawford can substantiate it or not, I canna say. But I propose he speak out.'

'An indictment?' The French King's general in Scotland was totally at sea. 'Against whom?'

'Against Sir Graham Reid Malett,' said Lymond gently, and placed both hands on the bright brass rail at his back. 'Look around you, Sir Graham. There are all your accusers.'

And there, Jerott saw, one by one, their friends were filtering in, dusty from hard riding, come by prearranged plan to the one place where they would be safe. Fergie Hoddim of the Laigh slipped in, waved, and sat down. Beside him was the broad person of Guthrie and beyond them, Nicolas de Nicolay, the French cosmographer. He saw Archie, and the black face of Salablanca, and Cuddie Hob's knotted grin, and wondered by what bribery or trick they had induced the watch to let them all in.

Beside him, Gabriel said, '*Indictment!*' in bewildered distress, and flinging into a stall the plumed helmet he had carried from the church door, he walked forward, the altar candles molten gold on his hair. He looked up into Francis Crawford's face and said, 'I beg you. Innocent people have suffered enough. Drag no more names in the mud to rescue your own. Let us go in peace; and take your courage instead, and seek your own salvation like a man.'

'It is beyond the testimony of angels,' quoted Lymond, gazing into Gabriel's shining, troubled blue eyes. 'It is beyond the word of recording saints. It is a matter, if I have not already made it clear, of hard proof. You are, sir, a traitor, a murderer and a foresworn monk of your Order; and there is nothing I should like better, at this moment, than to hear you try to deny it.'

For a long moment, Sir Graham Malett sustained that direct gaze. Then he turned away, and finding d'Oisel near him, addressed him quietly. 'The young man is losing his mind. I have known it for some time. I have spoken to the Queen Dowager about this tragic contingency; and she has been kind enough to trust my discretion. Allow me to carry him with me now. I myself will stand surety for his behaviour, and with Holy Church's help, will give him the nursing he needs.'

'M. d'Oisel. . . .' Jerott Blyth, his hand on his sword, moved forward into his self-appointed place again, at Gabriel's side. 'Witnesses present just now can substantiate all Mr Crawford has to say, and will swear also as to his sanity. In fairness, Sir Graham should allow him to speak.'

'I am only concerned,' said Malett wearily, 'with sparing the emotions of all those whom our friend has so peremptorily involved. Of course I have no objection. I should like, however, to show just how much weight you may place on this accusation by stating my own discoveries about Mr Crawford.'

'Sisters, I knew him far away by the redness of his heart under his silver skin. State your discoveries,' said Lymond. 'And like a crone on a creepie-stool, I shall sit here and marvel.' And dropping lightly to the steps he waited, hugging his knees.

Perhaps because of Jerott Blyth, Gabriel began his indictment, in a rich, deep voice that carried to every corner of the great church, with Lymond's actions in Malta. With a detachment shaken only now and then, when his hands clenched and the white cross on his breast rose and fell with his breathing, Graham Malett told again the story of the Turkish attack, only picking out the constant of Lymond's treachery.

'The Order should vanish from the face of the earth. . . . Do you remember saying that?' asked Gabriel of Lymond where he sat, his hands lightly clasped at his knees. 'You came to Malta straight from the French King, with orders to that effect. From the start, the Turks were your allies. . . . Do you recall, Jerott, his attempt to join the Turkish attack at Gozo? Who do you suppose arranged the seduction of that foolish man de Césel, Gozo's Governor, by Francis's own former mistress? Who did his best, at Mdina, to escape over the wall to the Turks to warn them to ignore the false message coming from Sicily . . . and would have done so, too, had I not been privileged to stop him. How did Nicholas Upton die? How was Francis on such close and friendly terms with a well-known pirate?

'At Birgu he would have liked to have overloaded us with useless mouths; on the eve of the sailing for Tripoli he hid in the hospital rather than leave. And once in Tripoli, don't you remember how he bribed the Calabrian soldiers to let him out of imprisonment—the Calabrians, with whom he was so friendly, and who finally tried to blow up the castle and desert the Order by sea? Don't you remember the mysterious spy who informed the Turks to fire on the St Brabe bulwark, not the St James? . . . Who paid him, do you suppose? Who, do you remember, tried to get the French knights in the garrison again and again to rise against the Marshal and the Spanish knights and to hold Tripoli by themselves alone? How long, do you suppose, would they have troubled to hold out? Who found it so simple, when he wished, to escape the city with his band of freed slaves and reach the Turkish camp unharmed? Who escaped to the Turks again, leaving his mistress to drown?

'*I* wanted no sovereignty!' cried Gabriel, his deep voice rising in his distress. 'Before the battle on Malta, as anyone will tell you, I was asked to lead, and I refused. I took my oath to obey only one master on earth, and to that I hold. But this . . . this animal in spangles, this bright, malicious harlot . . . this furious and fatuous young man, would take a great Order, and now attempts to take a great nation and with his puny, ill-informed fingers, crumble it into rubble on which he may strut. . . .' He raised his voice against a sudden uproar that floated in through the open, packed doors and merged, muttering, with the congregation already within. 'Shall I go on? Need I go on?'

'Please do,' said Lymond politely, his eyes suddenly bright. 'And forgive the clamour outside. Half the French troops, it appears, have gone off hunting Kerrs and we have been joined by a large part of our friends from St Mary's. Also by my family from Midculter. And also by Madame Donati.'

'Evangelista?' said Malett slowly. 'Crazed by the death of my sister? What kind of witnesses are these? In any case, we have no need of them. We all know how Will Scott came to die. And now his father, killed because he knew too much. What was in George Paris's papers, I wonder? Evidence that as a friend of Thompson you were also a traitor with Paris, so that at Falkland you even told Cormac O'Connor that the Queen Dowager was aware of Paris's misdemeanours, to prevent him telling her the truth? The sapphire you have been wearing—strangely missing today—was given you by Thompson—why? A hard-headed corsair gives nothing for nothing.'

Before Lymond could speak Jerott, ill-advisedly, had answered that one. 'He bought a woman from him. I was there.'

Malett looked round, disgust on his face. 'For a jewel of that price! And why, then, is it hidden today?'

'It isna hidden.' Plain, uncompromising, it was the voice of Janet Beaton, her strong-boned face queer and puffy with weeping but her step firm and her chin high as she came down the nave, her sister hesitant behind. At Gabriel's side she halted, and looking up to the altar steps she said in a changed voice, 'I hae come from my slaughtered husband, Francis Crawford, with something to give you. This I took from his hand: it was his son's ring and I mean you to have it. This'—and in the steady glow of the candles she held up a sapphire, the fire in it burning through and through--'this was not on his fist when he left Branxholm. Is it yours?'

'Yes,' said Lymond; and nothing more. But Jerott, with sudden illumination, remembered stumbling over that silent, kneeling figure in the Luckenbooths, and seeing Lymond, rising, replace Buccleuch's thick, blood-streaked hand at his side with long, gentle fingers that hid what they had done.

But whatever Lymond's reason had been, he had no intention, clearly, of giving it; and no need. Janet's gesture, fresh from her husband's bier, was enough. And when she turned from Lymond's still face to the fair, concerned features of Gabriel, her whole manner commanded, although her eyes were wet and her nose swollen and red. 'I heard from Robert,' said Janet Beaton contemptuously, 'how you filled the Dowager's ears with bonny tales of Lymond's deficiencies, for all ye defended him so nobly in public. No doubt ye did the same at St Mary's. No doubt they've all heard how Will Scott died because Francis Crawford was whoring at Dumbarton and drunk at Liddesdale and for all their work, they had to go into action ill-managed, ill-trained and ill-led.'

She spun round, her voice hoarse, and addressed not only Graham Malett but the rapt faces in the recesses of the wide church behind her. 'Shall I tell you,' she said, 'how and why Will Scott died? And shall I tell you how and why Buccleuch died like a dog in the gutter today?'

And so the story of the Hot Trodd was told, and was supported, voice to voice, where they sat, by those who had evidence of its truth. And after that, Janet turned to Lymond and, cool-voiced, he described the events of that day and how, deliberately, the Kerrs had been sent to murder Buccleuch. Wat Scott knew nothing—and Lord Provost Hamilton, rising stiffly, confirmed it—of any crime committed by Kerrs which would be revealed by Paris's papers. The Kerrs had been dispatched into Edinburgh in the hope that they would do murder; and on their exit, word had been sent to d'Oisel that Buccleuch was dead, though in fact he was not dead, and no one except the Kerrs actually involved knew he was stabbed.

'You knew George Paris was a double agent,' said Lymond, his calmly modulated voice breaking in again. 'You contrived in London to obtain his money and papers—Mistress Somerville can testify to that. And, staying with Ormond, you found it easy to approach Cormac O'Connor and sound him out about the betrayal of Paris. Because of course you knew who Paris was—you had seen him in France at least once, although he did not know you. Thomas Wishart knew that. His task, from the moment you left Malta, was never to let you out of his sight. Jerott thought he was following him, but that was not so. We wished to know, Sir Graham, exactly what you did, and what you did was most interesting.

'In any case,' said Lymond, and unclasping his hands he rose slowly to his feet and stood, head bent, looking down at Gabriel. 'In any case, Tosh was killed, and by your men. Trotty Luckup, too, was killed, because she knew too much about Joleta.... Madame Donati has told us all we need to know about that. And because Philippa Somerville had the same piece of information, she also was attacked and is lucky to be alive.... Of all these things we have proof.'

Gabriel stirred. 'Must I hear this?' he said. 'With the jewels you obviously have, with whatever wealth you have earned as your wages, you can bribe whom you like to say what you like. What you did on Malta and in Tripoli cannot be condoned. Nothing you fabricate now can obliterate it.'

'Shall I ask Nicolas de Nicolay to speak?' said Lymond softly. 'Or would you care to see this, that I took from your clothing the day that *you*, not I, tried to escape to the Turkish camp at Mdina? A piece of white paper, Sir Graham. A dirty, bloodstained piece of white paper with a message in English of the most loyal intent on one side. And on the other, a note in your own handwritten Arabic, giving them all the information they needed about the Receiver's false message from Sicily.'

It was defeat. His eyes wet for the annihilation of what had never truly existed, Jerott Blyth saw Gabriel draw himself up, as he seldom did, to his full magnificent height, the golden head high; all his thoughts, all his attention on the younger man standing still above him on the carpeted steps.

'Dear me,' said Gabriel mildly, the great voice pitched for Francis Crawford alone. 'What an importunate young man you are. You have just cost me, I believe, a quite excessive amount of my time. I shall be interested to pursue the matter with you, on some other occasion. At the moment . . . de Seurre!'

Then Jerott realized that he was going to appeal to St Mary's. The great company whose allegiance he had so confidently set out to command was here, deployed round St Giles, brought there at the first opportunity by its officers after d'Oisel's full escorting corps had been removed. One would trust de Seurre and des Roches and the rest to have done that without bloodshed. Their aim was not to escape but to see justice done, to be present at what touched them so vitally: the *Vehmgerichte* of their two leaders.

But they would not expect to escape mortal issues if they placed themselves now in Gabriel's hand. The axe was too sharp and too sweetly polished to fail. Good as the French were, if the Order now clove to its own: if the knights stood firm in their devotion to Gabriel; if Plummer, if Tait, if all the souls Graham Malett had enchanted now came at his call, and brought their army with them, the French would melt as agate on the hot blade, and the weapon Lymond had forged would be loose, under Gabriel, in the world.

So, 'De Seurre,' said Graham Malett, his voice firm, his fair face sober and set. 'Antichrist is here. I can do no more against him, or against these poor souls who malign me. Give me your hand. Come with me. Add your great spirit and your prayers to mine, and bring with you all who would come, pure and loyal and unsullied, before the great Throne of God. . . . Absolve, we beseech Thee, O Lord,' said Graham Malett, and tall and still at the foot of the steps he faced the high altar, his fair head flung back, his eyes on the Cross.

'Absolve the souls of thy servants from the chain of their sins, that being raised in the glory of the Resurrection, they may live among the saints and their elect.'

The echoes of the magnificent voice, mouthing from pillar to pillar, grew muffled and died. No one spoke. Outside, the crowd had fallen into a murmurous silence, and the men of St Mary's, taut at their posts, watched the great doors of the church where their officers stood, listening to the Order calling its knights.

Then de Seurre stirred. Tough, prosaic, deeply religious, he had been Gabriel's strongest support in all the cold, unseen struggle of ethos against ethos, and his face, hairless as limed leather, showed nothing of the conflict that indictment and appeal, so closely following, must have produced. As he neared Gabriel, M. d'Oisel, aware, Jerott knew, of the full menace St Mary's represented, said nevertheless, calmly, in his excellent English, 'For Sir Graham to leave now is out of the question. The charges on both sides are far too serious to ignore. Both Sir Graham Malett and Mr Crawford will kindly give up their swords.'

Graham Malett did not even look at him. 'Well?' he said to de Seurre.

The Chevalier de Seurre looked round. There, watching silent and tense in the nave, were the men who had abandoned Graham Malett for Lymond: Blacklock, Guthrie, Hoddim, Salablanca and Abernethy. By the door, equally intent, were those who, like himself, had stayed staunchly by their beliefs and their vows. He waited a moment, drawing from them whatever silent support he needed, and then turned. 'Sir Graham. In the name of justice we believe you must stay and answer these charges,' said the Chevalier. 'We cannot in conscience join you or follow you now.'

The fine aquamarine eyes stretched open. The pure skin, draining first, flushed next to carnation pink as Graham Malett's golden brows rose and his lips and chin flattened against his clenched teeth. Then, '*Must!*' he said smiling, on a note no one present had heard before. 'Must, fool . . . fat, God-sodden blunderer? There is nothing Graham Malett *must* do except clear the lice from his path.'

Beside him, Jerott Blyth drew a long, shuddering breath, his gaze turning to Lymond. But Lymond had eyes for no one but Gabriel and the Chevalier. His voice, saying sharply '*De Seurre!*' cut across the sudden rising note of excitement both inside and outside the church, as thus abruptly, swift and terrible as a fissure in ice, the soulless, loving imposture came to an end.

Lymond exclaimed; but Michel de Seurre took one second too many to react. As he turned, Gabriel's sword, naked in his hand, cut through de Seurre's scabbard and disarmed him, in one vital movement, while at the same time with his free hand Graham Malett twisted the

490

Chevalier's arm high and tight on his spine and held him, a living shield, before him. Then, instead of advancing, back exposed, into the crowded church, Gabriel backed, his blade before him scanning the air, until he was on the steps and just out of sword's reach of Crawford.

If he were quick, he might just manage to slip inside and round the altar, past the Chapel of the Holy Cross, and out of the church by the Lady Steps without meeting more opposition than he could handle. To do that, he had somehow to put both Lymond and de Seurre out of action. As he backed, the Chevalier must have felt Gabriel's muscles tense, and although he himself was fighting with every inch of packed muscle he possessed, must have known that with his great advantage of breadth and height, his Grand Cross could pick him up bodily if he chose, unarmed as he was, with one arm almost wrenched off at his back.

Then, like some chill, periastral missile, Lymond launched himself from the altar rails. The unexpectedness of it took more than de Seurre by surprise. Letting go his victim, rocked to his knees with the force of the blow as Lymond landed, Graham Malett staggered back, bent, and sword in hand, sprang. De Seurre, rolling out of the way, blundered into his own sawn-off scabbard and, sitting up, was attempting quickly to unsheath and rise when the Sieur d'Oisel's hard hand stayed his wrist. 'No. This is a case for single combat, if one ever existed. Start more, and the whole church will become a battlefield. This had to come, I would guess, some time. Let us listen and watch.'

And struggling to his feet, de Seurre moved back beside Jerott Blyth, back with the recoiling crowd, M. d'Oisel and the pick of his French troops forming a restraining cordon at its head, until within the altar rails, on the steps, on the fine Turkey carpet before the steps, there was no one but the two men facing one another from a space of a few yards, steel in hand.

And more than a hundred feet above their heads, above the choir roof vaulting, above the thronged, yellow-lit thread of the High Street, among the crowded Doric gables, sending its message of mourning round Edinburgh's small hills and out into the dark spaces where the river Forth rolled, the Moaning Bell started to toll.

His massive, golden head flung back, his broad shoulders braced under their black cloak lightly laced over his white shirt, his sword firm and light in his hand, Graham Malett, Knight Grand Cross of the Order of St John, Sigad id Din of Dragut's prophecy, looked across at his fated opponent, met that expressionless blue gaze above Lymond's sword, balanced between his two hands, and smiled. 'Sweet, hot-blooded creature,' he said. 'I had no idea you had a brain. You should have joined me. I would have made you a little prince.'

491

He sighed, his clear blue eyes tender. 'And now I must find another.' He moved his hand and the point of his blade, searing in the banked candlelight, described a gentle, impatient pattern in the still air. 'Come, my flower. No one will interfere. You have not yet quite proved your innocence and I have not yet quite proved my guilt but I cannot afford—you are right, surprisingly right—to be detained while they find out how just are your guesses. Ah, sir, *you meddle!*'

It was addressed to the Deacon, his old face white, his courage gripped hard under the cloth of gold, who ignoring d'Oisel's exclamation, ran forward between the two fair-headed men and laid a hand on Gabriel's arm. 'This is a House of God, sir! And you with the Cross on your breast draw naked steel before Our Lord's altar! Put up! And you also!'

Lymond's gaze did not leave Graham Malett's. 'Willingly,' he said. 'If the Knight Grand Cross will do the same.'

'Willingly,' repeated Gabriel at once. He made only a little movement, but the tip of his sword, entering the old man's shoulder, drove home with a speed that sent the deacon reeling back into d'Oisel's arms, his sparkling vestment running with blood. Stepping back, all his bright blade dulled, Gabriel turned again, smiling, to Francis Crawford.

'It is sheathed,' he said. 'As I was saying, no one will interfere. And only one man besides myself requires his freedom and has no objection to killing you first . . . *Randy!*'

Then they all saw the movement behind the octagonal pillar to the left of the altar. They all watched, helpless, as, dodging out of the shadows, sword drawn, Randy Bell, physician and Will Scott's assassin, drove straight for Lymond's unwitting back.

But because of Gabriel's shout, as Gabriel was fully aware, Lymond had a little forewarning: just enough to meet Bell sword to sword, as he backed up the steps, his eyes flickering from Malett on the one side to Bell on the other.

Bell was afraid. Catching the glint of his eye as he thrust at Lymond, dodged and thrust again, Jerott remembered where he had seen that look before. It was on the face of Joleta, in the streaming dark courtyard of St Mary's, when she read Gabriel's intention in his eyes.

But Randy Bell had no alternative. If he stayed, he would hang. And in supporting Gabriel lay his only chance of escape. Only Gabriel, playing his own amusing game, closing in a little, forcing Lymond, now fully engaged with Bell's blade, to watch his own sword; from time to time thrusting with intention so that Lymond had to guard himself, breathing quickly, on two sides at once, knew what outcome he planned. For Lymond was Randy Bell's master with the sword and Bell, looking desperately for help to Gabriel's playful blade, knew it. Only Gabriel was not supporting Randy Bell's attack. He was merely bent, Jerott saw suddenly with incredulous loathing, on having the inconvenient doctor neatly killed for him, while sapping Lymond's own strength.

It was not a game that Lymond, either, proposed to play. As Jerott watched, he suddenly put extreme pressure on Bell, his sword thrusting and flashing, arching always to the left, where Gabriel followed him up. Then at length Bell, chest heaving, the dark blood high in his face, stepped back just below the great standing candelabra at the top right of the steps. He saw it just as it came toppling over him, thrust by Lymond's shoulder and knee and, struck across the shoulders, slithered and bounced down the remaining steps to the carpet where he rolled to d'Oisel's feet.

Few watched while rough hands were laid on him and, below Janet Beaton's stony gaze, Randy Bell was dragged through the press to the north door to take his place in the Tolbooth. Instead, swaying, calling, they saw Lymond drop instantly on one knee, and dodging Gabriel's first, unconsidered drive of fresh anger, strike forward and up with his left hand.

Graham Malett rolled back along the altar rail, angry surprise in his lucid blue eyes and blood wet on his white shirt, where Lymond's dagger, slipped at speed from his belt, had slit the garment from end to end in a long raking thrust that ended deep by one clavicle. Bare under his black cloak, the stained skin of his breast heaved as he collected himself, his sword flickering as he parried Lymond's quick, following attack until, his forces gathered again, he stood firm and was able, in a moment, to disengage, his back to the rail. Then Jerott, and all those near enough, saw what the torn shirt revealed, pricked, white-scarred with the passage of time, on his breast.

Lymond saw it too, and his sickened understanding must have shown, for Gabriel's amusement lit all his fine, fresh-coloured face. 'Why so prim, sweeting? Surely Evangelista told you? But for Trotty, the Sisters of Sciennes might have had a rare child to nurture. ... Which reminds me. ...' The smiling eyes under the cropped golden hair considered Lymond. 'I have a little news for you, my brash child. But not yet. Not yet. First, Francis Crawford, I must teach you and others like you to keep out of my way.'

His arm steady, Lymond parried that first stroke. To Jerott, to all his men, to Sybilla, watching, her heart struck cold by Gabriel's words, his blue and level gaze was no more or no less than they had often seen it, in armed combat with someone whose skill he respected, or at the beginning of some subtle and delicate action. He said, speaking clearly and directly, 'There is no certainty in your sword, and no escape at the end. You are fighting for your pride, but I haven't done what I have done to die here, under your blade. Only a fool, Malett, *or a man losing his mind*, makes the same mistake twice.'

It was done deliberately, no doubt. It touched, Jerott saw, on what was probably the only fear that Gabriel knew. There was, in that open, tolerant face, a flowering of cold anger such as Jerott had never seen, even at the whipping-post at St Mary's; and Graham Malett, his eyes alight, said softly, *'Jabatek ummek wahad f'il-dunya. . . .* Thy mother made thee unique in the world; a true word, lout, usurper, hurd without name. You would meddle with me? You would lay your half-made hands on my life?' He broke off, his white teeth flashing. 'Come here, Francis Crawford, who worships, I am told, two things himself: power and music. Don't be afraid. I am not going to kill you. But the armbone of St Giles, who can cast out demons, will have company before very long. . . . First I shall sever your right hand, my dear. And in due time, the left. . . .'

And smiling still, he attacked.

Almost no one, of the crowded men of St Mary's who watched, murmuring and jostling from the body of the church, had ever seen these two men fight. It was something Francis Crawford had instinctively avoided, Jerott realized. Opposed often enough at the butts or the tilt, they had never been matched body to body in physical combat. And that, shortly, was what they were doing, for Gabriel, superb in height, reach and confidence, made the one small mistake he had made over and over: he underestimated his opponent. Richard Crawford, who better than anyone there knew Lymond's gift for the sword, drew in his breath as Gabriel, moving round and round the scuffed carpet, springing from step to step, up, sideways and down, his point intent on Lymond's bright sword and quick, skilful hands; his dagger left-handed matching Lymond's, overreached himself for one second too long. The fist of Lymond's dagger hand thrust up; his long blade came down, and Gabriel's sword, hooked from his grasp, flashed past the brass rail, and slitting the red silk of the altar, sank quivering into the carved wood behind.

Following its flight, Lymond almost missed the spurred foot rising with all Gabriel's weight to his groin. There was only one way he could jump: he hurled himself down the wide steps and was caught, deep in the sword-arm, by Gabriel's dagger. Adam Blacklock, gripping the child Philippa's shoulder, saw Lymond stumble, his hand loosening on the sword, and Gabriel's dagger pull out and flash downwards, its razor edge flying to the blood, flesh and tendons of that long, slender-boned hand. Then Lymond, dropping the sword, snatched his hand back, blood pouring from his right arm, and sought left-handed and nearly reached Gabriel's exposed ribs.

In the effort, both men overbalanced. With the effective use of only

494

one arm Lymond could not wholly control his manner of falling. He took the brunt on his shoulder, as Gabriel did, but rolling back to regain his feet, half his back must have been pressed hard against the thin edge of the steps, and when he found Gabriel, half-risen, on him again, his dagger high in his hand, Lymond did not parry, but instead, holding his dagger left-handed, he grappled close, pressing hard on the high wound of Gabriel's chest while quickly, unobtrusively, he sought the grip that would do what he wanted.

Pain Graham Malett had never feared. He would have withstood it, with massive strength, until Lymond tired, if Lymond's fingers, scored and bleeding where he had not always contrived to miss that teasing sword-point, had not found and pressed on the one nerve that mattered. No amusement at all on his face, Graham Malett dropped his last weapon and brought his two powerful hands to bear on wresting the remaining knife from Lymond's grip.

Watching, in a fellowship of craning heads and jostling, shouting bodies, among whom, marked by their silence, were Lymond's own officers and men, Jerott saw the two men crash again to the floor, and rolling over and over, stain the altar-carpet with their blood. There was a brutal, effective repertoire which he knew, and Gabriel in his day also had used against men taught to wrestle in the *bagnios* of Constantinople. He saw Gabriel begin the familiar moves with a kind of loving care, while the muscles of his left arm rose under his torn shirt as he kept Lymond's dagger hand in chancery. With only his feet left to use, Lymond used them, in a deft move quite as unforgivable as Gabriel's and entirely successful, since Gabriel had not expected it. You forgot, thought Jerott, that Lymond had not sailed the Mediterranean pacing the poop deck; he had been below, in shackles, where to exist you had to fight like a cur.

Because of it, now, he had broken Gabriel's grip on his thighs and, more important still, on his left hand holding the dagger. With a thrust that sent the big man hurtling in turn on to his back, Lymond followed him with the same hard deliberation, using knees, feet, the chopping edge of his hand in a sequence no one there could follow: a sequence that brought a husky growl from the golden throat, a rising flush to the mellow skin, a white-rimmed blaze of hatred to the pale blue stare of Graham Malett. Using his splendid body he arched his muscles and fought, fending off the blows that palsied his limbs and dissected his nerves, bent now on nothing but escape, revenge and total destruction. With the great advantage of his weight he would have succeeded, in no more than a moment, except that Lymond, releasing him choking from a blow on the windpipe, raised his left arm and hurled his one weapon, the dagger, after Gabriel's sword to the altar. Then, setting his teeth, Francis Crawford closed the fingers of his crippled arm fast on one of the thick white silk cords of Gabriel's torn and crumpled knight's garment, and seizing the other in his good left hand, pulled the cord tight.

To maintain a grip when your arm has been torn through with cold steel and when with feet and hands the man below you is attempting for his life to maim and overthrow, needs a special kind of endurance. Lymond was helped, perhaps, by the fact that Gabriel was tired and injured, as he was; and that by blow and pressure he was already at the start half-deprived of air and therefore full consciousness. But the punishment Lymond took as the cord tightened and the handsome, suffused face opened, gasping, for air, was made possible only by his training and the particular kind of way, Jerott thought, that his mind happened to work, notwithstanding the weaknesses of the past few weeks.

Then there came the moment when Graham Malett's big hands, still loosely flailing, fell to his sides and his bloodshot eyes closed; and Lymond then, releasing him, groped, his face half-blind with pain, and finding the dagger, placed the sharp blade, held by the heel of his hand, across the stretched tendons of Gabriel's empurpled throat.

Slowly, the air returned to Graham Malett's drained lungs; slowly the saintly blue eyes opened, and understood the meaning of the cold line at his throat, and comprehended, incredulously, his defeat. For a long moment, in the big church there was silence, barred only, second by second, with the slow muffled strokes of the bell. Then Lymond said, his strained and breathless voice strange to all their ears, 'I take upon me your execution, Graham Malett. I take you all to witness that if I must suffer for it, the crime is no one's but mine. The venue I cannot help . . . except that under this roof, Gabriel, your corpse is more seemly than your body. For Will Scott, for Wat Scott his father, for Thomas Wishart and Trotty Luckup, for the pain you occasioned the Somervilles and the corruption and death of your sister, for what, above all, you hoped to do to this realm of Scotland, I call your life forfeit.'

Soft from the body of the church came de Seurre's voice, chiming with Lymond's in its frozen intensity. 'For what you did in Malta and in Tripoli, I call your life forfeit.'

'For what you did to the peoples of the Borders, who will hardly knit now for a generation,' said Lymond's pale voice, resuming. 'For what you did to the men under your cure, who became less than men; for the lives you risked and the lives you wasted; for the emotion you fostered and fed on, and the values and beliefs you have left wrecked and cheapened by your masquerade; for the army that might have made us a whole nation and the Queen Mother deceived of her strong arm; for all your crimes against humanity and those far higher than human, Graham Malett, I call your life forfeit. . . .'

With difficulty; with breath that must have seared his lacerated

496

throat as it rose, Sir Graham Malett said hoarsely, 'I forgot, my winsome darling, that you were taught by the scum of the seas. What a pity that your Irish trollop and her grovelling bastard will never know what they've missed.'

Standing small, staunch and shivering beside her son Richard, Sybilla heard the words spoken to Francis at last. Jerott, understanding also, bent his head and covered his aching eyes with his hands. The men who had come to know Lymond well—Hoddim, Guthrie—stirred uneasily where they stood; and Adam Blacklock's long artist's hands tightened round Philippa who stood, looking at no one, misery in her dark-ringed eyes.

The bell tolled. Then Lymond said, the knife steady still in his hand, 'I see. I could not quite understand your confidence. You had better tell me, in undecorated English, what you mean.' And as Graham Malett smiled, his fine, long-lashed eyes on the knife, and said nothing, Lymond slowly withdrew it from his throat and sitting back on his heels, the dagger point aimed unwaveringly at Gabriel's heart, said, 'Speak.'

Graham Malett pulled himself up to his elbow. Round his neck, the furrow left by the cord showed plain among the swollen, purple flesh; beneath torn cloak and torn shirt the blood coursed steadily over the marked skin; but blotched, bruised and grazed, short of breath, hoarse of voice, the fine, fresh skin suffused and the short, guinea-gold hair dark with sweat and dust, he looked magnificent still: a fallen angel; an avenging god. 'Did you think, peasant, that the woman O'Dwyer really died?' said Gabriel with thick contempt. 'She lived on to give birth to a child. But understood, of course, that Francis Crawford's proud destiny should not be disturbed by the knowledge. . . .'

'It is true,' said Nicolas de Nicolay's voice, uncommonly sober, from behind d'Oisel's shoulder. Lymond did not look round.

'It is true,' Gabriel agreed, smiling. 'I have two letters here, from Dragut, which will prove it.' Reaching under his cloak, slowly because of the dagger, he found and threw down two dog-eared packets, their superscription written in Arabic. 'You will read them with close interest, I am sure. From them, you will learn that I have purchased the child who has been reared with his mother under Dragut's roof by my request. By now, also at my request, the woman O'Dwyer and her infant will have been removed from the palace to a place of greater security. . . .

'Are you interested?' said Graham Malett, lazily, his blue eyes sustaining the locked stare above him. 'You should be. Because the child isn't Cormac O'Connor's. You will see, when you read. It is a boy, five months old, branded with Dragut's mark, I am told, and given the name of Khaireddin. He is your son.

'But no doubt,' added Graham Malett softly, and made himself a little more comfortable as he lay, 'you have got several such, unheeded equally. If so, your remedy is under your hand. Kill me, and the woman and child will both be quietly disposed of. Let me go, and you may find them yourself.'

Lymond drew back, controlled still by his schooled, fighter's instincts. His face showed nothing. His hand, steadied now on one upraised knee, held the knife as before, perfectly still. But Sybilla, who knew him best, thought she saw his heart stop.

Oonagh O'Dwyer had not died through his agency. She could imagine what that meant to him. But what did it mean to know that he had left that proud woman behind to bear his child as a common possession of the Armenian sea-thief Dragut Rais; and that the child itself, the first and only son of his blood, instead of blossoming in that careful, careless affection which he had given already, so endearingly, to Kevin, had been bought like an animal, and branded like an animal, and was now being bartered, like some dirty, unconsidered coin, for Gabriel's life?

She saw Francis begin, automatically, to breathe again. Above the dishevelment, the blood, the useless arm, the cold threat of the knife, his face was still, and old beyond its years. Yet for all his forced maturity and all his arts, Francis Crawford did not possess Gabriel's true, impermeable mask, to speak, and smile and pray for him. The shock, the half-believing agony of mind showed now as he stared, shaken by the quiet force of his breathing, his brow lined, at Gabriel's smiling, satisfied eyes.

The bell was stopping. Within the church, the silence had the quality of a forest at night. Whisperings, shufflings, jostlings, rustled through the herb-laden air, warmed by many bodies, and by the tapers, hissing and guttering in their diminishing clusters before every quiet shrine. Behind the two men, on the high altar, the massive silver-gilt plate glistened under the candelabra, and the crimson velvet, stirred by the draught from the open doors, nudged the candle flame into remote genuflection. The bell had stopped.

'No,' said Lymond at length; and his voice, though thick, was painstakingly distinct. 'No . . . and again No. This time you have guessed wrongly. I am ready to give anything . . . even what is not mine to give . . . to see you dead. I think Oonagh O'Dwyer would have the courage to agree. For the child. . . . If there is a child. . . . If it is mine. . . . I must answer elsewhere.'

And a child's voice, echoing his in turn, said, '*No!*'

Adam Blacklock, catching in vain at Philippa's cloak as she wrested herself from his arms, saw Lymond's face tighten, though he did not look round as the child ran forward, her strong voice calling, her brown twisted hair slapping her face.

'No, Mr Crawford!' cried Philippa forbiddingly, and ducking under the snatching arms that tried to prevent her, she ran forward. 'No! What harm can Sir Graham do now? What might the little boy become?' And sinking on her knees, she shook, in her vehemence, Lymond's bloodstained arm.

'You castigate the Kerrs and the Scotts and the others, but what is this but useless vengeance? He can do us no harm; he can do Scotland no harm; he can do Malta no harm. There is a *baby*!' said Philippa, very loudly and insistently and desperately, as if Lymond could not hear her, or were too tired or too simple to understand. 'There is a *baby*. You can't abandon *your son!*'

It was Gabriel who answered, his light blue eyes smiling at Lymond, although it was to Philippa he spoke. 'He won't abandon him,' he said. 'He will go with him. Don't you see? He will kill me, and then turn the knife on himself. Otherwise it would be a little too much like sacrificing Joleta, wouldn't it? *Wouldn't it, my treasure?*'

'What in God's name . . . ?' said Jerott under his breath. It sounded as if Gabriel wanted to be killed, this mocking monotony of insistence.

Beside him, the Sieur d'Oisel spoke. 'None of this is in God's name,' he said. 'He is working on M. Crawford's friends in the hope that they will persuade him to save the woman and child, and let Sir Graham go free.'

'Stop it, then,' said Jerott in a low voice. 'Take Malett to the Tolbooth. Surely he can be made to say where the child is.'

D'Oisel turned. 'Do you think so?' he said. 'I do not. If Malett comes with me to the Tolbooth, he must know that knight or not, he will hang. He bargains here for his life. Whether he tells the truth now or not, while Gabriel lives, there is hope of finding the infant. . . . If M. le Comte spares his life, Malett has at least some chance of escaping the Church. The Crown recognizes as much, and the Crown leaves the decision to M. Crawford. He has earned the right, God knows, to make it.'

Moving forward quietly to Jerott's side, Adam Blacklock had heard. 'Don't you understand? The authorities are afraid of them both,' he said gently. 'Why do you supose this cordon is here, which only an unarmed girl was allowed to pass through? Lymond, loyal to Scotland, might be a threat to French power greater than even Gabriel, one of these days—*Philippa!*'

And a wordless shout, like a cry at a cockfight, rose among the stone pillars and sank muffled into the old, dusty banners above the choir roof. For Philippa Somerville, who believed in action when words were not enough, had leaned over and snatched the knife from Lymond's left hand.

It was all that Gabriel had been waiting for. Rolling sideways he sprang to his feet and hurled himself up the steps to the altar rail and over it to the sacred table beyond. On his face, triumphant, intent, there was no awareness of the bond between that high crucifix and the cross on his breast; of the years spent masquerading in prayer, of the great offices so humbly, so mockingly performed; the great names so familiarly mouthed. The massive monstrance with its golden bells, encrusted with pearls, stood firm at his hand. Bracing his great shoulders Graham Malett lifted it, and raising it high above his head, sent it crashing over the rails to where Lymond raced at his heels, the recovered dirk in his hand.

The heavy box caught him on the shoulder. As Philippa, a few steps below, shouted out, Lymond stumbled and half in company with the great battered casket, rolled and tumbled down to the foot.

'Did you think,' said Graham Malett, 'this great enterprise of my life could be pinched out by a halfpenny pedlar of arrows? Go seek your son. You won't find him. Nor will Cormac O'Connor, who claims Oonagh as his wife . . . and any child of hers as his son . . . is it not a matter for wit?'

The vessel had come to rest. Lymond stirred, and Gabriel, smiling, turned and using both hands, drew from the broken altar the long, shining blade of his sword. 'You won't find him,' he said, 'because he is going to have a new master. He will know the whipping-post, sweetheart, as you never knew it. He will learn to carry my filth, and when it pleases me, to sleep in my bed. It will teach you,' said Gabriel, and holding the sword, he began walking, slowly, towards the shadows by the Lady Steps and the door. 'It will teach you to remember Graham Malett.'

There must have been a horse waiting outside. There was, they found afterwards, a ship riding close in Leith roads. And because the French King's Lieutenant in Scotland did not want trouble with the French King or the Order; and because he suspected that Lymond's presence in Scotland might be an embarrassment to him, the order to pursue did not come as readily as it might, and Graham Malett caught both the horse and the ship.

Lymond had pulled himself to one knee, Philippa's frightened face at his shoulder, when the men of St Mary's realized that Graham Malett was being allowed to escape and, like sand sucked by the tide, they began to pour through the pillared vaults of the church to where the French still held their barrier firm.

Of those in the front, Jerott was the first to act. His white face blazing, he knocked up the sword-arm of the Frenchman standing before him and had begun to run forward, three men, sword in hand, flinging themselves on his heels, when Lymond, swaying, got to his feet and seizing Jerott as he passed, swung him round and held him to face the surging, shouting throng.

'*Stop!*' His voice, using all he knew of science to give weight to its weakness, cut through the uproar. 'Stop, you cob-headed fools. Are you an army or a rabble, brawling here with your allies?' He paused, and when Philippa suddenly took his arm, he did not shake it off. 'You had a leader who betrayed you. He has answered to me, on behalf of all of you, for that. For the rest, the law, in M. d'Oisel's hands, will act . . . is acting.'

Behind him, at last, their captain leading, d'Oisel's troops were deploying, sword in hand, from the church. D'Oisel himself, his orders given, waited on in the choir. He waited until, under Lymond's tongue, the impulse to violence died and his men came to a halt, uncertainly, eyeing each other and their officers, and those among them who had chosen Graham Malett to lead.

'I am indebted,' said M. d'Oisel abruptly. 'And dumbfounded. I had thought it would be the work of many months to get these men once more under control.'

Lymond's face was totally without colour. 'You owe me nothing,' he said. 'Your duty, as you saw it, was to let Graham Malett escape. These men of St Mary's know him now as a blaspheming impostor. If your men and mine had met in that race, Graham Malett's death would have cost more than any one man is worth. . . . Let him go. I, too, have taken precautions. We may not stop him, but we may manage to keep track of him somehow. . . . We must.'

'All the more I salute your most praiseworthy discipline. It is a warning though, is it not,' said M. d'Oisel crisply, 'of what might happen to such a tool as St Mary's in the wrong hands?'

Something—what?—thought Jerott, about these words was familiar. Then he remembered. Long ago, in Malta, Lymond had said something of the sort to Graham Malett, speaking of the condition of the Order. 'You are now what every sect potentially becomes when it loses leadership. A tool.' He had recognized and taunted them with the weakness of the Order; but then in creating St Mary's, had he not brought the same prospect of evil to his own country, with the same risk of other less able, less disinterested hands to guide them in future? A great and chivalrous Order, with their common religion to bind them, had become warped and debased in the hands of one corrupt Grand Master. Without those vows, those ideals, that spiritual discipline, how much more vulnerable was this force?

Some of this, in his dry, accented voice, d'Oisel was already saying. 'You chose to fight your duel with Graham Malett here, in this land. You drew this great and ruinous power from Malta and brought its real nature to light. . . . Many lives have been lost, many souls disillusioned; many in rejecting Gabriel will also now reject all Gabriel professed. I do not say,' said the King of France's General, his long face shadowed in the failing candles, 'that you could have prevented Graham Malett from following you, or that if you had asked for help earlier you would have met with anything but disbelief. But this nucleus force, so brilliantly organized for quick expansion, was the weapon Malett would have used in the end against all of us, and possibly, too, against Malta.'

'But he failed to use it,' said Lymond quietly. 'Because although we have men of religion among us, we use also other yardsticks of thought. I said once, I think, that the best thing the Order could do would be to offer the Osmanlis free passage and thereby force the warring countries of Christendom to unite. Had they not been smothered under the easy blanket of their vows, the Order should have learned that there is one thing more important by far than uniform piety . . . *peace*.'

'All right,' said Jerott suddenly. 'But for what do you substitute the great ideals, the discipline of the Church? Every army follows something. You know your own power. In a month you will have all the men of St Mary's in your hand. Is hero-worship any better? And what if the next leader they follow is Gabriel or his like?'

'There will be no successor,' said Lymond abruptly. 'That is the *sine qua non*. When I can no longer control it, St Mary's disappears. I have made every possible provision; in the officers I have chosen, and in the financial arrangements I have made. Only if the company had gone to France as part of a national army could Gabriel have afforded to have armed and maintained it, and even then, a good third would, I believe, have rejected him and stayed behind. . . . It was dangerous.

'Of course it was dangerous. I thought, I believe, to repay a debt by giving my own land for a few months the security it had lacked for forty years. . . . But we are still infants, where emotion finds outlet in force and force is met by emotion, and people cannot conceive of themselves even yet as nations instead of as families . . . and certainly not as a brotherhood of nations, when even sister religions bring their armies against one another. . . . Take heart,' said Lymond at last, with cold, exhausted irony. 'I shall convey them abroad.'

D'Oisel watched him. 'You could, if you wished, stand at the Queen Mother's right hand.' And Jerott, hearing, wondered if he guessed why Francis Crawford had been sent to Malta by Montmorency of France: to remove him, perhaps for all time, from the influence of the de Guises. Lymond had put his life, for that short space, at the disposal of the Knights of St John—his life, but nothing else. He had chosen a different destiny. And that, now, had brought him the offer that the Constable, long ago, had foreseen.

Lymond shook his head. The blood he had lost, the long bouts of alternate violence and strain, the patience and self-control he had had

502

to bring, now, to this deliberate and studied examination in the midst of dizziness and physical pain and all the devastating reaction of the news he had just received had, together, brought him at last to the end of the long night. He said, 'No.... We are not, either, a royal tool. If you are short of violent and persevering men to fight your battles in France ... send the Kerrs. Jerott ... the men should get back to their quarters. I shall join you all shortly. Philippa, my dear lass. ...'

Philippa Somerville, standing back a little, did not withdraw her arm. In her white face, a shadow of motherly irritation appeared. 'Has no one here any sense? Be quiet and sit down. The world will look after itself for a night, without your hand on the rim.'

'I'll take care of it,' said Richard Crawford quietly, and Lymond lifted his head. 'Oh, Richard. Timely as ever. I want. ...'

'I know what you want,' said Lord Culter comfortably, and hooked an arm under his brother's stained shoulders.

'I doubt it,' said Lymond drily. 'I want you to take me across the church. Is Sybilla. ...?'

'She is waiting for you,' said Richard. 'Later, when you are ready. Where do you want to go, for God's sake? You can hardly. ...'

'Over there,' said Francis Crawford. 'To Lauder's chapel. Can you help me, do you think?'

He got there, in the end, to the small and beautiful chapel against St Giles's south-west wall, founded, sixty years back, by Alexander Lauder of Blyth in honour of God, the Virgin Mary, and the Archangel Gabriel.

And there, while the great church emptied and his brother waited, his face grim, outside, Francis Crawford walked forward, and genuflected, and laid on the altar the shining ribbon of his sword, Graham Malett's blood dark on the blade. Then he spoke, his voice clear and low, before the shrine he had chosen, to affirm to his brother, his mother, and all those in the dimming vaults of the church who dared not come close, that the altar prevailed, eternal, untarnished, over the memory of the enemy who carried its name.

'My son ... my son,' said Francis Crawford before the blurred, failing candles, their light searching over his disordered, bent head and closed eyes and the long, scarred lines of his hands, laid flat on the steel.

'So small a spirit, to lodge such sorrows as mankind has brought you. Live ... live.... Wait for me, new, frightened soul. And though the world should reel to a puny death, and the wolves are appointed our godfathers, I will not fail you, ever.'

Edinburgh, October 1963—*February* 1965.

THE LYMOND CHRONICLES

BY DOROTHY DUNNETT

"The finest living writer of historical fiction."
—*Washington Post Book World*

THE GAME OF KINGS

Dorothy Dunnett introduces her irresistible hero Francis Crawford of Lymond, a nobleman of elastic morals and dangerous talents whose tongue is as sharp as his rapier. In 1547 Lymond returns to defend his native Scotland from the English, despite accusations of treason against him. Hunted by friend and enemy alike, he leads a company of outlaws in a desperate race to redeem his reputation.

Fiction/0-679-77743-1

QUEENS' PLAY

Once an accused traitor, now a valued agent of Scottish diplomacy, Lymond is sent to France, where a very young Queen Mary Stuart is sorely in need of his protection. Disguised as a disreputable Irish scholar, Lymond insinuates himself into the glittering labyrinth of the French court, where every courtier is a conspirator and the art of assassination is paramount.

Fiction/0-679-77744-X

THE DISORDERLY KNIGHTS

Through machinations in England and abroad, Lymond is dispatched to Malta, to assist the Knights Hospitallers in the island's defense against Turkish corsairs. But he shortly discovers that the greatest threat to the knights lies within their own ranks. In a narrative that sweeps from the besieged fortress of Tripoli to the steps of Edinburgh's St. Giles Cathedral, Lymond matches wits and swords against an elusive villain.

Fiction/0-679-77745-8

PAWN IN FRANKINCENSE

Lymond cuts a desperate path across the Ottoman empire of Suleiman the Magnificent in search of a kidnapped child, an effort that may place this adventurer in the power of his enemies. What ensues is a subtle and savage chess game whose gambits include treachery, enslavement, and torture and whose final move compels Lymond to face the darkest ambiguities of his own nature.

Fiction/0-679-77746-6

THE RINGED CASTLE

Between Mary Tudor's England and the Russia of Ivan the Terrible lies a vast distance indeed, but forces within the Tudor court impel Lymond to Muscovy, where he becomes advisor and general to the half-mad tsar. In this barbaric land, Lymond finds his gifts for intrigue and survival tested to the breaking point, yet these dangers are nothing beside those of England, where Lymond's oldest enemies are conspiring against him.

Fiction/0-679-77747-4/Available in September 1997

CHECKMATE

Francis Crawford returns to France to lead an army against England. But even as the soldier scholar succeeds brilliantly on the battlefield, his haunted past becomes a subject of intense interest to forces in both the French and English courts. For whoever knows the secret of Lymond's parentage possesses the power to control him—or destroy him.

Fiction/0-679-77748-2/Available in September 1997

Available at your local bookstore or call toll-free to order:
1-800-793-2665 (credit cards only).